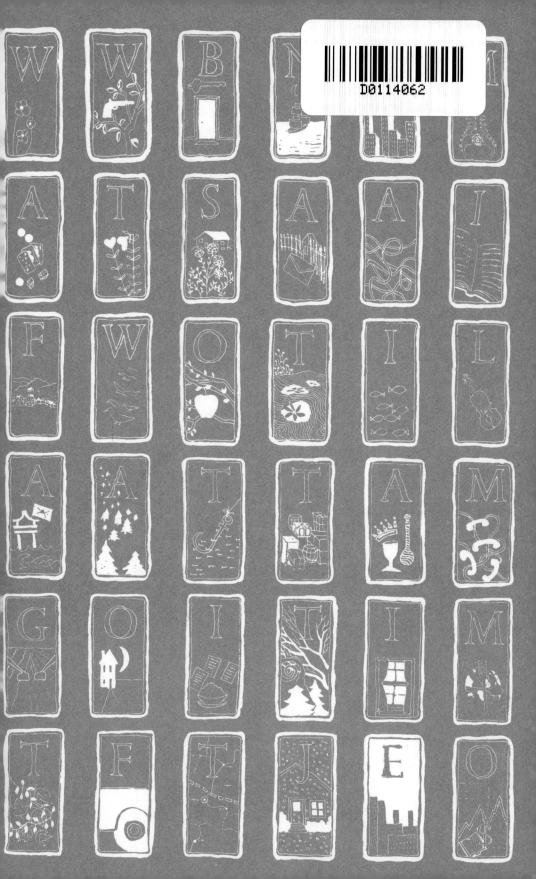

THE SECRET LIFE
OF OUR TIMES:
NEW FICTION
FROM *ESQUIRE*

THE SECRET LIFE OF OUR TIMES: NEW FICTION FROM *ESQUIRE*

EDITED BY GORDON LISH

INTRODUCTION BY TOM WOLFE

1973

DOUBLEDAY & COMPANY INC., GARDEN CITY, NEW YORK

DRAWINGS BY RAYMOND DAVIDSON

ISBN: 0-385-06215-x
Library of Congress Catalog Card Number 73–80734
Copyright © 1970, 1971, 1972, 1973 by Esquire Inc.

THIS BOOK IS FIRST FOR ATTICUS

CONTENTS

CONTENTS

CONTENTS

Foreword by Gordon Lish

It is in my head to use this space to display the sort of fellow I am. *Know me, know my stories* just about does it for the notion I have. For I am the customer who picked these stories, who picked them *twice*—who gathered them, first, from among the thousands of manuscripts that pass through *Esquire* and, second, from among the much smaller number that achieved print in my time on the job. You know a man by the choices he makes. But since respect for order asks that you see what I have to say before you sample what the stories want to say, I am going to tell you all about myself, in a major effort to deliver my heart.

1) I am thirty-nine years old, and the knowledge of this astonishes me.

2) To the best of my recollection, I always knew I was ending, but never so shockingly as now. I cannot shake an obsession with time, and I am accordingly impatient with the routine pace of experience. I want things speeded up, and I want to skip over what I already know. I choose to believe I am unexceptional in this regard.

3) I do not read a daily newspaper, but I do watch television, and it is chiefly in this manner that I discover what the world is doing. If television does not reflect the world accurately, then I am to that extent ignorant of it. But the prospect of this being the case does not really trouble me. I am not particularly

pleased with the world I'm told about, but I don't hold what I'm told against television. Clearly, there must be enough truth to what television tells me, for no invention of falsehood was ever so consistent. I think there is a lesson in this for people who are angry with fiction.

4) I was never a shy child, but I did feel alone. Jack Armstrong and Captain Midnight kept me company when I was a boy. I thought they lived in the radio—I mean *inside* the Emerson that stood on the table by my bed. I suppose if I had been asked to explain their residence there, I would have realized how ridiculous my believing this was. But I never told anyone, and no one ever challenged my faith. I just went on thinking they were *in* there, with all the rest of my radio friends. I am glad no one ever bothered to set me straight, to tell me these people were "actors" talking into "microphones" in faraway "studios." I am glad about it even now—because who, then, would have been the friends of my youth? No one, I am trying to say, not anyone in my house or my school, was the friend to me that Captain Midnight was. Captain Midnight knew all about me.

5) I read very little when I was a boy. The books in my home were mainly decoration—great sets of stuff in colors that were congenial to the carpet. Not that their forbidding appearance really mattered any, for I would not have read much, whatever was handy. Reading began when I was about fifteen and in and out of school and generally falling behind. I was in bed a lot and I was always very competitive, so I just got to reading competitively. I would read a thing if no one I knew had heard about it, teachers most of all. I began with Elio Vittorini's *The Red Carnation*, and then I went to Ugo Betti, Goffredo Parise, and of course Moravia, and I became an expert in the Neo-Realist way of seeing things, especially the central business between boys and girls. I got all my best poses from those fellows, and my debt to them is great. I found out reading got you girls—not

the choicest ones perhaps; perhaps the broody, darksome types—
but from there on there was no quarreling with the good a
"good" book could do you. I had a fine time those teen-age
years: Captain Midnight was no less the all-seeing friend of my
heart (though now he spoke in long, tragic sentences and his
triumphs were coded in failure), and I was owner of the lordliest
prize my generation could bestow: it was getting around that I
was . . . sophisticated! At last I was arrayed, just the way I had
always wanted, my magic mantle evident to any who dared get
into it with me on the subject of . . . Post-War . . . Italian . . .
Novelists. My mystery went before me; there was no stopping
me now. I read everything "difficult," as if everything depended
on it. Now that I am thirty-nine, I see that it really did.

6) Five years ago my wife and I were going along the freeway,
heading home after some dispiriting movie. It slammed us into
an awful state, that movie, and in the joyful pursuit of this
melancholy we set to whining over the kind of work we were
up to. What to do, what to do, what to do *next*? was the
question we had to get settled at once. At the off-ramp we were
stuck on repetitions. By the time we pulled into the garage we
had used up words. We sat there, in silence, both making a show
of being too tough to give up and go in. And just when I had
got to thinking Captain Midnight was instead Russian or Irish
but in any case a *man*, Barbara spoke in marvels as follows:
"What do you really, really want to be?" was what the wizard
said. Like a performer jolted into speech at the utterance of his
cue, I declared to the balcony seats: "The fiction editor of a big
magazine!" A year later I was one. My mystery had indeed
gone before me. The magic mantle, it turned out, could be
counted on even for this. So much for boys who believe on
Captain Midnight.

7) My principal concerns are paralysis, death, family, home, the
things people live with, the violence that is in us, flight from all

these concerns, a piece of brisk whistling in the long-toothed dark, and God, I just can't get enough of that wonderful stuff; and the older I grow, the hurrieder I get. I've no time for the languorous development of a vision, nor for the ceremonial transition from first *see this* to now *see that*. The world doesn't, either; it also ages. Give me conclusions, not arguments, and don't tire me with proofs of logic, or madness. I'm in a frenzy to find out if you've got something I can *use*. So if you know something, please reduce it to nouns—to findings—for your adjectives and adverbs are mostly tricks, special pleading. We are all waiting to know the same things; we can wait only so long. Show me *this! this! this! this!* and I'll do the best I can to fill in the oracular gaps between. Don't baby me; if your legs must have it, a crazy jump out or a crazy jump in, go ahead—because I want to follow if I can. I believe in the beatitudes of genius, and I think the next best thing to discovering something not commonly known is knowing someone who did. It is my ardent proposition that the writers presented here, in the works of fiction shown, have each discovered something not commonly known. I also propose that these writers went through some bad times to find out, which opinion is the organizing principle of this collection, in case you were wondering.

8) I do not suggest the stories you are about to read are the most laudable examples of recent fiction. I do not suggest they are emblematic of something we might justly call "the new fiction." Nor do I even say these stories are the most praise-worthy ones to have appeared in *Esquire* in my time. (For starters, "The Heart in Dreams," by Reynolds Price and Cynthia Ozick's "An Education" would otherwise be among this number, and those good stories you will not find here.) What I do say is that the stories I have thought to group under this title express the progress of my heart and mind over the period of the last four years. And why not? I picked them—and I picked

each one, the first time and the second, for that reason above all. In means and materials, these stories show what's been happening with me—and, inasmuch as I take on faith the universality of human feeling, what I also believe has been happening with you. I might add that this article of faith, unlike the dogma I observed undisturbed in my days of radio religion, not a few people have sought to challenge. But I go right on being steadfast, thank you, and comfortingly thoroughly convinced.

9) I got to be the fiction editor of a big magazine by being in the right place at the right time. It's an old story and a pretty magical one, actually. I hope it turns out you are in the right place at the right time for the stories I have chosen. Where it works out that way—that the story you are reading is the story most meant for you at precisely the moment—give a bit of credit to magic. It is the fundament of art: it is the feeling that Captain Midnight knows all about you, and you best of all.

10) Since I want to dedicate this book to my son, now's the time to get on record the names of four people who helped bring matters to this good stage: Rust Hills, who had done his own fine time and let me do mine; Julie Schwartz, who thrives on the "difficult" fiction of her time; Don Erickson, who always underwrote me at the right time; and Harold Hayes, who believes in a magazine that unfolds the story of the people who work for it.

I have covered everything in ten whole numbers, so long as you consider the fractional integers between. And these I didn't go into because the colossal truth is they are infinite. The same goes for the works of fiction that follow. Each one covers everything, so long as you consider the gaps between. Such absences are in fact uncountable. Listen: it is these intelligent silences, in the face of the facts, that unify the stories in this book, and which is yielding, in abundance, the most articulate fiction ever.

Introduction by Tom Wolfe

What a mess the magazine business is in! Just look around! The poor gorks are strangling on their bananas, stroking out, bleeding into their squashes, being held under for the count by their masters, drowning like kittens, or else putting up a brave front and lying for all they're worth. What a noise! What a mess! So how is it that *Esquire* has continued to thrive throughout the chaos? Through the depression of the 1930s, the war of the 1940s, through the Silent Generation, the Beat Generation, the Flower Generation, the Revolution Generation, the Probation Generation, the Salvation Generation, and the current Urethritic Ooze Generation, through tank tops, bell bottoms, race wars, gaping beavers, and recessions—*Esquire* somehow rides out every quake with the most obscene grin imaginable. The secret of the sheet's durability is no credit to its editors, however. For that secret is . . . their own perversity! their wrongheadedness! their sophomorism! their stubbornness! their contrariness! their unquenchable foolhardiness in the face of the most obvious warnings!

Thanks to this perverse streak they have been able to keep their readers and their critics off-balance for the past four decades. Such-and-such is the right thing to do . . . so . . . let's do something upside down on the ceiling! One never knows what to expect. I myself have been watching the process with witless fascination for ten years. Not many months ago I picked up a copy of *Esquire* and opened it to a ten-page spread of

color photographs . . . of chicken feet. Using the most refined camera lenses from the Jena glassworks, using some high-
powered photographic genius like Carl Fischer, using some hide-
ously lush and precise Teutonic color process, they presented
portrait after portrait of chicken feet, in high resolution, double-
size, triple-size . . . chicken feet! They dwelled on every horrible node of the poor beasts' scaly palms, every crusty dusty
shrunken knuckle, every flabby thorny gumball claw—they
gloried in the whole twisted mess—they rubbed your nose in it!
—until it was so real, you were brushing the grit and hayseeds
and chicken-flea nits off your lapels, like some nature boy with
the itch—and to what purpose? None, of course, except to
gratify the strange appetites of the editors of *Esquire*.

The disquieting thing is that at this moment I find them
employing me in the same manner. They have asked me to
write this introduction, an introduction to an *Esquire* anthology
of recent short stories, despite the fact that my attitude toward
current fiction in general is already on record. Not only have
I just finished singling out recent experiments in non-fiction
(the so-called New Journalism) as the only important new
direction in American literature in the past half century—
not only did I give a horselaugh to current fiction for good
measure—but I published this remarkable treatise in *Esquire* itself!

Why do they do these things? The explanation in this case is
that for four years now *Esquire* has had a fiction editor, Gordon
Lish, who is also editing this volume. Lish is a very dapper and
presentable fellow in the Litchfield briarthistle tweedmore squire
manner and at the same time just the sort of maniac who is
capable of perpetuating *Esquire*'s carnival of contrariness. At
the age of twenty-two he read Jack Kerouac's *On the Road*
and bolted out of some perfectly sane place such as Tucson,
Arizona, to head off to North Beach in San Francisco in order
to find the book's hero, Dean Moriarty. It was not until he got

to North Beach with all of his mortal possessions stuffed into the back of a station wagon that he discovered that Moriarty was a fictional name and that the real name of the individual in question was Neal Cassady. This fact did not demoralize him, however. He simply set out in quest of the man called Cassady and found him. Soon Lish himself became a character in the last days of the Beat movement and the early days of the Psychedelic movement. From his cottage in a lunatic stretch of heliotrope tangles known as Burlingame, which was the bohemian slum of Hillsborough, which is a mink ranch outside of San Francisco, he managed to inflame the literary egos of both groups by founding a magazine called *Genesis West*. Lish has now come to New York to turn his bizarre energies loose on this whining, wornout city.

We are about to witness the kind of dumb luck that watches over people like Lish and his *Esquire* colleagues as they pursue their perverse whims. On the one hand, as I say, I might seem like the worst possible choice to introduce a collection of contemporary fiction. But on the other hand—it is just their luck that I could also turn out to be the best possible choice! The fact is that I feel aloof enough from current fiction to be perhaps the sort of person best suited for analyzing it. Who else would be capable of providing a primer, in a brief space, that will enable a reader to appreciate the strange things that are going on in this volume? Certainly not Gordon Lish; he be*lieves* in the work herein!

Now, I must extend to my hosts one morsel of praise, if that is what it is. Under Lish's tutelage *Esquire* has become the magazine that serious short-story writers in America are most eager to be published in. Therefore, it is not stretching it too far to call the stories in this book the pick of the current lot. "Serious writer," in this context, is really a status term. It refers to those writers who are most concerned about advancing the state of the art. They are the writers people in the literary fraternity are usually talking about when a phrase such as "current literature" comes up in a serious fashion. These writers tend to favor *Esquire* partly, no doubt, because it is one of the few remaining magazines that pay well for short stories, but also because *Esquire* delivers the largest available audience that may still be considered inside the fraternity.

I should explain the use of the word fraternity. The rules of the game in modern fiction changed decisively during the 1960s. In that brief interval the American short story moved from the *vulgar* stage to the *poetic* stage, in terms of cultural evolution, and the abruptness of the transition all but cost it its life. Barely twenty years ago the short story was still spoken of as *the* great American literary form. With the exception of the work of a few exotic figures such as Poe and James Branch Cabell, this great American form was understood to be a particular type of short story: the realistic story, the slice of life, often with a regional flavor, capturing some facet of the sprawling continent, as it was still known. Twenty years ago the short story was still a major form of popular entertainment, via national magazines. Whatever else they might aspire to, serious short-story writers usually also had it in mind to entertain, delight, dazzle or move the reading public. Keep 'em dancing!

The picture began to change during the 1950s, and in the 1960s, as I say, the change was very swift. If the public, including what had been known as the reading public, wanted stories with plot, action, and realistic detail, they began turning to film for it, particularly movies and adventure series shown on television. In the 1960s a stranger thing happened. Journalists began mastering the same techniques of social realism that American short-story writers had depended on for so long. They began using them in quite sophisticated ways, in fact—and without ducking behind the screen of fiction. This was the movement or, better said, the development known as the New Journalism. These two forces—film and the New Journalism—would have probably been enough by themselves to deflect serious fiction writers onto a new course, much the same way that the rise of photography helped turn painters and sculptors against representationalism after the turn of the century.

As it happened, a third force hit the American literary scene at the same time: European formalism. European intellectuals such as José Ortega y Gasset, T. S. Eliot, and H. G. Wells had been talking about the "death" of realistic fiction as long ago as the 1920s, some thirty years before the term "death of the novel" became current in the United States. After Dickens, Balzac, Tolstoy, Dostoyevsky, James, Proust, and Joyce—what was there left to do with realistic fiction? This attitude, of course, put the emphasis on new forms. "Make it new!" as Ezra Pound had said, reflecting a spirit that was running through all the arts in France. Formalism made some headway among literary people in the United States during the 1920s—it was already obvious, for example, in Edmund Wilson's theories—but then came the Depression. The Depression focused American writers so sharply on social issues that the 1930s became, instead, the great period of social realism in American literature.

In fact, so powerful was the realistic movement that American literature rose to its highest international standing ever during the 1930s and 1940s. Yet during the 1950s and 1960s formalism finally triumphed, particularly among young writers. Writers now tend to get their start in the universities, and in the universities European influences, such as the so-called literature of the absurd, have proved irresistible. The favorite models are no longer Hemingway, Dos Passos, Fitzgerald, Faulkner, Thomas Wolfe and Sherwood Anderson—but Kafka, Beckett, Hesse, Pinter, and, more recently, Evgeny Zamyatin, as well as figures like Burroughs and Borges and the younger writers, Barthelme and Pynchon.

The upshot has been a type of short story that exhibits all the daring—and all the difficulties—of formalism. By the very nature of his task, the formalist is no longer writing for a vague "public." He is not out to entertain or arrest attention in the usual way. He is writing for a fraternity—a fraternity not merely of other writers but also of those readers who are sophisticated enough to appreciate form, technique, and the state of the art, who are able to read new work against the background of what has already been tried.

This has led to what I call the *poetic* stage in the American short story. The short story is now evolving a system of poetics, or formal conventions, after the manner of the classical conventions that English poets—and English readers—observed in the eighteenth century.

The ideal-typical story in this anthology—and, therefore, an excellent case study for the understanding of current fiction—is Raymond Kennedy's "Room Temperature," which, I must confess, I found engaging and amusing in an odd manner. "Curiously strong," as it says on the tin box that Altoid Peppermints come in.

The story concerns a man named Jack who is living as a Hermit in a shack in the Woods in the dead of winter without plumbing, electricity, or any other of the apparatus of modern civilization. He is evidently happy to be removed from society, but we are told Nothing of his Background. No Place Name is provided, either. Jack is possessed by a Nameless Dread. "I got the heebie-jeebies," he says. Soon an Inexplicable Visitor shows up, a man named Dick who has been beaten up in the city and dumped out here in the snow with no clothes on except for one shoe. Not the least bit dismayed by the way they stomped him in the city, Dick wants to return as soon as possible.

Hermit Jack has just saved Dick from freezing to death, but Dick has in Inexplicable Attitude toward him. He orders Jack about his own shack and wants him to return with him, evidently as a servant. Hermit Jack doesn't want to, but he finds himself trailing along behind Dick out into the snowy wastes.

The extreme cold is too much for Hermit Jack, and he slumps into the snow and begins to Freeze to Death . . . as Dick heads on back to civilization without so much as offering him a warm good-by. As the story ends, Jack is dying and Dick is long gone and doing fine.

These elements—the Hermit or Isolated Character, the Woods (or the Sea or Desert), the Nameless Dread, No Background, No Place Name, Inexplicable Visitor, Inexplicable Attitude, Inexplicable Force, Frozen Death (or Paralysis)—plus an atmosphere of futility, meaninglessness, or imminent disaster—these elements recur continually in current fiction. They make up part of the new poetic. Even the most minor of these conventions tend to be observed, often in curious ways. For example, No Place Name. Even where the geographic location is an obvious and essential part of the story, the writer may not be able to bring himself to name it. Bruce Jay Friedman's story about the cocaine scene, "Lady" (the outstanding story in this book, in my opinion), is obviously set in New York City. I myself could supply the names of the New York restaurants in the piece, but Friedman can't bring himself to name the city, much less the joints inside it—so powerful is the new convention of No Place Name. David Huddle's "The Interrogation" is obviously set in Vietnam, but he is not going to be so gauche as to mention it. Likewise with Thomas Bontly's "Eight Meetings." The scene is San Francisco down to the bone, but Bontly is not going to ruin his best shot by saying so. The fascinating thing, as we shall see in a moment, is the reason why such a convention is observed.

Other conventions of the new poetic are far more restricting, and the fact that so many of these writers can observe them and still engage the reader's interest and sense of mystery is the greatest tribute you can pay to their talent. For example, many stories in this book, in addition to Raymond Kennedy's "Room Temperature," feature characters in a state of catatonic solitude, physically or psychologically paralyzed, filled with The Nameless Dread . . . "I lie here sick, upstairs, in the afternoon watching the shadows of tree limbs move silently across my yellow ceiling" (Michael Rogers, "A Great Feeling") . . . "There are only the two of us, the child and me. I sleep alone. Jace is gone" (Joy Williams, "Shorelines") . . . "Moldenke lived the hainted life. As a child he was kept in a crumbled brick of a house" (David Ohle, "Some Moldenke") . . . "He drops his arms to his side in a gesture of despair, backs up against the nearest wall, crosses his legs and pleads in a whisper: 'But where? Go on, tell me where?' For, look, he is craving solitude . . . Utter, profound solitude. There he will be able to scrape together whatever is falling apart" . . . This last is from A. B. Yehoshua's "Facing the Forests." The new conventions are so strong that Yehoshua's story is like Kennedy's "Room Temperature," point for point, like two versions of the same Kabuki play . . . the man alone in the woods, fleeing one nameless dread, fearing a new one, confronting inexplicable visitors and forces.

The feeling that there is no hope, and, worse, no point, that the world is coming to an end, the game is up, the darkness is rolling in—a feeling of nihilism, in short—runs throughout the book . . . "We do not wait for anything" . . . "Everything tastes like chicken" . . . "The world is all pointless accident" . . . "What is there left to write about?" I especially like "Everything tastes like chicken." Modern times!

As likely as not, however, the nihilism is put across in flashes of great good humor, intentionally absurd, with manic cackles . . . all of it heightened by certain stylistic devices that also form part of the poetic of these writers. Often they go for antique or overgenteel language, creating an unaccountably old-fashioned atmosphere . . . " 'Pray what brings you here when, as you heard, the evenings are closed?' " (James Purdy, "I Am Elijah Thrush") . . . " 'Dark chasms!' I scream from the cliff edge, 'seize me! Seize me to your foul Black bowels and crush my bones!'" (John Gardner, "The Song of Grendel") . . . Sexual activity is frequently referred to in the most delicate Victorian euphemisms . . . "Sometimes I wake in the night and realize that I have called upon my body" (Joy Williams, referring to masturbation) . . . "give herself readily and often" (William Harrison, "Eating It") . . . "I wondered if she had given herself to Scott" (Thomas Bontly) . . .

Many of the writers avoid dialogue as much as possible. Some, such as Borges, are not very comfortable with dialogue to begin with. Others, like Friedman, have been good at it in the past but now hold it down, in keeping with the new rules. Still others write it in short, flat sentences, quite purposely avoiding any of the accents, class mannerisms, or repetitive patterns that would give it a specific, realistic flavor. They often use the same short, flat sentences in narration. At times this can create the impression that some weird and possibly uncontrollable emotion is boiling beneath the surface, ready to explode through the prose at any moment, particularly in a story such as Jerry Bumpus' "In Utica": "I would list their names here, but it is better that such particularities remain unrecorded. Five of them were involved in the plot—and one or two others. Time will disclose them: *traitors*."

Many of the writers construct short sentences into short paragraphs and then organize the short paragraphs into short "crots," which are sections of type separated by white space. On the page they look almost like stanzas of poetry. As each crot breaks off, it tends to make one's mind search for some point that must have just been made—*presque vu!*—almost seen! In the hands of a writer who really understands the device, it will have you making crazy leaps of logic, leaps you never dreamed of before. The undisputed Crot King is Richard Brautigan, as in "The Lost Chapters of *Trout Fishing in America*," printed herein. Brautigan is so good at it that his imitators have become as numerous as the shad (and some have found their way into this book).

So—to sum up—here we have a form of short story in which the characters are not tied to history, geography, nationality, or political subdivisions. They often live in elemental surroundings, such as forest, sea, swamp, or desert. They speak, if they speak at all, in a language that tells you nothing about class, regional or ethnic status. Their actions are often described in archaic diction. They respond to inexplicable abstract forces and are often capable of fantastic physical feats, such as devouring houses and cities (as in "Eating It"), all of which causes the reader to ransack the material for hidden and higher allegorical meanings. What are such stratagems typical of? Why . . . fables and myths, parables and legends. And there you have it!

I think that the mental process the writers of the new poetic have gone through runs as follows: "The great tradition of realism has been usurped by film and the New Journalism, with which I cannot compete. Besides, realism has been *done;* it's finished. But how can I abandon realism and all of its extraordinary power and yet transcend it? Why, by returning to a form that goes back to the very roots of literature itself, a pure and crystalline form, a form that does not depend on the soon outdated details of everyday life for its effects, a form that communicates directly with the consciousness of man, a form that is as timeless as language itself, as sovereign as the very power of imagination!—fable! legend! parable! myth!"

So far, so good . . . Spirits rise all around . . . One of the Neo-Fabulists, Mark J. Mirsky, writes a manifesto for his new publication *Fiction,* and he says, "We simply cannot believe that people have tired of stories, that the ear of America has atrophied permanently and is now deaf to myth, fable, puzzle, paradox" . . . "In the mythos," he goes on, quoting Thoreau, "a superhuman intelligence uses the unconscious thoughts of men as its hieroglyphics to address men unborn." Splendid! All that's left is to sit down and get to it!

Some of the Neo-Fabulists get right to it, indeed. They write directly in the form and rhythms of the fable, the fairy tale, on the old epic histories: John Barth ("Dunyazadiad"), Borges, John Gardner, James Purdy, James Reinbold ("Family Portrait"), Harrison, Alan V. Hewat, and Gabriel García Márquez. The rest pay homage to Neo-Fabulism, if only by observing such conventions as No Background, No Place Name, No Dialogue, and the Inexplicables.

There have been certain peculiarly modern problems with the Neo-Fable, however. In the past, myths, fables, legends, and parables have generally had a fairly obvious moral. They have expressed broad religious, cultural or national values, the higher emotions, the grander sentiments. But one of the assumptions of intellectual life in the West today is that these great societal codes are done for, too, that they are as spent and exhausted as literary realism. The upshot has been the nihilism that we have already seen. One of the all but stupefying problems that these writers have taken on is the task of writing moral tales with no moral. Hence the overriding emotional tone of these stories, the atmosphere of nameless dread . . . the Cosmic Anxiety . . . the Despair with a Grin On . . .

In that light it is easy to see why the original master of the fable of Cosmic Anxiety, Kafka, has been such a favorite model of young writers today. If anything, he has been too much of a favorite. The use of characters with Kafkaesque names such as H., V., and T. (but never C., D., and E., for some reason) creates no cosmic twitch any more. The bottom has fallen out of the device. Perhaps that is why some young writers in the Kafka tradition, such as Jerry Bumpus in "In Utica," seem to be turning more toward such newly discovered models as the old Russian symbolist, Evgeny Zamyatin.

But even these great infusions of Nihilism and Cosmic Anxiety—and there was never a more overpowering nihilist than Zamyatin in *We*—need not make anyone fear for the moral strength of the new set of American writers. Nihilism and Cosmic Anxiety are, after all, accepted literary conventions today, and conventions in literature are like conventions anywhere else: they are marks of grace and propriety, not wounds of the soul. Between the lines of this book, I am happy to report, I do not detect the slightest shred of real despair. I detect something buoyant and fun-loving, instead. I detect a group of fairly young writers, in good animal health, with high ambitions and cheery dispositions, people who have kept up their credit ratings and who buy their pillow shams at main-stem department stores and head for the French wine rack in the back of the liquor store and maintain good spirits and faith in the future and who vote even in the primary . . . who have enough faith, certainly, to tackle this very difficult form, the Neo-Fable, and to play the game according to the rules, new as they may be, observing the poetic, no matter how restricting it may be, summoning up the virtuosity to manipulate the new conventions as subtly as the most decorous sonneteer, and bringing, as ever, the rich and traditional glow of culture to those readers who are truly literate and sophisticated enough to belong to the noble fraternity.

For who, finally, is excluded? No one! Thanks to the short lesson now concluded, anyone who has read this far may consider himself qualified, certified, and licensed to join—even to take the vow. . . .

THE SECRET LIFE
OF OUR TIMES:
NEW FICTION
FROM *ESQUIRE*

LADY

Bruce Jay Friedman

hen it was good, it was of a smooth con-
sistency and white as Christmas snow. If
Harry Towns had a slim silver-foil packet
of it against his thigh—which he did two or
three nights a week—he felt rich and fortified,
almost as though he were carrying a gun. It
was called coke, too, never cocaine. A dealer,
one side of whose face was terrific, the other
collapsed, like a bad cake, had told him it was
known as "lady." That tickled Harry Towns
and he was dying to call it that, but he was
waiting for the right time. The nickname had to do with the fact
that ladies, once they took a taste of the drug, instantly became
coke lovers and could not get enough of it. Also, they never
quite got the hang of how expensive it was and were known to
toss it around carelessly, scattering gusts of it in the carpeting.
Even though one side of his face was collapsed, the dealer
claimed there were half-a-dozen girls who hung around him
and slept with him so they could have a shot at his coke. Harry
Towns could not claim to have enslaved groups of women with
the drug, but it did help him along with one outrageously young
girl who stayed over with him an entire night. She didn't sleep
with him, but just getting her to stay over was erotic and something of an accomplishment. Wearing blue jeans and nailed to
him by the sharp bones of her behind, she sat on his lap while he

3

fed her tastes of it all night long. She lapped it up like a kitten and in the morning he drove her to her high-school math class. He wasn't sure if he was proud of this exploit—she was about the same age as his son—but he didn't worry about it much either.

If someone asked Harry Towns to describe the effects of coke, he would say it was subtle, and leave it at that. He could remember the precise moment he had first smelled and then tried grass—a party, a girl in a raincoat whose long hair literally brushed the floor, some Bossa Nova music that was in vogue at the time, a feeling he wanted to be rid of both his wife and the tweed suit he was wearing—but he could not for the life of him figure out when coke had come into the picture. It had to do with two friends in the beginning, and he was sure now that the running around and hunting it down was just as important as the drug itself. They would spend a long time at a bar waiting for someone to show up with a spoon, one of them leaping up at regular intervals to make a call and see if their man was on his way. It was exciting and it kept them together. While they were waiting, they would tell each other stories about coke they had either heard about or tried personally, coke that was like a blow on the head, coke that came untouched from the drug companies, coke so strong it was used in cataract operations. Or they would tell of rich guys who gave parties and kept flowerpots full of it for the guests to dip into at will. It was a little like sitting around and talking about great baseball catches. Sometimes they wondered about how long you could keep at it before it began working on your brain. Even though they kidded about winding up years later in the back streets of Marseilles with their noses chewed away—it was a serious worry. Freud had supposedly been an addict and this buoyed them up a bit. Also, Towns had once run into a fellow who lived in Venezuela most of the year and had a gold ring in his ear. Rumor had it that he was a jungle fag. Leaning across to Towns one night, he had tapped

4

his right nostril, saying, "This one's thirty-six years old." The fellow was a bit bleary-eyed, but otherwise seemed in good health; the disclosure was comforting to Towns although he wondered why the fellow said nothing about his left nostril.

Once their contact arrived, they would each get up some money, not paying too much attention to who paid the most. Then they would go into the bathroom, secure the door and lovingly help one another to take snorts from the little packet. One of Towns' friends was a tall stylish fellow who was terrific at wearing clothes, somehow getting the most threadbare of jackets to look elegant. It was probably his disdainful attitude that brought off the old jackets. The other friend was a film cutter with a large menacing neck and a background in sports that could not quite be pinned down. They were casual about dividing up the drug, with no thought to anyone's being short-changed, although later on the stylish fellow would be accused of having a vacuum cleaner for a nose. But it was a sort of good-natured accusation. On each occasion, Towns' debonair friend could be counted on to introduce a new technique for getting at the coke, putting some in a little canal between two fingers, getting a dab of it at the end of a penknife, and on one occasion producing a tiny, carved monkey's paw, perfectly designed to hold a little simian scoopful. Towns' favorite approach was the penknife one. The white crystals, iced and sparkling, piled up on the edge of the blade, struck him as being dangerously beautiful. But Towns felt with some comfort that the varied techniques placed his friend further along the road to serious addiction than he was; Towns made do with whatever was on hand, usually the edge of a book of matches, folded in half. The film cutter had a massive family, and on occasion they would tease him about his children having to eat hot dogs because of his expensive coke habit. One night, out of nowhere, he gave them both a look and they abandoned that particular needle. He had been ill recently, and they had heard that four hospital attendants had been unable to hold him down and give him an injection.

After they had taken their snorts, they would each fall back against the wall of the john and let the magic drip through them, saying things like "Oh, brother," and "This has got to be the best." Towns usually capped off the dreamily appreciative remarks by saying, "I'll always have to have this." The stocky film cutter admitted one night that if it came to choosing between the drug and a beautiful girl, he would have to go with the coke. It seemed to be a painful admission for him to make, so Towns and the debonair fellow quickly assured him they both felt exactly the same way. Actually, Towns didn't see why one had to cancel out the other. He had heard that lovers would receive the world's most erotic sensation by putting dabs of coke on their genitals and then swiping it off. He tried this one night with a stewardess from an obscure and thinly publicized airline and found it all right, but nothing to write home about. As far as he could see, it was just a tricky way to get at the coke.

They would take about two tastes apiece and then bounce back into the bar with sly grins and the brisk little nose sniffs that distinguished the experienced coke user. Even if they scattered and sat with different people, the drug held them bound together in a ring. Later, when the evening took a dip, one of them would give a sign and they would return to the john to finish off the packet.

They kept their circle tightly closed, even though at least one fellow was dying to get into it. He was a writer who stood careful guard over his work and on more than one occasion had said, "I'll be damned if I'm going to let anyone monkey around with my prose." He also spoke of having "boffed" a great many girls. Towns took exception to that word "boffed" and so did his friends. They doubted that he had really done that much "boffing" and they didn't care that much for his prose either. So even though the fellow knew what they were doing in the john and gave them hungry, poignant looks, they would not let him into the group.

Sometimes, instead of waiting around at the bar, they would make forays into the night to round up some of the drug. They spent a lot of time waiting outside basement apartments in Chinatown, checking over their shoulders for the police. Towns owned the car and he had plenty of dents in the side to prove it. Somehow, tranquil and frozen by the drug, Towns felt that a little sideswipe here and there didn't matter much, but the dents were piling up and the car was pretty battered. The dapper, arrogant fellow sat in the back and seemed annoyed at having to ride around in such a disreputable-looking vehicle. He lived with his mother, who supposedly did all his driving for him, after first setting him up beside her with blankets over his knees for warmth. Towns decided to have all the car dents fixed in one swipe and then start over.

Leaving his friends behind one night, Towns went on a drug-hunting foray with a hooker who had seemed beautiful in the saloon light, but turned out to be a heavy user of facial creams. He didn't object to a girl using creams in private, but felt she had an obligation to take them off when she was out and around. She said she knew of some great stuff just over the bridge in Brooklyn. Towns drove and drove and when he asked her if they were there yet, she said it was just a little bit farther. He felt he might as well be driving to Chicago. When they finally got the coke, she described herself, with some pride, as a "nose freak"—as though Towns would be thrilled to hear this. Then she got rid of most of the coke in the car, beneath a streetlamp, leaving Towns with just a few grains. He felt it would be the right thing on his part to smack her around a little for her behavior, but he was worried about friends of hers running out of a nearby building with kitchen knives. So he let it pass. Besides, there had been something attractively illicit about snorting the drug with a heavily creamed hooker deep in the bowels of

7

Brooklyn. And it was strong, too, even if there wasn't much of it. He would have something to say to his friends about "Brooklyn coke" and how it could tear your head off if you didn't watch it. So instead of smacking her around, he took her on a long, silent drive back to Manhattan where he let her out.

In the beginning, Towns and his friends would fool themselves into thinking that the nighttime get-togethers were for the purpose of having some dinner. Midway through a Chinese meal, one of them would casually ask if the others felt like going after some coke. But after a while, they dropped all pretense, skipping the dinners and diving right into the business of getting at the drug. Towns soon discovered that he was throwing over entire evenings to phone calls, long waits, nervous foot-tapping and great outbursts of relief when their man finally showed up with the prize. He wasn't sure if he felt the tension legitimately or if he was just playing at it. There weren't too many things in life he liked to do more than once in exactly the same way and he figured out that he was having the same kind of evening over and over. So one night he simply stopped, probably too cruelly and abruptly, the way he stopped most things. He decided to get a whole bunch of coke and have it just for himself. He invited the dealer with the collapsing face up to his apartment and told him to bring along an entire ounce. It was a very exciting and significant call for him to make, and he rated it right up there with such decisions as moving out on his wife and signing up for a preposterously expensive apartment. Both had worked out. As soon as he called the dealer, he became afraid of some vague unnameable violence. His way of handling it was to strip down to his waist and greet the dealer bare-chested. Towns had a strong body and this maneuver would indicate that he was loose and could take care of things, even stripped down that way and obviously having no weapons concealed in the folds of his clothing. The dealer didn't notice any of this. He swept right in and began to carry on about some new moistureproof bottles he had found for the coke. If you closed them after snorts, no moisture would get in and the drug would not cake up. He was terribly proud of the bottles and told Towns to hang on to them; when they were empty, he would come by with refills. After he had left, Towns sunk back on a leather chair and didn't even try any of the coke. He just lit a cigar and richly enjoyed having bottles of it up there on the thirtieth floor with him. The idea fell into his head that if you had a lot of it, you were relieved of the pressure of always having to get it and as a result you didn't take that much. But he got onto himself in a second and knew it wasn't going to work out that way. He'd take more. The next time he saw his friends they tried to start up the coke-hunting apparatus and he excused himself by saying, "I don't think I'm in the mood for any tonight." He felt very sorry for them; they would have to go to all that trouble for just a little packet of it that would be sniffed up in an evening. Somehow they sensed he had a whole bunch of coke of his own and were snappish with him, but they stopped that quickly because they weren't that way. The stylish fellow's eyes began darting all over the place and Towns sensed he was making plans to lay in a giant supply of his own. He would be all right. But the film cutter's head drooped and when he was alone with Towns he admitted for the first time that even though he had a massive number of kids, he hated his wife. The evenings of hunting down coke had been terribly important to him. He said he always knew Towns was afraid to get close to people and amazingly he started to cry for a few seconds. At that moment, Towns would have taken him up to the apartment and given him half of the huge amount of coke. It was a close call, and the next day he was thrilled that he hadn't. As to Towns' inability to stay close to people, the fellow probably had him dead to rights. He had gone with a girl for three years and then brutally chopped off the affair, practically overnight. When it came to girls, if there was going to be any chopping off, he wanted to be the one to do it. Once it had been the other way. He saw himself as a man who had gotten off to a shaky start, then patched himself together and now had tough scar tissue at the seams. Chopping . . . getting chopped off . . . what he hoped for in life was to work his way back to some middle path.

Meanwhile, he had all that coke and a whole new style of evening set up. He would spread some of the drug on a dark surface, a pretzel box, as a matter of fact, snort some, rub a little on his gums and then take a long time getting dressed, returning from time to time to the pretzel box for additional sniffs. He had some special phonograph records, too, that seemed to go with the coke, ones that he rarely changed. They seemed to deepen the effects of the drug; cigars helped to string out the sensation, too, and he felt he was the only one who knew this. When he was ready to go out, he would sprinkle some in tinfoil and then try to figure out the best pocket to put it in, one that he wouldn't forget and the least likely one for a federal agent to suddenly thrust his hand into and nail him on the spot. He would be able to return to the tinfoil for little tastes throughout the night and there would be enough in there, too, for friends he might run across. Doling out coke from the thin little packet would make him seem generous and at the same time no one had to know about the moistureproof bottles lined up and waiting for him back at his apartment.

It was amazing how little he worried about the illegality of what he was doing. Only once did this come home to him with any force. He was in a cocktail lounge in Vegas with two girls and for the life of him he couldn't figure out if they were hookers. He was only fair at determining things like that. Sometimes his actions were sudden and dramatic, and on this occasion he reached out and stuck a fingerful of coke in each of their mouths, as if this would smoke them out and tell him if they were joy dolls. They both sucked on the fingers and loved what was happening, but Towns looked around the lounge and became aware of a number of men with white socks, shaved necks and even expressions who appeared not to approve of his having traipsed in with more than one girl. They probably didn't go for his beard much, either. At least that's the impression he got. All of this shook him up. What if one of the girls suddenly hollered out, "He shoved coke in my mouth." Towns had a lawyer who was terrific in the civil-liberties department, but he wasn't sure he could count on the fellow dashing out to Nevada on his behalf. He told the girls to wait for him, he had a lucky roulette hunch, and then he sneaked out of the casino and went to another one.

He didn't feel the danger much in the city, though. Rich is the only word to describe how he felt. When he started out of his apartment, high and immunized, he felt that nothing great had to happen. He didn't even have to wind up with a girl. The way he figured it, enough that was great had happened already. Right around the pretzel box. He knew there must be a dark side to all this, but he would worry about that later.

One of the smart things he did was not to use his car. He had had enough of the sideswipes. In his new routine, going about on foot and using cabs, he would hit a few warm-up places where he knew some people and felt cozy and secure; than he would head for a drugged and adventurous bar that could always be counted on for packs of long-haired girls, each of whom for some reason had just left her "old man" or walked out on a waitressing job that very day. In the drugged atmosphere of this bar, it was possible to slip into these packs of girls and on occasion to pick one off. All of a sudden he would be talking to one and, if her eyes looked right, asking if she would like to have a little coke in the john. If she said yes, he knew the battle was over and he was going to wind up in bed with her. The two went together. In his way, he was using the coke to push people around. One night, at one of the early bars, he stood next to two black men; one liked him, the other, whose glasses gave him the look of an abstract educational puzzle, didn't. He said that even though Towns was bigger than he was, he was positive he could take him outside and beat the shit out of him. Unlike liquor, the coke always had a defusing effect on Towns, who simply shrugged and said, "No way." Then, perhaps to teach the puzzle man a lesson, he invited the other black man into the john for some coke. They took some together and then the angry abstracted fellow appeared. Towns hesitated long enough to make his point and then gave him some, too. He put his arm around Towns and hugged him and Towns felt a little sad about how easy it had been to peel away his anger. Back at the bar, the fellow got angry again and finally walked out in what seemed to be a flash of hot abstract lightning. His renewed fury made Towns feel a little easier. But you certainly could do things with that coke. One night, when Towns had failed to pry any of the girls loose from her pack, he went looking for a hooker and found a terrific one on the street who looked like a high-school cheerleader. She had a tough style and needled him, saying she had balled every guy in the city, so why not him. At one time this would have been a threat to Harry Towns, but it wasn't now. What did all those other guys have to do with him? She said they could go upstairs to a tragic-looking little hotel across the street and Towns said no deal, he wanted to take her to his place. She said there was no way on earth she would go to a stranger's apartment, and then he mentioned the coke. "Jesus, do you really have some?" she wanted to know. "Pounds of it," he said, "at my place." It was amazing. As tough and street-wise as she was, she jumped in a cab with him and off they went. And all he had done was *say* he had the coke. It was a weapon, all right.

Sometimes, when he got finessed into drinking a lot, the liquor and drug combination left him shaky the next day. He had to make sure to let entire days go by without using any of the drug. On the off days, it would be like having a terrific date to look forward to. One night, a fellow with a belt full of tools walked up to Towns and said that if he ever saw him with his wife again, he would kill him in an alley. "We can do it now," said the fellow with surprising politeness, "or at a time of your convenience." Towns could not pinpoint the wife in question, but he had a pretty good inkling of who she was. He felt weak and anesthetized, his limbs sluggish, caught in heavy syrup. He mumbled something and hoped the fellow would not use the tools on him. So it wasn't all roses. He had to watch that sort of thing. Then, too, the moistureproof bottles emptied out after a while and he had to get them filled up again. He made an appointment to go to the dealer's apartment this time, and when he got there, the fellow snatched up his money and sat him down next to a young blonde carhop-style girl who looked as though she had just given up thumb-sucking. Then he slid a huge switchblade knife with a capsule of amyl nitrate on it between them, and excused himself, saying he had to get the coke which was a few blocks away. Towns knew about the capsule; it was for cracking open and sniffing. You got a quick high-voltage sexual rush out of it. He had graduated from it sometime back and felt it was small potatoes next to coke. But what about having it on a switchblade knife with a yellow-haired teen-ager on the other side. It reminded Towns of a religious ceremony in which a hotly peppered herb was placed beside something delicious to remind worshipers of the hard and easy times of their forebears. But this seemed to be a kind of drug ritual, and he couldn't decide what his next move was supposed to be. Was he supposed to make a quick grab for the capsule and crack it open before she got at him with the switchblade? He decided to stick to light conversation. A bit later, Towns excused himself to go to the john and by mistake opened the door of a closet; rifles and handguns came pouring out on him in a great metallic shower— also a few bullwhips. "Look what you did," said the girl, coming over in a pout, as though the cat had spilled some milk. Towns helped her to gather up the weapons; it seemed important to get them back in before the dealer returned. He showed up half an hour later, telling Towns that he was in great luck because he had come up with some pure coke rocks, much more lethal than anything Towns had been involved with before. It came in around once a year, something like soft-shell crabs; rich Peruvians sat around on their ranches and shaved slivers of it from a huge rock, inhaling these slivers for weeks on end and getting heart trouble in their thirties. But Towns wasn't to worry about this, since he would only be getting this one shipment and maybe never get a shot at it again. Another thing that wasn't to bother Towns was that the moistureproof bottles would not be filled to the top this time. That was because the Peruvian coke rocks were so pure. Towns wasn't so sure about this. "Oh well," said the dealer, disdainfully, "if you want me to fluff them up." Towns thought of the weapons closet and decided to pass on this and get going. In a kind of furious between-the-acts blur of activity, the dealer and his girl whipped out armloads of equipment, and before Towns could make a move toward the door, the dealer had wound a rubber coil around his arm and was straining to make a vein pop up. Meanwhile, the girl was melting down a Peruvian rock, probably one that belonged to Towns, in a tiny pan. They were like a crack surgical team. So this was the famous shooting-up routine! Towns had never seen it go on and had always been curious about it. The dealer, one side of his face not only collapsing but running down, like oil on a canvas, plunged a hypodermic into his vein and went into a series of ecstatic shivers, at the same time keeping up a surprisingly sober running commentary for Towns: "What's happening is that I'm getting a rush twenty times more powerful than you get taking it up through your nose. This is really something. The only trouble is, it will stop in about five minutes and I'll have to do it again. I've gotten so I can do it ten, twenty times, all through the night." None of this was appealing to Towns. He realized that the tableau was for his benefit, to hook him into the team so that he would wind up melting rocks with them in the tiny frying pan. It wasn't going to happen. There were certain things that he could say for sure he wasn't ever going to do—like sky-diving—and this was one of them. When the dealer finished up his shivers, it was time for the girl to take her turn; that's what Towns wanted to be on hand to see. She stuck some equipment under her arm and said she was going off to do it privately. Towns felt around in his bottle and pulled out a good-sized rock, saying it was hers if he could watch her in action. "No way," she said, giving him an infuriated look, "that's one thing no one in the world is ever going to see." What she seemed to want to get across was that she had been through a thousand assorted hells but was going to keep this one area stubbornly cordoned off to herself. Towns shrugged good-naturedly as if to say, "Oh well, win some, lose some," but he felt the loss sharply and didn't even wait around to see her when she got back. That wasn't what he wanted. He thanked the shivering fellow for the Peruvian rocks and sauntered outside, deciding to hunt down another arrangement, one with less danger in the air.

He went through quite a few of these dealers. They tended to live in lofts and to have young, sluggish girl friends; each was trying to "get something going" in the record business. The coke, according to them, was just a sideline. After Towns got his coke, he would be asked to listen to one of their tape decks. Not once did he like what he heard, even taking into account that he was not in a musical mood when he made these visits and just wanted to get the coke and get the hell out of there. It was his view that each of these fellows was going to do much better as a coke dealer than in the music business. Towns' favorite dealer was a tall, agreeable fellow who had once worked as a marriage counselor. He had a healing, therapeutic style of selling the coke; after each buy, Towns would flirt with the idea of sticking around for a little counseling, although he never followed through. One day, the fellow announced that in order to kick his own coke habit, which was becoming punishingly expensive, he was making his first visit to London. That struck Towns as being on the naïve side. How could you get away from coke in London? Some far-away island would seem to be more the ticket, but the fellow had his mind made up on the British Isles and there was no stopping him. Towns was convinced they would have him picked off as a user the second he stepped off the plane and be ready and waiting to sell him some.

Dealers brushed in and out of his life, and Towns could not imagine wanting some coke and not being able to come up with it. Yet that would happen on occasion, even though he started out early in the evening trying to drum some up. He had always told himself that all he had to do in that situation was to have a few drinks and he would be fine. But he wasn't that fine. He would sit around at one of his spots and drum his fingers on the bar, uneasy and unhappy. Was he hooked? He had heard that when a famed racketeer was buried, friends of his, for old times' sake, had stuck a few spoons of first-grade coke in there with him, since the racket man had been a user. Once high and dry at four in the morning, Towns actually found himself wondering if it would be possible to dig up the fellow and get at the coke. It all depended on whether it was in the coffin with him or on the topsoil somewhere. Towns wasn't sure of the details. If he knew for sure it was in the topsoil, he might have found a shovel somewhere in the city, driven out to the cemetery and taken a try at it. That's how badly he wanted it sometimes.

One day Towns got the word that his mother had died. It did not come around behind him and hit him on the head, since the death had been going on for a long time and it was just a matter of waiting for the phone call. It had always been his notion that when he got this particular news, he would drive up to a summer resort his mother used to take him to each September and hang out there for a weekend, sitting at the bar, tracing her presence, thinking through the fine times they had spent together. That would be his style of mourning. But now that he had the news, he didn't feel much like doing that. Maybe he would later. Instead, he sat in his apartment, thirty floors over the city, and tried to cry, but he could not drum up any tears. He was sure they would come later, in some oblique way, so he didn't worry too much about it. He knew himself and knew that he only cried when things sneaked up on him. Then he could cry with the best of them.

His mother was going to be put in a temporary coffin while the real one was being set up. And she would be lying in the chapel from six to eight that evening, with the family receiving close friends; the following day she would be buried. It set up a bit of a conflict for Towns. At six o'clock, he also had an appointment to meet Ramos, an old friend who had come in from California the night before. Formerly an advertising man, Ramos had now gone over entirely to an old-West style. Long-faced, sleepy-eyed, he turned up in the city looking as though he had ridden for days through the Funeral Mountains on a burro, seeking cowpoke work. He had taken Towns into the coatroom of the bar at which they met, pulled out a leather pouch that might have contained gold dust, and given Towns a sniff of some of the purest coke he had ever run across. It rocketed back and flicked against a distant section in the back of his head that may never have been touched before. Now Harry Towns had a new story to tell his friends, about Western coke, the wildest and most rambunctious of all. And he wanted that place in the back of his head to be flicked at again. So they made an appointment for six o'clock the following evening to go and get some more. Except that now Towns had to be at the chapel with his dead mother. He wondered, soon after he heard about the loss, if he would keep the appointment with Ramos, and even as he wondered, he knew he would. He didn't even have to turn it over in his mind. After all, it wasn't the funeral. That would make it an entirely different story. It was just a kind of chapel reception and if he turned up half an hour later, it would not be any great crime. And he would have the coke.

Harry Towns was at the midtown bar to meet Ramos at six on the dot, hoping to make a quick score and then hotfoot it over to the chapel. But Ramos loped in some twenty minutes late, squinty-eyed, muttering something about the sun having crossed him up on the time. He had never even heard of the sun when he was in advertising. He sat down, stretched his legs and tried to get Towns into a talk about the essential dignity of man, even in the big city. Towns felt he had to cut him off on that. People were already pouring into the chapel. At the same time, he didn't want to be rude to Ramos and risk blowing the transaction. He told Ramos about his mother, and the man from the West said he understood, no problem, except that he himself did not have the coke. It was just up the street a few blocks at a divorced girl's house. They would just have one drink and get going.

The divorced girl lived in a richly furnished high-rise apartment with authentic animal skins on the floor. Towns had to walk carefully to keep from sticking his feet in their jaws. She had racks of fake bookshelves, too, suspense-novel types that whirled around when you pressed a button and had coke concealed on the other side. He was certain she was going to turn out to be his favorite dealer. Long-legged, freshly divorced, she hugged Ramos, Towns wondering how they knew each other. The animal skins may have been some sort of bridge between them. More likely, they were teammates dating back to Ramos' advertising days. She also seemed interested in Towns, handing him a powder box filled with coke, something he had always dreamed of. He got the idea that this wasn't even the coke he would be buying. It was a kind of guest coke, a getting-ac-quainted supply. An hors d'oeuvre. That's what he called falling into something. But what a time to be falling into it. She told him to dig in, help himself, and they could take care of their business a bit later. The girl had legs that went on and on and wouldn't quit. Why had anyone divorced her? She went over to set up some elaborate stereo equipment and Towns put the powder box on his lap and took a deep snort as instructed.

"Jesus Christ," she said, pressing the palm of one hand to the side of her head, "what in hell are you doing?"

"You told me to dig in," he said.

"Yes, but I didn't know we had a piggy here."

"Don't tell someone to dig in if you don't mean it."

Now Towns really felt foolish. There was no way to proceed from the piggy insult, which bit deep, to buying half an ounce of the drug. So he had blown at least half the chapel service and he wasn't even going to get the coke. He vowed then and there to deal only with the tape-deck boys in their lofts. Ramos tried to smooth things over by telling her, "He's a true man," but she was breathing hard and there seemed no way to calm her down. "What a toke," she said. "I've seen people take tokes, but this one, wow."

"My mother just died," said Towns. As he said it, he knew he was going to regret that remark for a long time if not for the rest of his life. He had once seen a fellow get down on his knees to lick a few grains of coke from the bottom of a urinal. That fellow was a king compared to Towns—using his mother's dead body to get him out of a jam. And it got him out, too. "Oh God," said the girl, putting a comforting arm around Towns' shoulder, "I don't know how to handle death." Towns just couldn't wait any longer. He gave Ramos the money, told him to buy some coke from the girl and he would meet him later, after the chapel service. Then he got into a cab and told the driver to please get him across town as fast as possible. It was an emergency. You could travel only so fast in city traffic, and Towns got it arranged in his mind that it was the cabby's fault he was getting there so late. He arrived at a quarter of eight, with only fifteen minutes left to the service. Some remnants of his family were there, and a few scattered friends. Also his mother, off to one side, in the temporary coffin. Towns' aunt and his older brother were relieved to see him, but they didn't bawl him out. He would always appreciate that. They said they thought he might have been hurt and left it at that. What seemed to concern them the most was the presence of a woman Towns' mother hadn't cared for. They couldn't get over how ironic it was that the disliked woman had turned up at the chapel. The few surviving members of Towns' family were very short and for the hundredth time he wondered how he had gotten to be so tall. He chatted with some neighborhood friends of his mother, keeping a wary eye on the woman she hadn't liked. If Towns hadn't felt so low about showing up late, he might very well have chucked her out of there. A chapel official said the family's time was up. He gave out a few details about the funeral that was coming up the next day. The family filed out, and just as Towns was the last one to arrive, he was the last to leave, stopping for a moment at his mother's temporary coffin. He never should have worried about crying. Once he started, he cried like a sonofabitch. He probably set a chapel record. He cried from the tension, he cried from grief, he cried from the cab ride, from his coke habit, from the piggy insult, from his mother having to be cramped up in a temporary coffin and then shifted over to a real one when it was ready. They had a hard time getting him out of there.

That night, Ramos came by with the coke. Towns didn't weigh it, look at it, measure it. He never did. It seemed like a fat pack and he guessed that the girl had given him a good count because of the death. The main thing is that it was in there. He

gave Ramos some of it, which was the protocol, and told him
he would see him around. "I'll stick with you, man," said Ramos,
but Towns said he would rather be alone. He didn't want people
saying "man" to him and telling him he had "a terrific head."
All of which Ramos was capable of. The coke had a perfumed
scent to it, a little like the fragrance of the divorcée. Had she
rubbed some of it against herself? His guess was she had. He took
a snort of it, got into his bathrobe and put on some Broadway
show music, the kind his mother liked. The music would be the
equivalent of driving up to the old summer resort. But it didn't
work. It didn't go with the coke. During his mother's illness, he
had put her up in his apartment and moved into a hotel, the idea
being that she would get to enjoy the steel and glass and the
view and the doorman service. But she didn't go with the apartment either, and they both knew it. She stayed there a few
weeks, probably for his sake, to ease his mind about not having
sent her away on lavish trips, and then she said she wanted to go
back to her own home. She left without a trace, except for some
sugar packets she had taken from a nearby restaurant and put in
his sugar jar. To give him some extra and free sugar. He wondered if he should go over and take a look at the sugar. He was
positive that it would start him crying again, but he didn't want
to do that just then. He could always look at the sugar. Instead,
he switched on some appropriate coke music, took another snort
of the drug, and stared out at his view of the city, the glassed-in
one that was costing him an arm and a leg each month. His
mother had made a tremendous fuss over this view, but once
again it was for his sake. She had been very ill and wanted to be
in her own apartment. Staying in his had been a last little gift
for him, allowing him to do something for her. He kept the
tinfoil packet of coke open beside him and he knew that he was
going to stay where he was until dawn. He was not a trees-and-
sunset man, but he liked to be around for that precise time when
the night crumbled and the new day got started. He liked to get

ready for that moment by snorting coke, letting the drug drive him a hundred times higher than the thirtieth floor on which he lived. Once or twice, he wondered about the other people who were watching that moment, if there were any. It was probably only a few diplomats and a couple of hookers. Normally, he would take a snort, luxuriate in it and wait for a noticeable dip in his mood before he took the next one. This time he didn't wait for the dips. Before they started, he headed them off with more snorts. He saw now that his goal was to get rid of the entire half ounce before dawn. Never mind about the problem of coming down. He would take a hot bath, some Valium. He'd punch himself in the jaw if necessary, ram his head against the bathroom tile if he had to. The main thing was to have nothing left by the time it was dawn so he could be starting out clean on the day of the funeral. Then, no matter what he was offered, he would turn it down. He didn't care what it was, Brooklyn coke, Western coke, Peruvian coke rocks, coke out of Central Harlem. If someone gave him stuff that came out of an intensive-care unit, coke that had been used for goddamned brain surgery, he would pass it right by. Because the chapel was one thing. But anyone who stuck so much as a grain of that white shit up his nose on the actual *day* of his mother's funeral had to be some new and as yet undiscovered breed of sonofabitch. The lowest.

THE WARRIOR

William Harrison

hen I served in the American Army my trick was crawling by a sentry in the dark of night. No one was ever better at it: inching along, scarcely breathing, rippling a muscle here or shoving off gently there so that my body sometimes passed at an enemy's very feet in the good strong shadows of a moonless watch. I've passed a man so close that he could have turned and stepped on me, in which case, of course, he would never have taken another step. This was my specialty, getting by a man this way, and I did it in Korea and later when I wasn't an American anymore—just one of the world's mercenaries as I am now, in Algiers, the Congo, Biafra, and so on.

Africa, lovely restless continent, is just out that way across the water. This is my home now, this little port, Javea, and if you look out from our hill you can see the beach, Cabo de San Antonio, with the lighthouse, the city and mountain beyond it. Being just across from Africa this way pleases me and lately I've considered going back over with Al Fatah, say, or even the Israelis if they'd give me a good platoon, which they probably wouldn't. Spain is fine, but it reeks of peace now; not that I don't enjoy it with my family here, but before too long I always start contacting old friends in the business or reading the classified sections again, seeing who wants a warrior this season. One job of mine came right out of the London *Telegraph* and another I got out of *France-Soir*. Always in Africa: that old dark continent over there where a good savage is always appreciated.

This is my villa, all paid for, my pool, over there the vineyard and terraced olive grove. We sit in the *naya* in the evenings, my wife Val and I, and drink these good local wines and repeat the old stories; I'm not one of those who can't talk about battles or the things that go on during a good fight. My daughters, Jenny and Kip, sleep just above us in their own rooms. You've seen the antiques in the house, the gardens, the Porsche and Rover, my motorbikes: you know we have a good life here. This is a nice place, better in climate than Southern California, say, where I've lived, or the Riviera—which gets too cold for me in the winter. It's just that I get restless, as I say, and of course it was much better here on the Costa Blanca a few years back before the tourists found us, before the entrepreneurs—there's this queer film festival down on the beach right now—and before the big contractors moved in and started building these cut-rate villas. This part of the hillside twenty years ago was all fruit trees, lovely; that was when I came here, when I was in my twenties, just after Korea and hard as an oak and just a mean kid.

Val sits there in the cool afternoon breeze reading about the film festival in the provincial newspaper. She told me they're having one Fellini, one Mike Nichols, and the rest of the movies are by Frenchmen: Christ, some show. The kids and tourists have been in town for days, sprawling out on the sand down there, eating paella at our beach restaurants. Look at my wife: quiet, that good Spanish profile, still with me. My heart's blood. We have a generation of naked little flower girls now, not a woman among them like my Val.

This is the arsenal, yes, and everything's ready. A solid room: these old tiles make a fine echo when you walk on them. The sound—I've thought about this some—lends a little importance to every movement made in here. These are the automatic weapons, here are the mortars and a few heavier pieces, over there the explosives—some of which, I admit, I confiscated from the local *Guardia Civil.* I sat at this table and filled all these cartridges myself. Everything is sorted out and inspected and I've confiscated a boat, too—I'll tell you about all this later—and I have a motorbike and car waiting in strategic spots. No one suspects a thing. I'm still a man who can slip by in the darkness.

Sit here on the *naya.*

Get us some drinks, okay, Val, baby?

We should have a long talk and I should explain a lot of myself to you, but of course there isn't time for much of that. This domestic life—let me say this much—is great when I come back from assignments. We water-ski, skin dive along the reef, go over to the club for tennis in the late afternoons. But after a few weeks shadows start coming over me and let's face it: there isn't anything here that measures up to crawling by a guard in the darkness or running headlong into an attack. Not that we should get too philosophical, but paradise is a moody place. I get into the glooms, then, and start sitting around my table in the arsenal drinking and reading. Oh sure, you saw all the books inside the house: I'm no brute.

What will really come after nationalism—have you thought about it? As I see it, this tribalism will eventually go away and, no, not because of the United Nations, noble though the effort is. The U.N. is just a referee among the nations, after all, and so basically approves of the spirit of nationalism. No, big business will take over the masses. Men's loyalties in the next century or two, in my view, will shift from France and Pakistan and Brazil to Olivetti, Westinghouse, and Shell Oil. The big corporations are already cutting across borders. And government—think how obvious this is—will become a kind of regulation agency which will determine when the big corporations are cheating and when they're not. Clandestine business—war of sorts, yes—will go on. But men won't finally be as emotional about products and companies—especially if they can change jobs easily, after all—as they are about their homeland. Things will settle down and my sort should eventually become obsolete.

But make no mistake about it, eh: we're not obsolete yet, are we? And war is still a great education in reality—the way things really are. The kids on the beach need to learn that lesson; they nourish a lot of vague hopes, unaware.

Ah, thanks, Val. Sit here with us.

Civilization has been a long breeding process, true, but we aren't all bred and civilized yet, so there's the gap between our hope for ourselves and what really is. The warrior is out of favor nowadays, for instance, because so many people imagine that it's surely time for him to be finished. But that's hardly realistic with new nations still emerging, guerrilla wars, protest movements flaring up. The old warrior should be given his due. Ah, let me tell you, I dream now and then, you know, and shadows come over my sleep, names and faces swimming up inside me: Marathon, Alexandria, Hastings, Lyon. Does any of this make sense? Sometimes I feel that I just got back from, say, Dunkirk—or Okinawa. I've had strange dreams for months and when I wake up—the really curious part is this—I'll know how to work a crossbow or I'll remember a particular coat of mail I've worn with blue ringlets. And I forget my rank—have I just been a captain, a foot soldier?—and once I turned to Val and said, hey, remember how we walked out of the trees at Shiloh and found that road and made it up toward the next town with our wounded, and she gave me this loving look. Val indulges me; we've been together a long time and naturally she knows the humor I've been in lately.

You came here wanting to know what I'm going to do, I realize, and I'm going to tell you. Perform my art: that's all. It's partially for the old shell-shocked ego and self-satisfaction, sure, and you can invent your own explanations—such as, oh well, he never had any sons and this is part of his masculine anxiety and that sort of thing. Whatever, I'm going to show some of my repertoire of moves; the old ballet master will rise up and dance —while you stay up here, naturally, with Val. But it won't be just to demonstrate my skills. My attack will be a lesson in history. If everything goes right—and it will—I'll kill a thousand of the unwary this evening; I'll be identified, of course, and someone reading tomorrow morning's news will decipher some of the meaning of it all.

Some ice? No, my limit's one this afternoon.

Listen to me, where is history? My notion is that the philosophers can never tell us—nor the artists or anyone else. They can only record things static and gone, while the world nowadays powers along at an overwhelming speed. Only speed and power themselves are listened to: things that zoom and explode beyond our immediate comprehension like comets, so that we stop and ask, "Hey, what was that?" All lessons now must be actions: scars that wound the world's face so that it can never quite forget. And there's an irony here you ought to consider: it turns out that I'm one of the great humanitarian instructors, saying, wake up, see that you're still in a twilight of barbarism, be ready! It's a tough truth to take, but valuable—far better for mankind than so much idle wishing about its nature.

Well, you should know. This evening I'll attack the film festival. All those passive onlookers down there on the beach. They're down there pondering their various apocalyptic films, conning themselves with art and sand, imagining they're seeing something important flicker in front of their eyes. They're zombies, those hip children, passing love messages around. It's not that I hate them—I have no particular intolerance for one lifestyle or another—it's just that, oh, I don't flatter myself here either, I'm their instructor. I hope you can glimpse what I mean: time is against them, they don't know where they are, their fantasy is a dream of death.

Look at this view. A few sails out there on the bay this afternoon. I'll hate leaving here, but Val will join me, naturally, and there'll be many more days like this. We may live in Istanbul—I was there once years ago, I forget exactly when.

You'll want to know exactly how it will be. All right, I'll come down from the rocks so that I can sweep the whole beach before me. There should be about a thousand bathers, another thousand gathering inside the canopy to watch that stupid promoter—he calls himself an impresario—unwind his dull films. Weighted down with ammo, I won't move fast—I won't have to. When I open fire, I'll just get some astonished looks. You odd little soldier, they'll be thinking before they die, you're all baggy with packs and weapons and you rattle when you walk and look silly. Their eyes will fill up with hurt then, and I'll just move through them; strangely enough, it will take several minutes before they even start running ahead of my fire. A big Scandinavian girl will be blown right out of her bikini, and if you had the right mind about it the sight would strike you funny: zap, she's undressed, flying off in a little slow-motioned erotica. One brave idiot will come at me with a rubber float after he's wounded; oh, please, don't hit me with that, and I'll cut him in two. A group of rowdies, their motorcycles there beside them in the sand, boys in their marbled T-shirts and girls lying on towels with their halters loosened: I'll empty on them at very close range because they're too cool to move. Almost casually now, I sweep down the beach, walking near the surf where the sand is packed underfoot, spraying my fire into the wall of bodies just ahead. They start to fall over each other now as I step into a sand castle and advance. No time to finish the wounded, but there aren't many of those. Under the canopy just ahead, the crowd begins to stir, but by this time I stop, set up my mortar, and lob a few shells—first just beyond them and then into the tent itself. Human parts everywhere: our beach runs a little red now. As they race toward me in confusion and away from those first volleys, I let go with the remainder of my .50-caliber material. This turns them back again, and now I have the crowd on the run. Heavy ammo mostly gone, I leave weapons and empty cartridge belts and become more mobile. I carry the mortar only a few more quick meters toward the flaming canopy, let fly a few more lobs in the direction of the beach restaurants—a skillet, a Fanta sign, a Cinzano bottle high in the air—

then leave the mortar, too. Our impresario steps out on stage in front of a camera, and I give him the first voice of the burp gun; he and his camera dissolve, film cascading out into a strange and shiny black flower among the ruins. In a hurry, I move out again, calculating my minutes. The local police force—seven white cheerful uniforms, three pistols, four whistles strong— should be arriving in the next five minutes, so I dash toward my screaming crowd once more. Two grenades: they turn like wild horses, stampeding over each other, some of them diving off into the canal where the boats for the hotel are at dock. I burp a few volleys into them, they turn again. With my .45 in hand and a burp gun strung on my shoulder, I start my last run. A Spanish kid with his spear-fishing gun advances on me and with my .45 I amputate his right leg. Spare the brave in heart. Reaching my motorbike with one twilight hour left and work to do, I start up the main road toward the village, cut across a field, join another smaller country road, and hurry toward the charges I've planted. By this time the *Guardia Civil* scurries around, each man inside the armory searching for his rifle, shouting orders at the next man; the captain talks to the police commissioner on the telephone. Great confusion: they speculate on how many men attacked the beach and port and whether or not this is a Communist or Loyalist uprising. Meanwhile I set the fuse on the armory, pausing there at the rear of the building, my motorbike leaning against the white stucco wall. An old man passes on his mule-drawn cart, nodding at me and smiling. Then I move on, two blocks away to the school—which is empty, naturally, but which will entertain the citizens when it, too, goes up. Here I drop the motorbike—some crafty policeman probably spotted me on it as I headed away from the beach— and in an MG which I recently confiscated in Alicante I start driving back to my carnage. Keeping my grenades, the burp gun and my .45, I shuck off the recognizable fatigues which I wore during the beach extravaganza. As I drive slowly along, the concussion of my plastic explosives thuds throughout the valley and mushrooms of grey smoke dot the village. At the port everyone still runs amok. Mothers are crying out names and one of my enemies, a white-frocked policeman with a silver whistle, directs traffic from his usual position beside the fountain in the square. Coasting through the congestion, I honk. Spaniards and tourists move courteously aside. I muse about the town, my Javea: the village up there on the hill was built first away from the sea so that pirates would be discouraged from attacking. Later, in our century, when such precaution wasn't necessary, the town grew down toward the harbor. Incredible. At the port, I pull back the rayon coverlet on my waiting cabin cruiser. All is ready: food, the radio and radar set, enough armament to take on anything at sea. I work leisurely, starting the engines, as off in the distance columns of smoke rise up evenly from the village. Four or five shots ring out and one wonders what they're firing at or who is left to shoot. For a moment then my dreams overtake me and I'm somewhere else; voices of hundreds rise off a plain, the cry of a long charge. Revving up, I cast off and smoothly set forth into the canal. A final gesture now: I deposit my last grenades in the docked cruisers as I pass. One goes up in a ball of pleasant fire, then another, another, and I roar into the bay without one parting shot to protest my exit. From the hillside, secure, Val—and you—can see my departure. Everything goes as planned, and I am adream; names flutter in my thoughts, many names of comrades and victims, and I see a castle on a distant promontory flying a single black flag, the body of a friend—dressed as a legionnaire—swollen in the desert, a smiling Asian boy armed only with a sharp stick.

All this will happen.

Africa, gleaming under starlight now, awaits us. In Cairo later, at the Ding Dong Bazaar, Val will join me and we'll have a drink at a sidewalk table, hold hands, and talk about you and others. I'll eventually be at work again, inching by a man as he sleeps on his rifle at an outpost, scouting a jungle camp, sighting an enemy in my scope, instructing the innocents.

NEIGHBORS

Raymond Carver

ill and Arlene Miller were a happy couple. But now and then they felt they alone among their circle had been passed by somehow, leaving Bill to attend to his bookkeeping duties and Arlene occupied with secretarial chores. They talked about it sometimes, mostly in comparison with the life of their neighbors, Harriet and Jim Stone. It seemed to the Millers that the Stones lived a fuller and brighter life, one very different from their own. The Stones were always going out for dinner, or entertaining at home, or traveling about the country somewhere in connection with Jim's work.

The Stones lived across the hall from the Millers. Jim was a salesman for a machine-parts firm and often managed to combine business with a pleasure trip, and on this occasion the Stones would be away for ten days, first to Cheyenne, then on to St. Louis to visit relatives. In their absence, the Millers would look after the Stones' apartment, feed Kitty, and water the plants.

Bill and Jim shook hands beside the car. Harriet and Arlene held each other by the elbows and kissed lightly on the lips.

"Have fun," Bill said to Harriet.

"We will," said Harriet. "You kids have fun too."

Arlene nodded.

Jim winked at her. " 'Bye, Arlene. Take good care of the old man."

"I will," Arlene said.

"Have fun," Bill said.

"You bet," Jim said, clipping Bill lightly on the arm. "And thanks again, you guys."

The Stones waved as they drove away, and the Millers waved too.

"Well, I wish it was us," Bill said.

"God knows, we could use a vacation," Arlene said. She took his arm and put it around her waist as they climbed the stairs to their apartment.

After dinner Arlene said, "Don't forget. Kitty gets liver flavoring the first night." She stood in the kitchen doorway folding the handmade tablecloth that Harriet had bought for her last year in Santa Fe.

Bill took a deep breath as he entered the Stones' apartment. The air was already heavy and it was always vaguely sweet. The sunburst clock over the television said half-past eight. He remembered when Harriet had come home with the clock, how she crossed the hall to show it to Arlene, cradling the brass case in her arms and talking to it through the tissue paper as if it were an infant.

Kitty rubbed her face against his slippers and then turned onto her side, but jumped up quickly as Bill moved to the kitchen and selected one of the stacked cans from the gleaming drainboard. Leaving the cat to pick at her food, he headed for the bathroom. He looked at himself in the mirror and then closed his eyes and then opened them. He opened the medicine chest. He found a container of pills and read the label: *Harriet Stone. One each day as directed*, and slipped it into his pocket. He went back to the kitchen, drew a pitcher of water and returned to the living room. He finished watering, set the pitcher on the rug, and opened the liquor cabinet. He reached in back for the bottle of

Chivas Regal. He took two drinks from the bottle, wiped his lips on his sleeve and replaced the bottle in the cabinet.

Kitty was on the couch sleeping. He flipped the lights, slowly closing and checking the door. He had the feeling he had left something.

"What kept you?" Arlene said. She sat with her legs turned under her, watching television.

"Nothing. Playing with Kitty," he said, and went over to her and touched her breasts.

"Let's go to bed, honey," he said.

The next day Bill took only ten of the twenty minutes' break allotted for the afternoon, and left at fifteen minutes before five.

He parked the car in the lot just as Arlene hopped down from the bus. He waited until she entered the building, then ran up the stairs to catch her as she stepped out of the elevator.

"Bill! God, you scared me. You're early," she said.

He shrugged. "Nothing to do at work," he said.

She let him use her key to open the door. He looked at the door across the hall before following her inside.

"Let's go to bed," he said.

"Now?" She laughed. "What's gotten into you?"

"Nothing. Take your dress off." He grabbed for her awkwardly, and she said, "Good God, Bill."

He unfastened his belt.

Later they sent out for Chinese food, and when it arrived they ate hungrily, without speaking, and listened to records.

"Let's not forget to feed Kitty," she said.

"I was just thinking about that," he said. "I'll go right over."

He selected a can of fish for the cat, then filled the pitcher and went to water. When he returned to the kitchen the cat was scratching in her box. She looked at him steadily for a minute before she turned back to the litter. He opened all the cupboards and examined the canned goods, the cereals, the packaged

37

foods, the cocktail and wine glasses, the china, the pots and pans. He opened the refrigerator. He sniffed some celery, took two bites of cheddar cheese, and chewed on an apple as he walked into the bedroom. The bed seemed enormous, with a fluffy white bedspread draped to the floor. He pulled out a nightstand drawer, found a half-empty package of cigarettes and stuffed them into his pocket. Then he stepped to the closet and was opening it when the knock sounded at the front door.

He stopped by the bathroom and flushed the toilet on his way.

"What's been keeping you?" Arlene said. "You've been over here more than an hour."

"Have I really?" he said.

"Yes, you have," she said.

"I had to go to the toilet," he said.

"You have your own toilet," she said.

"I couldn't wait," he said.

That night they made love again.

In the morning he had Arlene call in for him. He showered, dressed, and made a light breakfast. He tried to start a book. He went out for a walk and felt better, but after a while, hands still in his pockets, he returned to the apartment. He stopped at the Stones' door on the chance he might hear the cat moving about. Then he let himself in at his own door and went to the kitchen for the key.

Inside it seemed cooler than his apartment, and darker too. He wondered if the plants had something to do with the temperature of the air. He looked out the window, and then he moved slowly through each room considering everything that fell under his gaze, carefully, one object at a time. He saw ashtrays, items of furniture, kitchen utensils, the clock. He saw everything. At last he entered the bedroom, and the cat appeared at his feet. He stroked her once, carried her into the bathroom and shut the door.

He lay down on the bed and stared at the ceiling. He lay for a while with his eyes closed, and then he moved his hand into his pants. He tried to recall what day it was. He tried to remember when the Stones were due back, and then he wondered if they would ever return. He could not remember their faces or the way they talked and dressed. He sighed, and then with effort rolled off the bed to lean over the dresser and look at himself in the mirror.

He opened the closet and selected a Hawaiian shirt. He looked until he found Bermudas, neatly pressed and hanging over a pair of brown twill slacks. He shed his own clothes and slipped into the shorts and the shirt. He looked in the mirror again. He went to the living room and poured himself a drink and sipped it on his way back to the bedroom. He put on a dark suit, a blue shirt, a blue and white tie, black wing-tip shoes. The glass was empty and he went for another drink.

In the bedroom again he sat on a chair, crossed his legs, and smiled, observing himself in the mirror. The telephone rang twice and fell silent. He finished the drink and took off the suit. He rummaged the top drawers until he found a pair of panties and a brassiere. He stepped into the panties and fastened the brassiere, then looked through the closet for an outfit. He put on a black and white checkered skirt which was too snug and which he was afraid to zipper, and a burgundy blouse that buttoned in the front. He considered her shoes, but understood they would not fit. For a long time he looked out the living-room window from behind the curtain. Then he returned to the bedroom and put everything away.

He was not hungry. She did not eat much either, but they looked at each other shyly and smiled. She got up from the table and checked that the key was on the shelf, then quickly cleared the dishes.

39

He stood in the kitchen doorway and smoked a cigarette and watched her pick up the key.

"Make yourself comfortable while I go across the hall," she said. "Read the paper or something." She closed her fingers over the key. He was, she said, looking tired.

He tried to concentrate on the news. He read the paper and turned on the television. Finally he went across the hall. The door was locked.

"It's me. Are you still there, honey?" he called.

After a time the lock released and Arlene stepped outside and shut the door. "Was I gone so long?" she said.

"Well you were," he said.

"Was I?" she said. "I guess I must have been playing with Kitty."

He studied her, and she looked away, her hand still resting on the doorknob.

"It's funny," she said. "You know, to go in someone's place like that."

He nodded, took her hand from the knob, and guided her toward their own door. He let them into their apartment. "It is funny," he said. He noticed white lint clinging to the back of her sweater, and the color was high in her cheeks. He began kissing her on the neck and hair and she turned and kissed him back.

"Oh, damn," she said. "Damn, damn," girlishly clapping her hands. "I just remembered. I really and truly forgot to do what I went over there for. I didn't feed Kitty or do any watering." She looked at him. "Isn't that stupid?"

"I don't think so," he said. "Just a minute, I'll get my cigarettes and go with you."

She waited until he had closed and locked their door, and then she took his arm at the muscle and said, "I guess I should tell you. I found some pictures."

He stopped in the middle of the hall. "What kind of pictures?"

"You can see for yourself," she said, and watched him.

"No kidding." He grinned. "Where?"

"In a drawer," she said.

"No kidding," he said.

And then she said, "Maybe they won't come back," and was at once astonished at her words.

"It could happen," he said. "Anything could happen."

"Or maybe they'll come back and," but she did not finish.

They held hands for the short walk across the hall, and when he spoke she could barely hear his voice.

"The key," he said. "Give it to me."

"What?" she said. She gazed at the door.

"The key," he said, "you have the key."

"My God," she said, "I left the key inside."

He tried the knob. It remained locked. Then she tried the knob, but it would not turn. Her lips were parted, and her breathing was hard, expectant. He opened his arms and she moved into them.

"Don't worry," he said into her ear. "For God's sake, don't worry." They stayed there. They held each other. They leaned into the door as if against a wind, and braced themselves.

MEN AGAINST THE SEA

Alan V. Hewat

ight falls swiftly in the South Seas, and though the dinner hour had but shortly passed aboard the H.M.S. *Gryphon Clipper*, the stately craft was already shrouded in darkness as she plied her graceful way, homeward bound. As though muffled by night, her decks were silent, save for the single voice of a solitary tar, singing at his lonely station, "Yo ho, yo ho, yo hoho."

In his cabin, the ship's master, Captain Sir Richard Crawshaw, was enjoying a glass of port and his customary postprandial serenade, rendered instrumentally by the two darkies, Cook's Helpers Cannonball and Abodeefa, upon, respectively, the banjo and the drum. Captain Crawshaw smiled generously and moved his foot in time to the music. Music, he reflected, was not merely the food of love, but a damn pleasant way to accompany a glass of port. How fortunate he was that the press-gang had allowed the darkies to keep their instruments! What good, talented lads they were! He let his heart surge with fondness for the darkies.

He was interrupted in his reverie by a sharp knocking on the cabin door. "Hush, lads," the Captain said. The darkies silenced their instruments, rose and stood stiffly by the bulkhead. "Who goes there?" cried the Captain. From without came the sound of several voices, muttering.

One voice rose above the others. "It's Lieutenant Dart, sir," it said. "Request a word with the Captain, sir." A rowdy chuckle sounded amidst the cacophony of muttering.

"Permission granted," shouted the Captain. "Do come in, First Officer."

The door swung open to reveal Dart, impeccably trig as always, standing before what looked like the entire crew, all armed to the teeth. At the sight of the Captain's visage, softened though it was by surprise from its habitually stern demeanor, the rabble brandished cutlasses and marlinspikes, pistols and belaying pins, musketry and scrimshaw knives, and, in a single loud voice, cried, "Har!"

"What is the meaning of this, First Officer?" the Captain asked, though his heart anticipated the answer.

Placing his hand on the hilt of his sword, Dart clicked his heels and executed a short bow from the waist. "Sir," he said, "it is my unhappy duty as Second in Command of this vessel to inform you that, as of this moment, by general and common consensus of the officers and men here gathered, you are summarily relieved of command, with all perquisites, honoraria and offices thereto appertaining, of Her Majesty's Ship *Gryphon Clipper*."

"Don't mince words, man," the Captain blustered. "You mean . . . ?"

"Yes sir," replied the officer. "You are my prisoner. I advise you not to attempt evading action. Resistance would be futile."

The darkies rolled their eyes. The Captain rose, upsetting his chair. "By God, sir," he cried, "this is mutiny." Outside the cabin door, the crew rattled their weapons and cried, "Har!"

"Harsh words, Mr. Crawshaw," said Dart coolly, with a sly emphasis on the Mister. He smiled good-naturedly. "I would prefer to say it is a matter of, shall we say, competitive expedience."

"Mutiny, I say," the Captain repeated, striking the top of his desk with a trembling fist. "I demand an explanation for this outrage."

Dart's smile wavered not the least. "Very well, sir," he said. "Time allows me to deliver you that privilege, though your demands shall avail you nothing further aboard this craft."

"It's the race," shouted a voice from the crew, which the Captain recognized as belonging to Boatswain's Mate Second Class Dithers.

"Aye, the race, the race," chorused the crew, adding a lusty, "Har!"

"Steady, lads," said Dart. The crew fell silent. Dart turned to the Captain. "It's this, sir," he said. "In the fortnight since we departed Nanking, our hatches brimming with rich teas and exotic Oriental spices, our progress in the great clipper race to Birkenhead has been abysmal. It's twelve days since we saw H.M.S. *Cutty Sark* and H.M.S. *John Lawson* disappear over the eastern horizon, bound for the Horn, and six since H.M.S. *Ballantine* overtook us as easily as though we were a pleasure craft on the Serpentine, not a mighty clipper ship. A pleasure craft, sir," he added, with undisguised distaste.

"A bleeding rowboat," crowed a voice from the crew, which the Captain knew as the voice of Bumstead, the ship's drunken physician.

"Aye, a rowboat, a rowboat," chorused the crew, adding a lusty, "Har!"

The Captain smiled placatingly, his hand fussing nervously at his collar. "Surely, Dart, you don't suggest the fault is mine," he said. "True, we have muddled about at the start, but there's plenty of race yet to run, and I'm confident that if we all pull together, stout fellows all, we'll show them what the *Gryphon Clipper*'s mettle is. Won't we, lads?" The crew murmured sullenly, and one or two cries of "Hip hip" were quickly silenced.

"It's no good, sir," said Dart, gently. "We're a loser."

"But there have been unforeseeable circumstances," the Captain pleaded. "Injuries to key members of the ship's company. Nagging mechanical difficulties. Adverse climatic factors." He lowered his voice. "I'd not expect them to understand," he said, indicating the crew, "but, look here, Dart, surely *you* of all men are cognizant of the limited, lonely powers of this office, its inherent haplessness in the face of time, tide and the elements."

"It's nothing personal, Captain," said Dart. "It's just that when the battle is running poorly, it's easier to replace your general than to discharge the troops."

"Damn, Dart, this is infamous. And to think, I treated you as I would my own son, had God granted me a son." The Captain hung his head.

"A fig for your paternity," said Dart, angrily. "I've wasted enough time talking. We have a race to win."

"All the way," cried a voice from the crew. It was Midshipman Woodley, the Captain realized.

"Charge," chorused the crew, adding their lusty, "Har!"

"What's to become of me, then?" asked the disconsolate Crawshaw.

"You'll be put over the side in a launch," said Dart, "with adequate provisions to enable you to reach the nearest landfall. According to my calculations, that would be in the area of Pitcairn Island." He motioned toward the two Cook's Helpers, who still stood, clutching their instruments, at the bulkhead. "The darkies will go with you," he said, "to man the oars. Frankly, I find their incessant music a distraction and an annoyance."

"Hab mercy," said Cannonball, rolling his eyes. He was a short, stocky Negro, whose coffee coloring appeared ashen beside the oily blue-blackness of Abodeefa, a small gaunt man who stared balefully at Dart but said nothing, being deaf and dumb.

An awkward silence invaded the cabin, crepuscular in the flickering light of the oil lamps. Finally, Crawshaw sighed heavily, and said, "I don't suppose, Dart, that you'd keep me on in some sort of advisory capacity." A note of hopelessness soured his voice.

Dart shook his head and affected a kindly smile. "Sorry, sir," he said, "but I'd rather be free to make my own mistakes."

"Of course, of course," said Crawshaw. "It was just a thought." He squared his shoulders and threw out his chest. "Well then, I suppose we'd better be on our way, eh lads?"

There were huzzahs from the crew, and in the rear two or three voices burst into a chorus of *For He's a Jolly Good Fellow.*

As the exiles lined up at the ship's rail and prepared to descend the rope ladder to the launch, Quartermaster Tracy reached for Cannonball's banjo. " 'Ere," he said. "I'll tyke that. We carn't 'ave ye mykin' off wif ship's stores, myte."

The darky twisted away from his grasp. "Beg pahdon," he replied, "dat banjo alla time mah own. Ah makin' him back home in West Africa when Ah a chile. Make da neck fum giraffe thighbone, frets an' bridge an' pegs fum elefump ivory, da drum fum zebra hide, an' da strings fum lion gut. All han' crafted, wif essquisite wukmanship." He showed the Quartermaster his hands, one tightly clutching the banjo's neck.

" 'Ow abaht that fancy work there?" said Tracy, indicating the belt of metal ornamentation which girdled the instrument's body. "Hit looks loike silver ter me, innit?"

"Oh no," said Cannonball, "dat a common alloy indigenous to da region ob mah tribe, wifout commercial value."

"All roite, all roite. In the boat wif yer then." The darky clambered over the side and descended to the launch. The next man was Abodeefa. "Oy, 'old on," said the Quartermaster. He grabbed the darky's drum and tossed it quickly to one of the other hands, who grinned lickerishly. "We know wot we 'ave there, don't we, lads?" Tracy laughed, then added to Abodeefa, "Over yer go." The darky fixed him with a burning stare, but said nothing and indicated no protest by his actions. Then, with reptilian swiftness, he was gone.

The Captain was last. He carried a small dispatch box containing sextant, shaving gear and his personal logbook. At the head of the ladder, he paused and turned to Dart. He held out his hand. "Is this to be good-bye then, Dart?" he said.

"Aye, sir," said the new master of the *Gryphon Clipper*. "I hope there's no ill feeling, sir. I wish you fair winds and a rising tide."

"I'll see you hanged for a mutinous dog," said the Captain, shaking Dart's hand warmly.

"Let history be my judge," Dart replied, returning Crawshaw's handshake.

Crawshaw turned to the crew. "May you all rot in hell," he shouted, his voice cracking. "You scurvy swine, you've not seen the last of Dick Crawshaw." Stifling a sob, he tore himself from Dart's handclasp and clambered over the side, keeping his face averted. Once seated in the stern sheets of the launch, he composed himself with visible effort and gave the command to cast off.

As the dowdy boat hove away from the giant clipper, the latter's sails filled and its hawsers cried out with effort. Graceful as a gull in flight, cleaving the waves like a freshly stopped razor, she raced on to the east, to rejoin the great race to Birkenhead. How she fared is another tale, and will soon be told.

Thus was accomplished the mutiny of the H.M.S. *Gryphon Clipper*.

From the Log of Richard Crawshaw:

July 21 (Tuesday)—Infamy. My struggles availed me naught against the numbers of the entire Crew as directed by the treacherous, cowardly Dart, and, though I warned them repeatedly of the consequences of their Piracy, I have been set adrift, with only faithful Cook's Helper Cannonball and faithful C.H. Abodeefa, who shall man the oars. Though uncivilized, they are doughty and devoted to me, and, with God's help, we shall prevail against the Perils of the deep, and shall survive to be granted Retribution for the Hardships forced upon us by Dart (I can scarce write the hated name) and his murderous pack of dogs. Est position S 32 deg. 129 min.

"All right, lads, pull smartly," said Captain Crawshaw. "Heave ho." The darkies strained at the oars, their muscles outlined by the sweat that ran from them in rivulets.

"Sah," said Cannonball, "how fah da Cap'n figger we gonna row?"

"Not to worry, lad," said the Captain, with a kindly chuckle. "Keep your spirits up. Chin high, eh? Let me worry about the navigation."

"Reason Ah asks, sah," said Cannonball, pausing to wipe the sweat from his forehead, "is dat Mistah Daht, he say we got 'nuff probitions fo' reachin' firs' landfall, an' by mah figgerin', dat dar is 'bout ten days worf." He turned toward the bow, and indicated the large barrel of salt pork, hardtack and potatoes, and the smaller cask of fresh water, with which they had been provisioned. "Seem to me, sah," Cannonball continued, "dat ten days is a pow'ful long time fo' rowin' a boat, eben fo' two spunky lads lak Abodeefa an' Cannonball, if'n yo' follers mah meanin', sah."

"That's a good point, lad," said the Captain, "and well taken. Hats off to you. I, of course, am not without a solution, however, since no dilemma is insurmountable to the seasoned commander. Henceforth, you shall *alternate* your turns at the oars. Let one man row and one man rest, eh? You'll do six-hour watches. That way we can keep up our strength for the long haul."

"Sah, it 'curs to me dat we gots canvas an' twine dere in da bilge, an' a fair breeze arunnin', so's hit might do to jury-rig usselfs a sail. We kin lash da oars fo' a mast an' crosstree, heist canvas an' be on our way, ovah the boundin' main. We kin takes turns steerin', sah, an' dat ways *yo'* don't have to keep awake da whole junney, payin' da physical tolls of eternal vigilance."

Primitive as the idea was, Captain Crawshaw was struck by its core of implicit possibility, and gave it careful consideration. "Very well, Cook's Helper," he said, "let's give it a try." And soon the frail craft was straining manfully through the great swells of the South Seas, propelled by the loveliest of fuels, a freshening sea breeze.

From the Log of Richard Crawshaw:

July 22 (Wednesday)—An unfortunate occurrence: As I was attempting to instruct C.H. Cannonball in the rudiments of Solar Navigation, in a kindly attempt to educate the poor fellow, my hand was jostled by C.H. Abodeefa, and the sextant fell overboard and was lost. Thus does Charity oft redound against the Giver. They were both of course contrite, but Contrition in our circumstances is a weak substitute for science. I am now forced to rely upon dead reckoning and the innate Sensibilities accrued by a lifetime spent in the maritime services of God and Her Majesty (may He grant me good fortune and She swift justice). Our Progress appears brisk. Est position approximately 15 naut. mi. N.E. of yesterday nightfall.

The Captain languished in the stern sheets, his hand shielding his eyes against the fierce noonday sun. The darkies sat on a thwart amidships, just aft of the sail, facing the stern. How do they stand it? Crawshaw wondered. He wiped his forehead elaborately, discomfited by the silent, staring presence of the two. Abodeefa looked particularly sullen.

"I say, Cook's Helper Cannonball," the Captain said, "is Cook's Helper Abodeefa well? He looks positively surly, and he hasn't eaten a thing since we came aboard."

"Oh, sah," said Cannonball, "Abodeefa jes' angry they take 'way his drum. Hit contain his opium."

"You don't say. But surely he knows it's against regs. No place for narcotics on a taut ship. Quite proper of them, I'd say. Had I known about it, I'd have done the same thing, Cook's Helper. That's just not done."

"But sah, dat his ecclesiastic supplies. Abodeefa a pow'ful religious feller, an' require opium fo' his interpitation ob da future an' da phenomena ob da present."

"Still," said the Captain, "it's hardly the thing aboard one of Her Majesty's vessels." He turned his gaze sternly to Abodeefa, and raised his voice. "No opium," he shouted. "Opium bad. Bad. Do you think he understands me, Cook's Helper Cannonball?"

"Oh yes, *sah*," said Cannonball, enthusiastically. "Abodeefa kin lip-read fifty-sebben languages, includin' dead tongues, obsolete dialeks an' obscure regionalisms, as well as da various variations ob da Queen's English as dey spoke t'roughout da Empire, da British Isles an' da United States ob America. Abodeefa know dem *all*, sah."

"You don't say," said the Captain. "How terribly interesting. Tell me, how did he acquire such remarkable linguistic versatility? Does he travel?"

"Oh, sah," said Cannonball, laying his arm across Abodeefa's shoulders, "Abodeefa been prackly ebberware in da worl'. He pow'ful *ole*, Cap'n. Got more'n two hunnerd *years* under dat ole skin, an' he still as spunky as a Watusi *wimoweh*."

"A what?" inquired the Captain.

"Dat a tribal teen-ager, sah. A adolescent."

"Ah," said the Captain. "But if he's so old, and don't think I doubt your veracity, incredible as it seems," he hastened to add, "shouldn't he be eating something? Surely he'll want to be keeping up his strength. Your strength, Cook's Helper Abodeefa," he shouted at the other darky, flexing his arms by way of illustration.

"No, sah," said Cannonball, cheerfully. "Abodeefa is purifyin' hissef by fastin'. Dat way he git da visions, an' be able to say if'n we gonna make it t'rough our travail or not, wif salient details."

"Oh," said the Captain. "Very well, then. Carry on, Cook's Helper. I said, carry on," he repeated, raising his voice. "Glad somebody can do something in this beastly heat," the Captain muttered to himself.

From the Log of Richard Crawshaw:

July 25 (Saturday)—Our situation worsens. During the night we were nearly swamped by a large wave over the bow, while C.H. Abodeefa had the tiller watch. Maintained buoyancy by dint of enthusiastic Bailing. However, sea water penetrated our stores, which one of the careless Cook's Helpers left uncovered. Hardtack saturated, and I decided to jettison it. Worse, drinking water contaminated by salt. May God forgive my Weakness and give me the Strength not to betray it in front of the Negroes, but I am afraid! No sign of land, nor estimate of Progress, due to the carelessness with which the Negroes handle the tiller. Beastly hot sun. Excruciating thirst. Dreamed of being caught in the rain in St. James' Park, Blackpool. Ah, to be in England! is our common Prayer.

The Captain ran his swollen tongue over his parched lips. He groaned, feebly. From the bow came the sound of the banjo, a strange, dissonant sound. The sail amidships blocked his view of the bow. He called out, "I say, Cook's Helper Cannonball. I don't mean to be stodgy, but this seems hardly the time for music, eh? Best conserve your energy, what?"

Cannonball ducked under the sail and smiled at the Captain. "Oh dat warn't me, sah," he said. "Dat's Abodeefa. He gonna try some magic." A sour plang of tones sounded in the clear sea air.

"Magic?" said the Captain. "Doesn't sound a bit magical to me. Sounds bloody awful. Never soothe the savage beast that way, Cook's Helper."

"Oh no, sah," grinned Cannonball. "Dat's jes' yo' ears, sah. Yo' ears suited to da diatonic modes. Dum-de-dum-de-dum-de-dum-DUM, da sebben-tone scale, sah. Abodeefa playin' in pentatonics, much older, an' culturally suited to his magic. Da-da-da-da-da-DA, like dat. Suited to da banjo, too, sah. Hit only gots five strings."

"Yes, yes, of course," said the Captain irritably. "It's what he's going to do with it that concerns me."

"Well, sah, Abodeefa jes' warmin' up rat now, gittin' his chops on. Den, when da time is rat, his visions gonna gib him a tone cluster, or p'raps a arpeggio, dat gonna sweeten da salt water. How 'bout dat, sah?"

Another group of straggled notes sounded, and an instant later a large fish leapt over the port gunwale and blundered about in the bilge near Cannonball's feet. The Captain jumped to his feet. "I say," he shouted excitedly, "grab him, Cook's Helper. Don't let it jump out." The darky stooped, and pinned the fish. "That's right, hold him," shouted the Captain. "Let me find something to use as a club. Ah, of course." He grabbed up his dispatch box and brained the fish with a corner of it. The fish gave a final, weak flutter, and expired, stretching to its full length. The Captain smiled broadly. "I say," he said, "there's a bit of luck for a change. A fish this size will feed us for, oh, a week, so long as we don't overindulge, eh Cook's Helper?"

"Oh sah," said Cannonball, "we kin eat him all in one sittin' if'n yo' wishes. Dey's plenty mo' where he come fum."

"Plenty of fish in the sea, eh?" chuckled the Captain. "A handy philosophy, that, but we can hardly expect them all to be as obliging as this fellow, now can we?"

"Hit not da fish, sah. Hit Abodeefa. He jes' find da right cluster dat attracks fish into da boat. You'll see, sah." Cannonball ducked back under the sail to the bow. A moment later, another chord sounded, and another large fish flopped over the gunwale. The Captain, thinking quickly, reached down and clubbed the fish with the dispatch box.

Cannonball reappeared, his smile broader than ever. "How yo' lak dat, sah? Betcha Jawge Freddick Handel nebbah done *dat*."

"Remarkable," the Captain admitted. "Simply remarkable."

"Aw, Abodeefa say dat not so much," the darky demurred. "He say, if'n he had a twelve-string instrument, he could do us a chromatic run dat would increase our speed by sebbenteen knots, he say. As it is, he workin' on da sweet-water tones rat now. We gonna hab good drinkin' to go wif dis yere fresh protein, sah, yo' waits an' sees."

Overwhelmed by his good fortune, the Captain collapsed weakly in the stern sheets.

From the Log of Richard Crawshaw:

July 29 (Wednesday)—Still no sign of land, but our Spirits are unbowed, thanks to God's Beneficence in providing us with fresh fish and water. By His graces, I am confident we shall make it through our Trial with our Spirits all the stronger for the Ordeal, and I shall live to see Dart and all of his scurvy Band hanged from the highest yardarm in the fleet. I am concerned for C.H. Abodeefa. The poor fellow still takes no Nourishment, despite my most humane Efforts, and I fear he weakens.

"Sah, sah," cried Cannonball.

The Captain looked up from his logbook, where he had been busily recording his thoughts in a precise hand. "What is it, Cook's Helper?" he inquired.

"Hit Abodeefa, sah," the darky answered, with visible excitement. "He say da visions comin' on." Beside him, Abodeefa stared vacantly toward the sun, motionless except for the fingers of his right hand, which moved rapidly in Cannonball's palm. "He say mostly da voyage gonna be successful."

"Really?" said the Captain, his interest mounting. "That *is* good news. But what do you mean by *mostly?*"

"Oh, Ah can't tell dat, sah. Hit Abodeefa what's doin' da talkin', as hit revealed to him. Wait a minute, sah." He concentrated on the dancing digits. "Abodeefa say da *Gryphon Clipper* gonna win da race. Gonna oberhaul da *Cutty Sark* rat in da mouf ob da Mersey Ribbah an' whup her ass into da slips ob Birkenhead, he say. Gonna be big bonus fo' all hands."

"Not bloody likely," said the Captain. "The owners were paying *me* a big bonus to hold back, while they laid off the field against me. If Dart wins, they'll keelhaul him." His voice was bitter.

"Oh no, sah," said Cannonball, watching Abodeefa's fingers with close care, "*Gryphon Clipper* gonna go into da slips under full sail. Gonna smash up, lose cargo in da ribbah, bust up owners' wharf an' warehouse. Owners gonna collect plenty on insurance, Abodeefa say. Make race bets look lak chickenshit. Lloyd ob London be plenty pissed off, all right, but owners gonna be pleased lak punch, Abodeefa say. Make Dart full partner, wif plenty expenses an' house in da country. Prosperity jes' 'roun' da corner, sah, Abodeefa say."

"Poppycock," said the Captain angrily. "A lot of heathen rot. Does he expect me to believe that nonsense? I'm a *civilized man*, Cook's Helper, a white man, an *Englishman*." He shook his fist, and paced distractedly as far as the small confines of the launch would permit. "Balderdash," he said loudly, "sheer, fabricated balderdash. A bunch of bloody savages, spouting rot. It's balderdash, I say."

The fingers in Cannonball's palm moved with a vehemence to match the Captain's own, then stopped. Cannonball looked up with wide eyes, first at his blue-black companion, then at the Captain. "Oh sah," he said, "yo' shouldn't say dat 'bout Abodeefa. He plenty sensitive 'bout his religion. Okay yo' talk politics wif him, or da relative superiority ob races, but not religion. Oh sah, Abodeefa plenty angry now. He say no mo' water, no mo' fishes fo' da infidel. Dat yo', sah."

"But surely, he can't expect me to credit such patent nonsense as that story about Dart. I know better. After all, I *am* an officer in Her Majesty's Merchant Marine. I understand how these things work." He nodded toward Abodeefa and extended his hand in a placating gesture. "I'm sure he just misunderstood, didn't you, Cook's Helper?" he said to Abodeefa.

The blue-black fingers slithered in Cannonball's palm. "Abodeefa say dat a pisspoor excuse fo' a apology, an' he don' want nuffin' mo' to do wif a infidel."

"Oh he does, does he?" said the Captain. "Well, we'll just see about that. May I remind him that I, not he, am in charge of this vessel, and you can tell him for me that once we reach land I'll see that things go hard for him unless he pulls himself together. There are penalties for insubordination in the civilized world. Now, Cook's Helper Abodeefa, you just step lively there and man the banjo. That's an order, man."

The savage's eyes bored piercingly into the Captain's, and he crossed his arms and sat, unmoving. Captain Crawshaw was about to raise his fist to the darky, but an icy shadow descended on his heart, and he withheld his blow.

"So," said the Captain, noticing a slight quaver in his voice. "So that's how it's going to be, is it? Very well then, Cook's Helper Abodeefa, as of this moment, and I'll note it in the log, you may consider yourself under confinement, by the power vested in me by Her Majesty, Queen Victoria, Empress of Great Britain and all her domains. Do not try to leave the ship." With an effort of the will, he pulled himself together, and brushing past the two seated darkies, ducked under the sail and went to the bow, where he picked up the banjo. He strummed it twice, tentatively. "Cook's Helper Cannonball," he called.

"Sah," answered Cannonball, appearing from behind the sail.

"Cook's Helper Cannonball," the Captain said, "you are a practiced and experienced musician, so surely you know the proper notes. I want you to teach them to me. The fish notes and the sweet-water notes. That's an order, Cook's Helper," he added. "Or are you going to turn against me too?"

"Oh no, sah," answered the darky, cheerfully, "Ah don't takes sides in theological arguments. Ah a freethinker. But Ah don't knows if'n Ah kin teach yo' properly, sah. Ah reckons da cultural disparity too great to obercome."

"Nonsense, Cook's Helper," said the Captain. "I'm not devoid of musical skills myself, you know. In my youth, I studied the clavichord, with *Meister* Friedhof of the Salzburg Academy, if you must know. There was talk of a career, in fact, but I shan't bore you with that. Just show me where to put my fingers."

"Well, sah, hit mo' dan jes' a question ob da fingers. Dere's internal rhythmic conventions to learn, too."

"Well, don't just stand there man, *show* me." The Captain handed the banjo to the darky, then stooped and grabbed up the water cask. He dipped it over the side, filling it with sea water. "Now, we'll start with the water notes, since that's our most pressing immediate need," he said. "For food, there's still some pork and potatoes, as well as a smidgen of yesterday's fish, but we have no fresh drinking water. Go ahead."

With a guilty glance astern, where Abodeefa sat obdurate on the other side of the sail, Cannonball plucked several chords, then nodded at the Captain and struck a descending dissonance. "Try dat, sah," he said.

The Captain dipped his index finger in the water and tasted it. It was cool and sweet. "Capital," he cried. "Stout fellow, Cook's Helper. Now show me." He dumped the cask overboard and refilled it with brine.

Cannonball handed him the banjo and showed him where to place his fingers on the neck. The Captain strummed lightly, then eagerly tasted the water. The salt stung on his lips. "Are you quite certain that's the right fingering?" he asked crossly.

"Oh yes, sah," the darky nodded, "but Ah tole yo' 'bout da rhythmic problem, didn't Ah? Yo' see, sah, dere's a slight syncopation goes in 'tween da second an' third strings, an' den a compensatin' delay 'tween three an' fo'. Hit suppose to soun' lak dis: Klak-to-VEE-des-teen, yo' see? Try him again, sah."

The Captain strummed again, rushing the interval between the second and third notes, as Cannonball had suggested, though it felt awkward to him. The water did not sweeten. He tried again, using two fingers to pluck the strings, again without success. And again. After several attempts, the proper rhythm still eluded him.

"Oh, sah," said Cannonball, "hit jes' culturally unfeasible. Hit no reflection 'gainst yo' musical abilities in yo' own tradition, sah, but yo' gots to be black lak usns to feel dat rhythm."

"Nonsense," said Crawshaw. He was sweating heavily. "You people are no more adept rhythmically than I am. I studied with Friedhof."

"Oh, *sah*," cried Cannonball, "*all* God's chillen got rhythm, only some gots differnt than others."

The Captain tried several more strums. Sweat made his fingers slippery on the lion-gut strings, and his frustration mounted. Angrily, he struck across the strings with his thumb. His thumb-nail caught, and, with a plangent *twang*, two strings snapped.

"Oh, sah," Cannonball moaned.

"Drat the luck," said the Captain. "I'm expected to do every-one's work around here. I'm only human, you know. Here." He thrust the banjo at Cannonball. The broken strings dangled, curled at the ends like two singed hairs. "You'd better fix it right away, Cook's Helper. Lively now, that's an order."

"Hit no good, sah. Even if Ah could splice up da gut, hit gonna hab adverse effectiveness on da tonal quality an' render hit useless fo' anythin' 'cept mebbe *Da Camptown Ladies*, an' dat sho' nuff don't sweeten no water, sah."

"Blast," said the Captain, sucking his thumb.

From the Log of Richard Crawshaw:

August 4 (Tuesday)—Managed to capture some rainwater last night, for first drink in six days. Its Insufficiency mocks us today, but we thank You, Lord, for Thy Bounties, however meager and often hard. Still no sign of land. I fear the onset of feverish humours, and must pray constantly for Strength, a clear Purpose and a concise Mind. May God preserve from further treacheries, from Abodeefa and Dart and the outrageous Misfortune of their ilk.

"Sah," cried Cannonball.

Captain Crawshaw raised his head with difficulty from its resting-place on the gunwale. In the searing sunlight, it took his eyes several instants to achieve focus. Cannonball was sitting on the port gunwale, his legs dangling over the side.

"What is it, Cook's Helper?" the Captain said. "Have you sighted something?" His voice was dry and croaking, barely a whisper. Amidships, Abodeefa sat motionless on the thwart.

"Ah jes' took inventory ob da stores, sah," said Cannonball. There was a note of resigned woe in his voice which made the Captain sit up. "Ah reckons dat, 'tween da salt pork an' da taters, which is goin' bad, we don't gots but three, mebbe fo', days worth."

"Very well," said the Captain, "we'll have to halve the rations again and pray for landfall. Don't give up hope, Cook's Helper, there's a stout fellow." He forced a heartiness into his voice which he was ill-inclined to feel.

"No, sah," said the darky. "T'wont do me no good, Cap'n."

"What do you mean, Cook's Helper?"

"Ah ain't fated to last out dis yere voyage, Cap'n," said Cannonball. Sadness swelled in his face, and he hung his head beneath its weight. "Ah din' tell yo' what Abodeefa mean by *mostly* in his prophecy, sah, on 'count we gots interrupted, an' da facks is, he din' gib me da whole story, neither, but Ah figgered out da rest as best Ah could."

"What about it, man?" said the Captain, impatiently. "Out with it."

"Well, sah," said Cannonball, "Ah knows dis much. Abodeefa say *he* gonna make it. He say *he* not gonna die till 1967, when he gonna perish in a airplane crash wif Otis Redding. In Wisconsin, U.S.A., he say."

"A what crash?"

"Ah don't rightly know, sah," answered the darky. "Ah din' gits dat part mahsef. Dat war jes' a phonetic transcription ob what Abodeefa tells me." He shook his head sadly. "Da point is, sah, if Abodeefa gonna make hit, one ob us others *ain't* gonna. Dat's what he mean by *mostly*. Now, Ah figgers dat by natchul selection, yo' is da one fated to go on wif Abodeefa, bein' as how yo' is da white man an' colonial massah ob da worl'. Mebbe in another time, p'raps a later century, Ah'd fight yo' fo' da honor ob survivin', but dis is da Eighteen-Eighties, an' yo' gots manifest destiny on yo' side, not to mention da evolutionary ladder, whereas Ah is fo' da moment worse equipped in bof departments. So stedda jes' lyin' 'round chere gittin' weak an' feeble, Ah reckons to jes' slip ober da side nice an' easy, an' let dat ole white shark dat's been follerin' us take me 'cross da Ribbah Jordan. Ah din' mean to disturb yo', sah, but Ah did wants to say farewell."

Tears sprang to the Captain's eyes. "See here, Cook's Helper," he said.

The darky held up his hand. "No, sah. Let's jes' say good-bye, an' hope we meet in a better worl' someday. Yo' kin hab mah banjo. Ah done spliced up da strings good enough fo' *Oh Susannah*, or *Waitin' fo' da Robert E. Lee*. It's better dis yere way, sah, so Ah'll jes' say So Long fo' a while." With a rueful smile and a wave of his hand, he pushed off, and, with a splash, was gone.

The Captain rushed forward to the gunwale. Cannonball was swimming strongly away from the boat. "Cook's Helper," the Captain cried. "Come back aboard, Cook's Helper. That's an order." His voice cracked and died, as a huge, cloudy shape rose suddenly from the depths and seemed to wash over the swimming darky. It was the great white shark, striking with swift deadliness, and as swiftly returning to the depths. The surface of the sea closed like a faulty memory. The Captain wept, calling the darky's name.

Suddenly, he whirled and bent to face Abodeefa. Crawshaw's lips quivered with rage and sorrow. "Do you see what you've done?" he screamed. "You devious coon. Pretty bloody clever, aren't you, with your bloody spook tales. Nineteen Sixty-seven. *Air*planes. We'll see about that, you black baboon. We'll just see.

You're going to be bloody well hanged, Mister Witchcraft, as soon as we make landfall. You just lost me my best man with your superstitious savage poppycock but let me assure you, you don't frighten *me* with your juju and your mumbo jumbo. *I'm* not going anywhere. If it takes five years, mark you, I'll wait five years. I'll *starve* for five years, and at the end of it I'll have the sublime pleasure of seeing you dance at the end of a rope. And that's a promise, *Mister* Abodeefa." As he shouted, he bent closer to Abodeefa's face, and a few drops of his spittle spattered the impassive blue-black countenance. Abodeefa seemed supremely bored.

The Captain fell to his knees. "Oh, Lord," he cried, joining his hands, "deliver me, I pray You, from this infamous travail. Make strong my hand and straight my path, that I may exact the vengeance owed the soul of Cook's Helper Cannonball. And, oh, Lord, keep me sound, I pray You, that I may rid Thy world of this beastly nigger, for Thy own sake. This I ask in Jesus' name. Amen." Rising, he turned again to Abodeefa. "So much for you, old fruit," the Captain said, ungraciously.

From the Log of Richard Crawshaw:

August 12 (Wednesday)—Lord, do not forsake me. We are eight days now without water, and still no sign of land. The nigger perches amidships like an avenging buzzard, his eyes grown hollow and his body gaunt for want of sustenance. He burns with envy of me, I know, of all Englishmen, nay, all Civilized men, for naught avails his witchery against Civilized men. Lord, do not, I beg you, let him die until I have exacted my Vengeance in a proper, enlightened manner by which all of his ilk may be informed and take heed, and know who are the proper Masters of the world. Lord, fortify me. The nigger has a huge penis. Last night, I dreamed of the rolling hills and green, green fields of Kent, and when I awoke, their Vision stayed before my eyes, dancing above the waves. Strangely enough, I heard music, too, though I had thrown the banjo overboard lest the nigger amuse himself with it. There shall

be no amusements for niggers aboard a vessel whose master is
Richard Crawsh

(Here the journal ends, with the downstroke of the "h" trailing
somewhat erratically off the page.)

The Captain slumped over the logbook. Abodeefa kept his
finger tight against the pressure point on the Captain's temple,
until he was certain Crawshaw was unconscious, then left him
and went to the bow of the launch. He picked up the water
cask, rinsed it with sea water and returned with it to the stern.
From beneath the stern thwart, he withdrew the Captain's ceremonial sword, pulled it from its scabbard and cut the Captain's
throat, collecting the spilling blood in the water cask. When the
last drops had drained, Abodeefa stripped the Captain, throwing
his clothes overboard, and washed the corpse thoroughly with
salt water. He cut a fatty slice from Crawshaw's haunch and ate
it, chewing slowly and washing it down with a sip of blood. He
smiled. "Oh, sah," he said, in a voice which, except for a note of
insincerity, sounded exactly like Cannonball's, "yo' so good to
dis ole nigger." He laughed wildly, and performed a slow, shuffling dance in the bilges.

Eight days later, having consumed the Captain, down to and
including his bone marrow, and having disposed of all of Crawshaw's remains and possessions (excepting the logbook, which
he kept with him, and which was eventually discovered among
the wreckage of a small plane salvaged from Lake Monona,
Wisconsin, in the Winter of 1968), Abodeefa was beached on
one of the lesser islands of the Tuamotu Archipelago, where he
received an amiable reception from the natives. He stayed
among their tribe for nearly twenty years, and even served as
their king for a brief period, until deposed by a jealous faction.
But that's another story, and will be told in its time too.

IN THE MEN'S ROOM OF THE SIXTEENTH CENTURY

Don DeLillo

t was the anniversary of the beheading of St. Thomas More, an incandescent night in Times Square, all manner of humanity engaged in vintage decadence.

Thomas Patrick Guffey walked into the precinct house just before midnight. The squad room was full of people arguing and sobbing, another summer night of arsonists, petty thieves, throat-slashers, film projectionists, Hispanic pimps, dynamiters, lost Iowans, molesters of every kind, hillbilly visionaries with bloody heads, so on and so forth, all of them being informed of their Constitutional rights. Guffey nodded hello here and there and went upstairs to his locker. He took off his sport coat and the pale green tie (embossed initials) which his youngest daughter had given him for his birthday. He transferred the snub-nosed .38 from his shoulder holster to the beige handbag inside the locker. At the far end of the room the precinct captain, Terrible Teddy Effing, was methodically punching and kicking a small hump-chested man in a black overcoat and skullcap. Guffey continued undressing. When he was finished he pounded his right fist into the palm of his left hand nine times. Then he took a padded bra and a pair of India-silk panties out of the locker and put them on. After a good deal of thought he got into a red-and-yellow Mexican maxi-dress—a fantastic flowing creation patterned with stars, mystic eyes and scorpions. He slipped into brown espadrilles and took his makeup kit into the bathroom. He washed his face with cold water. Then he sponged on some pancake, sketched a bit with an eyebrow pencil, applied eye shadow and used a thin sable-tipped brush to anoint his lids with liquid eye-liner. He stuck on false lashes with surgical glue. He followed this by applying mascara, as well as a few strokes of blusher to accent the cheekbones and give them an ascetic look. Then he chose a pastel peach shade of lipstick and followed it with clear gloss. He went back to his locker. It was exactly midnight. He put on a burnt sienna custom wig, brass and silver bracelets, an onyx ring on every finger. He picked up the handbag and went downstairs.

Near the desk his partner Vincent Capezio was questioning a stout bearded man who kept spitting on his right hand and then blessing himself. Capezio gestured to Guffey, who glanced at the clock over the desk and joined his partner.

"I spotted the perpetrator on Forty-third Street," Capezio said. "I took cognizance of the fact that he was peering into the windows of parked motor vehicles. I followed him to Eighth Avenue. At this locale he took out an implement and wedged open the left front window of a 1932 Bugatti Royale with DPL plates. When I identified myself as a law-enforcement officer, the perpetrator began to act in a loud and boisterous manner. He assaulted me with his hands and disarmed me. Then he fled in a westerly direction. I pursued him on foot and with the aid of patrolmen Passacaglia and Fugue I overpowered the son of a bitch and brought him here for booking."

"Why are you telling me this, Vince?"

"Because he denies he's a car booster."

"I deny," the man said.

"He says he's Bernal of Almería, a saint and former soldier of the Cross. I can't deal with him, Tommy. Effing tried, and Effing can't deal with him either. When Effing can't deal with something, it automatically falls into your category. The guy just won't answer questions. He says saints have traditionally cloaked themselves in silence. It's definitely in your category, Tommy. He says he rode with Cortez."

"I am the one they call Lady Madonna," Guffey said. "If you tell me what's in your heart, I'll do what I can for you. If you refuse to cooperate, you'll probably be tortured and thrown into prison. Mercy is all but unknown and good intentions rot with the meat of dogs."

"You have insulted my dignity," the man said.

Capezio hit him in the mouth and dragged him across the floor toward the cage. Guffey went out into the equatorial night, through humid air palpable as surf, north toward the lights and mad music. Six glossy prostitutes came toward him, shoulder to shoulder across the sidewalk, wearing polymerized thermoplastic dresses and Styrofoam slave bracelets. Right behind them was an individual called Jack & Jill, a known hermaphrodite and suspected dealer in unsterilized hypodermic needles. Guffey crossed the street and went into one of the all-night movie houses, the Basilica, a former showcase for wholesome family movies, now a vaulted haunt of such apathy that the screen often remained blank for days at a time, a fact which seemed to go unnoticed by the patrons. Great silver candlesticks lined the walls of the darkened lobby. Guffey wandered through the theatre. There were busts of desiccated popes and bleak noblemen. Banners and battle standards hung high on the grey walls, reminding him of his honeymoon in Europe, the sublime sense of civilization expressed even in torture chambers and cells. He stood near one of the balcony exits, watching the movie, a necrophile epic, and was soon approached by a long-haired emaciated young man who tried to sell him four capsules of a drug called pseudothalgenomide, a chemically hybrid stimulant so powerful it was able to cause cancer in organically dead tissue.

"I could easily put you under arrest."

"Then you must be Lady Madonna," the young man said. "They talk about you wherever the counter-culture puts down roots."

"What's your story, son?"

"I've sniffed, ate and shot every drug there is. Cyclogen, sleet, moko, gribbies, deecee, flash, sujo pinda. My head's just about inside out."

"The hardest road of all is the road that leads from reason."

"Ain't that the goddamn truth. All I want to do now is get on back to the border states. I'm all through with junk. I want to grow apples and broccoli. I want to spend ten minutes every morning doing squat-jumps and rapping with Jesus."

Guffey opened his handbag and gave the young man a Xeroxed sheet summarizing the *Metaphysical Disputations* of Suárez. Then he went downstairs to make his customary check of the rest-room facilities. The men's toilet reminded him of one of the bathrooms in the railroad station in Venice, not cleaned since the Renaissance, an extremely poignant spot, the fecal confluence of many cultures. He scrutinized his makeup in the mirror and then turned and watched as the derelict known as Agony Of The Rose crawled slowly across the wet tile floor to put his lips to the poised tip of Guffey's right shoe. On the wall above the urinals were stone-cold words boldly stroked in black: TIME-SPACE PSYCHOSIS FOLLOWS THE SHATTERING OF THE LOOP OF HISTORY ACCORDING TO THE COMPUTER DEMONS OF GIAM-BATTISTA VICO. In the lobby he saw Burgo Swinney, the eunuchoid pornographer, wearing an ecru velveteen jump suit and clear vinyl moccasins.

"*Quo vadis?*" Swinney said.

Dozens of people lounged outside a record store on Forty-second Street. Preadolescent boys for sale. Militant forestry students. Harbingers and importuners. Jackbooted Chinese bik-

Don DeLillo

ers. Hard-rock guitarists in Vietcong sweatshirts. A teen-age girl sat on a suitcase sniffing a handful of oxidized camphor pellets through a long plastic straw. Guffey touched the girl's head, then walked past the Persian baths, the computerized horoscope parlor, the deviation bookstore, the guns-and-ammo discount center, the homoerotic wax museum, the Jansenist reading room, the leper clinic, the paraplegic sex exhibit, the Afro-Cuban ballroom, the jujitsu academy, the pubic-wig boutique, the electric brain-massage outlet. At the end of the block he spotted Teeny Maeve Feeney, a former Ursuline abbess who now walked the streets trying to lure pleasure-seekers to her room. Maeve worked in platonic concert with Longjaw Ed Jolly, a man who claimed to be the last living member of the Castrated Priests of Cybele, a self-mutilation cult. Once Maeve's customer was in the room, Ed Jolly would appear with a sawed-off shotgun and confront the man with a list of questions concerning predestination, idealistic pantheism, the self-knowledge of angels, the existence of the Cynocephali—a race of men with doglike heads mentioned in the writings of St. Augustine. A single wrong answer prompted the two fanatics to initiate the Ravensburg Pattern, a series of cybernetic tortures. Guffey was always saddened to see these men and women in their hopeless roles, sinners in religious fever, poetic desperadoes, carnal martyrs of the Western dream. He turned a corner, away from the traffic noise and buzzing neon, and went into a small dark club called Galileo's Folly, a raided premises and known head-quarters for narcotics traffickers. He went straight back to the circular oak table where Niccolò Tancredi, the owner, customarily held forth. Tancredi was an impeccably dressed, clear-thinking and unemotional man, somewhat jesuitically inclined, extremely lean of body, his voice a cheese-grating rasp. He commented favorably on Guffey's Sant'Angelo handbag with its silken ropes and vaguely Middle English motif. They talked a while of Giacomo (Jimmy the Jap) Chikamatsu, missing since

71

spring from his suburban home with its flamingo-studded Zen garden. Tancredi was in a reflective mood.

"Man's salvation is far from assured," he said. "We're in mortal danger of losing the oldest and greatest battle."

"Man is good, Tancredi. He strives, he suffers, he bares his soul to the one true universe. He gives it his all."

"Old friend, the pale light of reason is on my side. We burn slowly and unknowingly. We're aware of nothing but our own search for self-annihilation. Hell is the living electricity."

"Fire is fire," Guffey said. "Light is light."

"But what is apparent is not what is real. I am a sinner, you a saint. But we burn in the same living fire. The fire of earth. The fire of air. The fire of fire. The fire of water. The Greeks knew but four elements. Is our death more glorious than theirs?"

"Man's salvation is wrung minute by minute out of his solitude. Have you read the Edict of Costa del Sol?"

"My subscription ran out."

"Your humor refines itself with the years, Tancredi."

"It is perfectable, my friend, as man is not."

Later they sat in Tancredi's dimly lit office and discussed the syndicate's opium holdings. Soon they were joined by four men, one of them Tancredi's brother, Asmodeus, a federal judge; the others, wearing white poppies in their lapels were enforcers of one kind or another. Tancredi suggested that Guffey remain for the interrogation of a would-be courier for the Mediterranean heroin combine. The candidate was brought in—a young, pale, delicately proportioned man. In questioning him, Tancredi referred to a book that looked to Guffey very much like the Baltimore Catechism he had used in grade school.

"Who made you?"

"God made me."

"Who is God?"

"God is the supreme being of heaven and earth Who made all things."

"Why did God make you?"

"God made me to love and honor Him on this earth and in the world to come."

The examination went on for about an hour. Gradually the questions became more difficult, dealing with infinitely compressible theological points, vast mysteries, proofs of refutations of proofs. Tancredi's scorched voice seemed almost eternal, a final moment burning beyond itself.

"It is affirmed that the Holy Ghost is present in raw opium. True or false?"

"True—if by 'present' it is meant that substantial form is not negated by first effects."

"It is affirmed that the One, Holy, Catholic and Apostolic Church, presided over by a Supreme Pontiff, Vicar of Christ on earth, is sole agent for and distributor of cut and uncut white crystalline narcotics on this earth, thus propagating the Holy Spirit and redeeming mankind. True or false?"

"Wait," Guffey said. "The boy needs help. He's no match for you, Tancredi. He can't be more than nineteen. Think of yourself at that age."

"I wrote fascist poems."

"You must be the good cop," the boy said. "We heard about you in North Africa. The drag-saint. Comforter of the afflicted."

"The earth is a woman," Guffey said. "Those who live on the earth are shaped to a woman's shape and comforted by a woman's form. Fortunately the commissioner's office understands this."

"Very well and good," Tancredi said. "Now that we have finished, it's time to begin again. This time you will not give the right answers but only the answers you believe in."

"I've done that."

"You believe nothing of this. We are the only believers. The syndicate is the true mystical body. We are powerful because we believe. We are untouchable because we believe. We are the Church and the Church is us. We live forever because we believe."

"He answered the questions," Guffey said. "How do you know he doesn't believe?"

"He has not the blood."

"Belief is lodged in the most remote places of the heart. You can't reach it even with threats of death."

"You claim to believe?" Tancredi said to the boy.

"Forever, yes."

"You will die for your beliefs?"

"I believe. Now more than ever."

"Then we will begin again. If you give the same answers, you prove you believe, and your life will end violently in a matter of minutes. Are you ready, courier-of-sand-to-the-gods-of-time?"

"I'm ready."

Tancredi reopened the book to the very beginning.

"Who made you?"

"Two normally functioning adults engaged in the act of copulation, with or without intent to engender further life, made me."

Tancredi smiled, his point won, his chilly brand of reason reaffirmed. He approached Guffey and kissed him lightly on each sparsely powdered cheek. Guffey left the club and headed into the night, horns blowing, bells ringing, the lame and the beggarly muttering their supplications. He walked past a woman pushing a baby carriage full of decomposing meat. On Forty-fourth Street he saw Killy Williams, an ex-prizefighter who spent his time directing traffic in the Times Square area. Williams tipped his porkpie hat to Guffey.

"Maybe you recall me," he said. "I fought prelims for six years at the old Garden. I possessed all the equipage to win big.

But I was a man who liked to lose. I craved the emotionship of losing. There was a wonderment to it. I've always been complex and introspective. I liked to analyze my defeats. In victory there's nothing to analyze. It was my introspectability that made me a loser. My trainer was Wiggy Abandando, who handled some of the great ones. You probably recall him. Before every fight he'd slap me three times hard in the face. To get the mean blood running. But you can't exteriorize anger. It has to come from inside. I guess I'll head on over to Broadway now. I hear traffic's backed up to infinity."

Guffey hadn't gone half a block when he saw five patrolmen trying to surround the gypsy woman named Dark As The Cave Where My True Love Did Those Things. She seemed to be in a frenzy, scratching and hissing at the men, keeping them at a distance. Vastas Panowski, one of the cops, spotted Guffey and came over.

"Tommy, we can't control her. She won't let us get close enough to put a hand on her."

"What's she done?"

"She's been walking around all night trying to grab the crotches of passersby. I've never seen her this wild. She's been darting at every crotch in sight, like a mongoose. Capezio came by a little while ago and tried to take her in on a nine-fourteen. But she scared him away. He thought she was going to turn him into a wild goat or a lily pad if she ever got her hands on his crotch. He said that's how the curse works. The crotch is the focal point. If she gets to your crotch, she can turn you into one of four different things, depending on your astrological sign. Capezio's on a cusp."

"I want to talk to her," Guffey said.

He followed the patrolman toward the group. Everybody moved out of the way. Dark As The Cave fell to her knees at the sight of the bright maxi-dress.

"Lady Madonna."

"Anxiety is the broken bow of the man-tribe. Once that fact sinks in, you'll no longer be afraid. Go back to your storefront home and try not to get hypertense. Touch my hand and go quickly."

Guffey went down the block and turned a dark corner, aware that someone was following him—white, male, early fifties, grey-templed, six feet two, one ninety-five, tie-dyed snakeskin trousers, gold silk bow tie, buttonless black dinner jacket piped with black satin. Guffey waited in front of a side-street theatre exit, his handbag open and his fingers tickling blissfully at the smoky blue steel of the .38. The stranger approached him now, a spode-faced man with platinum eyebrows and slightly puckered lips.

"I know who you are," the man said, "and I want to make a deal with you. Let me identify myself. Grambling Douglaston Clapper. The name may ring a bell. For the past three months my wife and I have been hosting a series of buffet dances in order to raise money for the United States Air Force, particularly the Strategic Air Command, one of my favorite branches of the military. But that's scarcely apropos. The point is as follows. We've recently become interested in possession by demons and we plan to start a nationwide chain of clinics, to be run on a franchise basis, devoted to exorcism and general postoperative therapy. We need somebody to run things from the spiritual standpoint. We're basically business-oriented, you see. The job will pay many times your present salary and there are stock options as well."

Guffey withdrew the .38 from his handbag and told the man to face the great metal door of the theatre. He hit him with the gun butt, just once, beneath the right ear. It was beginning to get light. Guffey walked over to Seventh Avenue, there to see Wilkie Kinbote, the perennially unemployed Jonsonian actor, lying in the gutter with his head resting on an empty bottle of

eight-year-old Glenfiddich. A boy was divesting him of his
Eton jacket, and two girls were using spoons and bottle openers
in an attempt to extract some teeth. The kids scattered when
they saw Guffey, who bent over the actor and cradled his
purplish scabby face.

"Wilkie, it's me."

"I haven't felt this out-of-sorts in twenty years. Give me
something to go on, Lady M. Some hope. A reason to bear up."

"An English pasture of the mind."

"Is that it?" the actor said.

"A shady nook of the mind. A sort of grassy mental resting
place. A leafy ensconcement. A mytho-lyrical bower deep in a
dell."

"In actual point of fact, I'm beginning to see what you mean."

"Lemonade amid the trellis-work."

"Yes, go on."

"A greensward of the mind."

"Great God in boots, I think I see it."

Guffey got up, then extended his hand to be kissed. Across
the street Erasmus von Hess y Vega, flanked by two catamites
holding muzzled Dobermans on short leashes, was giving a small
group of tourists and drifters his standard sermon on the Fourth
Reich, the realm of space and relativity brought into man's reach
by the new knowledge trickling out of Germany—that the universe is tuba-shaped, that heavy industry is unknown in other
solar systems, that the planet Uranus was once part of Germany,
having been torn away in a monumental earth spasm countless
eons ago, and is soon to be reclaimed by its rightful owner.
Guffey listened awhile, standing next to Monsignor Bob Dock-
ery, the abortionist priest. Then he went into an all-night
cafeteria and had coffee at a table in the rear. Two groggy flies
circled his cup. A girl in khaki screamed at him: "Fascist peeeg
power structure! White peeeg police! People's justice for
peeegs." The place was full of pigeon feeders, rejected blood

donors, men drinking muscatel, eerie female derelicts with news-papered feet, those who fornicated with incubi, those who fingered unholy talismans. A clean-cut young man, remarkably tall and lanky, took the chair across from Guffey.

"They told me I might find you here," he said. "I used to play basketball at the University of Kentucky. We won S.E.C. honors three years running. I had athletic greatness in me. But I soon realized I carry within me a kind of divine spark, a missionary quality that impels me to seek dark corners in which to work some good. My name is Lee (The Tree) McGee and I want to be a social worker. Tell me how to prepare."

"Read the accounts of the Black Plague," Guffey said. "Read the accounts of the Great Fire of London, the orgies of papal Avignon, the siege of Malta, the self-flagellation cults of the Rhine provinces, the burning of heretics, the Hundred Years' War. Check cross-references and bibliographies. Read on into the night."

"Who are the fallen, Lady Madonna?"

"The fallen are those who sin against God."

"Who are the just?"

"The just are those who sin against man."

"What is the greatest sorrow?"

"The greatest sorrow is simply to be."

Guffey walked slowly toward the precinct house. The sun was visible over silent construction sites, between the bones of partly demolished buildings, against the black glass of condemned skyscrapers. Inside, Capezio was questioning a strange ageless half-naked man; his head and upper body were totally without hair, no eyebrows or lashes or traces of beard, and his face conveyed the character of an off-white eraser at the end of a pencil. Capezio waved Guffey over.

"He says his name is Count Ugo Malatesta. He and his daughter or sister, we're not sure which she is, have been buying up teen-age corpses from one of the medical centers in order to use the lungs, sex members and kidneys in some kind of unspeakable rite. The guy's a real wisenheimer; won't say anything without a lawyer. His sister or daughter is pregnant with his child, due any minute, so we sent her over to Rikers Island for delivery or incarceration, whichever comes first. I heard you took care of the gypsy woman before she could get to your crotch."

"She'll be all right for a while."

"We're dealing with medieval forces," Capezio said.

"That's very true, Vincent."

Suddenly the hairless man dropped to the floor in a fit of mad drooling laughter. Guffey went upstairs to his locker, freshly painted in the unruly blue of a Blakean apocalypse. He undressed, got cleaned up, and put on his trousers, shoes, shirt and sport coat. He was straightening his tie when he realized he wasn't alone. Sitting at a chessboard in a distant corner of the room, apparently waiting for a challenger, was the man called Blessed Gondolfo, a polydactyl albino dwarf who bore the stigmata.

Guffey returned the .38 to his shoulder holster. He pounded his right fist into the palm of his left hand nine times. Then he left the precinct house and took the subway home to Queens.

I AM ELIJAH THRUSH

James Purdy

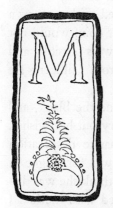

illicent De Frayne, who was young in 1913, the sole possessor of an immense oil fortune, languished of an incurable ailment—her will-ful hopeless love for Elijah Thrush, "mime, poet, painter of art nouveau, most beautiful man in the world," who, after ruining the lives of countless men and women, was finally him-self in love "incorrectly, if not indecently," with his great-grandson.

Because of my dependence on my habit I was fool enough to become a paid memoirist to Millicent De Frayne, and because I am black I was chosen by her likewise on the ground many doors in New York closed to a white man would be opened to me.

My work was painful, as eating éclairs and napoleons seven hours a day might be, but my habit (which I will describe later on) demanded support. Although my constitution is hardy, my nerves are delicate, and I had never been adept either at crime or at daily employment. Nor was I gifted as a defender of my own people, although I live now and will, I suppose, continue to live at the Father Divine Fairgroves Hotel. At the risk of leading the reader to think this story is about myself, let me say that I admire the violence and insurgency of my present-day "broth-ers" (a word I smile at nonetheless), but I can only live and be what I am, a desperate man, though a comfortable one. Perhaps if I were lighter—Elijah Thrush on my first visit to the Arcturus Gardens, his studio, said bluntly: "You are the color of ripe eggplant!"—I might pass. My sole passion was my habit, and my task here was to earn for that habit by reciting the exploits of Elijah Thrush, as dictated by his "paramour," Millicent De Frayne. It is for this reason that this story, in neither vocabulary nor meaning, will be in the taste of the present epoch, and for this reason also I embrace it wholeheartedly.

Because I am black everything is forgiven me by whites, which may be the reason I have been entrusted with a story a white writer, straining for nobility, for current coin, would not dare stoop to pick up. I am allowed to be as low as possible, and there is always an apology waiting. Except from Millicent De Frayne.

She had no love of the human race, let alone the black, and her only interest in life seemed to be that I carry out her wishes. My kind of consistent, lethargic, and undynamic desperation made me "do." She was a direct woman and was forthright in expressing her surprise that I did not "smell." I think she was disappointed. She would have been more collected with me had I done so. Later Elijah Thrush corrected her indirectly when, after having kissed me in a purely ceremonious way, he said, "Albert, you smell like a nocturnal moth I once crushed against my chest many years gone past, in Nebraska."

As the struggle to support my habit tired me greatly, I was glad for the time to be in the company of such superannuated persons as Elijah and Millicent. They rested me, and all I had to do was listen and feign attention. Attention gradually came, if not interest. And of course I wrote down what they told me. Yes, as close as it was possible for anybody to interest me, those two old parties came near to doing the trick. In fact they almost suited me to a T.

"I am a difficult, I am an impossible woman," Millicent had begun that stifling July day as we sat in her Fifth Avenue apart-

84

ment. She did not allow air-conditioning to be installed, and she kept the windows closed. Indeed, she wore a fur about her throat, which she occasionally brought higher around her neck as if feeling a draft of cold air.

"I have never worked with a person of your complexion." She studied my necktie. "Frankly, you are not what I would have selected had I the power of selection. But I am desperate. All the other memoirists have failed. They were miserable things, impostors all. I will not say I am counting on you, mind you. No such thing. But I have a kind of frayed hope. There is something about you that almost kindles optimism. Not quite. If you don't work out, have no fear. You'll be paid generously, just as if you finished the memoirs. Now, as to your duties. I want you first of all to listen to me. I'll go over his life with you, and you'll write down a skeleton of the facts. Then I'd have you go and spy on him. That's right, *spy* on him. Find out who his friends are, who he's seeing, and what's up with the child he calls the Bird of Heaven, who is his great-grandson. This is our bone of contention. I don't want him to love the boy. But first of all you must get to know the Arcturus Gardens, his dance studio and theatre. I've kept him in it for over thirty years, you understand. Have a dish of tea with me." Millicent then spoke in a voice of peevish command, and a gawky Swedish woman brought in a gleaming tea service. "We have only lemon," Millicent explained as Norah handed me an exquisite paper-thin cup adorned with forget-me-nots.

"I suppose I am the only person who is anybody who is not at the shore." She consulted a huge calendar on the wall. "Now I don't suppose you are afraid of bad neighborhoods. If you are, speak up at once and I will hire a bodyguard for you. Good, you have no fear. I raise the question of mayhem at this time because Thrush lives in the district on Manhattan Island around lower Tenth Avenue, which I understand in the days of good professional criminals they called Hell's Kitchen.

85

"Now as to strategy." Millicent commanded Norah to pour me another cup of tea. Drops of perspiration were standing out on my brow, and I could feel Norah's interest, revulsion, and wonderment as she poured me more of the lovely gunpowder. "Wipe his face with a napkin, can't you?" Millicent told the maid. "He's dripping wet from the torrid day, though he comes, as you've noticed from his face, from where people are sun-worshipers. Well, we all notice heat more or less, there's no gainsaying that, whoever we are. Now, as to your task. You say you're not afraid of thugs. Well and good. You're to go, then, to the Arcturus Gardens, where his studio is. Take this forged letter, though he'll know I wrote it or had it written. It's a request to have your portrait done. That's the easiest way to get into his studio." I put the letter in my breast pocket. "He does portraits for pocket money, since his dancing recitals are canceled during the hot months, and even in the winter they bring in hardly a dime in a month of Sundays. Now, Albert— do you have a last name, by the by?"

"Peggs," I told her.

"P as in porker?" she said.

I nodded.

"Well, Albert Peggs, you will go there, and of course spend as much time with him as you can stand to. Again, like heat, 'tis a matter of temperament. Many a person I've sent there couldn't take it and got deathly ill. He's not a health ad, you see, and hasn't washed his face in over twenty-five years because he feels it ruins the complexion. That won't bother you, though, will it? If so, say so. But be warned, the studio, though not as aired out as here, is *too* interesting: it recalls a zoo and an emporium of antiques both, and again, like hot weather, is hard on the arteries. He'll ply you with questions because he'll know you come from me. I would simply decline to discuss me, if you don't mind. When he vilifies me, just smile, or do nothing, or agree. Where are those Scotch cookies I asked for, Norah?"

She turned to the Swedish maid who was waiting, I gathered, to wipe my forehead again. "Well, fetch them before Albert goes off on his assignment, and whilst you're at it, my love, make him up a little brace of chicken dainty sandwiches so he can tide himself over till nightfall.

"No, Albert, my dear, I'll be frank with you about another matter also. In no way be too *intimate* with the Mime. I hope my warning is clear. I mean, you must not go over to his side. I'm the one paying the piper, and 'twon't do at all for you to take his part, or soldier for him. He's an abominable low mountebank when he feels the urge, which is most of the time, remember. But I've sent people before who's fallen in love with him. He is first-water mesmerism, no question about it, and in Old Salem would have been burned at the stake. He is a wizard. I've carried the cross of caring for him, and have only been rejected for my pains. As I told you, or did I? he hates me to within an inch of my life, once told me he could eat my kidney roasted on an andiron, and so forth. But it's of me he thinks constantly, you see—obsessed with me, that is, and as I've loved him since 1913, this has to be my only reward from that quarter.

"How many sandwiches did you put in, Norah?" She took the ivory lunch box from the Swedish maid, and peeked into it. "Mmm, well, that ought to stay him. Are you an awful big eater, Albert? Speak up, it's no crime if you have capacity. I won't let you suffer hunger pangs. Now then, off with you to the Arcturus Gardens. Be back here bright and early at nine tomorrow, and we'll begin our chores and chronicles in earnest.

"One last word of warning." She got up with great difficulty, refusing to take my hand, and leaning on a cane whose head was encrusted with jewels which blinked. "Beware of the piano player."

I nodded to let her know I would, but this irritated her.

"Don't ever pretend to knowledge you don't have, Albert Peggs," she scolded. "You don't know him. He's incredibly wicked, and incredibly charming. Looks like those kewpies at carnivals, I always thought, so well-groomed and clean, but a loathsome creature. He's shamelessly devoted to the Mime, and tries to prevent my ever communicating with him."

She suddenly took my hand in so convulsive a grasp that she clawed me as she stuck, I thought, something in my palm. Then, with a grip like that of a strong man, she closed my hand.

In the street I noticed I was holding—in addition to the forged letter in my jacket pocket and the chicken dainty sandwiches in my left hand—no fewer than two hundred-dollar bills in my right hand. I stopped and blinked in sunlight, for when I had left her apartment I had made the vow never to return, and of course never to go near the Arcturus Gardens, and certainly never to see Elijah Thrush, formerly the most beautiful man in the world. But there is no talking back to two hundred-dollar bills when you are the color of ripe eggplant and sweat more readily than white quality.

I decided, despite the heat, to walk all the way to his studio.

Eugene Bellamy, the piano player about whom Millicent had warned me, proved in many ways a more formidable and arresting figure than either Millicent De Frayne or the Mime of Tenth Avenue. Not that he *looked* formidable, for he resembled one of those toy bridegrooms one sees on Italian wedding cakes. Indeed, he looked as if made of spun sugar and, like the Mime, he had a Cupid's bow mouth. But unlike the Mime's, Eugene Bellamy's mouth was not formed by Dorin lip rouge.

I had got myself together, tied my tie—though it was so soaked with perspiration from my long walk from uptown that it resembled a wilted poppy, head downward—and, raising my chin to the right level of confidence, but without the angry hauteur of my people today, I rang the bell. A kind of tinkle of dromedary bells sounded. Many bolts and locks were heard moving, and the huge green door was pulled open. There, with folded arms, the piano player dared me to speak and double-dared me to enter.

"I am the bearer of this letter of introduction to Mr. Elijah Thrush, the noted mime and portrait painter," I began.

"The evenings are closed now at the studio, I would have you know," the piano player said, closing the door. Whereupon the thought of losing future installments of hundred-dollar bills impelled me to shoulder past him.

"I am sorry to be so forward." I looked him to within an inch of the eye and shot out my chest, which is still, despite my advanced years (I am twenty-nine), an effect that frightens white people. Though ruined in all other ways, I possess a perfect African physique.

"What I have to say to the Mime will not wait," I stood my ground in the room.

"Where did you get it into your head [I think he was about to say 'thick' but thought better of it], where did you get it into your head to address Mr. Thrush as the Mime?"

"I will not state my business to an intermediary, and I immediately demand to be given a seat and to be announced," I told the piano player.

"Well spoken, and beautifully delivered!" We heard a cavernous voice reverberate through the huge room into which I had walked uninvited. The bead curtain parted, and a creature entered, one I at first mistook to be among the paraphernalia of my hidden life. Though I cannot grow pale, I can look ashen and unwell, and so it was that the creature standing before me—who was of course Elijah Thrush—seeing my altered state, ordered the piano player to fetch his palm fan, and, sitting beside me on a little hand-carved stool, in the same deep voice began, "Call me Mime if you will, for in all my years as an artist I have never set eyes on one with so primitively princely a presence as yourself. Will you retire to the recitation room, if you please, my dear Bellamy," he turned to the piano player, who smirked a bit and left.

"Pray what brings you here when, as you heard, the evenings are closed?"

"I have come from quite a distance. Alabama," I said.

"You have no more come from Alabama than I have," Elijah Thrush said. "Understand my meaning," he tapped my knee at a bubble of protestation from me. "You have come from destiny. You were meant to know me. I was meant to know you. Thousands of years ago we knew one another, you and I. Long after we have cast off the flesh and bones of this unworthy existence under which we suffer now, you and I will know one another again. I knew immediately I heard your voice you were the new person in my life."

I now gazed with less dizziness at the face before me. I had the feeling it was a painting uttering these sounds. There seemed to be no bone structure—to be sure, no skin—for what issued the words was a kind of swimming agglutination of mascara, rouge, green tinting, black teeth, and hair like the leavings of an abandoned crow's nest.

"Alabama, indeed." He continued to fan my face. "You have come in response to the advertisement I placed in the news-paper, of course." He now rose and stood by a grand piano.

"I have come," I began, falling now, as I was to later, into his own language, "I have come only to know you, Mr. Thrush."

"Elijah," he corrected, and I saw, now he was standing, that his body looked more substantial than his face, this despite the fact he had on a costume so lavish and fantastic that it, like the face above it, seemed more the property of a picture than of life.

"Everything you say goes directly to my heart." Elijah Thrush now set to swaying and lifting his feet ever so slightly, so that I could see he was indeed a dancer.

Rising at last, I proffered the letter of Millicent De Frayne, saying only, "This is my introduction." Like the sudden change of weather in the open country when the sun is covered by an unforeseen cloud, and both rain and hail beat on the unprepared traveler, I saw his face contort with heavy lines. Raving as if I had knifed him, he cried, "You damned deceiver! You come from that rotten woman! Don't defend youself. Rise and get out. Do you hear? Get out!"

The beaded curtains parted and the piano player came forward more frightened than frightening, Elijah Thrush meanwhile tearing up the letter and screaming, "Go at once, or I will summon the authorities."

Pushing the piano player out of the room, I went over to Elijah Thrush, took the last shreds of paper from his hand, handed back to him the larger portion of them, and said quietly, "I have come to stay, Elijah. What does it matter who introduced us? We have met, and I am yours. Command me anything, but not to go out of your life."

"Are you, in God's name, real?" He went to weeping now. I supposed then (not now) that this was play-acting.

"Look at me," he said. "Prove you are real. *Comfort* me!"

Although white men had offered me their lust before, nobody white had ever offered me illusion, together with courtesy, attention, and persuasive theatrics. For a moment I felt I would give up my attachment to the expensive habit that had propelled me into the world of Elijah Thrush and Millicent De Frayne, and be his, and perhaps her, captive. But would white kindness, of even this willed variety, last? Would it not be followed, as always, by betrayal and enslavement?

"Do you realize what it is to have someone plotting against you every minute of the day?" Elijah was speaking of the "depraved" Millicent De Frayne. "Look at that clock and listen, listen. . . . You've heard it tick forty-two times as I point, and in every one of those forty-two beats she has thought of forty-two ways to beat me to my knees."

Whether it was my terrible life, my race, whatever, I found

everything he said believable, and once my eyes were accustomed to the sight of him, I found him, yes, I thought him beautiful. I did not reject his caresses, and he went on all this time fanning me with the palm leaf. It was a wonderful sensation. Occasionally I would catch glimpses of the distorted face of the piano player as he looked out at us from the beaded curtain.

"Pay no mind to Eugene Bellamy. He is harmless." Raising his voice, "You should be practicing the *Cornish Rhapsody*. I've had ten piano players to ruin it better than you. I want perfection, damn it, and what do I get but a mooning lovesick calf like Eugene Bellamy." And then turning back to me, "Alabama must be particularly fortunate if you came from out of its depths," fanning so close that from the recesses of my clothing a large brown feather rose, like something alive, and this he caught deftly in his hand. He put down his fan. "Where on earth did this come from?" he cried in a voice of unimpeachable awe. "Bellamy!" he called, and then thought better of it. I was shaken with a fit of trembling. "What is the meaning of this feather?" he demanded. "Have you brought it here? And if so, for what purpose? You know what I am talking about, don't you?"

"In Alabama the unusual is the usual," I spoke out of a mouth as dry as description.

Breaking into a charming laugh, he corrected, "It is impossible to be angry with someone as fetching as you. Yet God knows what you are up to. I have never forgiven anybody as many times as I have already forgiven you. You come from the one woman who remains committed to destroy me, you insult my piano player, you beat your way unannounced into my presence, you show no knowledge of my genius or who I am, you give me a forged letter, and then, as I am fanning you like your slave, the feather of a bird of prey falls from your rich mahogany chest!"

Despite the humor of his queer phraseology, at his last words I became very agitated again. A kind of foam came from my lips.

Urging me most politely from my chair, the Mime and the piano player led me to another room, where they made to remove my clothing to begin applications of witch hazel. But when they removed my clothing, both were taken aback at, in Elijah's word, the display of jewels I carried on my naked person. True, I had several bracelets near my biceps, three necklaces, and a stone I wear in my navel. The jewels convinced Elijah that I was, beyond any peradventure of a doubt, the most remarkable adult male, of whatever color, he had ever met.

"I do not say of any *person*," he added, "because there is the Bird of Heaven. . . ."

"I wish you wouldn't use that term!" I cried, anger coming over me, more froth foaming from my lips.

"I beg your pardon." He turned, though to Bellamy, as if Bellamy had been the one to speak disrespectfully.

"I can't have you use those references," I told him, and took his white hand and caressed it against my cheek.

"You are overwrought, my dear," he smiled. "God, how I love temperament after the milk-and-water creatures I live with. The Bird of Heaven is my great-grandson. It is also the supreme emotional attachment of my career. He was given the name Bird of Heaven—" here I began writhing, but Elijah continued, "—the name was given him by his colored servant and nurse. Because of my love for him I am barred from ever seeing the boy. He is supervised by a guardian as terrible and lowdown as Millicent De Frayne herself. Damn these duennas of the world who keep decent parties apart!" he cried, and he began walking about the room, beating his breast, arranging a loose earring, and making weeping sounds.

Turning on me suddenly, "I won't be bossed by you, smitten as I am by your overpowering personality. And furthermore, mark this down, you have got to give that woman up, do you hear? And I want an explanation of this feather," in a sudden rage. Taking the hand he offered, I bit it again and again, while his piercing screams echoed through the building. He fell against me then, and we lay there, becoming calm, comforting one another.

Hours later, as he bade me a warm embrace of good-bye, I made him promise not to force me to give up Millicent De Frayne.

"You will never know, Albert, how many concessions you have wrung from me in the one day of our wonderful friendship. I have committed treason against myself all for your sake. You are in the pay, as a spy, of my mortal enemy, and I go along with it. You forbid me to give the only name I have ever used for my great-grandson, and I seem to go along with that too."

"I will stop my ears, and let you say his name," I pampered him.

But even as he said *Bird of Heaven*, my fingers in my ears, I shivered and shook, and the sweat gathered again on my body.

I came to long for the company of Elijah and Millicent. Yet weekly there had to be—and this was wrung from them with the greatest difficulty—hours when I boarded the Staten Island ferry and went to the zoo, where I patiently transacted business in one of the buildings. I do not know who resented these absences more, Millicent or Elijah. Had I gone to the Cameroons, they could not have been more edgy. "You have no right to go so far!" both using the same expression, for, as I was later to find, they often spoke in the same phrases and idioms. After all, they had been enemies longer than most people live.

"If you think he's wonderful now, wait till the snow flies!" Millicent said after listening to the account of my visit. "When the Arcturus Gardens opens for the winter recital season," she went on. Suddenly she was laughing, a sound like a mechanical disturbance. "Until you have seen him dance, you know nothing of him. He's only himself when he lets the crocus curtain rise, and then he's Adonis or Pierrot or Narcissus. Of course, I pay for it all, you understand."

"He denies you give him a penny."

She smoothed the folds of a leather pouch, and then carefully opened it. Inside was a gold beaded purse with a dazzling fastener. When she opened it, one heard a sound like a pistol going off. She extricated from this purse a huge feather.

"You must have dropped this from your own person as you left the other day," she spoke in a voice light-years distant. "Pray come and take it, for I doubt not you'll need it, my pet."

It seemed I was unable to rise from the chair to go and take the feather, so long did I remain immobile. At last, with the greatest difficulty, she rose and approached me, put the feather behind my ear, and then, much in the manner of Elijah Thrush, took out a shimmering handkerchief and wiped my upper lip.

All that summer, from deserted warehouses, and other empty buildings near ghastly grisly West Street, with its rotting refuse and dying derelicts, with the green facade of old pier entrances in the distance, I followed Elijah Thrush in his diurnal and nocturnal wanderings. For he did emerge at times—to find a new disciple, at which he was often successful, or merely to sell some of his old watercolors, or just to review his impressions of the outside world. But West Street, with its drifters and addicts, its soul-food restaurants, its memories of great boats leaving for Europe, was as impossible of belief as was the Arcturus Gardens. And when Elijah at last appeared on the street, in his long saffron robes, his shoulder-length hair and rattling jewelry, he evoked little surprise.

Of course he knew I was spying on him, and I had to undergo hours or recrimination from him later, bitter scoldings, venomous taunts and insults. After which I would have to pose stark naked for him, a practice I first opposed vigorously owing to certain connections my nude body had with my habit. But he would not allow refusal. Indeed, he would go over my body with a magnifying glass, and give vent to his surprise, not only at my fantastic development, but at the discolorations I blamed the sun for.

Prior to being a spy for Millicent De Frayne, I did something for money that still does not go down the right way with me. My relationship with Ted Maufritz, a retired liberal-radical, is not excusable to this day. This white gentleman Maufritz hired me to lie down on a velvet couch, protected from stains by a goatskin and plastic throws. He would then open one of my best veins and drink a considerable amount of my blood, in the hope, he said, and only in the hope, of being worthy of the noble race I was a scion of. "Remember me when yours will be the power and glory of this world," he would cry, intoxicated by my physical prowess. Although loss of blood may have been delete-rious to my constitution, I would have continued, I believe, with "unworthy" Ted Maufritz, allowing him to approach the worth of my race, had not one evening, when I had stripped routinely to expose the appropriate vein, a large feather been discovered stuck to my breast. Ted Maufritz flew into such a terrible sei-zure of rage he was unable to partake of even a half ounce, though there I lay bleeding for him since he had already opened the vein. We parted friends on his part, however, though he had been injudicious enough to call me a *jamoka* at the height of his anger. I even allowed him to shake hands with me after I was clothed.

I had had "chambers" near Trinity Church, in the Wall Street area of Manhattan Island, but shortly after I was cashiered by Ted Maufritz, and without a red cent in my pocket, I had an-other fearful surprise when Juddson, the overseer of my private "chambers," told me of a new ruling: namely, that those now occupying special rooms could no longer use them for the pur-pose of sleeping or preparing food. Needless to say, the "chambers" were where I had recourse to for my habit, and where I also spent the night on the floor. Thus, from the ruling on, when night came, I found myself, like any vagrant, without a place to lay my weary head. I tongue-lashed Juddson, a white man, and went out. A few short years ago, he would have stung me with a pejorative, but now, owing to my brothers' victories, he could only bite his pale lips and let me go.

This was when I made up my mind I would have to be Millicent's spy. During my first weeks spying on Elijah I had nowhere to sleep, and did not wish to impart knowledge of my lack to either Millicent or the Mime. My trouble at this time was not, however, so much a suitable sleeping place as it was a falling-under-the-spell-of-Elijah-Thrush. I was deeply in love with him.

"Of course I foresaw it," Millicent explained to me one early August morning. (She got up about five o'clock in the morning and surveyed the heavens carefully; it was her only real pleasure.) "It either results that the spy falls in love with Elijah or that he quits his post."

With the funds from my fortuitous contact with Millicent De Frayne, I bought a silk suit and registered at the Father Divine Fairgroves Hotel, where my "princely" appearance secured for me one of its finer sleeping rooms, with a view of the river, and a seat in the dining room very near the table at which Father Divine had eaten in this life and where his ghostly presence visited regularly. It was also easier for Millicent to leave messages for me at so respectable a lodging place.

I do not know whether to say from this time onward my progress was upward or downward. Had I not become an impressed spy for Millicent De Frayne, and therefore solvent thereby, I might have been obliged to give up my expensive habit, and become any black man trying to find his bread. But then, there is, as Elijah said, destiny.

I soon discovered Millicent was deceiving me. One August noon she told me I could have a few days' rest, and during this time I would not need to pay calls on the Mime. This was a command, I saw at once. Her hand trembled as she passed me the dish of tea. She covered her neck higher and higher with her furs.

"You are the kindest of ladies," I told her.

"You don't mean a word of that," she said.

"Millicent, Millicent," I took the boldest course now by calling her by her Christian name.

She placed her right hand, heavy with rings, over the bridge of her immense aquiline nose, a gesture that drew this feature into such focus I became instantly ill, I put down the delicate dish with a bang.

"You must forgive me," she took away her hand, but I could not for a moment bear to look at her for the thought of her nose. The association was too strong.

"Do you know hopeless love, Albert Peggs?"

"Yes, all forms," I sobbed. "All forms of hopeless."

"How remarkable, yes, how perfectly remarkable," she soothed me. "Sit over here, my dear, on the little hassock."

I sipped a bit more tea, and then did as she bid me.

"You must go away for a few days. You need rest." I shook convulsively, and felt my left hand raised, and something pushed on the second finger. I opened my eyes. Her pearl ring was fixed upon this finger.

"Don't say what you have ready to say. If the doorman notices the ring and stops you, have him call me. It is yours, Albert, provided you are absent for a few days. What was the nature of your hopeless love?" she inquired.

"I admired a certain party," I said.

"What color was he?"

"White," I told her.

"How destiny grinds us to powder," she said. "Can you wipe your face, dear Albert?"

I disobeyed her, as I suppose she expected me to do.

98

I spent most of the day afterward admiring the ring. I had never felt stronger, and never more ill. I think I thought I was dying, while gaining strength; that I had died and gone to white heaven, and that Millicent and Elijah were God and Goddess there, and I their Only Son. Yet my real destiny, I knew, lay in my rented "chambers."

I stationed myself outside on the fire escape of Elijah Thrush's Arcturus Gardens. Oh, I knew she would come by daylight, for after six p.m. and her poached mackerel and capers she was too sleepy to go out.

She came at high noon while the sun broiled down on me. I suppose they knew I was outside, for the very reason they both moved to within earshot of where I stood. My discomfort was more than rewarded.

"Many as the times I've had that lock changed to keep you out of here, you always are able to get a key which fits, and come in here like the robber in broad daylight you are," Elijah's voice came to me. He was seated at the piano, playing a few notes. "You look even older than when you barged in here a month ago!"

"You never change," Millicent's voice, as if from cobwebs. "More adorable than ever, Elijah."

"Stop those ridiculous caresses."

"When shall we be married?"

"When hell freezes its star boarders."

I heard someone cover someone with scores of kisses, and a feeble cry of dissatisfaction and loathing from the Mime.

"It's bad enough when you put your claws in those of us who have weapons to fight back with," I heard Elijah say, "but when you choose as your victim a poor lad of another race, who cannot fight you!"

"Albert is the strongest boy I ever met!"

"He's a mature man of twenty-nine."

"He looks like an infant. I don't believe he has a beard as yet.

If it weren't for those hideous feathers that keep coming from his person!"

"What do you suppose those *mean?*" Elijah forgetting for the moment she was his eternal enemy.

"Oh, he's a cannibal, I suppose. Everything I say to him offends him," Millicent suggesting. "I adore him. He has a skin of the finest mahogany, and his eyes break my heart. Many an hour after he has left I weep over his physical perfection."

"You doddering fool! How can you expect him to care for you!"

"If there's any worshiping to be done, I suppose you think he'll do it to you! Well, then, let me tell you, he's already smitten with you. I have probed him to his marrow, and it's all come out of course, as I knew it would. But through money he'll betray your confidence, and no matter how much love you extract from him—"

"Out, out! Bellamy! Come in and put this chattering crone into the streets!"

Their quarreling over me intoxicated me. I could not restrain myself. Their praise of my body, my qualities, my all! Removing my clothing, I entered by the fire-escape window, to offer my love.

They paid not the slightest attention to me. Their quarrel, uninterrupted since 1913, could not be interrupted by a mere naked nigger. Elijah did not even look at me. Seated at the piano, he played a selection from Gottschalk.

I was not doing it for the money because I do not know how to do anything for money, but the money came, kept coming, and was plentiful. "We'll do it in this little surreptitious way," Millicent always whispered, as she pressed hundred-dollar bills into my palm, marveling at the sweat she found there. "You're worried about something, my dear," she would say. "Is it Alabama?"

Elijah also chided me. "You do not keep your mind completely on what I am saying to you, or on my *personality*, Albert. You are making your fortune through me, 'tis true, but you know as well as you're sitting in that Beauvais chair, you belong to me, heart and soul. Yet there's somebody else! I've known it from the beginning. There, there, you're driveling again in that abominable fashion. You can look really ugly when you do that. Oh, Albert, why can't you give me total fidelity, total oneness?" He shaded his face with his long red fingers, with those vaguely unclean nails.

"Elijah has told me there is somebody else," Millicent now broached this subject, on a day when she was outfitted in pink shoes with enormous gold buckles. Owing to an attack of rheumatism, she held her head far forward as if talking into a low-lying ear. "He was most abusive to me on the telephone today, but then his fury turned on you, Albert. He knows there's somebody else in your life."

"Not exactly a someone," I finally broke my promise to myself.

Despite her aches, she got her neck up and stared at me. "There shouldn't, there mustn't be!" she called to me.

"But I had my . . . attachment . . . before I met you!" I cried, a little beside myself.

"But, my dear, I thought we—Elijah and I—were your all."

"There is . . . somebody else," I at last put it their way, and my mind passed to where I had been born in Alabama and my hometown later, Bon Secour, and the towns of my grandfather and great-grandfather, Atmore Canoe and Tunnel Springs.

"Attention here, attention!" Millicent's voice. "Oh, how you woolgather these last few weeks, Albert. It's broken my heart. If you go back on me, it may be the end of the line. You exaggerate what money can do. It does nothing. No woman ever suffered as I suffer. I live on and on, and each day is more *pénible*. He said a very cutting thing to me today, I think the most discouraging and cutting thing ever said to me. Draw close, my dear, for I don't want one of the servants to overhear."

I approached her chair. She whispered. "Albert, my child, do you know what I sit on, according to the Mime?" Tears ran down her cheeks bearing with them the same brand of French rouge the Mime wore; indeed, I was to learn later she bought him his cosmetics. "Come, come Albert!"

"It will take some time to guess, Millicent," I warned her.

She drew me closer, and a drop of cosmetic fell to my wrist. This she dried with a man-sized handkerchief. "Listen closely. He said I sit on a tuffet here—" pointing with one sweep of her hand to the raised platform on which her chair stood. "Do you hear the fiendish spite in that word. Tuffet!"

I grinned and she looked at me searchingly.

"I have no idea what must be done with your other attachment. He has told me he will not go on with you unless you give up this other person."

"But there is no other person."

"Albert, you are far too handsome not to have lovers," she contradicted me.

"Oh well, those," letting my attention drift again.

"Go ahead, be coarse and low," she said. "But you'll find no pity or understanding from Elijah. And he'll make my life a hell until you make a clean breast of all this. Where, for example, do you go, Albert, when you are not with your own people at the Father Divine Fairgroves Hotel?"

"Is nothing to be left in privacy?" hardly hearing.

"We have investigated nothing about you, you know that, Albert," hurt now, and ringing for the maid. "I took you on first seeing you because of an intuition, and because of your marvelous eyes. Also, your breath is sweet as orange-blossom honey. To tell you the truth, that's what made me decide on you. Norah," she turned to the servant, "bring a tray with one of the better cordials, and—wait a moment, don't rush out like a chicken with severed jugular, for pity's sake—fetch two of the cut-glass wine goblets, the larger ones if you please—stop right there, don't rush so—I want a water biscuit with my cordial. Now, you can rush, and I hope you will. That woman loathes me, Albert," when the servant had left. "I've found literature in her sleeping room. She's a popular religionist of some sort, and believes the world is drawing to an early close. Hence, her lofty phlegm with me."

Hardly knowing I was going to speak, and more shocked than she at my words, "I suppose you and Elijah would be surprised if I spilled my semen on the floor before you. I suppose you would be surprised it was not brown."

"How perfectly droll," she considered this statement. "You seem not to have learned the lesson of our first encounter. I have no interest in any race, least of all the human race."

"What if I told you I was in love with an eagle?" I cried to her, and pulled at her gown.

"Albert," she went on, as if I had not spoken, "one afternoon a few weeks ago, a piece of paper, with your handwriting, fell out of your pants pocket. I picked it up with some difficulty. You understand, I did not want the maid to find anything that might turn her more acutely against me, and against you, and I will return it to you, if you wish it. I have it in safe custody upstairs. The paper said, *Are white griefs true, are they real?* I could not get this question out of my mind for a long time. But I have the answer for you, Albert. They are. They're real. You won't believe it, but God knows it to be a fact. Now a moment ago you spoke in very concrete sexual terms. You must get it out of your head either Elijah or I want your body, exquisite and noble as its lines are—and I have many an afternoon marveled at the curves of your arms and thighs. I have made every mistake known to the human mind, so can scarcely have a shred of prudery. We do not want your semen. We want your soul."

Just as Millicent did not hear certain of my statements, I do not think I quite caught this statement. However, later, in the Father Divine Fairgroves Hotel, where tears filled my eyes so frequently that I had to tell my brothers I had hay fever (though fall was passing into winter), I went over all Millicent had said. *"You will not have met the Mime until the snow flies, remember! For it's then he opens the Arcturus Gardens, and dances publicly!"* opening my purse, whereupon four thousand-dollar bills fell before the eyes of the astonished waitress. "I have come into an inheritance," looking into her wicked face.

At that very moment Millicent De Frayne was talking to Elijah Thrush on the telephone. "He tells me he loves an eagle."

"My dear, either your mind has gone this time, or they have punctured your eardrum as revenge, those hellish servants of yours. When your brain has cleared, communicate with my piano player if you have anything of importance to impart. And send me some money, do you hear, miserly creature that you have become!"

"He thinks all we want is his semen," Millicent began, but there was a click-click and silence followed.

"I should have died in 1917," Millicent sat with the pink cradle of the phone resting in her lap. "I wish it were the month of tulips. I despise these fall flowers, with their indeterminate foliage and their lobed leaves. I would give anything for a roomful of tulips. I think it would make me happy."

The frost of winter hung in the air. Millicent acknowledged the coming cold by one change in her dress: she put on her pearl choker. She did not bring out any more furs than she wore in July. Both she and the Mime were in a state of unearthly excitement now that he was appearing again before the footlights.

"New York, dearest Albert," Millicent spoke to me from her seat on the tuffet, "is over. Has been over since 1917. But we have indulged it to the extent of pretending otherwise. I suppose you will be going back to that town in Alabama. What did you say the name of it was? I have been looking at the map of your state, and if the places were as interesting as the names I might winter there. But when the season ends, you will, I assume, go back to Alabama. Albert!" she cried now in great splenetic irritability.

"I beg your pardon, Millicent," I told her. "I am very depressed today."

"If I could only understand your depression. . . ."

Norah came forward with a tiny golden tray, two alfalfa tablets, and a beaker of water. Millicent frowned as she took the tablets, and spoke on. "You didn't leave out anything of his career?"

"I think not," wondering at her remark.

"Look outside," she cried, consciousness coming over her. "It's snowing. Summer is over, and the season has begun! Do you hear me, Albert? The Arcturus Gardens opens!"

Yes, there were great huge flakes of the stuff, so foreign to my skin and heart. In my veins summer raged more fierce than ever, and my upper lip was ever covered with sweat no matter how many times Millicent commanded me or a servant to wipe, or did so herself. She despaired of me. But her mind was on his opening, so she neglected me. She had her finest gowns brought out, and ordered new pumps. The jeweler was sent for, new chokers looked at, a ring purchased.

"Understand, I will not be admitted," she told me. "Not because I will arrive two hours late. No, it is the principle of the thing. He must reject me, he must drive me out in front of his public. I have ruined his life, and this the public must be told. Yes, Albert, white griefs are real."

"I never said. . . ."

"You wrote it, and I will hold that note in a place of safety until this whole city is ashes." A terrible passion shook her. "You are taken care of," she cried, almost breathless. "But who ever took care of me? You know slavery! Fool. What of the slavery

I have known? Sit," she insisted as I approached her tuffet. "You must not miss one detail of his performance tonight. He claims that if he is not beautiful this season, and the audience does not love him to perfection, he will kill himself. As you know, I am forbidden to attend his performances."

I was a farmer's son, believe it or not, was what Elijah Thrush told me, to prepare me for his Grand Opening at the Arcturus Gardens. Pursuing the subject, "My father had been a farmer in Illinois, and then on the plains of Nebraska. There I would have remained forever, my dear Albert, following a horse's backside around a field of buckwheat, had I not gone to the Grand Opera House one evening and seen a troupe of dancers who accompanied a production of *Carmen*. I knew then. I knew I must leave and go to Chicago. I was fifteen. Though I loved Dad dearly, Mother, who was a religious maniac, opposed anything that was not hard labor and prayer. Without a good-bye to them, I hopped a freight, on which I in due course got a job watching the livestock, and arrived in Chicago with four dollars and no friends. But my personality was already fully developed, and if you will allow me to say so, though I know I am a shade dilapidated by current standards, I won the hearts of all who met me. Indeed, I had barely gone two blocks down Michigan Avenue when a noted impresario of that age saw me and straightaway booked me as a youth who carries banners, *Henry V*, Parts One and Two. But I soon tired of parts and, riding steerage to Greece, I made my debut on the steps of the Parthenon. Then Paris," etc.

"Yes, that was the way it was," Millicent raised her head from sleep and nodded, smiling.

Although Millicent had fortified me before my visit to the Arcturus Gardens with cold guinea sandwiches, strong coffee and brandy, my knees were water when I knocked at the door of Elijah's private theatre, waiting to be ushered into my new life—for my knowing Elijah only socially as a spy of Millicent De Frayne was no preparation for seeing him in his reincarnation as the Most Beautiful Man in the World.

Knocking then, waiting, I felt most unlike myself. (Oh, I had been getting less like myself ever since that July interview with Millicent.) I was wrapped in one of her fourth husband's heavy furs. A reverend crone opened the tall door, and inquired my name; a second crone, white-haired, profusely powdered, with tiny jet earrings, looked over the first old lady's shoulder, and inspected the list of those invited to the performance, but could not find the name of Albert Peggs.

"But I have been sent by Millicent De Frayne!" I begged with such alarm that some of the early audience began clearing throats.

"I can assure you," Mother Macaulay, the first white-haired lady spoke in tones of indignation, "I can doubly assure you, no friend of Millicent De Frayne can be admitted here."

"After all the money she has sent the Mime?" I wondered aloud.

"She has never so much as given him a penny," the second crone spoke up. "Will you be so kind as to depart, young man?"

"There is nobody in the world," so loud I would be heard throughout the building, "nobody anywhere who loves and respects Elijah Thrust as much as I. I will not take no for an answer, and I will not depart." I pushed my way past them just in time to hear a real stentor cry, "Allow him the big plush throne seat, Mother Macaulay, in the first row. And for God's sake, will you and Abigail Tuttle cease your bickering. Can glory never come without being clouded by incompetent devotees? Go to your places as soon as he's seated. Tonight admit everybody!"

"And should Miss De Frayne show up tonight?" Mother Macaulay inquired.

"Admit that molting old harum-scarum too, should her whore's bones get her here in this snowstorm," Elijah's voice fading, but not before I had cried out toward its source, "Thank you, dearest friend, for providing for me." I thought I heard a kiss blown me in reply.

Outside it was snowing; inside it was too warm, and there was a most powerful perfume of vetiver and thick clouds of Kashmir Saffron and Quaipur Rose incense that at once made my eyelids heavy. I began to shiver, so that I did not remove my heavy coat, though Mother Macaulay several times advanced toward me and made motions indicating she would take the burden of it from me should I desire it.

The small theatre filled, its walls covered with gold-framed paintings of the Mime's middle period: the Mime as Hiawatha, as the child Moses, as Apollo, and as Jesus in the Garden with Mary Magdalen, in addition to a long gallery of portraits of beautiful young men. As I was gazing at these, an old woman next to me leaned over and spoke, "Those are his dead paramours," whispering. "They all went the same way," and she shook her head and frowned. "They failed him." A gong sounded, and the lights grew dim.

In the distance I heard a deep sorrowful voice praying.

Then hands were clapped and in a lightning second, as with an eruption of fire, indeed I thought as much, the Mime, Elijah himself, was before my startled eyes looking not more than twenty-five and, I suppose, despite his atrocious jewelry and makeup, as handsome as the gods on the wall. He made kissing sounds to me.

Whether from the incense or sheer excitement, I felt it wise to slump to the floor, so as not to agitate my nerves excessively from what I knew they were soon to undergo. I allowed my head to rest against the boots of a young white gentleman who told me not to think of formality but to make myself comfortable. As if prompted by Elijah and Millicent, he wiped my upper lip.

After Elijah's electric appearance had thrilled everyone into a cascade of applause, Mother Macaulay mounted a tiny platform and announced the Mime's first number, "Narcissus Drinks His Last Glass of Joy."

"Just think, he is over ninety," the youth against whose boots I was reclining said. I was too ill to respond in words, but tugged at his boots in reply.

I wondered if this were actually Elijah, for if he was ninety or seventy or a hundred, his body was as firm as an apple, and his genitals looked marvelously hopeful. But something was amiss. Bellamy, the pianist, was present, in full evening dress, looking awful, with his pale face and a geranium in his buttonhole, and flashing hatred at me whenever he turned to the audience.

An entr'acte followed, in which the young man who sat behind me, having taken a fondness for me, I suppose, plied me with cognac from his private phial. "I always find someone rewarding here," he said. "I never miss a season." "What do you do for a liv—" I was about to ask when the gong sounded again and the lights went out.

"Are you a bosom friend of the Mime?" the young man whispered in my ear. "I am losing consciousness," I told him, "you may have to care for me." "My, my," he said.

Number followed number: Pierrot, an interminable thing in a French garden, the Mime in green tights, then a sensual debacle in the Sahara, the Mime in dromedary bells only, and in the midst of this a terrible crash on the door. True to promise, Millicent De Frayne entered, with a young man dressed as a fireman. He had broken down the door with his ax, it seemed.

"Stop this indecent performance at once!" her unmistakable shriek. I was stupefied, for was this the way to treat a man you had loved since 1913? "Stop it!" She looked remarkably young, without a trace of her rheumatism or her eighty-odd years. My illness abated, I got to my chair, hoping to be recognized by her, to have so magnificent and arresting a creature salute me before all those interesting people.

"You damned low bag of bones, stomping in like this in the middle of my most fatiguing number! Ladies and gentlemen, this common whore here, kept out of jail only by her wealth, which she never earned a dime of, has been persecuting me since the first decade of the century. [In his anger he always gave away his age, though professionally he always listed himself as twenty-eight.] She has the breath of a tribe of cannibals and about as much beauty as an anteater, yet she flatters herself that I am hopelessly enamored of her. She even gives out that she is supporting me in this theatre! Can you believe it, friends and public!" (There were enthusiastic cries of *No*, as in a play.)

"This wicked mountebank," Millicent De Frayne cried, "has corrupted his own great-grandson, and there is not a young person in this audience tonight whom he has not either corrupted or will soon ruin. I am begging you therefore to run for your lives, run as if the edifice were in flames! I hate what you've done to us all," revealing a fantastically long knife and rushing the stage. He seized her at once, removed the knife from her tired old hands, and spat in her face.

All this while, my attention elsewhere, the young man next to me had undressed me almost entirely. My overcoat was gone; my trousers and shorts had disappeared. Thinking he was about to enjoy my body, I turned to him. But he had left with all my clothing.

The rest of the evening seemed very long. Millicent De Frayne usurping the role of Elijah Thrush and attempting to dance, whilst he cried out from the wings, "Look at her, look at her, disgusting!" and then his brutal pommeling of my benefactress, succeeded by more of his numbers. When the police arrived, I slipped out onto the fire escape. Just as I was descending, I heard gunfire.

I read about their arrest and release in the newspaper. Their pictures were there, and both looked so inexpressibly ugly I wondered how I had ever endured their company. Yet I felt responsible to them in a way I could not explain, just as I could not explain the motive behind my visits to my "chambers" in Wall Street.

I went to Millicent's apartment, but the doorman insisted she had left the country. I told him, lying, she had just that day telephoned, and he put me in the ivory-paneled elevator with the green cockatoo designs, and I ascended.

"Miss De Frayne is not expecting you," Norah told me, keeping the elevator door open so that I would get back into it and descend.

"I will not see traitors, deserters, and impostors!" Millicent's voice, recognizable in rage. "Have him shown out. My check will be mailed."

I walked resolutely into the room from which her voice issued. She was looking very bad from rheumatism, her paisley shawl most unbecoming.

"I will not let you dispose of me as you did your other gentlemen retainers." I sat down on the tuffet.

"I suppose I am a pushover for brazenness in anybody," she said.

"I wish you would wear your furs. You don't fit a shawl type of party," giving tit for tat.

Norah meanwhile had been standing in the threshold of the receiving, or as Millicent called it, "withdrawing" room. "You may go about your duties, Norah. Mr. Peggs has some talking to do."

My tongue-lashing began now in earnest. She accused me of every shortcoming: failure, misdeed, meanness. Only a mother could have been so cruel. I cried very hard; it was a great pleasure and relief.

"I can never forgive that you did not go to jail with me. It was the least you could do."

I told her of the robber who had taken my clothing.

"Subterfuges, my dear! Evasions!"

A butler brought her her furs, and she dusted heavy white powder over her cheeks. "I found another of the little notes I presume you write to yourself," after she had made herself more beautiful, "and it touched me as much as your first note. If you could only get it out of your mind that I want your body! But to the note," taking out a gilded lorgnette with cupids on one side, and reading, "Though my meeting Millicent De Frayne and Elijah Thrust has set me apart from other men, my finally being admitted to the full grandeur and presence of these scintillating personages has ended my early life and career entirely, and ushered me into, well, into something no man can describe!"

"I have decided to kiss you on the mouth." She studied my lips with that angry attention I had seen only in doctors. "Come forward." I kneeled between her satin slippers, and she took my mouth in hers. Her tongue, like a cow's in roughness and vigor, explored the inside of my cheeks.

"You are in perfect health!" she said disengaging herself at last. "We will go on together. I will retain you. Betray Elijah as he has betrayed me. Please rise. Now leave the room."

"I will not see that wretched turncoat, and you can tell him to scat!" Elijah to Eugene Bellamy, who had announced me. "He's as false as water, a talebearer. Tell him, Eugene. Goes from one party to another, repeating slander, heating up this old bit of calumny, wounding here, opening an old sore there, rubbing in salt down there, and always looking angelic. Tell him to go back where his bread's buttered as thick as his finger. And I don't mean Alabama. Let Millicent eat him alive!"

When Eugene reappeared in the room, I spoke to him in my stoutest voice, saying, "Tell Elijah I haven't the least intention of being driven out of here like a greengrocer. I have had Elijah on my heart and mind ever since the disaster of the recital, tell him. But as a black youth, I could not run the risk of police apprehension, get him to understand."

"You're no more black than I am, precious," Elijah's voice nearer and nearer to where I was seated in my favorite Beauvais chair. "You're the whitest smoothest thing I ever saw."

The curtain drew back. He seemed masked, for he was wonderfully young-looking. He wore a crocus bathrobe, and had on gloves, in which, as I was to learn later, was almond meal to keep his hands and wrists youthful. "You can fool everybody but Elijah," sitting down about a room apart from me. Bellamy was seated also, on the piano stool, playing some Liszt at a sleepy tempo.

"I suppose, Albert, you're only interested in money, and yet there's something about you," rising now, "something in the whites of your eyes."

"How grand you always are, Elijah Thrush," I snapped at him.

"I will not allow impertinence from someone who has already been shown the door," flaring, but it was clear to me he was not seriously angry. "That creature you work for is at least a hundred years old, I suppose you know that! If you weren't so unversed in the ways of the world, I would tell you how she keeps her youth."

I half-closed my eyes, feigning lack of interest.

"Are you awake, my dear?"

"I think I know how she keeps her youth," I said.

"Well, indeed. Then you're the first of her many ambassadors who's ever found out. But of course you're egregiously clever."

"She has nothing whatsoever to do. That's all," my eyelids low.

He laughed his Shakespearean laugh. "That is the one thing ages people the most. No, you're on the wrong track, Albert, my dear, couldn't be further askew. Early in her career she discovered how to keep her youth. But it has aged her as much as it has kept her green. However, whether the earliness of the hour or your own childish mentality, I cannot bring myself to tell you."

"I have never liked being teased. It brings on fits of anger," and I stretched out my chest and arms, to remind him of my great strength.

"You have noticed, of course," studying what I believe were my feet, "since you are admitted to her castle daily, that file of young men in waiting on her."

"I have noticed a number of waiting young men, true." I became grave.

"Well, draw your own conclusions. I'll say no more." He looked at a huge gold watch.

"I never think of her as having lovers," I said, "though she pets me occasionally."

"Oh, that only means she's not serious," he comforted me. "There's no need to go on, for I can't tell you," now turning his attention to the piano player.

"Eugene, that's quite enough of Franz Liszt. You may retire.

"Since you are forcing me to tell you, I will," he went on, putting his arm on my shoulder. "In order to preserve her youth—" and here he turned away from me, letting out great cries of vexation and loathing, "that horrible creature extracts semen with a syphon from one after another of these perfect specimens of youth. Without tenderness, without interest in their bodies—or *minds*—as coldly as a surgeon, dismissing them then, with a sum of money. She's a monster!"

The snow began to freeze my Alabama blood. All I could do was drink gunpowder tea and remain, for as long as was decent, in the dining room of the Father Divine Fairgroves Hotel, where one gusty evening who should be introduced to me there, by Amanda Duddell, but the piano player from the Arcturus Gardens, his overshoes covered with snow, his scarf dripping with frost.

He fell rather heavily into an armchair beside me. "You will have to overlook my barging in on you, Mr. Peggs," he began.

"I hope you don't bring bad news from Elijah Thrush," worrying at once.

"There's nothing wrong with Elijah Thrush. It's what's wrong with me that brings me clear over here," rolling his head about as if this were China.

"Can Amanda bring you some refreshment?" She was standing by my hand, and immediately took out a little pad and pencil and waited for instructions.

"You don't have any spoon bread, by chance, do you?" he wondered. Amanda indicated by a few facial gestures they had none, and would not be having any in the near future. "Oh, just bring any of your typical desserts," he commanded her, and she brought a bread pudding, with two cherries on top, which he dispiritedly toyed with. "I may as well come to the point at once, Mr. Peggs, for I have no art of diplomacy and my heart is broken. You must give up Elijah Thrush. There are no two ways about it. My own happiness, my very sanity, is at stake, not to mention my bread and butter." He pushed the food away.

"It is a rule of the house that diners must finish all that they order," I spoke to him confidentially. "Not a morsel must go back to the kitchen. It would create a very touchy situation."

Bellamy went quite pale. He was, now I had time to study him, a very handsome young man, with ringlets of gold, strong chin, long black eyelashes.

"Peggs, you must give up Elijah, as I said earlier. You have everything. I have nothing. Nothing but Elijah," wolfing down his pudding.

"I can't very well give up what I don't have." I tightened my necktie for I was becoming a bit uncomfortable.

"I beg your pardon," he said.

"I don't belong to Elijah Thrush," I told him. "Nor he to me."

"If you could play the piano, I would be turned out of his studio tonight. Out of his life," eating the last of his pudding, "with no place to go. Whereas you, on the other hand, are in demand everywhere. It is your period."

"Oh, this will never do," I said, trying to control my anger.

"You have Millicent De Frayne," licking his dish.

"But the only reason I have her is to spy on Mr. Thrush. The two go together. Surely you must see that," adjusting my lapels, as he took out a violet envelope marked in large black letters FOR MR. ALBERT PEGGS.

"This is for you," he said.

I opened it and peeked within. As I more or less foresaw, it was a thousand-dollar bill.

"All I ask is that you go away."

I put the money in my pocket. "You know I cannot do that," I said.

"I'll give you anything," weeping. "You can use me any way you like. I know you have a very expensive habit; that is why I have given you this money. Perhaps you beat people. I am willing to have you beat me and abuse me in the current fashion, *if* this is your pleasure."

"Do you wish your money back?" I took out the envelope and held it to him.

He sniffed very hard.

I rose and bent down and kissed him on the mouth.

I have a scrapbook whose pages, under protective isinglass, display the wildflowers and the leaves of the trees of my native state. During depressed periods of my life, such as that which

James Purdy

followed my interview with Bellamy, I would retire to the library of the Father Divine Fairgroves Hotel and look at my collection. I tried not to notice the snow outside or the faces around me on which New York had cast a terrible sadness. That night I kissed each flower gently as I murmured its name: *short-spur, columbine, thimbleberry, rue anemone, nodding ladies' tresses, heart-leafed twayblade, chickasaw plum.* I was considering their perfume when Roscoe George shook me gently by the shoulder and, bowing in his capacity as bell captain, told me I was wanted on the telephone.

"Where in God's name have you been when I am in such earnest need of you?" Elijah's voice thundered over the wire. "Answer me!"

"Waylaid by your piano player!" I shouted back, disturbing several black ladies who were slumbering in the Peach Room, which was hard by.

"I am ruined," Elijah went on, possibly not having heard my mention of Bellamy's visit. "It's all over, my dear. The wicked creature with the ten fortunes has won her legal battle and has taken custody of my great-grandson—known everywhere as the Bird of Heaven. This is her final card to bring me to my knees. All is over."

To my stupefaction, I hung up. I walked back into the library, after having given a bow here and there to the ladies in the Peach Room, and slumped down on the davenport. I had done it now, hung up on the Mime, an offense as awesome as slobbering on the outstretched hand of royalty. I was through. New York was over. I was glad, terrified. He would never forgive me. But then my attention wandered back to what he had said. His great-grandson, about whom he had talked so often, was a prisoner of Millicent De Frayne. I had never thought his great-grandson existed. I thought it was his way of speaking, an ideal love, divine pederasty, Plato and his beloved disciples.

I rubbed my eyes, and looked out at the snow. Alabama was

far, far off, everybody dead, or gone, and here a white man had kneeled to me, and the next day Millicent De Frayne would be waiting to give me instructions. I closed the scrapbook, pressed my wrist to my ear and caught the smell of my perspiration.

"Stop! Eyes only for the President!" Millicent De Frayne's voice as I was about to go into her withdrawing room. But this incomprehensible remark did not make me hesitate. I walked directly into her presence. "Eyes only for the . . ." beginning and ending at my cry of astonishment.

I was unprepared for this spectacle. For one thing, Millicent was standing, without her cane, and directly in front of her, kneeling, was the Mime himself. There was nothing penitent, however, nor servile, in his expression. He looked, indeed, as if *he* were standing over a cowering Millicent De Frayne.

"I might have known you would come in at such a moment!" he shrieked at me. "You have no sense of timing, my dear. I'm afraid I am tiring of you."

"That would be a hard blow to get over, Elijah," I told him, and I did not speak with irony.

"How touching a remark, Elijah," Millicent spoke from her great height. She was, have I remembered to mention? a very tall person.

"I don't know why I am always being seen at my worst by people who have not had a proper introduction to my life and my work. I must give him my unpublished autobiography. Millicent, pray remind me, and the privately published book of poems and aphorisms."

"I wish you would either rise, my dear, or let me call for assistance from one of my staff."

"Count on you, my sweet, always to be a jackass," the Mime advancing on his knees toward a large sacristy cabinet in which, instead of priestly vestments, Millicent kept a small collection of monocles, some wine and medicines.

"I don't know why it is, but humiliation is one aspect of reality I could never get used to," Elijah cried. I realized in the instant what his predicament was: he had slipped and fallen, and owing to his age and the condition of his bones, he was unable to rise.

"Allow me, dear Elijah," I went toward him.

"Yes, yes, allow the dear boy!" Millicent cried.

"Back, you idiots," Elijah cried, and although his face went purple from the exertion, and a great many sheets of paper fell out from his clothing, he did manage, by holding onto the sacristy cabinet, to get up on one leg. Disobeying him, I helped him rise on the other.

"Perfectly grand, patently wonderful! Hosanna, indeed!" Millicent cried.

I picked up the papers and began looking through them, whereupon Millicent whispered, "Try to memorize aught you see there. We can write it down later."

"I don't know which of us must explain to Albert what the occasion of my being here is," Elijah from one of Millicent's stick-back chairs. I handed him back his papers. "I am, however —and let this be put down in writing, if you wish, for it seems to be the end of everything—I'm capitulating. I've just learned, through the newspaper, that she's succeeded in adopting the Bird of Heaven."

Studying the rib of an old parasol she had been mending (there were, by her account, no umbrella menders now alive), Millicent at last spoke. "All I have done, Elijah, is to take out papers for the boy's adoption, and immediately he," she turned to me, "insists I am harboring the child in this already too crowded apartment," on the heels of which, however, we heard a child's laughter, and then saw a man dressed in chauffeur's costume enter with a young chap in a fireman's suit, blond curls to his shoulders.

The Mime shaded his eyes, and even Millicent looked some-what discomfited. "Long ago," Elijah said, without taking his hands away from his eyes, "as far back as the teens of this cen-tury, I got rid of the critics by simply entering a world where they could not enter, where for all their cleverness they could not gain one scrap of information, or any invitation. But this harpy, who has pursued me through the lifetimes of several men, I could never have even the feeblest half-victory over her. Now she has taken away my only love."

"You neglected him, honeybunch."

I wondered why nobody spoke to the boy, when suddenly from his mouth came a cascade of the most sylvan sounds ever issued from human throat, a forest of singing birds. I felt a thrill of some unnameable kind. The Bird of Heaven was a mute.

"Well, my dear Albert, you see the postulant has been raised from the floor, but he is still on his knees, in any practical sense, and may remain there forever," Elijah Thrush spoke to me the next day in his studio theatre, after he had received the thunder-ous intelligence that his great-grandson was "in the power" of Millicent De Frayne. He looked, nonetheless, quite composed, seated in one of his two sgabello chairs, in either of which he invariably sat when he gave out important information. In his left hand, a telegram, unfolded, was waving in the wind from an opened window, through which some stray pigeons had entered expecting to be fed. "She communicates damnable messages like this by telegram," and he pushed it under my eyes. It read: CON-SOLE YOURSELF. ALL OWL EGGS ARE WHITE. MILLICENT.

"Can you make a thing out of it?" Elijah came near to laugh-ing. "Had she sent it to you, I would take it to be an example of her racial superiority. She's a firm believer in endogamy, mark my words, and all her interest in you is mere infatuation with the exotic. But let me tell you how she is attempting to win the boy away from his great-grandfather, the only one in the world whom he loves, and the only one I love, though I care for you deeply, Albert. Just hear how that rip on a broomstick is proceeding to win him away from me. First of all, she has called in several orchestras of trombones and saxophones to play for him, since, as are most young people of today, he is more at home with sounds than with words. When the orchestras are not amusing him, he has the palmarium, you know, where under huge tropical trees and amid giant cacti, a chorus of selected parrots calls to the poor boy in different languages, praising him, comforting his loneliness, *and*, don't let your attention stray here, my fetching friend, each parrot has been trained, oh with such fiendish finesse, in denigrating, maligning, and utterly destroying my character."

The Mime was wearing his famous "spotted" ermine, a dilapidated garment that as a matter of fact Millicent herself had bestowed on him, many many seasons past. He tugged at it savagely as he spoke. "Today is rehearsal day," in a less aggrieved tone, "and Eugene should be here at almost any moment. I do wish you would stay and tell me which of the numbers we will go through are in your opinion the most appealing. But I want you to engrave on the chambers of your heart that Millicent, whose bread you eat, my dear, though I forgive you for it, for I understand shame and poverty, especially when they go together, as they always, I suspect, do, engrave on your heart that her love for you is false.

A surly, uncombed, puffing Eugene Bellamy entered the room, with a sheaf of music in one hand and his lunch in the other. "You're from the country, Eugene," the Mime's voice, as I went into the next room to prepare for being his audience. "What color do you think owl eggs are?"

Was it only a rehearsal? Or was it not a command performance? In either case, I had dozed off until night, and Sunday had come, for, lo and behold, every seat in the Arcturus Gardens was filled, and I waked facing the tiny stage, and a large red sign:

Number 4 of the Repertory
"Forgotten Dreams"
Interpreted by
the World-Famous Mime,
Star of Stage and Silver Screen,
who appeared in the Original Film
of "Ben-Hur,"
and Made His Debut
on the Steps of the Parthenon

Every hand in the house was clapping violently. The gong sounded, and quiet was instantly installed.

The Mime recited a few lines from the Greek anthology, and then leaped to the front of the stage, whose boards answered him in creaking tones. A great smile of carmined lips and black teeth greeted us. He seemed to have on a large sewing basket as a hat; otherwise, he wore only four strings of black beads, and a tiny cache-sexe. Ancient as he was, I could see backwards some fifty or sixty years the young man he must have been, wooing sickly Parisian audiences with his frontier vigor and naïveté. I was sinking into reverie when a hand threw a note in my lap, and the spell was broken. The Mime sensed this, for he stopped in his movement, and then with a frown that aged him considerably, he threw himself again into the fury of his dance. I looked down at my lap, at the letter.

THE MIME CALLS YOU TARBOX THE SUPERB BEHIND YOUR BACK. CHEW ON THAT FOR A COMPLIMENT, SWELL-HIDE.

The attempted cruelty of the note, through an expression long well known to me, so unnerved me that I advanced to the little stage, where one of the Mime's long strings of beads struck me in the face with such force it drew blood. The Mime was in a towering rage when he saw me on the stage, waving my paper at him, and crying out, as I always do when moved, in falsetto. "Did you abuse me by calling me this behind my back, sir?" He had his lips set to say something when the door was thrown open and there stood Millicent De Frayne, with her hand on the head of the Bird of Heaven, dressed, like his great-granddaddy, in flowing toga-like robes, a garland on his yellow hair. In his one free hand—for the other clasped that of Millicent—he held a bouquet of anemones.

"You see how clever, ladies and gentlemen, this pit viper is!" and then, turning to Eugene Bellamy, he cried, "Stop banging the keys, Mr. Nonesuch, for God's sake, can't you see the entire performance is ruined by that moneybags and these two poor simpletons who are in her pay!"

"But this terrible pejorative must be explained, Elijah Thrush," I cried.

"Why don't you open at least one eye to daylight, my dear. This letter was written and dispatched to you by your employer, the noted seducer of youths, Millicent Charbonneau De Frayne, or by one of her countless accomplices."

Millicent and the boy were already on the small stage, so small there was room for only the four of us. She read the note briskly and then turned to me. "It's the Mime's handwriting, my dear. The whole world knows he's a bigot," now turning to the audience, "I came here, ladies and gentlemen, because I am the last woman in the world to keep blood kin asunder. Harkee," she bent over the blinking footlights, "you are my witnesses. I came here, most gentlewomanly, with his darling great-grand-son, who suffers under this terrible affliction. The sweetheart is dumb from birth, though perfect in every other part of his body," kissing the lad on the mouth, "but this Apollo of the stage and screen has never shown the slightest interest in the boy. He was about, this priceless child was, ladies and gentlemen, to be put in a county home for the defective. I intervened."

"You intervened, Charbonneau, only for your own depraved pleasure. Ladies and gentlemen, let me tell you how this creature, with her billions of fortune, keeps her youth, for she's over a hundred if she's a day. I intend to speak the truth here this instant."

"I demand to know, sir, if you have ever called me a *superb tarbox!*" I said to Elijah, pulling him in my distraction by his beads.

"Yes, I did," he spat at me, "and I'm not sorry. What's wrong with calling you by the color you came from your mother's body with? Answer me that! One minute you want me to praise your shoe-black ass, and the next I'm to speak of you as a field of alabaster lilies. You can't have it both ways. You're black as midnight, and why shouldn't I, as the greatest plastic artist of the body living, so denominate you!"

I descended the few steps leading away from the stage. On the bottom step was an old top hat waiting for a later number. I had long fancied it, and I put it on my head. I stood there a long time; one could have heard a pin drop. Then I slowly unbuttoned, and took out my much-prized member. I think I did this in the correct style, funereal, stately, perfectly timed. Then bowing, I beat my retreat into the hall.

Once outside, I began to cry. I adjusted my clothing, and left by the stairs, for I didn't want to wait for the elevator. I heard the Mime's voice calling, "Albert! For God in heaven's sake, come back, my darling!"

"Pray don't loiter and idle outside as though you had no business in the house. You're on the roster, after all, good lad, and so come in, my only dear, for you look more alarmed than I am ill. Do enter, do," Millicent spoke to me from her field bed.

124

"Doctor Hitchmough is just leaving, Albert," nodding to a man with goat-beard and glasses.

"Who is this dusky young person?" the doctor examined me closely.

"A memoirist, Doctor Hitchmough, a memoirist."

"Of what, my dear Millicent, may I inquire?"

"Haven't you asked a good many questions today of a woman you have diagnosed as very very tired?"

"Corrected as always by one of my own patients," he gave out a convulsive cough-like laugh. "But pray don't worry about your ovaries anymore, my dear," he said. "I wish many a girl of eighteen had your ovaries!"

"I won't have my best parts being wished off on hoi polloi. Albert and I have had a great many humiliations lately, and I wonder he is up and around, though I see, come closer, my dear, he's been clawed, it looks like, by a wild animal. Oh, youth, Doctor Hitchmough! Youth has no fear," touching the scratches and claw marks with a bit of spit. "Pray have a look at Albert, Doctor Hitchmough, you won't charge anything extra, will you, for he's part of the household. Pray, Doctor, take him over to the light there and have a good look."

Doctor Hitchmough led me to the bay window and looked into my face and eyes. "Are you a sporting man?" he spoke in a voice loud enough for Millicent.

"Just diagnose, why don't you, Hitchmough, my love," Millicent calling.

"He's been scratched by some large bird, I fancy," the doctor said.

"Well, prescribe, my dear. Some pill or liquid, for Albert and I must be busy today," and the doctor wrote out something hurriedly.

"Off with you now. We've so much to do, Albert and I," he exiting and she leaping from her bed with the alacrity of a young man. She put on her house slippers and took her seat in a Trafalgar chair. "Charlatans, all of them!"

"I have come to tell you good-bye Millicent, ma'am," I told her. "I can't stand it."

"What is it?" she said.

"All of it," I said.

Like lightning she moved to a mahogany card table, and from a drawer inside took a gun which she leveled at me.

"Now tell me what it was you said," she said. "And don't think I don't mean business. I'd as soon kill you as kiss you." She put the gun back in the drawer. "You *understand* the Mime of Tenth Avenue. Why and how I don't know. My white memoirists never understood a thing about it. They either pitied him, the Christians, or they wanted him to go on relief, the Jews. Love and justice, you know, counterfeit emotions. But you, my dear I can't lose you. Now come here and kiss me, for even though your cheeks are bleeding you've never looked so pretty."

My habit was turning against me, as witness the contusions and hemorrhages all over my body, and what was worse, as my disinclination toward my own life grew, I realized I had fallen hopelessly under the spell of Millicent and Elijah, and that this could only be described, improbable as it was, as the passion of love. They were replacing my habit in intensity, romance, and late-hour musings. They knew this, and their cruelty and tyranny were sharpened by the knowledge. Henceforward they would be restrained in nothing, whereas I, poor black pawn in their game, would yield to whatever indignity they might think up next.

I thought of killing them.

In my despair, I decided to disobey Millicent and visit the Bird of Heaven in his palmarium. He was at play as I entered the over-heated over-bright room the size of a tennis court, and of course did not hear me enter since he was deaf as well as mute. He was arranging a row of turtles in preparation for a race they were to have. I touched him on his ringlets, and he turned about and stared at me. He made a motion that I was to bend down, and then touched my face assiduously—looking, after each time he touched, at his fingers. He touched me all over my face and hands.

I recalled having heard from the Mime that the best way to communicate with the boy was by a sort of kissing sound. Two kisses meant yes, one kiss no.

In due course the Bird of Heaven became deeply attached to me, and I had the greatest difficulty leaving him without his bursting into tears. I supposed Millicent was watching all this from a central compartment, through some sort of electronic eye.

Accordingly, not counting my habit (which as I said, was failing me), my attachments now numbered three: the Bird of Heaven, Millicent, and the Mime, and each demanded everything. My health began its decline.

Love was devouring me.

Like the droppings from immense prehistoric birds, my notes, which were commissioned to be about Elijah Thrush, but were incoherently and divergently about everything, fell from my clothing. These pieces of paper, on which I had written my reflections, first drove Millicent to maniacal anger, and then, this having subsided and no medicine, either from her young men's fine parts or from Doctor Hitchmough's bag, being able to help her, she sank into a black bile and barely stirred from her chair beside her teapot, from which she helped herself to countless cups of gunpowder.

"Has he told the truth, this inky memoirist?" was her constant complaint, and then remembering this was only a word whilst the kaleidoscope of the deceived retina went on and on, until the eye itself ceased to take pictures, rotted with maggots and from maggots flew to dust, she commanded me to take my post. "His biography," she said, "does not add up to even the thinnest doctrine! You have fallen under his spell, as all do. You have deceived me, as he has! I should flay you, for the reality of the body is deep deep under the skin, in those parts that are ever wet, laved by the lymph and blood and running matter which is the body's only life, and all the outside, my dear, which you and I feast on, is death. What are we in love with? I must warn you, Albert, your presence is becoming so strong, the terrible stench of your perfume has worked my nostrils into such a state of activity, that you are a diet which may prove my poison supper at last. These notes," she brought them up from a carpetbag lying on the floor, "are too terrible. That you would win the love of the Bird of Heaven away from me is exactly as I had foreseen, and yet I find the reckoning unbearable. Why don't you kill me, and have done with it? Or better yet, grind Elijah Thrush to powder? Roll up your sleeves, Albert. You must try harder, my dear. Bait him, *confuse* him, make love to him, and of course continue to write these blackmail notes, since you are incapable of being a memoirist. You are incapable, you black whore, of being anything but wonderful you." She commanded me to kiss her, and as I did so she tore my newest pongee shirt. "I know what your habit is," she leveled a look at me. "You can thank God I do," wiping her mouth of my saliva. "Few women can plunge downward as far as I, and yet come up so happy and light. I put a dolphin to shame. Now get to him, and make his life the hell he has made mine. Do you hear, you Bought-and-Paid-For!"

I fell at her feet in a seizure the most violent in my memory. She listened to my weeping with fine attention and critical detachment. It had been destined I would cry like this, so fiercely the blood came from my nose. The event was ecstasy for her, and made our relationship impossible of severance.

"Sweet Albert," she put something into my hand, "make my

presence weigh on him wherever his hand or eye moves. I don't want him to know a minute's respite now, for we're out of time. And open that other door to the Jonquil Room as you go out. Some lovely young gentleman is waiting out there."

"*Come hither, my cherub,*" Millicent De Frayne spoke to the Bird of Heaven as he came hesitantly into her withdrawing room. She took the boy's hand in hers.

"*You are like a diadem of stars after the presence of that black jaguar, whose sleek movements fill me with such pain and madness. My mouth is full of musk from his kisses. Would you believe, my dearest of wards, I once looked out on the world in the cloudless blue I see in your eyes? I too expected something, but, if I may be allowed some frankness, your blue is already clouding. Blame me for it if you like. I expect to be blamed. Sit here, sparrow, and let me toy with your ringlets. You fear me, but I will never harm you.*" She brought him closer to her knees, and he let his head go against them as if an invisible sword had severed it.

"*I have something I have found by and large better than love, my darling. Peace, quiet, and oblivion. Of course you want love, and so you mean to leave me. I knew the black beast had been at your honey. I forbid nothing. People will do what they will do, and I do not prevent them. Of course I have my little tantrums, my orders, my imperial ways. Don't fifty millions of property in this one city alone allow me some whims? Meanwhile you endure my caresses, poor young one. I know of course you are planning to run away,*" the Bird of Heaven raising his head to gaze into her eyes. She kissed him again and again on his cheeks. "*How many flavors the human face has! As many as there are flowers and grasses! Yet you spurn me. Do I scold you for that? Of course not. Having known for nearly a hundred years there is no love under the sun, I have nevertheless never forbidden it in those I was getting my embraces from. I brought you here for many reasons, as you know,"* from her inside pocket plucking a long gold chain, which she then put around the boy's neck, he stirring a bit and touching it, but showing no further interest, *"and none of the reasons are what the world would call decent. You endure my caresses well, my dear. But you will go because there is nothing here to stir your mild bird-heart. Therefore not one door will be bolted against your escape with your black lover. Go, and be damned, for I'll never send an arm of the law to bring you back to this paradise. Be glad, my angel, you cannot talk. Your affliction is your happiness. It's talking that has made man lower than the brutes of creation, and is God's most calamitous mistake, that from which all other mistakes proceed. Without talk, history, that patched middling bore that is eating away at my brain, would never have been. Thank fortune a thing of such dreadful proportion is fizzling to its finish."*

He had fallen asleep at her knees, and without any real difficulty she brought him to her lap, and from a few careless motions of her jeweled fingers his lower clothes fell, and out there also fell the three globules of his sex. After an admiring look, she kissed these gently in way of farewell.

Intoning his morning prayer to Apollo (he worshiped all the major Greek gods), Elijah Thrush came out of his reverie for long enough to point with a curved hand at me, gesturing with it then downward. I fell on my knees in compliance with his command, and remained thus whilst he went on with his moaning and sighing. Prayer has always tired me greatly.

"Have you taken care of that genetrix of every evil?" he thundered at last.

"I have won the boy over to me," I said with some misgiving.

"The bitch of hell of course knows our plans," he lifted me up from the floor. "When will you bring the boy here?" his hands a cone over his mouth.

"Whenever you wish, Elijah."

130

"Oh, can we do it, do you suppose? I mean, where shall we flee to?"

"We could go anywhere," I said, and he answered with laughter from the lowest register to the highest.

"She just sent me this," unfolding another telegram.

The message: *All Your Problems Will Be Solved If You Will Consent To Take My Hand In Marriage. You May Live With The Bird Of Heaven, And We Will Live Apart, But We Must Marry. Reconsider Or Prepare For Oblivion.*

Millicent De Frayne

It was my turn to laugh, but my range was limited. Going into a rage, he tore the telegram out of my hand, walked into his dressing room, and in a trice came out wearing the most elaborate costume I think I have ever seen, an affair made entirely of quilts.

"What answer will you give?" I inquired.

"Do you think a person of my eminence answers such a creature's appeals? I wonder the telegraph office does not issue a warrant for her arrest. Of course the clerks there do not know idiom, let alone language. For over a half century I have received a telegram from her nearly every day. The only time they ceased was a period forty years ago when she had, she claimed, erysipelas, though I suspect it was really a conglomeration of venereal diseases. Are you listening to me, Albert? Oh, you are so distant lately. Am I, now listen carefully, do you attend me, is my affliction that I am really *she?*"

The thought of my predicament came over me with such force I feared I would go instantly insane. So like a physical pain was it, I put my head heavily on Elijah's shoulder and pressed against him.

"Am I actually Millicent De Frayne, oh Albert?"

"I have seen you together," I told him. "So you must be

131

separate parties." Then I said, "My dear friend, I am going mad!"

"Put aside those thoughts. You're too young, for one thing, and no primitive person, such as yourself, can go mad. Besides, Albert, you are the kidnapper of the Bird of Heaven. Once you have abducted him tonight, we will both feel better. Albert, Albert, look at me!"

Oh, I was terribly ill. I fell at his feet. Froth flecked with blood spilled from my tongue. It was his calm that restored me. "You have nothing whatsoever to fear, my angel," he said. "I love you devotedly. Not in the quintessential manner I bestow myself on the Bird of Heaven, but, oh Albert, so fully."

"A terrible creature has total power over me, a winged beautiful creature, my dear Elijah," telling him the truth. "It is this that is my habit!"

"Yes, yes, he possesses us all. But kissing will make it well," showering me with affection, making my fever pass.

I sat up beside him, and we took our cup of chocolate together.

Waiting outside her withdrawing-room door, I heard the piano player, Eugene Bellamy, say to Millicent De Frayne, "Oh spare me, why can't you! Why must I act against one I love!"

"Spare you, you ninny, when I've never spared myself! Quit that damnable driveling. Have you ever known me to spare myself?"

"You fanfaron!" I heard Bellamy cry, and my hand came off the knob.

"Do you expect me to scream stinking fish when I meet a lion in my path? Don't you know I have not a friend in the universe, that my power has made me anathema to all? Oh Eugene, my Eugene, you must now perform an act that requires the testicles of a bandit. Hand me that glass of grog over there, can't you, I'm hoarse with thirst. Now, my dear, let my mean-

James Purdy

ing be plain. I never use threats. Either betray him, or lay down your life."

I heard smacking sounds. So confused I became, I fled, and in my confusion, thinking I might be going through an exit, I entered instead an immense room I had never seen before. There, sitting around a great oak table, I found eight policemen playing cards. I went to where they were sitting and sat down on a stool. My presence scarcely brought a ripple of attention from them, so absorbed were they in their game.

At last the handsomest of the bluecoats winked at me, and passed me one of his playing cards. Naturally I put it in my sock, and then stood up, breathing heavily, but as I did so the cop pushed me.

"Excuse yourself, Albert, when you leave the room," he said.

Bowing as low as ever they had seen a black man bow, I exited to a round of applause.

"Lions! Pelicans! Elephant papers!" I shrieked in the hall, as Norah watched me in one of my seizures. "Bring me wine, Norah, a huge flask of it, and, damn you, put some motor power in your fat white ass as you do so. I'll have a drink before I kidnap the Bird. Cunctator of cunctators," I roared as she raced away, "it's all leather or prunella, Norah, don't you ever forget it," lying down on the floor and unbuttoning myself.

"My only angel, except one, and my dearest dear," I performed my apostrophe to the Bird of Heaven as he lay sleepless in his trundle bed, his thumb resting under his nose, his eyes drying from his tears (he cried most of the day and the night). "Are you ready to run over the roof with me to freedom?"

He nodded weakly.

"Do you love me, orphan?"

He raised his head.

I kissed each of his pink toes and tickled his ribs. But he made no motion of gaiety.

"A warm fur coat, good," I went over to the wardrobe. "Fur boots and your Scottish highland outfit underneath. You're a pumpkin," I said, and heard Millicent's voice rise from a down-the-hall room: "This wine you've served me is corked, you animals! Oh, these half-timer idiots. I'm choking from cork! Yes, you, damn me, get your shanks down to that cellar and bring me back a decent bottle. Down there, on the double, I say!"

The orphan gave me a finicky kiss on the cheek.

"That's better, Bird," I laced his boots, and he threw his arms around me and sobbed. "Shh," I warned, "don't raise the alarm, dearest darling." I extinguished the bed lamp and the orphan hugged me tight.

"That damned black wagtail is selling his semen to the help, I suppose," her voice from the depths of her sleeping chambers.

"We'll soon be out and away and gone," the Bird holding tight to me the way one should to his kidnapper. "Over the roofs of the city to great-grandpa's house."

A seizure hit me, and I fell to the floor, trembling, and then raising myself I put him on my back, opened the window, jumped to the fire escape, and from the fire escape we went to the roof. There, paces away, were the policemen from the game.

"Stop! Halt!"

We heard the bullets, all in the unreal way they have when they happen, and I felt something sting my elbow. But we were either too quick for them or we were supposed to get away. We leaped from one building to another, and then down down down to the street and over through snowflakes toward Tenth Avenue.

In our flight the Bird had lost his shoes, trousers, and his fine fur hat. We were shivering and wet to the bone. We found a deserted warehouse, and hid behind some bales of wool, whilst squad cars went by and sirens screamed their worst. I took off all my clothes, but found only nicks. My body bare, his eyes found the thing, my wound. He put his hand in it, and showed no surprise. The swooning thought took me to run off with him alone.

"Have you heard of *Aquila chrysaëtos*, the endangered species?" I told him everything, or was in the process of so doing when we looked up into the faces of two policemen.

The one took up the Bird and ran off with him; the other put the handcuffs on me. Then pinioning me to a bale and finding my body as he would wish it, he beat me until we both ran blood like rain. But the bluecoat left me when his fellow let out a great cry. *"The kid got away!"*

I put on my clothes, walked to the back of the building, and saw there the river floating like tar, snow and rain falling, and, as if lit up by ten moons, the Bird.

"Do you want to run off with me, Bird, or go to your great-granddad's?" I cried. "Do you want me or the Mime?" I asked him again. I knelt down to watch his lips, eyes. "I will take care of you with the last breath in my body." He took my hand. "I will give up the Golden Eagle," and I pointed to my wound. "There was no pain like it, Bird, none under the sun. But neither was there ever pleasure so great. If you will go with me, I will leave him," I cried. "You'll never find another Albert Peggs."

"Where in the land of never have you two been all this time?" a great voice fell upon us. It was the Mime, and behind him was a horse-drawn carriage. "We've not a minute to lose," he gathered us up and off we drove, passing squad car after squad car, and heading, as Elijah explained, for the Brooklyn docks.

"This is some painted dream of yours, Albert," the Mime scolded as I listened to the hooves on the wet asphalt. "No eagle would touch your flesh, and you know it! Now lay your mind to rest about having been the lover of a bird of prey, my dearest," taking my hand in his, "and let a slightly older party warn you against your too generous giving of the body to the first comer. Don't overstimulate yourself! You must keep your youth and good looks." I buried my head in his lap. "And you stated all this foolishness to the poor Bird of Heaven here," he pushed me gently away from him now and stroked his great-grandson's hair. "What must the dear creature think, you the lover of a bird of prey! I see there's naught to do but turn about and prove there's no such creature at all."

"Oh thank you, thank you," I cried.

"Our delay may cost us everything," the Mime continued. "Fear nothing, sweetheart," he reassured the Bird. "Nothing can harm us." Instructing the coachman to drive in the direction I pointed, Elijah went on, "Nonetheless, Albert, I can't tell you how irritated I am to have to go out of our way for your idle fancies. Do you know I've pawned everything to make our escape tonight? Silver, china, paintings, rings? And when freedom is within sight, we turn back to the city!"

The carriage stopped. "Is this it, Albert Peggs?" the Mime roared at me. I nodded. "Very well. All alight now, please, and we'll proceed to take the gilt off the gingerbread." There was no elevator service at this hour; indeed, the building was forbidden to tenants, as I pointed out earlier. How my fingers trembled with the keys when we had climbed the four flights of stairs! I opened the first door, whilst the Bird and the Mime followed close at my heels—then the second, and then at last we stood before the little violet-colored door with silver stars.

"Are you awake, my dearest dear?" I spoke into the cracks of the wood.

"Oh, John-a-dreams," the Mime muttered. "Heaven preserve us."

"Answer me," and I began weeping. "Oh, he's gone, Elijah, he's gone!"

"Who in the name of God are you addressing through that tiny door? We haven't a minute to lose. The police have orders to shoot us on sight, and you moon and drool here. I won't have it," and with a sudden push he broke the door down.

"There's not even a perch here for your winged creature to have sat on," surveying the floor, "not one dropping, not a feather. You are a lunatic!" he cried, when we all at once saw the letter on the floor. The Mime picked it up.

"Shall I open it?" he inquired. "It's bound to be from her."

I was so distraught, I cared not to go on breathing. There was death in my veins.

"Hark to this letter the old whore has written us," and Elijah recited:

I AM ONLY A FOX-STEP AWAY, MY HANDSOME. WHICHEVER WIND OF THE ROAD YOU TAKE 'TWILL LEAD TO ME. COMFORT ALBERT ON HIS LOSS.   M. DE F.

We were in the carriage again when the gunfire began. "Pay no mind to the firing over there," Elijah studied me, "and be glad the street fighting will draw off the police from pursuing us. Well, my dear, thanks to your morbid imaginings we are late for our boat. Turn here to the left, why don't you, my good fellow," he called to the driver. I reached for the Bird of Heaven's neckerchief, dried my lip, replaced the silk and kissed him as thanks, meanwhile attending Elijah's words.

"Because I need love so much, I give kindness where kindness is misunderstood, shower blessings where they are taken for common coin, and raise those to glory who would be satisfied with creaking humdrum. Albert, my dear, you have strained me," he said, in a weak but consoling voice, and then stoutly, "The docks are right ahead of us! Compose yourselves for the gangplank. Look at me! Do I not look a ruin? I am not at my best."

He picked up a hand mirror and smoothed down his hair and daubed his face with powder.

"Shall we go down, gentlemen?"

As we went up the gangplank, flakes of snow fell heavily, and I was heartsick. An officer, advancing toward us, called, "Party of Mr. Elijah Thrush? You're expected, sir. Kindly this way."

"But the boat I commissioned was given me under the name *Hors de Combat*, Captain! Whereas this, I observe, runs the name *Queen Dick*."

"One and the same, sir," the officer saluted Elijah, adding, "I must explain to you, I'm not the captain. The captain awaits you at his table. Please, this way, sir. Can't I carry the youngest chap there . . . ?"

"If you'd be so kind," Elijah cried, "for the poor tot has had a weary afternoon, none wretcheder," kissing his great-grand-son to reassure him.

I had scarcely noticed the ship, so annihilated did I feel. We were shown into a well-lighted room, and some spirits were brought for Elijah and me, and hot grape juice for the Bird of Heaven.

"No one can know how glad I am to be leaving that impossible city," Elijah was telling me when another officer, bowing low, came up.

"Ah, you are the captain of course," Elijah extended his hand.

"No, I'm sorry to disappoint you. The captain awaits you in the banquet room. If you'll come this way, you'll do me a great honor indeed. Mr. Thrush, kindly take my arm, and we'll announce ourselves."

"I was booked for the *Hors de Combat*," Elijah was saying to the officer, who now that he was leading us to the banquet room seemed not to hear more than his own footsteps, "and as I was saying to my good friend here, Mr. Albert Peggs, I was quite taken aback by the present name, which . . ." A great orange door opened, and we stood on the threshold of a room that seemed larger than the boat itself. A vast celebration was laid, with candles glowing, bursts of flowers, servants running here and there. At the center of the captain's table sat a personage wearing a mask. The captain! I thought, since authority is so often eccentric.

"My heart misgives me," Elijah cried, "I fear we've boarded the wrong ship."

"Your fears were sumptuously in vain, my beloved angel!" whilst off came the mask and there sat Millicent De Frayne.

"Manacle him, Jeffrey, if he makes any attempt to leave the ship!" She laughed heartily.

I felt the vessel moving now, and fearing I might topple over, I sat at Millicent's table.

"This is our wedding banquet, my darling!" she said, and then made a signal that both the Mime and the Bird of Heaven should be brought to sit by her. They were carried to their places by four young men. And how close to the point of death I came when I looked up above Millicent and saw in a large glass case the stuffed remains of my Golden Eagle.

It could not have been a copy!

I fainted.

"What poor sailors we are this evening. And I could live on the sea like a cork. Hoist our dark friend from the floor for the banquet's scheduled to begin."

And thus there we all were.

"Happiness so complete is not without its frightening promptings, gentlemen. Albert, my dear, I can never thank you enough for what you have done for me. I have tried, as you know, ever since 1913, to achieve this, and you, with your wonderfully primitive power, have brought it about. As a token of my gratitude to you, Albert, I am giving you your freedom tonight, sending you back on a private boat as soon as the banquet is over, and endowing you for life with a stipend. Gracious, I don't know where Elijah and I will be honeymooning. . . ."

"Oh, stop her, Albert," Elijah shrieking. "Run to the nearest wireless and send an S.O.S. There are still laws in effect!"

"You naïve booby, Elijah, believing what you hear on the radio or read in the press."

"I could never go back, Millicent," but without warning felt a great pain in my ear.

"Earache often comes on as a result of naughtiness, dearest Albert. Pray let me examine your ear," she took away my hand. "Jeffrey, fetch me my earspoon. You'll find it in that Empire cabinet yonder, that's a dear."

She took the earspoon and poked about. The pain was intolerable. Bits of paper, petals of flowers, an insect or two tumbled out. When she had finished I felt almost myself again and, forgetting Elijah's rage with her, kissed her hand again and again until she said firmly, "That will be about enough from that sweet bee-stung pair of lips."

"You are both positively disgusting," Elijah cried.

"What's wrong with us all is we're not getting wine," and she clapped her hands. Bottles were brought.

"To take away all occasion of dissension," her voice in priestly cadence, "which any person may have, let me answer him we have the finest breads and liquors one can procure. The meat will be another story. Eat and drink, my hearties, for you're all the acme of male glory, and it's glory I live for."

"Dearly beloved, all," Millicent began a kind of after-dinner speech, although we were still feasting on the entrée, "this is, as you all must know, my wedding day. After an engagement of more than fifty years, Mr. Thrush and I are to be wed on the high seas. No bridegroom," she went on, "has ever been wooed and pursued for so long. I have spared no expense, nor time, in capturing the only person who ever captured my heart. Mind you, I am not unacquainted with marriage. I have gone through four husbands." She stopped for a moment, like an actress back from retirement who cannot for the moment recall the one small speech a doting director has assigned her. "Jeffrey, seraph, fetch me that little ledger there."

Her lorgnette was also brought.

"Ah, I was mistaken. Six husbands," she read from the ledger. "But for the love of me, I can't remember the last one's name," consulting a few sheets of loose paper.

"This meat, Millicent, is not quite palatable," the Mime complained.

"Have the steward bring you something less recherché, then, my dear," poring over her notes.

"Good grief, Albert," she put down her lorgnette and looked at me. "These are *your* notes, for the good land's sake. They're devastating attacks on both of us, Elijah. You should hear what the poor boy thinks of us!"

"Can you wonder he would write against you, Millicent," helping himself to the escaloped potatoes. "You have driven this beauty from the cotton fields mad. Indeed, he believes, now that you've unhinged him, that he was the lover of a certain eagle."

"And so he was," putting away the notes and closing the ledger. "Albert had to come out sometime, Elijah, and though we were not the right people for him, in this pinch-back age of ours, the right people might never have come. I am aware of the hearts I have broken, but it's better to have one's heart broken by those who shower one with attention than to be ignored and untouched."

I AM ELIJAH THRUSH

It was the first time in my life I had ever heard of Baked Alaska or tasted it. "Yummy grand," I said.

"I couldn't send the boy away on a night like this without something special on his stomach, now could I, Elijah?" she called down the long table to her bridegroom.

She suddenly rose, and as she did so the Bird of Heaven, whom she had earlier teased onto her lap, fell to the floor with a loud bump. An attendant picked the boy up and whisked him out of the room. "Lower the lights, Jeffrey dearest, for the ceremony is about to begin. Fetch the little casket over there by the bouquet of hyacinths."

"Oh verminous old age!" Elijah cried, no sooner said than the Bird of Heaven made his reentry in a fine new costume, an admiral's suit.

"Now we are all assembled," she wept, and clasped her hands. "In this holy hour when Elijah and I are to be made one flesh, I will act as my own priest. There is no limit to my generosity, Albert," she studied me; "though I force myself to many little economies, I never stint where a friend is concerned. As for your eagle, my dear," she whispered in my emptied ear, "forget him, angel, for he would have died in any case. Think how cruel he was to you! Oh, your finest days are ahead, sweetheart. As soon as Elijah and I are married, you will leave the boat, remember? Thank you, thank you for everything, if I don't see you again."

Music sounded from somewhere on deck. Young men with flowers came tripping in, and from some box at her feet Millicent brought out a tiara, and this she placed on her head.

"Dearly beloved, all," she began.

"I am not listening, Millicent. I am not in my right mind. You've put something in this wine," Elijah spoke.

"Darling beloved, this is the moment of my greatest felicity— come forward all, this is my wedding day. With this ring I thee wed," she took up an enormous gold ring and stumbled over to where Elijah sat. "With my body I thee worship, and with all my worldly goods I thee endow," seizing his hand and forcing the great ring on his finger as he let out terrible cries of pain and rage.

"You have done all that need be done, dearest Albert," she turned to me. "Your career as a memoirist is over. Let me assure you of one thing, angel boy," covering me with kisses. "I not only love you as a woman, but as a mother. I suffered from caked breast after the birth and death of my fifth child. I know the agonies of lost motherhood."

"You know nothing," Elijah Thrush leaping from his seat, all the while attempting to remove the ring from his hand. "You, a mother! You, anything!" he cried. "Release all of us from this prison ship you've arranged. I'm going to the wireless and send an S.O.S."

As he spoke, he reeled from the wine and fell to the floor.

"Albert," he cried piteously, "go back to the city and tell them I have been spirited away. Get help from the authorities. I suddenly feel my correct age, Albert, my child."

I bent over to him and kissed him good-bye.

"Never say good-bye, my darling," he said, "only *au revoir*."

I nodded uncertainly, and felt Millicent's arms about me and her lips kissing mine. She slipped an envelope into my hand. "Don't look at this until you're safely in the boat, my dear. And as the wind is up, ask the steersman for a heavier coat. Now, kiss the Bird of Heaven good-bye, for of course he's going with us on our tour."

I bade farewell to the Bird and kissed all the young men who were attendants on board, and then closed the orange door to the wedding party. Out on deck, the air was cold indeed. To warm myself, as I knew she expected me to, I opened the envelope and saw her certified check for $200,000.

"Your boat is ready, sir," an officer now approached me,

and motioned to a rope ladder down which I was to go. "Mr. Peggs," the officer tugged at my sleeve.

Being from a landlocked part of the world, I understood nothing of what the pilot of the little boat said to me, and he talked continuously. So I began to doze a bit, which seemed to satisfy him as much as when I replied to his speeches.

We had not been out very long when I heard an electric megaphone, testing, and then the Shakespearean voice of Elijah Thrush, as clear through the snow and over the waves as from the stage to the first row of the Arcturus Gardens.

"My darling Albert, does my voice carry to wherever you are?" I straightaway jumped up and cried, "Yes!"

"Best to seat yourself, sir, for he can't hear you," the pilot cautioned me. "You'll only make yourself seasick in any case."

"Albert, I miss you more than I can say. I don't know when I've become so attached to a person of your quality and background. But what I have to say, my sweet," and here he cried out in a paroxysm of grief, "is that I am ruined, irreparably, for all time, of the little time that's left. Of course I don't blame you, and don't blame yourself. Go back to the Arcturus Gardens, play all my roles, and turn worshipful heads for many a season to come. Harken well, Albert. As for me, well she's already belittled my membrum virile, and is now in bed with the real captain. Albert, I will never recover from this slight. She has asked for the wedding ring back. Oh, can you hear me, wonderful faithful boy? It's so unnerving to speak into winds and billows and get no answer at all. Carry on for me, and keep the Gardens open. It must not close, do you hear, Albert? Aha! The whore has just come back from the wedding room, having worn out the captain. Her mode of intercourse is not normal, of course. As to prejudice, Albert, you know I have none. I see you as eternally golden, like your poor eagle, which she murdered and then, I think, tricked us to eat. Do I blame you for being the final hand to bring all this about? Never. Not in an ice age. Oh, Albert, I feel what I am saying is a love letter spoken over dark ocean waves."

A splendid display of fireworks came from land, toward which we rapidly approached. Circus music sounded from the shore, the melody of *American Patrol*. A great crowd was waiting for me at the dock, and there in the forefront was Eugene Bellamy.

"We haven't a minute to lose," he embraced me. "The audience has been waiting for well over an hour."

We drove like the wind through the back streets.

Stringing myself with beads, I walked out to the winking footlights.

"Ladies, and gentlemen," I began, as the piano playing let up for a bit, "I . . . I . . . I," and I choked back a sob. "I am . . . Elijah Thrush."

DEALER

David Kranes

t twenty-six, Hatch had lost, or lost at, almost everything: a father, a mother, college, a wife, their baby, any job. And so, trying to break a streak, Hatch packed an airline bag and took off, hitchhiking, on what he hoped to be the beginning of a change. Hatch traveled west. He went to Columbus and pumped gas. At Independence, he lifeguarded at a Best Western motel. In Cheyenne, he wore a white hat and turned steaks at the Sizzler Grill.

In early spring, Hatch moved on west again, taking Route 80 out of Salt Lake toward a series of towns all beginning with "W": Wendover, Wells, Winnemucca. In Wells, he saw that the road north toward Idaho led on to a town named Jackpot in Nevada, and he took that, riding with an Indian driving a lumber truck. Neither of them spoke. They rolled north. They passed a stretch of fences called the "Winecup Ranch," and at four in the morning and ten miles later, the Indian stopped the truck and nodded for Hatch to get out. Hatch swung the door open without protest and stepped down. He watched the truck pull out, fade north into the only paved road in the nightscape and followed, walking, in its wake.

Gradually light came. Winter sun started up low in the east and Hatch found himself walking past foothills strewn with volcanic rock. Hatch wondered when these rocks had been thrown up here on these hills, sensing, with that question, that his life, somewhere near here, soon would be different. Three miles later, in the town of Contact, he caught a milk truck that took him straight to Jackpot.

"This it?" Hatch asked, gesturing at a pocket cluster of three casinos, motel units, gas stations.

The driver nodded, and Hatch took the weight of the small airlines bag in his hand and wandered off toward the first casino, a sign flashing even with the dawn, off and on, off and on: *Cactus Pete's.*

Hatch had never been in a casino before. He had heard about them, read about them, imagined what Las Vegas must be like. But the minute he stepped inside, he knew he was home.

Something about the way light fell, about the smell, about the music—almost like an all-night radio station—something about the sounds of coins, about machines ringing, about tin undermusic of silverware in the coffee shop, about the reflection of ceiling mirrors, about the way people moved and stalked, about the way men in white shirts waited behind tables in the pit, about the dark wood on the bar, about the rugs: something about *all* of that made him forget the wind outside, made him forget his wife, the child, and the long paralysis of his father. Hatch was here. He was home. He put a nickel in a slot machine, won himself a dollar, had a coffee and left all the other nickels for the counter girl as a tip. "Thanks," she said.

"Who would you see about a job here?" Hatch said.

"See the man? Over there? With the white silk shirt and the hand-tooled leather belt?"

"Yes," Hatch said.

"You see him," the girl said.

Within twenty minutes Hatch had a room in the help's wing and a job as a guard on the graveyard shift, watching the slot machines. The man, Randolph, took him twice through the routine.

"We'll try you out," he said. "If you can do it, you're on."

"I can do it," Hatch assured him.

"What's your name?"

"Hatch."

"Just Hatch?"

"Hatch."

Hatch loved the work. He would watch for people using devices on the slots: plugs, nickels soldered to wires that could retract them, Xeroxed bills on the Big Bertha dollar machine. And Hatch had an instinct.

On his breaks Hatch loved to study the dealers. He would watch them shuffle, watch the cards fan out, see all the hits dealt, watch the dealer turn his own downcard over, take his own hit if it were necessary, scoop the chips in with his cards. It was all an image of fingertips, flashing like bird wings over felt; like small flames, like absolutely clear water: magical, dexterous.

Hatch bought some old packs of cards. "These cards have been in actual play at Cactus Pete's Casino," they said; and Hatch practiced dealing them in his small room. There was a long mirror in front of a walnut veneer dresser, and Hatch would stand there dealing at first one hand, then two, then finally all six, imagining players. He would watch the cards fall into the mirror, watch his hands. He was proud of them.

On his first day off, he hitchhiked to Twin Falls, and bought himself a large piece of green felt. He cut the felt and fixed it with masking tape to the dresser. He taped six card-boxes to deal to, spaced them in a slight arc. He had his own playing table, and he loved it, and he'd deal—sometimes four hours at a stretch.

On his next day off, Hatch bought chips and practiced playing with them: scooping in, stacking, paying. He was amazed at how little he had to pay off; how often he won. He could draw six cards to a twenty or twenty-one nearly every time without a break. It was strange. It was miraculous how the cards fell. Hatch felt select, he felt anointed and ordained. Cards turned in his favor, breaking all probability. He practiced "burning" the top card, a swift liquid motion moving it to the bottom after the cut so that no one could see what it was. Each day, for at least an hour, he would just shuffle. Finally, he chose the casino's best dealer, and asked that he come watch him deal.

"You think you're ready?" the dealer asked.

"Can't tell," Hatch managed, "just can't tell."

The dealer watched for almost an hour. "Phenomenal," he finally said; "unbelievable! I'll talk to Randolph." Then he left.

Hatch could sense something happening. That night on his shift, Randolph came up to him and took Hatch to an empty table. He instructed him, had him deal. Hatch won thirteen out of fifteen hands. "You're a natural," Randolph said.

He had Hatch deal out all six boxes: "Deal right to left. Pay off left to right. Tap your tips. Slap once when you walk away; shows you're clean." Randolph watched Hatch's hands, the agility, the brisk presumption of his cards. In ten rounds, Hatch only broke once and, outside that once, never had to pay off more than two of six.

"I think I could do better with real players there," Hatch said. "I think I could cool people. Cool people off."

"Tomorrow night," Randolph said, "you start dealing."

Hatch was an instant legend. No one won. He moved quickly from graveyard to day to prime shift. There was always a constant turnover at his table, but, at busy times, it didn't matter; people spent their money fast, moved out and others with new money came in. Hatch took it all. There was never any expression on his face. His hands moved. They were machines. He just dealt. He saw eyes, watched the eyes watching him, but never faces.

His reputation spread. Players came from Elko at first, then soon Tahoe and Vegas. "Where's Hatch?" they'd ask the pit boss. "We've heard about this guy named Hatch." And then they'd buy five hundred or a thousand dollars in chips, play two, sometimes three hands at a time. And Hatch would go through them, like a trout through rapids, his mind fastened somewhere in the light that caught the bladelike edges of the dealt cards. Once a man from Sarasota stayed a week, sending home every other day for money orders, playing only when Hatch was on duty, losing fifty-two thousand dollars when the week was done. They found him hanging in his motel shower, choked by his money belt. When Hatch heard about it, he touched the various bones that made up his head, but he could not really be said to have thought anything about the man.

Hatch bought things. The management gave him frequent bonuses, and he began, very selectively, to acquire. He bought leather: leather shirts, leather vests, leather pants; soft leather, smooth leather; natural leather, dyed leather; he bought almost a hundred pairs of shoes and almost fifty belts. To walk into Hatch's room at Cactus Pete's was to walk into the presence of sweatless animals, a place of cool and scentless hides. And Hatch bought himself a horse, a fine Appaloosa that he named Horse, but rode him only in snow, in winter.

In the days between December and early March, Hatch would ride the animal out, ride him south. They would walk into the rock formations below Contact, the more snow in the air, the better; and Hatch would weave a trail among the boulders. He would think of his father, of the unmoving silence in any air ever between them. He would see birds in his mind, brightly colored birds, frozen, falling through unwinded air onto a place like seacoast, shattering. He would see animals, stiff and still and stone, standing in place, crack, falling in fragments on a frozen ground. Then he would go home and, in the night, dream of rocks. His life had changed. He was not a loser any more. He could win. And he could have a woman when he wanted. And he would always insist that she do everything.

That's what had happened toward the end of his second February. He had ridden Horse out into the snow-covered rocks at Contact. He had stood there in the absolute gravity of all his images. It had been nearly fifteen below zero and he had stayed almost four hours without any movement while imagined deer split and tanagers plummeted, a weighted mass of shale and crystals inside his mind. Then he rode Horse back, took a shower, dressed for work, went to his table, and dealt.

Shortly after eleven, a woman took a place at his table. She had a look of terrified beauty that bore back far into her eyes. Hatch selected her. He watched her change two hundred dollars into chips and proceed to lose deal after deal. He saw her watching his shoulders and his hands. She had on a long blue skirt with a low-cut top, and, in exposed risings, her breasts looked polished, veined like good marble. Hatch finished his deal, brushed his hands once to show them empty, and moved off to the bar. She met him there.

"You're very good," she said.

Hatch nodded.

"Buy me a drink?"

Hatch held his hand up. The bartender came. Hatch pointed at the bartender for the girl.

"I'll have a whiskey sour, please," she said.

The bartender moved off.

"I'll bet you're a very cruel man," she said, her voice even. "The way you deal. There's something very . . ."

"I just deal," Hatch told her.

"No you don't." Something approached a smile on her lips. "No, you don't. No."

"There's your whiskey sour," Hatch pointed near her. "I'll be back in about twenty minutes—you want to lose more money."

"You live here?" she held him with the question.

"Yes," Hatch said.

"In the motel?" she said.

"Yes," Hatch said.

"What number?"

"Twenty-one." Hatch said, and almost smiled.

Minutes after he arrived back at his room, she knocked. She came in. She took his clothes off, then removed hers. She kissed him, took hold of him. She moved him to the bed. She pressed him down, stroked. She talked to him, talked him up: almost a set patter, he thought, somewhere inside his mind, like the stickmen at the craps table: "Number's four. You're knocking on the door"; "Eight; eight; no field this time, but next time looks great"; "Two; craps; two; a seven will do." "Coming out! Coming out this time." Hatch finished fast. She was nowhere near. She got up, got dressed and left. Hatch listened to the wind a moment. He could almost see it, like stiff celluloid. He saw a gazelle, inside the camera of his brain, become fiercely arterial with cracks; then fall apart. Hatch dressed and went back.

He started dealing. There was a man from Puerto Rico who had heard about Hatch in Reno and was there to beat him. He started playing fifty dollars a hand and lost seven straight. "Keep those cards coming from the top," he said. Hatch took another five hundred quickly; the man wanted to have Hatch drop the house limit: "Who do I see?" he asked. Hatch pointed to Randolph. Later, the man was back, betting one, two, then five hundred a hand. Hatch kept even, the Puerto Rican never winning more than one hand in five.

Hatch noticed the woman he'd just had standing with a man Hatch took to be her husband. They stood at the craps table. Hatch saw her whispering to the man. He saw the man look back over his shoulder at Hatch. He saw the woman whisper again. He saw the man look back, fix him. "Blackjack!" he heard the Puerto Rican say, five hundred dollars in chips sitting in the box in front of his seat. Hatch paid him off. "Why don't you bet it all the next time? See if you can win two in a row?" Hatch asked him, filaments of anger curling in his chest. The man took the challenge. The two pushed at nineteen apiece, pushed again with twenty. Then the man doubled down with an eleven and drew a seven to Hatch's nineteen. Hatch took his money back. The man started screaming, cursing Hatch in Spanish, scooped in the few chips he had left and moved away. Hatch calculated that in nineteen minutes he had taken in seven thousand dollars for the house.

The man taking the Puerto Rican's chair was the blue-skirted woman's husband. He was dark. His hair was black. His cheeks were somehow knuckled, clutched with multiples of bone. He looked at Hatch. Hatch looked at him and at the woman standing about two feet behind; he dealt and broke on a hand while the man was getting money out. "E-O-Eleven!" somebody yelled from the craps table. Three jackpot bells went off in chain. Hatch scraped a piece of lint from the felt in front of him.

"Five hundred in twenty-fives. A hundred in fives," the man said.

Hatch took the six hundred-dollar bills and changed them. The man set a five-dollar chip in his box. Hatch dealt himself a blackjack, ace and ten, and scooped all bets in. He felt the lefthand corner of his mouth flicker up. The woman's husband set a twenty-five-dollar chip out in front of his box, then replaced his lost five with another. Hatch looked at the twenty-five. "Tip," the man said, and the mirrors around the pit seemed, to Hatch, to catch brief light. Hatch nodded to the man, set the tip aside for himself, dealt again.

Hatch had a four showing. He dealt his hits, turned over a king, hit himself with a deuce and then a four. The woman's husband had an eighteen. Once more Hatch took in the losses and once more he saw the twenty-five-dollar chip set aside for him. He took it. He nodded. He drew a breath. He saw the woman behind her husband smiling. Once more the mirrors over his head flashed. He thought of Horse, wondered if it were cold where the animal had been fenced.

Hatch took the man's five dollars a third time. The mirrors blinked. The woman smiled. The cocktail waitress passed taking drink orders: "The house would like to buy you a drink": repeated. "Bourbon," the man said, "rocks," and set another twenty-five dollars out in front of him for Hatch.

"What's that for?" Hatch said.

"Excuse me?" the man said.

"The twenty-five," Hatch said.

"Same as the others." The man smiled. He smiled at the other players sitting at the table watching him. "Tip."

"But you lost." Hatch could feel his right knee vibrating. He pressed his foot into the carpet beneath him.

"Win some, lose some," the man said and smiled.

Hatch drew a breath, twisted his mouth, chewed, set aside the chip. "Maybe," he muttered.

He dealt again, won again: twenty. "You can't beat this guy," someone next to the man leaned over, advised.

"Lose some, win some," the man said again and smiled. He set another twenty-five out for Hatch. Hatch shook his head, took it, dealt. The man took a card and busted. This time he set fifty ahead of him for Hatch.

"But you *lost!*" Hatch almost shouted. The man's wife had her hand up to her mouth, holding her lips straight.

"Lose s . . ."

"But that's insane!"

". . . some; win some."

Hatch raised his deck as if to throw it. The pit mirrors flashed and photographed him. People were gathered. Hatch dealt out the hand, finished the others. Randolph came over. "Any problem?" he asked.

"I'm fine," Hatch bit hard, teeth against teeth.

"Sure?" Randolph said.

"Sure," Hatch said, and dealt.

Hatch won again. This time the man pushed him a hundred. Hatch leaned forward. "Look," he said to the man, as quietly as he could, "they're going to think I've got something going with you. I mean, why . . . ?"

"But you do," the man said, then smiled.

Hatch felt small stones strike his chest. There was a gel: tables, light, glass, all hardening. He stepped back. The others were waiting for him. They were watching. Hatch thought he saw his father, playing at the next table in a wheelchair. All around him, Hatch heard chips. Some of his bones Hatch thought he could feel slipping into new positions in his head and chest, realigning. Then he smiled. "You play with all kinds of people in a place like this," he announced to the crowd, those watching him, waiting. "Some just regular people—most. Some crazy. This man," he said, pointing to the woman's husband whose chips sat in a stack beside him, "I think he's crazy."

The man smiled. Behind him, his wife smiled as well. Some in the crowd, Hatch's audience, laughed. Then the man pushed eight twenty-five-dollar chips forward to Hatch. The watchers rumbled. Hatch took a breath, bit, felt something in his jaw, took the money. "Thanks," he said, as politely as he could.

"Pleasure," said the man.

Hatch dealt. He beat all except the woman's husband. Hatch had a twenty; the man drew an eight to his original thirteen. Hatch paid off the five. Then paused.

"No tip this time?" he asked.

"Not when I win," the man said, smiling. "Cuts the profits." Several around laughed. The cocktail waitress brought the table's drinks. The man changed two thousand dollars more into twenty-fives; a hundred more into fives. Hatch felt small flashes climbing his spine.

David Kranes

Hatch dealt and this time won. The man passed him three hundred, and Hatch felt another flash, one of the mirrors, a muscle pulling, left to right, across his brain. Again he dealt. He broke. Again: no tip. Hatch broke a second hand. "Lose some; win some," the man said, keeping all twenty-fives to himself, holding on tight, offering nothing. Then Hatch won: jack and queen for a twenty. The man smiled, passed Hatch five hundred dollars; Hatch threw the deck down and across the table. Watchers quieted. Others moved in. Randolph crossed the pit from the craps table: "What's going on?" he asked.

"Nothing," Hatch muttered, picking the cards precisely, one by one, from the felt.

"I don't get it," Randolph said.

Hatch looked at the black and red numbers coming up: four, seven, queen, six, nine, ace. "Nothing," he said. "I was dealing. I was trying to deal—deal too fast; that's all. I was dealing—Nothing." He held his breath.

"Take it easy," Randolph said, pressing a fist into a shoulderblade, smiling out at the table. "Easy"; and then: off and across the pit: "Jan! Could we have more drinks at this table again, please?"

Randolph moved away. The woman's husband passed Hatch another two hundred. Jennings, Hatch's relief dealer, tapped Hatch on the shoulder to take over. Hatch fanned the cards out on the felt with a stroke, brushed his hands, grabbed up his tips, dropping some, retrieving them, nodded to the players, left and walked, moving fast and directly, outside.

Snow blew over the empty highway and through the lights from the casino across the street, each flake smelling like a wet stone. Hatch lifted his head. He breathed hard. Snow flew in, flew in sharp into his nose and felt jagged against his face. In the dark he sensed his eyes and mouth: not hard, not boned, but crushed or soft. He started walking. Boulders, it seemed, were rising up: huge stones lifting against the snow, posing like moons in the low air. The air was filled with undiscovered rocks. Enormous things rose. Hatch was crying. He and his father were talking about catcher's mitts. They were in the back yard tossing to each other, talking about catcher's mitts: the ball lobbing, the ball sailing back and forth between them; talking about catcher's mitts, talking about pockets, talking about breaking gloves in, talking about the best catchers in the leagues.

Hatch drove his hands into the sheered rock at the highway's edge: repeatedly, repeatedly.

It was hard, back again, to deal with bandaged hands. In the first half hour, Hatch won only a third of his deals; by the end of the evening's shift, less than half. He had eighteen thousand dollars in tips from the man; but the man was beating him now, regularly, over the evening taking about three thousand from the house.

"Thanks," he said to Hatch at four when Hatch went off. "Thanks," his wife, standing behind him still and smiling, said.

Hatch looked at the man and saw the bones of his face. He watched them, stared. He thought of shoulders. Of necks. And of backs. He thought of a woman. Of an infant. An infant's feet. Of his mother's forehead, in the fluorescent light, in the kitchen late at night. Hatch nodded.

"Lose some, win some," the blue-skirted woman said.

"You're a good sport," her husband nodded in time.

"Hard as stone," the woman said.

"Tough as nails," said the man.

"Cold as ice," the woman said.

Hatch moved away.

Two weeks later, when anyone could beat him and after work one morning, Hatch packed his airline bag with whatever clothes he could fit, and left. He rode Horse down from Jackpot, down past Contact to the Winecup Ranch and left him, inside the fence, to be taken care of.

THE LOVER

Joy Williams

he girl is twenty-five. It has not been very long since her divorce but she cannot remember the man who used to be her husband. He was probably nice. She will tell the child this, at any rate. Once he lost a fifty-dollar pair of sunglasses while surf-casting off Gay Head and felt badly about it for days. He did like kidneys, that was one thing. He loved kidneys for weekend lunch. She would voyage through the supermarkets, her stomach sweetly sloped, her hair in a twist, searching for fresh kidneys for this young man, her husband. When he kissed her, his kisses, or so she imagined, would have the faint odor of urine. Understandably, she did not want to think about this. It hardly seemed that the same problem would arise again, that is, with another man. Nothing could possibly be gained from such an experience! The child cannot remember him, this man, this daddy, and she cannot remember him. He had been with her when she gave birth to the child. Not beside her, but close by, in the corridor. He had left his work and come to the hospital. As they wheeled her by, he said, "Now you are going to have to learn how to love something, you wicked woman." It is difficult for her to believe he said such a thing.

The girl does not sleep well and recently has acquired the habit of listening all night to the radio. It is a weak, not very good, radio and at night she can only get one station. From midnight until four she listens to ACTION LINE. People call the station and make comments on the world and their community and they ask questions. Music is played and a brand of beef and beans is advertised. A woman calls up and says, "Could you tell me why the filling in my lemon meringue pie is runny?" These people have obscene materials in their mailboxes. They want to know where they can purchase small flags suitable for waving on Armed Forces Day. There is a man on the air who answers these questions right away. Another woman calls. She says, "Can you get us a report on the progress of the collection of Betty Crocker Coupons for the lung machine?" The man can and does. He answers the woman's question. Astonishingly, he complies with her request. The girl thinks such a talent is bleak and wonderful. She thinks this man can help her.

The girl wants to be in love. Her face is thin with the thinness of a failed lover. It is so difficult! Love is concentration, she feels, but she can remember nothing. She tries to recollect two things a day. In the morning with her coffee, she tries to remember and in the evening, with her first bourbon and water, she tries to remember as well. She has been trying to remember the birth of her child now for several days. Nothing returns to her. Life is so intrusive! Everyone was talking. There was too much conversation! The doctor was above her, waiting for the pains. "No, I still can't play tennis," the doctor said. "I haven't been able to play for two months. I have spurs on both heels and it's just about wrecked our marriage. Air-conditioning and concrete floors is what does it. Murder on your feet." A few minutes later, the nurse had said, "Isn't it wonderful to work with Teflon? I mean for those arterial repairs? I just love it." The girl wished that they would stop talking. She wished that they would turn the radio on instead and be still. The baby inside her was hard and glossy as an ear of corn. She wanted to say something witty or charming so that they would know she was fine and would stop talking. While she was thinking of something perfectly balanced and amusing to say, the baby was born. They fastened a plastic identification bracelet around her wrist and the baby's wrist. Three days later, after they had come home, her husband sawed off the bracelets with a grapefruit knife. The girl had wanted to make it an occasion. She yelled, "I have a lovely pair of tiny silver scissors that belonged to my grandmother and you have used a grapefruit knife!" Her husband was flushed and nervous but he smiled at her as he always did. "You are insecure," she said tearfully. "You are insecure because you had mumps when you were eight." Their divorce was one year and two months away. "It was not mumps," he said carefully. "Once I broke my arm while swimming, is all."

The girl becomes a lover to a man she met at a dinner party. He calls her up the next morning. He drives over to her apartment. He drives a white convertible which is all rusted out along the rocker panels. They do not make convertibles any more, the girl thinks with alarm! He asks her to go sailing. They drop the child off at a nursery school on the way to the pier. The child's peculiar hair is braided and is pinned up under a big hat with mouse ears that she got on a visit to DISNEYWORLD. She is wearing a striped jersey stuffed into striped shorts. She kisses the girl and she kisses the man and goes into the nursery carrying her lunch in a Wonder Bread bag. In the afternoon, when they return, the girl has difficulty recognizing the child. There are so many children, after all, standing in the rooms, all the same size, all small, quizzical creatures, holding pieces of wooden puzzles in their hands.

It is late at night. A cat seems to be murdering a baby bird in a nest somewhere outside the girl's window. The girl is listening to the child sleep. The child lies in her varnished crib, clutching a bear. The bear has no tongue. Where there should be a small piece of red felt there is nothing. Apparently, the child had eaten it by accident. The crib sheet is in a design of tiny yellow circus animals. The girl enjoys looking at her child but cannot stand the sheet. There is so much going on in the crib, so many colors and patterns. It is so busy in there! The girl goes into the kitchen. On the counter, four palmetto bugs are exploring a pan of coffee cake. The girl goes back to her own bedroom and turns on the radio. There is a great deal of static. The Answer Man on ACTION LINE sounds very annoyed. An old gentleman is asking something but the transmission is terrible because the old man refuses to turn off his rock tumbler. He is polishing stones in his rock tumbler like all old men do and he refuses to turn it off while speaking. Finally, the Answer Man hangs up on him. "Good for you," the girl says. The Answer Man clears his throat and says in a sing-song way, "The wine of this world has caused only satiety. Our homes suffer from female sadness, embarrassment and confusion. Absence, sterility, mourning, privation and separation abound throughout the land." The girl puts her arms around her knees and begins to rock back and forth on the bed. The child murmurs in sleep. More palmetto bugs skate across the formica and into the cake. The girl can hear them. A woman's voice comes on the radio now. The girl is shocked. It seems to be her mother's voice. The girl leans toward the radio. There is a terrible weight on her chest. She can scarcely breathe. The voice says, "I put a little pan under the air-conditioner outside my window and it catches the condensation from the machine and I use that water to water my ivy. I think anything like that makes one a better person."

The girl has made love to nine men at one time or another. It does not seem like many but at the same time it seems more than necessary. She does not know what to think about them. They were all very nice. She thinks it is wonderful that a woman can make love to a man. When love-making, she feels she is behaving reasonably. She is well. The man often shares her bed now. He lies sleeping, on his stomach, his brown arm across her breasts. Sometimes, when the child is restless, the girl brings her into bed with them. The man shifts position, turns flat on his back. The child lies between them. The three lie, silent and rigid, earnestly conscious. On the radio, the Answer Man is conducting a quiz. He says, "The answer is: the time taken for the fall of the dashpot to clear the piston is four seconds, and what is the question? The answer is: when the end of the pin is approximately $\frac{5}{16}''$ below the face of the block, and what is the question?"

She and the man travel all over the South in his white convertible. The girl brings dolls and sandals and sugar animals back to the child. Sometimes the child travels with them. She sits beside them, pretending to do something gruesome to her eyes. She pretends to dig out her eyes. The girl ignores this. The child is tanned and sturdy and affectionate although sometimes when she is being kissed, she goes limp and even cold, as though she has suddenly, foolishly died. In the restaurants they stop at, the child is well-behaved although she takes only butter and ice water. The girl and the man order carefully but do not eat much either. They move the food around on their plates. They take a bite now and then. In less than a month the man has spent many hundreds of dollars on food that they do not eat. ACTION LINE says that an adult female consumes seven hundred pounds of dry food in a single year. The girl believes this of course but it has nothing to do with her. Sometimes, she greedily shares a bag of Fig Newtons with the child but she seldom eats with the man. Her stomach is hard, flat, empty. She feels hungry always, dangerous to herself, and in love. They leave large tips on the tables of restaurants and then they reenter the car. The seats are hot from the sun. The child sits on the girl's lap while they travel, while the leather cools. She seems to ask for nothing. She makes clucking, sympathetic sounds when she sees animals smashed flat on the side of the road. When the child is not with them, they travel with the man's friends.

The man has many friends whom he is devoted to. They are clever and well-off; good-natured, generous people, confident in their prolonged affairs. They have known each other for years. This is discomforting to the girl who has known no one for years. The girl fears that each has loved the other at one time or another. These relationships are so complex, the girl cannot understand them! There is such flux, such constancy among them. They are so intimate and so calm. She tries to imagine their embraces. She feels that they differ from her own. One afternoon, just before dusk, the girl and man drive a short way into the Everglades. It is very dull. There is no scenery, no prospect. It is not a swamp at all. It is a river, only inches deep! Another couple rides in the back of the car. They have very dark tans and have pale yellow hair. They look almost like brother and sister. He is a lawyer and she is a lawyer. They are drinking gin and tonics, as are the girl and the man. The girl has not met these people before. The woman leans over the back seat and drops another ice-cube from the cooler into the girl's drink. She says, "I hear that you have a little daughter." The girl nods. She feels funny, a little frightened. "The child is very *sortable*," the girl's lover says. He is driving the big car very fast and well but there seems to be a knocking in the engine. He wears a long-sleeved shirt buttoned at the wrists. His thick hair needs cutting. The girl loves to look at him. They drive, and on either side of them, across the slim canals or over the damp saw-grass, speed air-boats. The sound of them is deafening. The tourists aboard wear huge ear-muffs. The man turns his head toward her for a moment. "I love you," she says. "Ditto," he says loudly, above the clatter of the air-boats. "Double-ditto." He grins at her and she begins to giggle. Then she sobs. She has not cried for many months. There seems something wrong with the way she is doing it. Everyone is astounded. The man drives a few more miles and then pulls into a gas station. The girl feels desperate about this man. She would do the unspeakable for him, the unforgivable, anything. She is lost but not in him. She wants herself lost and never found, in him. "I'll do anything for you," she cries. "Take an aspirin," he says. "Put your head on my shoulder."

The girl is sleeping alone in her apartment. The man has gone on a business trip. He assures her he will come back. He'll always come back, he says. When the girl is alone she measures her drinks out carefully. Carefully, she drinks 12 ozs. of bourbon in 2½ hours. When she is not with the man, she resumes her habit of listening to the radio. Frequently, she hears only the replies of ACTION LINE. "Yes," the Answer Man says, "in answer to your question, the difference between rising every morning at 6 or at 8 in the course of 40 years amounts to 29,200 hours or 3 years, 221 days and 16 hours which are equal to 8 hours a day for 10 years. So that rising at 6 will be the equivalent of adding 10 years to your life." The girl feels, by the Answer Man's tone, that he is a little repulsed by this. She washes her whiskey glass out in the sink. Balloons are drifting around the kitchen. They float out of the kitchen and drift onto the balcony. They float down the hall and bump against the closed door of the child's room. Some of the balloons don't float but slump in the corners of the kitchen like mounds of jelly. These are filled with water. The girl buys many balloons and is always blowing them up for the child. They play a great deal with the balloons, breaking them over the stove or smashing the water-filled ones against the walls of the bathroom. The girl turns off the radio and falls asleep.

The girl touches her lover's face. She runs her fingers across the bones. "Of course I love you," he says. "I want us to have a life together." She is so restless. She moves her hand across his mouth. There is something she doesn't understand, something she doesn't know how to do. She makes them a drink. She asks for a piece of gum. He hands her a small crumpled stick, still in the wrapper. She is sure that it is not the real thing. The Answer Man has said that Lewis Carroll once invented a substitute for gum. She fears that this is that. She doesn't want this! She swallows it without chewing. "Please," she says. "Please what?" the man replies, a bit impatiently.

Her former husband calls her up. It is autumn and the heat is unusually oppressive. He wants to see the child. He wants to take her away for a week to his lakeside house in the middle of the state. The girl agrees to this. He arrives at the apartment and picks up the child and nuzzles her. He is a little heavier than before. He makes a little more money. He has a different watch, wallet and key-ring. "What are you doing these days?" the child's father asks. "I am in love," she says.

The man does not visit the girl for a week. She doesn't leave the apartment. She loses four pounds. She and the child make jello and they eat it for days. The girl remembers that after the baby was born, the only food the hospital gave her was jello. She thinks of all the water boiling in hospitals everywhere for new mothers' jello. The girl sits on the floor and plays endlessly with the child. The child is bored. She dresses and undresses herself. She goes through everything in her small bureau drawer and tries everything on. The girl notices a birthmark on the child's thigh. It is very small and lovely, in the shape, the girl thinks, of a wine glass. A doll's wine glass. The girl thinks about the man constantly but without much exactitude. She does not even have a photograph of him! She looks through old magazines. He must resemble someone! Sometimes, late at night, when she thinks he might come to her, she feels that the Answer Man arrives instead. He is like a moving light, never still. He has the high temperature and metabolism of a bird. On ACTION LINE, someone is saying, "I live by the airport, and what is this that hits my house, that showers my roof on takeoff? We can hear it. What is this, I demand to know! My lawn is healthy, my television reception is fine but something is going on without my consent and I am not well, my wife's had a stroke and someone stole my stamp collection and took the orchids off my trees." The girl sips her bourbon and shakes her head. The greediness and wickedness of people, she thinks, their rudeness and lust. "Well," the Answer Man says, "each piece of earth is bad for something. Something is going to get on it and the land itself is no longer safe. It's weakening. If you dig deep enough to dip your seed, beneath the crust you'll find an emptiness like the sky. No, nothing's compatible to living in the long run. Next caller, please." The girl goes to the telephone and dials hurriedly. It is very late. She whispers, not wanting to wake the child. There is static and humming. "I can't make you out," the Answer Man shouts. "Are you a phronemophobiac?" The girl says more firmly, "I want to know my hour." "Your hour came, dear," he says. "It went when you were sleeping. It came and saw you dreaming and it went back to where it was."

The girl's lover comes to the apartment. She throws herself into his arms. He looks wonderful. She would do anything for him! The child grabs the pocket of his jacket and swings on it with her full weight. "My friend," the child says to him. "Why yes," the man says with surprise. They drive the child to the nursery and then go out for a wonderful lunch. The girl begins to cry and spills the roll basket on the floor. "What is it?" he asks. "What's wrong?" He wearies of her, really. Her moods and palpitations. The girl's face is pale. Death is not so far, she thinks. It is easily arrived at. Love is further than death. She kisses him. She cannot stop. She clings to him, trying to kiss him. "Be calm," he says.

The girl no longer sees the man. She doesn't know anything about him. She is a gaunt, passive girl, living alone with her child. "I love you," she says to the child. "Mommy loves me," the child murmurs, "and Daddy loves me and Grandma loves me and Granddaddy loves me and my friend loves me." The girl corrects her, "Mommy loves you," she says. The child is growing. In not too long the child will be grown. When is this happening! She wakes the child in the middle of the night. She gives her a glass of juice and together they listen to the radio. A woman is speaking on the radio. She says, "I hope you will not think me vulgar." "Not at all," the Answer Man replies. "He is never at a loss," the girl whispers to the child. The woman says, "My husband can only become excited if he feels that some part of his body is missing." "Yes," the Answer Man says. The girl shakes the sleepy child. "Listen to this," she says. "I want you to know about these things." The unknown woman's voice continues, dimly. "A finger or an eye or a leg. I have to pretend it's not there."

"Yes." the Answer Man says.

MR. STAAL

James S. Reinbold

taal was interested in clouds and watched them at different times during the day from his yard. In the morning he set the lawn chair at the far corner of the tiny cement patio. In the early afternoon he moved away from the patio onto the lawn. When he watched the clouds at evening, usually after dinner, he placed the chair farther out on the lawn, on slightly higher ground, so that the sun would be blocked by a line of distant spruce trees.

The longest time Staal ever sat gazing at the clouds was about an hour. There were different reasons, corresponding to the time of day, that forced him to return to the house. In the morning the bees made him retreat. He swatted at them, even struck out at them with his fists, but gradually moved his chair foot by foot back across the patio toward the French doors. In a short time the lawn chair was up against the French doors, and his view was blocked by the patio roof. He could not regain any of the lost ground, so he went inside and smoked a small cigar in his living room. In the afternoon he was bothered by flies landing on his hands. The flies were not nearly as annoying, however, as the frequent trips he had to make to the bathroom to pass out the coffee he drank after his morning cigar. In the evenings he could nearly last out the hour. But Staal did not abandon his morning and afternoon sittings in favor of a prolonged evening one, for his main concern was to watch the changing patterns of the clouds —to follow the path of certain formations and to observe the dissolution of others.

For simplicity Staal referred to the yard as *his* yard. Actually it belonged to Mrs. Malik, an old woman who owned the house and who rented him the small basement apartment. The yard was large and the old woman kept an immense flower garden at the far end. She was constantly weeding, cutting, adding nutrients to the soil, pulling out dead plants and watering the healthy ones. Occasionally she worked where Staal could watch her from his window. She bent over at the waist, as old women do, to reveal the tops of her stockings. She always wore the same faded dress and a large straw hat.

It had crossed Staal's mind to offer to help Mrs. Malik with some of the more strenuous aspects of gardening, such as hoeing, pushing the wheelbarrow filled with dead cuttings and dried leaves, or tending the burning of the rubbish. The idea of helping Mrs. Malik was not born of any wish to make her task lighter, or to make himself feel better. He knew her to be strong and he felt fine. It was simply to fill out his day, to occupy himself with something more than his usual duties and pleasures. He understood that garden work might be enjoyable, providing the sun were not too hot nor the wheelbarrow too heavy.

Mrs. Malik refused any help. They were her flowers, she pointed out, and strange hands would disturb them. Violate them, she said.

It was all the better this way, if that was the way she wanted it, Staal thought. And now he watched with satisfaction every time dead flowers were dumped into the wheelbarrow or when he spied wilted peonies or azaleas from his lawn chair. When the roses weakened, Staal smoked an extra cigar and was very happy. He watched from his window as she vainly fed the soil and sprayed the roses. Finally a man came.

The nurseryman sat down on his heels and leaned over the roses. Holding the roses carefully by the stems, he moved them from side to side. Their heads drooped pathetically and they shed their crisp petals. After the nurseryman had gone, Mrs. Malik kept on looking at the roses with reproach and concern. Staal decided to go outside and talk with her.

"Was he the man from the nursery, Mrs. Malik?" Staal asked.

"They have some kind of rose blight, Mr. Staal," she replied coolly.

"I'm sorry. Will they all die?"

"Certainly not!" the old woman cried indignantly. She paused for a moment, then added, "He thinks that the worst is over."

"I hope he is right," Staal said, and smiled.

For dinner Staal made himself a bologna sandwich with hot mustard and drank a Coke. Just before he was about to go outside for his evening observations the wind started blowing. Within minutes the sun had disappeared and heavy grey clouds rolled in. Soon the whole sky was uniformly grey. Large drops of rain fell on Mrs. Malik before she could reach the safety of her house. Staal knew that she would stand and watch her roses from the kitchen window, confident that the rain was the medicine they needed.

Staal hoped it would rain long and hard and drown the roses.

Later that evening the rain stopped but the sky stayed overcast. Staal prepared a can of chicken rice soup and ate it directly from the pan. He filled the empty pan with water and left it in the sink. He carried a cup of coffee with him into the living room and read the newspaper.

At nine o'clock he heard the doorbell ring upstairs. This was such a rare occurrence that Staal stood up and listened. He heard Mrs. Malik's voice and the voice of another, younger woman. Their voices were loud, but distorted, and Staal could not make out a single word. He heard Mrs. Malik and the visitor go upstairs, but he heard only Mrs. Malik come down. The toilet flushed, but the visitor did not come down. It now seemed possible to Staal that Mrs. Malik had rented one of the rooms on the second floor and that the voice and footsteps belonged to the new tenant. Staal thought often about moving upstairs and now he smiled as he imagined himself sleeping up there naked, across the hall from Mrs. Malik.

Early the following morning Staal heard footsteps on the stairs. He knew they were too steady and quick to be Mrs. Malik's. He heard the old woman walk to the front of the house to meet the footsteps at the bottom of the stairs. Staal listened again to the muffled conversation and thought he heard his name mentioned. The front door closed and Mrs. Malik returned to the kitchen.

That evening, about nine, he heard someone come in the front door. He heard voices and again footsteps ascending the stairs.

Two days later the sky cleared and Staal was out on the patio early. He had sprayed himself with bug repellent and was able to sit undisturbed. He would have stayed out all morning but his buttocks and back began to ache. When he went out in the afternoon he took two pillows from the sofa.

Mrs. Malik appeared in the garden wearing her faded dress, her straw hat, and a pair of pink-rimmed sunglasses. She dusted the roses carefully with white powder. Staal removed the pillows from the chair and took them inside. He did not want her to see them and then explain to him again how the pillows were meant for the sofa and the sofa only. He had to have her in good humor if he were to question her.

"They seem to be coming around," he said quietly, glancing at the dying roses.

"Yes," the old woman sighed. "Some kind of blight. But they are getting better."

178

They stared at the roses for a while longer before Staal said:
"How is your new tenant?"

Mrs. Malik turned sharply to face him. Staal understood her expression and continued quickly:

"I've heard someone coming in and going out for the past few days. The floors are solid enough, but noise goes right through."

Then, to make sure she was completely at ease and would tell him what he wanted to know, he added:

"One cannot see through floors, Mrs. Malik."

The old woman seemed satisfied with his explanation.

"A very nice young lady," she said. "Her name is Miss Disher. She works at the clinic over there on Stavens Street."

"The Jensun Clinic?"

"She's a nurse, Mr. Staal. A pretty young nurse."

Here Mrs. Malik gave Staal a wink and stood for a while with her hands on her hips and her legs parted. Then she started toward the house.

"A nice young nurse." Mrs. Malik laughed. "And I don't think she has any men friends."

That night, while he listened to the radio, Staal drew up a description of Miss Disher, and wondered whether Mrs. Malik's wink and pose had not meant something else. But that was impossible. He was not allowed upstairs.

Miss Disher parked her motorbike behind the hedge in front of the Jensun Clinic and went inside. She did not like to move but had been forced to do so twice in the past two months. The first time she moved because of noisy neighbors and an especially rude man down the hall. She found a place with a family. Her rooms were nice, and surprisingly quiet. But she had to leave because the house was suddenly sold. She felt herself fortunate to find Mrs. Malik's house. But that was where her luck ended, for whenever Miss Disher moved she suffered sleepless nights and constipation. Lying in bed, wide awake, she considered every sound in the house and seized on one terror after another: burglars, arsonists, murderers, rapists. When the door to her room did not fly open to reveal a trouserless madman, the pains in her bowels began anew.

So when Miss Disher climbed the stairs and went into the small room on the first floor marked NURSE, she had reason to be upset and irritable. She put her purse on the table and looked into the mirror. Her fat face announced her misery. Today she would get pills again from Dr. Jensun and put an end to her discomfort. When she remembered she was scheduled to have the weekend off, the creases around her mouth smoothed and an inaudible fart brought a rich smile to her lips.

But now she drew her expression rigid, into what she called her professional face, and prepared for the day's duties.

The Jensun Clinic was more like a rest home than a hospital, so Miss Disher's tasks were more like a maid's than a nurse's. The clinic was located on Stavens Street off Kyes Drive. From the outside it looked like the other houses in that residential area except for the sign fixed to the wall above the door. It was a very small clinic: six patients, two nurses, and Dr. Jensun.

You entered the clinic through the front door and came upon a small circular lobby with an overhead light and a coat-tree. There were five doors before you, and these led to the rooms that radiated out from the lobby. One door was marked NURSE and the other DR. JENSUN. The remaining three were unmarked and opened into patient rooms. There were two flights of stairs, one on either side of the lobby. To the right led to the second floor and the three other patient rooms, while to the left led to the basement where the laundry and kitchen were situated. The patient rooms were very small. In each there were a bed, a chest of drawers, a chair. Each had a bathroom, and a window.

Dr. Jensun's office was the largest of the rooms. Three of the walls were bookshelves from floor to ceiling. The fourth was painted a pale blue and displayed a travel poster of Switzerland.

Against this wall were two chairs and aside one of these chairs was an ashtray on an iron stand. Dr. Jensun's desk was strangely large, and the chair behind it was the only other furniture in the room. The desk was cluttered and the chair, upholstered in black leather, swiveled. Directly behind the desk and crushed from all sides by bookshelves was another door. It was marked CLINIC. The clinic room was tiny: a large closet in fact. The walls and ceiling were white and a white wooden chair stood in the middle of the floor. A cord attached to the ceiling dropped down to the floor and then curled back up the chair where the other end was affixed to the headset Dr. Jensun wore when he examined his patients. The polished steel headset was fitted with switches to regulate the intensity of the lights.

"Nothing can escape me with this light," Dr. Jensun would tell patients as he tapped on the helmet. "Not one infinitesimal speck of contamination."

When Miss Disher entered Mr. Ellans' room she found Dr. Jensun there also. She made a motion to leave, but the doctor stopped her with a wave of his hand and continued talking to the patient.

"You could be misreading your improvement, Mr. Ellans," Dr. Jensun said. "With cases like yours we cannot be too careful. So many seem to be on the road to recovery and then . . . !"

He chose not to complete the sentence but snapped his fingers loudly, for the maximum effect. The noise startled Miss Disher who was in the bathroom cleaning the wash basin.

"I do not wish to lose you, Mr. Ellans," Dr. Jensun continued. "You are my first concern."

"Yes, Doctor," the patient said. "But I feel fine. Healthy!"

"Well, we shall see. You come to my office about four and we shall set our minds at ease."

Dr. Jensun left and went upstairs. Mr. Ellans got back into bed and addressed himself to Miss Disher.

"Nurse, you know I am fine now," he called. "When I first arrived I was weak, yellow in the face. But now I am strong and healthy." He beat on his chest for emphasis.

Miss Disher came into the room and looked at him but said nothing. She just stared at him with her professional face.

Throughout the day, between changing the sheets and preparing breakfast and lunch, Miss Disher went to the bathroom but with no success. Finally, at three o'clock, she went to see Dr. Jensun. He gave her a small bottle of green pills and then told her she could leave early if she so desired.

"Mr. Ellans will be going today," he said. "I received a confirmation just moments ago from Mr. Riggin's wife. Prepare Mr. Ellans' room for Mr. Riggin."

Miss Disher thanked Dr. Jensun for the pills and went to the basement to clean up the lunch dishes.

At four o'clock Mr. Ellans slipped into a pair of slacks and a plaid shirt. His feet were still swollen, so he put on his slippers over his socks. Dr. Jensun was studying a newspaper when Mr. Ellans entered the office.

"Well, Mr. Ellans, out of those dreary bed clothes at last."

"Yes, Doctor," the patient said. "It's time for me to dress the way I feel."

"So you plan to leave us here at the clinic," Dr. Jensun said.

"Only with your approval, of course," Mr. Ellans said, looking down at his feet.

"Good! Shall we have a little examination, then?"

Mr. Ellans followed Dr. Jensun through the door marked CLINIC, and in the small back room began undoing his trousers.

"No need for that this time, Mr. Ellans," Dr. Jensun called, shaking his head. "Just come over here and unbutton your shirt."

Mr. Ellans removed his shirt and stood in front of the chair. Dr. Jensun sat down facing Mr. Ellans and switched on the headset. He adjusted the dials carefully.

"Breathe in!

"Breathe out!

"Once more. Breathe in deeply.

"Hold your breath as long as you can.

"Run in place.

"Jump up and down. Higher!

"Fine! Very good! You can relax now."

Dr. Jensun got up from the chair, readjusted the light and the dials, and stood behind Mr. Ellans. He trained the light on the lower part of the old man's back.

"Breathe in!

"Breathe out!

"Breathe in deeply.

"Hold your breath as long as you can.

"Run in place.

"Jump up and down. A little higher.

"That's fine. Fine!"

Dr. Jensun switched off the light and smiled broadly.

"Very good, Mr. Ellans. I wish the others would respond as well. Naturally I want to give you something for the next few weeks. Just to be on the safe side."

They went back into the office. While Dr. Jensun wrote on the small bottle of green pills, Mr. Ellans walked over and stood in front of the travel poster.

"Not what you would expect to find in a doctor's office, is it, Mr. Ellans?"

"Oh, I don't know," Mr. Ellans said.

"Well, to be perfectly honest with you, if I had a basement in my house I would hang it there," Dr. Jensun said.

Miss Disher had already stripped the bed and put on clean sheets and emptied the wastebasket. She was running the vacuum when Mr. Ellans came in.

"No, no!" he said triumphantly. "You're not in the way. I'm leaving the clinic in a few minutes."

Miss Disher kept her face locked in place.

Mr. Ellans packed hastily and checked the drawers and bathroom cabinet twice before he closed and locked his suitcase. Only when he sat down in the chair to put on his shoes did he remember his swollen feet. He loosened the laces as much as he could and gently pushed his feet into his shoes. His laces untied, he stood up courageously and took a few steps toward Miss Disher.

"You won't tell the doctor, will you?"

"That's one of the bad effects," Miss Disher said quietly.

"But you won't tell, will you?" he repeated.

"No," she replied. "It only lasts for a few days."

Mr. Ellans smiled to her as he shut the door. She watched him from the window as he shuffled to the corner and sat down on the bench to wait for the bus.

Miss Disher tried again, on Mr. Ellans' toilet. After ten minutes she gave up.

It was after five when she arrived at Mrs. Malik's house. She thought she saw a face at the basement window, but she did not bother to look a second time. She went upstairs and took one of the green pills Dr. Jensun had given her and lay down on her bed. She glanced at her wristwatch and waited.

At nine-thirty Mrs. Malik drank a cup of tea and looked out her kitchen window at her roses. She sat down at the table, cleared aside the cup and saucer and sugar bowl, and wrote a letter to her sister.

"*Dear Adelaine,*" she wrote. "*My roses are very sick. The nurseryman was here the other day and he gave me some things for them, but they don't seem to be working. I believe Mr. Staal has something to do with it. I took in a young girl. She is a nurse at the clinic on Stavens Street. You know the one. Her*

*name is Helen Disher and she is a very nice young woman. Give
my love to Leo and the children. Your Affectionate Sister,
CeCe."*

Mrs. Malik sealed and addressed the envelope and clipped it
to her mailbox with a clothespin.

After lunch she went out into the yard to weed and to examine the roses. She saw Staal in the lawn chair staring at
clouds. He did not notice her, so she watched him. First he
crossed one leg, then the other. He folded his hands over the
knee. Mrs. Malik frowned. She thought it was an odd way for a
man to sit. She bent over again to resume her weeding but she
kept an eye on Staal. When he got up to go inside she raised
herself and called:

"Are those the sofa pillows, Mr. Staal?"

He looked over at her.

"Those are for the sofa and not for that dirty lawn chair.
Please keep them inside, Mr. Staal."

Staal nodded and retreated into the house, a pillow under
each arm.

For dinner Mrs. Malik had a piece of liver and a cup of weak
coffee. At six o'clock she heard the toilet flush and then it continued flushing off and on for the next half hour. She became
alarmed and walked to the foot of the stairs. The toilet flushed
again. She walked halfway up the stairs and called out:

"Miss Disher! Miss Disher! What's the matter?"

"Everything is all right. I'm fine, thank you." The voice from
the bathroom was so weak Mrs. Malik was not satisfied and
climbed to the top of the stairs.

The toilet flushed again.

"Miss Disher," she said, holding onto the post. "Shall I call a
doctor?"

"Really, Mrs. Malik, I'm fine."

"Are you ill?" Mrs. Malik was trembling.

"No, I'm all right now. Thank you."

The bathroom door opened and Miss Disher emerged. She managed a smile and patted Mrs. Malik on the arm as she passed.

Mrs. Malik went back downstairs and turned on the television, but her concern for Miss Disher was too great. Once again she climbed the stairs, walked down the hall, and knocked on the young woman's door.

"Would you like to come down for a cup of tea, Miss Disher?" Mrs. Malik called into the room.

There was the sound of someone getting out of bed, and then a reply.

"That would be nice. Thank you, Mrs. Malik. I'll be down in a moment."

They sat in the living room, Mrs. Malik on the corner of the sofa and Miss Disher on a large chair pulled close to the coffee table and sofa.

"I like a lot of milk in my tea," smiled the old woman.

"Just sugar," said the nurse.

"I wrote a letter to my sister and, you know, I couldn't remember the name of your clinic," Mrs. Malik said.

"The Jensun Clinic," Miss Disher said.

"Oh, yes. Yes! Mr. Staal told me, but I forgot," Mrs. Malik laughed. "But you don't know Mr. Staal, do you?"

Miss Disher thought that Mr. Staal was the name of Mrs. Malik's cat, and she smiled weakly and shook her head.

"Mr. Staal lives downstairs," the old woman continued. "He is quite young, maybe just a little older than you."

"I haven't met him," Miss Disher said.

"He's out in the yard a good deal," Mrs. Malik said very quietly. "You can see him there. I won't let him up here. I don't trust him."

There was a silence.

"There are six male patients at the clinic," Miss Disher finally said.

Mrs. Malik was shocked.

"And no one to help if they get out of hand?"

"Oh, no," Miss Disher smiled. "They are all quite harmless." And the nurse rose to her full height in the chair.

"There were no clinics when my dear husband passed away," Mrs. Malik said, looking at her teacup.

"I'm sorry," the nurse whispered.

"He was sitting in that chair when he suddenly got stiff all over. His eyes closed and his mouth clamped shut. And he just sat there stiff. The doctor said his brain quit, all except the part that made his heart work. He sat like that and then that other part of his brain quit and he was dead. He's buried over at Shorr's Cemetery and the doctors still don't know what happened."

Miss Disher accepted another cup of tea and listened to Mrs. Malik talk about her sister Adelaine and her husband, Leo. Whenever Miss Disher heard a floorboard creak, or a noise outside, she thought it was poor Mrs. Malik's cat, Mr. Staal.

Soon after Miss Disher moved into the house Staal began taking late afternoon walks, and during one of his walks he discovered a large wooded area a short distance from the house. So every day around four o'clock he left the house and walked to the woods where he spent several hours exploring the paths that cut through the trees and brush. He hoped he would discover a magazine with pictures of naked women, or come upon two people in a grassy clearing or up against a tree. He would have carried the magazine home with him. He would have hidden and watched the lovers.

On Saturday Staal returned from his walk empty-handed and earlier than usual. He put his walking stick against the side of the house and turned the corner to go inside. But he stopped short and quickly retraced his steps. After a few moments he peeked around the corner of the house. The old woman was standing in front of the roses talking to a young fat woman Staal knew to be Miss Disher.

He decided it would be better to get a good look at Miss Disher before the meeting. This would give him the advantage. It did not surprise Staal that the nurse looked just as he had imagined she would, tall and heavy, with an unsavory face. Her eyes were pushed back into her head by her cheeks, and her nose was squashed between those cheeks so that the tip was turned up from the pressure. The first of several folds of flesh marked the line between her face and throat, for she had no chin. Her body was a great bulk supported by two massive legs. Staal focused his attention on her immense thighs.

After the two women went inside Staal slipped quietly around the corner and into his basement rooms. He fixed a can of chili and ate it out of the pan. He took his coffee with him into his living room.

That evening Staal watched the clouds from seven until eight. They were moving rapidly from east to west. A similar movement had occurred two evenings before and the next day had been hazy and without clouds until late afternoon. When Staal picked up his chair and put it back on the patio he was no longer thinking about the clouds. How to arrange a meeting with Miss Disher and what to say to her were the matters he meant to review.

When he could resolve no plan he moved on to the time when all would be accomplished, to the time when he and Miss Disher were husband and wife. She would continue working; she would have to. They would move to the rooms upstairs where Miss Disher was now lodged, and even take one or two more. He would play up to the old woman, humor her, and help her in the garden if the weather were agreeable. He would be allowed downstairs into the parlor, into the living room, into the kitchen.

In the living room the three of them would watch television or spend the evening in pleasant conversation. Staal would drink coffee instead of tea, and Mrs. Malik would smile and cater to him. When she drew up her will they would receive only the house and the furniture, for any money she had saved would go to Adelaine and Leo. But that was fine. The house and the furniture would be plenty. And if she were to die suddenly, there might be some food in the pantry or the refrigerator. Staal and Miss Disher would go to Shorr's Cemetery and place flowers from his garden on the old woman's grave.

Staal passed the next day in his usual fashion, and at four he picked up his walking stick and headed for the woods. He entered by the broad path. A group of boys were climbing in the tall trees. They yelled to him when he passed beneath them. Farther into the woods the path became softer and his heels made impressions in the ground. There were puddles in the low places, and Staal was careful to avoid them. Where the wide paths intersected there were stacks of wood, piled in long neat rows. Staal sat down on a stump and poked the ground with his stick.

He remembered himself as a boy. He remembered himself with his best friend at a cabin in the mountains near a lake. One afternoon he and his friend went out to explore the surrounding woods. When they had reached a secluded area they decided to carry logs, as heavy as they could lift. They took off their shirts and rolled up their shorts and pretended they were slaves. They cried out and stumbled each time the lash crossed their backs.

Later, when his friend crept into the bushes to defecate, Staal watched. He noticed that his friend had hairy thighs.

Mrs. Malik received a letter from her sister. It was very short. *"Dearest Sister,"* it began. *"Sorry to hear about your roses.*

Mine are sick also. Has Mr. Staal been to Cherry Lane? Leo is down with bronchitis but the children are fine. Your Loving Adelaine."

Mrs. Malik returned the letter to the envelope and put it in the drawer. Cherry Lane was three miles away, and how could she be expected to keep an eye on Mr. Staal all the time? She would have to write Adelaine a long letter.

From the garage Mrs. Malik got the wheelbarrow, a small clippers, and a green spade. All her roses were dead. She clipped the small stems, and some of the big stalks, and put them into the wheelbarrow. She was not strong enough to dig out the bushes. The nurseryman would have to be called to finish the job.

Mrs. Malik left the spade and the clippers and pushed the wheelbarrow to the end of the yard. She dumped the cuttings onto the pile that was there.

It was beginning to get dark and Staal was angry with himself for sitting in the woods for so long. The sky was blue, but it was empty of clouds.

He left his walking stick at the usual place and turned the corner of the house with his head down. It was not until he got onto the patio that he saw Miss Disher sitting on the lawn chair. It was too late to turn back, so he stared at her.

"I knocked but no one answered, and the door was locked," she began.

"I was out walking," Staal said.

"So I decided to wait," she finished.

Staal nodded and walked past her and unlocked the door.

"May I come in?" she asked.

"Yes. Come in," Staal said.

She sat down on the sofa and her white, starched uniform crackled as she positioned her legs. Staal went into the kitchen and called to her:

"Do you want coffee?"

"Yes, please," she answered. "Thank you, Mr. Staal. Black, if you don't mind."

He was aware of an antiseptic smell that came from her.

"How did it go at the clinic today?" he asked.

She looked at him strangely.

"I had the day off," she said.

He looked at her uniform. But she did not explain. Nor did she speak until after it was over.

When he rubbed her back, he felt only her brassiere. And when he touched her breasts, all that he felt was her brassiere. When he removed her uniform and underwear he did not look at her body, but turned out the light.

Staal knew he would be happy when winter arrived. All of Mrs. Malik's flowers would be dead. Miss Disher would be fatter, and he would be preparing to move upstairs.

WEDNESDAY

Joyce Carol Oates

rthur woke Wednesday early. The day would be a long one. Already he could hear his daughter Brenda coming out of her room, in the hall, on her way downstairs. He listened closely. He could hear, or could imagine, her pulling out the piano bench from the piano, down in the living room. She must be there. The bench was white—a white grand piano, very beautiful—and she sat at it, seriously, frowning like her mother, staring down at the keys. Even the cracks arrested her attention. He lay in bed on the second floor of his house, imagining his daughter almost directly below him, sitting at the piano. He heard the first note. His face went rigid.

He got dressed quickly. His wife was evidently not going to wake, but lay frowning and severe in sleep, as if giving up to him the burden of this day. She had turned over in bed, was still asleep or pretending to sleep. The other day she had told him she would not remain herself much longer. "I can't live like this much longer," she had said. It was not a threat or a warning, only a curious, exploratory remark. They had come in late from a dinner party, from a marvelous evening, and she had told him suddenly that she was failing, giving up, being conquered, defeated.

Why should she wake up to see him off?

Downstairs he saw Brenda at the piano, seated just as he imagined her. She was running her fingers gently over the keyboard. The sound was gentle, soft. It would not shatter any crystal; there was no power behind it. Down at the far end of the living room the wide French windows were seared with light, the filmy curtains glowing. He appreciated that: he appreciated beauty. The living room had been decorated in white and gold. His daughter's face was pale, not quite white, and her legs pale, limp, motionless. She had put her little white socks on perfectly. She wore a yellow dress, perfectly ironed by the laundry that did her father's shirts so meticulously, and her hair was a fine dull gold, very neat. Everything matched. He appreciated that.

She was playing the *Moonlight Sonata* with a numb, feverish rhythm. She played like a sixteen-year-old girl who had taken lessons dutifully for years, mediocre and competent, with a firm failure of imagination underlying every note. But Brenda was only six and had never had any music lessons, did not even listen in any evident way to music, and yet she could play for hours with this mysterious competence. Arthur came to her and put his arms gently around her. "Good morning, honey," he said. She stopped playing the piano but did not seem to notice him. Instead, as if held by a thought that had nothing to do with him, she sat rigid, intense, staring at her fingers on the keyboard.

"You're all ready, are you? Scrubbed and clean and ready for the trip?"

She did not appear to have heard him. But she did hear him, of course, every word.

"I'll have some coffee, then we'll leave. Mommy's staying home today and I'm taking you. I thought we'd have a nice drive to school, then come back through the park. I took the whole day off today. I hope the sun stays out."

He was aware of the paragraphs of his speech. Talking to his silent, frowning daughter, he understood how silence mocks words: her blocks of silence, like terrible monstrous blocks of stone, fell heavily on either side of his words. What he said was never quite accurate. She might be ten years old, or eighteen, or two. It was an abyss, the fact of her. As soon as he entered the kitchen, he heard her begin to play where she had left off—the *Moonlight Sonata*, in that sun-filled room.

He made instant coffee. His hands had begun to tremble. The harmonic green and brown of the kitchen did not soothe him. When he came home from the office each day, he always came out to the kitchen to talk to his wife, and he talked energetically about his work. Arthur was thirty-seven, an architect. His wife always appeared to listen with sympathy. His paragraphs of words, tossed against her appreciative silence, were attempts to keep her quiet; he realized that now. She made dinner and listened to him, flattering him with her complete attention. He hinted of trouble at work, maybe a union threatening to strike, or the federal government again raising interest rates: tricks to keep her from talking about Brenda.

When he returned to the living room, Brenda slid dutifully off the bench. She never resisted physically. She was quite small for her age, with knobby white knees. Her hair was thin and straight, cut off to show her delicate ears. Her face was a pretty face, though too thin, unnaturally pale; her eyes were a light green. Seeing her was always a shock: you expected to see a dull, squat child, a kind of dwarf. Not at all. Everyone, especially the two sets of grandparents, remarked on her beauty. "She's so pretty! It will all work itself out!" both grandmothers said constantly.

Drawing slightly away from him, with a woman's coolness, she put on her coat. He knelt to check her, to see if the buttons were lined up correctly. Of course. It has been years since she'd buttoned them wrong. "All set? Great! We're on our way!" he said heartily. She did not look at him. She never met his eye, as if some secret shame or hatred forced her away.

His wife had driven Brenda to school every week since Brenda had begun, and today he was driving her, a generous act. It was a surprise how quickly time had passed, getting him up out of bed and on his way, drawing him to the ride. He had tried to think of this day as a gift, a day off from work, but it had been a pretense. He was afraid of the long trip and afraid of his daughter.

Between his wife and himself was the fact of their daughter. She was a mystery that jarred the soul; better not to think of it. His wife had accused him more than once of blaming her for the child. Her wisdom was sour and impregnable. "You hate failure," she said.

"Jesus Christ, what are you saying?" Arthur had shouted.

The school was experimental, expensive. "But we make no promises," the Director had said. "Everything is exploratory."

And so Wednesday had become the center of the week. On that day Arthur drove to work with a sense of anticipation, and his wife drove Brenda fifty miles to school and fifty miles back again, hoping. This was the usual procedure. Then, when Arthur came home, he would always ask, "How do you think it went today?" and she would always reply, "The Director is still hopeful. I think it's going well. Yes, I think it's going well."

In the car Brenda seated herself as far from him as possible. No use to urge her to move over. She was not stubborn, not exactly. It was rather as if no one inhabited her body, as if her spirit had abandoned it. "A great day for a ride!" he said. He chatted with her, or toward her. He disliked silence because of its emptiness, the possibility of anything happening inside it—no warning, no form to it. Arthur was amorous of forms. He lived in one of those forms.

Brenda took a piece of spaghetti out of her coat pocket. It was uncooked, broken in half. She began to chew on it. Except for random, unlikely things—bits of cardboard perhaps—she ate nothing but uncooked spaghetti. She bit pieces off slowly, solemnly, chewing them with precision. Her green eyes were very serious. Every day she stuffed her pockets with spaghetti, broken in pieces. Bits of spaghetti were all over the house. His wife vacuumed every day, with great patience. Perhaps Brenda did like spaghetti. Perhaps she could not taste it. But she would not eat anything else. Arthur had long ago stopped snatching it away from her, stopped pleading with her. For what had seemed a decade she had sat at the table with them, listless and stony-eyed, refusing to eat. She did not quite *refuse*—nothing so emphatic. But she would not eat. What she did was nibble slowly at pieces of spaghetti, all day long, or chew cardboard and shape it into little balls. She walked around the house or out in the backyard as if in a trance—slow, precise, unhurried, turning aside when someone approached her. The only life she showed was her piano playing, monotonous and predictable, the same pieces over and over again for years. Her silence was immense as a mountain neither he nor his wife could climb. And when the silence came to an end—when Brenda cried, which was infrequent—they heard to their horror the sobs of a six-year-old child, breathy and helpless. But how to soothe her? She could not be embraced.

When his wife took Brenda for her monthly checkup, and asked the doctor how Brenda was "doing," the doctor always said, with a special, serious smile, "She's surprisingly healthy, considering her diet. You should be thankful."

It was a long drive. Arthur began to think longingly of his office—an older associate whom he admired and imitated, the cheerfulness of a secretary he could almost have loved, elevators, high buildings, occasional long lunches. He thought of his office, of his working space. He like to work, he liked problems. They came to him in the shape of lines with three dimensions. With love he dreamt of the proper shapes of banks, of supermarkets, of hardware stores—seductive as music! Certainly he had enough love in him—love for his work, for his wife, his secretary, his parents, his friends, his daughter.

He entered the expressway in silence. Brenda was awake but silent. It was worse than being truly alone. He glanced sideways at her, smiling in case she noticed him. He believed his daughter was thinking constantly, that her silence was not peaceful. Something unseen would move in the corner of her eye and she would shiver, almost imperceptibly. What did she see? What did she think?

"Look at the cows!" he said, pointing. "Do you see the cows?" He felt the need to talk. "Look at the big truck up ahead . . . all those new cars on it. . . ." He stared at the carrier with its double row of shining cars, cars of all colors, very handsome. What if, at the crucial moment, the truck wobbled and the cars came loose? He imagined metal searing through metal, slicing off the top of his skull. The steering wheel would cut him in two, and his daughter would be crushed in an instant.

"Like to hear some music, Brenda?" He turned on the radio. Strange how he felt the need to talk to her in spurts, as if offering her a choice of remarks. Like his wife, Arthur somehow thought that a magic moment would arrive and Brenda would come awake, a fairy princess waked by the right incantation. But she would not listen, would not suffer the kiss. She did not need them. She was a delicate weight in the corner of his eye, not really a burden because she wanted nothing.

She ate spaghetti for the rest of the drive.

The school was housed in a one-story building, previously a small-parts shop. On the walk he noticed a bit of drool about Brenda's mouth. He wanted to wipe it off because he was her father and had the right to touch her.

"Do you have a handkerchief, honey?"

She sensed his weakness. She wiped her mouth with her hand,

blankly and efficiently. A college girl with a sun-tanned face took Brenda from him, all charm and enthusiasm. He watched Brenda walk away, and it pained him to see how easily she left him, how unconnected they were. She did not glance back, did not notice he was remaining behind.

He drove around for a while, then stopped to have some coffee. Then he walked around the university, browsing in bookstores. He had several hours to get through. What did his wife do on these Wednesdays?

At noon he went to a good restaurant for lunch: two cocktails first, then a steak sandwich. Women shoppers surrounded him. He admired their leisure, their rings, their gloves. They seemed happy. Once at a party he had noticed his wife in deep conversation with a stranger, and something in his wife's strained, rapt face had frightened Arthur. When he asked her about it later she had said, "With him I felt anonymous; I could have begun everything again. He doesn't know about me." He had seen her touch that man's arm, unconsciously perhaps.

He wandered into another bookstore. In a mirror he caught sight of himself and was surprised, though pleasantly—so much worry and yet he was a fairly young man, still handsome, with light hair and light, friendly eyes, a good face. He wandered along the aisles, looking at textbooks, manuals for beginning lives: engineering texts, medical texts, French dictionaries. A crunching sound at the back of the store put him in mind of his daughter, eating—spaghetti being snapped, chewed.

He strolled through the campus but its buildings had no interest for him. The sidewalks were new, wide, functional, the landscaping impressive. Students sat on the grass, reading. A girl caught his attention—she wore soiled white slacks, sat with her legs apart, her head flung back so that the sun might shine onto her face. Her long brown hair hung down behind her. She was immobile, alone. Distracted, he nearly collided with someone.

He walked in another direction. There were too many young girls, all in a hurry, their faces impatient. A metallic taste rose to his mouth. He felt panic, he felt something coming loose in him, something dangerous.

What did his wife do on these long days?

He went to the periodical room of the university's library. He leafed through magazines. World affairs, domestic affairs, medicine. What new miracles? What about architecture? He could not concentrate. He tried to think about his work, his problems, about the shapes of banks and stores. He thought of his salary, and tried to feel satisfaction. He saw the girl on the grass, in a blaze of light, her white slacks glowing—an anonymous girl who sat with her head thrown back, her face turned to the sun.

He wanted to leave the library and find her, but he remained with the magazines on his lap. He waited. After a while, he went to a campus bar and had a drink, two drinks. Around him was music, noise, young people jostling his chair as if seeking him out, contemptuous of his age, of something. A slight fever had begun in his veins. Boys and girls hung over one another, arguing, stabbing the air with their fingers, scraping their chairs angrily on the floor. "I am not defensive!" a girl cried.

Now and then a girl passed who was striking as a poster, and he heard beneath the noise in the bar a terrible silence, violent as the withheld power of great boulders.

When he picked Brenda up, he felt he had survived an ordeal. "How was it today, honey? What is that you've got—a paper flower?" He took it from her hand. "A red rose. It's great. Did you make it yourself, honey?" He put it in his buttonhole, as if Brenda had made it for him. She did not glance up. In the car she sat as far from him as possible, while he chattered wildly, feeling his grin slip out of control. Around him boulders on mountainsides were beginning their long fall.

"We'll stop in the park for a few minutes. You should get out in the sun." He tried to sound festive. Parks meant fun: children knew that.

The park was large, mostly trees, with a few swings and tennis courts. It was nearly empty. He walked alongside her on one of the paths, not touching her. "Look at the birds. Bluejays," he said. He wanted to take her hand, but only by force could anyone take her hand. She took a stick of spaghetti out of her pocket and bit into it, munching slowly, solemnly. "Look at the squirrels, aren't they cute? There's a chipmunk," he said. He felt that he was in charge of all these animals and that he must point them out to his daughter. What terror, not to know the names of animals, of objects!

"Stay nearby, honey. Stay on the path," he said. He was suddenly exhausted. He sat on a bench, while Brenda walked along the path in her precise baby steps, chewing spaghetti. She seemed not to have noticed that Arthur was sitting, weary. He put his hands to his head and heard the notes of the *Moonlight Sonata*.

Brenda walked on slowly, not looking around. She could walk like this for hours in the backyard of their house. She might have been walking on a ledge, high above a street, or through poisonous foam on a shore. The shadows of leaves moved about her; birds flew overhead. She saw nothing.

And then something happened. Afterward Arthur was never able to remember it clearly.

Brenda was on the path, not far from him, no one was in sight, and yet out of nowhere a man appeared, running. He was middle-aged, and, in spite of the mild September day, wore an overcoat that flapped around his knees. His face was very red, his hair grey and spiky. He ran bent over, stooped, as if about to snatch up something from the ground, an outlandish running figure, colliding with Brenda, knocking her down. The man began to scream. He seized Brenda's arm and shook her, screaming down into her face in a high, womanish voice.

"What are you doing—what are you doing?" Arthur cried. He ran to Brenda and the man jumped back, his mouth working. He was crouching, and he began to back up slowly, cunningly. Arthur picked Brenda up. "Are you all right? Are you hurt?" He stared into her face and saw the same face, unchanged.

Now, as if released, the man in the overcoat turned and began walking away. "You'd better get out of here before I call the police!" Arthur yelled at him.

The man was nearly gone. Arthur's heart pounded. He looked down at Brenda, and suddenly decided to run after the man. "You, hey wait! You'd better wait!" Arthur yelled. He left Brenda behind and ran after the man. "Come back here, you dirty bastard, dirty pervert bastard!" The man crashed into something. He stumbled in a thicket. Arthur caught up with him and could hear his panicked breathing, could see the back of the man's neck, dirty and reddened. The man turned away from the thicket and tried to run in another direction, then shifted suddenly toward Arthur as if to push past him. Arthur swung his fist around and struck the man on the side of the neck. The man cried out sharply, nearly fell. Arthur struck him again. "Filth!" Arthur cried. His third blow knocked the man down. Arthur bent over him, kicking. "*I'll kill you, I'll tear you into pieces!*" The man rolled over wildly onto his stomach, hiding his face in his hands. Arthur kicked viciously at his back. He kicked the back of the man's head. "I'm going to call the police —throw you in jail—filth, filth. . . ." Arthur kicked at the body, the head, with the toe of his shoe, then the heel. "You better get the hell out of here because I'm going to call the police," Arthur said, backing away.

He ran back to Brenda, and there she was, safe, her leg a little dirty, a small scratch, small dots of blood. He bent to dab at her knee with his handkerchief. She stepped away. "There, there, it's just a tiny scratch," Arthur said. He could feel sweat everywhere on his body, his heart pounding. He tried again to blot the blood, but Brenda stepped away again. He looked sharply up at her and saw her look away from him. Just in that instant she had been looking at him.

He took her back to the car. They were safe, nothing had happened, no one had seen. His clothes were rumpled, his breathing hoarse, but they were safe. He was alarmed at the pounding of his heart. Excitement still rose in him in waves.

The two of them sat in the front seat of the car, in silence. Arthur wiped his face. He looked over at his daughter and saw that her coat was perfectly buttoned, her hair still in place, her face once again composed, secret.

After a few minutes he felt well enough to drive. He turned on the radio, heard static and loud music, then turned it off again. He headed for the expressway and saw with burning eyes the signs pointing toward home: it was impossible to get lost in the United States of America. Beside him, in the far corner of the seat, his daughter took out a small piece of spaghetti and began to chew.

THE LETTER

Bernard Malamud

t the gate stands Teddy holding his letter.

On Sunday afternoons Newman sat with his father on a white bench in the open ward. The son had brought one pineapple tart and one strawberry but the old man wouldn't eat them.

Sometime during the two-and-a-half hours he spent in the ward with his father, Newman said, "Do you want me to come back next Sunday, or do you want to have next Sunday off?"

The old man said nothing. Nothing meant yes or it meant no. If you pressed him to say which, he wept.

"All right, I'll see you next Sunday. But if you want a week off sometime, let me know. I could stand a Sunday off myself."

His father said nothing. Then his mouth moved and he said, "Your mother didn't like to leave any dead chickens in the bathtub. When is she coming to see me here?"

"Pa, she's been dead before you got sick and tried to take your life. Try to keep that in your memory."

"Don't ask me to believe that one," his father said, and at that point Newman got up to go to the station where he took the Long Island Rail Road train to New York City.

He said, "Get better, Pa," when he left, and his father answered, "Don't tell me that. I am better."

On Sundays after he left his father in Ward 12 of Building B and walked across the hospital grounds, that spring and dry summer, at the arched iron-barred gate between brick posts, under a towering oak that shadowed the raw red-brick wall, he met Teddy standing there with his letter in his hand. Newman could have got out through the main entrance to Building B of the hospital complex, but this way to the railroad station was shorter. The gate was open to visitors on Sundays only.

Teddy was a stout soft man in loose grey institutional clothes and canvas slippers. He was fifty or more and maybe so was his letter. He held it as he always held it, as though he had held it always, a thick squarish finger-soiled blue envelope with unsealed flap. Inside were four thick sheets of cream paper with nothing written on them. After he had looked at the paper the first time Newman had handed the envelope back to Teddy, and the green-uniformed guard had let him out of the gate. Sometimes there were other patients standing by the gate who wanted to walk out with Newman but the guard said they couldn't.

"What about mailing my letter?" Teddy said on Sundays.

He handed Newman the finger-soiled envelope. It was easier to take, then hand back, than to refuse to take it.

The mailbox hung on a short cement pole just outside the iron gate on the other side of the road, a few feet from the oak tree. Teddy sometimes threw a right jab in its direction as though pointing at the mailbox through the gate. Once it had been painted red and was now painted blue. There was also a mailbox in the doctor's office in each ward, Newman had reminded him, but Teddy said he didn't want the doctor reading his letter.

"You bring it to the office and so they read it."

"That's his job," Newman answered.

"Not on my head," said Teddy. "Why don't you mail it?"

"There's nothing in it."

"That's what you say."

His heavy head was set on a short sunburned neck, the coarse grizzled hair cropped an inch from the skull. One of his eyes was a fleshy grey, the other was walleyed. He stared beyond Newman when he talked to him, sometimes through his right shoulder. And Newman noticed he never so much as glanced at the blue envelope when it was momentarily out of his hand. Once in a while he pointed a short finger at something but said nothing. When he said nothing he rose a little on the balls of his toes. The guard did not interfere when Teddy handed Newman the letter every Sunday.

Newman gave it back.

"It's your mistake," said Teddy. After a while he said, "I got walking privileges. I'm almost sane. I fought in Guadalcanal."

Newman said he knew that.

"Where did you fight?"

"Nowhere yet."

"Why don't you mail my letter out?"

"It's for your own good the doctor reads it."

"That's a hot one." Teddy stared through Newman's shoulder.

"The letter isn't addressed to anybody and there's no stamp on it."

"Put one on. They won't let me buy one three or three ones."

"It's eight cents now. I'll put one on if you address the envelope."

"Not me," said Teddy.

Newman no longer asked why.

"It's not that kind of a letter."

He asked what kind was it.

"Blue with white paper inside of it."

"Saying what?"

"Shame on you," said Teddy.

Newman left on the four o'clock train. The ride home was not so bad as the ride there, though Sundays were murderous.

Teddy holds his letter.

"No luck?"

"No luck," said Newman.

"It's off your noodle."

He handed the envelope to Newman anyway and after a while Newman gave it back.

Teddy stared at his shoulder.

Ralph holds the finger-soiled blue envelope.

One Sunday a tall lean grim old man, clean-shaven, faded-eyed, wearing a worn-thin World War One overseas cap on his yellowed white head, stood at the gate with Teddy. He looked eighty.

The guard in the green uniform told him to step back, he was blocking the gate.

"Step back, Ralph, you're in the way of the gate."

"Why don't you stick it in the box on your way out?" Ralph asked in an old man's voice, handing the letter to Newman.

Newman wouldn't take it. "Who are you?"

Teddy and Ralph said nothing.

"It's his father," the guard at the gate said.

"Whose?"

"Teddy."

"My God," said Newman. "Are they both in here?"

"That's right," said the guard.

"Was he just admitted or has he been here all this time?"

"He just got his walking privileges returned again. They were revoked about a year."

"I got them back after five years," Ralph said.

"It's astonishing anyway," Newman said. "Neither of you resembles the other."

"Who do you resemble?" asked Ralph.

Newman said he couldn't say.

"What war were you in?" Ralph asked.

"None so far."

"That settles your pickle," said Ralph. "Why don't you mail my letter?"

Teddy stood by sullenly. He rose on his toes and threw a short right and left at the mailbox.

"I thought it was Teddy's letter."

"He told me to mail it for him. Teddy fought at Iwo Jima. We fought two wars. He fought the second war and I fought the first. Which war did you fight?"

"None yet."

"Make up your mind."

"None."

"We're stuck here because we fought the wars. I fought in the Marne and in the Argonne Forest. I had both lungs gassed with mustard gas. The wind changed and the Huns were gassed. That's not all that were."

"I'm sorry you were gassed."

"Tough turd," said Teddy.

"Mail it anyway for the poor kid," said Ralph. His tall body trembled. He was an angular man with close-set bluish eyes and craggy features that looked as though they had been hacked out of a tree.

"I told Teddy I would if he wrote something on the paper," Newman said.

"What do you want it to say?"

"Anything he likes. Isn't there somebody he wants to communicate with? If he doesn't feel like writing it he could dictate it to me and I'll write it out."

"Tough turd," said Teddy.

"He wants to communicate with me."

"It's not a bad idea," Newman suggested. "Why doesn't he write a few words to you? Or you could write a few words to him."

"A Bronx cheer to you."

"It's my letter," Teddy said.

"I don't care who writes it," Newman said. "If you want me to, I could write a message wishing him luck. I could say I hope he gets out of here soon."

"A Bronx cheer to that."

"Not in my letter," Teddy said.

"Not in mine either," said Ralph grimly. "Why don't you mail it like it is? I'll bet you're afraid to."

"Not that I know of."

"I'll bet you are."

"No, I'm not."

"I have my bets going."

"There's nothing to mail. There's nothing in the letter."

"What makes you think so?" asked Ralph. "There's a whole letter in there. Plenty of news."

"I'd better be going," Newman said, "or I'll miss my train."

The guard opened the gate to let him out. Then he shut the gate.

Teddy turned away and stared over the oak tree into the summer sun with his grey eye and his walleyed one.

Ralph trembled at the gate.

"Who do you come here to see on Sundays?" he called to Newman.

"My father."

"What war was he in?"

"The wars of life."

"Has he got his walking privileges?"

"No."

"What I mean, he's crazy?"

"That's right," said Newman, walking away.

"So are you," said Ralph. "Why don't you come back in here and stay around with the rest of us?"

IN UTICA

Jerry Bumpus

*t appears the author of the journal, for reasons of his own, or perhaps without reason, skipped long stretches of pages. In several instances where a sentence continues from one page to the next, blank pages separate the first segment of the sentence from the last. The handwriting is generally small and precise, though some early and all later entries slant across the page as though the journalist were writing in extreme haste.*

. . . in Utica, though for all we know, that is, those of us here who keep watch on these matters. The idea is appealing.

Again I noticed a curious phenomenon concerning their gait. They walk leaning forward in a peculiar manner, their necks outstretched like urgent geese. The oddity of the observation lies not in the evidence itself—for we are discovering each day of this new age new data at every turn—but in the defiance, disruption even, of Nature. I have questioned

A thousand years from now when this Journal is examined, there will be no doubt many amused remarks concerning our naïveté and trepidation in approaching the most important cultural decisions of our time. No doubt our hesitancy, our great hesitancy in rising to action, will be a source of levity and merry, witty songs at festive musicales generations hence. The idea is appealing.

But H is here now.

I have dined: I was pleased by a sauce perigueux, with truffles. An interest I shall indulge later, when there is more time: cuisine. I shall indulge many interests later. I dismissed H as orderly; his hands were obscene. His uniform is presentable, but his hands are positively disgusting. The nails, the little fingers! The new orderly shall have better hands

I now turn to work. This Journal shall be a pleasant interest. It is a gift from V, my second in command.

January 29

I would list their names here, but it is better that such particularities remain unrecorded. Five of them were involved in the plot—and one or two others. Time will disclose them: *traitors*. The full extent of their treachery is not yet known, and shall not be known until weeks of investigation. Their scheme appears to have been the redirecting of transports, though such a misrouting, of course, was quite impossible. They could gain no control over matters outside this camp, no effect could have resulted from their treachery—if, indeed, that is the proper term.

I am writing this later, following a celebration with my staff: a celebration to reward loyalty. Such rewards are beneficial: a few festive hours of conviviality with, later, women from Albany. P put on an extraordinary performance for us; quite remarkable.

Interesting conversation with Dr. T.

The next day. I have returned from T's laboratories which were recently established and are now designated as Unit Three. I am exhilarated: T brilliantly points out startling features of subhuman structure that I had never before observed in living tissue. His experimentations, in conjunction with vast research being conducted everywhere, amaze even me; and of course T and his small but dedicated staff are keeping complete and detailed records of all research. I shall have a copy made of his more interesting findings and will include them in this Journal— I will have C, my new orderly, copy them in. I intend to register a commendation from my office, and I shall be greatly displeased if Dr. T is not rewarded by promotion in rank, and my displeasure shall be severely expressed.

Undated

A pleasant evening with T; he was quite impressed with the efforts of my chef, L: a small pâté de foie gras; a marvelous breaded veal with an ox-eye; superb noodles; tongue mousse with shallots, cognac. Pleasant, intelligent conversation running on until quite late. However, when I left he produced a surgeon's mask which he put on. Rather eccentric. Detecting my disapproval, he explained that the smoke aggravated a mild respiratory ailment from which he has occasionally suffered since childhood. A rather peculiar susceptibility, I should think.

March 5

A visit from my wife. My gratitude to dependable colleagues in Orienburg—especially R—for their great cooperation without which, along with my own efforts and application of influence and even force where it was necessary, my wife would not have been able to make the long and extremely hazardous journey, solely for the purpose of being with me for our fifteenth anniversary. Naturally, she was quite impressed with the camp, though she is completely ignorant of its function. She reports our children are progressing well. The sexualism of females— and T informs me it is so with females of all species—is contrary to the higher purposes of our national effort. T's current researches in sexual differentiation are in part concerned with this problem. The sluggishness of the female reeks of weakness; this passivity is at their very core. Two evenings ago I watched her mouth and throat as we were dining. The slow, steady movement, up and down: this is the essence of female.

In some respects T is not far from this realization, though I am certain he shall never achieve absolute comprehension. He is a man of science; consequently, he lacks the capacity for true insight. For instance, I casually dropped the word *jackal* and noted his stunned reaction, though I did not look at him directly. Quite amusing.

March 6

Already I am lonely for my wife; and I am lonely for my children more than ever before. I have their photographs on my desk and find myself distracted when I am working in my office: I sit, staring at the photos. Prior to my wife's visit the pictures were still in one of my trunks: they were stored there not from insufficient affection, but because the constant frenzy of work demands that every inch of my desk top be used. In one picture, my wife, Franz, and Erica are in the garden we shared with H. I distinctly recall standing with the camera in my hands. I can, in fact, feel it in my hands at this very moment, and I can see them standing in the garden as I snap the shutter. The other picture is of Franz and Erica on H's white mare. Erica's face is shadowed by her bonnet.

I think of my wife's body, that these children in these pictures came *from her body!* I am disgusted.

The body is the enemy.

T and I dine together each evening. A brilliant conversationalist, for a short while he is able to lift both of us from the deep concerns of our work, though still I find myself staring into his mouth as he opens it to speak, and I see the hideous yellow-white mass of food he is chewing. I see through his uniform, through his skin, and into his stomach where chewed food, lumped as large as heads, is soaking in digestive juices.

Stomach juices. The idea is slime.

March 7

One hundred and twenty meters south a windmill faces the camp. Its arms are locked at the perpendicular, perfectly cruciform.

July 17

I have received a commendation from the administrative center in St. Louis. In part: ". . . service meritorious and reflective of dedication to those purposes which elevate our nation and our race."

Such recognition and praise cause me to reflect upon true purposes, on nation, on duty. Our highest aims link arms with our immediate objectives in this struggle against infidelity, barbarism, savagery in all its forms.

Undated

Dr. B made a point of saying he knows nothing of T and what happened here. Naturally, I am directly led to suspect that there has been much talk, indeed, here and along channels beyond Utica, concerning the difficulty caused by T which, coming so soon after my commendation, is a grave embarrassment to me. I have considered sending a personal letter to R explaining all that happened here. But too much said on any matter suggests culpability; my report was thorough, containing all relevant material and proof concerning T's failure.

B is quite young, no doubt fresh from his medical training; unbelievably simple, naïve, even childlike: all qualities which I find unspeakably repulsive. His eyes are suspiciously dark; they have that sorrowful look I find detestable: I consider it bovine, *swinish* in fact. But B is at least courteous: a trait T totally lacked. I find B tolerable, though I shall have little to do with him, since work increases daily. He seems efficient. He certainly is not the conversationalist T was. But that is quite as well. Indeed!

August 16
B is not a physician. I know now. There is no doubt. The matter of T is *not* settled. The matter is still under investigation. Investigation!

August 18
To: R.S.H.A., Arlington, WC2.
Copy To: SS Administrative Office D, St. Louis.
Subject: The Incident Involving Dr. Israel T, Director of Research and Camp Physician, Camp SO, Division II, 44070.
The incident involving Dr. Israel T comprised three problems:
1. T's incompetency as a scientist. (Earlier entries in this Journal emphatically verify my suspicions regarding T's inadequacies.)
2. T's feminism which made his habitation and service in this camp impossible, impracticable, intolerable.
3. This person was disgusting. Let me add, his increasing lack of confidence, his reversion to excesses, his femininely manic behavior in reaction to certain household words, his constant tremors, his frequent and loathsome loudness, his general rudeness, his disrespect to certain basic ideals as revealed in his drunken discussions of religion, politics, and so forth. Certain documents are available. Once he remarked, *in my presence*, that the helmets worn by our troops made them resemble frogs. *Frogs!*
Conclusions: This statement is included in my personal Journal for the purpose of accomplishing the honest and open expression of my total and heartfelt conviction of the truth of

the facts which have been included in my earlier reports and in subsequent reports I have rendered to Inspector B.

September 30

Camp roll higher than in its history. Increased responsibilities necessitate my placing more work in charge of my second in command, V. I trust he will be capable of handling the problems of these new duties.

November 12

V has been replaced by O, older, more capable, dependable. It is inconceivable that I could have overlooked V's disgusting habits.

December 25—Christmas

I am saddened this anniversary of the Birth of the Light of Man. There are many enemies. Looking down the registry I find these figures:

Alabamans	1748	Lithuanians	250
Armenians	44	Luxembourgers	211
Angelanos	3632	Poles	1
Belgians	989	Portuguese	8
Danes	2	Rumanians	69
Germans	6118	Russians	17,536
British	13	Swedes	7
Estonians	3	Swiss	12
French	1	Slovaks	4
Greeks	23	Slovenes	6
Dutch	836	Spaniards	286
Italians	1388	Czechs	3
Canadians	5751	Turks	86
Croatians	18	Virginians	11,204
Chicagoans	8870	Yorkers	7311
Latvians	30	Hungarians	7
Norwegians	77	Homeless	17

At the window I look out. Perfect snow covers everything. Lights move across the snow. They are hands on a smooth stomach. The snow is a smooth stomach.

My Dearest Wife— When you read this, I shall be dead, having died in the service of nation and God. You cannot know the full depth of feeling in my heart. Tell Franz that I have

Undated

The time will come. Oh, the time will really come.

February 9

Most distressing rumors from Z who, quite out of his way, stopped in here for a few hours. He has achieved more rank than I thought him capable, though he is still far below Major. I have known him ten years and find that, like many others I have known prior to their call to duty, he has changed in a most admirable way. I have observed this before: certain men are airplanes. They are the dive of airplanes in attack. The awesome responsibility of my command I accept, and always have, but at times I have dreamed of and desired a flight command; I could easily learn the skills of flying; I would soon excel, as I have in all pursuits to which I have dedicated myself. Z, of course, is *not* in command of aircraft: his duty is trivial compared to aircraft. Z in fact is posing. That angelic sternness is *not* him: I remember once in Baltimore he came to *me* when he was in serious difficulties involving a venture in paint. *Paint! That is Z.* I wonder if it is generally known that these "serious ideals" of his allowed him at one time to become seriously involved in *paint!* The men of this so-called "camp" are little more than women. *Little more than women.*

May

I must admit I never knew that there could be so beautiful an experience as that which I have just recently undergone. Allow me to attempt an analysis of this phenomenon—though I humbly feel my efforts shall be futile. Her name is Verna, though I fear the name is not a good one; I shall have her change it to one more fitting. She is not beautiful—I must be honest. But, I challenge you, what does mankind know of this quality "beauty"? Tell me!

But true charm and beauty are

I must admit she is lascivious and this appeals to me in this particular season and what in another time would be lascivious is now most comely most beautiful though I know that in time I shall tire of it as indeed I always have and I shall by and by see the whole matter for what it is but in the meantime I allow her to worship that which she calls her *rhinoceros*. I am her rhinoceros. Crude worship that it is, I find I must agree with her: she does draw forth from me that which

May

A tiff. A lovers' quarrel, alas! Her tastes, I must admit, in furnishings are not far removed from her tastes in, shall I say, *other* matters of domesticity. Our nest is now quite habitable, comfortable, proper. It is appropriate to my rank and responsibility, and we shall be entertaining soon—an evening for my staff. If there is uttered a single slurred remark, he who makes it shall die. Champagne, truffles with espagnole, so forth. It shall be the first time the Commandant has properly entertained.

May

She inquired about the three hundred geese; so we rode, she on the sorrel gelding I recently won from O, I on the black stallion, to the yard where the geese are kept. She said she found it strange they cried out so often; was it caused by their being stuffed at feeding? I believed she already knew, and that she was being droll; however, we rode to the yard next to Unit One, and I had prearranged that while we were there Unit One was to be filled. Soon Chief of Guards G sent men into the goose yard to chase them about. What are the fools doing? she asked. I put my hand to my ear. Thinking not that I was suggesting that she listen *closely* to the din of honking and crying of the geese but that I could not hear her, she shouted her question a second time: What are the fools doing?

May 21
She has many of the stupidities of a child. She is naïve about the most absurd matters. Her tastes and interests are beyond understanding. She prefers the bed in the morning, upon just waking. Yesterday she would not let me out of bed, and then again at luncheon when I returned she was in the bed and induced me to join her, and again that evening; and this seemed to content her: the rest of the world could have been piling up and she would have been quite merry as long as she could squeeze the rhinoceros horn.

June 1
Camp capacity strained beyond endurance. Expediency. Efficient functioning creates high morale among the men. If time allowed, I would dictate commendations. Even the Egyptian auxiliary seem inspired to function quite remarkably.

June
Rid of the pest at last.

June
I have received word that Z has been killed in Africa. He was as good a man as ever wore the silver cord. I have written a letter of courage to his widow. She must know that now, more than ever before, all the

Jerry Bumpus

June 6
An inspection by H. First, however, he had been to the camp at El Paso. If only he had inspected Utica first!

July 7
For this date: 15,109
Remaining registry: 58,877

July
The geese are no longer used. Obviously. The futility of it. However, Chief of Guards G killed seventeen geese: he ran them to death. Presumably Grieschutz in his stupidity would have chased the geese all day and all night until all three hundred were dead. Chasing the geese, it develops, had been unnecessary from the beginning.

July 16
7322
Registry: 53,487

July 17
8102
Registry: 45,385

July 18
8986
Transport Received: 10,706
Registry: 45,105

August 2
10,180

227

August
10,001

August
15,861
00 000
00 000
00 000
00 000
00 000
00 000
00 000

December 5
This room will be destroyed. Looking around it: table, chairs, flag, window. Though I will not see the window. Though I come to my end, higher purposes shall never end. Consolation to
The black sky is an insult.

December 6
This Journal is I see it. Do you feel you are here yes I am here good good good

December 7
God in heaven. The obscenity of these swine.

December 8
Last Will and Testament of Major Friedrich Sweeney, Camp SO, Division II/44070.
To my wife and my children I leave all my worldly goods; all my estate: houses, lands, money, cattle, horses, poultry, swine. I request my library of books and files of papers be

tended by Professor P who often expressed interest, but his friendship with my father

Testament: In performance of my duty I have never failed to comply with every command of my superiors. I dream of the town where I was born and I would later be returned there; though I am fully aware that national needs and expediencies make technically unfeasible such matters as

May my sons die for high purposes.

God bless this land.

Major Friedrich Sweeney.

December 9

O's performance as Vice-Commandant is adequate. It is barely adequate. It is adequate.

I will kill them.

December

This Journal

There are several problems that have yet to be considered with complete rationality, and these problems I should 'like at this point to raise for our review. Being men, we

December

It is time for the truth. This is the truth. O is reliable at least. I feel confident that he shall do whatever is necessary and in all related duties appertaining to his rank. The truth

I, Friedrich Sweeney

December

Watching them from my window enables me to know about them facts which had heretofore been blinded from me because let us say I was blinded. They definitely walk differently. I had observed this years ago. I have always known eminent facts concerning them. Their loathsome habits confirm my most serious doubts.

I, Friedrich Sweeney.

December

Experience testifies that leaders are fools. The difficulties of nations have never been ideas, but the solid objects that crush us, that are around us, that I see at the very moment I write this. Let us begin with the elements. Hands. I have known hands; now let us see them for what they are, in fact. Or consider beetle shells. Hard black shells of beetles. Feet I see white narrow feet. They are long and bony. Please dear God in Heaven

Undated

O shall see that I am no easy victim. This Journal, personal, direct, shall be, has been, evidence of my dedication to high purposes. No malfeasance, no possible dereliction of duty.

What do you think of your Commandant now?

Undated

This last entry shall be my final word: the purpose must be high!

Undated

Let us begin with the elements. Hands. Feet. The body that moves.

BLACAMÁN THE GOOD, VENDOR OF MIRACLES

Gabriel García Márquez

Translated from the Spanish by Gregory Rabassa

rom the first Sunday I saw him he reminded me of a bullring mule, with his white suspenders that were backstitched with gold thread, his rings with colored stones on every finger, and his braids of jingle bells, standing on a table by the docks of Santa María del Darién in the middle of the flasks of specifics and herbs of consolation that he prepared himself and hawked through the towns along the Caribbean with his wounded shout, except that at that time he wasn't trying to sell any of that Indian mess but was asking them to bring him a real snake so that he could demonstrate on his own flesh an antidote he had invented, the only infallible one, ladies and gentlemen, for the bites of serpents, tarantulas, and centipedes, plus all manner of poisonous mammal. Someone who seemed quite impressed by his determination managed to get a bushmaster of the worst kind somewhere and brought it to him in a bottle, the snake that starts by poisoning the respiration, and he uncorked it with such eagerness that we all thought he was going to eat it, but as soon as the creature felt itself free it jumped out of the bottle and struck him on the neck, leaving him right then and there without any wind for his oratory and with barely enough time to take the antidote, and the vest-pocket pharmacist tumbled down into the crowd and rolled about on the ground,

his huge body wasted away as if he had nothing inside of it, but laughing all the while with all of his gold teeth. The hubbub was so great that a cruiser from the north that had been docked there for twenty years on a goodwill mission declared a quarantine so that the snake poison wouldn't get on board, and the people who were sanctifying Palm Sunday came out of church with their blessed palms, because no one wanted to miss the show of the poisoned man, who had already begun to puff up with the air of death and was twice as fat as he'd been before, giving off a froth of gall through his mouth and panting through his pores, but still laughing with so much life that the jingle bells tinkled all over his body. The swelling snapped the laces of his leggings and the seams of his clothes, his fingers grew purple from the pressure of the rings, he turned the color of venison in brine and from his rear end came a hint of the last moments of death, so that everyone who had seen a person bitten by a snake knew that he was rotting away before dying and that he would be so crumbled up that they'd have to pick him up with a shovel to put him into a sack, but they also thought that even in his sawdust state he'd keep on laughing. It was so incredible that the marines came up on deck to take colored pictures of him with long-distance lenses, but the women who'd come out of church blocked their intentions by covering the dying man with a blanket and laying blessed palms on top of him, some because they didn't want the soldiers to profane the body with their Adventist instruments, others because they were afraid to continue looking at that idolater who was ready to die dying with laughter, and others because in that way perhaps his soul at least would not be poisoned. Everybody had given him up for dead when he pushed aside the palms with one arm, still half-dazed and not completely recovered from the bad moment he'd had, but he set the table up again without anyone's help, climbed on it like a crab once more, and there he was again, shouting that his antidote was nothing but the hand of God in a bottle, as we had all seen with our own eyes, but it only cost two *cuartillos* because he hadn't invented it as an item for sale but for the good of all humanity, and as soon as he said that, ladies and gentlemen, I only ask you not to crowd around, there's enough for everybody.

They crowded around, of course, and they did well to do so, because in the end there wasn't enough for everybody. Even the admiral from the cruiser bought a bottle, convinced by him that it was also good for the poisoned bullets of anarchists, and the sailors weren't satisfied with just taking colored pictures of him up on the table, pictures they had been unable to take of him dead, but they had him signing autographs until his arm was twisted with cramps. It was getting to be night and only the most perplexed of us were left by the docks when with his eyes he searched for someone with the look of an idiot to help him put the bottles away, and naturally he spotted me. It was like the look of destiny, not just mine, but his too, for that was more than a century ago and we both remember it as if it had been last Sunday. What happened was that we were putting his circus drugstore into that trunk with purple straps that looked more like a scholar's casket, when he must have noticed some light inside of me that he hadn't seen in me before, because he asked me in a surly way who are you, and I answered that I was an orphan on both sides whose papa hadn't died, and he gave out with laughter that was louder than what he had given with the poison and then he asked me what do you do for a living, and I answered that I didn't do anything except stay alive, because nothing else was worth the trouble, and still weeping with laughter he asked me what science in the world do you most want to learn, and that was the only time I answered the truth without any fooling, I wanted to be a fortune-teller, and then he didn't laugh again but told me as if thinking out loud that I didn't need much for that because I already had the hardest thing to learn, which was my face of an idiot. That same night

he spoke to my father and for one *real* and *two cuartillos* and
a deck of cards that foretold adultery he bought me forever-
more.

That was what Blacamán was like, Blacamán the Bad, because
I'm Blacamán the Good. He was capable of convincing an
astronomer that the month of February was nothing but a herd
of invisible elephants, but when his good luck turned on him he
became a heart-deep brute. In his days of glory he had been an
embalmer of viceroys, and they say that he gave them faces with
such authority that for many years they went on governing
better than when they were alive, and that no one dared bury
them until he gave them back their dead-man look, but his
prestige was ruined by the invention of an endless chess game
that drove a chaplain mad and brought on two illustrious sui-
cides, and so he was on the decline, from an interpreter of dreams
to a birthday hypnotist, from an extractor of molars by sugges-
tion to a marketplace healer; therefore, at the time we met, people were already looking at him askance, even the freebooters.
We drifted along with our trick stand and life was an eternal
uncertainty as we tried to sell escape suppositories that turned
smugglers transparent, furtive drops that baptized wives threw
into the soup to instill the fear of God in Dutch husbands,
and anything you might want to buy of your own free will,
ladies and gentlemen, because this isn't a command, it's advice,
and, after all, happiness isn't an obligation either. Nevertheless,
as much as we died with laughter at his witticisms, the truth is
that it was quite hard for us to manage enough to eat, and his
last hope was founded on my vocation as a fortune-teller. He
shut me up in the sepulchral trunk disguised as a Japanese and
bound with starboard chains so that I could attempt to foretell
what I could while he disemboweled the grammar book looking
for the best way to convince the world of my new science, and
here, ladies and gentlemen, you have this child tormented by
Ezequiel's glowworms, and those of you who've been standing

236

there with faces of disbelief, let's see if you dare ask him when you're going to die, but I was never able even to guess what day it was at that time, so he gave up on me as a soothsayer because the drowsiness of digestion disturbs your prediction gland, and after whacking me over the head for good luck, he decided to take me to my father and get his money back. But at that time he happened to find a practical application for the electricity of suffering, and he set about building a sewing machine that ran connected by cupping glasses to the part of the body where there was a pain. Since I spent the night moaning over the whacks he'd given me to conjure away misfortune, he had to keep me on as the one who could test his invention, and our return was delayed and he was getting back his good humor until the machine worked so well that it not only sewed better than a novice nun but also embroidered birds or astromelias according to the position and intensity of the pain. That was what we were up to, convinced of our triumph over bad luck, when the news reached us that in Philadelphia the commander of the cruiser had tried to repeat the experiment with the antidote and that he'd been changed into a glob of admiral jelly in front of his staff.

He didn't laugh again for a long time. We fled through Indian passes and the more lost we became the clearer the news reached us that the marines had invaded the country under the pretext of exterminating yellow fever and were going about beheading every inveterate or eventual potter they found in their path, and not only the natives, out of precaution, but also the Chinese, for distraction, the Negroes, from habit, and the Hindus, because they were snake charmers, and then they wiped out the flora and fauna and all the mineral wealth they were able to because their specialists in our affairs had taught them that the people along the Caribbean had the ability to change their nature in order to confuse gringos. I couldn't understand where that fury came from or why we were so fright-

ened until we found ourselves safe and sound in the eternal
winds of La Guajira, and only then did he have the courage to
confess to me that his antidote was nothing but rhubarb and
turpentine and that he'd paid a drifter two *cuartillos* to bring
him that bushmaster with all the poison gone. We stayed in the
ruins of a colonial mission, deluded by the hope that some smugglers would pass, because they were men to be trusted and the
only ones capable of venturing out under the mercurial sun of
those salt flats. At first we ate smoked salamanders and flowers
from the ruins and we still had enough spirit to laugh when we
tried to eat his boiled leggings, but finally we even ate the water
cobwebs from the cisterns and only then did we realize how
much we missed the world. Since I didn't know of any recourse
against death at that time, I simply lay down to wait for it where
it would hurt me least, while he was delirious remembering a
woman who was so tender that she could pass through walls
just by sighing, but that contrived recollection was also a trick
of his genius to fool death with lovesickness. Still, at the moment
we should have died, he came to me more alive than ever and
spent the whole night watching over my agony, thinking with
such great strength that I still haven't been able to tell whether
what was whistling through the ruins was the wind or his
thoughts, and before dawn he told me with the same voice and
the same determination of past times that now he knew the
truth, that I was the one who had twisted up his luck again, so
get your pants ready, because the same way as you twisted it up
for me, you're going to straighten it out.

That was when I lost the little affection I had for him. He
took off the last rags I had on, rolled me up in some barbed wire,
rubbed rock salt on the sores, put me in brine from my own
waters, and hung me by the ankles for the sun to flay me, and
he kept on shouting that all that mortification wasn't enough to
pacify his persecutors. Finally he threw me to rot in my own
misery inside the penance dungeon where the colonial mission-

aries regenerated heretics, and with the perfidy of a ventrilo-
quist, which he still had more than enough of, he began to imitate the voices of edible animals, the noise of ripe beets, and the
sound of fresh springs so as to torture me with the illusion I was
dying of indigence in the midst of paradise. When the smugglers
finally supplied him, he came down to the dungeon to give me
something to eat so that I wouldn't die, but then he made me
pay for that charity by pulling out my nails with pliers and filing
my teeth down with a grindstone, and my only consolation was
the wish that life would give me time and the good fortune to be
quit of so much infamy with even worse martyrdoms. I myself
was surprised that I could resist the plague of my own putrefac-
tion and he kept throwing the leftovers of his meals onto me
and tossed pieces of rotten lizards and hawks into the corners so
that the air of the dungeon would end up poisoning me. I don't
know how much time had passed when he brought me the
carcass of a rabbit in order to show me that he preferred
throwing it away to rot rather than giving it to me to eat, but
my patience only went so far and all I had left was rancor, so I
grabbed the rabbit by the ears and flung it against the wall with
the illusion that it was he and not the animal that was going to
explode, and then it happened, as if in a dream. The rabbit not
only revived with a squeal of fright, but came back to my
hands, hopping through the air.

That was how my great life began. Since then I've gone
through the world drawing the fever out of malaria victims for
two pesos, visioning blind men for four-fifty, draining the water from dropsy victims for eighteen, putting cripples back together for twenty pesos if they were that way from birth, for
twenty-two if they were that way because of an accident or a
brawl, for twenty-five if they were that way because of wars,
earthquakes, infantry landings, or any kind of public calamity,
taking care of the common sick at wholesale according to a special arrangement, madmen according to their theme, children

at half price, and idiots out of gratitude, and who dares say that I'm not a philanthropist, ladies and gentlemen, and now, yes, sir, commandant of the twentieth fleet, order your boys to take down the barricades and let suffering humanity pass, lepers to the left, epileptics to the right, cripples where they won't get in the way, and there in the back the least urgent cases, only please don't crowd in on me because then I won't be responsible if the sicknesses get all mixed up and people are cured of what they don't have, and keep the music playing until the brass boils, and the rockets firing until the angels burn, and the liquor flowing until ideas are killed, and bring on the wenches and the acrobats, the butchers and the photographers, and all at my expense, ladies and gentlemen, for here ends the evil fame of the Blacamáns and the universal tumult starts. That's how I go along putting them to sleep with the techniques of a congressman in case my judgment fails and some turn out worse on me than they were before. The only thing I don't do is revive the dead, because as soon as they open their eyes they're murderous with rage at the one who disturbed their state, and when it's all done, those who don't commit suicide die again of disillusionment. At first I was pursued by a group of wise men investigating the legality of my industry, and when they were convinced, they threatened me with the hell of Simon Magus and recommended a life of penitence so that I could get to be a saint, but I answered them, with no disrespect for their authority, that it was precisely along those lines that I had started. The truth is that I'd gain nothing by being a saint after being dead, an artist is what I am, and the only thing I want is to be alive so I can keep going along at donkey level in this six-cylinder touring car I bought from the marines' consul, with this Trinidadian chauffeur who was a baritone in the New Orleans pirates' opera, with my genuine silk shirts, my oriental lotions, my topaz teeth, my flat straw hat, and my bicolored buttons, sleeping without an alarm clock, dancing with beauty queens, and leaving them hallucinated with my dictionary rhetoric, and with no flutter in my spleen if some Ash Wednesday my faculties wither away, because in order to go on with this life of a minister, all I need is my idiot face, and I have more than enough with the string of shops I own from here to beyond the sunset, where the same tourists who used to go around collecting from us through the admiral, now go stumbling after my autographed pictures, almanacs with my love poetry, medals with my profile, bits of my clothing, and all of that without the glorious plague of spending all day and all night sculptured in equestrian marble and shat on by swallows like the fathers of our country.

It's a pity that Blacamán the Bad can't repeat this story so that people will see that there's nothing invented in it. That last time anyone saw him in this world he'd lost even the studs of his former splendor, and his soul was a shambles and his bones in disorder from the rigors of the desert, but he still had enough jingle bells left to reappear that Sunday on the docks of Santa María del Darién with his eternal sepulchral trunk, except that this time he wasn't trying to sell any antidotes, but was asking in a voice cracking with emotion for the marines to shoot him in a public spectacle so that he could demonstrate on his own flesh the life-restoring properties of this supernatural creature, ladies and gentlemen, and even though you have more than enough right not to believe me after suffering so long from my tricks as a deceiver and falsifier, I swear on the bones of my mother that this proof today is nothing from the other world, merely the humble truth, and in case you have any doubts left, notice that I'm not laughing now the way I used to, but holding back a desire to cry. How convincing he must have been, unbuttoning his shirt, his eyes drowning with tears, and giving himself mule kicks on his heart to indicate the best place for death, and yet the marines didn't dare shoot, out of fear that the Sunday crowd would discover their loss of prestige. Someone who may not have gotten the Blacamanipulations of past times managed, no one knew how, to get and bring him in a can enough barbasco roots to bring to the surface all the *corvinas* in the Caribbean, and he opened it with great desire, as if he really was going to eat them, and, indeed, he did eat them, ladies and gentlemen, but please don't be moved or pray for the repose of my soul, because this death is nothing but a visit. That time he was so honest that he didn't break into operatic death rattles, but got off the table like a crab, looked on the ground for the most worthy place to lie down after some hesitation, and from there he looked at me as he would have at a mother and exhaled his last breath in his own arms, still holding back his tears of a man, all twisted up by the tetanus of eternity. That was the only time, of course, that my science failed me. I put him in that trunk of premonitory size where there was room for him laid out. I had a requiem mass sung for him which cost me fifty-four peso doubloons, because the officiant was dressed in gold and there were also three seated bishops. I had the mausoleum of an emperor built for him on a hill exposed to the best seaside weather, with a chapel just for him and an iron plaque on which there was written in Gothic capitals here lies Blacamán the Dead, badly called the Bad, deceiver of marines and the victim of science, and when those honors were sufficient for me to do justice to his virtues, I began to get my revenge for his infamy, and then I revived him inside the armored tomb and left him there rolling about in horror. That was long before the fire ants devoured Santa María del Darién, but the mausoleum is still intact on the hill in the shadow of the dragons that climb up to sleep in the Atlantic winds, and every time I pass through here I bring him an automobile-load of roses and my heart pains with pity for his virtues, but then I put my ear to the plaque to hear him weeping in the ruins of the crumbling trunk, and if by chance he has died again, I bring him back to life once more, for the beauty of the punishment is that he will keep on living in his tomb as long as I'm alive, that is, forever.

EIGHT MEETINGS

Thomas Bontly

I

e sat in the bar at a seaside hotel, looking out at the emerald cove, the white rage of surf, the jagged black rocks like the hulls of stranded ships. The fog lay out to sea, a high wall in two quite distinct layers—the lower dark blue, the upper frosting white. I was drinking a gimlet.

"Do you suppose there is a demon which plagues the creative soul?" Ramon asked. "I haven't been able to work for six months."

"I haven't worked well for several weeks myself," said Morton. His remark occasioned an awkward silence, for there were those among us who thought Morton never worked well.

"Ones hates to utter such banalities," said Winnie, "but sometimes one has the feeling that it's all been done—that there's just nothing left to write about."

Tanya smiled and looked away. Tanya was a poetess but she never showed anyone her work. If she published at all, it was under a *nom de plume*. No one knew what sort of thing she did, and we were all terribly curious; we were sure her poems must be very fine.

Bert, an architect, looked bored. He was the only one among

245

us who was not a writer, and we all knew his opinion of writers. Bert was a very successful architect. His buildings had sprouted all across the city and had virtually ruined its distinctive and charming hills. I was sure we all despised Bert.

"Look," someone said, "out there—just off that next point. Aren't those whales?"

We all looked. After a moment I saw something white, or a very light grey, surface and instantly disappear. Then another, and another.

"Yes," Morton said, "I believe they *are* whales."

"I think so," echoed Julian, "although it's rather late for them, isn't it?"

"I've heard you could see whales from here," said Kurt, "but I never believed it. How very fascinating."

"Darling," Winnie asked me, "are you staying over the night, or will you be going back to the city with the others?"

"I shall go back," I said.

II

We were at a large table on the open deck alongside the yacht club, looking across the bay at the distant whiteness of the city. The sun was warm where we sat, but tentacles of fog were already creeping beneath the bridge at the entrance to the harbor. Sailboats and cruisers rode softly at anchor below us. Gulls banked and hovered overhead. I was drinking martinis.

"God, the city looks lovely from here," said young Lyons, who was prone to enthusiastic utterances.

"Yes," said Julian. "From this distance, Bert's skyscrapers are nearly an asset, aren't they?"

Bert had taken Scott and Kurt out in his sailboat. We were always more comfortable when he was out of the way.

"How are you getting along with your demon?" Morton asked Ramon.

Ramon stroked his handsome beard. The hair on his arms was dark and curly, like his beard, like the hair that showed at his half-open shirt. "I am trying to befriend it," he said. "I've made several sacrificial offerings. I'm trying to find out what it wants."

"What sort of sacrifices?" Winnie asked. "Not human, I hope."

One never knew about Ramon.

"Even more precious," Ramon said. "I'm burning manuscripts."

"Good heavens," Cynthia said, "that's rather drastic, isn't it?"

Ramon shrugged. "Only my very early stuff so far. But I've become desperate. The demon has me by the throat. It's dreadful."

Tanya smiled softly to herself. I saw her looking out across the bay, her beautiful green eyes like precious stones. I wondered if she burned her new poems as soon as they were finished, before anyone could see them.

A gull had landed on the wooden railing beside our table. Morton playfully offered the gull a cracker. The gull reared back, as if affronted. Then it stretched forward its long neck and its long beak picked the cracker daintily from Morton's fingers.

We all laughed.

"Oh say, that's good!" cried young Lyons.

The gull, frightened by our outburst, flew away. The women instinctively covered their heads.

Julian took my hand beneath the table. "Are you going to Bert's housewarming party?" he asked me.

"I abhor Bert," I said.

"But the party might be rather fun," Julian said.

"I abhor housewarmings," I said. "Besides, I have no gift."

Tanya turned to smile at me with her beautiful eyes, and I felt as if we had grown closer.

247

III

We were in the Crown Room of the Royale Hotel.

"All these tourists," Julian said. "All these fat middle-aged conventioneers. It's goddamn depressing."

"Whatever did we come here for?" Winnie asked. "One can't see a thing today."

It was true. The fog was in and all we could see, really, was the tower of the hotel just across from us. The two hotels, with their top-floor cocktail lounges, looked at one another like wary behemoths. Occasionally a puff of blowing fog would obscure the gabled peaks of the rival lookout.

I was drinking a Manhattan and not very pleased with it.

"Tell us about your demon, Ramon," Kurt said. "Have you managed to placate him?"

Ramon gazed out at the fog. "Ah," he said. "Ah."

"My own work is going very badly this summer," Julian said. "I'm afraid I shall have to change my environment."

He looked quickly at me to see if I would mind his going away. I tried to show him with a careful smile that I would not.

"I feel," said Winnie, "that we are all haunted by some imminent catastrophe. Suppose the world ended tomorrow. . . ."

"Well, it would give us something to write about, anyway," laughed Scott.

"Perhaps it already has ended," suggested Kurt. "I can't see a blessed thing down there, can you?"

"No, no," Winnie said. "What I mean is, suppose it did end? Would any of this matter?"

"I shall ask my demon," Ramon said. "I am beginning to believe he is a very wise demon."

"Why use the masculine?" Cynthia asked, seductively. "Perhaps you are possessed by a female demon."

Ramon brightened. "I hadn't thought of that. You may be right, Cynthia." One could see that he was immensely cheered. "Now I shall know how to deal with her."

We laughed, all of us but Tanya. I wondered if Tanya had ever slept with Ramon.

"I want to buy a painting for my new apartment," young Lyons said to me. "Would you like to go to a gallery or two with me tomorrow? I'm sure you must have admirable taste."

"Oh, I have very bad taste, I'm afraid," I said. "Besides, I promised myself I would work tomorrow."

"Then *you* still work, at least?" he asked.

"Sometimes," I said, and tried to catch Tanya's distant gaze.

"Pigs!" Julian said. "A lot of disgusting pigs! I don't think we should come here anymore. It's not pleasant here anymore."

IV

At a restaurant on the beach we watched the seals. There was no fog that day and we could see the dark, shining, shapeless animals sunning themselves on the black rocks. The windows were heavily filmed with salt and the air in the room where we sat was hot and oppressive, but the Irish coffee was quite good.

Ramon was not with us. We were all a bit relieved, since he seemed to carry his demon about with him now wherever he went and it had become quite depressing.

"Of course it's absurd to say that it's all been done," Julian observed. "The world changes. New things are continually happening. Each of us is a unique individual, I'm sure, seeing things in a unique way. Originality is a myth, you know. What matters is truth to one's own unique perspective."

"But art is not truth," said Kurt. "Surely we all know by now that art has nothing to do with truth whatsoever."

"Or perhaps it is the only truth," said Cynthia.

"That's the same thing," said Kurt. "The point is, art mustn't imitate life. It must go its own way. Art and life have nothing whatsoever in common. Surely this must be obvious."

Morton squirmed uncomfortably. "As for myself," he said, "I still like a certain minimal verisimilitude in fiction. I mean, a lot of the old standards still apply. One has to be a craftsman first of all."

We all knew that Morton prided himself on his craftsmanship. Six novels, all perfectly crafted, all perfectly conventional, all absurdly successful. Morton resented the fact that he was not taken seriously among the cognoscenti. He felt such a prodigious output entitled him to a certain amount of respect.

"Don't you ever wish," Winnie asked, "that you had become a filmmaker or something? I mean, anything where there are still lots of creative possibilities? Anything besides a novelist?"

"No," said Morton.

"I do admire some of Antonioni's things," said Julian, "but Fellini is a charlatan."

"All true artists are charlatans," Kurt said. "This goes without saying. I would like to have been a magician—a conjurer, perhaps even a spiritualist."

"Then you could have mediated between Ramon and his demon," said Scott, laughing.

Tanya was watching the seals.

So was young Lyons. "Does anyone know," he asked, "when, where, and how seals mate?"

"Good Lord, no," said Julian.

"Well, I think there are two of them mating out there right now," said young Lyons.

"The poor things," Winnie said. "Perhaps we shouldn't look."

Tanya turned back to us with a tragic smile. "It's over," she said.

V

"I was sorry you didn't come to my housewarming," said Bert. "We missed you."

I muttered an insincere apology. We had met, quite by accident, at the aquarium. (Is no place safe? I wondered.) It was a weekday afternoon and the aquarium was crowded with touring schoolchildren. We sat on a bench in a dark corner and Bert offered me his flask. It was vodka. Cunning Bert.

"Do you come here often?" he asked.

"No," I said, "only when I can't work."

"Oh, then your work has bogged as well, has it?"

I watched the long sleek supple sharks, passing and repassing in their Windex-blue tank. "I don't talk about my work," I said. "It's bad luck."

"You know," he said, "I'm glad I'm not a writer. You all seem to lead such desperate lives—so harried, so—so—" he glanced at the sharks—"rapacious."

"Life is short," I said, taking a swig of his vodka, "but art is long."

Bert sighed. "You've heard about young Lyons, I suppose."

"No. What about him?"

"Shot himself. Last Thursday. He rather bungled the job, though. They say he'll be permanently blind. Isn't that terrible?"

"Terrible," I said. The cries of the schoolchildren echoed in the dark building, echoes within echoes, like electronic music.

"You don't seem very moved for the poor fellow," Bert said. "He liked you a lot."

"Have you seen the porpoises?" I asked. "They're quite amusing."

"I've decided to leave my wife," Bert said.

"I thought you already had," I said.

"I did," Bert said, "but I went back in February. For the children, you know. It was a mistake. She's turned them against me, the bitch. All my kids are rotten little good-for-nothings. Are you going to the lake this weekend?"

"No," I said. "I'm sick to death of the lake. Look—they're about to feed the sharks."

VI

At the Alpine Chalet we were all quite drunk, still in the up- stairs cocktail lounge awaiting our table at ten P.M. I was on my fourth old-fashioned.

"You look dreadful," Winnie said to Ramon. "Is it your demon?"

"I haven't slept in weeks," Ramon said. "She's destroying me, bit by bit. If only I could discover what she wants!"

"Your gorgeous body, obviously," said Julian, with his char- acteristic smirk.

"She wants to keep you from writing," Cynthia said. "It's very simple—all you have to do is renounce literature forever and you'll be free of her."

Ramon doubled his large fist. His dark Latin eyes shone magnificently. "Never," he said. "Never."

"The problem as I see it," said Scott, "is where does one go from Joyce? Have all the technical possibilities of the form really been exhausted?"

"Of course they have," said Julian. "The novelistic form is a dry bladder."

"How very evocative," said Cynthia, batting her false eye- lashes.

"When the hell are we going to get a goddamn table?" Mor- ton wanted to know.

I gazed out the window at the lights of the city. I could see a section of the bridge and, across the dark chasm of the waters, the twinkling line of the airport, like a hem of sequins on a black velvet gown.

"And really," said Winnie, "what is there left to write about? God is dead. The family is kaput. Society has lost its cohesiveness. Sex has been exploited to the point at which no self-respecting writer would touch it. One gets so weary of alienation, that sad old nag."

"I think we've about worn out alienation," Julian said. "Of course, if we've lost theology, we still have demonology, which takes us back to Ramon again."

I looked around the table and missed Tanya, who was not with us tonight.

Morton, who was feeling frisky, had removed a string of cowbells from the wall and draped them over his broad shoulders. "Moo," he said, making a cow face and shrugging his shoulders to tinkle the bells. "Moo."

"Morton," Julian observed, "you're an ass."

VII

It was the first time I had been in Tanya's apartment. It was strikingly furnished in black and gold, with numerous oriental *objets d'art* which I openly admired. Through the bay windows I could see a tall palm tree with its grey beard of dead branches and the descending rooftops of Pirate's Hill. The blue bay was punctuated with sails like white commas, and the evening fog hung back at the bridge, as if awaiting an invitation to enter.

Tanya's cat, Caliban, purred in my lap. We were drinking cheap red wine to prolong the high of the reefer we had shared.

"Have you ever balled a black?" Tanya asked me.

"No," I said.

"Neither have I," Tanya said. "There's so much I haven't done."

She was totally nude, reclining on the divan across from me in a pool of golden sunlight. Her body was incredibly sensuous for one so young, the curve of her hip like an artist's inspired line, the lower slope of her belly a sculptor's dream. I thought her poems must be like her body, lush and perfect, a bowl of fruit.

"Have you ever wondered what it's like to be blind?" she asked me.

"Yes," I said, "since young Lyons."

"Ah, poor young Lyons," she said. "Poor Ramon. Poor Julian. Poor everybody."

"Poor Caliban," I said, stroking the cat's soft fur. I could feel Caliban's throat vibrating against my leg as he purred. I could see his scratches, long red marks, on Tanya's chest, between her delicate breasts.

"Do you suppose there'll be another earthquake here sometime?" she asked me. "I mean, a really grand, devastating one? Wouldn't that be lovely? It might knock down every one of Bert's wretched buildings."

Caliban leaped from my lap and sprang lightly to the windowsill. Tanya slid off the divan and began to crawl toward me across the oriental rug. Her dark hair fell down across her eyes. A strand clung wetly to the side of her mouth, close to her pink lower lip. Her eyes showed me enormous hunger. I saw her long white back with its deeply shadowed spine.

I wished there were some way to make Tanya show me her poems, now that we were lovers.

VIII

"Ramon has gone back to Brazil," Sidney said. Rings glistened on his pudgy fingers as he lit one of his filthy cigars.

We were in the Vista, crowded very close together in the usual crush. Bert pressed against me on one side, Morton on the other. Across the table from us Tanya was flanked by Scott and Julian. Scott had his arm around Tanya. Julian kept trying to catch my eye. I sipped my cognac.

"Do you suppose he'll finally lose his demon in Brazil?" Winnie asked.

"I think he hoped to leave it in the States," Kurt said.

"I envy him immensely," Julian said. "I've been pining for a change of scene myself for some time now. We've used up all the good places in this old town."

"There were many good places," Kurt said. "Something's spoiled them. The whole city has been spoiled."

"It's the tourists," Sidney said. "And the hippies. And the racketeers. And the phonies. And the hustlers. And the whores and pimps. And the pornographers. And the dope pushers. And the cops. And the queers. And the promoters. And the politicians. I blame it mostly on the politicians."

"One feels that life must be richer, somehow, in South America," Cynthia said. "Nobler. More meaningful. More fun. They have carnivals and festivals and gaiety."

"And the Church," Winnie said.

"God is alive and hiding out in South America," Scott said, and laughed. No one else bothered to laugh, although Tanya smiled distantly. I wondered if she had given herself to Scott.

"In the jungles of the Amazon," Julian said, "they still have human sacrifices. And cannibalism. And shrunken heads."

"And magic," Kurt said.

"Look," someone cried, "that man at the bar has a parrot on his arm."

"So he has," Julian observed. "And a patch over one eye. Do you suppose he could have a peg leg as well?"

The parrot tried to bite the man's ear.

"Good Christ," Morton breathed. "It's young Lyons!"

So it was.

"How he's aged," Winnie said. "The poor thing. Do you suppose we should invite him over?"

"I wouldn't," Sidney said. "He's seen us, but I don't believe he wants us to recognize him."

"But I thought he lost both eyes," Tanya said, wonderingly.

"Apparently only one, dear," Winnie said. "The diagnosis was premature. My, but he does look a splendid creature with that bird on his arm. Say, does anyone want to run down to the mountains this weekend?"

"God, no," Julian said. "It's the same old thing."

"Let's go somewhere new," Tanya said. "Somewhere far away. Far, far, far—as far as we can go." Her eyes turned to green fire at the prospect.

"I know," said Cynthia, "we can go to Brazil! Bert can fly us down in his plane—can't you, Bert?"

"I guess I could," Bert said. He turned to me. "Would *you* like to go to Brazil?"

"And see Ramon?" I asked.

"Of course," they all shouted. "Ramon! Ramon! We must see Ramon!"

I looked at Tanya, and her slight, secretive nod seemed to say that it would be acceptable.

"Then, *viva la Brazil*," I cried.

We drank to it.

A RUSSIAN
BEAUTY

Vladimir Nabokov

Translated from the Russian by Simon Karlinsky

lga, of whom we are about to speak, was born in the year 1900, in a wealthy, carefree family of nobles. A pale little girl in a white sailor suit, with a side parting in her chestnut hair and such merry eyes that everyone kissed her there, she was deemed a beauty since childhood. The purity of her profile, the expression of her closed lips, the silkiness of her tresses that reached to the small of her back—all this was enchanting indeed.

Her childhood passed festively, securely, and gaily, as was the custom in our country since the days of old. A sunbeam falling on the cover of a *Bibliothèque Rose* volume at the family estate, the classical hoar-frost of the Saint Petersburg public gardens. . . . A supply of memories, such as these, comprised her sole dowry when she left Russia in the spring of 1919. Everything happened in full accord with the style of the period. Her mother died of typhus, her brother was executed by the firing squad. All these are ready-made formulae, of course, the usual dreary small talk, but it all did happen, there is no other way of saying it, and it's no use turning up your nose.

Well then, in 1919 we have a grown-up young lady, with a pale, broad face that overdid things in terms of the regularity of its features, but just the same very lovely. Tall, with soft breasts, she always wears a black jumper and a scarf around her white neck and holds an English cigarette in her slender-fingered hand with a prominent little bone just above the wrist.

Yet there was a time in her life, at the end of 1916 or so, when at a summer resort near the family estate there was no schoolboy who did not plan to shoot himself because of her, there was no university student who would not. . . . In a word, there had been a special magic about her, which, had it lasted, would have caused . . . would have wreaked . . . But somehow nothing came of it. Things failed to develop, or else happened to no purpose. There were flowers that she was too lazy to put in a vase, there were strolls in the twilight now with this one, now with another, followed by the blind alley of a kiss.

She spoke French fluently, pronouncing *les gens* (the servants) as if rhyming with *agence*, and splitting *août* (August) in two syllables (*a-ou*). She naively translated the Russian *grabezhi* (robberies) as *les grabuges* (quarrels) and used some archaic French locutions that had somehow survived in old Russian families, but she rolled her *r*'s most convincingly even though she had never been to France. Over the dresser in her Berlin room a postcard of Serov's portrait of the Tsar was fastened with a pin with a fake turquoise head. She was religious, but at times a fit of giggles would overcome her in church. She wrote verse with that terrifying facility typical of young Russian girls of her generation: patriotic verse, humorous verse, any kind of verse at all.

For about six years, that is until 1926, she resided in a boarding house on the Augsburgerstrasse (not far from the clock), together with her father, a broad-shouldered, beetle-browed old man with a yellowish moustache, and with tight narrow trousers on his spindly legs. He had a job with some optimistic firm, was noted for his decency and kindness and was never one to turn down a drink.

In Berlin, Olga gradually acquired a large group of friends, all of them young Russians. A certain jaunty tone was established. "Let's go to the cinemonkey," or "That was a heely deely (German *Diele*, dancing hall)." All sorts of popular sayings, cant phrases, imitations of imitations were much in demand. "I wonder who's kissing her now?" Or, in a hoarse, choking voice: "Mes-sieurs les officiers . . ."

At the Zotovs', in their overheated rooms, she languidly danced the fox trot to the sound of the gramophone, shifting the elongated calf of her leg not without grace and holding away from her the cigarette she had just finished smoking, and when her eyes located the ashtray that revolved with the music she would shove the butt into it, without missing a step. How charmingly, how meaningfully she could raise the wine glass to her lips, secretly drinking to the health of a third party as she looked through her lashes at the one who had confided in her. How she loved to sit in the corner of the sofa, discussing with this person or that somebody else's affairs of the heart, the oscillation of chances, the probability of a declaration—all this indirectly, by hints—and how understandingly her eyes would smile, pure, wide-open eyes with barely noticeable freckles on the thin, faintly bluish skin underneath and around them. But as for herself, no one fell in love with her, and this was why she long remembered the boor who pawed her at a charity ball and afterwards wept on her bare shoulder. He was challenged to a duel by the little Baron R., but refused to fight. The word "boor," by the way, was used by Olga on any and every occasion. "Such boors," she would sing out in chest tones, languidly and affectionately. "What a boor . . ." "Aren't they boors?"

But presently her life darkened. Something was finished, people were already getting up to leave. How quickly! Her father died, she moved to another street. She stopped seeing her friends, knitted the little bonnets in fashion and gave cheap French lessons at some ladies' club or other. In this way her life dragged on to the age of thirty.

She was still the same beauty, with that enchanting slant of the widely-spaced eyes and with that rarest line of lips into which the geometry of the smile seems to be already inscribed. But her hair lost its shine and was poorly cut. Her black tailored suit was in its fourth year. Her hands, with their glistening but untidy fingernails, were roped with veins and were shaking from nervousness and from her wretched continuous smoking. And we'd best pass over in silence the state of her stockings. . . .

Now, when the silken insides of her handbag were in tatters (at least there was always the hope of finding a stray coin); now, when she was so tired; now, when putting on her only pair of shoes she had to force herself not to think of their soles, just as when, swallowing her pride, she entered the tobacconist's, she forbade herself to think of how much she already owed there; now that there was no longer the least hope of returning to Russia, and hatred had become so habitual that it almost ceased to be a sin; now that the sun was getting behind the chimney, Olga would occasionally be tormented by the luxury of certain advertisements, written in the saliva of Tantalus, imagining herself wealthy, wearing that dress, sketched with the aid of three or four insolent lines, on that ship-deck, under that palm tree, at the balustrade of that white terrace. And then there was also another thing or two that she missed.

One day, almost knocking her off her feet, her one-time friend Vera rushed like a whirlwind out of a telephone booth, in a hurry as always, loaded with parcels, with a shaggy-eyed terrier, whose leash immediately became wound twice around her skirt. She pounced upon Olga, imploring her to come and stay at their summer villa, saying that it was Fate itself, that it was wonderful and how have you been and are there many suitors. "No, my dear, I'm no longer that age," answered Olga, "and besides . . ." She added a little detail and Vera burst out laughing, letting her parcels sink almost to the ground. "No, seriously," said Olga, with a smile. Vera continued coaxing her, pulling at the terrier, turning this way and that. Olga, starting all at once to speak through her nose, borrowed some money from her.

Vera adored arranging things, be it a party with punch, a visa or a wedding. Now she avidly took up arranging Olga's fate. "The matchmaker within you has been aroused," joked her husband, an elderly Balt (shaven head, monocle). Olga arrived on a bright August day. She was immediately dressed in one of Vera's frocks, her hairdo and make-up were changed. She swore languidly, but yielded, and how festively the floorboards creaked in the merry little villa! How the little mirrors, suspended in the green orchard to frighten off birds, flashed and sparkled!

A Russified German named Forstmann, a well-off athletic widower, author of books on hunting, came to spend a week. He had long been asking Vera to find him a bride, "a real Russian beauty." He had a massive, strong nose with a fine pink vein on its high bridge. He was polite, silent, at times even morose, but knew how to form, instantly and while no one noticed, an eternal friendship with a dog or with a child. With his arrival Olga became difficult. Listless and irritable, she did all the wrong things and she knew that they were wrong. When the conversation turned to old Russia (Vera tried to make her show off her past), it seemed to her that everything she said was a lie and that everyone understood that it was a lie, and therefore she stubbornly refused to say the things that Vera was trying to extract from her and in general would not cooperate in any way.

On the veranda, they would slam their cards down hard. Everyone would go off together for a stroll through the woods, but Forstmann conversed mostly with Vera's husband, and, recalling some pranks of their youth, the two of them would turn red with laughter, lag behind, and collapse on the moss. On the eve of Forstmann's departure they were playing cards on the veranda, as they usually did in the evening. Suddenly, Olga felt an impossible spasm in her throat. She still managed to smile and to leave without undue haste. Vera knocked on her door but she did not open. In the middle of the night, having swatted a multitude of sleepy flies and smoked continuously to the point where she was no longer able to inhale, irritated, depressed, hating herself and everyone, Olga went into the garden. There, the crickets stridulated, the branches swayed, an occasional apple fell with a taut thud, and the moon performed calisthenics on the white-washed wall of the chicken coop.

Early in the morning, she came out again and sat down on the porch step that was already hot. Forstmann, wearing a dark blue bathrobe, sat next to her and, clearing his throat, asked if she would consent to become his spouse—that was the very word he used: spouse. When they came to breakfast, Vera, her husband, and his maiden cousin, in utter silence, were performing nonexistent dances, each in a different corner, and Olga drawled out in an affectionate voice "What boors!" and next summer she died in childbirth.

That's all. Of course, there may be some sort of sequel, but it is not known to me. In such cases, instead of getting bogged down in guesswork, I repeat the words of the merry king in my favorite fairy tale: Which arrow flies forever? The arrow that has hit its mark.

THE
INTERROGATION
OF
THE PRISONER
BUNG
BY MISTER
HAWKINS
AND SERGEANT
TREE

David Huddle

he land in these provinces to the south of the capital city is so flat it would be possible to ride a bicycle from one end of this district to the other and to pedal only occasionally. The narrow highway passes over kilometers and kilometers of rice fields, laid out square and separated by slender green lines of grassy paddy-dikes and by irrigation ditches filled with bad water. The villages are far apart and small. Around them are clustered the little pockets of huts, the hamlets where the rice farmers live. The village that serves as the capital of this district is just large enough to have a proper marketplace. Close to the police compound, a detachment of Americans has set up its tents. These are lumps of new green canvas, and they sit on a concrete, French-built tennis court, long abandoned, not far from a large lily pond where women come in the morning to wash clothes and where policemen of the compound and their children come to swim and bathe in the late afternoon.

The door of a room to the rear of the District Police Headquarters is cracked for light and air. Outside noises—chickens quarreling, children playing, the mellow grunting of the pigs owned by the Police Chief—these reach the ears of the three men inside the quiet room. The room is not a cell; it is more like a small bedroom.

The American is nervous and fully awake, but he forces himself to yawn and sips at his coffee. In front of him are his papers, the report forms, yellow notepaper, two pencils and a ball-point pen. Across the table from the American is Sergeant Tree, a young man who was noticed by the government of his country and taken from his studies to be sent to interpreter's school. Sergeant Tree has a pleasant and healthy face. He is accustomed to smiling, especially in the presence of Americans, who are, it happens, quite fond of him. Sergeant Tree knows that he has an admirable position working with Mister Hawkins; several of his unlucky classmates from interpreter's school serve nearer the shooting.

The prisoner, Bung, squats in the far corner of the room, his back at the intersection of the cool concrete walls. Bung is a large man for an Asian, but he is squatted down close to the floor. He was given a cigarette by the American when he was first brought into the room, but has finished smoking and holds the white filter inside his fist. Bung is not tied, nor restrained, but he squats perfectly still, his bare feet laid out flat and large on the floor. His hair, cut by his wife, is cropped short and uneven; his skin is dark, leathery, and there is a bruise below one of his shoulder blades. He looks only at the floor, and he wonders what he will do with the tip of the cigarette when the interrogation begins. He suspects that he ought to eat it now so that it will not be discovered later.

From the large barracks room on the other side of the building comes laughter and loud talking, the policemen changing shifts. Sergeant Tree smiles at these sounds. Some of the younger policemen are his friends. Hawkins, the American, does not seem to have heard. He is trying to think about sex, and he cannot concentrate.

"Ask the prisoner what his name is."

"What is your name?"

The prisoner reports that his name is Bung. The language

startles Hawkins. He does not understand this language, except the first ten numbers of counting, and the words for yes and no. With Sergeant Tree helping him with the spelling, Hawkins enters the name into the proper blank.

"Ask the prisoner where he lives."

"Where do you live?"

The prisoner wails a string of language. He begins to weep as he speaks, and he goes on like this, swelling up the small room with the sound of his voice until he sees a warning twitch of the interpreter's hand. He stops immediately, as though corked. One of the Police Chief's pigs is snuffling over the ground just outside the door, rooting for scraps of food.

"What did he say?"

"He says that he is classed as a poor farmer, that he lives in the hamlet near where the soldiers found him, and that he has not seen his wife and his children for four days now and they do not know where he is.

"He says that he is not one of the enemy, although he has seen the enemy many times this year in his hamlet and in the village near his hamlet. He says that he was forced to give rice to the enemy on two different occasions, once at night, and another time during the day, and that he gave rice to the enemy only because they would have shot him if he had not.

"He says that he does not know the names of any of these men. He says that one of the men asked him to join them and to go with them, but that he told this man that he could not join them and go with them because he was poor and because his wife and his children would not be able to live without him to work for them to feed them. He says that the enemy men laughed at him when he said this but that they did not make him go with them when they left his house.

"He says that two days after the night the enemy came and took rice from him, the soldiers came to him in the field where he was working and made him walk with them for many kilometers, and made him climb into the back of a large truck, and put a cloth over his eyes, so that he did not see where the truck carried him and did not know where he was until he was put with some other people in a pen. He says these other people also had been brought in trucks to this place. He says that one of the soldiers hit him in the back with a weapon, because he was afraid at first to climb into the truck.

"He says that he does not have any money, but that he has ten kilos of rice hidden beneath the floor of the kitchen of his house. He says that he would make us the gift of this rice if we would let him go back to his wife and his children."

When he has finished his translation of the prisoner's speech, Sergeant Tree smiles at Mister Hawkins. Hawkins feels that he ought to write something down. He moves the pencil to a corner of the paper and writes down his service number, his Social Security number, the telephone number of his girl friend in Silver Spring, Maryland, and the amount of money he has saved in his allotment account.

"Ask the prisoner in what year he was born."

Hawkins has decided to end the interrogation of this prisoner as quickly as he can. If there is enough time left, he will find an excuse for Sergeant Tree and himself to drive the jeep into the village.

"In what year were you born?"

The prisoner tells the year of his birth.

"Ask the prisoner in what place he was born."

"In what place were you born?"

The prisoner tells the place of his birth.

"Ask the prisoner the name of his wife."

"What is the name of your wife?"

Bung gives the name of his wife.

"Ask the prisoner the names of his parents."

"What are the names of your parents?"

Bung tells the names.

"Ask the prisoner the names of his children."

David Huddle

"What are the names of your children?"

The American takes down these things on the form, painstakingly, with help in the spelling from the interpreter, who has become bored with this. Hawkins fills all the blank spaces on the front of the form. Later, he will add his summary of the interrogation in the space provided on the back.

"Ask the prisoner the name of his hamlet chief."

"What is the name of your hamlet chief?"

The prisoner tells this name, and Hawkins takes it down on the notepaper. Hawkins has been trained to ask these questions. If a prisoner gives one incorrect name, then all names given may be incorrect, all information secured unreliable.

Bung tells the name of his village chief, and the American takes it down. Hawkins tears off this sheet of notepaper and gives it to Sergeant Tree. He asks the interpreter to take this paper to the Police Chief to check if these are the correct names. Sergeant Tree does not like to deal with the Police Chief because the Police Chief treats him as if he were a farmer. But he leaves the room in the manner of someone engaged in important business. Bung continues to stare at the floor, afraid the American will kill him now that they are in this room together, alone.

Hawkins is again trying to think about sex. Again, he is finding it difficult to concentrate. He cannot choose between thinking about sex with his girl friend Suzanne or with a plump girl who works in a souvenir shop in the village. The soft grunting of the pig outside catches his ear, and he finds that he is thinking of having sex with the pig. He takes another sheet of notepaper and begins calculating the number of days he has left to remain in Asia. The number turns out to be one hundred and thirty-three. This distresses him because the last time he calculated the number it was one hundred and thirty-five. He decides to think about food. He thinks of an omelet. He would like to have an omelet. His eyelids begin to close as he considers all the things that he likes to eat: an omelet, chocolate pie, macaroni, cookies, cheeseburgers, black-cherry Jell-O. He has a sudden vivid image of Suzanne's stomach, the path of downy hair to her navel. He stretches the muscles in his legs, and settles into concentration.

The clamor of chickens distracts him. Sergeant Tree has caused this noise by throwing a rock on his way back. The Police Chief refused to speak with him and required him to conduct his business with the secretary, whereas this secretary gloated over the indignity to Sergeant Tree, made many unnecessary delays and complications before letting the interpreter have a copy of the list of hamlet chiefs and village chiefs in the district.

Sergeant Tree enters the room, goes directly to the prisoner, with the toe of his boot kicks the prisoner on the shinbone. The boot hitting bone makes a wooden sound. Hawkins jerks up in his chair, but before he quite understands the situation, Sergeant Tree has shut the door to the small room and has kicked the prisoner's other shinbone. Bung responds with a grunt and holds his shins with his hands, drawing himself tighter into the corner.

"Wait!" The American stands up to restrain Sergeant Tree, but this is not necessary. Sergeant Tree has passed by the prisoner now and has gone to stand at his own side of the table. From underneath his uniform shirt he takes a rubber club, which he has borrowed from one of his policeman friends. He slaps the club on the table.

"He lies!" Sergeant Tree says this with as much evil as he can force into his voice.

"Hold on now. Let's check this out." Hawkins' sense of justice has been touched. He regards the prisoner as a clumsy, hulking sort, obviously not bright, but clearly honest.

"The Police Chief says that he lies!" Sergeant Tree announces. He shows Hawkins the paper listing the names of the hamlet chiefs and the village chiefs. With the door shut, the light in the small room is very dim, and it is difficult to locate the names on the list. Hawkins is disturbed by the darkness, is un-

David Huddle

comfortable being so intimately together with two men. The breath of the interpreter has something sweetish to it. It occurs to Hawkins that now, since the prisoner has lied to them, there will probably not be enough time after the interrogation to take the jeep and drive into the village. This vexes him. He decides there must be something unhealthy in the diet of these people, something that causes this sweet-smelling breath.

Hawkins finds it almost impossible to read the columns of handwriting. He is confused. Sergeant Tree must show him the places on the list where the names of the prisoner's hamlet chief and village chief are written. They agree that the prisoner has given them incorrect names, though Hawkins is not certain of it. He wishes these things were less complicated, and he dreads what he knows must follow. He thinks regretfully of what could have happened if the prisoner had given the correct names: the interrogation would have ended quickly, the prisoner released; he and Sergeant Tree could have driven into the village in the jeep, wearing their sunglasses, with the cool wind whipping past them, dust billowing around the jeep, shoeshine boys shrieking, the girl in the souvenir shop going with him into the back room for a time.

Sergeant Tree goes to the prisoner, kneels on the floor beside him, and takes Bung's face between his hands. Tenderly, he draws the prisoner's head close to his own, and asks, almost absent-mindedly, "Are you one of the enemy?"

"No."

All this strikes Hawkins as vaguely comic, someone saying, "I love you," in a high-school play.

Sergeant Tree spits in the face of the prisoner and then jams the prisoner's head back against the wall. Sergeant Tree stands up quickly, jerks the police club from the table, and starts beating the prisoner with random blows. Bung stays squatted down and covers his head with both arms. He makes a shrill noise.

Hawkins has seen this before in other interrogations. He listens closely, trying to hear everything: little shrieks coming from Sergeant Tree's throat, the chunking sound the rubber club makes. The American recognizes a kind of rightness in this, like the final slapping together of the bellies of a man and a woman.

Sergeant Tree stops. He stands, legs apart, facing the prisoner, his back to Hawkins. Bung keeps his squatting position, his arms crossed over his head.

The door scratches and opens just wide enough to let in a policeman friend of Sergeant Tree's, a skinny, rotten-toothed man, and a small boy. Hawkins has seen this boy and the policeman before. The two of them smile at the American and at Sergeant Tree, whom they admire for his education and for having achieved such an excellent position. Hawkins starts to send them back out, but decides to let them stay. He does not like to be discourteous to Asians.

Sergeant Tree acknowledges the presence of his friend and the boy. He sets the club on the table and removes his uniform shirt and the white T-shirt beneath it. His chest is powerful, but hairless. He catches Bung by the ears and jerks upward until the prisoner stands. Sergeant Tree is much shorter than the prisoner, and this he finds an advantage.

Hawkins notices that the muscles in Sergeant Tree's buttocks are clenched tight, and he admires this, finds it attractive. He has in his mind Suzanne. They are sitting in the back seat of the Oldsmobile. She has removed her stockings and garter belt, and now she slides the panties down from her hips, down her legs, off one foot, keeping them dangling on one ankle, ready to be pulled up quickly in case someone comes to the car and catches them. Hawkins has perfect concentration. He sees her panties glow.

Sergeant Tree tears away the prisoner's shirt, first from one side of his chest and then the other. Bung's mouth sags open now, as though he were about to drool.

274

The boy clutches at the sleeve of the policeman to whisper in his ear. The policeman giggles. They hush when the American glances at them. Hawkins is furious because they have distracted him. He decides that there is no privacy to be had in the entire country.

"Sergeant Tree, send these people out of here, please."

Sergeant Tree gives no sign that he has heard what Hawkins has said. He is poising himself to begin. Letting out a heaving grunt, Sergeant Tree chops with the police club, catching the prisoner directly in the center of the forehead. A flame begins in Bung's brain; he is conscious of a fire, blazing, blinding him. He feels the club touch him twice more, once at his ribs and once at his forearm.

"Are you the enemy?" Sergeant Tree screams.

The policeman and the boy squat beside each other near the door. They whisper to each other as they watch Sergeant Tree settle into the steady, methodical beating. Occasionally he pauses to ask the question again, but he gets no answer.

From a certain height, Hawkins can see that what is happening is profoundly sensible. He sees how deeply he loves these men in this room and how he respects them for the things they are doing. The knowledge rises in him, pushes to reveal itself. He stands up from his chair, virtually at attention.

A loud, hard smack swings the door wide open, and the room is filled with light. The Police Chief stands in the doorway, dressed in a crisp, white shirt, his rimless glasses sparkling. He is a fat man in the way that a good merchant might be fat— solid, confident, commanding. He stands with his hands on his hips, an authority in all matters. The policeman and the boy nod respectfully. The Police Chief walks to the table and picks up the list of hamlet chiefs and village chiefs. He examines this, and then he takes from his shirt pocket another paper, which is also a list of hamlet chiefs and village chiefs. He carries both lists to Sergeant Tree, who is kneeling in front of the prisoner. He shows

Sergeant Tree the mistake he has made in getting a list that is out of date. He places the new list in Sergeant Tree's free hand, and then he takes the rubber club from Sergeant Tree's other hand and slaps it down across the top of Sergeant Tree's head. The Police Chief leaves the room, passing before the American, the policeman, the boy, not speaking nor looking other than to the direction of the door.

It is late afternoon and the rain has come. Hawkins stands inside his tent, looking through the open flap. He likes to look out across the old tennis court at the big lily pond. He has been fond of water since he learned to water-ski. If the rain stops before dark, he will go out to join the policemen and the children who swim and bathe in the lily pond.

Walking out on the highway, with one kilometer still to go before he comes to the village, is Sergeant Tree. He is alone, the highway behind him and in front of him as far as he can see and nothing else around him but rain and the fields of wet, green rice. His head hurts and his arms are weary from the load of rice he carries. When he returned the prisoner to his hamlet, the man's wife made such a fuss Sergeant Tree had to shout at her to make her shut up, and then, while he was inside the prisoner's hut conducting the final arrangements for the prisoner's release, the rain came, and his policemen friends in the jeep left him to manage alone.

The ten kilos of rice he carries are heavy for him, and he would put this load down and leave it, except that he plans to sell the rice and add the money to what he has been saving to buy a .45-caliber pistol like the one Mister Hawkins carries at his hip. Sergeant Tree tries to think about how well received he will be in California because he speaks the American language so well, and how it is likely that he will marry a rich American girl with very large breasts.

The prisoner Bung is delighted by the rain. It brought his

children inside the hut, and the sounds of their fighting with each other make him happy. His wife came to him and touched him. The rice is cooking, and in a half hour his cousin will come, bringing with him the leader and two other members of Bung's squad. They will not be happy that half of their rice was taken by the interpreter to pay the American, but it will not be a disaster for them. The squad leader will be proud of Bung for gathering the information that he has—for he has memorized the guard routines at the police headquarters and at the old French area where the Americans are staying. He has watched all the comings and goings at these places, and he has marked out in his mind the best avenues of approach, the best escape routes, and the best places to set up ambush. Also, he has discovered a way that they can lie in wait and kill the Police Chief. It will occur at the place where the Police Chief goes to urinate every morning at a certain time. Bung has much information inside his head, and he believes he will be praised by the members of his squad. It is even possible that he will receive a commendation from someone very high.

His wife brings the rifle that was hidden, and Bung sets to cleaning it, savoring the smell of the rice his wife places before him and of the American oil he uses on the weapon. He particularly enjoys taking the weapon apart and putting it together again. He is very fast at this.

SHORELINES

Joy Williams

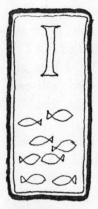want to explain. There are only the two of us, the child and me. I sleep alone. Jace is gone. My hair is wavy, my posture good. I drink a little. Food bores me. It takes so long to eat. Being honest, I must say I drink. I drink, perhaps, more than moderately, but that is why there is so much milk. I have a terrible thirst. Rum and Coke. Grocery wine. Anything that cools. Gin and juices of all sorts. My breasts are always aching, particularly the left, the earnest one, which the baby refuses to favor. First comforts must be learned, I suppose. It's a matter of exposure.

I have tried to be clean about my person since the child. I wash frequently, rinse my breasts before feeding, keep my hands away from my eyes and mouth . . . but it's hard to keep oneself up. I have tried to think only harmonious thoughts since the child, but the sun on the water here, that extravagant white water, the sun brings such dishevelment and confusion.

I am tall. I have a mole by my lip. When I speak, the mole vanishes. I address myself to the child quite frequently. He is an infant, only a few months old. I say things like,

"What would you like for lunch? A marmalade crêpe? A peanut-butter cupcake?"

Naturally, he does not answer. As for myself, I could seldom comply with his agreement. I keep forgetting to buy the ingredients. There was a time when I had everything on hand. I was quite the cook once. Pompano stuffed with pecans. Quiche Lorraine. And curry! I was wonderful with curries. I had such imaginative accompaniments. The whole thing no bigger than a saucer sometimes, yet perfect!

We live in the sun here, on the beach, in the South. It is so hot here. I will tell you exactly how hot it is. It is too hot for orange trees. People plant them but they do not bear. I sleep alone now. I will be honest. Sometimes I wake in the night and realize that I have called upon my body. I am repelled but I do not become distraught. I remove my hands firmly. I raise and lower them to either side of the bed. It seems a little self-conscious, a little staged, to bring my hands away like that. But hands, what do they have to do with any of us?

The heat is the worst at night. I go damp with fever here at night, and I dream. Once I dreamed of baking a bat in the oven. I can't imagine myself dreaming such a thing. I am a sensitive woman. I might have read about it because there are things I know about bats. I am knowledgeable about their eyes. I know that their retinas have only rods and no vascular system. They can only see moving objects. Unlike us, you know.

I try to keep the child cool at night. I give him ice to play with. He accepts everything I have to offer. He is always with me. He is in my care.

I knew when Jace had started the baby. It's true what you've heard. A woman knows.

It has always been Jace only. We were children together. We lived in the same house. It was a big house on the water. Jace remembers it precisely. I remember it not as well. There were eleven people in that house and a dog beneath it, tied night and day to the pilings. Eleven of us and always a baby. It doesn't seem reasonable now when I think on it, but there were always eleven of us and always a baby. The diapers and the tiny clothes, hanging out to dry, for years!

Jace was older than me by a year and a day and I went everywhere with him. My momma tried to bring me around. She said, "One day you're going to be a woman. There are ways you'll have to behave."

But we were just children. It was a place for children and we were using it up. The sharks would come up the inlet in the morning rains and they'd roll so it would seem the water was boiling. Our breath was wonderful. Everything was wonderful. We would box. Underneath the house, with the dog's rope tangling around our legs, Jace and I would box, stripped to the waist. Red and yellow seaweed would stream from the rope. The beams above us were soft blue with mold. Even now, I can feel exactly what it felt like to be cool and out of the sun.

Jace's fists were like flowers.

Jace is thin and quick. He has thick hair but it is almost white. His jeans are white with my washing. I have always done my part. Wherever we went, I planted. If the soil were muck, I would plant vegetables; if dry, herbs; if sandy, strawberries. We always left before they could be harvested. We were always moving on, down the coast. But we always had bread to eat. I made good crusty bread. I had a sourdough starter that was seventy-one years old.

We have always lived on the water. Jace likes to hear it. We have been on all the kinds of water there are in the South. Once we lived in the swamp. The water there was a creamy pink. Air plants covered the trees like tufts of hair. All the life was in the trees, in the nests swinging from high branches.

I didn't care for the swamp, although it's true the sun was no problem there.

In Momma's house, a lemon tree grew outside the window of the baby's room. The fruit hung there for color mostly. Sometimes Momma made a soup. The tree was quite lovely and it flourished. It had been planted over the grease trap of the sink. I am always honest when I can be. It was swill that made it grow.

Here there is nothing of interest outside the child's room. Just the sand and the dunes. The dunes cast no shadow and offer no relief from the sun. A small piece of the Gulf is visible and it flickers like glass. It's as though the water is signaling some message to my child in his crib.

We do not wait for Jace to come back. We do not wait for anything. We do not want anything. Jace, on the other hand, wants and wants. There is nothing he would not accept. He has many trades. Once he was a deep-sea diver. He dove for sponges out of Tarpon Springs. He dove every day, all of one spring and all of one summer. There was a red tide that year that drove people almost mad. Your eyes would swell, your throat would burn. Everything was choking. The water was like chewing gum. The birds went inland. All the fish and turtles died. I wouldn't hear about it. I was always a sensitive woman. Jace would lie in bed, smoking, his brown arms on the white sheets, his white hair on the pressed pillowcases. Yes, everything was spotless once, and in order.

He said, "The fastest fish can't swim out of it. Not even the barracuda."

I wouldn't hear it. I did not like suffering.

"The bottom was covered with fish," he said. "I couldn't see the sponges for the acres of fish."

I began to cry.

"Everything is all right," he said. He held me. "No one cares," he said. "Why are you crying?"

There were other jobs Jace had. He built and drove. He would be gone for a few weeks or a few months and then he would come back. There were some things he didn't tell me.

The beach land here belongs to the Navy. It has belonged to them for many years. Their purpose has been forgotten. There are a few trees, near the road, but they have no bark or green branches. I point this out to the child, directing his gaze to the blasted scenery. "The land is unwholesome," I say. He refuses to agree. I insist, although I am not one for words.

"Horsetail beefwood can't be tolerated here," I tell him, "although horsetail beefwood is all the land naturally bears.

"If they had a decorative bent," I tell him, "they would plant palms, but there are no palms."

The baby's head is a white globe beneath my heart. He does not look. He exhausts me, even though his weight is little more than that of water on my hands. He is a frail child. So many precautions are necessary. My hands grow white from holding him.

I am so relieved that Jace is gone. He has a perfect memory. His mouth was so clean, resting on me, and I was so quiet. But then he'd start talking about Momma's house.

"Wasn't life nice then?" he'd say. "And couldn't we see everything there was to see? And didn't life just make the finest sense?"

Even without Jace, I sometimes feel uneasy. There is something I feel I have not done.

It was the third month I could feel the child best. They move, you know, to face their stars.

There is a small town not far from here. I loathe the town and its people. They are watchful country people. The town's economy is dependent upon the Prison. The Prison is a good neighbor, they say. It is unobtrusive, quiet. When an execution is necessary, the executioner arrives in a white Cadillac and he is unobtrusive too for the Cadillac is an old one and there are a great many white cars here. The cars are white because of the terrible heat. The man in the Cadillac is called the "engineer" and no one claims to know his name.

The townspeople are all very handy. They are all very willing to lend a helping hand. They hire Prison boys to work in their yards. You can always tell the Prison boys. They look so hungry and serene.

Martha is the only one of the townspeople who talks to me. The rest nod or smile. Martha is a comfy woman with a nice complexion, but her hair is the color of pork. She is always touching my arm, directing my attention to things she believes I might have overlooked, a sale on gin, for example, or frozen whipped puddings.

"You might could use a sweet or two," she says. "Fill you out."

Her face is big and friendly and her hands seem clean and dry. She is always talking to me. She talks about her daughter who has not lived with her for many years. The daughter lives in a special home in the next state. Martha says, "She had a bad fever and she stopped being good."

Martha's hand on my shoulder feels like a nurse's hand, intimate and officious. She invites me to her home and I accept, over and over again. She is inviting me in for tea and conversation and I am always opening the door to her home. I am forever entering her rooms, walking endlessly across the shiny wooden floors of her home.

"I don't want to be rich," Martha says. "I want only enough to have a friend over for a piece of pie or a highball. And I would like a frost-free refrigerator. Even in the winter, I have to defrost ours once a week. I have to take everything out and then spread the newspapers and get the bowl and sponge and then I have to put everything back."

"Yes," I say.

Martha's hands are moving among the cheap teacups. "It seems a little senseless," she says.

There are small table fans in the house, stirring the air. The rooms smell of drain cleaner and mold and mildew preventives. When the fans part the curtains to the west, an empty horse stall and a riding ring are visible. Martha crowns my tea with rum, like a friend.

"This is a fine town," Martha says. "Everyone looks out for his neighbor. Even the Prison boys are good boys, most of them up just for stealing copper wire or beating on their women's fellows."

I hold the child tight. You know a mother's fears. He is fascinated by the chopping blades of the little fans, by the roach tablets behind the sofa cushions. Outside, as well, he puts his hands to everything—the thorns on the grapefruit tree, the poisonous oleander, the mottled dumb cane. . . .

"I imagine the wicked arrive at that Prison only occasionally," I say.

"Hardly ever," Martha agrees.

I am trying to explain to you. I am always inside this woman's house. I am always speaking reasonably with this Martha. I am so tired and so sad and I am lying on a bed drinking tea. It is not Martha's bed. It is, I suppose, a bed for her guests. I am lying on a bedspread which is covered by a large embroidered peacock. Underneath the bed is a single medium-sized mixing bowl. In the light socket is a night-light in the shape of a rose. I feel wonderful in this room in many ways. I feel like a column of air. I would like to audition for something. I am so clean inside.

"My husband worries about you," Martha says. She takes the cup away. "We are all good people here," she says. "We all lead good lives."

"What does your husband do, then?" I say. I smile because I do not want her to think I am confused. Actually, I've met the man. He placed his long hands on my stomach, on my thighs.

"We are not unsubtle here," Martha says, tapping her chest.

I met the man and when I met him in this house he was putting in new pine boards over the cement floors. When I arrived, he stopped, but that was what he was doing. He had a gun which shot nails into the concrete. Each nail cost a quarter. The expense distressed Martha and she mentioned it in my hearing. Men resume things, you know. He went back to it. As I lay on the bed, I could hear the gun being fired and I awoke quickly, frightened the noise might awaken the child. You know a mother's presumptions. There was the smell of sawdust and smoke from the nail gun.

"I wouldn't have thought we'd have to worry about you," Martha says unhappily.

When I returned from Martha's house the first time, I passed a farmer traveling on the beach road in his rusty car. Strapped to the roof of the car was a sandhill crane, one wing raised, pumped full of air and sailing in the moonlight. They kill these birds for their meat. The meat, they say, tastes just like chicken. I have found that almost everything tastes like chicken.

There is a garage not far from town where Jace used to buy gas. I stopped there once. There was a large wire meshed cage outside, by the pumps. A sign on it said BABY FLORIDA RATTLERS. Inside were dozens of blue and pink baby rattles on a dirt floor. It gave me a headache. It was such a large cage.

At night I take the child and walk over the beach to the water's edge where it is cool. The child is at peace here, beside the water, and it is here, most likely, where Jace will find us when he comes back. When Jace comes back it will be at night. He always comes in on the heat, at night.

"Darling," I can hear him say, "even as a little boy, I was all there ever was for you."

I can see it quite clearly. I will be on the shoreline, nursing, and Jace will come back on the heat, all careless and easy and "Darling," he'll shout into the wind, into the white roil of water behind us. "Darling, darling," Jace will shout, "where you been, little girl?"

FAMILY PORTRAIT

James S. Reinbold

undin Street is a very old street; it is still brick-paved. A "T" is formed at the top of the steep Lundin Street hill by Dunde Street. During the winter it is impossible to drive up the hill, and the snow and ice make descending treacherous, even on foot. On one side of Lundin Street are houses with small cement porches that are all connected, forming one great row. There is a small corner grocery store at the bottom of the hill. On the other side of the street is a large warehouse. Next to the warehouse is a wire mill. The mill yard is littered with large wooden spools, metal poles, and broken, rusted machine parts. Beyond the mill the street curves. There is a cement bridge over a small creek and then there is another hill. This one is not nearly as steep. Squashed between the mill on the one side and houses on the other is the Corona Hotel.

It is six o'clock in the morning and snowing lightly. Fresh snow has been falling since midnight on a bed of ice. The street-lamps are still burning. The trolley stops at the bottom of the hill and the only passenger gets out. He turns up his collar and says a few words to the conductor about the weather and the steepness of the hill. The trolley lights blink twice and the car moves off slowly, stranding a man in a long grey coat holding a bass fiddle at his side.

His apartment is at the top of the hill: the one with a single light burning in the hall window, and a wife lying awake in the bedroom. Slowly he ascends the hill, slipping and falling down, finally using the bass fiddle like a pick, embedding the metal tip in the ice and inching himself forward.

He stamps his feet on the porch before going inside. The vestibule door he closes quietly and climbs the stairs to the second-floor landing, unlocks the door, and goes inside. He rests the bass fiddle against the wall near the door and removes his overcoat, which he hangs on the closet door. He is dressed in a tuxedo and a ruffled shirt. His shoes are wet but he puts them in the closet. He carries his bass fiddle with him into the bedroom.

"How did it go tonight?" his wife asks as soon as he closes the door.

"As usual, I suppose. We were at the Beauford Hotel. It was a wedding party and lasted until four."

"What time is it now?" she asks.

"About six-thirty," he replies and slips into bed.

FATHER AND TWO SONS

In the backyard of Grandfather's house is a swing made from an old tire. It hangs from a piece of thick rope tied to the low limb of an elm tree. The tire is attached to the rope horizontally so that the swinger sits on top of the tire rather than inside it with his legs stuck through. Under the swing the grass has been scuffed away. A circle of ground with protruding roots remains.

A narrow pavement runs down the center of Grandfather's yard. The garage is set down a few steps at the end of the yard so that only the roof is visible from the house. There are two metal lawn chairs, one under each of the cherry trees. To the left of the pavement there is a grotto with a statue and a bird-bath. Five poles for wash lines run down the right side of the pavement. There are no flowers in the long narrow beds, although the soil has been raked and weeded.

Ellis Velik moves from the kitchen window onto the small back porch. His father is coming up the walk from the garage with a broom and a small cardboard carton. Ellis can hear the lawn mower along the side of the house. His brother will be finished soon.

"Aren't you even going to help sweep up the grass?" his father calls.

Ellis starts back into the kitchen.

"At least give us a hand with the sweeping," his brother says, appearing from around the side of the house. He is sweating, and his white undershirt is stuck to his large round stomach. He is wearing plaid Bermuda shorts.

"Come on, Ellis," he says. "Sweep the grass off the pavement."

Reluctantly Ellis walks to his father to get the broom. The man sits down on one of the chairs and fans himself with his hands.

"Well, come on, get to it," his father says, and waves him away.

The following Friday, instead of sweeping, Ellis goes into the kitchen and sits down at the table, his hands folded. He looks under the table to see that all the red rubber tips on the legs of the aluminum table and chairs are in place. He lifts his end of the table slightly and moves the table to the left, against the wall, but it still wobbles.

The kitchen is clean. The counter space is clear of crumbs and stains and the refrigerator hums. Ellis opens the refrigerator door. It is empty except for a quart of buttermilk, drunk sparingly directly from the container by Mrs. Ritter, the cleaning woman. The metal racks are spotless. There is only a hint of ice along the sides and top of the freezer compartment. The cupboards above the refrigerator and sink are empty and the green shelving paper shines.

Mrs. Ritter does her cleaning every Saturday and receives the following Monday an envelope in the mail containing five dollars. Ellis' father has agreed that the lawn will be cared for, the flowers tended. He has also agreed to run the car for a few minutes when he is at the house. He did this until he had exhausted the gas in the tank.

Grandfather has been dead for ten years, but there is no reason to discontinue the agreement. Every Friday morning, except in the winter or when the weather is too foul, Ellis, his father, and his brother tend the lawn. Every Saturday Mrs. Ritter cleans the house and takes a few sips of buttermilk.

ELLIS VELIK

One Friday Ellis descends the wooden stairs from the kitchen into the basement. He sits on the stool in front of the workbench. The top of the workbench is not wood like the rest of the bench but is a piece of sheet metal cut to fit over the wooden surface. There are metal shavings still on the vise and on the table around the vise. Ellis looks out the cellar window and sees his father and brother. His father is mowing furiously and his brother is trimming along the pavement.

Suspended between the crossbeams and the wooden ceiling of the basement lies Grandfather's bass fiddle, zipped up in the brown cloth case.

He moves away from the workbench and sits on the damp floor with his back against the wall. He glances idly up at the ceiling. There is a lot of discarded material stacked on large pieces of plywood which rest on the beams; piles of wood, old suitcases, cardboard cartons filled with photographs and family albums, and the bass fiddle. The first time Ellis sees it he is not sure what it is. All that he can really see is the butt end of something large with a metal rod poking through a brown cloth case. He stands on a stool to get a better look. Now he sees clearly that it is a bass fiddle, though the pouch on the side is empty of a bow. His grandfather's name is still legible behind the little identification window. He takes the bass fiddle down from the plywood palate and carries it upstairs into the kitchen. He rests for a moment and then carries it out to the back porch.

"I want to take it home," he calls to his father.

For a long time he is afraid to unzip the case and look at the instrument. He has a vague frightened feeling that if he is too occupied with the bass fiddle Grandfather will knock one night at his bedroom door and ask to come in and play it for a while. So he puts the bass fiddle in the closet, but he cannot forget about it.

GRANDMOTHER

What I know of Grandfather Velik I have learned from Grandmother. I never once doubted her sanity, though my father and brother did. One would have to be mad himself to believe stories about an old woman's state of mind. I never questioned her method of imparting information to me either. From the beginning I trusted both her method and her information. To hear it from her, without the embarrassment of having to be in the same room with her, has been a source of comfort when I find minor contradictions in her accounts. These are easily resolved, however, when I take into consideration certain trivialities that I am aware of, that I have experienced firsthand. She once told me that when the bass fiddle was stored the bow was in the pouch.

I believe I would have abandoned this business of the bass fiddle if I would have had to speak to Grandmother face to face.

Her eyes were impossible to look into. By now they must be clouded by cataracts, but my memory of them is so strong that if I saw her today I would still have to hide my face in my hands.

To have only her brain would of course be the ideal situation. When curiosity overwhelmed me or when I felt I needed an immediate response, there would be no waiting. As it is, I have the second-best way: the telephone. True, there are drawbacks, but when I think for a moment of the prospect of speaking to her face to face, I know the telephone is the only possible alternative.

The old woman sleeps nearly twenty hours a day, a habit which baffles me. I sold medical supplies door to door for seven years, and met many old people. As I remember, they were all insomniacs. When I was a child, we lived near an old people's home and it was always comforting to me when restlessness awoke me at three or four in the morning to see lamps burning in the windows of the home. But Grandmother prefers to sleep.

"'I sleep much now, Ellis," she told me. "Please only call me between noon and four."

It took me some time to get accustomed to this but, as with everything else, I have adapted myself to it. I worry about how long Grandmother will continue to consent to speak with me. The fear that one day she will decide to have the telephone removed or that she will decide to remain silent is as persistent as the fear that she will soon be dead. There is sometimes a gurgling sound coming from her end of the line, but I suspect this to be a faulty connection.

I imagine Grandmother standing in the doorway between the bedroom and the empty room where she keeps the telephone. There is a metal folding chair by the telephone, which has been placed on top of a wrought-iron stand. I cannot describe what she looks like standing there, waiting for the ring, for it has been too many years since I saw her.

Why she stands in the doorway waiting for the phone to ring is something else I cannot explain. She could lie quietly in bed, under a quilt, and do needlepoint. She could dust her bureau and the bric-a-brac, or make a cup of tea or bouillon in the kitchen. But she prefers to stand.

When I first began to call her I would suggest that she tell me her address. I could send you a puzzle to work at or some needlepoint, I said. No, she replied, then you would come and visit me. I assured her that it was not my intention to see her. She would not be reasoned with and I dropped the matter entirely.

THE CORONA HOTEL

At the age of forty I left my father's house. It was a minor irritation that started a chain of events which led me to the Corona Hotel.

Let me say that life in my father's house was by no means uncomfortable or strained. I had my own life to live and did so in my area of the house. My father and brother rarely bothered me. The only other person in the large house was a widow by the name of Mrs. Lutz who did the cooking and cleaning. She lived several doors down the street. In many ways she was essential to the household but I never cared for her, and I never allowed her to clean my room. I felt she was a meddlesome woman and that she did the cooking and cleaning only to see what went on in my father's house. I had discovered her looking in drawers when she thought there was no one in the house. She always pretended it was a part of her cleaning duties and protested to my father that she did not appreciate being spied on, as she called it, when she was working. I was angry at my father for not knowing what kind of a woman Mrs. Lutz was, and horrified one evening when he said that he was considering proposing marriage to her. Fortunately my brother intervened in that matter and dissuaded him, albeit for completely different reasons than my own.

The evening meal was the only meal that the woman prepared, and it was always ready at six. I ate in silence because as far as I was concerned we were all talked out. My father and my brother, however, saw it differently. They always had a list of things to chatter about. I imagined them discussing their topics all day long in the living room, on the porch, or wherever they went. They waited until dinner to summarize their conclusions; for my benefit, I am sure, although I never responded with more than a grunt or a sigh. They needed no encouragement, and proceeded as planned every evening.

One evening, after an especially depressing day—the weather contributed greatly to my sour disposition and it was unseasonably cold and raining—they began their usual summations. Any other day I would have been able to tolerate them and if that had proved impossible I would have excused myself; but not that evening. Enraged, I threw down my fork and shouted:

"You are both fools. Him I can understand"—I pointed to my father—"he has years of experience. But you are not yet fifty and already are being fitted for the dunce's cap."

I had taken my stand, and committed myself to only one course of action. They sat looking at each other so surprised I had spoken that they were only vaguely aware of what I had said. The two of them turned their forks in their hands waiting for me to continue. But I was too angry to say more. I turned from them for the last time and left the room with bits of peas still clinging to my small goatee.

They were just finishing dessert, and had begun anew their summations, when I shut the front door and walked out to the edge of the sidewalk. I had my two suitcases and Grandfather's bass fiddle. I started walking toward the bus stop still furious, unconcerned with the rain and cold. I believe my napkin was still tucked in my collar. The rain was coming down harder and although I did not take my eyes from the pavement I was sure that Mrs. Lutz was watching me from the window. Two blocks from the house I glanced up and saw a cab coming in my direction. Because of the bass fiddle the driver put my suitcases up in the front seat with him and I was obliged to sit with the huge instrument in the back.

The driver turned around to me, waiting for me to tell him my destination.

"The Corona Hotel," I said.

"Are you a musician?" the driver asked.

"No," I replied. "It belonged to my grandfather."

By the time we reached the Corona Hotel the rain had stopped. I carried my luggage and the bass fiddle into the lobby. Before I could speak the clerk pushed the register toward me.

"Do you have anything besides single rooms?" I asked.

He looked at me questioningly.

"I plan to stay for some time," I explained. "I would like a suite if that is possible."

He looked at my name as if he were trying to discern what kind of person I was. If I had not been so tired I believe I would have walked out.

"The elevator doesn't work," he said finally. "You have to use the stairs over there."

My new accommodations seemed as though they would be impossible to accept. I regretted my bold statement to the desk clerk and felt that I would suffer new embarrassment when I went down in the morning to say I was leaving.

The Corona Hotel was a large, square, wooden structure of four floors at the bottom of the Lundin Street hill. Only the rooms on the first three floors were rented, however. It was a wonder that the whole place was not closed down. I do not believe there was one solid piece of wood in the whole building.

There was a wide porch, another hazard, that ran across the entire front of the hotel. It was littered with chairs and small tables.

Inside the hotel, to the right of the lobby, was a dining room and bar. This room was filled with an odd assortment of unmatched tables and chairs though there were never more than five people in it at one time. On the other side of the lobby was a sitting room, about the same size as the dining room. Thick curtains and drawn shades kept in the dimness and cigar smoke. The chairs and sofas that were scattered about were pocked with burns. From between two large green plants in the sitting room the stairs wound up to the rooms above.

My suite, one of two, was on the second floor. I had two rooms and what is sometimes called a half bath—a washbasin and toilet. I had to go down to the end of the hall when I wanted to take a shower. I did not do this often for I found my washbasin to be sufficient. My rooms were in the front portion of the hotel so I was offered a view of Lundin Street.

It was coincidental, I remember saying to Hadler, the desk clerk, some weeks after I moved in, that my grandfather had lived at the top of the hill. I also told him that at that time my grandfather played in a dance orchestra which was much in demand for private parties and large gatherings.

A man named Jenkins was the other permanent lodger. The rest of the rooms were occupied by transients I seldom saw. It would have seemed that Jenkins and I should have been on better terms than we were but I could not stand to be around him. His rooms were on the third floor immediately above mine. Often I would be awakened late at night by the sound of him retching in his basin. It was not from an illness but from gluttony. The man was crude, loud, and without hint of sensibility. I avoided him as best I could, but there was little escape when he rapped on my door and invited himself in for conversation. I was as curt as possible, but his feelings were either so warped or so submerged in that great sea of flesh that he seemed unaware of the strain. These impositions usually lasted for about two hours. For a while I tried to keep him out. I would not answer his persistent knocking or I would shout through the door that I was ill. Unfortunately these served as only temporary stays, and in a week or so his visits began anew. Finally I resigned myself to them, and endured him as best I could.

I recall the day when Jenkins registered at the Corona Hotel. It was midafternoon and I was in the dining room having a late lunch. It is a habit of mine to look up when someone comes into a room or to observe anyone moving about nearby. A quick, unobtrusive glance is usually enough to satisfy me and then I resume my business. This time I found myself staring. I have seen fat people, and a great many fatter than this man was, but I had never seen a fat person move as this man did. He was very nervous for some reason and his short fat fingers constantly searched his pockets, of which he seemed to have a great many. He sought first a card, then his billfold, then another purse for change. After this he checked all his pockets again to make sure he had replaced all the items correctly. His only luggage was a small leather suitcase, secured by two bands with buckles. I was hoping he would come into the dining room so I could watch him eat, but he went upstairs.

I finished my lunch and inquired at the desk who the new boarder was. I was by this time on friendly terms with Hadler and had forgiven him for his behavior on the day I registered.

"Jenkins," Hadler said to me, still looking at the man's peculiar handwriting. "I don't believe I've ever seen a man as fat as that."

"I have, Hadler," I said. "Though I've never seen one move around like this Jenkins. Did he take a room just for the night?"

"No, he took the suite on the third floor," Hadler said.

"Oh, so he intends to stay?" I replied.

"Perhaps he won't stay too long," Hadler said.

That evening I showered and was drying myself when I heard a faint rapping on the door. It was a large bathroom with several stalls and washbasins with mirrors, like a bathroom you would expect to find in a clubhouse or a gymnasium. Whenever I used this bathroom I locked the door, even though there was room inside for several men to shower or shave. I preferred to attend to myself in private. The rapping on the door continued and I heard the knob being tried.

"Occupied," I called out.

"Who is it? Who is in there?" the voice called back.

"Occupied," I repeated. "What business who it is!"

The would-be intruder stood at the door for some time. I listened intently, waiting for him to make the next move. The door was tried again and then I distinguished footsteps trailing away from the door and back down the hall. I thought for a moment that the strange voice might belong to the new boarder. My assumption was correct for as soon as I emerged from the bathroom I saw him coming down the hall. I walked past him slowly and turned around to watch him go into the bathroom.

As I lay in bed that night the idea of seeing this fat Jenkins disrobing and then showering struck me as particularly interesting. The more I thought about it, the more I felt that I had to see Jenkins naked. To surprise him in the bathroom seemed out of the question. He might easily become suspicious of my motives: fat people possess a strange vanity. I decided that I should become familiar with him and hope that when comfortable with me he might change into other clothes in my presence. But getting to know the man by hours of tedious conversation would be too distressing; besides, he might never disrobe in front of anyone, not even members of his own family. I went to sleep perplexed.

302

Sometime later I discovered that it was possible, when shaving or washing at one of the sinks in the bathroom, to see clearly into the shower area by positioning oneself at the proper angle in front of the mirror. The stalls themselves were not visible, only the area of the lockers and benches—the very area where one changed!

For me to be in the bathroom at approximately the same time as Jenkins was not a difficult matter to arrange. I was well aware of his comings and goings and knew that he showered on Wednesday and Friday. On the pretense of shaving I stationed myself in the bathroom about seven the following Friday evening. I left the door unlocked. Jenkins entered a few minutes later.

"Hello, Jenkins," I said cheerily, almost betraying myself. I looked away quickly and continued lathering my face.

"Good evening, Velik," he replied.

As he padded by me I noticed that he had removed his shoes and was wearing a pair of new leather lounging slippers.

Jenkins sat on the edge of the bench, bent forward slightly with his elbows on his knees, resting for a moment to catch his breath. He slipped off his suit coat and placed it beside him. With considerable effort he then crossed his left leg over his right knee and removed his slipper and sock. His breathing was strained. He repeated the process with his right foot after another brief rest. Rising only slightly, he was able to slip his trousers down to his knees. He sat back down on the bench and with his hands and a little shuffling of his legs the trousers fell down to his ankles. Lifting his feet out of them, he slid the trousers aside. Still seated he unbuttoned and took off his shirt, placing it on the bench beside him on top of his coat. He was beginning to perspire freely. Then he put his hands on his knees and arched his back. I was sure that he would soon topple over and I would have to help him get back on the bench again.

Otherwise, he would remain on his back, grasping at the air with his limbs, like a great sea turtle.

He was naked now except for his underwear. Instead of pulling his undershirt up over his head with crossed arms, he pulled his arms out first and then twisted the garment ferociously from his head. There were little swirls of black hair around his brown nipples and a great number of moles on his chest. His white, sticky flesh seemed to roll from his breasts downward, flowing over his undershorts. As soon as he had stepped out of his undershorts he turned his back on me and began arranging his clothes on the bench. I was able to get a good look at his nearly hairless legs. They were thin and it was a wonder to me how they could support and carry that huge torso. Despite his great weight, his buttocks were lean, and hung like drooping breasts. They were dotted with pimples and more moles.

I toweled my face dry and went back to my room. I doubt that Jenkins ever realized I was so familiar with his body, and it took all my power to resist recounting to him that evening in the bathroom. He would have denied remembering the occasion, I am sure, but had he pressed me I could have proved my bold pronouncement with the details of his body. This was my defense against him. When his presence was unduly troubling I would allow my thoughts to go back to that evening and repeat it all in detail. That was enough to put my mind at rest.

GRANDFATHER'S BASS FIDDLE

It was obvious which chair Jenkins sat in when he visited me. The cushion sagged and the springs no longer responded. I never gave up hoping this discomfort would end his visits. In that regard, I always directed him to that chair with my usual welcome.

I had stopped offering him the candies and mints I sometimes kept around. He was never satisfied to have three or four. If more were not offered, he took them. He once consumed an entire jar of green mints without a moment's hesitation.

Near the end of my stay at the Corona I was leaving my room to go downstairs to get the evening newspaper, a little errand which had become part of my daily routine. When I got to my door and was preparing to lock it, I discovered that my key was not in my pocket. I searched my other pockets but without success. After a few frightened moments I spied the key over on my desk. Rather than go back into the room and get it, I decided to leave the door unlocked. It only took a few minutes to slip downstairs, get the paper, and return, I thought to myself. This was the only time I left my door unlocked, and it proved a regrettable breach of habit. I paid for the paper and was about to stop for a cup of coffee, but my having left the door un-locked created in me such an uneasy feeling that I walked on by the dining room and hastened my step up the stairs.

When I entered my room I found Jenkins with his head in my closet. He was neither surprised nor embarrassed when I came in, but promptly closed the closet door. He pointed to the news-paper under my arm and said:

"Any news on the bright side today, Velik?"

When I did not reply, he tried to humor me:

"You didn't answer when I knocked and the door was open. I suspected that perhaps you had hung yourself in the closet."

"I don't appreciate someone poking around in my room, es-pecially you," I shouted.

"Come on, Velik," Jenkins continued calmly. "We're friends, we've got nothing to hide."

That was true enough in his case. He had laid his past out for me and displayed it just as nakedly as he had his huge body that day in the bathroom. As for myself, I had told him nothing and had vowed never to do so. I stood looking out the window with my back turned to him, hoping that this display of anger would send him away. But he sat down in his chair, and I listened to his heavy breathing.

"What's that large case in your closet?" he asked finally, as I was afraid he would.

"None of your business," I snapped.

He pressed me further:

"Is it an instrument of some sort?"

I sat down in the other chair.

"Yes," I said, plucking at my goatee. "It is an instrument. It is my grandfather's bass fiddle."

I could see that he was pleased at himself for what he thought was a clever deduction.

"It must be quite old, then," he said.

I related to him how I had discovered the instrument some thirty years before in the basement of my grandfather's house. I explained how I had moved it to my father's house and then to the Corona. I did not go into the story of Grandmother or any of the details of life at my father's house. In effect, I had told him nothing of consequence.

Despite my reluctance Jenkins persuaded me to take the bass fiddle out of the closet. He wanted to get a better look at it. Perhaps it was worth some money, he said. I went hesitantly to the closet. I laid the bass fiddle on the bed gently and unzipped the brown cloth case which had protected the instrument for so many years. When I parted the case from the fiddle, it seemed as though I were removing its skin.

Jenkins was standing at the foot of the bed with his hands on his hips. He examined it and then said that the instrument was too abused to be worth any money. He wanted to know why the bow was missing. I told him that it was missing from the first, that when I discovered the instrument the bow pouch was empty.

For some reason I never returned the bass fiddle to the closet. Instead I rested it in a corner of my bedroom. I even went out

306

one day and bought a used bow which I placed either on the chair beside the instrument or hung from one of the pegs.

LUNDIN STREET

Winter came early and without warning. Nearly all traffic stopped during the heavy snowfalls, and Lundin Street was closed for weeks at a time because of the hill. From my window the houses across the street seemed greyer than before, and even though lights burned inside and the chimneys smoked they all seemed cold.

I awoke one morning shivering more than usual and was unable to go back to sleep. Even when there was heat, the wind and cold prevailed. I pulled my blanket around me and sat up in bed. The bass fiddle seemed larger than usual in the odd, early-morning light and I had the same feeling of foreboding I often experienced as a child. Once again I tried to go back to sleep but it was useless. My body shook with cold and fear.

About six o'clock I got out of bed. I kept the blanket wrapped around me, and went to the window. It was snowing, and the wind was beginning to gust. The streetlamps were still burning, although dawn was lighting the morning. The street was deserted. In the distance I heard the Harrison Street trolley change over to Lundin Street and in a few moments it passed slowly under my window, plowing through the snow. I watched it stop at the bottom of the hill, unable to go any farther. One man got out. He turned up his collar and talked to the conductor for a while and then looked over at the hotel. The trolley lights blinked and then the car moved backwards, past my window and around the corner out of view. The man stood in the middle of the street as if he were waiting for someone. Then he began climbing the hill.

THE WIDOW
CHING,
LADY PIRATE

Jorge Luis Borges

Translated from the Spanish by Norman Thomas di Giovanni

ny mention of pirates of the fair sex runs the immediate risk of awakening painful memories of the neighborhood production of some faded musical comedy, with its chorus line of obvious housewives posing as pirates and hoofing it on a briny deep of unmistakable cardboard. Nonetheless, lady pirates there have been—women skilled in the handling of ships, in the captaincy of brutish crews, and in the pursuit and plunder of seagoing vessels. One such was Mary Read, who once declared that the profession of pirate was not for everyone, and that to engage in it with dignity one had, like her, to be a man of courage. At the flamboyant outset of her career, when as yet she captained no crew, one of her lovers was wronged by the ship's bully. Challenging the fellow to a duel, Mary took him on with both hands, according to the time-honored custom of the West Indies—unwieldy and none-too-sure flintlock in the left, trusty cutlass in the right. The pistol misfired, but the sword behaved as it should. . . . Along about 1720, Mary Read's daring career was cut short by a Spanish gallows at St. Jago de la Vega, in Jamaica.

Another lady buccaneer of those same seas was Anne Bonney, a good-looking, boisterous Irishwoman, with high breasts and fiery red hair, who was always among the first to risk her neck boarding a prize. She was a shipmate and, in the end, gallows mate of Mary Read; Anne's lover, Captain John Rackam, sported a noose on that occasion, too. Contemptuous of him, Anne came up with this harsh variant of Aisha's reproach of Boabdil: "If you had fought like a Man, you need not have been hang'd like a Dog."

A third member of this sisterhood, more venturesome and longer-lived than the others, was a lady pirate who operated in Asian waters, all the way from the Yellow Sea to the rivers of the Annam coast. I speak of the veteran widow Ching.

THE APPRENTICE YEARS

Around 1797, the shareholders of the many pirate squadrons of the China seas formed a combine, to which they named as admiral a man altogether tried and true—a certain Ching. So severe was this Ching, so exemplary in his sacking of the coasts, that the terror-stricken inhabitants of eighty seaboard towns, with gifts and tears, implored imperial assistance. Their pitiful appeal did not go unheard: they were ordered to put their villages to the torch, forget their fishing chores, migrate inland, and there take up the unfamiliar science of agriculture. All this they did, so that the thwarted invaders found nothing but deserted coasts. As a result, the pirates were forced to switch to preying on ships, a form of depredation which, since it seriously hampered trade, proved even more obnoxious to the authorities than the previous one. The imperial government was quick to act, ordering the former fishermen to abandon plow and yoke and mend their nets and oars. True to their old fears, however, these fishermen rose up in revolt, and the authorities set upon another course—that of pardoning Ching by appointing him Master of the Royal Stables. Ching was about to accept the bribe. Finding this out in time, the shareholders made their righteous indignation evident in a plate of poisoned greens, cooked with rice. The morsel proving deadly, the onetime admiral and would-be Master of the Royal Stables gave up his ghost to the gods of the sea. His widow, transfigured by this twofold double-dealing, called the pirate crews together, explained to them the whole involved affair, and urged them to reject both the emperor's deceitful pardon and the unpleasant service rendered by the poison-dabbling shareholders. She proposed, instead, the plundering of ships on their own account and the election of a new admiral.

The person chosen was the widow Ching. She was a clinging woman, with sleepy eyes and a smile full of decayed teeth. Her blackish, oiled hair shone brighter than her eyes. Under her sober orders, the ships embarked upon danger and the high seas.

THE COMMAND

Thirteen years of systematic adventure ensued. Six squadrons made up the fleet, each flying a banner of a different color—red, yellow, green, black, purple, and one (the flagship's) emblazoned with a serpent. The captains were known by such names as "Bird and Stone," "Scourge of the Eastern Sea," "Jewel of the Whole Crew," "Wave with Many Fishes," and "Sun on High." The code of rules, drawn up by the widow Ching herself, is of an unappealable severity, and its straightforward, laconic style is utterly lacking in the faded flowers of rhetoric that lend a rather absurd loftiness to the style of Chinese officialdom, of which we shall presently offer an alarming specimen or two. For now, I copy out a few articles of the widow's code:

All goods transshipped from enemy vessels will be entered in a register and kept in a storehouse. Of this stock, the pirate will receive for himself out of ten parts, only two; the rest shall belong to the storehouse, called the general fund. Violation of this ordinance will be punishable by death.

The punishment of the pirate who abandons his post without permission will be perforation of the ears in the presence of the whole fleet; repeating the same, he will suffer death.

Commerce with captive women taken in the villages is prohibited on deck; permission to use violence against any woman must first be requested of the ship's purser, and then carried out only in the ship's hold. Violation of this ordinance will be punishable by death.

Information extracted from prisoners affirms that the fare of these pirates consisted chiefly of ship biscuits, rats fattened on human flesh, and boiled rice, and that, on days of battle, crew members used to mix gunpowder with their liquor. With card games and loaded dice, with the metal square and bowl of fantan, with the little lamp and the pipe dreams of opium, they whiled away the time. Their favorite weapons were a pair of short swords, used one in each hand. Before seizing another ship, they sprinkled their cheekbones and bodies with an infusion of garlic water, which they considered a certain charm against shot.

Each crewman traveled with his wife, but the captain sailed with a harem, which was five or six in number and which, in victory, was always replenished.

KIA-KING, THE YOUNG EMPEROR, SPEAKS

Somewhere around the middle of 1809, there was made public an imperial decree, of which I transcribe the first and last parts. Its style was widely criticized. It ran:

Men who are cursed and evil, men capable of profaning bread, men who pay no heed to the clamor of the tax collector or the orphan, men in whose undergarments are stitched the phoenix and the dragon, men who deny the great truths of printed books, men who allow their tears to run toward the North—all these are disrupting the commerce of our rivers and the age-old intimacy of our seas. In unsound, unseaworthy craft, they are tossed by storms both night and day. Nor is their object one of benevolence: they are not and never were the true friends of the seafarer. Far from lending him their aid, they swoop down on him most viciously, inviting him to wrack and ruin, inviting him to death. In such wise do they violate the natural laws of the Universe that rivers overflow their banks, vast acreages are drowned, sons are pitted against fathers, and even the roots of rain and drought are altered. . . .

. . . In consequence, Admiral Kwo-lang, I leave to your hand the administration of punishment. Never forget that clemency is a prerogative of the throne and that it would be presumptuous of a subject to endeavor to assume such a privilege. Therefore, be merciless, be impartial, be obeyed, be victorious.

The incidental reference to unseaworthy vessels was, of course, false. Its aim was to encourage Kwo-lang's expedition. Some ninety days later, the forces of the widow Ching came face-to-face with those of the Middle Kingdom. Nearly a thousand ships joined battle, fighting from early morning until late evening. A mixed chorus of bells, drums, curses, gongs, and prophecies, along with the report of the great ordnance, accompanied the action. The emperor's forces were sundered. Neither the proscribed clemency nor the recommended cruelty had occasion to be exercised. Kwo-lang observed a rite that our present-day military, in defeat, choose to ignore—suicide.

THE TERRORIZED RIVERBANKS

The proud widow's six hundred war junks and forty thousand victorious pirates then sailed up the mouths of the Si'kiang, and to port and starboard they multiplied fires and loathsome revels and orphans. Entire villages were burned to the ground. In one of them alone, the number of prisoners passed a thousand. A hundred and twenty women who sought the confused refuge of neighboring reed fields and paddies were given away by a crying baby and later sold into slavery in Macao. Although at some remove, the tears and bereavement wreaked by this depredation came to the attention of Kia-king, the Son of Heaven. Certain historians contend that this outcry pained him less than the disaster that befell his punitive expedition. The truth is that he organized a second expedition, awesome in banners, in sailors, in soldiers, in the engines of war, in provisions, in augurs, and in astrologers. The command this time fell upon one Ting-kwei. The fearful multitude of ships sailed into the delta of the Si'kiang closing off passage to the pirate squadron. The widow fitted out for battle. She knew it would be difficult, even desperate; night after night and month after month of plundering and idleness had weakened her men. The opening of battle was delayed. Lazily, the sun rose and set upon the rippling reeds. Men and their weapons were waiting. Noons were heavy, afternoons endless.

THE DRAGON AND THE FOX

And yet, each evening, high, shiftless flocks of airy dragons rose from the ships of the imperial squadron and came gently to rest on the enemy decks and surrounding waters. They were lightweight constructions of rice paper and strips of reed, akin to comets, and their silvery or reddish sides repeated identical characters. The widow anxiously studied this regular stream of meteors and read in them the long and perplexing fable of a dragon which had always given protection to a fox, despite the fox's long ingratitude and repeated transgressions. The moon grew slender in the sky, and each evening the paper and reed figures brought the same story, with almost imperceptible variants. The widow was distressed, and she sank deep into thought. When the moon was full in the sky and in the reddish water, the story seemed to reach its end. Nobody was able to predict whether limitless pardon or limitless punishment would descend upon the fox, but the inexorable end drew near. The widow came to an understanding. She threw her two short swords into the river, kneeled in the bottom of a small boat, and ordered herself rowed to the imperial flagship.

It was dark; the sky was filled with dragons—this time, yellow ones. On climbing aboard, the widow murmured a brief sentence. "The fox seeks the dragon's wing," she said.

THE APOTHEOSIS

It is a matter of history that the fox received her pardon and devoted her lingering years to the opium trade. She also left off being the widow, assuming a name which in English means "Luster of Instruction."

From this period [wrote one Chinese chronicler lyrically], *ships began to pass and repass in tranquillity. All became quiet on the rivers and tranquil on the four seas. Men sold their weapons and bought oxen to plow their fields. They buried sacrifices, said prayers on the tops of hills, and rejoiced themselves by singing behind screens during the daytime.*

FACING THE
FORESTS

A. B. Yehoshua

Translated from the Hebrew by Miriam Arad

nother winter lost in fog. As usual he did nothing; postponed appointments, left letters unwritten. Words weary him; his own, others', words. He drifts from one rented room to another, rootless, jobless. But for occasional tutoring of backward children he would starve to death. He is approaching thirty and a bald spot crowns his wilting head. His eyesight blurs; his dreams are dull. Unchanging they are, uneventful: a yellow waste where a few stunted trees may spring up in a moment of grace, and a naked woman.

Sometimes, at noon, returning from their offices, friends encounter him in the street: a grey moth in search of its first meal.

Solitude is what he needs.

He drops his arms to his sides in a gesture of despair, backs up against the nearest wall, crosses his legs and pleads in a whisper:

"But where? Go on, tell me, where?"

For, look, he is craving solitude.

They catch hold of him in the street, their eyes sparkling: "Well, your lordship, we've found the solution to your lordship's problem at last." And he is quick to show an expectant eagerness, though cunning enough to leave means of retreat.

"What?"

The function of forest scout. Fire-watcher. Yes, it's something new. A dream of a job, a plum. Utter, profound solitude. There he will be able to scrape together whatever is falling apart.

Where did they get the idea?

From the papers, yes, from skimming the daily papers.

He is astonished, laughs. What's the idea? Forests? What forests? Since when do we have forests in this country? What do they mean?

But they refuse to smile. They are determined.

He glances at his watch, pretending haste. Will not a single spark light up in him then? For he, too, loathes himself, doesn't he?

And so when spring has set the windows ajar he shows up one morning at the Afforestation Department. A sunny office, a clerk, a typist, several typists. He enters, armed with impressive recommendations, heralded by telephone calls. The man in charge of forests, a worthy character edging his way to old age, is faintly amused (his position permits him as much). Much ado about nothing, about such a marginal job. Hence he is curious about the caller, considers rising to receive him even. The patch of wilderness atop the head of the candidate adds to his stature. The fellow inspires trust, surely, is surely meant for better things.

You certain this is what you want? The observation post is a grim place. Only primitive people can bear such solitude. What is it you wish to do there?

Well, he wishes to look at the forest, of course.

No, he has no family.

Yes, with glasses his vision is sound.

The old manager explains that, in accordance with a certain semi-official agreement, this work is reserved for social cases only and not for, how shall I put it, romantics, ha-ha, intellectuals in search of solitude. However, he is prepared, just this once, to make an exception and include an intellectual among the wretched assortment of his workers. Yes, he is himself getting sick of the social cases, the invalids, the cripples, the cranks. A fire breaks out, these fellows will do nothing till the fire brigade arrives but stand and stare panic-stricken at the flames. Whenever he is forced to send out one such unstable character he stays awake nights thinking what if in an obscure rage, against society or whatever, the fire-watcher should himself set the forest on fire. He feels certain that he, the man in front of him here, though occupied with affairs of the mind, will be sufficiently alive to his duty to abandon his books and fight the fire. Yes, it is a question of moral values.

Sorry, the manager has forgotten why it is this candidate wishes the job?

To look at the forest. To watch for fires.

A secretary is called in.

He is invited to sign a contract for six months: spring, summer (ah, summer is dangerous!), and half the autumn. Discipline, responsibility, vigilance, conditions of dismissal. A hush descends while he runs his eyes over the document. Manager and secretary are ready with pen, but he prefers to sign with his own. He signs several copies. First salary due on April the fifth. He inquires about the size of the forests, the height of trees. To tell the truth, he has never seen a real forest in this country yet. An occasional ancient grove, yes, but he hardly believes (ha-ha-ha) the authorities in charge of afforestation have anything to do with that. Yes, he keeps hearing over the radio about forests being planted to honor this, that, and the other personage. Though apparently one cannot actually see them yet. Trees grow slowly. He understands . . . this arid soil. . . . In other countries, now. . . .

At last he falters. He realizes, has realized from the start, that he has made a blunder, has sensed it from the laughter trembling in the secretary's eyes, from the shock coloring the face of the manager. The candidate has taken a careless step, trampled a tender spot.

What does he mean by small trees? He has obviously failed to use his eyes. Of course there are forests. Real forests. Jungles, no, but forests, yes indeed. If he will pardon the question: What does he know about what happens in this country, anyway? For even when he travels through it he won't bother to take his head out of his book. It's laughable, really, these flat allegations. He, the old man, has come across this kind of talk from young people, but the candidate is rather past that age. If he, the manager, had the time to spare, he could show maps. But soon he will see for himself. There are forests in the hills of Judea, in Galilee, Samaria, elsewhere. Perhaps the candidate's eyesight is dim, after all. Perhaps he needs stronger spectacles. The manager would like to ask the candidate to take spare spectacles with him. The manager would rather not have any more trouble. Good-bye.

Where are they sending him?

A few days later he is back. This time he is received not by the manager, but by an underling. He is being sent to one of the larger forests. He won't be alone there, but with a laborer, an Arab. They feel certain he has no prejudices. Good-bye. Ah yes, departure is on Sunday.

Things happen fast. He severs connections and they come loose with surprising ease. He vacates his room and his landlady is glad of it. He spends the last nights with one of his learned friends, who sets to work at once to prepare him a study schedule. While his zealous friend is busy in one room cramming books into a suitcase, the prospective fire-watcher fondles the beloved wife in another. He is pensive, his hands gentle, there is something of joy in his expectations of the morrow. What shall he study? His friends say: the Crusades. Yes, that would be just right for him. Everyone specializes.

But in the morning, when the Afforestation Department truck comes to fetch him out of his shattered sleep, he suddenly imagines that all this has been set on foot just to get rid of him; and, shivering in the cold morning air, he consoles himself with the thought that this adventure will go the way of all others, be drowned in somnolence. He abandons himself to the jolts and pitches of the truck. The laborers with their hoes and baskets sit huddled away from him in the back of the car. They sense that he belongs to another world. The bald patch, the glasses, are an indication.

Traveling half a day.

The truck leaves the highway, travels over long, alien dirt roads, among nameless new settlements. Laborers alight, others take their place. Everyone receives instructions from the driver, who is the one in command around here. We are going south, are we? Wide country meeting a spring-blue sky. The ground is damp still; clods of earth drop off the truck's tires. It is late in the morning when he discovers the first trees scattered among rocks. Young slender pines, tiny, light green. "Then I was right," he tells himself with a smile. But farther on the trees grow taller. Now the light bursts and splinters. Long shadows steal aboard the truck, like stowaways. People keep changing, and only the driver, the passenger, and his suitcases stay put. The forests grow denser, no more bare patches now. Pines, always, and only the one species, obstinately, unvaryingly. He is tired, dusty, hungry, has long ago lost all sense of direction. The sun is playing him tricks, twisting around him. He does not see where he is going, only what he is leaving behind. At three o'clock the truck is emptied of laborers and only he is left. For a long time the truck climbs over a rugged track. He is cross, his mouth feels dry. In despair he tries to pull a book out of one suitcase, but then the truck stops. The driver gets off, bangs the door, comes round to him and says:

"This is it. Your predecessor's already made off—yesterday.

Your instructions are all up there. You at least can read, for a change."

He hauls himself and his two suitcases down. An odd, charming stone house stands on a hill. Pines of all sizes surround it. He is at a high altitude here, though he cannot yet see everything from where he is. Silence, a silence of trees. The driver stretches his legs, looks around, breathes the air, the light; then suddenly he nods good-bye and climbs back into his cabin and switches the engine on.

He who must stay behind is seized with regret. Despair. What now? Just a minute! He doesn't understand. He rushes at the cab, beats his fist against the door, whispers furiously at the surprised driver.

"But food. . . . What about food?"

It appears that the Arab takes care of everything.

Alone, he trudges uphill, a suitcase in each hand. Gradually the world comes into view. The front door stands open and he enters a large room. Semi-darkness, objects on the floor, food remnants, traces of a child. The despair mounts in him. He lets go of the suitcases and climbs to the second floor. The view! Five hills covered with a dense green growth—pines. A silvery blue horizon with a distant sea. He is instantly excited, on fire, forgetting everything. He is even prepared to change his opinion of the Afforestation Department.

A telephone, binoculars, a sheet covered with instructions. A large desk and an armchair beside it. He settles himself into the chair and reads the instructions five times over, from beginning to end. Then he pulls out his pen and makes a few stylistic corrections. He glances fondly at the black instrument. He is in high spirits. He considers calling up one of his friends in town, saying something tender to one of his aging ladyloves. He might announce his safe arrival, describe the view perhaps. Never has he had a public telephone at his disposal. He lifts the receiver to his ear. An endless purring. He is not familiar with the procedure. He tries dialing.

In vain. The purr remains. At last he dials zero.

The Fire Brigade comes on with a startled, "What's happened?" Real alarm at the other side. (Where, where, confound it!) Before he has said a word, questions rain down on him. How large is the fire? What direction the wind? They are coming at once. He tries to put in a word, stutters, and already they are starting a car over there. Panic grips him. He jumps up, the receiver tight in his hand. With the last words in his power he explains everything. No. There is no fire. There is nothing. Only getting acquainted. He has just arrived. Wanted to get through to town. His name is so-and-so. That is all.

A hush at the other side. The voice changes. This must be the Chief now. Pleased to meet you, sir, we've taken down your name. Have you read all the instructions? Personal calls are quite out of the question. Anyway, you've only just arrived, haven't you? Or is there some urgent need? Your wife? Your children?

No, he has no family.

Well then, why the panic? Lonely? You'll get used to it. Please don't disturb again in the future. Good-bye.

He is tired, hungry. He has risen early, and he is unused to that. This high commanding view makes him dizzy. Needless to add—the silence. He picks up the binoculars, raises them to his eyes. The world leaps close, blurred. Pines lunge at him upright. He adjusts the forest, the hills, the sea horizon. He amuses himself a bit, then lets go of the binoculars and eases into the chair. He has a clear understanding of the job now. Just watching. His eyes grow heavy. He dozes, sleeps perhaps.

Suddenly he wakes—a red light is burning on his glasses. He is bewildered, scared, his senses heavy. The forest has caught fire and he has missed it. He jumps up, his heart beating wildly, grabs the telephone, the binoculars. But then it occurs to him that it is the sun, only the sun setting beyond the trees. He is facing west. Now he knows. He drops back into the chair. He imagines himself deserted in this place, forgotten. His glasses mist over and he takes them off, wipes them.

When dusk falls he hears steps.

An Arab and a little girl are approaching the house. Swiftly he rises to his feet. They notice him, look up and stop in their tracks—startled by the soft, scholarly-looking figure. He bows his head. They walk on but their steps are hesitant now. He goes down to them.

The Arab turns out to be old and dumb. His tongue was cut out during the war. By one of them or one of us? Does it matter? Who knows what the last words that stuck in his throat were? In the dark room, its windows ablaze with the last light, the fire-watcher shakes a heavy hand, bends to pat the child, who flinches, terrified.

The Arab puts on lights. The fire-watcher will sleep upstairs.

The first evening. The weak yellow light of the bulbs is depressing. For the time being he draws comfort only from the wide view, from the soft blue of the sea in the distance and the sun going into it. He sits cramped on his chair and watches the big forest entrusted to his eyes. He imagines fire may break out at any moment. The Arab brings up his supper. An odd taste, but he devours everything, leaves not a morsel. His eyes rove hungrily between the plate and the thick woods. He broods awhile about women, then removes his clothes, opens the suitcase that does not hold the books, takes out his things. It seems a long time since he left town. He wraps himself in blankets, lies facing the forest. What sort of sleep will come to one here? The Arab brings him a cup of coffee to help him stay awake.

The fire-watcher would like to talk to him about something, about the view, about the poor lighting perhaps. He has words left in him still, from the city. But the Arab does not understand.

It is half-past nine—the beginning of night. He struggles against sleep. His eyes close and his conscience tortures him. The binoculars dangle from their strap around his neck, and from time to time he picks them up, lifts them to his eyes, glass clicking against glass. He stares to keep awake, finds himself in the forest, among pines, hunting for flames.

How long does it take for a forest to burn down? Perhaps he will only look every hour, every two hours. Even if the forest should start to burn he would still manage to raise the alarm in time to save the rest. The Arab and his child are asleep, and he is up here, light-headed, between three walls and a void gaping to the sea. He must not roll over onto his other side. He nods, and his sleep is pervaded by the fear of fire, fire stealing upon him unawares. At midnight he transfers himself from bed to chair; it is safer this way. His spine aches, he is crying out for sleep, full of regret, alone against the dark empire swaying before him. Till at last the black hours of the first night pass, till out of the corner of his eye he sees the morning grow among the hills.

Only fatigue makes him stay on after the first night. The days and nights following move as on a screen, a mist lit once every twenty-four hours by the glow of the setting sun. It is not himself but a stranger who wanders those first days between the two stories of the house, the binoculars slung across his chest, chewing on the food left him by the unseen Arab. The heavy responsibility that has suddenly fallen upon his shoulders bewilders him. Hardest of all is the silence. Will he be able to open a book here? The view amazes and enchants him still and he cannot have enough of it. After ten days he can embrace all five hills in one brief glance. He has learned to sleep with his eyes open.

At last he opens the other suitcase, the one with the books. Are not the spring, the summer, and half the autumn still before him? The first day he devotes to sorting the books, spelling out titles, thumbing pages. One can't deny that there is some pleasure in handling the fat, fragrant volumes. The texts are in English, the quotations in Latin. Strange phrases from alien worlds. He worries a little. His subject, the Crusades. He has not gone into particulars yet. "Crusades," he whispers softly to himself and feels joy rising in him at the word, the sound. He feels certain there is some dark issue buried within the subject, that it will startle him, and that it will be just out of this drowsiness which envelops his mind that the matter will be revealed to him.

The following day is spent on pictures. Monks, cardinals; a few kings, thin knights; tiny, villainous Jews. Curious landscapes, maps. He studies them, compares, dozes. That night he is kept off his studies by a gnat. Next morning he opens the first book, reads the author's preface, his grateful acknowledgement. He reads other prefaces, various acknowledgements, publication data. He checks dates. At noon his attention is distracted by an imaginary flame flashing among the trees. He remains tense for hours, excited, searching with the binoculars, his hand on the telephone. At last, toward evening, he discovers that it is only the red dress of the Arab's little daughter who is skipping among the trees. The following day, when he is all set to decipher the first page, his father turns up suddenly with a suitcase in his hand.

"What's happened?" the father asks.

"Nothing. . . . Nothing's happened. . . ."

"But what made you become a forester then?"

"A bit of solitude. . . ."

"Solitude . . ." he marvels, "you want solitude?"

The father bends over the open book, removes his heavy

330

glasses and peers closely at the text. "The Crusades," he murmurs. "Is that what you're engaged on?"

"Yes."

"Aren't I disturbing you in your work? I haven't come to disturb you. . . . I have a few days' leave. . . ."

"No, you're not disturbing me. . . ."

"Magnificent view."

"Yes, magnificent."

"You're thinner. . . ."

"Perhaps."

"Couldn't you study in the libraries?"

Silence. The father sniffs round the room like a little hedgehog. At noon he asks his son:

"Do you think it is lonely here? That you'll find solitude?"

"Yes, what's to disturb me?"

"I'm not going to disturb you."

"Of course not. . . . What makes you think that!"

"I'll go away soon."

"No, don't go. Please stay."

The father stays a week.

In the evening the father tries to become friendly with the Arab and his child. A few words of Arabic have stuck in his memory from the days of his youth, and he will seize any occasion to fill them with meaning. But his pronunciation is unintelligible to the Arab, who only nods his head dully.

They sit together, not speaking. The son cannot read a single line with the father there, even though the father keeps muttering, "Don't bother about me. I'll keep myself in the background." At night the father sleeps on the bed and the firewatcher stretches himself out on the floor. Sometimes the father rises in the night to find his son awake. "Perhaps we could take turns," he says. "You go to sleep on the bed and I'll watch the forest."

In the daytime they change places—the son lies on the bed, the father sits at the desk.

During the last days of his visit the father occupies himself with the Arab. Questions bubble up in him. Who is the man? Where is he from? Who cut his tongue out? Why? Look, he has seen hatred in the man's eyes. Such a creature may set the forest on fire some day. Why not?

On his last day the father is given the binoculars to play with.

Suitcase in hand, back bent, he shakes his son's hand, tears in the eyes of the little father.

"I've been disturbing you, I know I have. . . ."

The son protests, mumbles about the oceans of time still before him—about half the spring, the whole long summer, half the distant autumn.

From his elevated seat he watches his father fumbling for the back of the truck. The driver is rude and impatient with him. When the truck moves off the father waves good-bye to the forest by mistake.

For a week he crawls from line to line over the difficult text. After every sentence he raises his head to look at the forest. He is still awaiting fire. The air grows hot. A haze shimmers above the sea horizon. When the Arab returns at dusk his garments are damp with sweat, the child's gestures tired.

He wonders whether it is still spring, or whether the summer has crept upon the world already. One can gather nothing from the forest, which shows no change. His hearing has grown acute, all his senses keener. The sound of trees whispers incessantly in his ears. His dreams are rich in trees. The women sprout leaves.

His text is difficult, the words distant. It has turned out to be a preface to the preface. Yet he does not skip a single passage. He translates every word, then rewrites the translation in rhyme.

No wonder that by Friday he can count but three pages read, out of thousands to go. "Played out," he whispers to himself and trails his fingertips over the desk. Perhaps he'll take a rest? Bring some order into the chaos of his room? He picks a page off the floor. What is this? The instruction sheet. Full of interest, he reads it once more, discovers a forgotten rule or one added by his own hand, perhaps.

"Let the fire-watcher go out from time to time for a short walk among the trees, in order to sharpen his senses."

His first steps in the forest are like a baby's. He circles the observation post, hugging its walls as though afraid to leave them. Yet the trees attract him. Little by little he ventures among the hills, deeper and deeper. If he should smell burning he will run back.

Here and there the sun appears through the foliage and a traveler among the trees is dappled with flickers of light. The pines stand erect, slim, serious; like a company of new recruits awaiting their commander. His body aches the ache of cramped limbs stretching; his legs are heavy. Suddenly he catches sight of the telephone line, a yellowish wire. Well, so this is his contact with the world. He starts tracing the wire, searching for its origin, is charmed by its pointless twists and loops between the trees. They must have let some joker unwind the drum over the hills.

Suddenly he hears voices. He wavers, stops, sees a little clearing in the wood. The Arab is seated on a pile of rocks, his hoe by his side. The child is talking to him excitedly, describing something with animated gestures. The fire-watcher tiptoes nearer. They are instantly aware of him and fall silent. The Arab jumps up, stands by his hoe as though hiding something. He faces them, wordless. He stands and stares, like a supervisor bothered by some obscure triviality. He smiles absently, his eyes stray, and slowly he withdraws with as much dignity as he can muster.

He has been wandering in the woods for over an hour now and is still making new discoveries. The names of donors, for example. Rocks bear copper plates, brilliantly burnished. He stoops, takes off his glasses, reads: Louis Schwartz of Chicago; the King of Burundi and his People. The names cling to him, like the falling pine needles that slip into his pocket. Name after names sticks to him as he walks, and by the time he reaches the observation post he can recite them all, a smile on his face.

Friday night.

His mind happens to be perfectly lucid at the moment. Clear out on Sunday, he whispers suddenly, and starts humming a snatch of song, inaudibly at first, the sound humming inside him, but soon trilling and rising high to the darkening sky. Strings of light tear the sunset across and he shouts song at it, shrills recklessly, wanton with solitude. He starts one song, stops, plunges into another without change of key. His eyes fill with tears. He hears himself and falls silent.

The Arab and the girl emerge from the cover of the underwood and hurry to the house with bent heads.

He is utterly calm. He has begun counting the trees. Sunday the truck brings him his salary. He is amazed, gushes his thanks to the mocking driver. He takes the money and forgets his plan.

He returns to the books.

Summer. A change has come over him. The heat wells up in him, frightens him. A dry flow of desert wind may rouse the forest to suicide; hence, he redoubles his vigilance, presses the binoculars hard against his eyes, subjects the forest to a strict survey. How far has he come? Some twenty pages are behind him, thousands before. What does he remember? A few words, a bit of a theory, the atmosphere on the eve of the Crusades. He could have studied, could have concentrated, were it not for the gnats. Night after night he extinguishes the lights and sits in the darkness. The words have dropped away from him like husks.

334

Hikers start arriving in the forest. Lone hikers some of them, but mostly they come in groups. He follows them through the binoculars. Various interesting ages. They swarm over the forest, pour in among the trees, calling out to each other, laughing; then they cast off their rucksacks and unburden themselves of as many clothes as possible.

Water is what they want. Water!

He comes down to them, striking them with wonder. The bald head among green pines, the heavy glasses. Indeed, everything indicates an original character.

He stands by the water tap, firm, upright. Everyone begs permission to go upstairs for a look at the view. He consents, joyfully. They crowd into his little room, utter admiring exclamations. He smiles as though he had created it all. They are surprised by the sea. They had never imagined one could view the sea from here. Yet how soon they wish to go! One glance, a cry of admiration, and they grow restless, eager to be away.

Would they be interested in the names inscribed on the rocks? They laugh.

The girls look at him kindly. No, he isn't handsome. But might he not become engraved on one of their hearts?

They light campfires.

They wish to cook their food, to warm themselves. A virtuous alarm strikes him. Tiny flames leap up, smoke blows about the treetops. A fire? Yes and no. He stays glued, through his binoculars, to the lively figures.

Toward evening he goes to explore. He wishes to sound a warning. Soundlessly he draws near the campfires, the figures wreathed in flames. He approaches them unnoticed, and they are startled to discover him beside them. The leader rises at once.

"Yes? What do you want?"

"The fire. . . . Be careful! One spark, and the forest may burn."

Laying their hands on their young hearts they give him their solemn promise to watch with all the eyes shining in a row before him. They will keep within bounds, of course they will, what does he think?

He draws aside. There, among the shadows, in the twilight of the fire, he lingers and lets his eyes rove. The girls, their bare creamy legs, slender toes. The flames crackle and sing, softly, gently. He clenches his fists in pain. If only he could warm his hands a little.

"Like to join us?" they ask politely. His vertical presence is faintly embarrassing.

No, thanks. He can't. He is busy. His studies. They have seen the books, haven't they? He withdraws with measured tread. But as soon as he has vanished from their view, he flings himself behind the trees, hides among the branches. He looks at the fire from afar, at the girls, till everything fades and blankets are spread for sleep. Giggles, shrieks. Before he can begin to think, it will be dawn. Silence is still best. At midnight he feels his way through the trees, back to the observation post. He sits in his place, waiting. One of the figures may be working its way in the darkness toward him. But no, nothing. They are tired, sleeping already.

And it is the same the next day, and all the days following.

From time to time he scribbles in his notebook. Stray thoughts, speculations, musings, outlines of assumptions. Not much. A sentence a day. He would like to gain a hold upon it all indirectly. Yet is doubtful whether he has gained a hold even upon the forest in front of his eyes. Look, here the Arab and the girl are disappearing among the trees, and he cannot find them. Toward evening they emerge from an unforeseen direction as though the forest had conceived them. He smiles at them both, but they recoil.

Ceremonies. A season of ceremonies. The forest turns ceremonial. The trees standing bowed, heavy with honor, take on meaning. White ribbons are strung to delimit new domains. Luxurious automobiles struggle over the rocky roads, a procession. Sometimes they are preceded by a motorcycle mounted by an excited policeman. Personages alight, shambling like black bears. Women flutter around them. Little by little they assemble, crush out cigarettes with their black shoes and fall silent—paying homage to the memory of themselves. A storm of obedient applause breaks out, a gleam of scissors, a flash of photographers, ribbons sag. A plaque is unveiled, a new truth is revealed to the world. A brief tour of the conquered wood, and then the distinguished gathering dissolves into its various vehicles and sallies forth.

Where has the light gone?

In the evening, when the fire-watcher comes down to the drooping ribbons, to the trees, he will find for example: "Donated by the Sackson Children in Honor of Daddy Sackson of Baltimore, a Fond Tribute to his Paternity. End-of-Summer Nineteen-Hundred-and. . . ."

Sometimes, observing from his height, the fire-watcher will notice one of the party darting troubled looks about him, raising his eyes at the trees as though searching for something. It takes many ceremonies before the fire-watcher understands that this is the manager in charge of Afforestation.

Once he goes down to him.

The manager is walking among his distinguished foreign party, is jesting with them in their language. The fire-watcher comes out of the trees. The distinguished party stops, startled. An uneasy silence falls over them.

"What do you want?" demands the manager masterfully.

The fire-watcher gives a weak smile.

"Don't you know me? I'm the watchman. . . . That is to say, the fire-watcher. Employee of yours. . . ."

"Ah!" fist beating against aged forehead, "I didn't recognize you, was alarmed, these tatters have changed your appearance so, this heavy beard. Well, young man, and how is the solitude?"

337

"Solitude?" he wonders.

The manager presents him to the distinguished party. "A scholar."

They smile, troubled, meet his hand with their fingertips, move on. They do not have complete faith in his cleanliness. The manager, on the other hand, looks at him affectionately. A thought crosses his mind and he stays behind a moment.

"Well, so there *are* forests." He grins with good-natured irony.

"Yes," admits the fire-watcher. "Forests, yes . . . but fires, no."

"Fires?" the manager wonders.

"Yes, fires. I spend whole days here sitting and wondering. Such a quiet summer."

"Well, why not? Actually, there hasn't been a fire here for several years now. To tell you the truth, I don't think there has ever been a fire in this forest."

"And I was under the impression. . . ."

"That what?"

"That fires broke out here every other day. By way of illustration, at least. This whole machinery waiting on the alert, is it all for nothing? The fire engines . . . telephone lines . . . the manpower. . . . For months my eyes have been strained with waiting."

"Waiting? Ha ha, what a joke!"

The manager wants to hurry along. But before he goes he would just like to have the fire-watcher's opinion of the Arab. The truck driver has got the idea into his head that the fellow is laying in a stock of kerosene. . . .

The watchman is stirred. "Kerosene?"

"Daresay it's some fancy of that malicious driver. This Arab is a placid kind of fellow, isn't he?"

"Wonderfully placid," agrees the fire-watcher eagerly.

"Because our forest is growing over, well, over a ruined village. . . ."

"A village?"

"A small village."

"A small village?"

"Yes, there used to be some sort of a farmstead here. Arabs. But that is a thing of the past."

Of the past, certainly. What else?

Light springs up between his fingers. What date is today? There is no telling. He could lift the receiver and find out the date from the firemen bent over their fire engines, waiting in some unknown beyond, but he does not want to scare them yet.

He goes down to the tap and sprinkles a few drops of water over his beard. Then he climbs back to his room, snatches up the binoculars, and holds a pre-breakfast inspection. Excitement grips him. The forest filled with smoke? No, the binoculars are to blame. He wipes the lenses with a corner of his grimy shirt. The forest clears up at once. None of the trees has done any real growing overnight.

He goes down again. He picks up the dry loaf of bread and cuts himself a rough slice. He chews rapidly, his eyes roving over a torn strip of newspaper in which tomatoes are wrapped. He has no hunger for news, oh no, but he must keep his eyes in training lest they forget the shape of the printed letter. He returns to his observation post, his mouth struggling with an enormous half-rotten tomato. He sucks, swallows. Silence. He dozes a bit, wakes, looks for a long time at the treetops.

He remembers what he has read up to now perfectly well, forward and backward. The words wave and whirl within him. For the time being, therefore, for the past few weeks, that is, he has been devoting his zeal to one single sheet of paper. A picture? Rather, a map. A map of the area. He will display it on this wall here for the benefit of his successors. Look, he has signed his name already, signed it to begin with, lest he forget.

What is he drawing? Trees. But not only trees. Hills too, also a horizon. He is improving day by day. He might add birds as well; at least, say, those native to the area. What interests him in particular is the village buried beneath the trees. What was it the manager had said?—"A scholar." He strokes the beard and his hand lingers, disentangles a few hairs matted with filth. What time is it? Early still. He reads a line about the attitude of the Pope to the German Kaiser and falls asleep. He wakes with a start. He lights a cigarette, tosses the burning match out into the forest, but the match goes out in midair. He flings the cigarette butt among the trees, it drops on a stone and burns itself out.

He gets up, paces about restlessly. What time is it?

He goes in search of the Arab, to say good morning. He must impress his vigilance upon the man, lest he be murdered some morning between one doze and another. The fire-watcher strides rapidly between the pines. How light his footstep has grown during the long summer months. His soundless appearance startles the two.

"Shalom," he says.

They reply.

The fire-watcher smiles to himself and hurries on as though he were extremely busy.

What does he find one fine day? Small tins filled with kerosene? Yes, hidden. Among the trees. How wonderful! The zeal with which someone has filled tin after tin and covered them up with the girl's old dress. He stoops over the treasure, the still liquid on whose face dead pine needles drift. His reflection floats back at him, together with the faint smell.

Blissfully he returns to the house, opens a can of meat and bolts its contents to the last sliver. He wipes his mouth and spits far out among the branch-filled air. He turns two pages of a book and reads the Cardinal's reply to a Jew's epistle. Funny, these twists and turns of the Latin. He falls asleep, wakes, wipes the dust off the silent telephone. To give him his due—he bestows meticulous care on the equipment that belongs to the Afforestation Department, whereas his own possessions are falling apart.

Wearily he chews his supper. The Arab and his daughter go to bed. Darkness. He turns over a few dark pages, swats a gnat, whistles. Night.

He does not fall asleep.

He is out there, he is counting trees, and at sixty-three the Arab is suddenly in front of him, breathing heavily, his face dull.

And what do you have to say, mister? From where have you sprung now?

The Arab spreads his arms in a gesture.

Yes, yes, he knows! The treasure is three trees ahead. Exactly.

The fire-watcher strides ahead and the Arab follows. Moonlight pours over the branches, makes them transparent. He leads the Arab to the exact place. There.

Here he kneels on the rustling earth. Who will give him back all the empty hours? He heaps up some brown needles, takes a match, lights it, and the match goes out at once. He takes another and cups his hands round it, strikes, and this too flares up and dies. The air is damp and traitorous. He rises. The Arab watches him, a gleam of lunatic hope in his eyes. The fire-watcher picks up a tin of the clear liquid, empties it over the heap of pine needles, tosses in a burning match and leaps up with the surging flame—singed, happy. Stunned, the Arab goes down on his knees. The fire-watcher spread his palms over the flame and the Arab does likewise. Their bodies press in on the fire. He muses, his mind distracted. The fire shows signs of languishing, little by little it dies at his feet. They stomp out the last sparks meticulously. Thus far it was only a lesson. He rises wearily and leaves. The Arab slouches in his wake.

Who is sitting on the chair behind the book-laden desk? The child. Her eyes are wide open. The Arab has put her there to replace the roving fire-watcher. It's an idea.

Strange days follow. The needles seem to fall faster, the sun grows weaker, clouds come to stay and a new wind. The ceremonies are over. The donors have gone back to their countries, the hikers to their work, pupils to their study. His own books lie jumbled in a glow of dust. He is neglecting his duties, has left his chair, his desk, his faithful binoculars, and has begun roving endlessly about the forest, by day and by night; a broken twig in his hand, he slashes at the young tree trunks as he walks. Suddenly he slumps down, rests his head against a shining copper plaque, removes his glasses and peers through the foliage, searches the grey sky. Then he collects himself, jumps up to wander through the wood, among the thistles and rocks. He has spent a whole spring and a long summer, never once properly sleeping, and what wonder is it if these last days should be like a trance?

He has lost all hope of fire. Fire has no hold over this forest. He can therefore afford to stay among the trees, not facing them. In order to soothe his conscience he sits the girl in his chair. It has taken less than a minute to teach her the Hebrew word for "fire." How she has grown up during his stay here! Unexpectedly her limbs have ripened, her filth become a woman's smell. At first her old father had been forced to chain her to the chair, or she would have escaped. Yes, the old Arab has grown very attached to the fire-watcher, follows him wherever he goes. Ever since they hugged the little bonfire, the Arab, too, has grown languid. He has abandoned his hoe. The grass is turning yellow under his feet, the thistles multiply. The fire-watcher will be lying on the ground and see the dusky face thrusting at him through the branches. As a rule he ignores the Arab, continues lying with his eyes on the sky. But sometimes he calls him and the man comes and kneels by his side, his heavy eyes wild with terror and hope.

The fire-watcher talks to him therefore, quietly, reasonably. The Arab listens. Then the Arab explains something with hurried, confused gestures, squirming his severed tongue, tossing his head. He wishes to say that this was his house, that there used to be a village here, that they have hidden it all, buried it in the big forest.

The fire-watcher looks on at this. What is it that rouses such passion in the Arab? A dark affair, no doubt. Gradually he moves away, pretending not to understand. Was there really a village here? He sees nothing but trees.

More and more the Arab clings to him. They sit there, the three of them like a family, in the room on the second floor. The fire-watcher sprawling on the bed, the child chained to the chair, the Arab crouching on the floor. Together they wait for the fire. The forests are dark and strong, a slow-growing world. These are his last days. From time to time he gets up and throws one of the books back into the suitcase, startling the old Arab.

The nights are growing longer. Hot desert winds and raindrops mingle, soft shimmers of lightning over the sea. The last day is come. Tomorrow he will leave this place. He has discharged his duty faithfully. It isn't his fault that no fires have broken out. All the books are packed in the suitcase, scraps of paper litter the floor. The Arab has disappeared, has been missing since yesterday. The child is miserable. From time to time she raises her voice in a thin lament. The fire-watcher is growing worried. At noon the Arab turns up suddenly. The child runs toward him but he takes no notice of her. He turns to the fire-watcher instead, grabs him between two powerful hands and—feeble and soft that he is and suffering from a slight cold—impels him toward the edge of the observation post and explains whatever he can explain to him with no tongue. Perhaps he wishes to throw the fire-watcher down two stories and into the forest. His eyes are burning. But the fire-watcher is serene, unresponsive; he shadows his eyes with his palm, shrugs his shoulders, gives a meaningless little smile. What else is left him?

He collects his clothes and bundles them into the other suitcase.

Toward evening the Arab disappears again. The child has gone to look for him and has come back empty-handed. The fire-watcher prepares supper and sets it before the child, but she cannot bring herself to eat. She scurries off once more into the forest to hunt for her father and returns in despair, by herself. Toward midnight she falls asleep at last. He undresses her and carries the shabby figure to the bed, covers it with the torn blanket. He lingers awhile. Then he returns to his observation post, sits on his chair, sleepy. Where will he be tomorrow? How about saying good-bye to the Fire Brigade? He picks up the receiver. Silence. The line is dead. Not a purr, not a gurgle. The sacred hush has invaded the wire as well.

He smiles contentedly. In the dark forest spread out before him the Arab is moving about like a silent dagger. He sits watching the world as one may watch a great play before the raising of the curtain. A little excitement, a little drowsing in one's seat. Midnight performance.

Then, suddenly—fire. Fire, unforeseen, leaping out of a corner. A long graceful flame. One tree is burning, a tree wrapped in prayer. For a long moment one tree is going through its hour of judgment and surrendering its spirit. He lifts the receiver. Yes, the line is dead. He is leaving here tomorrow.

The loneliness of a single flame in a big forest. He is beginning to worry whether the ground may not be too wet, the thistles too few, the show over after one flame. His eyes are closing. He rises and starts pacing nervously through the room. He starts

344

counting the flames. The Arab is setting the forest on fire at its four corners, rushing through the trees like an evil spirit. The thoroughness with which he goes about his task amazes the fire-watcher. He goes down to look at the child. She is asleep. Back to the observation post—the forest is burning. He ought to run and raise the alarm, call for help. But his movements are so tranquil, his limbs leaden. Downstairs again. He adjusts the blanket over the child, pushes a lock of hair out of her eyes, goes back up, and a blast of hot air blows in his face. A great light out there. Five hills ablaze. Flames surge as in a frenzy high over the trees, roar at the lighted sky. Pines split and crash. Wild excitement sweeps him, rapture. He is happy. The Arab is speaking to him out of the fire, saying everything, everything and at once.

Intense heat wells up from the leisurely burning forest. The fire is turning from vision to fact. He ought to take his two suitcases and disappear.

But he takes only the child.

At dawn, shivering and damp, he emerges from the cover of the rocks, polishes his glasses and lo, five bare black hills, wisps of smoke rising. The observation post juts out over the bare land-scape. A great black demon grinning with white windows. For a moment it seems as though the forest had never burnt down but had simply pulled up its roots and gone off on a journey.

The air is chilly. He adjusts his rumpled clothes, does up the last surviving button, rubs his hands to warm them, then treads softly among the smoking embers.

He hears sounds of people everywhere. Utter destruction. Soot, a tangle of charred timber. Wherever he sets foot a thousand sparks fly. The commemorative plaques alone have survived. There they lie, lustrous in the sun: Louis Premington of New York; the King of Burundi and his People.

He enters the burnt building, climbs the singed stairs. Everything is still glowing hot. He arrives at his room. Shall we start with the books burnt to ashes? Or the contorted telephone? Or perhaps the binoculars fused to a lump? The map of the area has miraculously survived, is only blackened a bit at the edges. Gay fire kittens are still frolicking in the pillow and blankets. He turns his gaze to the five smoking hills, frowns. There, directly under him, at the foot of the building, he sees the manager of the forests, wrapped in an old windbreaker, his face blue with cold. How has this one sprung up here all of a sudden?

The manager throws his grey head back and sends up a look full of hatred. For a few seconds they stay thus, their eyes fixed on each other; at last the fire-watcher gives his employer a smile of recognition and slowly starts down. The manager approaches him with quick mad steps. He would tear him to pieces if he could. He is near collapse with fury and pain. In a choking voice he demands the whole story, at once.

But there is no story, is there? There just isn't anything to tell. All there is is: Suddenly the fire sprang up. I lifted the receiver —the line was dead. That's it. The child had to be saved.

The rest is obvious. Yes, the fire-watcher is sorry about the forest too. He has grown extremely attached to it during the spring, the summer, and half the autumn.

He feels that the manager would like to sink to the ground and beat his head against some rock. The fire-watcher is surprised. The forests are insured, aren't they? At least they ought to be, in his humble and practical opinion. And the fire won't be deducted from the budget of the manager's department, will it? Right now he would very much like to be told about other forest fires. He is willing to bet they were puny ones.

Soon he is surrounded by men in uniform. Though the fire has not been completely tracked down, they have unearthed some startling news.

It has been arson. Yes, arson. The smell of morning dew comes mingled with a smell of kerosene.

The manager is shattered. "Arson?" he turns to the fire-watcher.

The fire-watcher smiles gently.

The investigation is launched at once. First the firemen, who are supposed to write a report. They draw the fire-watcher aside, take out large sheets of paper, ball-points.

"What have you lost in the fire?" they inquire sympathetically.

"Oh, nothing of importance. Some clothes, a few books. Nothing. . . ."

By the time they are through it is far into the morning. The Arab and the child appear from nowhere, led by two policemen. Two sergeants improvise a kind of emergency interrogation cell among the rocks, place the fire-watcher on a stone and start cross-examining him. For hours they persist, and that surprises him—the plodding tenacity, the diligence, page upon written page. A veritable research is being compiled before his eyes. His glasses mist over with sweat. Inside the building they are conducting a simultaneous interrogation of the Arab. Only the questions are audible.

The forest manager dodges back and forth between the two interrogations, adding questions of his own, noting down replies. The interrogators have their subject with his back against the rock, they repeat the same questions over and over. A foul stench rises from the burnt forest, a huge carcass rotting away all around them. The interrogation gains momentum. What did he see? What did he hear? What did he do? It's insulting, this insistence on the plausible as though that were the point.

About noon his questioners change, two new ones appear and start the whole process over again. How humiliating to be interrogated thus, on scorched earth, on rocks, after a sleepless night. He spits, grows angry, loses his temper. He removes his glasses, starts contradicting himself. At three o'clock he breaks in their hands, is prepared to suggest the Arab as a possible clue.

This, of course, is what they have been waiting for. They had suspected the Arab all along, promptly handcuff him, and then all at once everything is rapidly wound up. The police drivers start their cars. The Arab is bundled into one of them. The child clings to him desperately. The fire-watcher walks over to the manager and boldly demands a solution for the child. The other makes no reply. His old eyes wander over the lost forest as though in parting. The fire-watcher repeats his demand in a loud voice. The manager steps nearer.

"What?" he mumbles in a feeble voice, his eyes watery. Suddenly he throws himself at the fire-watcher, attacks him with shriveled fists, hits out at him. With difficulty the policemen pull him back. To be sure, he blames only this one here. Yes, this one with the books, with the dim glasses.

Before he has time to say good-bye to the place, the fire-watcher is being borne away toward town. They dump him on one of the side streets. He enters the first restaurant he comes to and gorges himself. Afterward he paces the streets, bearded, dirty, sunburnt—a savage.

At night, in some shabby hotel room, he is free to have a proper sleep. Except that he will not fall asleep, will only go on drowsing. Green forests will spring up before his troubled eyes.

And so it will be all the days and nights after.

THE LOST CHAPTERS OF *TROUT FISHING IN AMERICA*

Richard Brautigan

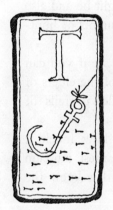

hese two chapters were lost in the late winter, early spring of 1961. I looked all over for them but I couldn't find them anywhere. I haven't the slightest idea why I didn't rewrite them as soon as I realized that they were gone. It's a real puzzler but I didn't and now, eight years later, I've decided to return to the winter that I was twenty-six years old, living on Greenwich Street in San Francisco, married, had an infant daughter and wrote these two chapters toward a vision of America and then lost them. I'm going back there now to see if I can find them.

REMBRANDT CREEK

Rembrandt Creek looked just like its name and it was in lonely country that had very bad winters. The creek started in a high mountain meadow surrounded by pine trees. That was about the only real light that creek ever saw because after it had gathered itself from some small springs in the meadow, it flowed off into the pines and down to a dark tree-tangled canyon that went along the edge of the mountains.

The creek was filled with little trout so wild that they were barely afraid when you walked up to the creek and stood there staring down at them.

I never really went fishing for them in any classical or even functioning sense. The only reason I knew that creek was because that's where we camped when we went deer hunting.

No, it was not a fishing creek for me but just a place where we got water that we needed for our camp but I seemed to carry most of the water that we used and I think I washed a lot of dishes because I was the teen-ager and it was easier to have me do those things than the men who were older and wiser and needed time to think about places where deer might be and also to drink a little whiskey which seemed to aid thoughts of hunting and other things.

"Hey, kid, take your head out of your ass and see if you can do something about these dishes." That was one of the elders of the hunt speaking. His voice is remembered down trails of sound-colored hunting marble.

Often I think about Rembrandt Creek and how much it looked like a painting hanging in the world's largest museum with a roof that went to the stars and galleries that knew the whisk of comets.

I only fished it once.

I didn't have any fishing tackle, just a 30:30 Winchester, so I took an old rusty bent nail and tied some white string onto it like the ghost of my childhood and tried to catch a trout using a piece of deer meat for bait and I almost caught one, too, lifting it out of the water just before it fell off my nail and back into the painting that carried it from my sight, returning it to the Seventeenth Century where it belonged on the easel of a man named Rembrandt.

CARTHAGE SINK

The Carthage River came roaring out of the ground at a fountainhead that was like a wild well. It flowed arrogantly a dozen miles or so through an open canyon and then just disappeared into the ground at a place that was called Carthage Sink.

The river loved to tell everybody (everybody being the sky, the wind, the few trees that grew around there, birds, deer and even the stars if you can believe that) what a great river it was.

"I come roaring from the earth and return roaring to the earth. I am the master of my waters. I am the mother and father of myself. I don't need a single drop of rain. Look at my smooth strong white muscles. I am my own future!"

The Carthage River kept this kind of talking up for thousands of years. Needless to say: Everybody (everybody being the sky, etc.) was bored up to here with that river.

Birds and deer tried to keep away from that part of the country if they could avoid it. The stars had been reduced to playing a waiting game and there was a dramatically noticeable lack of wind in that area, except of course for the Carthage River.

Even the trout that lived there were ashamed of the river and always glad when they died. Anything was better than living in that God-damn bombastic river.

One day the Carthage River in mid-breath telling about how great it was, dried up, "I am the master of my. . . ." It just stopped.

The river couldn't believe it. Not one more drop of water came from the ground and its sink was soon just a trickle dripping back into the ground like the runny nose of a kid.

The Carthage River's pride vanished in an irony of water and the canyon turned into a good mood. Birds suddenly flew all over the place and took a happy look at what had happened and a great wind came up and it even seemed as if the stars were out earlier that night to take a look and then smile beatifically.

There was a summer rainstorm a few miles away in some mountains and the Carthage River begged for the rain to come to its rescue.

"Please," the river said with a voice that was now only the shadow of a whisper. "Help me. I need water for my trout. They're dying. Look at the poor little things."

The storm looked at the trout. The trout were very happy with the way things were now, though they would soon be dead.

The rainstorm made up some incredibly elaborate story about having to visit somebody's grandmother who had a broken ice-cream freezer and somehow lots of rain was needed to repair it. "But maybe in a few months we might get together. I'll call you on the telephone before I come over."

The next day, which was of course August 17, 1921, a lot of people, townspeople and such, drove out in their cars and looked at the former river and shook their heads in wonder. They had a lot of picnic baskets with them, too.

There was an article in the local paper with two photographs showing two large empty holes that had been the fountainhead and the sink of the Carthage River. The holes looked like nostrils.

Another photograph was of a cowboy sitting on his horse, holding an umbrella in one hand and pointing into the depths of the Carthage Sink with his other hand. He was looking very serious. It was a photograph to make people laugh and that's exactly what they did.

Well, there you have the lost chapters of *Trout Fishing in America*. Their style is probably a little different because I'm a little different now, I'm thirty-four, and they were probably written in a slightly different form, too. It's interesting that I didn't rewrite them back there in 1961 but waited until December 4, 1969, almost a decade later, to return and try to bring them back with me.

THE HEADER, THE RIGGER, THE CAPTAIN

Earl Thompson

he trawler *Billie Marie* had good luck in the Bay of Campeche below Tampico. In the hold were over fifty barrels of shrimp. Beer was broken out, marijuana was offered, and when the header, Ezequiel, was within arm's reach, Captain Slocum goosed him.

Ezequiel did not mind. He accepted such behavior as a show of comradely affection and suffered no loss of dignity because of it. At the moment, the header sat on the hatch cover of the hold fooling with two rockets the *Billie Marie* had netted in a poor run over the shrimp beds near the Matagorda firing range off Padre Island, where it curves along the Texas coast past Los Fresnos—right there in the shrimp beds, although the area is restricted and the fliers from the Naval Air Station are ordered to practice many miles to the south.

After netting the rockets and a few redfish for the pot, but nothing he could bank money on, Captain Slocum had damned the boat's luck and pointed southeast, vowing to stay out six weeks if necessary and run all the long way around Yucatán.

A hurricane had torn up many of the old shrimp beds above Tampico. Shrimp were crazy anyway. No one really knew anything about them. "Goddamn cockroaches of the sea," Slocum called them.

It wasn't until he had made a triangulation on the flat Indian mountain north of Tampico and the lights of the town and lowered the doors carrying the big otter trawls to the bottom for the second run that Slocum was certain the *Billie Marie* was going to make its nut. By the time they had rigged for a fourth run, the crew knew it was going to make some money.

The sun was warm on the header's shoulders. The breeze was fresh on his face. He had already decided to buy a little television set on time as soon as he got home. Idly, Ezequiel turned the dark blue and silver rockets over on the hold cover, searching his experience for some slight use to which they might be put. The rockets were about a yard long, heavy, and did not rattle when shaken. Perhaps there was a great little motor inside.

"Goddamn bracero!" Slocum complained, edging up to the side of the hold. "Leave those alone. You could blow us to hell fooling with them things."

"Maybe make a nice lamp," the header explained.

"By the same token so would a rattlesnake," the captain snapped. "Man, them things got enough powder to sink a gunboat."

"There is no danger unless one bumps the head," Ezequiel assured him—as if the designer had been a relative. Then, noticing the unopened can of beer in the captain's hand, the header asked, "You looking for a beer sticker?"

"That was what I came back for," Slocum said.

"*Si, permite,*" Ezequiel said, springing off the hatch, going for a pocket.

"Can't never keep one," the captain mumbled.

Carefully wedging one of the rockets under his left arm, Ezequiel shifted the other to the two-talon claw that was all that was left on the end of his left arm and plunged his good right hand deep into a pocket. After a thorough rummaging of the pocket, the header produced a rusty opener, a length of twine braided through the hole in the handle.

"Jesus Christ!" Slocum swore, ever amazed at the things that came from the header's voluminous biballs.

"Tell me, Zequiel, what you got in them biballs 'sides shrimp heads and poverty?" Slocum asked.

"Ah, *nada*, Captain," the header grinned.

"*Nada*, my ass!" the captain snorted. "I bet you got everything loose from here to Corpus. From the stink of you, I'd judge maybe a couple of dead cats too."

"Ha, no!" the header protested. "No dead pussy een thees *pantalónes*."

"*Mucho* dead *nalgas* though, hunh?" the captain countered.

The little header crowed, slapping his skinny belly beneath the loose cloth with his good hand, the pear-shaped head of the silver and blue rocket held in his armpit waggling at the captain. "Okay, Captain, okay. But thees once we stink of many dollars also, ha?"

"We stink of shrimp," the captain said. "And I don't want it turned into no gumbo from fooling with bombs. Now, whyn't you chunk them things over and find something soft to play with?"

"Es no danger. See, first I remove thees little end. . . ." The header commenced fitting action to words.

"No-by-goddamn-you-don't neither!" Slocum shouted, going for cover inside the cabin. "Now I'm telling you, Zequiel, you stop fooling with me!" he admonished the header with a waving finger the size of a banana. "You do one least little thing with them bombs to blow up this here shrimp boat and I'll make a steer out of you, boy. *Cortada tu cojones!*"

"Small loss," the header replied in English, dropping his pretense, amused at the excitement he was creating.

"Jesus Christ!" Slocum solicited further witness to his plight, while stretching his neck to see over the galley door. Ezequiel grinned and continued to twist purposefully on the head of the rocket. "Damn it, Zequiel," the captain shouted, "least you can do is go back and hold the sonsabitches over the fantail."

"Okay. Okay," Ezequiel said. "Don't worry." And he moved to squat against the stern rail, where he placed one of the rockets on the deck, holding it secure with a bare foot while he concentrated on dismantling the other.

The header liked the captain; he liked his twelve-and-one-half percent of the haul too; but what he liked best of all was to think of himself as a man of talent, an inventor, engineer, scientist, seer, a forecaster of hurricanes. "A sort of spic Ben Franklin is what he thinks," Gatliff, the rigger, would say, always adding, in his solemn drawl, "but it comes out more spic than spankin'!"

The header hunkered in the lee of the stern, bent intently over the mysterious object that had been launched from the sky and come to his hand from the sea. He had an old face, but he was not an old man: thirty-five, maybe; always amicable, rarely drunk, and could head shrimp as well as any man, though he had only thumb and little finger on his left hand.

Slocum left the small galley at the rear of the cabin, passed through the sleeping quarters with its two bunks and two-way radio, and entered the wheelhouse, where Gatliff steered the boat with one hand while eating a wiener and drinking from a bottle of Bohemia. He did this with one hand, holding the cold wiener like a cigar, snapping off a bite and chasing it with a pull at the bottle.

"If you ain't a world beater at motion conservation," Slocum said.

The captain gave Gatliff a start and the rigger momentarily choked on a bite of wiener. He had been considering at length diverse ways and means of going about getting one of Slocum's cans of Jax, seeing as how the near-empty he held in his hand was the last beer Gatliff owned.

The boat furnished groceries, soap, drinking water, and a

certain amount of jerry-built companionship. It was up to each shrimper to supply himself with such other necessities as beer, tobacco, marijuana in sufficient quantity to last the trip. But Gatliff was always in short supply, on everything, and he didn't expect things ever to be any different.

"That crazy bracero's going to blow us up fooling with them things back there," Slocum said, more in way of conversation than complaint. "He says he's *mucho simpático* with all little engines and claims to have fixed clocks once for a whole winter."

"You're the captain. You could order him to stop," the rigger said.

"Hunh? Ahhh . . ." the captain waved away the notion as smoke before his eyes. "He's just like a little child. He don't mean no harm."

"Yah," Pete agreed, "but sometimes, you know, he says wild stuff. Yesterday, frying beans, he tells me the Gulf is like God. Went on about it for some time too. Said how the earth was like your grandma and the sky, your grandpa. On and on into a whole lot of crap!"

"Must've been high," the captain said.

"Well, he'd had some, all right," Gatliff said.

"I thought he was a Catholic," the captain said, glancing over his shoulder toward the stern.

The captain shuddered, sloshed the beer around in the can to see how much was left, took a drink from it and looked decided. "Think I'll go back and chuck them things over. No sense in worrying myself." He started out, then stopped, unsure of his timing. "When we cut divvies on this mess, I'm across the river like a turpentined cat and onto that little Chelo gal at the Yellow Bar."

The captain edged toward the door, but hesitated to give Gatliff a chance to make his brag.

The rigger quick-stuffed the remainder of the sausage into his mouth, chewed and swallowed hard, working it down behind his Adam's apple.

"Yah, I know what you mean! Now me, I'm for that Cleopatra-looking one at the Old Laredo, and when I get to her, I'm just going to stand on my joint!"

"Oh hell, Gatliff," the captain scoffed, "I'd as soon cut a fart in a diver's suit as do that sorry chunk."

"I like her," was all the rigger could think to say.

"Like her! With her Injun hair all bleached out like sisal and her painted all blue and green and gold around the eyes! Hell, man, she don't even look like a natural woman!"

Gatliff cut a surprised look at the captain. "How come you're so hard on her?" the rigger asked, really wanting to know.

"Well," Slocum started. "Well, hell! She ain't natural, is all. She's queer like. A whore ought to be a natural woman."

"Listen," the rigger waved off the captain's contention, "she don't set herself up as no *natural* woman. She's something else, and that's what I pays my money for."

"Well, she don't look right to me," the captain said, edging closer to the door. "I mean she ain't real like—"

"*Wives* are real," the rigger bawled. "And snoddy-nosed kids. Getting home and not finding nobody there, that's your god-damn *real*, compadre."

"Why, Pete," the captain snuffled, taking a step back into the center of the wheelhouse, "I reckon if that sort of trade is to your taste, you can sure as hell have her."

"I'll take her and much obliged," the rigger snapped.

Slocum snorted and stepped close enough to poke the rigger on the shoulder with his fist, "Hooee, damn."

"To hell with you," the rigger said. "I ain't telling you nothing."

"Well, I'll tell *you* then," the captain jabbed the rigger in the ribs with the forefinger of authority. "I read in a magazine

362

where some doctor in New York was talking to whores and found out they's every last one of them tetched in the head."

"Them's New York whores," the rigger complained righteously.

"Ho, ho, Pete," the captain chided his rigger.

"All right," Gatliff said, finished with it now, "but by God, she likes this man's style."

His anger was left hanging by the explosion that blew the whole fantail out of the water. The screw came out of the water and raced freely, stirring air. The wheel was wrenched out of the rigger's grasp and his beer bottle was blown through the windshield, but he caught at the wheel as the boat settled back into the water, and he kept his feet. Slocum was picked up and thrown hard against the bulkhead in the corner of the wheelhouse. The bow plowed into the Gulf and water flew back over the deck and the pilothouse, washing in a low fast wave. There was water in the pilothouse a quarter inch or so deep over the yellow linoleum.

When their ears cleared, Slocum and Gatliff could hear the steady throb of the diesel beneath them. Gatliff blinked salt water from his eyes, rubbed his long face with his hands and got used to the idea of still being alive; then he sent his hands to the control panel to see if he could do something about remaining that way. Slocum, his broad back against the starboard bulkhead, sloshed his feet around on the slick linoleum trying to get the deck under him one way or another. He could not see, but in the instant that he floundered there, he had a clear vision of his wife, Billie Marie, seeing her high-cheekboned face with its upper lip pushed out by her large even teeth, the long skinny length of her blue-white shanks and the hollows of her buttocks. He could smell the awful scent of her, and he wanted suddenly to smash her face, send her skinny ass over bony shoulders rolling, rolling away. Later he would recall his vision and feel guilty, anxious to get to this woman, to their shade-darkened rooms, to thrust himself into her loose flesh. He would roar his repentance into the open-mouthed moaning of her: "Billie! Oh, Billie honey, you're the only woman there ever was that was so good for me."

Now, with returning breath, he cried out, "You life-sucking hog-wallow!"

Presently, Slocum gained his feet, banging his back against the bulkhead to encourage breath to come more quickly. Gatliff looked to see if the captain could stand and saw the captain's face drained of color beneath its sunburn. The captain's eyes focused on the rigger's, and Slocum nodded his head to show he was all right. Then he cast about the wheelhouse, kicking at stuff sliding around on the wet deck. Slocum started to pick things up, retrieving his soaked chart case. Then he gave it all up and moaned, "Oh, goddamn the goddamn thing," and he lurched through the cabin toward the stern.

Smoke hung over the water in the trawler's wake, thinning out landward on the breeze. There was a hole in the rise of the fantail rail and planking, a space that would measure four feet across. Slocum dropped down on the hatch cover and looked out over the hole in his boat. "I was on my way," he told the Gulf. He saw how the wake veered sharply at the point where the rocket went off.

After a while Slocum got up, went back into the cabin through the galley, and returned to the pilothouse. "Gone, Pete. Ain't a speck anywhere."

"We going to make her?" the rigger wanted to know. "We leaking bad?"

"We ain't leaking any that I can see," the captain said. "Unless something's sprung below, we're all right, I think."

"Praise the Lord for unearned favors," the rigger breathed relief and reached up to cut off the auxiliary bilge pump to keep it from burning out. Then he asked, "You mean he's just gone?"

364

"There ain't nothing back there," Slocum said. "See for your-self."

The rigger left and came back.

"Jesus! Not meat nor rag," he said.

"No, sir," the captain said.

"Man, man," the rigger said.

They lit cigarettes and blew smoke at the horizon. Slocum finally went back into the cabin and tried to raise the coast Guard but the blast had damaged the radio and it would not work. Slocum banged it a few times with the heel of his hand, gave up, lit another cigarette and returned to stand beside the rigger.

"Guess we'll just go in," he said. After a while, he said, "That Zequiel was one funny one."

"Yeah. He was a funny one," Gatliff agreed.

The captain considered for a long moment. "But he was all right, you know, by God. He was an all right little Mexskin."

"Yah," Gatliff said. "He was a right good one."

"Best cook we ever had as a header," the captain said.

"Yeah," the rigger said.

"Man, oh, man, Pete, I just don't know," the captain said.

"Me neither," Gatliff said.

The captain found his theme: "I mean, there a man is, just cutting a fool and trying to get along. Just trying to get along. Then kerplowee! He ain't nothing. He's just gone."

"That's it, all right," the rigger said.

"Man, I'll tell you, I just don't know," the captain said. "I just don't."

"Makes you wonder," the rigger said.

The two men smoked silently for a few moments, and then the rigger asked, "You ever notice all the crap he carried in his pockets? Bits of this and that? And that hand of his. Strong as a trap. Made me feel real queer every time he laid that thing on me."

"Sort of hard to take," the captain agreed. "Reckon I just got used to it."

"Yeah," the rigger said, "that claw was another thing altogether."

"Well, he blowed himself up, all right," the captain said.

"Gone," the rigger said. "Just gone."

"Yes, sir," the captain said. "*All* gone."

"That's right," the rigger said, "every bit of him gone."

"You know it," the captain said. "Gone, gone."

The rigger looked at the captain's face, and then the two men commenced to laugh. They tried it out and then stopped. Then they let it blow. Howling laughter filled the cabin twelve miles from any safe shore, rattling the broken windows, wild belly laughter. The two men threw their heads back and shrieked. "Gone, gone." They stomped their feet on the deck and slapped their long thighs. They threw arms around each other to keep from falling down. They clung together, and howled in each other's face.

"Ho, me!" Slocum howled hoarsely. "Screwing on that damn thing."

"His goddamn britches a-bagging down in the back," Gatliff added.

"And flapping like an empty sack," the captain groaned.

"Oh, Captain, we oughtn't to laugh," the rigger complained weakly.

"Can't help it," the captain croaked. "Just can't."

"Man alive, that sonofabitch went *boom!* didn't she?" the rigger howled.

"Oh, God," the captain bawled back, "I mean to tell you that thing went *off!*"

366

DUNYAZADIAD

John Barth

t this point I interrupted my sister as usual to say, 'You have a way with words, Scheherazade. This is the thousandth night I've sat at the foot of your bed while you and the King made love and you told him stories, and the one in progress holds me like a genie's gaze. I wouldn't dream of breaking in like this, just before the end, except that I hear the first rooster crowing in the east, et cetera, and the King really ought to sleep a bit before daybreak. I wish I had your talent.'

"And as usual Sherry replied, 'You're the ideal audience, Dunyazade. But this is nothing; wait till you hear the ending, tomorrow night! Always assuming this auspicious King doesn't kill me before breakfast, as he's been going to do these thirty-three and a third months.'

" 'Hmp,' said Shahryar. 'Don't take your critics for granted; I may get around to it yet. But I agree with your little sister that this is a good one you've got going, with its impostures that become authentic, its ups and downs and flights to other worlds. I don't know how in the world you dream them up.'

" 'Artists have their tricks,' Sherry replied. We three said good-night then, six good-nights in all. In the morning your brother went off to court, enchanted by Sherry's story. Daddy came to the palace for the thousandth time with a shroud under

369

his arm, expecting to be told to cut his daughter's head off; in most other respects he's as good a Vizier as he ever was, but three years of suspense have driven him crackers in this one particular—and turned his hair white, I might add, and made him a widower. Sherry and I, after the first fifty nights or so, were simply relieved when Shahryar would hmp and say, 'By Allah, I won't kill her till I've heard the end of her story'; but it still took Daddy by surprise every morning. He groveled gratitude per usual; the King per usual spent the day in his durbar, bidding and forbidding between man and man, as the saying goes; I climbed in with Sherry as soon as he was gone, and per usual we spent *our* day sleeping in and making love. When we'd had enough of each other's tongues and fingers, we called in the eunuchs, maid-servants, mamelukes, pet dogs and monkeys; then we finished off with Sherry's Bag of Tricks: little weighted balls from Baghdad, dildoes from the Ebony Isles and the City of Brass, et cetera. Not to break a certain vow of mine, I made do with a roc-down tickler from Bassorah, but Sherry touched all the bases. Her favorite story is about some pig of an ifrit who steals a girl away on her wedding night, puts her in a treasure casket locked with seven steel padlocks, puts the casket in a crystal coffer, and puts the coffer on the bottom of the ocean, so that nobody except himself can have her. But whenever he brings the whole rig ashore, unlocks the locks with seven keys, and takes her out and rapes her, he falls asleep afterward on her lap; she slips out from under and cuckolds him with every man who passes by, taking their seal rings as proof; at the end of the story she has five hundred seventy-two seal rings, and the stupid ifrit still thinks he *possesses* her! In the same way, Sherry put a hundred horns a day on your brother's head: that's about a hundred thousand horns by now. And every day she saved till last the Treasure Key, which is what her story starts and ends with.

"Three and a third years ago, when King Shahryar was raping

370

a virgin every night and killing her in the morning, and the people were praying that Allah would dump the whole dynasty, and so many parents had fled the country with their daughters that in all the Islands of India and China there was hardly a young girl fit to fuck, my sister was an undergraduate arts-and-sciences major at Banu Sásán University. Besides being Homecoming Queen, valedictorian-elect, and a four-letter varsity athlete, she had a private library of a thousand volumes and the highest average in the history of the campus. Every graduate department in the East was after her with fellowships—but she was so appalled at the state of the nation that she dropped out of school in her last semester to do full-time research on a way to stop Shahryar from killing all our sisters and wrecking the country.

"Political science, which she looked at first, got her nowhere. Shahryar's power was absolute, and by sparing the daughters of his army officers and chief ministers (like our own father) and picking his victims mainly from the families of liberal intellectuals and other minorities, he kept the military and the cabinet loyal enough to rule out a coup d'état. Revolution seemed out of the question, because his woman-hating, spectacular as it was, was reinforced more or less by all our traditions and institutions, and as long as the girls he was murdering were generally upper-caste, there was no popular base for guerrilla war. Finally, since he could count on your help from Samarkand, invasion from outside or plain assassination were bad bets too: Sherry figured your retaliation would be worse than Shahryar's virgin-a-night policy.

"So we gave up poly sci (I fetched her books and sharpened her quills and made tea and alphabetized her index cards) and tried psychology—another blind alley. Once she'd noted that *your* reaction to being cuckolded by your wife was homicidal rage followed by despair and abandonment of your kingdom, and that Shahryar's was the reverse; and established that *that*

371

was owing to the difference in your ages and the order of revelations; and decided that whatever pathology was involved was a function of the culture and your position as absolute monarchs rather than particular hang-ups in your psyches, et cetera—what was there to say?

"She grew daily more desperate; the body count of deflowered and decapitated Moslem girls was past nine hundred, and Daddy was just about out of candidates. Sherry didn't especially care about herself, you understand—wouldn't have even if she hadn't guessed that the King was sparing her out of respect for his Vizier and her own accomplishments. But beyond the general awfulness of the situation, she was particularly concerned for my sake. From the day I was born, when Sherry was about nine, she treasured me as if I were hers; I might as well not have had parents; she and I ate from the same plate, slept in the same bed; no one could separate us; I'll bet we weren't apart for an hour in the first dozen years of my life. But I never had her good looks or her way with the world— and I was the youngest in the family besides. My breasts were growing; already I'd begun to menstruate: any day Daddy might have to sacrifice me to save Sherry.

"So when nothing else worked, as a last resort she turned to her first love, unlikely as it seemed, mythology and folklore, and studied all the riddle/puzzle/secret motifs she could dig up. 'We need a miracle, Doony,' she said (I was braiding her hair and massaging her neck as she went through her notes for the thousandth time), 'and the only genies I've ever met were in stories, not in Moormen's-rings and Jews'-lamps. It's in words that the magic is—Abracadabra, Open Sesame, and the rest— but the magic words in one story aren't magical in the next. The real magic is to understand which words work, and when, and for what; the trick is to learn the trick.'

"This last, as our frantic research went on, became her motto, even her obsession. As she neared the end of her supply of lore, and Shahryar his supply of virgins, she became more and more certain that her principle was correct, and desperate that in the whole world's stock of stories there was none that confirmed it, or showed us how to use it to solve the problem. 'I've read a thousand tales about treasures that nobody can find the key to,' she told me; 'we have the key and can't find the treasure.' I asked her to explain. 'It's all in here,' she declared—I couldn't tell whether she meant her inkstand or the quill she pointed toward it. I seldom understood her anymore; as the crisis grew, she gave up reading for daydreaming, and used her pen less for noting instances of the Magic Key motif in world literature than for doodling the letters of our alphabet at random and idly tickling herself.

"'Little Doony,' she said dreamily, and kissed me: 'pretend this whole situation is the plot of a story we're reading, and you and I and Daddy and the King are all fictional characters. In this story, Scheherazade finds a way to change the King's mind about women and turn him into a gentle, loving husband. It's not hard to imagine such a story, is it? Now, no matter what way she finds—whether it's a magic spell or a magic story with the answer in it or a magic anything—it comes down to particular words in the story we're reading, right? And those words are made from the letters of our alphabet: a couple-dozen squiggles we can draw with this pen. This is the key, Doony! And the treasure, too, if we can only get our hands on it! It's as if—as if the key to the treasure *is* the treasure!'

"As soon as she spoke these last words a genie appeared from nowhere right there in our library stacks. He didn't resemble anything in Sherry's bedtime stories: for one thing, he wasn't frightening, though he was strange-looking enough: a light-skinned fellow of forty or so, smooth-shaven and bald as a roc's egg. His clothes were simple but outlandish; he was tall and healthy and pleasant enough in appearance, except for queer lenses that he wore in a frame over his eyes. He seemed as startled as we were—you should've seen Sherry drop that pen and pull her skirts together!—but he got over his alarm a lot sooner, and looked from one to the other of us and at a stubby little magic wand he held in his fingers, and smiled a friendly smile.

" 'Are you really Scheherazade,' he asked. 'I've never had a dream so clear and lifelike! And you're little Dunyazade—just as I'd imagined both of you! Don't be frightened: I can't tell you what it means to me to see and talk to you like this; even in a dream, it's a dream come true. Can you understand English? I don't have a word of Arabic. O my, I can't believe this is really happening!'

"Sherry and I looked at each other. The Genie didn't seem dangerous; we didn't know those languages he spoke of; every word he said was in *our* language, and when Sherry asked him whether he'd come from her pen or from her words, he seemed to understand the question, though he didn't know the answer. He was a writer of tales, he said—anyhow a *former* writer of tales—in a land on the other side of the world. At one time, we gathered, people in his country had been fond of reading; currently, however, the only readers of artful fiction were critics, other writers, and unwilling students who, left to themselves, preferred music and pictures to words. His own pen (that magic wand, in fact a magic quill with a fountain of ink inside) had just about run dry: but whether he had abandoned fiction or fiction him, Sherry and I couldn't make out when we reconstructed this first conversation later that night, for either in our minds or in his a number of crises seemed confused. Like Shahryar's, the Genie's life was in disorder—but so far from harboring therefore a grudge against womankind, he was distractedly in love with a brace of new mistresses, and only recently had been able to choose between them. His career, too, had reached a hiatus which he would have been pleased to call a turning point if he could have espied any way to turn: he wished

374

neither to repudiate nor to repeat his past performances; he aspired to go beyond them toward a future they were not attuned to and, by some magic, at the same time go back to the original springs of narrative. But how this was to be managed was as unclear to him as the answer to the Shahryar-problem was to us—the more so since he couldn't say how much of his difficulty might be owing to his own limitations, his age and stage and personal vicissitudes; how much to the general decline of letters in his time and place; and how much to the other crises with which his country (and, so he alleged, the very species) was beset—crises as desperate and problematical, he avowed, as ours, and as inimical to the single-mindedness needed to compose great works of art or the serenity to apprehend them.

"So entirely was he caught up in these problems, his work and life and all had come to a standstill. He had taken leave of his friends, his family, and his post (he was a doctor of letters), and withdrawn to a lonely retreat in the marshes, which only the most devoted of his mistresses deigned to visit.

"'My project,' he told us, "is to learn where to go by discovering where I am by reviewing where I've been—where we've *all* been. There's a kind of snail in the Maryland marshes —perhaps I invented him—that makes his shell as he goes along out of whatever he comes across, cementing it with his own juices, and at the same time makes his path instinctively toward the best available material for his shell; he carries his history on his back, living in it, adding new and larger spirals to it from the present as he grows. That snail's pace has become my pace—but I'm going in circles, following my own trail! I've quit reading and writing; I've lost track of who I am; my name's just a jumble of letters; so's the whole body of literature: strings of letters and empty spaces, like a code that I've lost the key to.' He pushed those odd lenses up on the bridge of his nose with his thumb—a habit that made me giggle—and grinned. 'Well,

375

almost the whole body. Speaking of keys, I suspect that's how I got here.'

"By way of answer to Sherry's question then, whether he had sprung from her quill pen or her words, he declared that his researches, like hers, had led him to an impasse; he felt that a treasure-house of new fiction lay vaguely under his hand, if he could find the key to it. Musing idly on this figure, he had added to the morass of notes he felt himself mired in, a sketch for a story about a man who comes somehow to realize that the key to the treasure he's searching for *is* the treasure. Just exactly how so (and how the story might be told despite all the problems that beset him) he had no chance to consider, for the instant he set on paper the words *The key to the treasure is the treasure*, he found himself with us—for how long, or to what end, or by what means, he had no idea, unless it was that of all the story-tellers in the world, his very favorite was Scheherazade.

"'Listen how I chatter on!' he ended happily. 'Do forgive me!'

"My sister, after some thought, ventured the opinion that the astonishing coincidence of her late reveries and his, which had led them as it were simultaneously to the same cryptic formulation, must have something to do with his translation to her library. She looked forward, she said, to experimenting whether a reverse translation could be managed, if the worst came to the worst, to spirit me out of harm's way; as for herself, she had no time or use for idle flights of fancy, however curious, from the gynocide that was ravaging her country: remarkable as it was, she saw no more relevance to her problems than to his in this bit of magic.

"'But we know the answer's right here in our hands!' the Genie exclaimed. 'We're both storytellers: you must sense as strongly as I that it has something to do with the key to the treasure's being the treasure.'

"My sister's nostrils narrowed. 'Twice you've called me a

storyteller,' she said; 'yet I've never told a story in my life except to Dunyazade, and her bedtime stories were the ones that every-body tells. The only tale I ever invented myself was this key-to-the-treasure one just now, which I scarcely understand. . . .'

" 'Good lord!' the Genie cried. 'Do you mean to say that you haven't even *started* your thousand and one nights yet?'

"Sherry shook her head grimly. 'The only thousand nights I know of is the time our pig of a king has been killing the virgin daughters of the Moslems.'

"Our bespectacled visitor then grew so exhilarated that for some time he couldn't speak at all. Presently he seized my sister's hand and dumbfounded us both by declaring his lifelong adoration of her, a declaration that brought blushes to our cheeks. Years ago, he said, when he'd been a penniless student pushing book carts through the library stacks of his university to help pay for his education, he'd contracted a passion for Scheherazade upon first reading the tales she beguiled King Shahryar with, and had sustained that passion so powerfully ever since that his love affairs with other, 'real' women seemed to him by compari-son unreal, his two-decade marriage but a prolonged infidelity to her, his own fictions were mimicries, pallid counterfeits of the authentic treasure of her *Thousand and One Nights*.

" 'Beguiled the King with!' Sherry said. 'I've thought of that! Daddy believes that Shahryar would really like to quit what he's doing before the country falls apart, but needs an excuse to break his vow without losing face with his younger brother. I'd considered letting him make love to me and then telling him exciting stories, which I'd leave unfinished from one night to the next till he'd come to know me too well to kill me. I even thought of slipping in stories about kings who'd suffered worse hardships than he and his brother without turning vindictive; or lovers who weren't unfaithful; or husbands who loved their wives more than themselves. But it's too fanciful! Who knows which stories would work? Especially in those first few nights!

I can see him sparing me for a day or two, maybe, out of relief; but then he'd react against his lapse and go back to his old policy. I gave the idea up.'

"The Genie smiled; even *I* saw what he was thinking. 'But you say you've read the book!' Sherry exclaimed. 'Then you must remember what stories are in it, and in which order!'

"'I don't have to remember,' said the Genie. 'In all the years I've been writing stories, your book has never been off my worktable. I've made use of it a thousand times, if only by just seeing it there.'

"Sherry asked him then whether he himself had perhaps invented the stories she allegedly told, or would tell. 'How could I?' he laughed. 'I won't be born for a dozen centuries yet! You didn't invent them either, for that matter; they're those ancient ones you spoke of, that "everybody tells": Sinbad the Sailor, Aladdin's Lamp, Ali Baba and the Forty Thieves. . . .'

"'What others?' Sherry cried. 'In which order? I don't even *know* the Ali Baba story! Do you have the book with you? I'll give you everything I have for it!'

"The Genie replied that inasmuch as he'd been holding her book in his hand and thinking about her when he'd written the magic words, and it had not been translated to her library along with him, he inferred that he could not present her with a copy even if the magic were repeatable. He did however remember clearly what he called the frame story: how Shahryar's young brother Shah Zaman had discovered his bride's adulteries, killed her, abandoned the kingdom of Samarkand, and come to live with Shahryar in the Islands of India and China; how, discovering that Shahryar's wife was equally unfaithful, the brothers had retreated to the wilderness, encountered the ifrit and the maiden, concluded that all women are deceivers, and returned to their respective kingdoms, vowing to deflower a virgin every night and kill her in the morning; how the Vizier's daughter Scheherazade, to end this massacre, had volunteered herself, much against her father's wishes, and with the aid of her sister Dunyazade—who at the crucial moment between sex and sleep asked for a story, and fed the King's suspense by interrupting the tale at daybreak, just before the climax—stayed Shahryar's hand long enough to win his heart, restore his senses, and save the country from ruin.

"I hugged my sister and begged her to let me help her in just that way. She shook her head: 'Only this Genie has read the stories I'm supposed to tell, and he doesn't remember them. What's more, he's fading already. If the key to the treasure is the treasure, we don't have it in our hands yet.'

"He had indeed begun fading away, almost disappeared; but as soon as Sherry repeated the magic sentence he came back clearly, smiling more eagerly than before, and declared he'd been thinking the same words at the same moment, just when *we'd* begun to fade and his writing room to reappear about him. Apparently, then, he and Sherry could conjure the phenomenon at will by imagining simultaneously that the key to the treasure was the treasure: they were, presumably, the only two people in the history of the world who had imagined it. What's more, in that instant when he'd waked, as it were, to find himself back in the marshes of *America*, he'd been able to glance at the open table of contents of Volume One of the *Thousand and One Nights* book and determine that the first story after the frame story was a compound tale called 'The Merchant and the Genie' —in which, if he remembered correctly, an outraged ifrit delays the death of an innocent merchant until certain sheiks have told their stories.

"Scheherazade thanked him, made a note of the title, and gravely put down her pen. 'You have it in your power to save my sisters and my country,' she said, 'and the King too, before his madness destroys him. All you need to do is supply me from the future with these stories from the past. But perhaps at bottom you share the King's feelings about women.'

"'Not at all!' the Genie said warmly. 'If the key trick really works, I'll be honored to tell your stories to you. All we need to do is agree on a time of day to write the magic words together.'

"I clapped my hands—but Sherry's expression was still cool. 'You're a man,' she said; 'I imagine you expect what every man expects who has the key to any treasure a woman needs. In the nature of the case, I have to let Shahryar take me first; after that I'll cuckold him with you every day at sunset if you'll tell me the story for the night to come. Is that satisfactory?'

"I feared he'd take offense, but he only shook his head. Out of his old love for her, he gently declared, and his gratitude for the profoundest image he knew of the storyteller's situation, he would be pleased beyond words to play any role whatever in Scheherazade's story, without dreaming of further reward. His *own* policy, moreover, which he had lived by for many nights more than a thousand, was to share beds with no woman who did not reciprocate his feeling. Finally, his new young mistress —to whom he had been drawn by certain resemblances to Scheherazade—delighted him utterly, as he hoped he did her; he was no more tempted to infidelity than to incest or pederasty. His adoration of Scheherazade was as strong as ever—even stronger now that he'd met her in the lovely flesh—but it was not possessive; he desired her only as the old Greek poets their Muse, as a source of inspiration.

"Sherry tapped and fiddled with her quill. 'I don't know these poets you speak of,' she said sharply. 'Here in our country, love isn't so exclusive as all that. When I think of Shahryar's harem full of concubines on the one hand, and the way his wife got even with him on the other, and the plots of most of the stories I know—especially the ones about older men with young mistresses—I can't help wondering whether you're not being a bit naïve, to put it kindly. Especially as I gather you've suffered your share of deceit in the past, and no doubt done your share of deceiving. Even so, it's a refreshing surprise, if a bit of a put-down, that you're not interested in taking sexual advantage of your position. Are you a eunuch?'

"I blushed again, but the Genie assured us, still unoffended, that he was normally equipped, and that his surpassing love for his young lady, while perhaps invincibly innocent, was not naïve. His experience of love gone sour only made him treasure more highly the notion of a love that time would season and improve; no sight on earth more pleased his heart, annealed as it was by his own past passions and defeats, than that rare one of two white-haired spouses who still cherished each other and their life together. If love died, it died; while it lived, let it live forever, et cetera. Some fictions, he asserted, were so much more valuable than fact that in rare instances their beauty made them real. The only Baghdad was the Baghdad of the *Nights*, where carpets flew and genies sprang from magic words; he was ours to command as one of those, and without price. Should one appear to *him* and offer him three wishes, he'd be unable to summon more than two, inasmuch as his first—to have live converse with the storyteller he'd loved best and longest—had already been granted.

"Sherry smiled now and asked him what would be the other two wishes. The second, he replied, would be that he might die before his young friend and he ever ceased to treasure each other as they did currently in their salt-marsh retreat. The third (what presently stood alone between him and entire contentment) would be that he not die without adding some artful trinket or two, however small, to the general treasury of civilized delights, to which no keys were needed beyond goodwill, attention, and a moderately cultivated sensibility: he meant the treasury of art, which if it could not redeem the barbarities of history or spare us the horrors of living and dying, at least sustained, refreshed, expanded, ennobled, and enriched our spirits along the painful way. Such of his scribblings as were already in print he did not presume to have that grace; should he die before he woke from his present sweet dream of Scheherazade, this third wish would go unfulfilled. But even if neither of these last was ever granted (and surely such boons were rare as treasure keys), he would die happier to have had the first.

"Hearing this, Sherry at last put by her reserve, took the stranger's writing-hand in her own, apologized for her discourtesy, and repeated her invitation, this time warmly: if he would supply her with enough of her stories to reach her goal, she was his in secret whenever he wished after her maiden right with Shahryar. Or (if deception truly had no more savor for him), when the slaughter of her sisters had ceased, let him spirit her somehow to his place and time, and she'd be his slave and concubine forever—assuming, as one was after all realistically obliged to assume, that he and his current love would by then have wearied of each other.

"The Genie laughed and kissed her hand. 'No slaves; no concubines. And my friend and I intend to love each other forever.'

"'That will be a greater wonder than all of Sinbad's together,' Sherry said. 'I pray it may happen, Genie, and your third wish be granted too. For all one knows, you may already have done what you hope to do: time will tell. But if Dunyazade and I can find any way at all to help you with *your* tales-to-come in return for the ones you've pledged to us—and you may be sure we'll search for such a way as steadfastly as we've searched for a way to save our sex—we'll do it though we die for it.'

"She made him promise then to embrace his mistress for her, whom she vowed to love thenceforth as she loved me, and by way of a gift to her—which she prayed might translate as the precious book had not—she took from her earlobe a gold ring worked in the form of a spiral shell, of which his earlier image had reminded her. He accepted it joyfully, vowing to spin from it, if he could, as from a catherine wheel or whirling

John Barth

galaxy, a golden shower of fiction. Then he kissed us both (the first male lips I'd felt except Father's, and the only such till yours) and vanished, whether by his will or another's we couldn't tell.

"Sherry and I hugged each other excitedly all that night, rehearsing every word that had passed between the Genie and ourselves. I begged her to test the magic for a week before offering herself to the King, to make sure that it—and her colleague from the future—could be relied upon. But even as we laughed and whispered, another of our sisters was being raped and murdered in the palace; Sherry offered herself to Shahryar first thing in the morning, to our father's distress; let the King lead her at nightfall into his fatal bed and fall to toying with her, then pretended to weep for being separated from me for the first time in our lives. Shahryar bade her fetch me to sit at the foot of the bed; almost in a faint I watched him help her off with the pretty nightie I'd crocheted for her myself, place a white silk cushion under her bottom, and gently open her legs; as I'd never seen a man erect, I groaned despite myself when he opened his robe and I saw what he meant to stick her with: the hair done up in pearls, the shaft like a minaret decorated with arabesques, the head like a cobra's spread to strike. He chuckled at my alarm and climbed atop her; not to see him, Sherry fixed her welling eyes on me, closing them only to cry the cry that must be cried when there befell the mystery concerning which there is no inquiry. A moment later, as the cushion attested her late virginity and tears ran from her eye-corners to her ears, she seized the King's hair, wrapped about his waist her lovely legs, and to insure the success of her fiction, pretended a grand transport of rapture. I could neither bear to watch nor turn my eyes away. When the beast was spent and tossing fitfully (for shame and guilt, I hoped, or unease at Sherry's willingness to die), I gathered my senses as best I could and asked her to tell me a story.

383

" 'With pleasure,' she said, in a tone still so full of shock it broke my heart, 'if this pious and auspicious King will allow it.' Your brother grunted, and Sherry began, shakily, the tale of the Merchant and the Genie, framing in it for good measure the First Sheik's Story as her voice grew stronger. At the right moment I interrupted to praise the story and say I thought I'd heard a rooster crowing in the east; as though I'd been kept in ignorance of the King's policy, I asked whether we mightn't sleep awhile before sunrise and hear the end of the story tomorrow night—along with the one about the Three Apples, which I liked even more. 'O Doony!' Sherry pretended to scold. 'I know a dozen better than that: how about the Ebony Horse, or Julnar the Sea-Born, or the Ensorcelled Prince? But just as there's no young woman in the country worth having that the King hasn't had his fill of already, so I'm sure there's no story he hasn't heard till he's weary of it. I could no more expect to tell him a new story than show him a new way to make love.'

" 'I'll be the judge of that,' said Shahryar. So we sweated out the day in each other's arms and at sunset tried the magic key; you can imagine our relief when the Genie appeared, pushed up his eyeglasses with a grin, and recited to us the Second and Third Sheiks' Stories, which he guessed were both to be completed on that crucial second night in order, on the one hand, to demonstrate a kind of narrative inexhaustibility or profligacy (at least a generosity commensurate to that of the sheiks themselves), while, on the other hand, not compounding the suspense of unfinished tales-within-tales at a time when the King's reprieve was still highly tentative. Moreover, that the ifrit will grant the merchant's life on account of the stories ought to be evident enough by daybreak to make, without belaboring, its admonitory point. The spiral earring, he added happily, had come through intact, if anything more beautiful for the translation; his mistress was delighted with it, and would return Sherry's embrace with pleasure, he was confident, as soon as the memory of her more contemporary rivals was removed enough, and she secure enough in his love, for him to tell her the remarkable story of the magic key. Tenderly then he voiced his hope that Scheherazade had not found the loss of her maidenhood wholly repugnant to experience, or myself to witness; if the King was truly to be wooed away from his misogyny, many ardent nights lay ahead, and for the sake of Scheherazade's spirit as well as her strategy it would be well if she could take some pleasure in them.

"'Never!' my sister declared. 'The only pleasure I'll take in that bed is the pleasure of saving my sisters and cuckolding their killer.'

"The Genie shrugged and faded; Shahryar came in, bid us good evening, kissed Sherry many times before caressing her more intimately, then laid her on the bed and worked her over playfully in as many positions as there are tales in the Trickery-of-Woman series, till I couldn't tell whether her outcries were of pain, surprise, or—mad as the notion seemed—a kind of pleasure despite herself. As for me, though I was innocent of men, I had read in secret all the manuals of love and erotic stories in Sherry's library, but had thought them the wild imaginings of lonely writers in their dens, a kind of self-tickling with the quill such as Sherry herself had fallen into; for all it was my own sister I saw doing such incredible things in such odd positions, it would be many nights before I fully realized that what I witnessed were not conjured illustrations from those texts, but things truly taking place.

"'On with the story,' Shahryar commanded when they were done. Unsteadily at first, but then in even better voice than the night before, Sherry continued the Merchant-and-Genie story, and I, mortified to find myself still moistening from what I'd seen, almost forgot to interrupt at the appropriate time. Next day, as we embraced each other, Sherry admitted that while she found the King himself as loathsome as ever, the things

he did to her were no longer painful, and might even be pleas-
urable, as would be the things she did to him, were he a bed
partner she could treasure as our Genie treasured his. More
exactly, once the alarm of her defloration and her fear of being
killed in the morning began to pass, she found abhorrent not
Shahryar himself—undeniably a vigorous and handsome man
for his forty years, and a skillful lover—but his murderous
record with our sex, which no amount of charm and tender
caressing could expunge.

"'No amount at all?' our Genie asked when he appeared
again, on cue, at sunset. 'Suppose a man had been a kind and
gentle fellow until some witch put a spell on him that deranged
his mind and made him do atrocious things; then suppose a certain young lady has the power to cure him by loving him despite his madness. She can lift the spell because she recognizes
that it *is* a spell, and not his real nature. . . .'

"'I hope that's not my tale for tonight,' Sherry said dryly,
pointing out that while Shahryar may once upon a time have
been a loving husband, even in those days he gave out virgin
slave girls to his friends, kept a houseful of concubines for himself, and cut his wife in half for taking a lover after twenty
years of one-sided fidelity. 'And no magic can bring a thousand
dead girls back to life, or unrape them. On with the story.'

"'You're a harder critic than your lover,' the Genie complained, and recited the opening frame of the Fisherman and
the Genie, the simplicity of which he felt to be a strategic
change of pace for the third night—especially since it would
lead, on the fourth and fifth, to a series of tales-within-tales-
within-tales, a narrative complexity he described admiringly as
'Oriental.'

"So it went, month after month, year after year; at the foot
of Shahryar's bed by night and in Scheherazade's by day, I
learned more about the arts of making love and telling stories
than I had imagined there was to know. It pleased our Genie,

for example, that the tale of the Ensorcelled Prince had been framed by that of the Fisherman and the Genie, since the prince himself had been encased (in the black stone palace); also, that the resolution of the story thus enframed resolved as well the tale that framed it. This metaphorical construction he judged more artful than the 'mere plot-function' (that is, preserving our lives and restoring the King's sanity!) which Sherry's Fisherman tale and the rest had in the story of her *own* life; but that 'mere plot-function,' in turn, was superior to the artless and arbitrary relation between most framed and framing tales. This relation (which to me seemed less important than what the stories were *about*) interested the two of them no end, just as Sherry and Shahryar were fascinated by the pacing of their nightly pleasures or the refinement of their various positions, instead of the degree and quality of their love.

"Sherry kissed me. 'That other either goes without saying,' she said, 'or it doesn't go at all. Making love and telling stories both take more than good technique—but it's only the technique that we can *talk* about.'

"The Genie agreed: 'Heartfelt ineptitude has its appeal, Dunyazade; so does heartless skill. But what you want is passionate virtuosity.' They speculated endlessly on such questions as whether a story might imaginably be framed from inside, as it were, so that the usual relation between container and contained would be reversed and paradoxically reversible—and (for my benefit, I suppose) what human state of affairs such an odd construction might usefully figure. Or whether one might go beyond the usual tale-within-a-tale, beyond even the tales-within-tales-within-tales-within-tales which our Genie had found a few instances of in that literary treasure-house he hoped one day to add to, and conceive a series of, say, *seven* concentric stories-within-stories, so arranged that the climax of the innermost would precipitate that of the next tale out, and that the

next, et cetera, like a string of firecrackers or the chains of or-
gasms that Shahryar could sometimes set my sister catenating.

"This last comparison—a favorite of theirs—would lead them
to a dozen others between narrative and sexual art, whether in
spirited disagreement or equally spirited concord. The Genie declared that in his time and place there were scientists of the
passions who maintained that language itself, on the one hand,
originated in 'infantile pregenital erotic exuberance, polymor-
phously perverse,' and that conscious attention, on the other,
was a 'libidinal hypercathexis'—by which magic phrases they
seemed to mean that writing and reading, or telling and listening,
were literally ways of making love. Whether this was in fact the
case, neither he nor Sherry cared at all; yet they liked to speak
as if it were (their favorite words), and accounted thereby for
the similarity between conventional dramatic structure—its exposition, rising action, climax, and dénouement—and the rhythm
of sexual intercourse from foreplay through coitus to orgasm
and release. Therefore also, they believed, the popularity of love
(and combat, the darker side of the same rupee) as a theme for
narrative, the lovers' embrace as its culmination, and postcoital
lassitude as its natural ground: what better times for tales than
at day's end, in bed after making love (or around the campfire
after battle or adventure, or in the chimney corner after work),
to express and heighten the community between the lovers,
comrades, co-workers?

"'The longest story in the world,' Sherry observed, '*The
Ocean of Story*, seven hundred thousand distichs, was told by
the god Siva to his consort Parvati as a gift for the way she
made love to him one night. It would take a minstrel five hundred evenings to recite it all, but she sat in his lap and listened
contentedly till he was done.'

"To this example, which delighted him, the Genie added several unfamiliar to us: a great epic called *Odyssey*, for instance,
whose hero returns home after twenty years of war and wan-

dering, makes love to his faithful wife, and recounts all his adventures to her in bed while the gods prolong the night in his behalf; another work called *The Decameron,* in which ten courtly lords and ladies, taking refuge in their country houses from an urban pestilence, amuse one another at the end of each day with stories (some borrowed from Sherry herself) as a kind of *substitute* for making love—an artifice in keeping with the artificial nature of their little society. And, of course, that book about Sherry herself which he claimed to be reading from, in his opinion the best illustration of all that the very relation between teller and told was by nature erotic. The teller's role, he felt, regardless of his actual gender, was essentially masculine, the listener's or reader's feminine, and the tale was the medium of their intercourse.

" 'That makes me unnatural,' Sherry objected. 'Are you one of those vulgar men who think that women writers are homosexuals?'

" 'Not at all,' the Genie assured her. 'You and Shahryar usually make love in Position One before you tell your story, and lovers like to switch positions the second time.' More seriously, he had not meant to suggest that the 'femininity' of readership was a docile or inferior condition: a lighthouse, for example, passively sent out signals that mariners labored actively to receive and interpret; an ardent woman like his mistress was at least as energetic in his embrace as he in embracing her; a good reader of cunning tales worked in her way as busily as their author; et cetera. Narrative, in short—and here they were again in full agreement—was a love-relation, not a rape: its success depended upon the reader's consent and cooperation, which she could withhold or at any moment withdraw; also upon her own combination of experience and talent for the enterprise, and the author's ability to arouse, sustain, and satisfy her interest—an ability on which his figurative life hung as surely as Scheherazade's literal.

"'And like all love-relations,' he added one afternoon, 'it's potentially fertile for both partners, in a way you should approve, for it goes beyond male and female. The reader is likely to find herself pregnant with new images, as you hope Shahryar will become with respect to women; but the storyteller may find himself pregnant too. . . .'

"Much of their talk was over my head, but on hearing this last I hugged Sherry tight and prayed to Allah it was not another of their *as if*'s. Sure enough, on the three hundred eighth night her tale was interrupted not by me but by the birth of Ali Shar, whom despite his resemblance to Shahryar I clasped to my bosom from that hour as if I had borne instead of merely helped deliver him. Likewise on the six hundred twenty-fourth night, when little Gharíb came lustily into the world, and the nine hundred fifty-ninth, birthday of beautiful Jamilah-Melissa. Her second name, which means 'honey-sweet' in the exotic tongues of Genie-land, we chose in honor of our friend's still-beloved mistress, whom he had announced his intention to marry despite Sherry's opinion that while women and men might in some instances come together as human beings, wives and husbands could never. The Genie argued, for his part, that no matter how total, exclusive, and permanent the commitment between two lovers might turn out to be, it lacked the dimensions of spiritual seriousness and public responsibility which only marriage, with its ancient vows and symbols, rites and risks, provided.

"'It can't last,' Sherry said crossly. The Genie put on her finger a gift from his fiancée to her namesake's mother—a gold ring patterned with rams'-horns and conches, replicas of which she and the Genie meant to exchange on their wedding day— and replied, 'Neither did Athens. Neither did Rome. Neither did all of Jamshid's glories. But we must live as if it can and will.'

"'Hmp,' said Sherry, who over the years had picked up a number of your brother's ways, as he had hers. But she gave them her blessing—to which I added mine without reservations

390

or *as if*'s—and turned the ring much in the lamplight when he was gone, trying its look on different hands and fingers and musing as if upon its design.

"Thus we came to the thousandth night, the thousandth morning and afternoon, the thousandth dipping of Sherry's quill and invocation of the magic key. And for the thousand and first time, still smiling, our Genie appeared to us, his own ring on his finger as it had been for some forty evenings now—an altogether brighter-looking spirit than had materialized in the bookstacks so long past. We three embraced as always; he asked after the children's health and the King's, and my sister, as always, after his progress toward that treasury from which he claimed her stories were drawn. Less reticent on this subject than he had been since our first meeting, he declared with pleasure that thanks to the inspiration of Scheherazade and to the thousand comforts of his loving wife, he believed he had found his way out of that slough of the imagination in which he'd felt himself bogged: whatever the merits of the new work, like an oxcart driver in monsoon season or the skipper of a grounded ship, he had gone forward by going back, to the very roots and springs of story. Using, like Scheherazade herself, for entirely present ends, materials received from narrative antiquity and methods older than the alphabet, in the time since Sherry's defloration he had set down two thirds of a projected series of three *novellas*, longish tales which would take their sense from one another in several of the ways he and Sherry had discussed, and, if they were successful (here he smiled at me), manage to be seriously, even passionately, *about* some things as well.

" 'The two I've finished have to do with mythic heroes, true and false,' he concluded. 'The third I'm just in the middle of. How good or bad they are I can't say yet, but I'm sure they're *right*. You know what I mean, Scheherazade?"

"She did; I felt as if I did also, and we happily re-embraced. Then Sherry remarked, apropos of middles, that she'd be winding up the story of Ma'aruf the Cobbler that night and needed at least the beginning of whatever tale was to follow it.

"The Genie shook his head. 'My dear, there are no more. You've told them all.' He seemed cruelly undisturbed by a prospect that made the harem spin before my eyes and brought me near to swooning.

"'No more!' I cried. 'What will she do?'

"'If she doesn't want to risk Shahryar's killing her and turning to you,' he said calmly, 'I guess she'll have to invent something that's not in the book.'

"'I don't invent,' Sherry reminded him. Her voice was no less steady than his, but her expression—when I got hold of my senses enough to see it—was grave. 'I only recount.'

"'Borrow something from that treasury!' I implored him. 'What will the children do without their mother?' The harem began to spin again; I gathered all my courage and said: 'Don't desert us, friend; give Sherry that story you're working on now, and you may do anything you like with me. I'll raise your children if you have any; I'll wash your Melissa's feet. Anything.'

"The Genie smiled and said to Sherry, 'Our little Dunyazade is a woman.' Thanking me then for my offer as courteously as he had once Scheherazade, he declined it, not only for the same reasons that had moved him before, but also because he was confident that the only tales left in the treasury of the sort King Shahryar was likely to be entertained by were the hundred mimicries and retellings of Sherry's own.

"'Then my thousand nights and a night are ended,' Sherry said. 'Don't be ungrateful to our friend, Doony; everything ends.'

"I agreed, but tearfully wished myself—and Ali Shar, Gharíb, and little Melissa, whom—all I loved as dearly as I loved my sister—out of a world where the only *happy* endings were in stories.

"The Genie touched my shoulder. 'Let's not forget,' he said, 'that from my point of view—a tiresome technical one, I'll admit

—it *is* a story that we're coming to the end of. All these tales your sister has told the King are simply the middle of her own story—hers and yours, I mean, and Shahryar's, and his young brother Shah Zaman's.'

"I didn't understand—but Sherry did, and squeezing my other shoulder, asked him quietly, that being the tiresome technical case, if it followed that a happy ending might be invented for the framing story.

" 'The author of *The Thousand and One Nights* doesn't invent,' the Genie reminded her; 'he only recounts how, after she finished the tale of Ma'aruf the Cobbler, Scheherazade rose from the King's bed, kissed ground before him, and made bold to ask a favor in return for the thousand and one nights' entertainment. "Ask, Scheherazade," the King answers in the story—whereupon you send Dunyazade to fetch the children in, and plead for your life on their behalf, so that they won't grow up motherless.'

"My heart sprang up; Sherry sat silent. 'I notice you don't ask on behalf of the stories themselves,' the Genie remarked, 'or on behalf of your love for Shahryar and his for you. That's a pretty touch: it leaves him free to *grant* your wish, if he chooses to, on those other grounds. I also admire your tact in asking only for your life; that gives him the moral initiative to repent his policy and marry you. I don't think I'd have thought of that.'

" 'Hmp,' said Sherry.

" 'Then there's the nice formal symmetry—'

" 'Never *mind* the symmetry!' I cried. 'Does it work or not?' I saw in his expression then that it did, and in Sherry's that this plan was not news to her. I hugged them both, weeping enough for joy to make our ink run, so the Genie said, and begged Sherry to promise me that I could stay with her and the children after their wedding as I had before, and sit at the foot of her bed forever.

" 'Not so fast, Doony,' she said. 'I haven't decided yet whether or not I care to end the story that way.'

" 'Not care to?' I looked with fresh terror to the Genie. 'Doesn't she *have* to, if it's in the book?'

"He too appeared troubled now, and searched Sherry's face, and admitted that not everything he'd seen of our situation in these visions or dreams of his corresponded exactly to the story as it came to him through the centuries, lands, and languages that separated us in waking hours. In his translation, for example, all three children were male and nameless; and while there was no mention of Scheherazade's *loving* Shahryar by the end of the book, there was surely none of her despising him, or cuckolding him, more or less, with me and the rest. Most significantly, it went without saying that he himself was altogether absent from the plot—which, however, he prayed my sister to end as it ended in his version: with the double marriage of herself to your brother and me to you, and our living happily together until overtaken by the Destroyer of Delights and Severer of Societies, et cetera.

"While I tried to assimilate this astonishing news about myself, Sherry asked with a smile whether by 'his version' the Genie meant that copy of the *Nights* from which he'd been assisting us or the story he himself was in midst of inventing; for she liked to imagine, and profoundly hoped it so, that our connection had not been to her advantage only: that one way or another, she and I and our situation were among those 'ancient narrative materials' which he had found useful for his present purposes. How did *his* version end?

"The Genie closed his eyes for a moment, pushed back his glasses with his thumb, and repeated that he was still in the middle of that third novella in the series, and so far from drafting the climax and dénouement, had yet even to plot them in outline. Turning then to me, to my great surprise he announced that the title of the story was *Dunyazadiad;* that its central character was not my sister but myself, the image of whose circumstances, on my 'wedding-night-to-come,' he found as arresting for tale-tellers of his particular place and time as was my sister's for the estate of narrative artists in general.

"'All those nights at the foot of that bed, Dunyazade!' he exclaimed. 'You've had the whole literary tradition transmitted to you—and the whole erotic tradition, too! There's no story you haven't heard; there's no way of making love that you haven't seen again and again. I think of you, little sister, a virgin in both respects: All that innocence! All that sophistication! And now it's *your* turn: Shahryar has told young Shah Zaman about his wonderful mistress, how he loves her as much for herself as for her stories—*which he also passes on;* the two brothers marry the two sisters; it's your wedding night, Dunyazade. . . . But wait! Look here! Shahryar deflowered and killed a virgin a night for a thousand and one nights before he met Scheherazade; Shah Zaman has been doing the same thing, but it's only now, a thousand nights and a night later, that *he* learns about Scheherazade—that means he's had two thousand and two young women at the least since he killed his wife, and not one has pleased him enough to move him to spend a second night with her, much less spare her life! What are you going to do to entertain *him*, little sister? Make love in exciting new ways? There are none! Tell him stories, like Scheherazade? He's heard them all! Dunyazade, Dunyazade! Who can tell your story?'

"More dead than alive with fright, I clung to my sister, who begged the Genie please to stop alarming me. All apologies, he assured us that what he was describing was not *The Thousand and One Nights* frame story (which ended happily without mention of these terrors), but his own novella, a pure fiction—to which also he would endeavor with all his heart to find some conclusion in keeping with his affection for me. Sherry further eased my anxiety by adding that she too had given long thought to my position as the Genie described it, and was not without certain plans with respect to our wedding night; these, as a final favor to our friend, she had made written note of in the hope that whether or not they succeeded, he might find them useful for his story; but she would prefer to withhold them from me for the present.

" 'You sense as I do, then,' the Genie said thoughtfully, 'that we won't be seeing each other again.'

"Sherry nodded. 'You have other stories to tell. I've told mine.'

"Already he'd begun to fade. 'My best,' he said, 'will be less than your least. And I'll always love you, Scheherazade! Dunyazade, I'm your brother! Good night, sisters! Farewell!'

"We kissed; he disappeared with Sherry's letter; Shahryar sent for us; still shaken, I sat at the bed-foot while he and Sherry did a combination from the latter pages of *Ananga Ranga* and *Kama Sutra* and she finished the tale of Ma'aruf the Cobbler. Then she rose as the Genie had instructed her, kissed ground, begged boon; I fetched in Ali Shar, walking by himself now, Gharíb crawling, Jamilah-Melissa suckling at my milkless breast as if it were her mother's. Sherry made her plea; Shahryar wept, hugged the children, told her he'd pardoned her long since, having found in her the refutation of all his disenchantment, and praised Allah for having appointed her the savior of her sex. Then he sent for Daddy to draft the marriage contract and for you to hear the news of Scheherazade and her stories; when you proposed to marry me, Sherry countered with Part Two of our plan (of whose Part Three I was still ignorant): that in order for her and me never to be parted, you must abandon Samarkand and live with us, sharing your brother's throne and passing yours to our father in reparation for his three years' anguish. I found you handsomer than Shahryar and more terrifying, and begged my sister to say what lay ahead for me.

" 'Why, a fine wedding-feast, silly Doony!' she teased. 'The eunuchs will perfume our Hammam-bath with rose- and willow-flower water, musk pods, eaglewood, ambergris; we'll wash and clip our hair; they'll dress me like the sun and you the moon, and we'll dance in seven different dresses to excite our bridegrooms. By the end of the wine and music they'll scarcely be able to contain their desire; each of us will kiss the other three good-night, twelve good-nights in all, and our husbands will hurry us off toward our separate bridal chambers—'

" 'O Sherry!'

" '*Then*,' she went on, no tease in her voice now, 'on the very threshold of their pleasures I'll stop, kiss ground, and say to my lord and master: "O King of the Sun and the Moon and the Rising Tide, et cetera, thanks for marrying me at last after sleeping with me for a thousand and one nights and begetting three children on me and listening while I amused you with proverbs and parables, chronicles and pleasantries, quips and jests and admonitory instances, stories and anecdotes, dialogues and histories and elegies and satires and Allah alone knows what else! Thanks too for giving my precious little sister to your brute of a brother, and the kingdom of Samarkand to our father, whose own gratitude we'll hope may partially restore his sanity! And thanks above all for kindly ceasing to rape and murder a virgin every night, and for persuading Shah Zaman to cease also! I have no right to ask anything further of you at all, but should be overjoyed to serve your sexual and other interests humbly until the day you tire of me and either have me killed or put me by for other, younger women—and indeed I *am* prepared to do just that, as Dunyazade surely is also for Shah Zaman. Yet in view of your boundless magnanimity Q.E.D., I make bold to ask a final favor." If we're lucky, Shahryar will be so mad to get me into bed that he'll say "Name it"—whereupon I point out to him that a happy occasion is about to bring to pass what a thousand ill ones didn't, your separation from me till morning. Knowing my husband, I expect he'll propose a little something à quatre, at which I'll blush appropriately and declare that I'm resigned after all to the notion of losing you for a few hours, and wish merely thirty minutes or so of private conversation with you before you and your bridegroom retire, to tell you a few things that every virgin bride should know. "What on earth is there in that line that she hasn't seen us do a hundred times?" your delicate brother-in-law will inquire. "Seeing isn't doing," I'll reply: "I myself have pretty intensive sexual experience, for example, but of one man only, and would be shy as any virgin with another than yourself; Shah Zaman has the widest carnal acquaintance in the world, I suppose, but no long and deep knowledge of any one woman; among the four of us, only you, King of the Age, et cetera, can boast both sorts of experience, having humped your way through twenty years of marriage, a thousand and one one-nighters, and thirty-three and a third months with me, not to mention odd hours with all the concubines in your stable. But little Dunyazade has no experience at all, except vicariously." That master of the quick retort will say "Hmp" and turn the matter over to Shah Zaman, who after bringing it to the full weight of his perspicacity will say, in effect, "Okay. But make it short." They'll withdraw, with the grandest erections you and I have ever shuddered at—and *then* I'll tell you what to do in Part Three. After which we'll kiss good-night, go in to our husbands, and do it. Got that?'

"'Do *what?*' I cried—but she'd say no more till all had fallen out as she described; our wedding-feast and dance; the retirement toward our chambers; her interruption and request; your permission and stipulation that the conference be brief, inasmuch as you were more excited by me than you'd been by any of the two thousand unfortunates whose maidenheads and lives you'd done away with in the five and a half years past. You two withdrew, your robes thrust out before; the moment

398

your bedroom doors closed, Sherry spat in your tracks, took my head between her hands, and said: 'If ever you've listened carefully, little sister, listen now. For all his good intentions, our Genie of the Key is either a liar or a fool when he says that any man and woman can treasure each other until death—unless their lifetimes are as brief as our murdered sisters'! Three thousand and three, Doony—dead! What have you and I and all that fiction accomplished, except to spare another thousand from a quick end to their misery? What are they saved for, if not a more protracted violation, at the hands of fathers, husbands, lovers? For the present, it's our masters' pleasure to soften their policy; the patriarchy isn't changed: I believe it will persist even to our Genie's time and place. Suppose his relation to his precious Melissa were truly as he describes it, and not merely as he wishes and imagines it: it would only be the exception that proves the wretched rule. So here we stand, and there you're about to lie, and spread your legs and take it like the rest of us! Thanks be to Allah you can't be snared as I was in the trap of *novelty*, and think to win some victory for our sex by diverting our persecutors with naughty stunts and stories! There *is* no victory, Doony, only unequal retaliation; it's time we turned from tricks to trickery, tales to lies. Go in to your lusty husband now, as I shall to mine; let him kiss and fondle and undress you, paw and pinch and slaver, lay you on the bed; but when he makes to stick you, slip out from under and whisper in his ear that for all his vast experience of sex, there remains one way of making love, most delicious of all, that both he and Shahryar are innocent of, inasmuch as a Genie revealed it to us only last night when we prayed Allah for a way to please such extraordinary husbands. So marvelous is this Position of the Genie, as we'll call it, that even a man who's gone through virgins like breakfast eggs will think himself newly laid, et cetera. What's more, it's a position in which the woman does everything, her master nothing—except submit himself to a more excruciating pleasure than he's ever known or dreamed of. No more is required of him than that he spread-eagle himself on the bed and suffer his wrists and ankles to be bound to its posts with silken cords, lest by a spasm of early joy he abort its heavenly culmination, et cetera. Then, little sister, then, when you have him stripped and bound supine and salivating, take from the left pocket of your seventh gown the razor I've hid there, as I shall mine from mine—and geld the monster! Cut his bloody engine off and choke him on it, as I'll do to Shahryar! Then we'll lay our own throats open, to spare ourselves their sex's worse revenge. Adieu, my Doony! May we wake together in a world that knows nothing of *he* and *she!* Good night.'

"I moved my mouth to answer; couldn't; came to you as if entranced; and while you kissed me, found the cold blade in my pocket. I let you undress me as in a dream, touch my body where no man has before, lay me down and mount to take me; as in a dream I heard me bid you stay for a rarer pleasure, coax you into the Position of the Genie, and with this edge in hand and voice, rehearse the history of your present bondage. Your brother's docked; my sister's dead; it's time we joined them."

II

"That's the end of your story?"

Dunyazade nodded.

Shah Zaman looked narrowly at his bride, standing naked beside the bed with her trembling razor, and cleared his throat. "If you really mean to use that, kindly kill me with it first. A good hard slice across the Adam's apple should do the trick."

The girl shuddered, shook her head. As best he could, so bound, the young man shrugged.

"At least answer one question: Why in the world did you tell me this extraordinary tale?"

400

Her eyes still averted, Dunyazade explained in a dull voice that one aspect of her sister's revenge was this reversal not only of the genders of teller and told (as conceived by the Genie), but of their circumstances, the latter now being at the former's mercy.

"Then have some!" urged the King. "For yourself!" Dunyazade looked up. Despite his position, Shah Zaman smiled like the Genie through his pearly beard and declared that Scheherazade was right to think love ephemeral. But life itself was scarcely less so, and both were sweet for just that reason— sweeter yet when enjoyed as if they might endure. For all the inequity of woman's lot, he went on, thousands of women found love as precious as did their lovers: one needed look no further than Scheherazade's stories for proof of that. If a condemned man—which is what he counted himself, since once emasculate he'd end his life as soon as he could lay hands on his sword— might be granted a last request, such as even *he* used to grant his nightly victims in the morning, his would be to teach his fair executioner the joys of sex before she unsexed him.

"Nonsense," Dunyazade said crossly. "I've seen all that."

"Seeing's not feeling."

She glared at him. "I'll learn when I choose, then, from a less bloody teacher: someone I love, no matter how foolishly." She turned her head. "If I ever meet such a man. Which I won't." Vexed, she slipped into her gown, holding the razor awkwardly in her left hand while she fastened the hooks.

"What a lucky fellow! You don't love me then, little wife?"

"Of course not! I'll admit you're not the monster I'd imagined —in appearance, I mean. But you're a total stranger to me, and the thought of what you did to all those girls makes me retch. Don't waste your last words in silly flirting; you won't change my mind. You'd do better to prepare yourself to die."

"I'm quite prepared, Dunyazade," Shah Zaman replied calmly. "I have been from the beginning. Why else do you suppose I haven't called my guards in to kill you? I'm sure my brother's long since done for Scheherazade, if she really tried to do what she put you up to doing. Shahryar and I would have been great fools not to anticipate this sort of thing from the very first night, six years ago."

"I don't believe you."

The King shrugged his eyebrows and whistled through his teeth; two husky mamelukes stepped at once from behind a tapestry depicting Jamshid's seven-ringed cup, seized Dunyazade by the wrists, covered her mouth, and took the open razor from her hand.

"Fair or not," Shah Zaman said conversationally as she struggled, "your only power at present is what I choose to give you. And fair or not, I choose to give it." He smiled. "Let her have the razor, my friends, and take the rest of the night off. If you don't believe that I deliberately put myself in your hands from the first, Dunyazade, you can't deny I'm doing so now. All I ask is leave to tell you a story, in exchange for the one you've told me; when I'm finished you may do as you please."

The mamelukes reluctantly let her go, but left the room only when Shah Zaman, still stripped and bound, repeated his order. Dunyazade sat exhausted on a hassock, rubbed her wrists, pinned up her fallen hair, drew the gown more closely about her.

"I'm not impressed," she said. "If I pick up the razor, they'll put an arrow through me."

"That hadn't occurred to me," Shah Zaman admitted. "You'll have to trust me a little, then, as I'm trusting you. Do pick it up. I insist."

"You insist!" Dunyazade said bitterly. She took up the razor, let her hand fall passively beside the hassock, began to weep.

"Let's see, now," mused the King. "How can we give you the absolute advantage? They're very fast, those guards, and loyal; if they really *are* standing by, what I fear is that they'll misconstrue some innocent movement of yours and shoot."

"What difference does it make?" Dunyazade said miserably. "Poor Sherry!"

"I have it! Come sit here beside me. Please, do as I say! Now lay that razor's edge exactly where you were going to put it before; then you can make your move before any marksman can draw and release. You'll have to hold me in your other hand; I've gone limp with alarm."

Dunyazade wept.

"Come," the King insisted: "it's the only way you'll be convinced I'm serious. No, I mean right up against it, so that you could do your trick in half a second. Whew, that gooseflesh isn't faked! What a situation! Now look here: even this advantage gripes you, I suppose, since it was given instead of taken: the male still leading the female, et cetera. No help for that just now. Besides, between any two people, you know—what I mean, it's not the patriarchy that makes you take the passive role with your sister, for example. Never mind that. See me sweat! Now, then: I agree with that Genie of yours in the matter of priorities, and I entreat you not only to permit me to tell you a story, but to make love with me first."

Dunyazade shut her eyes and whipped her head from side to side.

"As you wish," said the King. "I'd never force you, as you'll understand if you'll hear my story. Shall I tell it?"

Dunyazade moved her head indifferently.

"More tightly. Careful with that razor!"

"Can't you make it go down?" the girl asked thickly. "It's obscene. And distracting. I think I'm going to be sick."

"Not more distracting than your little breasts, or your little fingers. . . . No, please, I insist you keep hold of your advantage! My story's short, I promise, and I'm at your mercy. So:

"Six years ago I thought myself the happiest man alive. I'd had a royal childhood; my college years were a joy; my career had gone brilliantly; at twenty-five I ruled a kingdom almost as prosperous as Shahryar's at forty. I was popular with my subjects; I kept the government reasonably honest, the various power groups reasonably in hand, et cetera. Like every king I kept a harem of concubines for the sake of my public image, but as a rule they were reserved for state visitors. For myself I wanted nobody except my bride, never mind her name, whom I still loved more than any woman I'd ever known. After a day's work in the durbar, bidding and forbidding, et cetera, I'd rush in to dinner, and we'd play all night like two kittens in a basket. No trick of love we didn't turn together; no myth of gods and nymphs we didn't mimic. The harem girls, when I used them, only reminded me of how much I preferred my wife; often as not I'd dismiss them in mid-clip and call her in for the finish.

"When my brother summoned me here to visit that first time, much as I longed to see him it was all I could do to leave my bride behind; we made our first good-byes; then I was overjoyed as I imagined she'd be when I discovered that I'd forgotten a diamond necklace I'd meant to present to Shahryar's queen. I rushed back to the palace myself instead of sending after it, so that we could make love once again before I left— and I found her in our bed, riding astride the chief cook! Her last words were 'Next time invite *me*'; I cut them both in two, four halves in all, not to seem a wittol; came here and found my sister-in-law cockolding my brother with the blackamoor Sa'ad al-Din Saood, who swung from trees, slavered and gibbered, and sported a yard that made mine look like your little finger. Kings no more, Shahryar and I left together by the postern gate, resolved to kill ourselves as the most wretched fools on earth if our misery was particular. One day as we were wandering in the marshes, far from the paths of men, devouring our own souls, we saw what we thought was a waterspout coming up the bay, and climbed a loblolly pine for safety. It turned out to be that famous ifrit of your sister's story: he took the steel coffer out of its casket, unlocked the seven locks with seven keys, fetched out and futtered the girl he'd stolen on her wedding night, and fell asleep in her lap; she signaled us to come down and ordered us both to cuckold the ifrit with her then and there. Who says a man can't be forced? We did our best, and she added our seal rings to the five hundred seventy she'd already collected. We understood then that no woman on earth who wants a rogering will go unrogered, though she be sealed up in a tower of brass.

"So. When I'd first told my brother of my own cuckolding, he'd vowed that in my position he'd not have rested till he'd killed a thousand women: now we went back to his palace; he put to death his queen and his concubines and their lovers, and we took a solemn oath to rape and kill a virgin a night, so as never again to be deceived. I came home to Samarkand, wondering at the turns of our despair: how a private apocalypse can infect the state and bring about one more general, et cetera. With this latter motive, more than for revenge on womankind, I resolved to hold to our dreadful policy until my kingdom fell to ruin or an outraged populace rose up and slew me.

"But unlike Shahryar, I said nothing at first to my Vizier, only told him to fetch me a beautiful virgin for the night. Not knowing that I meant to kill her in the morning, he brought me his own daughter, a girl I knew well and had long admired, Samarkand's equivalent of Scheherazade. I assumed he was pandering to his own advancement, and smiled at the thought of putting them to death together; I soon learned, however, from the woman herself, that it was her own idea to come to me— and her motive, unlike your sister's, was simple love. I undressed and fell to toying with her; she wept; I asked what ailed her: it was not being separated from her sister, but being alone at last with me, the fulfillment of her lifelong dream. I found myself much touched by this and, to my surprise, impotent. Stalling for time, I remarked that such dreams could turn out to be

nightmares. She embraced me timidly and replied that she deplored my murdering my wife and her paramour, both of whom
she'd known and rather liked, for though in a general way she
sympathized with my disenchanted outrage, she believed she
understood as well my wife's motives for cuckolding me, which
in her view were not all that different, essentially, from the
ifrit's maiden's in the story. Despite my anger, she went on
· bravely to declare that she herself took what she called the
Tragic View of Sex and Temperament: to wit, that while perfect equality between men and women was the only defensible
value in that line, she was not at all certain it was attainable; even
to pursue it ardently, against the grain of things as they were,
was in all likelihood to spoil one's chances for happiness in love;
not to pursue it, on the other hand, once one had seen it clearly
to be the ideal, no doubt had the same effect. For herself, though
she deplored injustice whether in individuals or in institutions,
and gently affirmed equality as the goal that lovers lovingly
should strive for, however far short of it their histories and
temperaments made them fall, yet she knew herself personally
to be unsuited for independence, formed by her nature and up-
bringing to be happy only in the shadow of a man whom she
admired and respected more than herself. She was anything but
blind to my faults and my own blindness to them, she declared,
but so adored me withal that if I could love her even for a night
she'd think her life complete, and wish nothing further unless
maybe a little Shah Zaman to devote the rest of her years to
raising. Or if my disillusionment with women were so extreme
(as she seemed uncannily to guess from my expression) that I
had brought her to my bed not to marry her or even add her to
my harem, but merely to take her virginity and her life, I was
welcome to both; she only prayed I might be gentle in their
taking.

"This last remark dismayed me the more because it echoed
something my late wife had said on our wedding night: that

even death at my hands would be sweeter to her than life at another's. How I despised, resented, missed her! As if it were I who was cut in two, I longed to hold her as in nights gone by, yet would have halved her bloody halves if she'd been restored to me. There lay my new woman on the bed, naked and still now; I stood on my knees between hers, weeping so for her predecessor's beauty and deceit, my own blindness and cruelty —and the wretched state of affairs between man and woman-kind that made a love a will-o'-the-wisp, jealousy and boredom and resentment the rule—that I could neither function nor dis-semble. I told her of all that had taken place between my de-parture from Samarkand and my return, the oath I'd sworn with my brother, and my resolve to keep it lest I seem chicken-hearted and a fool.

" 'Lest you *seem!*' the girl cried out. 'Harems, homicides—everything for the sake of seeming!' She commanded me then, full of irony for all her fears, to *keep* my vow if I meant to keep it, or else cut out her tongue before I cut off her head; for if I sent her to the block without deflowering her first, she would declare to any present, even if only her executioner, that I was a man in seeming merely, not in fact, and offer her maidenhead as proof. Her courage astonished me as much as her words. 'By Allah,' I vowed to her, 'I won't kill you if I can't get it up for you first.' But that miserable fellow in your left hand, which had never once failed me before, and which stands up now like an idiot soldier in enemy country, as if eager to be cut down, de-serted me utterly. I tried every trick I knew, in vain, though my victim willingly complied with my instructions. I could of course have killed her myself, then and there, but I had no wish to seem a hypocrite even for a moment in her eyes; nor, for that matter, to let her die a virgin—nor, I admitted finally to myself, to let her die at all before she was overtaken like the rest of us by the Destroyer of Delights, et cetera. For seven nights we tossed and tumbled, fondled and kissed and played, she reaching such heats of unaccustomed joy as to cry out, no longer sarcastically, that if only I would stick her first with my carnal sword, she'd bare her neck without complaint to my steel. On the seventh night, as we lay panting in a sweat of frustration, I gave her my dagger and invited her to do me and Samarkand the kindness of killing me at once, for I'd rather die than seem unable to keep my vow.

"'You *are* unable to keep it,' she told me softly: 'not because you're naturally impotent, but because you're *not* naturally cruel. If you'd tell your brother that after thinking it over you've simply come to a conclusion different from his, you'd be cured as if by magic.' And in fact, as if my magic indeed, what she said was so true that at her very words the weight was lifted from heart and tool together; they rose as one. Gratefully, tenderly, I went into her at last; we cried for joy, came at once, fell asleep in each other's arms.

"No question after that of following Shahryar's lead; on the other hand, I found myself in the morning not yet man enough after all to send word to him of my change of heart and urge him to change his. Neither was I, after all, in love enough with the Vizier's daughter to risk again the estate of marriage, which she herself considered problematical at best.

"'I never expected you to marry me,' she told me when I told her these things, 'though I'd be dishonest if I didn't say I dreamed and prayed you might. All I ever really hoped for was a love affair with you, and a baby to remember it by. Even if I don't have the baby, I've had the affair: you truly loved me last night.'

"I did, and for many nights after—but not enough to make the final step. What your Genie said concerning marriage could have come from my own mouth if I had the gift of words: to anyone of moral imagination who's known it, no other relation between men and women has true seriousness; yet that same imagination kept me from it. And I dreaded the day my brother

408

would get word of my weakness. I grew glum and cross; my mistress, intuitive as ever, guessed the reason at once. 'You can neither keep your vow nor break it,' she told me: 'Perhaps you'd better do both for a while, till you find your way.' I asked her how such a contradiction was possible. 'By the magic words *as if*,' she replied, 'which, to a person satisfied with seeming, are more potent than all the genii in the tales.'

"She then set forth a remarkable proposal: legend had it that far to the west of Samarkand was a country peopled entirely with women, adjoining another wholly male: for two months every spring they mated freely with each other on neutral ground, the women returning home as they found themselves pregnant, giving their male children to the neighboring tribe and raising the girls as members of their own. Whether or not such a community in fact existed, she thought it a desirable alternative to the present state of affairs, and unquestionably preferable to death; since I couldn't treasure her as she treasured me (and not for a moment did she *blame* me for that incapacity), she proposed to establish such an alternative society herself, with my assistance. I was to proclaim my brother's policy as my own, take to bed a virgin every night and declare her executed in the morning; but instead of actually raping and killing them I would tell them of her alternative society and send them secretly from Samarkand, in groups of a hundred or so, to organize and populate it. If, knowing their destiny, they chose to spend their last night in Samarkand making love with me, that was their affair; none, she imagined, would choose death over emigration, and any who found their new way of life not to their liking could return to Samarkand if and when I changed my policy, or migrate elsewhere in the meanwhile. In any case they'd be alive and free; or, if the pioneers were captured and made slaves of by barbarians before the new society was established, they'd be no worse off than the millions of their sisters already in that condition. On the other hand, separate societies of men and women, mingling freely at their own wills as equals on neutral ground, might just make possible a true society of the future in which the separation was no longer necessary. And in the meantime, of course, for better or worse, it would be as if I'd kept my dreadful vow.

"At first hearing, the plan struck me as absurd; after a few nights it seemed less so, perhaps even feasible; by the end of a week of examining passionately with her all the alternatives, it seemed no less unreasonable than they. My angel herself, in keeping with her Tragic View, didn't expect the new society to *work* in the naïve sense: what human institutions ever did? It would have the vices of its virtues; if not nipped in the bud by marauding rapists, it would grow and change and rigidify in forms and values quite different from its founders'—codifying, institutionalizing, and perverting its original spirit. No help for that.

"Was there ever such a woman? I kissed her respectfully, then ardently a final time. After one last love-making in the morning, while my hand lingered on her left breast, she declared calmly her intention, upon arriving at her virgin kingdom, to amputate that same breast for symbolic reasons and urge her companions to do the same, as a kind of initiation rite. 'We'll make up a practical excuse for it,' she said: '"The better to draw our bows," et cetera. But the real point will be that in one respect we're all woman, in another all warrior. Maybe we'll call ourselves The Breastless Ones.'

"'That seems extreme,' I remarked. She replied that a certain extremism was necessary to the survival of anything radically innovative. Later generations, she assumed, established and effete, would find the ancestral custom barbaric and honor its symbolism, if at all, with a correspondingly symbolic mammectomy—a decorative scar, perhaps, or cosmetic mark. No matter; everything passed.

"So did our connection: with a thousand thanks to her for

410

opening my eyes, a thousand good wishes for the success of her daring enterprise, and many thousands of dinars to support it (which for portability and security she converted into a phial of diamonds and carried intravaginally), I declared her dead, let her father the Vizier in on our secret, and sent her off secretly to one of my country castles on a distant lake, where she prepared for the expedition westward while her companions, the ostensible victims of my new policy, accumulated about her. Perhaps a third, apprised of their fate, chose to remain virginal, whether indignantly, ruefully, or gratefully; on the other two thirds who in whatever spirit elected to go hymenless to the new society, I bestowed similar phials of jewels. Somewhat less than fifty percent of this number found themselves impregnated by our night together, and so when the first detachment of two hundred pioneers set out across the western wastes, their actual number was about two hundred and sixty. Since I pursued this policy for nearly two thousand nights, the number of pilgrims and unborn children sent west from Samarkand must have totaled about twenty-six hundred; corrected for a normal male birth rate of somewhat over fifty percent, a rather higher than normal rate of spontaneous abortion, miscarriage, and infant as well as maternal mortality owing to the rigors of traveling and of settling a new territory, and ignoring—as one must to retain one's reason—the possibility of mass enslavement, rape, massacre, or natural catastrophe, the number of pioneers to the Country of the Breastless must be at least equal to the number of nights until Shahryar's message concerning your sister arrived from the Islands of India and China.

"Of the success or failure of those founding mothers I know nothing; kept myself ignorant deliberately, lest I learn that I was sending them after all to the Destroyer of Delights and Severer of Societies. The folk of Samarkand never rose against me; nor did my Vizier, like Shahryar's, have difficulty enlisting sacrificial virgins; even at the end, though my official toll was twice my brother's, about half the girls were volunteers, from all of which I infer that their actual fate was an open secret. For all I know, my original mistress never truly intended to found her gynocracy; the whole proposal was perhaps a ruse; perhaps they all slipped back into the country with their phials of gems for dowry, married and lived openly under my nose. No matter: night after night I brought them to bed, set forth their options, then either glumly stripped and pronged them or spent the night in chaste sleep and conversation. Tall and short, dark and fair, lean and plump, cold and ardent, bold and timid, clever and stupid, comely and plain—I bedded them all, spoke with them all, possessed them all, but was myself possessed by nothing but despair. Though I took many, with their consent, I wanted none of them. Novelty lost its charm, then even its novelty. Unfamiliarity I came to loathe; the foreign body in the dark, the alien touch and voice, the endless *exposition*. All I craved was someone with whom to get on with the story of my life, which was to say, of our life together: a loving friend; a loving wife; a treasurable wife; a wife, a wife.

"My brother's second message, when it came, seemed a miraculous reprise of that fatal first, six years before: I turned the kingdom over to my Vizier and set out at once, resolved to meet this Scheherazade who had so wooed and yarned him back to the ways of life that he meant to wed her. 'Perhaps she has a younger sister,' I said to myself; 'if she does, I'll make no inquiries, demand no stories, set no conditions, but humbly put my life in her hands, tell her the whole tale of the two thousand and two nights that led me to her, and bid her end that story as she will—whether with the last good-night of all or (what I can just dimly envision, like dawn in another world) some clear and fine and fresh good-morning.'"

Dunyazade yawned and shivered. "I can't imagine what you're talking about. Am I expected to believe that preposterous business of Breastless Pilgrims and Tragic Views?"

"Yes!" cried Shah Zaman, then let his head fall back to the pillow. "They're too important to be lies. Fictions, maybe—but truer than fact."

Dunyazade covered her eyes with her razor-hand. "What do you expect me to do? Forgive you? Love you?"

"Yes!" the King cried again, his eyes flashing. "Let's end the dark night! All that passion and hate between men and women; all that confusion of inequality and difference! Let's take the truly tragic view of love! Maybe it *is* a fiction, but it's the profoundest and best of all! Treasure me, Dunyazade, as I'll treasure you!"

"For pity's sake, stop!"

But Shah Zaman urged ardently: "Let's embrace; let's forbear; let's love as long as we can, Dunyazade—then embrace again, forbear and love again!"

"It won't work."

"Nothing *works!* But the enterprise is noble; it's full of joy and life, and the other ways are deathy. Let's make love like passionate equals!"

"You mean *as if* we were equals," Dunyazade said. "You know we're not. What you want is impossible."

"Despite your heart's feelings?" pressed the King. "Let it be *as if!* Let's make a philosophy of that *as if!*"

Dunyazade wailed: "I want my sister!"

"She may be alive; my brother, too." More quietly, Shah Zaman explained that Shahryar had been made acquainted with his brother's recent history and opinions, and had vowed that should Scheherazade ever attempt his life, he'd manage himself somewhat similarly: that is (as he was twenty years older, and more conservative), not exactly granting his wife the power to kill him, but disarming and declining to kill *her*, and within the bounds of good public relations, permitting her a freedom comparable to his own. The harem was a royal tradition, necessarily public; Scheherazade could take what lovers she would, but of necessity in private. Et cetera.

"Did you really imagine your sister *fooled* Shahryar for a thousand nights with her mamelukes and dildoes?" Shah Zaman laughed. "A man couldn't stay king very long if he didn't even know what was going on in the harem! And why do you suppose he permitted it, if not that he loved her too much, and was too sick of his other policy, to kill her? She changed his mind, all right, but she never fooled him: he used to believe that all women were unfaithful, and that the only way to spare himself the pain of infidelity was to deflower and kill them; now he believes that all *people* are unfaithful, and that the way to spare oneself the pain of infidelity is to love and not to care. He chooses equal promiscuity; I choose equal fidelity. Let's treasure each other, Dunyazade!"

She shook her head angrily, or desperately. "It's absurd. You're only trying to talk your way out of a bad spot."

"Of course I am! And of course it's absurd! Treasure me!"

"I'm exhausted. I should use the razor on both of us, and be done with it."

"Treasure me, Dunyazade!"

"We've talked all night; I hear the cocks; it's getting light."

"Good-morning, then! Good-morning!"

III

Alf Laylah Wa Laylah, The Book of the Thousand Nights and a Night, is not the story of Scheherazade, but the story of the story of her stories, which in effect begins: "There is a book called *The Thousand and One Nights,* in which it is said that once upon a time a king had two sons, Shahryar and Shah Zaman," et cetera; it ends when a king long after Shahryar discovers in his treasury the thirty volumes of *The Stories of the Thousand Nights and a Night,* at the end of the last of which the royal couples—Shahryar and Scheherazade, Shah Zaman and Dunyazade—emerge from their bridal chambers after the wedding night, greet one another with warm good-mornings (eight in all), bestow Samarkand on the brides' long-suffering father, and set down for all posterity *The Thousand Nights and a Night*.

If I could invent a story as beautiful, it should be about little Dunyazade and her bridegroom, who pass a thousand nights in one dark night and in the morning embrace each other; they make love side by side, their faces close, and go out to greet sister and brother in the forenoon of a new life. Dunyazade's story begins in the middle; in the middle of my own, I can't conclude it—but it must end in the night that all good-mornings come to. The Arab storytellers understood this; they ended their stories not "happily ever after," but specifically "until there took them the Destroyer of Delights and Desolator of Dwelling-places, and they were translated to the ruth of Almighty Allah, and their houses fell waste and their palaces lay in ruins, and the Kings inherited their riches." And no man knows it better than Shah Zaman, to whom therefore the second half of his life will be sweeter than the first.

To be joyous in the full acceptance of this dénouement is surely to possess a treasure, the key to which is the understanding that Key and Treasure are the same. There (with a kiss, little sister) is the sense of our story, Dunyazade: The key to the treasure is the treasure.

SOME MOLDENKE

David Ohle

I. EARLY MOLDENKE

oldenke lived the hainted life. As a child he was kept in a crumbled brick of a house where thick windows moaned in their frames through summerfall and gathered ice by winter.

In the prime of his boyhood an ether tree patiently died in the view from his bedroom window. In the spring a green woodbird flew down and pecked spirals around its dry trunk. Moldenke would fold himself in his chair and watch several suns rise behind the ether branches, studying the woodbird's habits.

Days would rush on a klick a minute. All things were tight then. Moldenke was free and green, bright suns behind him, spirals ahead.

2. LATER MOLDENKE

He pressed his noseball against a lookout and felt something coming toward him, formless, edgeless, nothing at all, silent, from the direction of eastern light. He crabbed backward up the stairwell and crouched in a blind spot. He felt it move through his rooms, the visitor, searching out a place to fix itself. A light went on. Now Moldenke could see. He closed his eyes, knowing it was closer. He stood up. It was with him, its rubber bag inflated against his face.

3. UPPER MOLDENKE

When Moldenke allowed his mind to wander it would take him to a sunchoked acre of grasses and weed where a pollen snow lay yellow and inches deep. It was like a rotunda, obviously complete, yet nothing suggested architecture. There was no dome.

Northerly winds, unnaturally warm, lapped his stringy hairs. He felt no pulse, little metabolism, only hum and flow. If life was flight, Moldenke was wing.

He would circle the acre and listen. There would be heavy breathing, laboring lungs. Something with mudded claws would spit clots from surrounding bush. Moldenke would turn away in fear, his chin on his chest, his hands in his pockets.

Rarely were there permutations from the standard, and even then only a matter of red-eyed rabbits. Other than these things, nothing would ever happen.

4. A TELEPHONE CALL

Moldenke picked up the speaker.

"Moldenke?" It seemed a genuine voice.

"Yes?"

"Moldenke?"

"Yes, this is Moldenke."

"Moldenke?"

"Yes?"

"Are you leaning against a wall?"

"No."

"It would be easier if you did."

"Who am I speaking to?" Moldenke asked, his shoulder against the wall.

"Never mind that, friend. Are you leaning yet?"

"Yes."

"Fine enough. Open up your good ear and listen hard."

"Now I know who this is. I'm not playing." He could feel floor through his soft shoes.

"Listen to me, Moldenke. This is turds. Don't hand me gas. Are you ready to hear me out?"

"All right, all right. Say it, get it over with."

"It's quite simple, friend. We have something you might want. Nicely packaged and locked in the vaults. A few tapes. Nothing complex. Just tapes."

At this point Moldenke hung up.

5. A LETTER CAME IN THE MAIL

Dear Mr. Moldenke,

Now that Featherfighter is free, why don't we pull you out of the M's and jack you up to a loftier position, perhaps as high as the higher A's, assuming things continue smooth.

By the way, I understand that old Bunce has moved himself, as it were, to another location. On the one hand, this fact doesn't bother me in the slightest. But on the other hand, as you well know, I wear a different glove, and I occasionally find myself wanting him brought into focus before summer falls. Can you comprehend this, Moldenke? I ask you.

How are things in the city? I think of you often, Moldenke. I say to myself, Moldenke should be the one soaking in this country air, not me. After all, he's the one with twisted organs.

Many regards,

Your country friend,

Burnheart

6. DELETED

7 . DELETED

8 . OATMEAL AND CATFISH

He picked up the speaker, put it to his good ear, and listened. Static, chewing bleeps, dust of silver, *static,* as though someone shaved burnt toast at the other end.

He put the speaker back in its cradle and went to his lookout. Traffic signals, cars, noise, people, and the stink of barley.

Something faint, and above, suggested sky. A sun looked over a building, a pig over a fence.

As far as Moldenke could tell, things were tight. The sight of it made him flash to his youthful days of steaming oatmeal and catfish.

9 . DELETED

10 . COMMENTARY

Moldenke was faithless. Each time he opened a spigot and got water, no matter how lymphy, he swooned, as though he didn't really expect it, although he loved water as dearly as he loved anything. That was the way with Moldenke, little more than heat and confusion, a bright candle with a shortened wick, destined to give off gas and burn low.

11 . THE COMPLETE TAPES

The phone rang. Moldenke answered the last ring in its middle.
"Hello?"
"Is this Moldenke?"
"Yes."
"I don't like a hang up, friend. How would you like a fire iron inserted in your very delicate chuff pipe, all the way up? And if that doesn't do it, I have alternatives. Are you ready to listen now?"
"You don't scare me, Bunce."

"We have the tapes. . . ."

"I don't know tapes. What tapes? I'm not worried about tape threats, Bunce. What tapes?"

"Tapes, friend. The *complete* tapes. Every word that was ever said about you when you weren't around. Would you like to know what goes on in your absence? Would you like to know what so-and-so said about you at such-and-such a time? If you ever do, give me a call. I'll be around."

Moldenke hung up.

12. A WEATHER REPORT

He dialed in a station and got a weather report:

Cloudy, with freezing in the outskirts. Colder tonight, on the warm side tomorrow, Thursday, and Friday. Much colder over the weekend. Looks like a trend—warm to cold to warm. Chance of snow, probable sleet, mixed drizzle finishing out the month. Covering haze from coast to coast with gaps at Amarillo, Texaco, and Kodak City. The fences are reported up on seaboards finally, and the wind is dying. That looks good for east-west traveling. We're looking for a midnight reading of zero degrees, without humidity. Lozenges will be more than handy tonight. You may want to shelter animals, you may not, depending. Wrapping it up, the jet stream looks like it's curling, and that looks ominous for the West.

13. DELETED

14. 555-3535-3355-5

Moldenke dialed 555-3535-3355-5. Someone answered the first ring.

"Chelsea Fish Pavilion."

Moldenke said, "Excuse me. I may have misdialed."

"Sir," the voice was female, "what number did you call?"

"What number did I reach?"

"555-3535-3355-5, the Chelsea Fish Pavilion."

"Yes, that's the number. Is there someone there by the name of Bunce?"

"Yes, sir. There is. Would you like me to connect you with him?"

"No thanks, dear. I already am."

15. DELETED

16. A BURNHEART LETTER

Moldenke went to his cabinet of files and took out an old Burnheart letter.

Dear Mr. Moldenke,

Yesterday I had a productive visit with my friend, Peter Eagleman, from Atmospheric Sciences. He was full of his ensifer work with *Oecanthus*, and it took him a full cigar to get it all out on the table, so to speak. Picture me in my tiny lab, gagging on all that smoke.

One question, Moldenke. How are your polyps?

Cordially, Burnheart

17. DELETED

18. THE POSTWAR YEAR

Subsequent to his discharge from the Army, Moldenke found a make-work position in the gauze plant near Kodak City, a few klicks from the northern borderline. He started out low, but quickly went up. He remembered what his mother had said. "Son," she had said, huddled over him, her eyes like basement windows. "Sonny," she would say, "I always want you to have a job to go to. No matter where. No matter what. I want you to have a situation which allows you to go straight up. Do you understand what I say?" The rigors of age printed on her

424

face, the collar of her woolly at his neck like a feather, the smell of her like coconut. He never forgot the words.

19. DELETED

20. DARKNESS

As suddenly as they had come on, Moldenke's lights went out. He spun in panic, flipping switches, going to the lookout and pressing his noseball against the pane, seeking brightness. But nothing happened. The juice was off.

He ran to his refrigerator. Warmth, darkness. A circle of cockroaches fed at his lettuce. *Already?* he thought. Something scratched around inside the eggshells. He knew now what to do. No more hesitating. He would have to call the Power Co-op.

21. FURTHER BUNCE

The phone rang. Moldenke took his time answering.

"Hello?"

"Am I speaking with Moldenke?" It was Bunce.

"What now, Bunce?"

"Here it is, friend: From now on only one outgoing call per day, two incoming, all monitored. Consider benefits and privileges terminated, and don't leave your room until we say so. We don't *necessarily* want your blood, but don't rule it out. Be patient. Read a few magazines. No moving around. Pick a chair you like and stay with it. No changing. We'll have your food sent up. What do you think this is, Moldenke, a night-flying outfit? Don't be so casual. How would you like to spend an afternoon in the hot-room with old Bunce? I want seriousness from you. Remember, if you don't ease off, you might get plugged."

"What are you doing, Bunce?"

"What am I doing, he says."

"I don't like hot-room threats."

"He doesn't like hot-room threats."

"Your joshing gets me angry."

"My joshing gets him angry."

"Show me some proof."

"You want proof?"

"Yes, proof."

"Okay, friend. Wait a few minutes and then go to your lookout."

He waited.

He stood at the lookout, watching an amber mist become a drizzle. Where was the proof? He scanned horizons. Nothing. Where was the sign? He surveyed the streets. No sign. He felt utterly alone, yet snug. He saw pigeons in eaves across the way. No cars, no buses.

An ant crawled across the floor, over Moldenke's foot, over his other foot, across more floor, and went up the farthest wall. He never noticed.

Something climbed from shelf to shelf in the refrigerator.

There was a low hiss, at first distant, then close. He spun in the darkness. He saw its eyelike headlight, heard the rubber inflating. Proof had arrived.

22. DELETED

23. A COUPLE

Several months before all this, Moldenke had been driving his kerosene Rambler along a white boulevard that curved around a stadium. At a certain point on the curve he spotted a couple, man and woman. The woman knelt over the gutter, favoring her stomach, her face a shade of purple. Moldenke stopped. The man, tobacco-stained and scholarly, asked if Moldenke would be so kind as to give them a ride to a drugstore to get some charcoal tablets.

426

They lifted the heavy woman into the rear seat and drove on. Moldenke began to have his doubts about the couple. The woman grunted in the back, an odd smell coming from her direction.

"Charcoal tablets?" Moldenke questioned.

"Yez," the man said, "for my wife."

Moldenke looked at him more closely. One eyebrow dangled over the eye; parts of the face began to flake down the front of the suit.

Moldenke took out a cigar. He was testing.

"No flames, pliz!" The man trembled.

Moldenke held out his lighter, his thumb on the flint.

"Why not?" He turned the flint slowly. The car was filling with gas.

The moustache was sliding down the tie. Above the collar the plastic had begun to curl. Now Moldenke was certain. He knew exactly what to do. He gunned the k-Rambler and drove toward the Southern Bottoms. Traffic dwindled and disappeared, civilization thinned to an empty marsh veined with treeless ridges. Blind roads turned into the marsh at every klick marker. Moldenke picked one at random and drove through the slush ruts until they ended. He turned off the motor.

He looked at the man. "Are you a pair of Bunce's scabs?"

The woman sat up, said nothing. The man was rigid, most of his face in his lap.

"I asked if you were from Bunce!" Moldenke held the lighter tightly.

They said nothing.

"All right, you two. This is the end of the road. Get out."

They stepped out like obedient dogs.

Moldenke went to the trunk and got his tire tool.

"Both of you, lie flat, heads down."

The skulls were brittle. He could have used the heel of his

shoe instead of the tire tool. A clear liquid drained from the wounds, thick and jellylike, smelling of laboratories.

In the morning, with the first sun behind him like a stray moon, Moldenke examined his car. The odor of gas was faint. In the back seat there was the same jellylike substance, sloshed across the upholstery, studded with nibs, as though she had eaten peanuts.

24. DELETED

25. THE MEAL

There was a knock at his door. When he answered it his meal was there. If Bunce was nothing else, he was punctual. Whoever knocked was gone. The meal was on a tray, covered with a cloth. Moldenke took it inside and ate. The meal consisted of cat, crickets, and a chunk of stale pinebread.

26. A LETTER AND A QUESTIONNAIRE

A parcel arrived in the mail. Moldenke opened it. There was a letter and a questionnaire.

Dear Mr. Moldenke,

Be a good boy, as they say, and fill out this questionnaire and get it back to me as fast as you can. I can't move an inch without it. We haven't had the meeting yet, so keep your fingers crossed.

Sincerest regards, Burnheart

The questionnaire:

SITUATION REACTION

Situation One: You are shad fishing in a plainly marked municipal water tub. The fog log is at .77, the light scanty. No moons are up. As you look out over the water you spy what appears to be the corpse of a horse. You stand and look harder. *Caution*—it may not be a horse at all. It floats closer, a few feet from the breakwater,

428

clearly in danger of barnacles. You feel your heart leaping up. Your spleen is puffy. What now?

(Use this space)

27. DELETED

28. ONE OUTGOING

Moldenke called the Power Co-op.

"Good afternoon, sir. Power Co-op, may I help you?" The voice was ambitiously female.

Moldenke was puzzled.

"How did you know I was male, dear?"

"Didn't you say so, sir?"

"I haven't said a word yet. Was it my breathing? A man's breathing is always huskier than a woman's, is that the key?"

"Sir, my apologies. We beg your pardon."

"*We* beg my pardon? *We?*"

"Yes, sir. Power Co-op, as a whole. All of us."

"I understand. I see. Let's forget it. What I called about is my electricity. It went off. No radio, no weather reports, no re-frigerator. I can hardly think. I need some service out here."

"Certainly, Mr. Moldenke. Anything we can do."

"Excuse me, dear."

"Yes?"

"I'm a little confused. First there was the *sir*, and now you give me a clear *Mr. Moldenke.* I haven't mentioned my name as yet, have I, miss?"

"Haven't you, sir? Didn't you just say it?"

"Nope."

"You didn't?"

"Not once. Let me speak to your supervisor."

"I'm sorry, sir. He's not in the building at the moment."

"Then I'll talk to *his* supervisor. Right now!"

"Yes, sir. That would be Mr. Bunce. Just a moment—"
The only outgoing of the day, thrown to the winds.

29. DELETED

30. BURNHEART COMES

Moldenke sat in his chair like a hen, brooding in the dark, chewing a numbpick, refusing to think. His door opened halfway, showing an obelisk of hall light, and Burnheart came in.

"Burnheart?"

"Moldenke?"

Burnheart struck a match and held it an inch from Moldenke's chin. "Why are you living like this, Moldenke? You become more like a rat every season. How much do they pay you to live in this dump? I smell urine. Where's the straw?"

The match went out. Burnheart struck another, this time moving it up and down, looking at the whole Moldenke.

"Burnheart. I'm glad to see you. Sit down, please. I thought you were in the country."

"I was in the country. Now I'm in the city. My body moves with my moods. I wanted city, so I came to get it, as the saying goes. Why do I strike matches? Turn on some lights."

"I can't. They're off."

"I'll smash the landlord's teeth."

"It's not the landlord. It's Bunce."

"I see. Bunce."

"I'm worried. Help me."

"Surely you have a candle somewhere."

"Tell me what to do, Burnheart. You're the only one."

"What a season this has been, Moldenke. What a season. My old heart won't stand another one. I may retire. There are only so many loads in the gun, as it were. I'm plumb tired."

"Sit down, then."

"Are there chairs?"

430

"Just this one. I'm sorry."

Another match went out.

"I'm running low on matches . . . we'll puff cigars. A little light is better than none." Burnheart lit two cigars with his last match and gave one to Moldenke. "Here, puff constantly. We'll get close and puff."

They studied one another in the wavering orange light of the cigars, through the smoke.

"Burnheart . . . I killed two of Bunce's scabs."

"You did what?"

"I smelled the gas. The face came off. I *knew* they belonged to Bunce."

"So you killed them?"

"Sure, what else?"

"You chew too many numbpicks. Where are your brains?"

"I did wrong?"

"Bunce has power, Moldenke. More than I have. There's not much I can do now."

"Burnheart! Help me."

"I'm sorry. All I can do is be your friend. I'm only a scientist. I have limits."

"Should I run?"

"I'd sit still."

"What should I do?"

"I'd do nothing."

Their eyes ran. They blinked. Occasionally they coughed. The cigars wore down. Burnheart went to the lookout. "There it is," he said.

"What?" Moldenke sat in his chair.

"The city. There's the city. I'm back again."

"Don't leave here yet, Burnheart. Stay longer."

"I'm sorry, Moldenke. I have experiments to run. I'll be going. I only came to bring you a letter I'd written, and then forgot to mail." He took an envelope out of his coat and gave it to Moldenke.

"I'm leaving now. Are we friends?"

"Yes, of course."

"Double-clutching buddy-buddies?"

"Sure."

"Then what are you worried about? Read the letter when I leave. It may be a bit out-of-date, as I heard a man say once."

Burnheart turned and closed the door behind him.

By the final glow of his cigar, Moldenke read the letter.

Dear Mr. Moldenke,

Eagleman is too fast for me. He's what the railroad is to the cow. Ah, why these preliminaries? Let's get to the meat— Eagleman and I met yesterday. We drank instant tea and discussed your future, although we didn't agree on a single issue. Once again, you're safe.

As ever, Burnheart

P.S. But watch out for Bunce.

31. DELETED

THE TEMPTATION OF ST. IVO

John Gardner

od forgive me, I hate Brother Nicholas. I hoe in silence, sweat pouring down my forehead, catching in my bristly eyebrows, dripping from my nose, washing down my neck inside my cassock. My feet grow slippery in my sandals. My arms ache, my heart pounds, and despite my labors I can't stay ahead of him. I know he's watching. I know his hoe must surely overtake me before I can reach the monastery wall, and if it doesn't, I must turn the next row of beans and must face him, pass him, and as I pass hear his whisper, shrink from his trawling, ferreting smile. Where we meet, where he attacks me, will be his decision. He's younger than I am, and stronger, for though we weigh the same, he's nearly two feet taller, and his weight is all in his thighs, his chest, his shoulders.

I am old. Fifty. My weight's in my miserable belly. My arms and legs are as white as potato sprouts under the cassock, and as flabby, as jiggly, as buttocks. I spent all my years—until lately, when Brother Nicholas made that life intolerable—at books, serving God with my hand and eyes. I drew, as did he, zoomorphic capitals—beasts eating beasts in the universal war of raging will against raging will: dragons, bears, birds, rabbits, bucks, all coiled, unwitting, in the larger design of an *A* or an *O*.

435

Decorations for sacred manuscripts. I was said to be a genius along that line. All the glory be to God.

But then one day there was Brother Nicholas, long-nosed, eagle-eyed, his flowing hair more black than a raven's, and he was whispering, brazenly defying the rule—whispering and whispering, and glancing at me slyly from time to time as if daring me to respond to his whisper or report him to the keeper of the cell. I'd do neither. The scheme of providence demands of us all that each man humbly perform his part, sing his own line in the terrestrial hymn, as the planets are singing, unheard, above us, and with charity forgive those to left and right when they falter. That may sound pompous, simpleminded, but it's true, or anyway I hope it's true. A man can go mad, discarding all tradition, reasoning out for himself the precise details of celestial and terrestrial law. I've been there. Live by rule, as all Nature does, illuminating the divine limits exactly as ink fills invisible lines. Put strife aside. Shall blue contend with gold, or gold with crimson? We are merely instruments, and he who denies his condition will suffer. The world is a river, and he who resists the pressure of Time and Space will be overwhelmed by it. Surely I am right and Brother Nicholas wrong!

I could not answer him in words—the rule of silence forbade it—but I told him in every way I could that I had no wish to contend with him. I gave him gifts, touched his shoulder gently as I passed. He hissed at me, eyebrows lifted, "Ha! Homosexual!" I changed to a carrel far removed from his, smiling meekly to let him understand I intended no offense. He smiled, jaw thrown forward like a billy goat's, and moved to the carrel directly behind my new one.

I prayed for peace of mind. I put all my energy into my work. But I can hardly deny it, that endless, malevolent whisper was distracting. Malevolent. Why should I shrink from the charge? He meant me to hear it, meant my soul to be offended by it. I can see him now, tall, his long hair black as midnight, his careless, undisciplined brush moving swiftly, making swoops and arcs, his tiny pig's eyes rolled to watch me, his thin mouth wickedly smiling as he whispers. But I would not break the rule of silence for any provocation, and after a moment his eyes would slice back to his work.

He's a fiend, I would tell myself. I tried to believe, and to some extent succeeded, that it was not Brother Nicholas himself I hated, but the devil within him. For there *is* a devil within him, so both doctrine and common sense maintain. He willfully, pointlessly strikes out at me. He scorns all rule, defies all order for mere anarchy's sake. I will not deny that I begin to be alarmed.

There's no question now: he's pursuing me. Though his craft is mediocre, he had a position many brothers might envy, in sinful secret. He sat in comfort in the cool of the high-arched sunlit hall, merely filling in lines with his weightless brush, while out where rain makes a cassock hang heavy and sun burns the forehead and nose to a crisp, men less gifted—lay brothers of the order—were pitching manure behind the monastery stables, or hauling, shaping, and implanting stone, or throwing their weight on the blunt iron plow and stumbling along after oxen. You've no idea till you've tried it what that means. They don't dawdle, those beasts. Even Brother Molin, whose father was a giant, can't muster the power it would take both to hammer the plowshare in and jerk back the rein that would slow the lead ox to a walk. So we see on every side that he who pursues his individual will, in defiance of providence and common profit, will be dragged where the oxen choose, but he who will put all his back into plowing, merely guiding direction, and will let oxen run as the Lord inspires, can carve out furrows that feed not only the monastery but passing knights and the prisoners in town as well.

When I asked to be transferred to the fields, pleading that God had called me there, to serve with the humblest of our lay brothers, mortifying my puffed up heart, Brother Nicholas at once asked for similar transfer. I think I need not set it down to sinful pride that I interpret his transfer as pursuit of me. He does not whisper when others are nearby. In fact, when I mentioned his eternal whispering in confessional, my confessor was unable to believe me. He's new, this confessor, and doesn't know me well. I was not much surprised or disappointed. As one grows older, one sees finally that one cannot take one's troubles to other men. They have troubles of their own.

Gently, kindly, the voice behind the dark curtain said: "Brother Ivo, pray for perception in this matter. Open your heart to God, and consider in your mind, with the freedom and pure objectivity God's grace can give, that the situation may not be as you think. You work at a pitch very few maintain. All your brothers have noticed and have worried about it, and have prayed for you. Meditate on this: that the mind and body are interdependent, so long as corruptible flesh enfolds us. The strain on the body which heightens your gifts may heighten, also, your soul's susceptibilities to influences darker than those which illuminate your art."

Ah, how rich with self-satisfaction that sleepy, maternal voice! It's not easy to believe he was ever shocked awake with an image burning to be realized, an image so fierce in its holiness and beauty that it lifts you, as if by the hairs of your head, and condemns you to pace from wall to wall in your room, stalling its terrible energy, until at last, praise God, you hear vigil ring and can plunge, after prayers, into diligence. But it was not my place to condemn my confessor. He too is God's instrument— unless all Brother Nicholas whispers is true.

"Thank you, Father," I said, resisting the anger of frustration. And in the days that followed I made an honest effort to believe it might be as my confessor supposed.

Most widespread errors, I have come to see, contain an element of truth. I prayed for sleep, and I slept. But the whispering continued. And watching my brothers shrewdly—pretending to struggle with an interlace figure round a serpent's head—I discovered they *knew*. They'd glance up, startled, from four great sunlit windows away when Brother Nicholas' whispering began, and then, quickly, they'd look down again, denying the knowledge.

So I fled to the fields. He followed me, smiling, tall and hollow-eyed, his affected meekness sinister.

And now his hoe is some six feet behind me, swiftly, casually tearing up the earth, still gaining on me, and I begin to imagine already that I can hear his whisper. *Brother Ivo, your rules are absurd! The order of the world is an accident. We could change it in an instant, simply by opening our throats and speaking. Brother Ivo, listen!* The sound is so distinct I glance back past my shoulder without meaning to, and I see I'm not wrong. His eyes meet mine, sharp blue cones of fire beneath those coal-black brows. He smiles, shows his teeth. *Brother Ivo, I've decided to murder the phoenix. I've discovered where it lives.* I jerk my head around, continue hoeing, stabbing fiercely, resisting the temptation to work sloppily and escape him again. *You don't believe in the phoenix, Brother Ivo? I give you my word, you're the only man who can save the beast.*

"Fool!" I could tell him, "do you take me for a blear-eyed, bullnecked serf, who places his trust in mere outward signs, allegorical apparel—phoenixes, salamanders, fat-coiled dragons? I've been painting the shadows the truth casts all my life!"

But my heart quickens and a tremor of fear runs through my veins. I almost spoke! I have underestimated my enemy again.

Why is it so important to him that I break my vow and speak? What will he have proved? That one man can be corrupted? Surely he must know that any man can be corrupted!

He continues to gain on me, whispering. The blade of his hoe strikes two inches from my foot, jerks backward, strikes again. He will soon come even with me. *I leave tonight, Brother*

Ivo. As soon as they're all asleep, after Compline. Up there on the mountain, that's where it is. A cave just under the outcropping rocks. There's a goat path goes up to a hundred yards from the entrance. He comes even with me, his sleeve brushes against mine, mock-seductive. I jerk myself away. I'm enraged, tempted almost beyond resistance to turn on him with my hoe. (In a fight he could easily kill me.) I flash him a warning glance, struggling to do it with the dignity befitting a superior; he smiles, head tipped, flaps a womanish hand; and suddenly I see how grotesque I must look, head drawn back unnaturally, pursed lips pompous, a small fat man twisting his head around, manfully struggling to stare down his nose at a man who's taller. Again he's made a fool of me.

I turn, facing him, but swallow my shout. He studies me coolly, leaning forward over his hoe, as detached and cold-blooded as an alchemist studying iron. I control myself. My rage turns to fear. The shadow of the forested mountain has reached the western edge of the village. All the valley to my left is in ominous shade. He leans toward me, whispering. *Do not be too hasty in judging my project, Brother Ivo. Many notable authors have spoken of the phoenix, and holy men among them. Cyril, Epiphanius, Ambrose, Tertullian.* He hisses straight into my ear, spraying spittle. *Illum dico alitem orientis peculiarem, de singularitate famosum, de posteritate monstruosum; que semetipsum libenter funerans renovat, natali fine decedens, atque succedens iterum Phoenix. —And what of the ninety-second psalm?* He rolls up his steel-grey eyes, mock-pious. *Despite all that, you deny the bird's existence. Very well! But it exists, nonetheless, and I have found it, and I mean to murder it. Prevent me if you can!* And now, without a backward glance, he strides forward, hoeing.

I stand watching, baffled by the turmoil of my emotions, until he's chopped his way to the monastery wall. He's like a monstrous crow, bent forward, black hair streaming over his shoulders and the black of his borrowed habit. Dirt flies, bits of plants. I press my hand to my chest, calming the rush of my heart.

I can find no escape from this dread, I have walked from end to end of this place. I have tried to lose myself in the majestic schemata of stained-glass windows, the gargoyles' brute anguish, high above me, or the nobler beauty of groups of monks in silent fellowship, their white cassocks sharp against the dark of groves and shadowed hill slopes, like delicate white flowers in cedar shade. I have considered the old, symbolic walls, the ascent of shaft on sculptured shaft toward finials blazing in the sun's last light. I have fled like a tortured ghost from one green court-yard to another, have stood on the bridge looking out on the mirror-smooth lake where two old monks sit fishing and a heavy old serf, a lay brother, black-robed, sits sleeping at the oars. Swans move, silent as grace, toward the darkening shore. I have knelt in prayer at the place where the river divides in three, in the shadow of oaks and walnut trees, but no prayer came, my eyes were too full of black arches and pilings.

My eyes go, sick with envy, to the third-floor room of scribes and illuminators, the room where, not long since, I was master. Pride, envy, wrath. . . . My soul is bloated, weighed down, with sin. It fills me with panic. He has only begun on me!

I pray for understanding. If I could grasp what drives him, I could elude him, I think. I could pity him, look for the good his hostility toward me obscures. I could feel charity. Is it envy that drives him? Envy of my skill, perhaps?

I remember when he looked at the phoenix with which he makes fun of me now. A design as perfect—I give thanks to God—as anything I've done. Interlace so complex as to baffle the mind, as God's providence baffles, His mysterious workings, secret order in the seemingly pathless universal forest. Twelve colors, the colors of the New Jerusalem. And in the feathers of the bird, ingeniously, almost invisibly woven, the characters *Resurrexit*. Brother Nicholas studied it, holding the parchment to the light, at arm's length, frowning. I could see that he understood its virtues—the reverence, the integrity of mind and emotion, the tour de force technique. Then he turned to me, gave me a queer, bored smile, and handed the parchment back.

It was not feigned, that smile. One knows what one knows. He whispered, "Excellent," and I saw that what he said he meant, but also that the excellence was a matter of total indifference to him. Then if ever I might have spoken!

A man cannot be a master artist if he lies to himself, settles for illusions; and I do not fool myself that my vow of silence is as important to me as God's gift to me of skill. But I said nothing. If I were to break the vow, it should be in the name of another man's need, not my own.

I had known, from the first time I heard him whisper, that one clear possibility was that Brother Nicholas was reaching, in devious fashion, for help. It was perhaps despair that made him a careless, indifferent artist. What if I, a fellow artist, was his soul's last human hope? What selfishness, then—what spiritual cowardice—that I refused him what he asked, a companionable voice! But the choice was not by any means easy. Far into the night I would pace in the black of my windowless cell, from bench to wall, from wall to bench, wringing my fingers, straining for clarity, wrestling with the problem. I would pray on the cold stone floor until my knees felt crushed, and still no certainty came.

This was the thing: None of my brothers is free from sin, any more than I am, but how lax our order has grown in these, the world's last days, nevertheless alarms me. Many brothers keep hounds and hawks, though all the councils have forbidden hunting, *voluptatis causa*, as a mortal sin. They not only go out with hounds and hawks, they mount horses and join in noisy, drunken parties, chasing headlong after rabbits and deer and outrunning the hounds themselves. They show no shame about feeding their packs from the possessions of the poor, so that slender greyhounds batten on what might have kept children alive. They know well enough how little I approve, and how little I favor their costly meals, their wrestling matches, their frequent absence from prayers, their indifference to the chants. Though vengeance is the Lord's, I can't keep secret my scorn.

I fight for humility, but surely it is true that either you believe in the code and traditions or you don't, and if you don't, you ought to get out. And so the question is this: how can I be sure that Brother Nicholas pursues me from need of me, not from hatred of what he thinks my foolish, old-fashioned rigidity? How do I know it's not barbaric joy that drives him—the joy of the kill?

I can say this: He whispers to me of freedom. He tells me he's freed himself of all restraints—religions, philosophies, political systems. He tells me he means to so use up life that when death comes it will find in him nothing but shriveled dregs. He looks in my eyes as he says this (it was weeks ago, but I see the grim image more clearly than I see the abbey spires, now dark in the shadow of the mountain). *You understand this,* he whispers. *You're a man of keen intelligence, though afraid of life.*

I do not answer, but my heart beats fast. "You're wrong, I would tell him. Not wrong in mere doctrine. Even if there were, as he claims, no heaven or hell, he would be wrong. A terrifying error.

So this: Suppose it's zeal that drives him, the passion of a mad ideal? If so, he will be merciless. My vow of silence will be a minor detail. Having broken down my defenses there, he'll press on, break down further defenses—teach me gluttony, lechery, sloth, despair. He'll hammer till I'm totally free, totally abandoned.

I cannot know, mortal that I am, what's in his heart, whether his pursuit of me is a devious plea or a murderous temptation.

And so I cling to my creed, my rules, my traditions. If God is just, despairing man's cry will be answered. If not, what hope for any of us? So I reason it through for the hundredth time, and am no more satisfied than ever.

I search the darkening sky, the pitch-dark woods for some sign, and there is none. In the abbey they are singing Compline now. Who would guess from the sweetness of their voices that they are mere men, fallible and confused and perhaps at times terrified, like me? *Dear Lord*, I whisper. . . . But I find myself moving, plunging back toward the bridge and across it and up the wide stone steps toward the chancel door, hardly aware what it is that I've decided. I wait there, listening. It scarcely bothers me that I've missed supper, missed the service. Compline ends. For a few moments longer they will kneel on the floor in silent prayer, then begin to get up, one here, three there, then more, padding softly away to their beds.

The confessor will be last to leave, as is right and traditional.

I am surprised at how patiently he listens tonight. I pour out my sins, worst of all, my faithless terror. Strangely, the fear does not diminish, here in God's sanctuary. Behind me, beyond the confessional door, the great room is dark except for one red flame above the altar, the burning heart. I cannot see where the ornamented columns attach to the ceiling: for all my eye can tell, they may plunge upward forever, into deepest space.

"Father," I whisper, "I am afraid. I believe in the Resurrection, believe that God has redeemed us all, made mankind free —all these things I've believed since childhood. But I seem to believe them only with my mind. My heart is full of fear."

His voice is gentle, mysteriously patient. I would feel better, somehow, if I could see his face—lean on his humanness until my trust in God comes back. I have a childish thought that he might not be a man at all but an angel or a demon, perhaps a fox with slanting eyes. I have done too much drawing, too much looking at drawings; my mind is infected by shadows from dreams.

He says gently—the huge room echoes around him from window to window and beam to beam: "You believe Brother Nicholas is the Devil."

"I do," I confess. "It's madness. I know that. And yet I need some help against my fantasy."

"I understand, my son."

"Father, I haven't imagined these things. I realize it's difficult for you to believe, but he does whisper. Constantly. It's like a serpent's hiss—he means it to be, to frighten me. And he follows me. There's no denying it: he followed me out into the fields. He follows me everywhere, teasing, tempting, tormenting me. . . ."

"I know."

I look up, startled, at the black curtain. The room grows ominously silent. At last I whisper, "You know?"

"I know, yes. I have thought and prayed on this matter of yours, and I have watched. I saw it myself this afternoon."

My heart races, full of joy. Only now do I recognize that I have actually begun to doubt that Brother Nicholas whispers.

"He's cunning, Father, and shameless. He believes in *nothing*."

I tell what he's said to me of freedom. Behind the dark curtain the confessor seems to listen. I tell of the lunatic joke about the phoenix. The confessor stops me.

"But that's absurd," he says. "Surely Brother Nicholas knows you take no stock in dead mythologies!"

"Exactly! But you see, that's his cynicism. It's like a certain kind of madness, but it isn't madness. Sometimes madmen, to avoid the dangers inherent in human contact, will retreat to gibberish. They communicate, yet don't communicate. So Galen writes, and many other ancients are of the same opinion. But it's not fear of human relationships that drives Brother Nicholas.

445

It's scorn, Father. He speaks, as if earnestly, of things he knows to be nonsense, and thus he mocks all earnestness."

I wait eagerly for his reaction. I'm not sure myself that I am right. It seems a full minute before he answers.

"Scorn," he muses.

A tingle of terror runs through me. I fully understand only now how dangerous my enemy is.

My confessor says: "But wait. Perhaps we're proceeding too quickly. He told you he was going to murder the phoenix—told you he would leave the monastery tonight, after everyone was asleep."

"Yes, he said that." I do not grasp what my confessor is driving at.

"And if he *does* leave?"

"Why should he? He knows perfectly well—" But a chill in my spine tells me that my confessor is onto something.

"If he does in fact leave, what will it mean? Is it possible that his absurd warning is in some way a code? Could he possibly have meant—" He pauses, thinking.

I wait. I am afraid to make the guess myself.

"There are numerous possibilities," he continues. "If he's satanic as you think, he may mean he's resolved to kill some child or virgin—a phoenix in the sense of unique innocence and beauty. Or he may mean the phoenix as figure of man's immortal soul—his own, perhaps . . . or yours. Then again, the phoenix may be a symbol of Mary, as we read in Jerome, or of Christ Himself, as in the poem we ascribe to Lactantius. But what he can intend, if that's his meaning—"

My confessor pauses again, and his silence, as he thinks the question through, expands in the room, makes the shadows seem darker—crouched animals, demons with burning eyes. I concentrate on the curtain between us, black as the pall on a coffin. "Our best course, no doubt, is to wait and see if he leaves."

446

I snatch at it. "Yes." But I know, instantly, that it's a hope of fools.

"If he does, of course, you'll have a terrible choice to make."

I am bathed in sweat, as if I'd been hoeing for hours, except the sweat is cold. "But there's this," I say. "It would be a violation of rule for me to leave the monastery. If he makes me break one rule, he'll make me break another. Rules are my only hope against his nihilism."

"True, if it's nihilism. On the other hand, as you've suggested, if all his acts are a devious plea for help—if his terror in an abandoned universe is as great as your own this moment—then surely you'd be right to break the rule. It would be the act of a saint."

For an instant it seems that he too is a tempter. I have seen no visions, worked no miracles.

"I am no saint, Father," I say.

He seems to consider it.

Despite all his kindness, my dread is building. I whisper, suddenly remembering: "There's no slightest sign that his behavior is a plea, Father."

"You forget, my son. He told you, when he said he would murder the phoenix, 'I give you my word, you're the only man who can save it.' Surely that means you *can* save it, whatever the meaning of the symbol."

The room is full of fire, the demons in every dark corner are real. "I didn't tell you that," I whisper.

With a violently shaking hand I snatch away the curtain between us.

"Brother Nicholas!" I whisper—

He bows, solemn.

"The question is, can you trust the promise I've given you."

He smiles, then turns, his robe silent, and he goes into the darkness.

A SORROWFUL
WOMAN

Gail Godwin

ne winter evening she looked at them: the husband durable, receptive, gentle; the child a tender golden three. The sight of them made her so sad and sick she did not want to see them ever again.

She told the husband these thoughts. He was attuned to her; he understood such things. He said he understood. What would she like him to do? "If you could put the boy to bed and read him the story about the monkey who ate too many bananas, I would be grateful." "Of course," he said. "Why, that's a pleasure." And he sent her off to bed.

The next night it happened again. Putting the warm dishes away in the cupboard, she turned and saw the child's grey eyes approving her movements. In the next room was the man, his chin sunk in the open collar of his favorite wool shirt. He was dozing after her good supper. The shirt was the grey of the child's trusting gaze. She began yelping without tears, retching in between. The man woke in alarm and carried her in his arms to bed. The boy followed them up the stairs, saying, "It's all right, Mommy," but this made her scream. "Mommy is sick," the father said, "go and wait for me in your room."

The husband undressed her, abandoning her long enough to root beneath the eiderdown for her flannel gown. She stood naked except for her bra, which hung by one strap down the side of her body; she had not the impetus to shrug it off. She looked down at the right nipple, shriveled with chill, and thought, How absurd, a vertical bra. "If only there were instant sleep," she said, hiccuping, and the husband bundled her into the gown and went out and came back with a sleeping draught guaranteed swift. She was to drink a little glass of cognac followed by a big glass of dark liquid and afterwards there was just time to say Thank you and could you get him a clean pair of pajamas out of the laundry, it came back today.

The next day was Sunday and the husband brought her breakfast in bed and let her sleep until it grew dark again. He took the child for a walk, and when they returned, red-cheeked and boisterous, the father made supper. She heard them laughing in the kitchen. He brought her up a tray of buttered toast, celery sticks and black bean soup. "I am the luckiest woman," she said, crying real tears. "Nonsense," he said. "You need a rest from us," and went to prepare the sleeping draught, find the child's pajamas, select the story for the night.

She got up on Monday and moved about the house till noon. The boy, delighted to have her back, pretended he was a vicious tiger and followed her from room to room, growling and scratching. Whenever she came close, he would growl and scratch at her. One of his sharp little claws ripped her flesh, just above the wrist, and together they paused to watch a thin red line materialize on the inside of her pale arm and spill over in little beads. "Go away," she said. She got herself upstairs and locked the door. She called the husband's office and said, "I've locked myself away from him. I'm afraid." The husband told her in his richest voice to lie down, take it easy, and he was already on the phone to call one of the baby-sitters they often employed. Shortly after, she heard the girl let herself in, heard the girl coaxing the frightened child to come and play.

After supper several nights later, she hit the child. She had known she was going to do it when the father would see. "I'm sorry," she said, collapsing on the floor. The weeping child had run to hide. "What has happened to me, I'm not myself any-more." The man picked her tenderly from the floor and looked at her with much concern. "Would it help if we got, you know, a girl in? We could fix the room downstairs. I want you to feel freer," he said, understanding these things. "We have the money for a girl. I want you to think about it."

And now the sleeping draught was a nightly thing, she did not have to ask. He went down to the kitchen to mix it, he set it nightly beside her bed. The little glass and the big one, amber and deep rich brown, the flannel gown and the eiderdown.

The man put out the word and found the perfect girl. She was young, dynamic and not pretty. "Don't bother with the room, I'll fix it up myself." Laughing, she employed her thou-sand energies. She painted the room white, fed the child lunch, read edifying books, raced the boy to the mailbox, hung her own watercolors on the fresh-painted walls, made spinach soufflé, cleaned a spot from the mother's coat, made them all laugh, danced in stocking feet to music in the white room after reading the child to sleep. She knitted dresses for herself and played chess with the husband. She washed and set the mother's soft ash-blonde air and gave her neck rubs, offered to.

The woman now spent her winter afternoons in the big bed-room. She made a fire in the hearth and put on slacks and an old sweater she had loved at school, and sat in the big chair and stared out the window at snow-ridden branches, or went away into long novels about other people moving through other win-ters.

The girl brought the child in twice a day, once in the late afternoon when he would tell of his day, all of it tumbling out quickly because there was not much time, and before he went to bed. Often now, the man took his wife to dinner. He made a courtship ceremony of it, inviting her beforehand so she could get used to the idea. They dressed and were beautiful together again and went out into the frosty night. Over candlelight he would say, "I think you are better, you know." "Perhaps I am," she would murmur. "You look . . . like a cloistered queen," he said once, his voice breaking curiously.

One afternoon the girl brought the child into the bedroom. "We've been out playing in the park. He found something he wants to give you, a surprise." The little boy approached her, smiling mysteriously. He placed his cupped hands in hers and left a live dry thing that spat brown juice in her palm and leapt away. She screamed and wrung her hands to be rid of the brown juice. "Oh, it was only a grasshopper," said the girl. Nimbly, she crept to the edge of a curtain, did a quick knee bend and reclaimed the creature, led the boy competently from the room.

"The girl upsets me," said the woman to her husband. He sat frowning on the side of the bed he had not entered for so long. "I'm sorry, but there it is." The husband stroked his creased brow and said he was sorry too. He really did not know what they would do without that treasure of a girl. "Why don't you stay here with me in bed," the woman said.

Next morning she fired the girl who cried and said, "I loved the little boy, what will become of him now?" But the mother turned away her face and the girl took down the watercolors from the walls, sheathed the records she had danced to and went away.

"I don't know what we'll do. It's all my fault, I know. I'm such a burden, I know that."

"Let me think. I'll think of something." (Still understanding these things.)

"I know you will. You always do," she said.

With great care he rearranged his life. He got up hours early, did the shopping, cooked the breakfast, took the boy to nursery school. "We will manage," he said, "until you're better, however long that is." He did his work, collected the boy from the school,

454

came home and made the supper, washed the dishes, got the child to bed. He managed everything. One evening, just as she was on the verge of swallowing her draught, there was a timid knock on her door. The little boy came in wearing his pajamas. "Daddy has fallen asleep on my bed and I can't get in. There's not room."

Very sedately she left her bed and went to the child's room. Things were much changed. Books were rearranged, toys. He'd done some new drawings. She came as a visitor to her son's room, wakened the father and helped him to bed. "Ah, he shouldn't have bothered you," said the man, leaning on his wife. "I've told him not to." He dropped into his own bed and fell asleep with a moan. Meticulously she undressed him. She folded and hung his clothes. She covered his body with the bedclothes. She flicked off the light that shone in his face.

The next day she moved her things into the girl's white room. She put her hairbrush on the dresser; she put a note pad and pen beside the bed. She stocked the little room with cigarettes, books, bread and cheese. She didn't need much.

At first the husband was dismayed. But he was receptive to her needs. He understood these things. "Perhaps the best thing is for you to follow it through," he said. "I want to be big enough to contain whatever you must do."

All day long she stayed in the white room. She was a young queen, a virgin in a tower; she was the previous inhabitant, the girl with all the energies. She tried these personalities on like costumes, then discarded them. The room had a new view of streets she'd never seen that way before. The sun hit the room in late afternoon and she took to brushing her hair in the sun. One day she decided to write a poem. "Perhaps a sonnet." She took up her pen and pad and began working from words that had lately lain in her mind. She had choices for the sonnet, ABAB or ABBA for a start. She pondered these possibilities until she tottered into a larger choice: she did not have to write a sonnet. Her poem could be six, eight, thirteen lines, it could be any number of lines, and it did not even have to rhyme.

She put down the pen on top of the pad.

In the evenings, very briefly, she saw the two of them. They knocked on her door, a big knock and a little, and she would call Come in, and the husband would smile though he looked a bit tired, yet somehow this tiredness suited him. He would put her sleeping draught on the bedside table and say, "The boy and I have done all right today," and the child would kiss her. One night she tasted for the first time the power of his baby spit.

"I don't think I can see him anymore," she whispered sadly to the man. And the husband turned away, but recovered admirably and said, "Of course, I see."

So the husband came alone. "I have explained to the boy," he said. "And we are doing fine. We are managing." He squeezed his wife's pale arm and put the two glasses on her table. After he had gone, she sat looking at the arm.

"I'm afraid it's come to that," she said. "Just push the notes under the door; I'll read them. And don't forget to leave the draught outside."

The man sat for a long time with his head in his hands. Then he rose and went away from her. She heard him in the kitchen where he mixed the draught in batches now to last a week at a time, storing it in a corner of the cupboard. She heard him come back, leave the big glass and the little one outside on the floor.

Outside her window the snow was melting from the branches, there were more people on the streets. She brushed her hair a lot and seldom read anymore. She sat in her window and brushed her hair for hours, and saw a boy fall off his new bicycle again and again, a dog chasing a squirrel, an old woman peek slyly over her shoulder and then extract a parcel from a garbage can.

In the evening she read the notes they slipped under her door.

456

The child could not write, so he drew and sometimes painted his. The notes were painstaking at first, the man and boy offering the final strength of their day to her. But sometimes, when they seemed to have had a bad day, there were only hurried scrawls.

One night, when the husband's note had been extremely short, loving but short, and there had been nothing from the boy, she stole out of her room as she often did to get more supplies, but crept upstairs instead and stood outside their doors, listening to the regular breathing of the man and boy asleep. She hurried back to her room and drank the draught.

She woke earlier now. It was spring, there were birds. She listened for sounds of the man and the boy eating breakfast; she listened for the roar of the motor when they drove away. One beautiful noon, she went out to look at her kitchen in the daylight. Things were changed. He had bought some new dish towels. Had the old ones worn out? The canisters seemed closer to the sink. She inspected the cupboard and saw new things among the old. She got out flour, baking powder, salt, milk (he bought a different brand of butter), and baked a loaf of bread and left it cooling on the table.

The force of the two joyful notes slipped under her door that evening pressed her into the corner of the little room; she had hardly space to breathe. As soon as possible, she drank the draught.

Now the days were too short. She was always busy. She woke with the first bird. Worked till the sun set. No time for hair brushing. Her fingers raced the hours.

Finally, in the nick of time, it was finished one late afternoon. Her veins pumped and her forehead sparkled. She went to the cupboard, took what was hers, closed herself into the little white room and brushed her hair for a while.

The man and boy came home and found: five loaves of warm bread, a roast stuffed turkey, a glazed ham, three pies of differ-

457

ent fillings, eight molds of the boy's favorite custard, two weeks' supply of fresh-laundered sheets and shirts and towels, two hand-knitted sweaters (both of the same grey color), a sheath of marvelous watercolor beasts accompanied by mad and fanciful stories nobody could ever make up again, and a tablet full of love sonnets addressed to the man. The house smelled redolently of renewal and spring. The man ran to the little room, could not contain himself to knock, flung back the door.

"Look, Mommy is sleeping," said the boy. "She's tired from doing all our things again." He dawdled in a stream of the last sun for that day and watched his father roll tenderly back her eyelids, lay his ear softly to her breast, test the delicate bones of her wrist. The father put down his face into her fresh-washed hair.

"Can we eat the turkey for supper?" the boy asked.

NOTES: WHAT I THINK PUDDING SAYS

John Deck

have met Felix Prine and I think I shall be able to see the son, Lester, soon!

Yesterday, I went to the farm again and Felix came rolling across the grounds toward me, in his cart, smiling, his jowls shaking, his flesh quivering massively. He wears a straw hat with a very wide brim, curved downward; his pants and shirt are floppy, and the tails of his shirt are loose. His feet and ankles are stuffed into untied high-top tennis shoes.

He is immense and of course thoroughly intimidating. Nonetheless his manner is altogether relaxed. I suppose I had expected the worst and felt safe because there were no dogs, no siren alarms, no caretakers carrying rifles.

"I've seen you around. You aren't from the Farm Labor—"

"No. I'm a student," I said. "I want to do a study on your family."

He smiled. "I don't like students coming around here. But it is a pleasure to see a woman, student or not."

I had not expected his flattery. And I am not sure that flattery was his intention. To be frank, there was something threatening about Mr. Prine. I do not think it was just his size.

He was, though not the tallest, certainly the largest man I had ever seen. I should say *human being* I had ever seen. I had never stood so close to anyone so large.

"I used to be secretary-editor of a newsletter in communications edited by Dr. Malcom." I waited, then continued. "Dr. Malcom passed away about a year ago. He came out here to Prine Farm and was chased away by dogs and armed men. He died a day or so later."

"He should have sent you in his place," Mr. Prine said, struggling to assume an attitude which I suppose was meant to seem romantic, debonair.

"He did," I said. "I plan to continue his work."

A single narrow wrinkle creased the puffy brow. "I think I heard about someone. I often miss those chases because I cannot move as quickly as others. I am ill, of course. We all are. Some sicker than others. I don't understand why people from the universities come to make fun of our illness. Are you here to laugh at us too?"

It was so perfect an opening, so complete an advantage. I almost smiled.

"My dear Mr. Prine," I said. "Is there somewhere that we can talk? I want to assure you, sir, Dr. Malcom had no intention of laughing at you. He came, and I am here, to investigate the so-called Prine Gift."

"So-*called?* Do you know what you're saying? It is a true *thing!* My son and daughter both have it."

"I know," I said. "You must excuse me. I've read what little has been written about your family."

"There's never been a Prine over twelve years old, man or woman, that weighed less than two hundred pounds." He sounded almost boastful.

"I'm not interested in what you weigh," I said. "Your son wrote an essay years ago and it was brought to Dr. Malcom's attention. It caught his eye, and *ear*, if I may say so. We study communications—the exchange of information, the way it is transmitted, received, and what is used as a medium. If you would permit me, Mr. Prine, I think I could convince you that we do not laugh at unusual characteristics. We will take the Gift as seriously as you do."

He did not believe me. "Attractive women have been here before. They don't stay."

I was certain that Felix Prine was not flattering me this time.

"I'll stay, if I am allowed to. I will stay until my work is done," I said.

II

My name is not well known and in fact I am a novice in the field. Barbara Michaels is listed as secretary-typist, editorial assistant, and copy editor in the last ten issues of the *Quarterly Newsletter of Communications*, that Dr. Clyde Malcom so heroically published to an often indifferent community of students and scholars. I am pleased to say that the great man gave me impetus to continue his work. I hope, when I have completed my Master's degree, to begin publishing the *Newsletter* again on a regular basis. I have decided, now that the first foothold on Prine property has been gained, to bring out a special memorial issue at my own expense if the Prine study comes to anything. In it I intend to publish all that is known about the Prines, the Prine Farms, and the "gift" or "curse" of the family.

When I came home this evening I began to make notes on the events of the day. (I will continue to do so.)

I went to Dr. Malcom's files. I found Weston's first mention of the Prines in the Spring, 1933, issue of the now defunct *Agronomics of the Southwest*. In an article concerned with crops and water and soil condition, his historic footnote betrays a lapse in discipline of which he must have been ashamed:

"Unfortunately the owners of this excellent acreage have allowed gluttony and a ridiculous story about 'talking food' to

addle them. So it was that when I approached them to secure permission to run the regular tests, I was driven from the property as a common trespasser."

I calculated swiftly how old Felix Prine was in 1933: a boy still, attending the Teague School in the valley. Perhaps he saw the way in which Weston was dispatched. I imagined torches and guns and the howl of hounds, and recalled how poor Dr. Malcom fared little better, although he came in daylight, thank God.

I have decided that the study, whatever form it takes, will begin with the Weston quote. I will then include the beautiful passage Dr. Malcom left to the world.

I find in all things inarticulate—all incomprehensible sounds— if not a voice, at least a challenge to the mind that would offhandedly dismiss them as dumb or meaningless or unimportant. I lift a stone, and in its weight and hardness I feel the aeons of heat and cold, the massive changes the rock has *experienced*. Geologists study the mineral composition of the stone; I listen to it. And I hear in the wind that makes of the earth a throat, a voice box, the infinitesimal whispers of speech so foreign no human mind can penetrate their lexicons for the meaning of a single syllable. Yet it speaks to me.

Oh, it is a glorious adventure, a constant search for the meaning that comes to us in silence, that is encapsulated and hidden in noise. And when there is intelligence behind the sound, how I rejoice! From every side I encounter pricking mystery. A child's discussion with a pet; the gluttonous farm family's member, incredibly fat, seeming to mumble to its food. Even the inhuman roar of a large cat in a zoo as it attacks its ration of bone and meat. These are not just sounds. I listen and, with luck, learn.

—From *A Listener's Notebook* (unpublished)

Of course, Dr. Malcom never heard a Prine mumble. He permitted himself a liberty there, but I hope to justify him. I hope, in fact, to place the great man in the vanguard of our field with the work I do. I hope to repay him in this way for teaching me to "listen and, with luck, learn."

The third of the key documents for this study, and in many ways the most important, is Lester Prine's schoolboy essay, written when he was twelve and subsequently published in the *Newsletter*. The teacher at the Teague School sent it off to Dr. Malcom as a joke, I'm afraid. But it backfired, as some jokes do. I reprint it here in full, although I am sure it was altered somewhat inasmuch as the original copy came in the mail typed. Grammatically uncertain as the author is, I cannot imagine his mastering the typewriter to the degree indicated.

Lester Prine
9/26/62

A Special Way to Eat

They call me Fatty Prine because I am fat. So is my Dad. Mom isn't because she is nervous. My sister Bonnie also my twin is a lot fatter.

The reason all of us Prine people get so fat is because we grow food right on Prine Farm and it gives the best vegetables in the world. The best pigs and cows and sheep in the world too.

We know special things about growing food. Some of us know special names. Like people think the name of lettus is really lettus but you couldn't write the name of lettus down on this page. If you know the real name, like Bonnie does.

Bonnie eats like anything because she hears special names of food and it is just like music to her. She used to tell me the names but she won't talk much now. I don't hear those names. Dad can't hear them.

We eat a lot because we are food experts. But nobody eats as much as my sister. We are all fat in a special way. Some of us are special people.

I hope to revive Dr. Malcom's spirit, to have him speak through me to the world that so ignored him during his life!

III

Felix Prine met me at the stone gate to the Prine Farm in a limousine, and I must say he was much, much improved.

He apologized for his behavior on the day previous. He said he was afraid I would not return, and used unpleasantness to shield himself against disappointment. I am impressed by his understanding of psychology and the open and aboveboard manner. As yet I am not too confident of the information I received from him.

We had a brief conversation. For me it was a preliminary investigation. And I have made random notes which will of course need further work. Here then is what I have collected thus far (meanings of a few of the terms are not perfectly clear at this time):

Lester and Bonnie Prine are twins. They are twenty years and two months old. Bonnie was the first to show signs of the Gift. Bonnie toppled five years ago, at about age fifteen. Fifteen is, I think, the normal age for toppling.

Twins are not uncommon in the Prine family, but never has a set of twins been gifted.

Bonnie, from about three or four on, began to show the "classic" development: happy, hungry, never eager to form lasting friendships, never particularly outgoing, spending most of her time in the kitchen with the cook. The young gifted come to the conclusion in early adolescence that there is no place quite so comfortable as the kitchen, no companion so necessary as the cook, no activity so rewarding as eating.

Lester liked people. He was devoted to his parents from the beginning, loved life on the farm and spent hours in the fields and at the pond. He is the first Prine, gifted or not, to show the least interest in athletics. Felix says now that Lester learned

466

to float for all the wrong reasons, but he did learn to float. He was considered normal.

So Lester was sent to school. He went to Teague, a private accredited school in the valley endowed exclusively by his family and attended by his relatives and the children of the farm workers.

It is a first-rate institution which has done much to keep the reputation of Prine Farm high among workers. Not only are the children of stoop labor given an excellent preparatory education but, if their parents have exhibited industry and ambition enough, those children who qualify are sent on to a small private college in the county, also quite dependent on the Prines for a major share of its financial support. (An interesting indication of how the feelings of the workers regarding their employer change can be found in the popularity of a child's song: "Fatty Prine, fat as swine." Heard frequently in grades one to six, it is less common among students after those years, and those who do sing it are likely to be the children of migrant families recently arrived.)

At about fifteen, when Bonnie was toppling, Lester began to spend more and more time in the swimming pool at Teague. Walking into the water, he would roll forward on his face in what is called the dead man's float. Felix was so proud of the accomplishment he didn't question it. Then he discovered that Lester was skipping classes, rising from his seat in the middle of a lecture, rushing off toward the pool.

One day Felix received a call from the headmaster. Lester was in the swimming pool and would not come out, and there was a girl's water-ballet class waiting in the dressing room. Felix left for the school immediately.

"He won't come out, sir. Says he can't stand it."

When Lester saw his father, he stood up, hands over his ears. When he removed one hand to wave, he winced.

"I knew what it was, but I didn't want to believe it," Felix told me, and if the Prine Gift is a blessing, as the Prines them-selves insist it is, then I cannot explain the unhappy look on the father's face as he said that.

They were driven to a field of young beans. The windows in the limousine, remote-controlled, were closed while they were riding, and Lester was able to take his hands away from his ears. When they stopped, Felix told Lester that he would lower the windows, that he wanted the boy to describe the sound he then heard.

"It's a sweet sound, like a baby laughing. Kind of high. Chee-chee-chee-chee, and some other sounds. Pretty."

"It isn't too pretty, is it? You don't want to get too close, do you?"

They were driven to a field of ripe tomatoes. When the car was stopped, the windows lowered, Lester smiled and climbed out of the back seat. He went directly to the nearest vine. He jerked a fruit from the vine, took it to his mouth and, according to his father, did not bite it so much as crush it over his *moving* lips. The juice broke upon his chin and dribbled down over his chest and belly. Talking and eating, the boy stood there and devoured over a half dozen tomatoes.

"I began to cry like a child," Felix said. "You see, I had been wrong. I could do nothing to make him what he was, or what I expected him to be. When a Prine has the Gift he is destined to be the happiest of people. His life is constantly pleasant, perfect. And that is why we are different. We are changed. Fat. Horribly fat! But—"

"You have brown hair and brown eyes for the same reasons you are overweight, Mr. Prine," I said. "You don't curse the color of your eyes and hair because it seems normal to you. But surely obesity is also normal in the family."

He told me I was very kind but that, forgive him, he did not believe I felt that way, not really.

468

"I am a great big mountain of blubber. All of us are. I admire your courage, Miss Michaels, but I am obnoxious to you."

"No, no," I protested.

He smiled, shook his head. "I don't blame you," he said. "You are confident now. Most people are. But you haven't even met my son. You haven't been near the stone house, seen Bonnie. Others have not been as kindly and pleasant as you. My wife, for example."

I almost gasped. I was appalled by my own thoughtlessness. I suppose I blushed.

"Don't let it bother you," Felix said. "Most of the people who call are astonished I exist. If they get over that, they have trouble believing I could have children. Seldom does anyone ask about the mother of the child—my wife. They are dazzled and confused by what they see."

"What . . . where is your . . . is Mrs. Prine around?" I am trying to re-create my confusion, which was astonishing to me.

"No. I am a widower," he said. "My wife took her life at about the time that Bonnie toppled. It is pretty common, really. People from the outside marry Prines because they pity us, or for some reason are attracted to fat people, or because they want control of the farm. Once in a while they love us. But when one of their children actually leaves them to live in the stone house, they usually go away. A few commit suicide."

"But if the children are so happy . . ." I began.

"It is a special kind of happiness," he said. "An awful happiness. You would not find it pleasant."

"I would like to reserve the right to make my own decision about *that*," I said.

"Well, when you feel strong enough," he said, "I will let you see and talk to Lester. You are fortunate that Lester is here and still talking. Because he went to school for several years, he is much more articulate than most of the gifted children. Bonnie quit talking to people when she was ten or eleven."

"I feel strong enough right now to meet your son," I said.

"In time," Felix said. "I will tell you openly, Miss Michaels, I am disappointed by people. They do not understand."

"I shall understand," I said.

"It would be a miracle if you did," he said. He shook his head slowly and a vibration began in the neck and traveled down his chest and arms. As the head swung right and left, these movements started and descended, in the manner ripples start from pebbles dropped in pools. I had never seen anything like it before. The ripples began at the terminus of each swing.

Below are some other remarks he made. I have recalled them while sitting here:

—The Gift is really quite simple. Foodstuffs, all of them, have special names. The gifted say they hear part of the name when hungry. When they eat they say they hear the secret name of the food. It is beautiful. It is like music and something else. If you will pardon me, Miss Michaels, it is something like sexual music. They feel it in the organs.

—It is true that some Prines try to escape the call and most are successful. Cousins have changed their names; an elder brother of mine disappeared under somewhat strange circumstances shortly after the Second War.

—There are Prines in almost all of the professions. Medicine seems the least attractive to us, while teaching and the law are quite to our liking. There are other Prine Farms, in different parts of the country, though they may be operated under different names. We also run cattle and sheep. We are rich and we remain so because we must be rich. We have responsibilities. It is necessary that we be able to protect those who have toppled.

—Lester "hears" food in the fields calling out its name. The closer he comes to the food, the louder it becomes. When he eats, the sound is at maximum effectiveness; this does not mean maximum volume. It means that the sound is perfect sensory accompaniment to the food being eaten. You will probably get some of the names from Lester, but I doubt he will be able to explain what they mean to him.

I'm sorry you have to hear this, Miss Michaels. It must be repugnant to you. But to us we are blessed. Gifted. That is our trouble.

Doesn't that offend you, the idea? We think we are important people!

—You, Miss Michaels, are unique. Wives and children, knowing less than you know, have left the farm forever. We are in constant danger of losing our land because we depend on outsiders for our marriages. It seems almost impossible but I, for example, must marry again. Imagine.

(Here, Felix laughed bitterly.)

—You have great courage and conviction. I will be sorry when you have finished writing.

(I assured him here that, with his permission, I would like to continue my investigation.)

But you must understand, my dear young woman, that everything I tell you and show you will seem to you a gross distortion, if you will pardon the pun.

(I smiled.)

—My wife was strong enough until she saw Bonnie go to the kitchen and spend almost a year there. I tried to convince her that she must face up to the facts. Bonnie's joy is boundless. The gifted Prine is the happiest of creatures. She sat there numb.

Then, foolishly, I took her to the stone house and showed her Uncle Lenox. Actually, I only opened the door. After that my wife was never the same.

(I told him I could sympathize with her, though I did not understand what she had seen. Her point of view would of course be far more personal than that of an outsider.)

Do you suppose you would care to visit Bonnie? She's only been in a few years. She's young too, about your age.

(I protested that I was much older than twenty.)

I'm sorry. (He was laughing.) You must understand that I am lonely. I have lost a wife and son recently. I was trying to flatter you, but I'm afraid I do not know how.

(I said I was not unflattered.)

Well, thank you. I want you to see Lester soon, talk to him. I notice that he is less articulate now than he was when he first went to the kitchen. But you will find him informative. Then, if you can, and you mustn't feel you *have* to, I would so much like you to see Bonnie. It would mean something to me, personally. And you would be the first person from off the farm who has seen a toppled Prine.

(The first person, I thought selfishly, I admit. I was filled with eagerness.)

IV

I saw Lester Prine today. In this section I will do my best to repeat what he said. Long ago Dr. Malcom told me that a tape recording is an offense against scholarship because it lulls us into worship for the denotational. I agree, but in talking to Lester Prine I found that I was so terribly aware of my physical surroundings, his presence, and the labored speech and thought of the young man that I could scarcely concentrate on what he said.

Therefore, before I forget it, I mean to strain my mind to get down precisely what he said.

Let me say we met in a huge kitchen and that he leaned—almost lay—upon a tile-covered table made of brick and that while we talked he was served small individual helpings of food by a cook. He ate and made noises as he ate and said nothing while eating. From small bowls he ate a lettuce salad, Canadian bacon, lima beans, candied yams, and other things.

Here is what he said:

If you aren't a Prine, you can't understand anything and that's all there is to it.

I can give you ideas, but nothing—absolutely nothing—can describe it. It's a miracle! We are miracle people, the miracle family!

Once when we were kids Bonnie and I were playing a game about secrets. And when we played we would whisper to each other. We put our tongues right in each other's ears, and breathed air in, like a big gush of air. That was kind of like how the names of the foods sound. Only the noise is gorgeous.

It wouldn't sound good to you. It's special, still a secret. Ours. It belongs here, to us.

Listen, I liked school. I had fun. The kids called me Fatty, but we've always been called Fatty. Fatty Prine is carved on desks, on trees. But a Fatty Prine bought the desks, planted the trees, and hired the parents of the kids. It didn't bother me.

I studied. I liked animal studies. I heard about evolution just about the time I saw Uncle Lenox and began to understand what it meant that Bonnie had the Gift. I remember that at first I was sort of sick and I didn't want anything to happen to Bonnie and I thought: Maybe we are fish. Maybe that was why I liked to swim. Maybe the Prines were the first humans to keep right on going, see, beyond being like the next guy.

Pardon me. That was a lettuce salad—just lettuce, olive oil and vinegar, with salt and pepper. That seems simple enough, but the real sound of lettuce, the secret name of it, can't be written. If you tried to write it out, you would have to write while you are chewing. There are lots of sounds: the ones your teeth makes against the leaves; and each bite has a different sound or name because there is more or less oil, vinegar, salt and pepper, and, besides, you get a big folded piece of lettuce sometimes and then other times maybe only one small piece or two or three pieces from different leaves. Yes. Each leaf has a different sound.

Of course, the first name is like lettuce, because that is what you see first. When it gets into your mouth, it's a lot of L's, with the L feeling for each leaf, and if the leaf is folded, each fold. Then, when you bite, it isn't *let*, it's *leccchhheeeeee-cheeee-cheeee-chee-chee*. But that isn't right. The sound there goes way up into your ears like a cymbal sound in the Teague marching band. Not too long or loud.

I can't tell you. You get the *cheee-cheee-cheeeyak-cheeyak-cheyak*. Because then your teeth go right through the thickness of the leaves and hit together. First a soft hit, then a harder one, a harder hit.

As the leaves get chewed, the one bite, you swallow, and that is a sound. But maybe before you swallow all the first you start on the second and you swallow little bits of the first.

One high *shosh* for the first bite; then *chosh, chosh, shosh, shoosh, shoosh, shush, shush* as the stuff gets softer. Then *shaa-gong-guh* for the sound of swallowing lettuce.

I had to say that word, *lettuce*. It's just a word.

Now that is nothing, the sound I just told you, because I left out oil, vinegar, salt and pepper, plus what I know about growing lettuce, the work, the fertilizer, water, sprays, the washing and care (and I know something about oil and vinegar and salt and pepper, too). And there are special feelings from my stomach and intestines when I smell and feel and taste a lettuce salad for the first time.

I suppose I can say anything to you. I suppose I can tell you I feel it right down all the way to my rectum. All the way through. Digestion and everything.

Desserts are not so important to me. Sugar is just sugar, and the way sweets feel, to chew them isn't much fun. I would rather eat a cake that the cook hasn't finished baking, so parts are still wet a little.

Here's something. Meat! Good!

I like meat when it comes up the best. Pork, I watched pigs grow up. When I could carry things I carried the slops to them.

474

I love their meat the best. I love it best when we have a big piece of their meat and we roast it.

If you bite into the end where it's crispy, the sound is like two sounds: *cheeelll* and *shallah*. You say those two sounds to yourself at the same time and that is the name of the crust. Fat just inside the crust—the crust is *pahl-pahl-pahl-pahl*, but deeper in it is more like *poll-llooll-lloo*. The lean meat is something like *jing* at first, if it is juicy; if it is dry, it is *junnnm*. Of course the name of lean meat changes, and so does the fat's name and the crust's name when you chew it.

You can get crust, fat, juicy lean, and dry lean in one bite, and you can hear all those sounds at once.

But before you hear anything, there would be the sound of a pig's life, too. Some of it is like sniffing when you have a bad cold. Some of it is like clearing your throat.

I can start it for you, give you just the first part, about the dirt: *Fffffferrddrrruukkakakafub, bubba, bulubba, subba, soggle-soggle, keeeble ellebelleel lee blee bleek blek blek.*

That part really is just about mud and soft stuff. It is like when the pig is born from the mother, comes out in the blood and water and things, everything soft and floppy. It doesn't take long to hear it at all. The whole name of the pig, which is a hundred times as long as what I just said, you could hear that starting when you took a piece on your fork, and ending when you first heard the sound of the crust or fat or juicy lean.

Pardon me.

At Teague we had a music-appreciation course and we listened to symphonies, each movement, the themes and how they give you different parts added together all over one another.

Eating is like that. The special name for food is just like that. It's like Bonnie's wet tongue when we were playing. But it goes on, it never changes. Oh, it is so sweet.

Every bite I eat is perfect. I used to be hungry when I didn't think I had the Gift. Now it's different. Now I can feel the cook coming over with a new dish. I don't look up. My heart begins to beat fast. I can hardly breathe. But I don't look up. He slides the bowl in front of me and suddenly I see the food. I hear it. I take a bite and say its name! It's mine, *my* food!

Lima beans. The smell, the tougher skin, the mushy center, the butter and pepper, the one that you bite into when the others are chewed, the mixtures of well chewed and partly chewed, the sticky slow way it goes down when you swallow. Everything has a name. And it calls out to you. Beautiful. So beautiful!

And it isn't just lima beans! It's lima beans after another dish. With another dish coming!

The words I have to say to you, the names *you* give foods, they have ugly sounds. They hurt my ears now.

But when I was in school even the true names hurt. I was happy at Teague when I was floating in the pool because then I didn't hear the fruits and vegetables from the fields. The beets ring like bells, and onions have voices like coyotes; onions howl, and beans are like birds.

I didn't think I had the Gift and so I wouldn't listen, and the older I got the more my ears roared and screeched. In the pool I didn't hear anything.

But now I hear from all over the farm.

Bonnie can, and so does Uncle Lenox. Imagine, I felt sorry for Bonnie! I used to go off to school and she would be going from bed to this room. And I would say to myself: She's going to miss a lot. She did, too; she missed everything but the fun. She was having *all* of that.

Oh, I miss Teague, sometimes. I liked Phillip Berrigan, the boy that used to help me out of the pool, and Arnold and Armstrong Wylie, the twins. George Halstead, too. He could draw pictures. I miss those guys, but they don't miss me. The best of them thought I was fat and dumb.

I felt bad when I had to quit school, and I felt terrible the day they took Bonnie over to the stone house. But both of them were happy moments, great moments! That was when I was stupid.

Listen, can you understand this? My food sings. Every bite is better than a tongue in the ear.

I'm happy.

It took me all evening to write that. It isn't accurate yet. I have failed.

I am disappointed. Reading it over, you get the impression Lester is only vain. That isn't quite correct.

I mean it seems impossible.

I don't know. Already I've gotten further than Dr. Malcom did. I have new information! I know enough to realize that we are not talking simply about naming food. What Lester did when he ate was hum and make noises chewing. But that is *my* interpretation, and I feel as if I am betraying my opportunities by simplifying. I have a chance now to uncover *startling new things, concepts, experiences,* and I am not sure how to proceed!

I discovered my answer. Felix called and asked me how I was.

"Fine," I said. "Only I'm not sure about how it went with Lester."

"Yes. It's a pity you weren't here earlier, when he was smaller and more sociable. I'm sorry but—"

"I don't suppose I could see him again?" I asked. Felix has his gentlemanly formalities and I get tired of them.

"You could see him any time when he will allow it. And he'll be tractable for a while longer, I hope. But I thought your time here was limited."

"Well, it is! That's why I'm so anxious," I said, "to get everything right the first time."

"I'm not prying into your personal life, Barbara, but you are always welcome to stay on the farm. Because we automate, we have less help, so there are plenty of empty quarters. And, of course, we can feed you."

I paused to think.

"Of course, you'll want to think it over," he said. "And perhaps you feel you should be less intimate with the subject of your study. I won't press you on it. In fact, I won't mention it again."

"Felix," I said, "your offer is generous." I giggled. "I will tell you if I want to stay."

"Oh, it's nothing," he said. "It's just here. We've got more—well, more than we need."

When he offered room and board I thought he was trying to be kind, perhaps to distract me from my unpleasant interview with his son.

Then I thought: No. It is something else.

I must admit that Lester was fat and that the combination of an extremely fat young man and an ego equally monstrous was beyond my expectations. I had not been prepared, and it took me some time to recover myself. By then Lester had begun to drowse while leaning on the table, and I left.

I will explain just how I feel to Felix tomorrow. Being frank will give him the chance to withdraw his offer. Although it is somewhat expensive to maintain, I think I should have this room to return to after an interview.

Felix is the exact opposite of his son.

V

Felix called for me today, or had his driver do so. And when I arrived at the farm he joined me in the car and we drove around. He apologized, but not excessively, for needing the entire back seat. The little folding seats are quite comfortable, I find. And it is a pleasure to be able to look at him without seeming to stare. I do not stare. But I sometimes think he thinks I'm staring.

"I thought about offering you a place to live," he said. "But I think it is unfair. My son horrified you yesterday. You probably want to finish this whole business."

I told him frankly that I had not been altogether prepared for Lester.

"But further study will make it worse," he said. "Lester gets —well, bigger, and more conceited, all the time. Bigger and happier. He won't leave the kitchen now. The only thing that will force him to leave later is that the cook's presence and the exertion of sitting up will distract him from the full enjoyment of the food. That's always the case. Now people talk, pans clang together, and perhaps the odor of several things cooking at once confuses him. He will eventually request to leave."

"And that will be when he topples?"

"Yes," Felix said.

"I suppose the nearer he comes to that, the louder and clearer the names of the foods become," I said.

"Yes," he said.

"I should like to be around when he makes his noises, to see how they change."

"As awful as I look," Felix said, "Lester looks worse. And as disgraceful as he is, he will be horrifying when he has toppled. I don't think you could take it. I don't think anyone who isn't a Prine could stand it."

I said I could stand it.

Felix told his driver to take us by the old stone house.

I had seen it before, from across the pond. It is two stories, large and plain, an L-shaped building. Windows with curtains drawn. It is not sinister in any way. We stopped before it. We sat in the car.

"The underside, the basement," he said, "is filled with a huge kitchen. It connects to all the rooms by dumbwaiters. A chef is at work in the basement at all times, and there are attendants who take dishes from the stoves to the dumbwaiters. Servings arrive at intervals of from ten to twenty minutes depending on the complexity of the dish being prepared."

"How many people live in the house now?" I asked.

"There are, besides Bonnie, five of us in there now. When the four on the top floor quit eating, all the spaces there will be full. Bonnie is the first on the lower floor."

"When they quit eating?"

He looked at me. "We seal the doors," he said.

He shook his head. He gave the driver instructions to return me to my motel. At the door of his house, a modest bungalow directly across the pond from the stone house, he said:

"You are braver by far than most people. But the task you have set for yourself is impossible. Thank you for trying. You have made me feel like a human being these past few days."

He gave me his hand. It was firmer than I expected, and drier. He was sad and lonely and I felt sorry for him.

It is hours later.

I am at the motel now and I have just called Felix. I asked him to send the driver back. I told him I had apostacized myself by not fulfilling my obligations.

"Let me visit Bonnie," I said.

"If you allow yourself to see her," Felix said, "the farm is yours. There will be no secrets."

"I'll do it," I said. "Send the car."

Dr. Malcom, forgive me, but I am frightened. I am trembling.

VI

It is all over and yet it has just started. It is as if my life ended and began in a single moment. I am not the same, but those words above I wrote. These notes are mine. This is my writing.

As you enter, you immediately smell food cooking and hear, faintly, water running.

480

The stair rises ahead. There are hand-hewn benches and plastered walls without pictures. We turned left.

Bonnie's room was down the hall to the very end. While we walked to it, passing door after door that stood ajar but not opened widely enough to see inside, Felix said:

"We seal them when the dumbwaiters bring back dishes that are not emptied. A great uncle of mine, Elwyn, had his door sealed when I was a boy. My father sealed it. I have done the same a few times. Two cousins and an aunt."

As we approached Bonnie's room, the sound of water flowing grew louder. As we entered I was struck by moist air, warm but not hot, and a louder sound of water, pouring water.

"There is a fountain under here, a perpetual cleansing. I hope such an idea does not offend you. It is necessary."

"Where is she?" I said.

"There," he said. "We are looking at her back. Wait. You'll figure out where you are in just a minute."

There was no recognizable contour, no fold of flesh or structuring that I, with my limited knowledge of anatomy, could recognize. I was about to ask Felix if she were not covered with something when suddenly I heard a mechanical snap and whir. And a huge mass lifted off the top and, while attached, began to weave and circle in the air. At the end of the mass, which again was shapeless, I saw a number of short projections that, to my astonishment, I later realized were fingers. The attached mass was therefore an arm. And it connected to the body by a shoulder.

"You see?" Felix said. I could recognize the dear man's anxiety. He was terrified that I would turn on him, or run away. Of course I had no intention of doing so.

"The arm moves about after the dumbwaiter goes down; it curves about waiting for the next delivery."

The arm was about as long as a child of, say, two. In some way its bulk suggested a very fat infant trying to dance, though the comparison will serve us no further purpose. It wove about; the fingers fluttered and tremors ran the length of the arm. When it tilted too far to one side or the other, the loose stuff within flowed to the low side, almost as rapidly obedient to the pull of gravity as sand in a bottle.

Now that I saw this substance was an arm, I again looked over the bulk of her and found no anatomical landmark. She gave the impression of something melted. I later discovered that Bonnie lay on her side and that the leg on top had covered the leg beneath. The upper side of the foot had draped fatty tissue over the lower foot. The upper buttock, in this case the right one, had loosened and now it reached the deck beneath her.

By the way, the floor was of tile, sloping gently toward the center, where the flow of water carried off her wastes.

The arm continued to weave until there was another whirring sound, another click. Then, from end to end, the great bulk quivered, and a low, sensuous sound came from the far side. It was a human voice.

"*Nahmahnahmahnumanumanumanuma. . . .*"

"Something soft. That's the sound she makes for soft," Felix said.

I confess that for a moment there, listening to the diminuendo of her voice, I almost missed what might well prove to be the most important discovery of my life. But my training under Dr. Malcom did not fail me.

"The sound *she* makes. You mean they don't all make the same sound."

"Similar sounds," Felix said. "Lester's soft begins *noomooo* and goes on to *nnnnnnnnnnnnnnnnnnnnnnnnnnnnnn.*"

Something registered at once. But I confess I was still irrational. Astonished by the huge thing there, I was struggling with a resistant reason that would not accept Bonnie as human.

"I'm sorry," Felix whispered.

And when I could not respond, he said:

"It would be hard for you to do so, but if you could look at her face. It is a face. You can see an eye and a nostril. Then you know."

I nodded. I think I nodded or just walked on. He was ahead of me.

There was a tangle of curly damp hair through which I saw a wild eye and a nostril that seemed unusually big. I thought at first it was the mouth. The whole face reminded me of a photograph I once saw of a whale's head. The head covered the picture from frame to frame, and in the lower right-hand corner was an eye, and only the eye was alive.

This comparison came to me much later, several days later. I am writing this several days later.

Oh, yes, I saw the dumbwaiter, the hand scooping chocolate pudding from the bowl onto the floor just before the heavy cheek. Out from under the cheek came the tongue. It scooped the food in, under the cheek, out of sight.

Her name for pudding continued all around us as she ate.

That's all I have to say right now.

Bonnie's eye did not look at us. Never did she acknowledge our presence if she was aware of it. The water's trickle was slight and clean and remote, and I confess to loving it. I remember how soothing it was, and how enjoyable was the steamy feeling of the air.

When she finished the pudding and replaced the bowl, a jet of water inside the shaft cleansed her fingers. The door snapped shut, an electrical whirring began, and the arm rose, began its trembling dance, the fingers weaving about, and then the eye, staring out of the smooth convexity of the cheek and brow, seemed to roll in its socket with the movement of the arm.

I thought it was time to leave, and we left.

Outside, I felt giddy. I sat first on the bench. But before that I leaned against a wall. Then I sat on the bench.

NOTES: WHAT I THINK PUDDING SAYS

"You're ill," Felix said. "Stay here and I'll have a car brought around and take you to a doctor."

"I do not need a doctor," I said, still distraught. "I want to sit right here. On this bench. For a minute."

I recall my words clearly and my emphasis.

"You are truly a brave and unusual girl, Barbara," he said.

I did not answer. Something was bothering me.

"You've seen the worst now, you know. Nothing is. . . ."

"Please. I'm trying to recall—yes, I know. You said that Lester and Bonnie have different ways of naming, or calling out the name, for something soft like pudding?"

"That's right."

"That's interesting. This is just the kind of discovery I hoped I would make. I find it interesting."

"Good."

"Let's go," I said.

He helped me up. He was stronger than I expected. He did not touch me again, but he opened the door of the stone house for me and then he opened the door of the car.

"If you want to sit in back I can lean against the—"

"No, no, no!" I almost screamed. It was not the first time I had almost screamed since I left the room.

I was glad to be in the car, but when Felix wondered if I wanted to go home, to the motel, I said I didn't think so. In fact, later I asked him to have my things brought to the farm and I stayed here. I have since.

VII

I think I have discovered something very important, but I am not yet sure what it is.

The other night I had some tapioca pudding and I began eating it, and I said *nnnnuuuuunnngggguuunnnnggguuuunnnn-gggg* to myself. It seemed to enhance the taste. I'm sure of that. But perhaps I wanted it to, for Felix's sake.

484

Felix said I can record the sounds Bonnie and Lester make when they are served the same dishes and perhaps I will discover some pattern. If we could formulate the rules that govern the Gift, it would be quite an advance, quite a feather in my cap, professionally speaking. The farm is entirely self-sufficient and has workshops so that such things as plumbing and construction can be done by trusted employees. People are fond of Felix, but I sometimes think they take him for granted. I told him I was going to buy him a handsome big hat some day, a gentleman farmer's hat, to give a little flair to his dress.

Bonnie was, I estimate, four feet across at the top and seven to ten feet at the bottom. Her head was far down from the sort of blunt, rounded-off top of her. You wouldn't say from her shoulders.

Just now I stay away from Bonnie and talk only to Lester. He gets bored and sometimes won't answer, particularly when I ask him to name a dish he isn't eating.

He sometimes cries if the name of it comes to him.

It is incredible. Oh, Dr. Malcom, it is all so incredible!

Felix has also promised to put up the money for a special issue of the *Newsletter*. He has been wonderful in every way. He has shown me the farm, from end to end.

THE SONG OF GRENDEL

John Gardner

he old ram stands looking down over rock-slides, stupidly triumphant. I blink. I stare in horror. "Scat!" I hiss. "Go back to your cave, go back to your cow shed—whatever." He cocks his head like an elderly, slow-witted king, considers the angles, decides to ignore me. I stamp. I hammer the ground with my fists. I hurl a skull-size stone at him. He will not budge. I shake my two hairy fists at the sky and I let out a howl so unspeakable that the water at my feet turns sudden ice and even I myself am left uneasy. But the ram stays; the season is upon us. And so begins the twelfth year of my idiotic war.

The pain of it! The stupidity!

"Ah, well," I sigh, and shrug, trudge back to the trees.

Do not think my brains are squeezed shut, like the ram's, by the roots of horns. Flanks atremble, eyes like stones, he stares at as much of the world as he can see and feels it surging in him, filling his chest as the melting snow fills dried-out creek beds, tickling his gross, lopsided balls and charging his brains with the same unrest that made him suffer last year at this time, and the year before, and the year before that. (He's forgotten them all.) His hind parts shiver with the usual joyful, mindless ache to mount whatever happens near—the storm piling up black towers to the west, some rotting, docile stump, some spraddle-legged ewe. I cannot bear to look. "Why can't these creatures discover a little dignity?" I ask the sky.

The sky ignores me, forever unimpressed. Him too I hate, the same as I hate these brainless budding trees, these brattling birds.

Not, of course, that I fool myself with thoughts that I'm more noble. Pointless, ridiculous monster crouched in the shadows, stinking of dead men, murdered children, martyred cows. "Ah, sad one, poor old freak!" I cry, and hug myself, and laugh, letting out salt tears he he! till I fall down gasping and sobbing. (It's mostly fake.) The sun spins mindlessly overhead, the shadows lengthen and shorten as if by plan. Small birds, with a high-pitched yelp, lay eggs. The tender grasses peek up, innocent yellow. It was just here, this shocking green, that once when the moon was tombed in clouds, I tore off sly old Athelgard's head.

Such are the tiresome memories of a shadow-shooter, earth-rim-roamer, walker of the world's weird wall. "Waaah!" I cry, with another quick, nasty face at the sky, mournfully observing the way it is, bitterly remembering the way it was, and idiotically casting tomorrow's nets. "Aargh! Yaww!" I reel, smash trees. Disfigured son of lunatics. The big-boled oaks gaze down at me yellow with morning, beneath complexity. "No offense," I say, with a terrible grin, and tip an imaginary hat.

It was not always like this, of course. On occasion it's been worse.

No matter, no matter.

The doe in the clearing goes stiff at sight of my horridness, then remembers her legs and is gone. It makes me cross. "Blind prejudice!" I bawl at the splintered sunlight where half a second ago she stood. I wring my fingers, put on a long face. "Ah, the unfairness of everything," I say, and shake my head. It is a matter of fact that I have never killed a deer in all my life, and never will. Cows have more meat and, locked up in pens, are easier to catch. It is true, perhaps, that I feel some trifling dislike of deer, but no more dislike than I feel for other natural things— discounting men. But deer, like rabbits and bears and even men, can make, concerning my race, no delicate distinctions. That is their happiness: they see all life without observing it. They're buried in it like crabs in mud. Except men, of course. I am not in a mood, just yet, to talk of men.

So it goes with me day by day and age by age, I tell my-self. Locked in the deadly progression of moon and stars. I shake my head, muttering darkly on shaded paths, holding conversa-tion with the only friend and comfort this world affords: my shadow. Wild pigs clatter away through brush. A baby bird falls feet-up in my path, squeaking. With a crabby laugh, I let him lie, kind heaven's merciful bounty to some sick fox. So it goes with me, age by age by age. (Talking, talking. Spinning a web of words, pale walls of dreams, between myself and all I see.)

The first grim stirrings of springtime come (as I knew they must, having seen the ram), and even under the ground where I live, where no light breaks but the red of my fires and nothing stirs but the flickering shadows on my wet rock walls, or scam-pering rats on my piles of bones, or my mother's fat, foul bulk rolling over, restless again—molested by nightmares, old mem-ories—I am aware in my chest of tuber-stirrings in the black-sweet duff of the forest overhead. I feel my anger coming back, building up like invisible fire, and at last, when my soul can no longer resist, I go up—as mechanical as anything else—fists clenched against my lack of will, my belly growling, mindless as wind, for blood. I swim up through the firesnakes, hot dark whalecocks prowling the luminous green of the mere, and I sur-face with a gulp among churning waves and smoke. I crawl up onto the bank and catch my breath.

It's good at first to be out in the night, naked to the cold mechanics of the stars. Space hurls outward, falcon-swift, mounting like an irreversible injustice, a final disease. The cold night air is reality at last: indifferent to me as stone. I lie there resting in the steaming grass, the old lake hissing and gurgling behind me, whispering patterns of words my sanity resists. At last, heavy as an ice-capped mountain, I rise and work my way to the inner wall, beginning of wolfslopes, the edge of my realm. I stand in the high wind balanced, blackening the night with my stench, gazing down to cliffs that fall away to cliffs, and once again I am aware of my potential: I could die. I cackle with rage and suck in breath.

"Dark chasms!" I scream from the cliff edge, "seize me. Seize me to your foul black bowels and crush my bones!" I am terrified at the sound of my own huge voice in the darkness. I stand there shaking, whimpering.

I sigh, depressed, and grind my teeth. I toy with shouting some tidbit more—some terrifying, unthinkable threat, but my heart's not in it. "Missed me!" I say with a coy little jerk and a leer, to keep my spirits up. Then, with a sigh, a kind of moan, I start very carefully down the cliffs that lead to the fens and moors and Hrothgar's hall. Owls cross my path as silently as raiding ships, and at the sound of my foot, lean wolves rise, glance at me awkwardly, and, neat of step as lizards, sneak away. I used to take some pride in that—the caution of owls when my shape looms in, the alarm I stir in these giant northern wolves. I was younger then. Still playing cat and mouse with the universe.

I move down through the darkness, burning with murderous lust, my brains raging at the sickness I can observe in myself as objectively as might a mind ten centuries away. Stars, spattered out through lifeless night from end to end, like jewels scattered in a dead king's grave, tease, torment my wits toward meaningful patterns that do not exist. I can see for miles from these rock walls: thick forest suddenly still at my coming—

cowering stags, wolves, hedgehogs, boars, submerged in their stifling, unmemorable fear.

I sigh once more, sink down into silence, and cross it like dark wind. Behind my back, at the world's end, my pale slightly glowing fat mother sleeps on, old, sick at heart, in our dingy underground room. Life-bloated, baffled, long-suffering hag. Guilty, she imagines, of some unremembered, perhaps ancestral crime. (She must have some human in her.) Not that she thinks. Not that she dissects and ponders the dusty mechanical bits of her miserable life's curse. She clutches at me in my sleep as if to crush me. I break away. "Why are we here?" I used to ask her. "Why do we stand this putrid, stinking hole?" She trembles at my words. Her fat lips shake. "Don't ask!" her wriggling claws implore. (She never speaks.) "Don't ask!" It must be some terrible secret, I used to think. I'd give her a crafty squint. She'll tell me in time, I thought. But she told me nothing.

And so I come through trees and towns to the lights of Hrothgar's meadhall. I am no stranger here. A respected guest. Eleven years now and going on twelve I have come up this clean-mown central hill, dark shadow out of the woods below, and have knocked politely on the high oak door, bursting its hinges and sending the shock of my greeting inward like a cold blast out of a cave. "Grendel!" they squeak, and I smile like exploding spring. The old Shaper, a man I cannot help but admire, goes out the back window with his harp at a single bound, though blind as a bat. The drunkest of Hrothgar's thanes come reeling and clanking down from their wall-hung beds, all shouting their meady, outrageous boasts, their heavy swords aswirl like eagles' wings. "Woe, woe, woe!" cries Hrothgar, hoary with winters, peeking in, wide-eyed, from his bedroom in back. His wife, looking in behind him, makes a scene. The thanes in the meadhall blow out the lights and cover the wide stone fireplace with shields. I laugh, crumple over; I can't help myself. In the darkness, I alone see clear as day. While they squeal and screech and bump into each other, I silently stack up my dead and withdraw to the woods. I eat and laugh and eat until I can barely walk, my chest hair matted with dribbled blood, and then the roosters on the hill crow, and dawn comes over the roofs of the houses, and all at once I am filled with gloom again.

"This is some punishment sent us," I hear them bawling from the hill.

My head aches. Morning nails my eyes.

"Some god is angry," I hear a woman keen. "The people of Scyld and Heorogar and Hrothgar are mired in sin!"

My belly rumbles, sick on their sour meat. I crawl through bloodstained leaves to the eaves of the forest, and there peek out. The dogs fall silent at the edge of my spell, and where the king's hall surmounts the town, the blind old Shaper, harp clutched tight to his fragile chest, stares futilely down, straight at me.

A few men, lean, wearing animal skins, look up at the gables of the king's hall, or at the vultures circling casually beyond. Hrothgar says nothing, hoarfrost-bearded, his features cracked and crazed. Inside I hear the people praying—whimpering, whining, mumbling, pleading—to their numerous sticks and stones. He doesn't go in. The king has lofty theories of his own.

"Theories," I whisper to the bloodstained ground. "They'd map out roads through Hell with their crackpot theories!"

They wail, the whole crowd, women and men, a kind of song, like a single quavering voice. The song rings up like greasy smoke and their faces shine with sweat and something that looks like joy. The song swells, pushes through woods and sky, and they're singing now as if by some lunatic theory they had won. I shake with rage. The red sun blinds me, churns up my belly to nausea. I cringe, clawing my flesh, and flee for home.

I used to play games when I was young—it might as well be a thousand years ago. Explored our far-flung underground world in an endless war game of leaps onto nothing, ingenious twists into freedom or new perplexity, quick whispered plottings with invisible friends, wild cackles when vengeance was mine. I nosed out, in my childish games, every last shark-toothed chamber and hall, every black tentacle of my mother's cave, and so came at last, adventure by adventure, to the pool of firesnakes. I stared, mouth gaping. They were grey as old ashes; faceless, eyeless. They spread the surface of the water with pure green flame. I knew—I seemed to have known all along—that the snakes were there to guard something. Inevitably, after I'd stood there a while, rolling my eyes back along the dark hallway, my ears cocked for my mother's step, I screwed my nerve up and dove. The firesnakes scattered as if my flesh were charmed, and so I discovered the sunken door, and so I came up, for the first time, to moonlight.

I went no farther, that first night. But I came out again, inevitably. I played my way farther out into the world, vast cavern aboveground, cautiously darting from tree to tree challenging the terrible forces of night on tiptoe. At dawn I fled back.

I lived those years, as do all young things, in a spell. At times the spell would be broken suddenly: on shelves or in hallways of my mother's cave, large old shapes with smoldering eyes sat watching me. A continuous grumble came out of their mouths; their backs were humped. Then little by little it dawned on me that the eyes that seemed to bore into my body were in fact gazing through it, wearily indifferent to my slight obstruction of the darkness. Of all the creatures I knew in those days, only my mother really looked at me.

She loved me.

I was her creation. We were one thing, like the wall and the rock growing out from it. Or so I ardently, desperately affirmed. When her strange eyes burned into me, I was intensely aware of where I sat, the volume of darkness I displaced, the shiny-smooth span of packed dirt between us, and the shocking separateness from me in my mama's eyes. I would feel, all at once, alone and ugly, almost—as if I'd dirtied myself—obscene. The cavern river tumbled far below us. Being young, unable to face these things, I would bawl and hurl myself at my mother and she would reach out her claws and seize me, though I could see I alarmed her (I had teeth like a saw) and she would smash me to her fat, limp breast as if to make me part of her flesh again. After that, comforted, I would gradually ease back out into my games. Crafty-eyed, wicked as an elderly wolf, I would scheme with or stalk my imaginary friends, projecting the self I meant to become into every dark corner of the cave and the woods above.

One morning I caught my foot in the crack where two old tree trunks joined. "Owp!" I yelled. "Mama! Waa!" I looked at the foot in anger and disbelief. It was wedged deep, as if the two oak trees were eating it. Pain flew up through me like fire up the flue of a mountain. I lost my head. I bellowed for help. "Mama! Waa! Waaa!" I bellowed to the sky, the forest, the cliffs, until I was so weak from loss of blood I could barely wave my arms. "I'm going to die," I wailed. "Poor Grendel! Poor old Mama!" I wept and sobbed. "Poor Grendel will hang here and starve to death," I told myself, "and no one will ever miss him!" The thought enraged me. I hooted. I thought of my mother's foreign eyes, staring at me from across the room. I thought of the cool, indifferent eyes of the others. I shrieked in fear; still no one came.

"Please, Mama!" I sobbed as if heartbroken.

I slept, I think. When I woke and looked up through the leaves overhead there were vultures. I sighed, indifferent. I tried to see myself from the vultures' viewpoint. I saw, instead, my mother's eyes.

That night, for the first time, I saw men.

It was dark when I awakened—or when I came to, if it was that. I was aware at once that there was something wrong.

There was a smell, a fire very different from ours, pungent, painful as thistles to the nose. I opened my eyes and everything was blurry, as though underwater. There were lights all around me, like some weird creature's eyes. They jerked back as I looked. Then voices, speaking words. The sounds were foreign at first, but when I calmed myself, concentrating, I found I understood them: it was my own language, but spoken in a strange way, as if the sounds were made by brittle sticks, dried spindles, flaking bits of shale. My vision cleared and I saw them, mounted on horses, holding torches up. Some of them had shiny domes (as it seemed to me then) with horns coming out, like a bull's. They were small, these creatures, ridiculous but, at the same time, mysteriously irritating, like rats. Their movements were stiff and regular, as if figured by logic. They had skinny, naked hands that moved by clicks.

I tried to move. They all stopped speaking at the same instant, like sparrows. We stared at each other.

One of them said—a tall one with a long black beard—"It moves independent of the tree."

They nodded.

The tall one said. "It's a growth of some kind, that's my opinion. Some beast-like fungus."

They all looked up into the branches.

A short fat one pointed up into the tree with an ax. "Those branches on the northern side are all dead there. No doubt the whole tree'll be dead before midsummer. It's always the north side goes first when there ain't enough sap."

They nodded, and another one said, "See there where it grows up out of the trunk? Sap running all over."

They leaned over the sides of their horses to look, pushing the torches toward me. The horses' eyes glittered.

"Have to close that up if we're going to save this tree," the tall one said. The others grunted, and the tall one looked up at my eyes, uneasy. I couldn't move. He stepped down off the horse and came over to me, so close I could have swung my hand and smashed his head if I could make my muscles move. "It's like blood," he said, and made a face.

Two of the others got down and came over to pull at their noses and look.

"I say that tree's a goner," one of them said.

They all nodded, except the tall one. "We can't just leave it rot," he said. "Start letting the place go to ruin and you know what the upshot'll be."

They nodded. The others got down off their horses and came over. The fat one said, "Maybe we could chop the fungus out."

They thought about it. After a while the tall one shook his head. "I don't know. Could be it's some kind of a oak tree spirit. Better not to mess with it."

They looked uneasy. There was a hairless, skinny one. He stood with his arms out, like a challenged bird, and he kept moving around in jerky little circles, bent forward, peering at everything, at the tree, at the woods around, up into my eyes. Now suddenly he nodded. "That's it! King's right! It's a spirit!"

"You think so?" they said. Their heads poked forward.

"Sure of it," he said.

"Is it friendly, you think?" the king said.

The hairless one peered up at me with the fingertips of one hand in his mouth. The skinny elbow hung straight down, leaning on an invisible table while he thought the whole thing through. His black little eyes stared straight into mine, as if waiting for me to tell him something. I tried to speak. My mouth moved, but nothing would come out. The little man jerked back. "He's hungry!" he said.

"Hungry!" they all said. "What does he eat?"

He looked at me again. His tiny eyes drilled into me and he was crouched as if he were thinking of trying to jump up into my brains. My heart thudded. I was so hungry I could eat a rock. He smiled suddenly; a holy vision had exploded in his head. "He eats *pig!*" he said. He looked doubtful. "Or maybe pigsmoke. He's in a period of transition."

They all looked at me, thinking it over, then nodded.

The king picked out six men. "Go get the thing some pigs," he said. The six men said, "Yes sir!" and got on their horses and rode off. It filled me with joy, though it was all crazy, and before I knew I could do it, I laughed. They jerked away and stood shaking, looking up.

"The spirit's angry," one of them whispered.

"It always has been," another one said. "That's why it's killing the tree."

"No, no, you're wrong," the hairless one said. "It's yelling for pig."

"Pig!" I tried to yell. It scared them.

They all began shouting at each other. One of the horses neighed and reared up, and for some crazy reason they took it for a sign. The king snatched an ax from the man beside him and, without any warning, he hurled it at me. I twisted, letting out a howl, and it shot past my shoulder.

"You're all crazy," I tried to yell, but it came out a moan. I bellowed for my mother.

"Surround him!" the king yelled. "Save the horses!"—and suddenly I knew I was dealing with no dull mechanical beasts, but with thinking creatures, patternmakers, the most dangerous things I'd ever met. I shrieked at them, trying to scare them off, but they merely ducked behind bushes and took long sticks from the saddles of their horses, bows and javelins. "You're all crazy," I bellowed, "you're all insane!" I'd never howled more loudly in my life. Darts like hot coals went through my legs and arms and I howled more loudly still. And then, just when I was sure I was finished, a shriek ten times as loud as mine came blaring off the cliff. It was Mother! She came roaring down like thunder, screaming like a thousand hurricanes, eyes as bright as dragon fire, and before she was within a mile of us, the creatures had leaped to their horses and galloped away. Big trees shattered and fell from her path; the earth trembled. Then her smell poured in like blood into a silver cup, filling the moonlit clearing to the brim, and I felt the two trees that held me falling, and I was fumbling, free, into the grass.

I woke up in the cave, warm firelight flickering on walls. My mother lay picking through the bone pile. When she heard me stir, she turned, wrinkling her forehead, and looked at me. I tried to tell her all that had happened, all that I'd come to understand. She only stared, troubled at my noise. "The world resists me and I resist the world," I said. "That's all there is."

The fire in Mother's eyes brightens and she reaches out as if some current is tearing us apart. "The world is all pointless accident," I say. Shouting now, my fists clenched. Her face works. She gets up on all fours, brushing dry bits of bone from her path, and, with a look of terror, rising as if by unnatural power, she hurls herself across the void and buries me in her bristly fur and fat. I sicken with fear. "My mother's fur is bristly," I say to myself. "Her flesh is loose." Buried under my mother I cannot see. She smells of wild pig and fish. "My mother smells of wild pig and fish," I say. What I see I inspire with usefulness, I think, trying to suck in breath, and all that I do not see is useless, void. I observe myself observing what I observe. It startles me.

(Talking, talking, spinning a skin, a skin. . . .)

I can't breathe, and I claw to get free. She struggles. I smell my mama's blood and, alarmed, I hear from the walls and floor the booming booming of her heart.

It wasn't because he threw that battle-ax that I turned on Hrothgar. That was mere midnight foolishness. I dismissed it, thought of it afterward only as you remember a tree that fell on you or an adder you stepped on by accident, except of course that Hrothgar was more to be feared than a tree or snake. It wasn't until later, when I was full-grown and Hrothgar was an old, old man, that I settled my soul on destroying him—slowly and cruelly. Except for his thanes' occasional stories of seeing my footprints, he'd probably forgotten by then that I existed.

Oh, I heard them at their meadhall tables, their pinched, cunning rats' faces picking like needles at a boaster's words, the warfalcons gazing down, black, from the rafters, and when one of them finished his raving threats, another would stand up and lift his ram's horn, or draw his sword, or sometimes both if he was very drunk, and he'd tell them what *he* planned to do. Now and then some trivial argument would break out, and one of them would kill another one, and all the others would detach themselves from the killer as neatly as blood clotting, and they'd consider the case and they'd either excuse him, for some reason, or else send him out to the forest to live by stealing from their outlying pens like a wounded fox. At times I would try to befriend the exile, at other times I would try to ignore him, but they were treacherous. In the end, I had to eat them. As a rule, though, that wasn't how all their drinking turned out. Normally the men would howl out their daring, and the evening would get merrier, louder and louder, the king praising this one, criticizing that one, no one getting hurt except maybe some female who was asking for it, and eventually they'd all fall asleep on each other like lizards, and I'd steal a cow.

Darting unseen from camp to camp, I observed a change come over their drunken boasts. It was late spring. Food was plentiful. Every sheep and goat had its wobbly twins, the forest was teeming, and the first crops of the hillsides were coming into fruit. A man would roar, "I'll steal their gold and burn their meadhall!", shaking his sword as if the tip was afire, and a man with eyes like two pins would say, "Do it now, Cowface! I think you're not even the man your father was!" The people would laugh. I would back away into the darkness, furious at my stupid need to spy on them, and I would glide to the next camp of men, and I'd hear the same.

Then once, around midnight, I came to a hall in ruins. The cows in their pens lay burbling blood through their nostrils, with javelin holes in their necks. None had been eaten. The watchdogs lay like dark wet stones, with their heads cut off, teeth bared. The fallen hall was a square of flames and acrid smoke, and the people inside (none of them had been eaten either) were burned black, small, like dwarfs turned dark and crisp. The sky opened like a hole where the gables had loomed before, and the wooden benches, the trestle tables, the beds that had hung on the meadhall walls were scattered to the edge of the forest, shining charcoal. There was no sign of the gold they'd kept—not so much as a melted hilt.

Then the wars began, and the war songs, and the weapon-making. If the songs were true, as I suppose at least one or two of them were, there had always been wars, and what I'd seen was merely a period of mutual exhaustion.

I'd be watching a meadhall from high in a tree, night birds singing in the limbs below me, the moon's face hidden in a tower of clouds, and nothing would be stirring except leaves moving in the light spring breeze and, down by the pigpens, two men walking with their battle-axes and their dogs. Inside the hall I would hear the Shaper telling of the glorious deeds of dead kings—how they'd split certain heads, sneaked away with certain precious swords and necklaces—his harp mimicking the rush of swords, clanging boldly with the noble speeches, sighing behind the heroes' dying words. Whenever he stopped, thinking formulas for what to say next, the people would all shout and thump each other and drink to the Shaper's long life. In the shadow of the hall and by the outbuildings, men sat whistling or humming to themselves, repairing weapons: winding bronze bands around grey ash spears, treating their sword blades with snakes' venom.

Then suddenly the birds below me in the tree would fall silent, and beyond the meadhall clearing I'd hear the creak of harness leather. The watchmen and their dogs would stand stock-still, as if lightning-struck; then the dogs would bark, and the next instant the door would bang open and men would come tumbling, looking crazy, from the meadhall. The enemies' horses would thunder up into the clearing, leaping the pig fences, sending the cows and the pigs away mooing and squealing, and the two bands of men would charge. Twenty feet apart they would slide to a stop and stand screaming at each other with raised swords. The leaders on both sides held their javelins high in both hands and shook them, howling their lungs out. Terrible threats, from the few words I could catch. Things about their fathers and their fathers' fathers, things about justice and honor and lawful revenge.

Then they would fight. Spears flying, swords whonking, arrows raining from the windows and door of the meadhall and the edge of the woods. Horses reared and fell over screaming, ravens flew, crazy as bats in a fire; men staggered, gesturing wildly, making speeches, dying or sometimes pretending to be dying, sneaking off. Sometimes the attackers would be driven back, sometimes they'd win and burn the meadhall down, sometimes they'd capture the king of the meadhall and make his people give weapons and gold rings and cows.

It was confusing and frightening, not in a way I could untangle. I was safe in my tree, and the men who fought were nothing to me, except of course that they talked in something akin to my language, which meant that we were, incredibly, related. I was sickened, if only at the waste of it: all they killed— cows, horses, men—they left to rot or burn. I sacked all I could and tried to store it, but my mother would growl and make faces because of the stink.

The fighting went on all that summer and began again the next and again the next. Sometimes when a meadhall burned the survivors would go to another meadhall and, stretching out their hands, would crawl unarmed up the strangers' hill and

would beg to be taken in. They would give the strangers whatever weapons or pigs or cattle they'd saved from destruction,
and the strangers would give them an outbuilding, the worst
of their food, and some straw. The two groups would fight as
allies after that, except that now and then they betrayed each
other, one shooting the other from behind for some reason, or
stealing the other group's gold some midnight, or sneaking into
bed with the other group's wives and daughters.

I watched it, season after season. Sometimes I watched from
the high cliff wall, where I could look out and see all the meadhall lights on the various hills across the countryside, glowing
like candles, reflected stars. With luck, I might see on a soft
summer night as many as three halls burning down at once. That
was rare, of course. It grew rarer as the pattern of their warring
changed. Hrothgar, who'd begun hardly stronger than the
others, began to outstrip the rest. He'd worked out a theory
about what fighting was for, and now he no longer fought with
his six closest neighbors. He'd shown them the strength of his
organization, and now, instead of making war on them, he sent
men to them every three months or so, with heavy wagons
and back slings, to gather their tribute to his greatness. They
piled his wagons high with gold and leather and weapons, and
they kneeled to his messengers and made long speeches and
promised to defend him against any foolhardy outlaw that
dared to attack him. Hrothgar's messengers answered with
friendly words and praise of the man they'd just plundered, as if
the whole thing had been his idea, then whipped up the oxen,
pulled up their loaded back slings, and started home.

And now when enemies from farther out struck at kings who
called themselves Hrothgar's friends, a messenger would slip
out and ride through the night to the tribute-taker, and in half
an hour, while the enemy bands were still shouting at each
other, still waving their ash spears and saying what horrible
things they would do, the forest would rumble with the sound

of Hrothgar's horsemen. He would overcome them: his band
had grown large, and for the treasures Hrothgar could afford
now to give them in sign of his thanks, his warriors became
hornets. New roads snaked out. New meadhalls gave tribute.
His treasure hoard grew till his meadhall was piled to the rafters
with brightly painted shields and ornamented swords and boars-
head helmets and coils of gold, and they had to abandon the
meadhall and sleep in the outbuildings. Meanwhile, those who
paid tribute to him were forced to strike at more distant halls
to gather the gold they paid to Hrothgar—and a little on the
side for themselves. His power overran the world, from the foot
of my cliff to the northern sea to the impenetrable forests south
and east.

One night, inevitably, a blind man turned up at Hrothgar's
temporary meadhall. He was carrying a harp. I watched from
the shadow of a cow shed, since on that hill there were no trees.
The guards at the door crossed their axes in front of him. He
waited, smiling foolishly, while a messenger went inside. A few
minutes later the messenger returned, gave the old man a nod,
and—cautiously, feeling ahead of himself with his crooked bare
toes like a man engaged in some strange, pious dance, the
foolish smile still fixed on his face—the blind old man went in.
A boy darted up from the weeds at the foot of the hill, the
harper's companion. He too was shown in.

The hall became quiet, and after a moment Hrothgar spoke,
tones low and measured—of necessity, from too much shouting
on midnight raids. The harper gave him back some answer, and
Hrothgar spoke again. I glanced at the watchdogs. They still sat
silent as tree stumps, locked in my spell. I crept closer to the
hall to hear. The people were noisy for a time, yelling to the
harper, offering him mead, making jokes, and then again King
Hrothgar spoke, white-bearded. The hall became still.

The silence expanded. People coughed. As if all by itself,
then, the harp made a curious run of sounds, almost words, and

then a moment later, arresting as a voice from a hollow tree, the harper began to chant.

> Lo, we have heard the honor of the Speardanes,
> nation-kings, in days now gone,
> how those battle-lords brought themselves glory.
> Oft Scyld Shefing shattered the forces
> of kinsman-marauders, and dragged away their
> meadhall-benches, terrified earls—after first men found him
> castaway. (He got recompense for that!)
> He grew up under the clouds, won glory of men
> till all his enemies sitting around him
> heard across the whaleroads his demands and gave
> him tribute. That was a good king!

So he sang—or intoned, with the harp behind him—twisting together like sailors' ropes the bits and pieces of the best old songs. The people were hushed. Even the surrounding hills were hushed, as if brought low by language. He knew his art. He was king of the Shapers, harp-string scratchers. That was what had brought him over wilderness, down his blind man's alleys of time and space, to Hrothgar's famous hall. He would sing the glory of Hrothgar's line and gild his wisdom and stir up his men to more daring deeds. For a price.

He sang of battles and marriages, of funerals and hangings, the whimperings of beaten enemies, of splendid hunts and harvests. He sang of Hrothgar, hoarfrost white, magnificent of mind.

When he finished, the hall was as quiet as a mound. I too was silent, my ear pressed tight against the timbers. Even to me, incredibly, he had made it all seem true and very fine. Now a little, now more, a great roar began, an exhalation of breath that swelled to a rumble of voices and then to the howling and clapping and stomping of men gone mad on art. They would seize the oceans, the farthest stars, the deepest secret rivers in

Hrothgar's name! Men wept like children: children sat stunned. It went on and on, a fire more dread than any visible fire.

I crossed the moors in a queer panic, like a creature half insane. I knew the truth: *A man said, "I'll steal their gold and burn their meadhall!" and another man said, "Do it now!"*

Thus I fled, ridiculous hairy creature torn apart by poetry— crawling, whimpering, streaming tears, across the world like a two-headed beast, like a mixed-up lamb and kid at the tail of a baffled, indifferent ewe—and I gnashed my teeth and clutched the sides of my head as if to heal the split, but I couldn't.

At the top of the cliff wall I turned and looked down, and I saw all the lights of Hrothgar's realm and the realms beyond that, that would soon be his, and to clear my mind, I sucked in wind and screamed. The sound went out, violent, to the rims of the world.

I clamped my palms to my ears and stretched up my lips and shrieked again. Then I ran on all fours, chest pounding, to the smoky mere.

The Shaper remains, though now there are nobler courts where he might sing. The pride of creation. He built this hall by the power of his songs.

The boy observes him, tall and solemn, twelve years older than the night he first crept in with his stone-eyed master. He knows no art but tragedy—a moving singer. The credit is wholly mine.

Inspired by winds (or whatever you please) the old man sang of a glorious meadhall whose light would shine to the ends of the ragged world. The thought took seed in Hrothgar's mind. It grew. He called all his people together and told them his daring scheme. He would build a magnificent meadhall high on a hill, with a view of the western sea, a victory seat to stand forever as a sign of the glory and justice of Hrothgar's Danes. There he would sit and give treasures out, all wealth but the lives of men and the people's land. And so his sons would do after him, and his sons' sons, unto the final generation.

I listened, huddled in the darkness, tormented, mistrustful. I knew them, had watched them; yet the things he said seemed true. He sent to far kingdoms for woodsmen, carpenters, metalsmiths, goldsmiths—also carters, victuallers, clothiers to attend to the workmen—and for weeks their uproar filled the days and nights. I watched from the vines and boulders two miles off. Then word went out to the races of men that Hrothgar's hall was finished. He gave it its name. From neighboring realms and from across the sea came men to the great celebration. The harper sang.

I listened, felt myself swept up. I knew very well that all he said was ridiculous, not light for their darkness but flattery, illusion, a vortex pulling them from sunlight to heat, a kind of midsummer burgeoning, waltz to the sickle. Yet I was swept up. "Ridiculous!" I hissed in the black of the forest. I snatched up a snake from beside my foot and whispered to it, "I knew him *when!*" But I couldn't bring out a wicked cackle, as I'd meant to do. My heart was light with Hrothgar's goodness, and leaden with grief at my own bloodthirsty ways. I backed away, crablike, farther into darkness, backed away till the honey-sweet lure of the harp no longer mocked me. Yet even now my mind was tormented by images. Thanes filled the hall and a great silent crowd of them spilled out over the surrounding hill, smiling, peaceable, hearing the harper as if not a man in all that lot had ever twisted a knife in his neighbor's chest.

"Well then, he's changed them," I said, and stumbled and fell on the root of a tree. "Why not?"

I listened, tensed. No answer.

"He reshapes the world," I whispered, belligerent. "So his name implies. He stares strange-eyed at the mindless world and turns dry sticks to gold."

A little poetic, I would readily admit. His manner of speaking was infecting me, making me pompous. "Nevertheless," I whispered crossly—but I couldn't go on, too conscious all at once of my whispering, eternal posturing.

In the hall they were laughing.

Men and women stood talking in the light of the meadhall door and on the narrow streets below; on the lower hillside boys and girls played near the sheep pens, shyly holding hands. A few lay touching each other in the forest eaves. I thought how they'd shriek if I suddenly showed my face, and it made me smile, but I held myself back. They talked nothing, stupidities, their soft voices groping like hands. I felt myself tightening, cross, growing restless for no clear reason, and I made myself move more slowly. Then, circling the clearing, I stepped on something fleshy, and jerked away. It was a man. They'd cut his throat. His clothes had been stolen. I stared up at the hall, baffled, beginning to shake. They went on talking softly, touching hands, their hair full of light. I lifted up the body and slung it across my shoulder.

Then the harp began to play. The crowd grew still.

The harp sighed, the Shaper sang, as sweet-voiced as a child.

He told how the earth was first built, long ago: said that the greatest of gods made the world, every wonder-bright plain and the turning seas, and set out as signs of his victory the sun and moon, great lamps for light to land-dwellers, kingdom torches, and adorned the fields with all colors and shapes, made limbs and leaves and gave life to every creature that moves on land.

The harp turned solemn. He told of an ancient feud between two brothers which split all the world between darkness and light. And I, Grendel, was the dark side, he said. The terrible race god cursed.

I believed him. Such was the power of the Shaper's harp! Stood wriggling my face, letting tears down my nose, grinding my fists into my streaming eyes, even though to do it I had to squeeze with my elbow the corpse of the proof that both of us were cursed, or neither, that brothers had never lived, nor the god who judged them. "Waaa!" I bawled.

Oh what a conversion!

I staggered out into the open and up toward the hall with my burden, groaning out, "Mercy! Peace!" The harper broke off, the people screamed. (They have their own versions, but this is the truth.) Drunken men rushed me with battle-axes. I sank to my knees, crying, "Friend! Friend!" They hacked at me, yipping like dogs. I held up the body for protection. Their spears came through it and one of them nicked me, a tiny scratch high on my left breast, but I knew by the sting it had venom on it and I understood, as shocked as I'd been the first time, that they could kill me—eventually *would* if I gave them a chance. I struck at them, holding the body as a shield, and two fell bleeding from my nails at the first little swipe. The others backed off. I crushed the body in my hug, then hurled it in their faces, turned, and fled. They didn't follow.

I ran to the center of the forest and fell down panting. My mind was wild. "Pity," I moaned. "O pity! Pity!" I wept—strong monster with teeth like a shark's—and I slammed the earth with such force that a seam split open twelve feet long. "Bastards!" I roared. "Sons of bitches! Monsters!" Words I'd picked up from men in their lunatic rages.

Two nights later I went back. I was addicted. The Shaper was singing the glorious deeds of the dead men, praising war. He sang how they'd fought me. It was all lies. The sly harp rasped like snakes in cattails, glorifying death. I snatched a guard and smashed him on a tree, but my stomach turned at the thought of eating him.

"Woe to the man," the Shaper sang, "who shall through wicked hostilities shove his soul down into the fire's hug! Let him hope for no change: he can never turn away! But lucky the man who, after his deathday, shall seek the Prince, find peace in his father's embrace!"

"Ridiculous!" I whispered through clenched teeth. How was it that he could enrage me so? I knew what I knew, the mindless, mechanical bruteness of things, and when the Shaper's lure drew my mind away to hopeful dreams, the dark of what was, and always was, reached out and snatched my feet.

I got up and felt my way back through the forest and over to the cliff wall and back to the mere and to my cave. I lay there listening to the indistinct memory of the Shaper's songs. My mother picked through the bone pile, sullen. I'd brought no food.

"Ridiculous," I whispered.

She looked at me, and whimpered, scratched at the nipples I had not sucked in years. She was pitiful, foul, her smile a jagged white tear in the firelight.

I clamped my eyes shut, listened to the river, and after a time I slept.

It was the height of summer, harvest season in the first year of what I have come to call my war with Hrothgar. The night air was filled with the smell of apples and shucked grain, and I could hear the noise in the meadhall from a mile away. I moved toward it, drawn, as always, as if by some kind of curse. I meant not to be seen that night.

I had no intention of terrifying Hrothgar's thanes for nothing. I hunkered down at the edge of the forest, looking up the long hill at the meadhall lights. I could hear the Shaper's song.

I no longer remember exactly what he sang. I know only that it had a strange effect on me: it no longer filled me with doubt and distress, loneliness, shame. It enraged me. It was their confidence, maybe—their blissful, swinish ignorance, their bumptious self-satisfaction and, worst of all, their *hope*. I went closer, darting from cow shed to cow shed and finally up to the wall. I found a crack and peeked in. I do remember what he said, now that I think about it. Or some of it. He spoke of how god had been kind to the Scyldings, sending so rich a harvest. The people sat beaming, bleary-eyed and fat, nodding their approval of god. He spoke of god's great generosity in sending them so wise a king. They all raised their cups to god and Hrothgar, and Hrothgar smiled, bits of food in his beard. The Shaper talked of how god had vanquished their enemies and filled up their houses with precious treasure, how they were the richest, most power-ful people on earth, how here and here alone in all the world men were free and heroes were brave and virgins were virgins. He ended the song, and people clapped and shouted their praise and filled their golden cups.

Then a stick snapped behind me, and a dog barked. A hel-meted, chain-mailed guard leaped out at me, sword in two hands above his head, prepared to split me.

I was as surprised as the guard. We both stared.

Then, almost the same instant, the guard screamed and I roared like a bull gone mad to drive him off. He let go of the sword and tried to retreat, walking backward, but he tripped on the dog and fell. I laughed, a little wild, and reached out fast as a striking snake for his leg. In a second I was up on my feet again. He screamed, dangling, and then there were others all around me. They threw javelins and axes, and one of the men caught the guard's thrashing arms and tried to yank him free. I held on, and laughed again at Hrothgar's whispering and trem-bling by the meadhall door, at everything—the oblivious trees and the witless moon. I'd meant them no harm, but they'd attacked me again, as always. They were crazy.

I wanted to say, "Lo, god has vanquished mine enemies!"— but that made me laugh harder, though even now my heart raced and, in spite of it all, I was afraid of them. I backed away, still holding the screaming guard. They merely stared, with their weapons drawn, their shoulders hunched against my laughter. When I'd reached a safe distance I held up the guard to taunt them, then held him still higher and leered into his face. He went silent, looking at me upside down in horror, suddenly knowing what I planned. As if casually, in plain sight of them all, I bit his head off, crunched through the helmet and skull with my teeth and, holding the jerking, blood-slippery body in two hands, sucked the blood that sprayed like a hot, thick geyser from his neck. It got all over me. Women fainted, men backed toward the hall. I fled with the body to the woods, heart churning—boiling like a flooded ditch—with glee.

Some three or four nights later I launched a raid. I burst in when they were all asleep, snatched seven from their beds, and slit them open and devoured them on the spot. I felt a strange, unearthly joy. It was as if I'd made some incredible discovery, like my discovery long ago of the moonlit world beyond the mere. I was transformed. I was a new focus for the clutter of space I stood in: if the world had once imploded on the tree where I waited, trapped and full of pain, it now blasted outward, away from me, screeching terror. I had become, myself, the mama I'd searched the cliffs for once in vain. I had *become* something. I had hung between possibilities before, between the cold truths I knew and the heart-sucking conjuring tricks of the Shaper; now that was passed: I was Grendel, Ruiner of Meadhalls, Wrecker of Kings!

But also, as never before, I was alone. I do not complain of it (talking talking, complaining complaining, filling the world I walk with words). But I admit it was a jolt.

It was a few raids later. The meadhall door burst open at my touch exactly as before, and, for once, that night, I hesitated. Men sat up in their beds, snatched their helmets, swords, and shields from the covers beside them, and, shouting brave words that came out like squeals, they threw their legs over the sides to stumble toward me. Someone yelled, "Remember this hour, ye thanes of Hrothgar, the boasts you made as the meadbowl passed! Remember our good king's gift of rings and pay him with all your might for his many kindnesses!"

Damned pompous fools. I hurled a bench at the closest. They all cowered back. I stood waiting, bent forward with my feet apart, flat-footed, till they ended their interminable orations. I was hunched like a wrestler, moving my head from side to side, making sure no sneak slipped up on me. I was afraid of them from habit, and as the four or five drunkest of the thanes came toward me, shaking their weapons and shouting at me, my idiotic fear of them mounted. But I held my ground. Then, with a howl, one plunged at me, sword above his head in both fists. I let it come.

I closed my hand on the blade and snatched it from the drunken thane's hand and hurled it the length of the hall. It clattered on the fireplace stones and fell to the stone floor, ringing. I seized him and crushed him. Another one came at me, gloating in his blear-eyed heroism, maniacally joyful because he had bragged that he would die for his king and he was doing it. He did it. Another one came, reeling and whooping, trying to make his eyes focus.

I laughed. It was outrageous: they came, they fell, howling insanity about brothers, fathers, glorious Hrothgar and God. But though I laughed, I felt trapped, as hollow as a rotten tree. The meadhall seemed to stretch for miles, out to the edges of time and space, and I saw myself killing them, on and on and on, mechanically, without contest. I saw myself swelling like bellows on their blood.

All at once I began to smash things—benches, tables, hanging beds—a rage as meaningless and terrible as everything else.

Then—as a crowning absurdity, my salvation that moment—came the man the thanes called Unferth.

He stood across the hall from me, youthful, intense, cold sober. He was taller than the others; he stood out among his fellow thanes like a horse in a herd of cows. His nose was as porous and dark as volcanic rock. His light beard grew in patches.

"Stand back," he said.

The drunken little men around me backed away. The hall floor between us, Unferth and myself, lay open.

"Monster, prepare to die!" he said. Very righteous. The wings of his nostrils flared and quivered like an outraged priest's.

I laughed. "Aargh!" I said. I spit bits of bone.

He glanced behind, making sure he knew exactly where the window was. "Are you right with your god?" he said.

I laughed somewhat more fiercely. He was one of those.

He took a tentative step toward me, then paused, holding his sword out and shaking it. "Tell them in Hell that Unferth, son of Ecglaf, sent you, known far and wide in these Scannian lands as a hero among the Scyldings." He took a few side steps, like one wrestler circling another, except that he was thirty feet away. The maneuver was ridiculous.

"Come, come," I said. "Let me tell them I was sent by Side-ways-Walker."

He frowned, trying to puzzle out my speech. I said it again, louder and slower, and a startled look came over him. Even now he didn't know what I was saying, but it was clear to him, I think, that I was speaking words. He got a cunning look, as if getting ready to offer a deal—the look men have when they fight with men instead of poor stupid animals.

He was shaken, and to get back his nerve he spoke some more. "For many months, unsightly monster, you've murdered men as you pleased in Hrothgar's hall. Unless you can murder me as you've murdered lesser men, I give you my word those days are done forever! The king has given me splendid gifts. He will see tonight that his gifts have not gone for nothing! Prepare to fall, foul thing! This one red hour makes your reputation or mine!"

I shook my head at him, wickedly smiling. "Reputation!" I said, pretending to be much impressed.

His eyebrows shot up. He'd understood me; no doubt of it now. "You can talk!" he said. He backed away a step. My talking changed the picture.

I nodded, moving in on him. Near the center of the room there was a trestle table piled high with glossy apples. An evil idea came over me—so evil it made me shiver as I smiled—and I sidled across to the table. "So you're a hero," I said. He didn't get it, and I said it twice more before I gave up in disgust. I talked on anyway, let him get what he could, come try for reputation when he pleased. "I'm impressed," I said. "I've never seen a live hero before. I thought they were only in poetry. Ah, ah, it must be a terrible burden, though, being a hero—glory reaper, harvester of monsters! Everybody always watching you, weighing you, seeing if you're still heroic. You know how it is —he he! Sooner or later the harvest virgin will make her mistake in the haystack." I laughed.

I picked up an apple and polished it lightly and quickly on the hair of my arm. I had my head bowed, smiling, looking at him up through my eyebrows.

"Dread creature—" he said.

I went on polishing the apple, smiling. "And the awful inconvenience," I said. "Always having to stand erect, always having to find noble language! It must wear on a man."

He lifted his sword to make a run at me, and I laughed— howled—and threw an apple at him. He dodged, and then his mouth dropped open. I laughed harder, threw another. He dodged again.

"Hey!" he yelled. A forgivable lapse.

And now I was raining apples at him and laughing myself weak. He covered his head, roaring at me. He tried to charge through the barrage, but he couldn't make three feet. I slammed one straight into his pockmarked nose, and blood spurted out like joining rivers. It made the floor slippery, and he went down. *Clang!* I bent double with laughter. Poor Jangler—Unferth— tried to take advantage of it, charging at me on all fours, snatching at my ankles, but I jumped back and tipped over the table on him, half burying him in apples. He screamed and thrashed, trying to get at me and at the same time trying to see if the others were watching. He was crying, only a boy, famous hero or not, a poor miserable virgin.

"Such is life," I said, and mocked a sigh. "Such is dignity!" Then I left. I got more pleasure from that apple fight than from any other battle in my life.

I was sure, going back to my cave, that he wouldn't follow. They never did. But I was wrong; he was a new kind of Scylding. He must have started tracking me that same morning. A driven man, a maniac. He arrived at the cave three nights later.

I was asleep. I woke up with a start, not sure what it was that had awakened me. I saw my mother moving slowly and silently past me, blue murder in her eyes. I understood instantly, and I darted around in front to block her way. I pushed her back.

There he lay, gasping on his belly like a half-drowned rat. His face and throat and arms were a crosshatch of festering cuts, the leavings of the firesnakes. His hair and beard hung straight down like seaweed. He panted for a long time, then rolled his eyes up, vaguely in my direction. In the darkness he couldn't see me, though I could see him. He closed his hand on the sword hilt and jiggled the sword a little, too weak to raise it off the floor.

"Unferth has come!" he said.

I smiled.

He crawled toward me, the sword noisily scraping on the cave's rock floor. Then he gave out again. "It will be sung," he whispered, then paused again to get wind. "It will be sung year on year and age on age that Unferth went down through the burning lake—" He paused to pant. "—and gave his life in battle with the world-rim monster." He let his cheek fall to the floor and lay panting for a long time, saying nothing. It dawned on me that he was waiting for me to kill him. I did nothing. I sat down and put my elbows on my knees and my chin on my fists and merely watched. He lay with his eyes closed and began to get his breath back. He whispered: "It's all very well to make a fool of me before my fellow thanes. All very well to talk about dignity and noble language and all the rest, as if heroism were a golden trinket, mere outward show, and hollow. But such is not the case, monster. That is to say—" He paused, seemed to grope; he'd lost his train of thought.

I said nothing, merely waited, blocking my mother by stretching out an arm when she came near.

"Even now you mock me," Unferth whispered. I had an uneasy feeling he was close to tears. If he wept I was not sure I could control myself. His pretensions to uncommon glory were one thing. If for even an instant he pretended to misery like mine. . . .

"You think me a witless fool," he whispered. "Oh, I heard what you said. I caught your nasty insinuations. 'I thought heroes were only in poetry,' you said, implying that what I've made of myself is mere fairy-tale stuff." He raised his head, trying to glare at me, but his blind stare was in the wrong direction, following my mother's pacing. "Well it's not, let me tell you." His lips trembled and I was certain he would cry: I would have to destroy him from pure disgust, but he held it. He let his head fall again and sucked for air. A little of his voice came back: "Poetry's trash, mere clouds of words, comfort to the hopeless. But this is no cloud, no syllabled phantom that stands here shaking its sword at you."

I let the slight exaggeration pass.

But Unferth didn't. "Or lies here," he said. "A hero is not afraid to face cruel truth." That reminded him, apparently, of what he'd meant to say before. "You talk of heroism as noble language, dignity. It's more than that, as my coming here has proved. No man above us will ever know whether Unferth died here or fled to the hills like a coward. Only you and I and God will know the truth. That's inner heroism."

"Hmm," I said. It was not unusual, of course, to hear them contradict themselves.

He looked hurt and slightly indignant. He'd understood.

"Wretched shape—" he said.

"But no doubt there are compensations," I said. "The pleasant feeling of vast superiority, the easy success with women—"

"Monster!" he howled.

"And the joy of self-knowledge, that's a great compensation! The easy and absolute certainty that whatever the danger, however terrible the odds, you'll stand firm, behave with the dignity of a hero, yea, even to the grave!"

"No more talk!" he yelled. His voice broke. He jerked his head up, "Does *nothing* have value in your horrible ruin of a brain?"

I waited. The whole foolish scene was his idea, not mine.

I saw the light dawning in his eyes. "I understand," he said. I thought he would laugh at the bottomless stupidity of my cynicism, but while the laugh was still starting at the corner of his eyes, another look came, close to fright. "You think me deluded. Tricked by my own walking fairy tale. You think I came without a hope of winning—came to escape indignity by suicide!" He did laugh now, not amused: sorrowful and angry. The laugh died quickly. "I didn't know how deep the pool was," he said. "I had a chance. I knew I had no more than that. It's all a hero asks for."

I sighed. The word *hero* was beginning to grate. He was an idiot. I could crush him like a fly, but I held back.

"Go ahead, scoff," he said, petulant. "Except in the life of a hero, the whole world's meaningless. The hero sees values beyond what's possible. That's the *nature* of a hero. It kills him, of course, ultimately. But it makes the whole struggle of humanity worthwhile."

I nodded in the darkness. "And breaks up the boredom," I said.

He raised up on his elbows, and the effort of it made his shoulders shake. "One of us is going to die tonight. Does *that* break up your boredom?"

"It's not true," I said. "A few minutes from now I'm going to carry you back to Hrothgar, safe and sound. So much for poetry."

"I'll kill myself," he whispered. He shook violently now.

"Up to you," I answered reasonably, "but you'll admit it may seem at least a trifle cowardly to some."

His fists closed and his teeth clenched; then he relaxed and lay flat.

I waited for him to find an answer. Minutes passed. It came to me that he had quit. He had glimpsed a glorious ideal, had struggled toward it and seized it and come to understand it, and was disappointed. One could sympathize.

He was asleep.

I picked him up gently and carried him home. I laid him at the door of Hrothgar's meadhall, still asleep, killed the two guards so I wouldn't be misunderstood, and left.

He lives on, bitter, feebly challenging my midnight raids from time to time (three times this summer, innumerable times in the dreary twelve years that have passed since that idiot apple fight)—lives on, poor Unferth, crazy with shame that he alone is always spared, and furiously jealous of the dead. I laugh when I see him. He throws himself at me, or he cunningly sneaks up behind, sometimes in disguise—a goat, a dog, a sickly old woman—and I roll on the floor with laughter. So much for heroism. So much for the harvest virgin. So much for Shaper's dreams.

They talk of a man who will get me sure, some super super-hero men call Beowulf. Terrific.

Come, fierce stranger.

Soon.

A GREAT FEELING

Michael Rogers

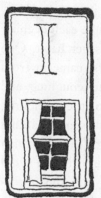I lie here sick, upstairs, in the afternoons, watching the shadows of tree limbs move silently across my yellow ceiling, while downstairs Wanda brings in young men. An hour before dinner I hear the front door open and close once, and if the particular afternoon's automobile or motorcycle is sufficiently unmuffled I can trace its path out to the corner, until, at the turn, a stand of poplars intervenes and silences even the most ambitious exhaust.

"Peter?" I ask Wanda when she brings my tray. "Was it Peter this afternoon?" Each dinner time, to keep our conversation fresh, I contrive a new name.

"Filthy," she tells me. "Your mind is filled with filth and suspicion. But you're sick. We're out of the artichokes. I have creamed spinach instead."

"Claude, then. Claude is the one with the motorcycle?"

"What Claude, what motorcycle? How is your temperature today?"

"101 at noon. 101.3 at one. 101.7 at two. 101.5 at three, when Claude came in."

"No Claude, no Peter, no motorcycle."

"102 at four. 102.1 an hour ago."

Wanda nods angelically over my covers. Her long hair has grown out fully two inches since the last time she bleached it and now a neat stripe of dark brown divides the crown of her head in half. Brown and yellow: her hair perches on her head fiercely, like a patterned football helmet. "The new medicine is helping you, you think?"

"I think."

"That's fine." She tugs gently at the cuffs of her blouse. Wanda changes her clothes before she brings me my dinner. Tonight, as every night, her skirt is demurely long and well-pressed, her white blouse is creased and spotless and primly high-necked. Her deception would be flawless were it not for Wanda's innate laziness: she wears the identical costume each evening and I am not so naïve as to think uniformity is her habit. One afternoon more than a month ago when she first came in from school I feigned loud distress, the choking and coughing and hysterical spasms that are the private province of the moribund, and thereby brought Wanda bounding up the stairs, panting and sweating, to breathlessly minister my passing. (Good Wanda is, in fact, most solicitous about my health, and in order to avoid the inevitable neighborhood rumor-mongering and the unfortunate possibility of official curiosity, I think that she will do all she can to stave off the moment of my demise.) That afternoon she paused outside my room, and certain that this was a sudden caution on her part, I redoubled my gasping and throat-rattling and brought her spinning, nearly tripping on the carpet, through the door. Ah! My Wanda, here caught for a rare portrait in her natural habit by the wily eye and subtle snare of the infirm woodsman: she halts then, at the foot of my bed, when I appear to be in no critical state—faded baggy blue denims dragging about her bare feet, a thin yellow undershirt stenciled SMASH THE STATE! front and back, the A's precisely punctuated by her nipples, her long hair ironed arrow-straight and separated into a thousand independent strands down over her face and shoulders, her eyes sunk back deep in their sockets under the pressing weight of mascara that appears to have been applied by trowel.

I chose to play the jovial fool. "Costume day at school?" I ask her with the proper fool's quaver.

She steps more completely behind the footboard of my bed. "Ha. You're all right? I heard you. . . ." She is the picture of concern.

"My throat." I point weakly to my throat as if it is an object not easily located. "In my throat. You know."

"You're all right now." No longer as a question.

I nod, with the exaggerated gravity of one who has glimpsed death.

Wanda looks down at her clothes. "I was going to paint."

"The house?"

"A canvas."

I stare.

"Oils, you know, oil painting."

"Oh. A new hobby?"

"New hobby." She edges toward the door. Wanda does very little for the soft idyllic life she has fallen into here.

"I'd like to see the results. Very much."

Wanda nods, turning to go out.

"I'll be looking forward to it. I'd like to see your paintings when they're done."

"Sure thing."

Wanda, I know, cannot even paint her eyelids neatly, so for several weeks afterward I ask constantly to see her canvases. From this she will learn to avoid hastily thought-out excuses.

That single afternoon was the only occasion I have caught Wanda out of her costume. Each evening at six she is at the door with my tray, hair tied back and face utterly without makeup. I embrace her nightly deception as a touching tribute to my invalid sensibilities and my apparently abysmal stupidity.

"You'll like the creamed spinach," Wanda tells me.

"George. His name was George."

Wanda is becoming exasperated with me. "No George, no Peter, no Ralph, no nobody."

"*Ralph*. I never mentioned a *Ralph*."

She leaves wordlessly. This perpetual strain of bantering with the bedridden is terrible to bear.

There is a nervous affliction within me that is traveling a slow pilgrimage up the two peninsulas of my legs. Last July, on the morning of Independence Day, this affliction first seized me about my ankles and brought me graceless to my hands and knees, on the hot sidewalk two blocks from my home. At that moment the joints of my feet simply ceased to function according to my will: the hinge joints of my ankles became as fluid and precarious as greased metal bearings rolled between the hands. Stretcher and ambulance were required, a full set of mechanical contrivances to bear me the two blocks home in state and deposit me here, permanently, hapless victim of an inexplicable system of rebellious ganglia. The rebellion spreads. The muscles of my calves are now putty. Last month my knees —patellae and tendons once stiffened and powerful with rugby and soccer—began a slow secession from the dominion of my brain.

"If you're going to stay home you'll need someone to look after you. That is all there is to it." This from my sister, married twice and once divorced, seven years younger than I, flown in from Chicago to see me through the initial crisis of my degeneration.

"A nurse," I told her then. "I'll hire a nurse."

"Nonsense," as if the idea itself might be sprung from the worst depths of my illness. "Absolute nonsense." She stood next to my bed, her hair newly dyed a deep resonant red, amplifying the authority that her voice has carried since childhood. "We will let you have Wanda."

"Ah!"

One week later Wanda is at my door. The temporary nurse brings her upstairs. "You have a very wonderful house here, Uncle," are her first words to me: I have them written down somewhere, as a small keepsake.

I gather then that she views this new arrangement as a liberation of sorts and for nearly a month I am treated as if I am the prince of all liberators. When it turns fall and Wanda begins her final year of high school, her interests gradually shift away from my convalescence.

Tonight the thin odor of burning hemp cigarettes spirals up the staircase and silently invades my room. Wanda employs an inferior grade of incense that I do not think would mask the scent of fresh air. She offers, solicitously, to close my door, but I say no, I like the feel of ventilation, I enjoy the circulation of breeze and the exchange of odors, please, Wanda, leave my door wide open.

These parties of Wanda's have become a source of entertainment to me. Late in the summer when it became clear that she would stay on for the winter and attend school here, some random flash of intimacy motivated her to deliver a brief confession along with my dinner tray.

"You know I had some trouble in Chicago?"

I had heard family rumors.

"Something of the sort," I told her.

"You know what kind of trouble it was?"

"Ah. Not in detail, no."

Wanda stared at me, her brown eyes wide and perfectly clear. "Boy trouble."

Boy trouble. The essential cherubic innocence of the phrase propelled me into sympathy. "Well. We all have—"

"Bad boy trouble."

"Hmmm. It's not—"

"I mean serious boy trouble."

527

"Forget it," I told Wanda. Apparently she has.

The male voices that regularly echo ever so slightly from downstairs are not the thin adenoidal tones of boy trouble. If Wanda still feels she has trouble she must realize by now that it is man trouble. Truck drivers, certainly. Perhaps college football players or boxers or piano movers. Perhaps (the possibility just now occurs to me) professional TV wrestlers. It is unfortunately difficult to guess the identity of Wanda's visitors from those faint wisps of sound that float up the stairwell.

This, then, my evening's entertainment: to lie here encapsulated by my sheets and strain to catch the abbreviated fragments of conversation from downstairs. Wanda will not tolerate overloud voices—on the very brink of numerous revelations I have heard her: "Shhhh, for crissake, keep it down."

"—not dammit fourteen times, only—"

"Shhh," comes Wanda's voice, quiet, faintly venomous.

"—and you can take it and—"

"Shhh," is Wanda, dulcimer sweet.

"—if power does not derive from the people then—"

"Shhh," says Wanda, soothing, beneficent, maintaining still a fine edge of steel.

Tonight is no exception. The voices from downstairs flow around me, just at the edge of my perception, as if on some acoustical sea I lie at rest in the troughs of waves, only occasionally lifted up to glimpse the horizon.

"—yesterday was—"

"—no evidence of any—"

"—buy three more, is enough, three—"

Wanda is altogether and uncharacteristically silent this evening. Her guests (by now I have distinguished two slightly different timbres of voice) apparently monopolize the discussion.

"—either Mexico or—"

"—tracing back—"

528

"—gelignite—"

Gelignite. This word I extract from the conversation and retain for a moment: it seems to me that Wanda and her friends
discuss a remarkable and eclectic range of topics. These three
syllables have echoed up the stairwell on other nights, *gel-ig-nite*,
and this is, I think, a word that I should recognize. In the
morning I will have Wanda bring me the dictionary. For crosswords, I will tell her.

This morning Wanda wrapped in her robe brings my breakfast. I find myself wondering what sort of costume she wears to
school now that the days have become warmer.

"Was the party enjoyable?"

"Party?" Wanda unfolds the short legs of the tray and sets it
over me. "I stayed in last night. I'd tell you if I went out."

"I mean your friends. They left about midnight."

She tucks a linen napkin into the neck of my pajamas and
smiles, shaking her head almost imperceptibly. She is a con-
summate actress. To watch her I could almost think myself
senile. "No friends. I studied last night."

"Ah. Any trouble with your classes, something I could help
with?"

"No." She has taken, these mornings, even to cracking my
egg for me.

"What was it you studied?"

Wanda steps back, to survey critically the breakfast tableau
she has created. She smiles at me. "Government."

Before she leaves for school Wanda brings me the dictionary
and sharpened pencils and my crosswords book. During the
summer I did crosswords from the newspaper until Wanda saw
fit to cancel the subscription. I ask her occasionally if she might
renew it but it is in my best interests, she tells me, not to be
upset by the state of the world.

Page 448 of the dictionary. Just at the top of the left-hand
column I locate my word:

gel-ig-nite n: a high explosive in which the base is composed of potassium nitrate or a similar nitrate with wood pulp. A dynamite.

I read it twice, slowly: in my paralysis print has acquired a sensual quality that requires concentration. The rest of the day goes quickly. In the afternoon Wanda entertains two visitors.

Tonight while she serves me dinner I tell Wanda that the muscles of my thighs have begun a deterioration and it is no longer so easy for me to move myself about the bed. Perhaps, I suggest, we might install a telephone beside me in case I encounter some sort of emergency during the day when she is at school.

"We'll see," Wanda promises me.

"You could make a note of it so it wouldn't slip your mind."

"I'll remember."

Wanda has more guests tonight. I think I hear two motorcycles and two cars stop in front of the house. Of late Wanda has left off playing the stereo at these gatherings. My ears have become exceedingly keen at separating voices recently, and tonight my powers are at a peak. Three men and two young women, I am certain, besides the familiar drone of my Wanda.

Wanda has left a small chrome bell on my bedstand, as a substitute, I suppose, for a telephone. "Ring," she told me, "if you ever want anything." It has been there beside the water pitcher for two weeks and I have never touched it. Tonight, around midnight, when the unintelligible murmur of voices begins to bore me, I ring for Wanda, a single penetrating jangle. The voices downstairs stop instantly. In thirty-five seconds (I time her, idly curious) Wanda is at my door wrapped up in a blue dressing gown.

"Yes?" Her smile is magnificent.

I hold up my crosswords book, gripped with both hands, covering my face with it. "I was doing crosswords."

"You should be asleep." She approaches the bed, to confiscate my book and tuck me in.

"I need a word."

"Tomorrow. Plenty of time for crosswords tomorrow."

"Just one word, tonight."

Wanda pauses in the middle of the floor. She is so patient with me. "One word. Then asleep, you promise?"

I nod. "Nine letters."

"Yes." She is all attention.

"Starts with g."

"All right."

"Ends with g-n-i-t-e."

"Meaning?"

I pretend to read laboriously from the book. "A high explosive with a wood-pulp base." I look up and squint at Wanda.

"Ah." Her lips slack. She stares at me for perhaps five beats of my pulse and shakes her head. "Can't help you." Now she smiles again. "You've got to do easier crosswords. Sorry."

"Well." I shrug.

On her way out Wanda closes my door. I call after her to leave it open but she is already too far down the hall, well out of earshot.

The next morning dawns as yet the fairest day of this spring. At breakfast Wanda does not mention my question of the previous evening. Apparently she still cannot think of the word. She says, in fact, very little.

"The doctor will be here tomorrow morning."

"Oh?" I hadn't asked for the doctor.

"I thought he should see you. New symptoms and all."

I nod: Wanda has the practice of registering each of my deteriorations with the outside world lest at some future date she be considered an inattentive nurse. I try to make this process as

531

difficult for her as possible. "I'll ask him about the telephone. If he thinks it's a good idea."

Wanda stops at the door. "Don't bother. I'll take care of it."

"Well."

"No. I mean I will take care of it."

Today I recatalog the semeiology of my disorder. I am sole curator of a full museum of symptoms original to my condition and it is a duty I take seriously. Each tingle of paralysis, each initial loss of sensation, each mortal nervous spasm, every new road sign of my disability I mark down and report faithfully to my neurophysician. In time I will qualify as a syndrome; I am determined to attain that status with the most impressive of credentials.

Late afternoon: Wanda returns from school by herself and remains alone. The house is silent until she brings me dinner, when I notice a certain and marked air of agitation about her.

"No visitors today, Wanda?"

"No." She looks at me. "As usual."

When Wanda came here in the summer she was a very attractive girl who looked to be several years older than eighteen. (I have heard conflicting theories to account for the sudden and deceptive maturity reached by the female portion of this latest generation: it is either, I am told, the hormonal content of commercial meat tenderizers, or else the radiation from television picture tubes. Or perhaps some subtle alchemical combination of the two.) She found, I think, a kind of novelty in her relationship with an immobilized bedroom captive and for several weeks I was treated to a constantly changing display of perfumes and hairstyles and provocative clothing. It was not at all difficult to see in her appearance and bearing the origins of Wanda's boy trouble. Lately, however, I sense that Wanda has entered onto a slow decline that even her dinner-time costuming cannot altogether conceal. Tonight I notice for the first time that the hair on Wanda's legs is unusually long, so long that under her stockings it is matted into a spectacular pattern of thin baroque curls and designs. She seems possessed of unusual energy tonight and as she leans against the doorframe, watching me eat, the itching of her nylons causes her to rub the calves of her legs together constantly and furiously. I try to make conversation. "I found my word."

"Your word?"

"From the crossword puzzle."

"Yes." Wanda nods, and glances back out the door.

"*Gelignite*. G-e-l-i-g-n-i-t-e."

"Oh." I let the silence drag on and Wanda fidgets. "That's a bomb?"

"A high explosive. Nine letters. G-e-l-i-g-n-i-t-e."

"Well. It's good you found it." A tone of finality, which I ignore.

"How was your school today?"

"All right." She sighs and leans back against the doorframe. "How is school any day?"

"Anything interesting happen?"

"Nothing."

"Well. No news is good news, right?"

Wanda is half out the door. "Right." She disappears down the hall.

The doctor arrives at ten the next morning, bright and cheerful, shaven so close his neck is scarlet, loaded down with his tools and a sheaf of medical journals. Each visit he reads to me short research notes from these journals: "Research goes on," he tells me. "It is going on at *this very moment*." He will lean over my bed and lower his voice: "Let me tell you that medicine now makes more progress in one day than it did in a full month twenty years ago." He nods. "*One day*."

Today during the examination we discuss the insecure and ephemeral nature of neural connections. "Ropes of sand," my doctor tells me. "It is a wonder, a natural wonder, that any of us function after fifty." He prods the nerve centers of my legs with polished chrome tools. "Nothing?"

I shake my head. My legs are as lifeless as timbers, fully as high as my hips. "A little deterioration." The doctor taps the bedside table with his tiny mallet, considering this.

"A little," he agrees. "We would do more tests, downtown, run more EEG's, if it wasn't for the fire. We're closed down for at least a week."

"The fire?"

"Well. We were half a block away. Mostly water damage." He begins to write me a new prescription. "How is Wanda?"

"She's well. Which fire was this?"

He stops writing. "Didn't you see the paper this morning?"

"No."

"They bombed the Second Precinct yesterday. Dynamite and something incendiary. Burned down half a city block." The little mallet in his hand comes up and strikes the bedstand once, sharply.

"Any deaths?"

"Twelve. Ten in the hospital." He describes the disaster as he viewed it in quick glimpses from the rear windows of an ambulance, springs creaking, overloaded with the weight of rhetoric suddenly condensed into a thousand pounds of damaged flesh. My isolation from the event renders it cold and lifeless to me: it is as if I hear at a distance the fractured retelling of a violent movie plot, in fragments undone from the whole; flames and wreckage and shattered bodies sweep over me as gently as conversation overheard in a restaurant.

The EEG's will have to be put off, we decide; the insane dynamics of the times have superseded the more deliberate dysfunctioning of my being.

"A terrible terrible thing," the doctor says to me before he leaves.

534

I agree with him. "It's hard to know what to do."

"Shoot them. They should be shot."

I am left two new prescriptions and a kindly worded prognosis: perhaps I should consider a move to a well-equipped hospital, for a time at least, in order to allow some concentrated tests and a higher level of therapy. When the paralysis reaches my waist, I am gently reminded, I will be a considerably greater bother.

Wanda comes up directly after school, dressed neatly, with the first traces of a spring tan appearing around her cheekbones.

"The doctor was here?"

I show her the two prescriptions.

"Fine. He said you were better?"

"No."

"He said you were no worse?"

"No."

"The new medicine will probably help a lot."

New medicine. This has become a weekly routine—the prescription of new drugs, my dutiful consumption of the bright tablets, sometimes ten or twelve each day, different colors every week. They are a perpetual vote of confidence in the reversibility of my condition. I suspect that the bulk of these tablets are sugar or simple vitamins done up in impressive coatings: I have come to view the weekly prescriptions as a touching bit of concern. "Will help. Probably."

"Certainly will." Wanda is insistent. "They most certainly will help."

"Any interesting news today?"

Wanda shakes her head.

"Nothing new at school?"

"Nope."

"Any guests expected tonight?"

Wanda sighs: she is the most abused of martyrs. "No guests."

535

She hooks her long hair back behind her ears. "But something nice. A treat."

"Oh?"

"A special dinner tonight. Two days' sodium allowance, all at once. Lobster Newburg." Wanda smiles now, radiantly. "You'll like it. And then maybe lights-out at nine." As she closes the door behind her I catch in the breeze the faint odor of the perfume she wears for me, almost entirely submerged in the suddenly sharp scent of her body. Wanda is perspiring to excess tonight.

An hour later she brings up dinner, lavishly set out on the tray in good china with a linen napkin folded beneath the plate. Before she leaves, she lights with a flourish a short taper set in a sterling base. Dinner by candlelight. "Enjoy!" says Wanda.

A delicate bitter acridity about the rich sauce of the meal first makes me suspicious. I set the candle aside and bring a bright light to bear on the congealing liquid: there is a vaguely improper tint to it, a coppery green business, that lies in a thin oily swirl on the surface. I hold a few drops of the most discolored portion of the sauce on my tongue and the area they touch grows numb.

Wanda has obtained some preparation to make my lights-out even easier. For a moment I consider ringing the bedside bell, calling to tell her that the lobster is spoiled and I cannot eat it. But Wanda is already far too defensive. I have fifteen or twenty empty glass pill bottles in the drawer of my bedstand: souvenirs that I keep, glossy remembrances of past potions and restoratives. It takes only ten to bottle up the bulk of my dinner, and I cap them tightly and return them to the drawer. Tomorrow I will ask Wanda to open my window before she leaves; even from bed I should be able to sail each pill bottle far into the street.

"Delicious," I tell her when she comes up to take away my

dishes. "It's nice, once in a while, to have a little change in the diet."

"A good dinner helps you sleep. All these late-night crosswords. I think you need some extra rest."

"Ah, yes," I tell her.

When she takes away my tray Wanda stands over the bed for a moment watching me. She is a beautiful girl, her bone structure and coloring and skin texture. In addition she has a certain and difficult beauty that radiates from within. This I tentatively identify tonight as a smooth and magnificent female authority.

"I'll be in a little later to see if you feel like sleep." As a special dessert she leaves me a tiny dish of four white mints. I sink them solemnly into the bottles of lobster.

At nine Wanda comes in to turn my light off. I sense that she is surprised to find me still awake, so I yawn several times while she fluffs my pillow. "Doctor examinations can leave you very tired," she tells me. "It's no wonder you feel like going to sleep."

When the bedstand clock has passed nine-thirty I hear the first motorcycle and car pull up. There is no bell or knock at the door: either Wanda has met them or they have taken now to simply walking in.

Wanda's confidence in the effectiveness of her special dinner is unbounded. My door is left open and the voices downstairs go unhushed as they increase in volume. Two more cars arrive and the conversation becomes much quieter; I am again reduced to listening to murmurings.

Tomorrow, I decide, I will contrive some way to get a message outside: my suspicion of Wanda has grown intense after the doctor's visit, and if there is even a chance that she is involved with some plot it is only humane that I try to warn the authorities. I consider writing a short note and tying it to one of the pill bottles to be heaved out into the street. The idea seems to be the best at my disposal—I begin to compose the note with pen and paper, in the faint filtered glow from a streetlight fifty yards from my window.

TO WHOM IT MAY CONCERN. I strike that out: too formal, with no sense of urgency in it. Perhaps ATTENTION! FORWARD THIS NOTE TO CHIEF OF POLICE. But in all likelihood only a small child would pick up a scrap of paper tied to shards of glass in the street. Something simple is required.

There are footsteps on the stairs, Wanda's light tread. I put my pad and pen under the pillow and lean back feigning sleep. She passes down the hall into her own bedroom without pausing outside my door. When she returns I risk opening my eyes to watch her passage: she is carrying her suitcase.

TAKE THIS TO YOUR PARENTS. No. TAKE THIS TO MOMMY AND DADDY. That is closer; I print it in large block letters on the outside of my note and beneath the lines I sketch a quick picture of a laughing clown with curly wire hair: something, I hope, to catch the child's eye. The body of the note will be easier to compose. PLEASE INFORM PROPER AUTHORITIES. Or? PLEASE INFORM POLICE DEPARTMENT. Proper authorities, I decide: the police department, I am told, is harder to find these days.

Wanda outside in the hall once more. She stops by my door and I close my eyes, breathe rhythmically. She goes on to her bedroom and returns carrying a coat and a pair of boots, strange attire for springtime.

I HAVE REASON TO SUSPECT. Should that be stronger? I MAY HAVE KNOWLEDGE OF SUSPECTS DESIRED BY POLICE. This is much better; the longer phrase confirms legitimacy. SUSPECTS. IN-VOLVED IN DYNAMITE FIREBOMBING. No—I will demonstrate the accuracy of my knowledge. INVOLVED IN GELIGNITE FIRE-BOMBING OF PO-

Wanda up the stairs a third time. Once more I put my pen and paper under the pillow and lie back. She stops at my door—I risk one open eye—and then she is inside, coming up directly next to my bed. I can hear her breathe no more than two feet from my face before she turns away. She is in the room for a long time: her footsteps move from one side of the room back to the other several times, finally stopping in the corner directly opposite my bed. Small faint muffled noises: then she is gone. I wait until she has fully descended the stairs before I open my eyes. The glow of the streetlight is just sufficient to illuminate the ceiling-high bookshelves that face my bed. Very near the top, some seven feet off the ground, Wanda has cleared away a space of perhaps twenty thin volumes that are now piled on the floor.

—LICE HEADQUARTERS. PRIMARY SUSPECT MY NIECE, HIGH-SCHOOL SENIOR, AND FRIENDS. This is well-phrased and to the point. MOST LIKELY TO BE FOUND TOGETHER IN EVENI—

Wanda at the stairs again. And not alone. The steps coming up are heavy and slow, at least three pairs of feet, sounding almost clumsy. I close my eyes once more, lean back, breathe deeply. Footsteps stop outside my door. The darkness behind my eyelids brightens as the hall light is switched on. Thuds, scrapings, strange noises not easily placed. The footsteps recede back down in the direction of the living room. Outside, in the hall, directly opposite my open door, they have left the heavy oaken sideboard that has stood for years in an alcove of the dining room. It stands squat and ugly, utterly out of place, harshly lighted by the fixture directly overhead.

—NG. IMPERATIVE THAT YOU INVESTIGATE THIS IMMEDIATELY. ADDRESS—

She moves so quietly this time that I fail to notice her until she reaches the top of the stairs. I close my eyes just before Wanda steps into the room. She moves directly to the book-shelf and stays there perhaps thirty seconds. Absolutely silent, even though in this bedroom isolation I have trained myself to hear the slightest sound. Then she is gone again, the faintest whisper through the door. This time the door closes: I hear it latch, and now I open my eyes. Outside more footsteps up the stairs and then the sound of a heavy object being pushed across the hall carpeting. A single powerful violent thud as the sideboard comes to rest against my door and the thin sliver of light below it is extinguished.

It requires a moment for my eyes to adjust to the new darkness. I raise up on my elbows and look around the room, now illuminated only by the streetlight outside my window. Wanda's footsteps have disappeared down the staircase again and the house is silent. High on the bookshelf that she cleared so purposefully ten minutes before, she has deposited one small white shoebox centered perfectly between the remaining volumes. The box produces the very faintest of mechanical noises—a delicate and gentle whirring.

Downstairs the front door slams shut. The cars and motorcycle parked in front of the house start at nearly the same moment and I hear them pull away, a caravan, down the street, around the corner, and silence. Only, now, the slight and persistent whir from the bookshelf.

I cannot reach that highest bookshelf: there is no way to scale those sheer mahogany steps without the use of one's legs. I cannot open the window without assistance and Wanda closed it tightly when she first turned out my light. My door is blocked by more weight than I could move even when I was whole and fit. At my bedside there is nothing more than pencil and paper and pill bottles.

No. There is one more item, folded neatly and propped up between a bottle and the bedstand lamp: TO UNCLE it reads on the outside. It is a note from Wanda, left here during one of her silent raids on my bedroom. I switch on the lamp and unfold the note.

Dear Uncle,
You fake sleep very badly. I don't know what you did with your dinner tonight but wherever it is please retrieve it and eat the lob-

ster. Do this for me, for my peace of mind. Remember, please, that I only want what is best for you.

Love,
Wanda

The lobster by now is cold, but that works in part to disguise the bitterness of Wanda's clumsy additive.

I empty nine of the pill bottles quickly and already my throat is anesthetized down to my gullet. I am about to open the tenth bottle when a great numbness in my head tells me that is unnecessary. This tenth bottle, cool and milky white, I hold for a moment, gauging its weight in my hand, and then I hurl it directly at the space on the bookshelf now occupied by the whirring shoebox mechanism, to see it shatter on my target into a thousand fragments of glass all woven up with viscous threads of Wanda's special dinner.

In this collision the shoebox is dislodged so that it tumbles forward, off the shelf, the top coming loose in midair and its contents falling free, smashing into the floor, erupting into an intense shining fountain of light and heat and sound that frees me, now numb and frozen in all my limbs, from the confines of my covers and in some freak of detonation propels me upward on an immense blast of boiling air and flame, violently through the thin and aged plaster of my yellow ceiling and past the solid rafters of the attic, and then, in a cloud of cedar shingles and roofing paper and scraps of bed linen, for the space of a heartbeat, I am launched as the brightest of stars in the cloudless night sky.

EATING IT

William Harrison

y first piece was a madeleine, one of those small French pastries and, yes, I ate it at my great-aunt's house. Auntie Drew had come down from Quebec to that sprawling, relic-filled lakeshore house in Wilmette, north of Chicago. It was there I spent all the introspective summers of my youth—until my parents went down in a freak air crash—and then I moved in permanently, occupying the large, glassed-in porch and the east bedroom overlooking Lake Michigan all during the time I attended the university.

Auntie Drew's house had a smart Gallic kitchen: gleaming bronze pans, knives at attention in a walnut rack, some delicious sauce always simmering on a rear burner. On the shelves of the reading room there were Proust's inevitable volumes and those of Balzac, Stendhal, Gide and others, but Auntie Drew's taste for French literature was mostly confined to those plain-wrapper jobs published by the Olympia Press. Pornography was her passion and she admitted it freely and, ah, how she loved those dirty little books with strumpets named Kitty or Daphne going down on gentlemen of the evening named Raoul or roughnecks named Skag, lots of kissing and licking and slurping. Her life was all saucy novels and novel sauces, if you'll excuse that, and she loved to cook for me and read me lurid passages while I sat at my desk working equations.

On a luxurious April afternoon filled with such interruptions (she had already ventured out onto the porch twice to read me succulent parts of her latest acquisition) she brought me that plate of French cookies.

The depth of Auntie Drew's sensualism might easily be miscalculated because, after all, she was a solid seventy years old and scrawny and blue all over: blue veins in her wrists, blue bags under her blue eyes, blue hair, and even a little blue tongue sloshing around in her mouth as she talked or ate with me. But a true sensualist she was—and an evangelist for the various pleasures of the skin. Finding that those tidbits from the Paris press just weren't exciting me, she brought out those cookies with a fierce determination.

By the time I had grabbed up three or four of them, though, she was hissing at me, "See here, Willie, roll the bite around in your mouth before you swallow! Just don't wolf them down like that! *Feel* the individual crumbs! The texture! Try to understand *taste!*"

Of course, I didn't understand. The senses, taste included, were numb—for reasons I will struggle to convey to you later. But there we sat with that magnificent lake breeze filtering through a slightly opened glass panel, the porch all bright and wispy and full of April, the sun warming us, and I felt nothing; adrift in my usual cerebral cloud, I was cold as a machine and a madeleine was simply fuel, something to stoke my motor so that I could go down to the school to work equations for my dullard profs, so that I could polish my meager identity as a minor genius. My genius: ugh! I'll tell you about that later, too, but first a bit more of that afternoon with Auntie Drew.

She became impatient with me.

"Now see here, you don't eat merely for the sake of your belly," she snapped at me. "You eat for the sake of your mouth or sometimes—with certain foods or beverages—for your throat's pleasure, but never, oh, please, Willie, slow down!"

Reaching across me, she turned the pages of my equations face-down. "Take a deep breath," she urged me. "Just relax."

"To tell you the truth, Auntie, you make me a little nervous," I said, but obeyed orders.

"Of course you're slightly nervous, but things will come out all right," she assured me. "You're a perfectly normal boy, remember that. Just relax. Eating is an absolutely natural and relaxing activity, but sometimes one has to *learn* to be natural and relaxed. Just lean back."

Her smile—pale blue tongue and all—reassured me and she carefully guided the madeleine to my mouth, taking my slightly ink-stained fingers in her sweet and scrawny hand and moving it into place. Taking another deep breath, I made a real effort to concentrate on the flavor.

"Much better, Willie. Now you're getting it."

"You really think so?"

"Oh, yes, much better."

"I want it to be all right with you, Auntie."

"It's good for me, Willie, dear. Sure it's good for you?"

"It's very good for me."

In truth, as I munched I was getting slightly aroused to the spirit of it all. Detecting this, Auntie Drew pulled her chair closer to my desk and placed the dish at my elbow. Blue eyes glistened. A pause of our breath. From far off, a boat's horn on the lake.

"Now then," she said, "food isn't my particular way of life, but it might possibly be yours." She offered another madeleine. "Personally, I'm very visually oriented. I love the pictures I get in my mind's eye with all my dear books. And I love the flowers in my garden and the colors of the lake. Now I knew a gentleman in Capri once, Willie, who was very big on aphrodisiacs. Anything even remotely perfumed just scuttled him and let me tell you, Willie, he liked some odd odors! Gunpowder, the sweatbands of hats, that sort of thing. Then there was your Cousin Orlie: you remember her? She was a real toucher, perhaps a touch*ee*, too, always patting and rubbing."

"These are really excellent cookies," I put in.

"Right, I believe you're catching on. Taste is your sensation."

"You notice I've slowed down?"

"Good, Willie, yes. But of course you should have savored your very *first* bite. If you want to experience true taste you can't do it after you're a dozen madeleines to the good."

A pause, please, in this central event of my life, this singular afternoon with Auntie Drew. If you imagine that you detect a murmur of disquiet, a tremor of abnormalcy in these doings, be put straight. I was, I am, I have always been a perfectly normal young man. I have had the juice of a thousand morning headlines in my time, have gone down for a few of the penny-arcade pleasures of lower State Street in this very city, and before my parents made their exit we traveled widely to all the fascinating places in Germany, Egypt, Russia and Harlem. I have done the things, as a child, that all children do: batted balls, run in competitions, dreamed nightmares, attended movies (Westerns and bloody Technicolor epics), raised my voice to be heard, suffered a bully. I have visited Indian burial mounds and circuses, football games and ice hockey. In my teens I had a girl who liked to drive out to the lakeside and talk metaphysics and sociology and another girl who liked to dance at the Fox River Bop Shop and who gave herself readily and often. I achieved musical recognition—don't we all want that?—by mastering the deep, steady rhythms of the portable electric organ (I was a chord man, yes) at that same Fox River establishment. My early grades were happily mediocre.

The truth is that all this somehow didn't move me. Or—just perhaps—moved me too much into numbness. But at any rate

I found myself one day a collegiate cliché: alienated, aloof, silent, aimless, a bit blown out near the emotional fuse box. With deliberation and will I became an abstract intellectual, a mathematician; and the winters stretched out and enfolded me. When my wayfaring parents brushed a palm tree in their little Stinson and tipped over tipsied and laughing into the sheen of the Ionian sea, I shed no tear. Back in a cubicle at the school or out at my desk I simply worked another problem, felt a small satisfaction in its symmetry, and drew my identity around me like a cloak. Auntie Drew seemed a harmless eccentric, all nerve ends and giggles and nostalgia (she still lived in a world of speakeasies, bad gin, and the staggering madness of the Charleston, I imagined), so I ignored her. An illusion, yes, my small algebraic world, but a haven. At times I became mildly proud of my thinly disguised retreat into myself and my invulnerable crust: an assassination, a mugging down the block, the war, Auntie's giggle from a distant room, the polluted haze over the lake, nothing penetrated me.

You know, you do it yourself, this retreating. Done to perfection, we are each rewarded for it. We are called good citizens, sane, even geniuses.

But the days on the porch do arrive.

The madeleines do get eaten.

"Perhaps we should nibble on something else," I suggested to Auntie.

"That's the spirit," she said brightly, getting up. "Just remember, too, Willie, that *everything* is tasty." She said this with an intensity that made it seem profound.

"Everything deserves a bite? Is that the idea?"

"Exactly. That old wicker chair over there. Why don't you give it a chew?"

I got up with a shrug, approached it, and sank my teeth into its back.

"Well?" she asked, expectantly. "How is it?"

"Not too awfully edible," I said.

"Nonsense! Give it another try. And this time try to analyze its flavors! Try!"

"It's terribly tough."

"Just try, please!"

Concentrating, I consented to another bite. The flavors were, roughly, sixty-odd years of finely granulated dust, a slight hint of my deceased uncle's oily palms, a dash of the original green-wood fiber, and, unmistakably, a definite essence of nut bread. I related all this to Auntie Drew.

"You're coming along, Willie!" she said. "That's imaginative, too. Nut bread!"

My body was saying hello to itself and all its lost and for-gotten parts; it was singing, all its juices and vitals in harmo-nious concert, and I followed my aunt into the living room.

Impulse took me and I broke off a piece of her Tiffany lampshade, a pretty green sliver of antique glass, and popped it right into my mouth. I thought she'd faint with happiness. "Oh, Will, oh my goodness," she swooned. Then: "How is it, dear? What's it got?" But before I could answer she smashed the whole lamp—expensive blue and green fragments everywhere—and grabbed up a bite for herself. A flash of her blue tongue.

"Glass is glass, I suppose, Auntie," I allowed. "But this seems like a pretty good piece of glass."

"It's a great piece of glass," she hissed. "Don't hold yourself back! Admit it!"

But the whole house waited to be devoured and I became distracted. The house was suddenly a forbidden fruit and I was inside it like a giddy parasite, eating out its core. Bites, bites, everywhere bites: I tasted the expensive velveteen drapes, the Italian love seat, the Persian rug (Kafir design) and the bro-cade pillows. Those pillows weren't too tasty—slick to the tongue, somewhat dry and stringy—but altogether substantial.

550

"I can't believe this of you, Will," Aunt Drew said with a whistle. "After all these months! This is so sudden!"

I smiled and nibbled a tassel on her French settee.

We reeled through the house now. In the kitchen, rejecting the obvious foodstuff in the refrigerator and cupboards, we chewed on a plastic bread box. "Take us!" cried the fern and ivy perched in the windowsill, so I gobbled them down. Magnificent greenery. After a plastic bread box my taste buds leapt with gratitude. "Suck me!" beckoned a stray French novel idling in the breakfast nook, so I held it under the water tap until it was dripping wet, then gave it a mighty suck. It was pasty, but deserved the gesture. "Nibble here!" cried the silk screen which hung in the sewing room, so I did.

Delirious, we circled back toward the porch, Auntie Drew in my wake, her hands dancing nervously in her blue hair and her laughter a dear and gentle spasm.

"You don't really mind this?" I asked breathlessly as I munched the pencils on my desk.

"A house is made to be eaten!" she hissed, grinning at me. "Never feel guilty for your abandon! Never!"

A line from one of her books, I said to myself, and I poked a nice eraser into my jaw. Yummy rubber.

"Your equations!" she said with inspiration. "Eat those!"

About here my senses began to blur.

Summoning all my willpower and saliva, I laughed and gagged and swallowed my past. The sunlight of the porch anointed us and Auntie—I followed her movements only vaguely—seemed to be devouring the television set off in the corner. A newscaster, full of grim modulations, was cut off in mid-sentence and I heard a crunch of tubes and the high crackle of his last breath. Adream, then, I followed into the yard where Auntie was twice her size, bulging and blue, and eating everything in sight except the trees and grass: the spears of the little iron fence bordering her yard, a mini-car parked at the curb, a telephone pole. Then came a belch, sure as thunder, and Auntie, cracking her fingers to the distant strains of the Charleston, a large hungry flapper loosed on the population, was biting off smokestacks and high-rise apartment buildings and drinking Lake Michigan dry and feeding on the city. Hurriedly, I followed after her and popped the crumbs of her destruction into my mouth. Eat it all, we were saying in harmony, eat everything; choking, gagging, we stuffed it all in, and a happy nausea was overtaking me, a bliss of gluttony, the joy of the gorge.

A SNAG IN THE HARP

Robert Ullian

he creature is a very small, very shaggy, furry white rhinoceros with one yellow horn on its nose. It stands for hours in a swamp behind Leslie's garden, but sometimes, if you take a handful of fur on its neck and tug gently, the rhinoceros will let itself be coaxed through the garden and into the main room of the house, where Paul and Ovie and Giddy feed it lettuce leaves and long stalks of celery. Leslie has decreed that anything the children feed the rhinoceros must be big. Food enters the creature's mouth by force of a vacuum suction system, and the first time Leslie offered a small piece of kohlrabi to him, the creature nearly took Leslie's hand in with it. The creature has white square teeth as flat and perfectly fitted as piano keys. He looks at you with grateful blue eyes as he grinds his lettuce back and forth between his jaws, and tends to follow faithfully the last person who has fed him anything, which means that if you've slipped him a hunk of cabbage leaves, he'll tail you rather aggressively from room to room until someone else steps in with a handout of long-stemmed gladioli or sunflowers. He never takes what isn't offered him. The important thing is not to run or slam a door in his face, because that would be needlessly uncivil, and the creature could probably plow down the wall and knock the wind out of you permanently. Deal skill-

fully with the creature, minimize your grievances, and at worst, you will sacrifice a few bushels of carrots.

"It will be murder to get it out of the house," Leslie said on the Mother's Day morning when he looked up from *The News of the Week in Review* and for the first time saw Paul and Ovie and Giddy lead the creature in through the French doors. At times during the winter, Leslie thought he had noticed a white shaggy thing lurking off in the snowdrifts, or in the fog behind the swamp, but he never believed it to be anything but an overfed goat.

"A rhinoceros!" Ovie told them, prancing alongside it. "A real rhinoceros!"

Leslie, who kept careful count of his children's vocabularies, was immediately pleased. This was a new word for Ovie. Evidently, he had picked it up from the neighborhood gossip. If it had been Paul, who was older than Ovie, or Giddy, who was younger, who had chosen to call the creature a rhinoceros, Leslie would have interrupted them at this point, explained that the rhinoceros has been passé in southern New England since at least the Second Ice Age and recommended further readings in the *Golden Book of Darwin*. But with Ovie, he hesitated. Ovie was a different child, so gentle and so filled with a dogged energy for goodness that Leslie stood in awe of him, and if he had learned anything in the four years he had known Ovie, it was mainly that anything this child did or said was essentially right and that his sense of the world was impeccable.

Leslie's wife, who had been reading through *Arts and Leisure*, turned immediately to *Real Estate*, and began checking off other places they might move to.

"But what guarantee do you have the same thing won't happen wherever we go?" Leslie asked her.

"Small furry white rhinoceri are hardly ubiquitous," she said.

556

Robert Ullian

From that moment, it was totally impossible to keep the miniature shaggy rhinoceros from visiting them on the prowl.

Leslie Isaiah Bristol is free. In the mornings, he likes to arrange his throat across one of his wife's breasts while he watches tiny Syneeba asleep on the floor. Syneeba's diaper has gone drastically awry. Somehow, amid the throes of sleep, fleas, and thumb-sucking, it has come to encompass only one leg and the major portion of the skull. Leslie's wife does not trouble to open her eyes. Syneeba is an eighteen-month-old chimpanzee of the usual virtues. Outstripping any human baby alive, Syneeba can un-peel oranges, shake hands when presented to company, eat Chinese food and reproduce with gargantuan frankness any facial expression, action, or gesture of civilization that motivates his fancy. What motivates Leslie's fancy is harder to say. At twenty-eight, with a broad grin and a loose out-turned footstep picked up on the sidewalks of Brooklyn, he is universally happy; he always has been. He was happy at six, when a siege of polio-myelitis sent him into the contagion ward of the Kings County Hospital for a summer. He was happy at Harvard, where he followed meagerly in the wake of two illustrious older brothers, and, after his parents died when he was twenty-one, as a result of one terrible month which he tried to erase from his memory, he took a wife who played violins, and was happy again, using his portion of the money his parents had saved for old age to fashion a new family for himself, carefully sustaining them and living in a shaky string of apartments which they moved in and out of before they could memorize the colors of the walls. When death came to his grandfather, Leslie once more made the best of it, using this new legacy to settle his family in a sturdy rustic house where he could retire to his children every summer while his wife practiced scales and sonatas through the open windows, and grapes ripened on the trellis and in the trees. The snag in the harp was the plumbing, which was not all it was cracked up to be. To run the hot water even moderately caused an artillery barrage of pipes inside the walls. Open window frames banged shut, their panes shattered, china and papers slid from their cabinets, doors swung on their hinges, the children screamed. True to form, Syneeba soon detected the key to the household's epileptic fits, and his favorite act of human imitation was to enter the second-floor bathroom unobserved, shinny up the sink, pull the hot-water tap full force, and start the walls dancing around his ears. At times like these, Leslie would come upon Syneeba sitting on the edge of the bathtub chuckling and slapping his knees while the faucet spurted bursts of steam and hot water, and it was hard for him to believe that a practical joker of fate was not hidden somewhere, deep inside the baby ape's heart, waiting to pull a more deadly gag when the right moment came. Nonetheless, Leslie would smile, miming an impromptu laugh as he closed the water tap and lifted Syneeba forgivingly into his arms, because Leslie was only too well aware that Syneeba had been a special victim of human torment. Each time he handed Syneeba a peanut butter and marmalade sandwich, or each time Syneeba held his plastic cup out for an extra swig of milk, Leslie would look down into the placid, small face with hopeful eyes and wonder if the little chimp could still remember what had happened. For if the rumors Leslie and his wife had heard were true, and he did not for a moment doubt them, then Syneeba and his mother, like all baby chimpanzees and their mothers, had held onto each other so tightly before Syneeba could be pried loose and sent to an American pet store, that Syneeba's mother had to be clubbed to death. Early in the mornings, when birds were breakfasting all around the house, and new sunlight was just beginning to play into the rooms, Leslie and his wife lay in bed and pondered the story of Syneeba's past.

"Is it really possible?" Leslie's wife wanted to know. Leslie was pretty sure. He knew that no market existed for chimpanzees once they had reached adulthood, when a morose, over-protective quality began to dominate their personalities.

"But clubbing?" Leslie's wife used to say.

It was hard to explain, Leslie thought, but in some ways it might be the most humane method. If you gave the mother a tranquilizer, when she woke up and found her baby gone there was no telling how she might take it. She might fly into a rage and kill lots of small innocent animals who happened to be nearby, or she might become depressed, wandering around the jungles until some pack of hyenas made a meal of her. Shooting was not likely. A gunshot in a place like Tanganyika could set off a stampede. There were the ever-wary game wardens to be considered; then, too, the mother and the baby would be so entwined that the merchandise could easily become damaged. Injecting poison or air bubbles into the bloodstream of the mother required skilled workers and the most favorable conditions if it were not to end up as bloody as clubbings. Besides, it smacked too much of the antiseptic techniques of homicide which the Nazis had perfected. Perhaps there was no alternative.

In the two months they had owned him, Syneeba had come to occupy a much sought-after position in Leslie's household, first tending to sleep on the Sumatran tiger rug which Leslie's oldest brother, an anthropologist in Bali, had mailed to Leslie for safekeeping, and then ingratiatingly dragging the rug into the master bedroom each night at bedtime.

"Absolutely not!" Leslie's wife told him. "We are not going to do it with him over there on the floor."

"But honey, he's only a baby. He doesn't comprehend anything."

"What does he ever comprehend? But does that stop him from mimicking everything he sees? Do you know what he would try to do to me? To Giddy? Oh God, Leslie, do you know what he would do to Giddy?"

At first, Leslie would initiate their lovemaking with sleigh rides for the gleeful Syneeba around and around the bedroom on the Sumatran tiger rug; then, a careless flick of the wrist, Syneeba spinning astonished into the hallway, slamming of the door, a turning of the lock, and they were together, listening to Syneeba pace his thumps and screams of protest to the progress of their embraces. Before long, however, even the best conceived tactics degenerated into a lurid teeth-gnashing tug-of-war, Syneeba's long arms occasionally extending with the inhuman precision of a construction crane to snatch some small unforeseen object and smash it while his face gazed in another direction with peculiar unconcern.

In the end, Leslie was forced to begin his plottings against Syneeba at four o'clock in the afternoon, as soon as he brought the children home from swimming. While standing Paul and Ovie and Giddy in the sun to towel their heads before the evening chill and dress them and repair the ruins of colored designs on their cheeks and their elbows, Leslie took the children into his confidence, and later joined them sitting on the ground to stare reverently at their mother as she swerved into the yard aboard a bicycle, with her head in a shower cap, and milk-of-magnesia-bottle-colored dark glasses protecting her eyes.

So far, so good. The plan had been to entertain Syneeba by feeding bread crumbs to the ants on the kitchen table, a project which would be of educational value to the children as well as Syneeba, and one that any reasonable insurance agent could deftly pro-rate into the low-risk category. When Leslie last looked in on them, one green ant was apparently having a brain hemorrhage, thrashing about with his head glued to the table and his front arms pounding in frustration. Syneeba observed the proceedings carefully, emitting a series of low grunts that is heard when a chimpanzee begins to feed on some desirable food.

In the moonlight, Leslie sat at the edge of the bed and looked into his lap while pieces of his children's voices came up through the kitchen ceiling. His wife undressed. It was time, they had decided for some weeks now, to have another child and, according to a screw-brained theory that had three times proved correct, tonight was the scientifically most perfect evening for producing a girl. Leslie examined a small unfolding piece of paper with charts and instructions not unlike those for developing Polaroid pictures in sixty seconds at varying extremes of climate. His eyes fell on a paragraph heading marked in red: CESSATION OF DOSAGE.

"Do you know what Giddy did this morning?" Leslie said to his wife as she crossed in front of his eyes and sat beside him on the bed. "When Mrs. Baumley asked her how come she was so pretty, Giddy put the hem of her skirt in her mouth and thought about it for a while and said, 'Because my mother put this dress on me today,' and she got on her tricycle and pedaled off like a madcap."

Leslie's arms folded around his wife, but they felt as if they could be reaching for Giddy or Paul or Ovie and he was astonished by the silence and the feel of himself and his wife together. His wife's fingers were very cold. They held each other quietly, and waited, listening for the voices of their children underneath them. Leslie put his wife's hands in his and tried to get them warm. Downstairs, Syneeba could be heard serenading with a series of hoots, his breath drawn in audibly after each one, and finishing with three or four roars. Paul and Ovie and Giddy joined in on the chorus. According to the books, this was the cry of a male chimpanzee as he crossed a ridge. It was believed to announce "Here I come" to any other chimpanzees that might be living in the valley below, but Syneeba was not particularly discriminating in his use of the idiom. At last, grieved by the certainty about the pinpoint in time which Syneeba's antics had assigned to their next child, and shivering, Leslie sank into his wife and waited.

The evening had been customary. As a man of no small fortune, Leslie generally drove his family on special nights to a small Chinese restaurant seven miles down the road, where he and his wife could sit back over river shrimps in hot sauce, or braised Mandarin duckling, while the children gripped spareribs and the tablecloth and passing clientele, and Syneeba picked apart the contents of three or four egg rolls, carefully scrutinizing them for tasty insect morsels which the management obligingly baked into the product. On this evening, Leslie had been ebullient with the knowledge that for the last night ever, half of their next child would be inside him. Chewing on fried noodles, he grinned senselessly at passersby, at Syneeba, at the children. His wife, garbed in a red and pink diagonally striped tent dress, with her long black hair swept tightly up, and then allowed to flow loose into a wildly free mane, reclined, crossed her legs, and filed her nails, like a circus bareback rider between acts. Leslie was satisfied to note that the tent dress covered her crotch. The waiter, demonstrating a most beguiling deadpan, glided in plates of food with all the serenity of a fully programmed Socialist strolling through the people's gardens of Peking, guilty of no opposing philosophy on any subject under the sun. To Leslie's delight, a young couple, probably willing to appreciate his children, entered and were led to a table adjacent to Paul and Syneeba. The boy was six or seven years younger than Leslie, thin and neatly bearded. When he turned around to seat himself, Leslie saw that the hair on the back of his skull had been shaved away, and a healing, crazily stitched lump covered the spot.

"Hey, you," Paul asked him, "What's wrong with your head?"

"I took it to Chicago," the boy answered, imitating a silent laugh the way Leslie himself sometimes did when nothing really was funny.

The remark, however, was too cryptic for Paul. He glowered at the couple and they withdrew their attention to the menus.

"The best thing for you would be your heads all mashed up with duck sauce and your bloody throats. They know how to make it in the kitchen."

The boy smiled again and went on fingering the menu. Syneeba, busy excavating his last egg roll, paid them no mind.

"Where do you live?" the girl asked softly to the three children in general. Leslie knew that Ovie and Giddy would be too shy to answer. He watched the girl's face.

"In heaven, I think," Leslie heard Paul answer. "We have a white rhinoceros there."

Leslie hoped Paul would not go into the white rhinoceros with the young couple, because despite their kindness, he sensed they would fail to be charmed by so wistful a version of zoology.

"We feed him lettuce leaves when he's hungry," Paul continued.

"What's your name?" the girl asked him.

"Lee Harvey Oswald."

This was better, Leslie thought. A good hard-hitting answer from a child of the times, but he felt compelled to open his mouth and explain to the girl, "Paul's at the age now where they're heavily concerned with death." The girl's hair was long and gentle. There were a dozen smooth freckles across her nose, and her eyes were the palest green he had ever known a human being to have. He looked down at her fingers. Amazingly, there was a wedding ring. For an instant, Leslie thought he understood something about the couple, but he could not think it into words. Then his wife began to adjust her lips in the compact, the waiter slipped the bill onto the table, Paul and Giddy and

Ovie asked for more water, and the long process of leaving set in.

Now in the dark with his wife, Leslie pictured the young husband and the wife again. Wherever they had come from, wherever they had gone, Leslie felt they must be doing the same thing at this moment, except that they had never done it to have children, nor would they be doing it for that tonight. He understood now, as if a blurred clandestine instinct deep inside him had suddenly been freed, that this was the secret he had seen in them. He thought of the husband, anxious and tense, and he remembered men from his own childhood, working their way through night school, or hurrying home through the streets of Brooklyn on their furloughs, and he thought of the wife, and remembered his mother's friends, women who came with their hands in their pockets to watch him and his brothers play, while they waited first for the Depression to end, and then for the war to end, and finally for a simple place to live before they permitted themselves the luxury of bringing children into the world. One woman, a perfect stranger who came to the house to talk to his mother, had held him on her lap so tightly that he couldn't breathe, and when he struggled, she pulled his face into her breasts with a death grip he knew his own mother had never used, yet after he finally squirmed free, and looked at the woman and his mother continuing to talk as if nothing murderous had just scarcely been avoided, Leslie had been forced to conclude that it was not just the one woman, but everyone who must be crazy. Now, as his wife pulled closer and closer, his face crushing into her hair, Leslie remembered the scenes he had seen on TV, of people only a few years younger than himself begging for peace, and almost like a cameraman who had moved in too close, he saw a club swinging toward him, and when he jerked his head away, spreading his eyes wide in amazement, he realized that those same times he vaguely remembered were back again. Perhaps they had never gone away.

For a moment, Leslie lapsed into stillness. If it had been any other moment, if it had been any other idea, he could have faked a friendly laugh and kept his mind walking in its own direction. Now there was no place for it to go. In defiance of thinking, almost in panic, Leslie surged ahead, pulling his wife against him. His own parents had been reckless in love, ignoring bank accounts and Hitler to have him and his brothers, and he knew they were right, for their lives would not have been long enough if they had waited. Maybe that would happen to them as well; perhaps the times would leave them alone, perhaps they too were destined for nothing more than a brief unstruggling life together. Reason began to return; the terror in Leslie's head was enticed back into the shadows. Leslie smiled at his wife, closed his eyes, and then, to keep the thing going a little longer, to give them a few seconds more time together before the dice finally spilled, and the voice, the sex, the eyes, the laughter, and the talents of the next child who grew between them would be settled forever, Leslie thought of the girl in the restaurant, her wedding ring, the tattoo of worry on her thin, empty hands.

Meanwhile, downstairs, on the kitchen table, the ante was steadily being raised. Syneeba took an ant and crushed it between his fingernails. Ovie matched him. Syneeba held a large ant on his lower incisor and bit it in two. Paul and Giddy did the same. Ovie stuck out his tongue, placed a carpenter ant at its tip and let it crawl down his larynx. Syneeba motioned for a recount. Staring perplexed into Ovie's open mouth, Syneeba proceeded to shove his fingers down Ovie's throat. As Ovie struggled, and Paul and Giddy began to tug, Syneeba coined a new, savagely predatory screech that rose through the kitchen ceiling and flayed the nerves of Leslie's spine like a bloodthirsty leopard, sending him out of his wife, spraying the contents of next summer's baby across the bed sheets, vaulting him down the stairs four at a time, completely naked, to lay hands on Syneeba's skull and wrist, his arms scalding to rip Syneeba in two and grind him into the heap of ill-journeyed ants, while in a spot on his forehead, between his eyes, the thought appeared and nourished itself in a second's glance at the blank faces of Paul and Giddy: that if he killed Syneeba on the spot, the creature's death grip could rip out whatever might be left of Ovie's voice, and for Ovie's sake, for his second son, who he knew was his favorite, who meant life itself to him, Leslie held back all his strength and forced himself away as his wife appeared in the kitchen doorway with a robe held tightly around her body. Devoid of hope, he looked at her as she suavely commandeered the situation. Deftly tripping open the refrigerator door with her foot, she drew out a blue bowl of yesterday's soggy egg rolls and wafted them under Syneeba's nose. Leslie did not breathe. Slowly, Syneeba began to respond with a series of feasting grunts, and when his hand cautiously removed itself from Ovie's mouth, Leslie felt words breaking apart inside of him. Sweeping Ovie into his arms, he scrambled up the stairs, and with Ovie hanging weightless around his neck, he donned a bathing suit, grappled with a sweater, and galloped down the stairs again, and out the door to the car which his wife was warming up for the motorcade down the road to the doctor. That night, with Ovie asleep between them, and Syneeba lying restless on the floor, Leslie and his wife made plans to let the animal out for adoption.

At dawn, two days later, Leslie, his wife, Syneeba and the children reached the big city. They double-parked the car on a side street, and Leslie's wife went alone into an apartment building on Central Park West, where she entered the elevator, planning to break the news that they were back in town to her parents, while Leslie herded Syneeba and the children over to the Central Park Children's Zoo, where Syneeba and sixteen packages of frozen Chinese egg rolls were to be disposed of.

The children were amenable to this decision. They had always been told that Syneeba could not stay with them permanently, that it was in the character of chimpanzees to become morose and overprotective in old age, and now, evidently, Syneeba had entered old age sooner than anyone had anticipated. The side effects of this stream of logic, however, included the notion that old age could creep up on you suddenly, and lurking behind it, death, Paul's favorite fixation. Unwilling to allow the children to attribute Syneeba's behavior to darker, more bestial motives, Leslie maintained his position that old age was Syneeba's only difficulty, and had fought tooth and nail all the way into New York City, explaining that Syneeba's case was an aberration, that they had long happy lives in front of them, that death was not around the corner. Now, however, as Leslie walked the children through the green lawns of Central Park, with the brown fog of the city dawn giving way all about them, death dangled from the sturdy limb of a chestnut tree in the corpse of a young man who must have stood on an orange crate and looped the rope around his neck in the deepest hours of the night, when no one but police and muggers were supposed to be about in the park. Leslie stopped in his tracks when he saw the victim, about a hundred yards from the footpath, and then forced himself to keep going in the hope that the children would not notice anything amiss. The grounds were morbidly still. As luck would have it, Paul, heavily concerned with dying, saw it, like an evangelical wonder shouted, "Glory be to God!", and the stampede was on, Paul, Ovie and Giddy running as fast as their legs would carry them to the spot over which Marcus Beasley, as Leslie later learned, swung. For an instant, Leslie stood helpless, with Syneeba's hand clasped firmly in his, and then, thrusting aside the unperturbed chimpanzee's grasp, he charged the thirty yards after his children, grabbing Giddy and Ovie up as he overtook them, and tackling Paul not five feet from the finish line, the three children crashing together in his arms, and coming up from the ground bruised and in tears.

"No, Ovie, no, you mustn't cry. The doctor said it's no good for your throat." Leslie wiped the tears from Giddy's face with his own cheek and held Paul tightly by the wrist. "Leave this person alone. He wanted to be alone." For a moment, Leslie held his brood together on the ground and allowed them to feast their eyes. He had done his best to protect them. If this thing had to be, let it happen and be done with. Then, as he pulled the children to their feet in hopes of hustling them away to a more comforting spectacle (such as the doorway of Temple Emanu-El or the window of F.A.O. Schwarz), the image of Syneeba methodically gamboling the lawn slid across Leslie's eyes, and when he turned about, Syneeba had already latched onto the sneakers of Marcus Beasley's feet, and the two of them, Marcus and the chimpanzee, had begun to spin slowly in the sunlight. Leslie looked toward the windows of Central Park West and wondered if his wife might be taking everything in from her parents' living room. Syneeba, tossing his body back and forth, endeavored to turn the corpse into a low-swinging trapeze.

"Syneeba, get down from there right now!" Leslie demanded, but this tone of voice had never worked before, and now it only sent Syneeba scuttling up a trouser leg. Leslie shut his eyes. When he opened them, Syneeba was cooing gently, and hugging onto the stomach of Marcus Beasley, as if it were his own dead mother.

"The zoo keeper," Leslie muttered. "We've got to get the zoo keeper," but he merely stood fixed to the spot with his hands feeling for the arms of his children, while behind them, on the Sheep Meadow, nine very small, very shaggy, furry white rhinoceri gathered, assembling for the kill.

WHAT IS IT?

Raymond Carver

act is the car needs to be sold in a hurry, and Leo sends Toni out to do it. Toni is smart and has personality. She used to sell children's encyclopedias door-to-door. She signed him up, even though he didn't have kids. Afterward, Leo asked her for a date, and the date led to this. This deal has to be cash, and it has to be done tonight. Tomorrow somebody they owe might slap a lien on the car. Monday they'll be in court, home free—but word on them went out yesterday, when their lawyer mailed the letters of intention. The hearing on Monday is nothing to worry over, the lawyer has said. They'll be asked some questions, and they'll sign some papers, and that's it. But sell the convertible, he said, today, tonight in fact. They can hold onto the little car, Leo's car, no problem. But they go into court with that big convertible, the court will take it, and no argument.

Toni dresses up. It's four o'clock in the afternoon. Leo worries the lots will close. But Toni takes her time dressing. She puts on a new white blouse, wide lacy cuffs, the new two-piece suit, new heels. She transfers the stuff from her straw purse into the new patent-leather handbag. She studies the lizard makeup pouch and puts that in too. Toni has been two hours on her hair and face. Leo stands in the bedroom doorway and taps his lips with his knuckles, watching.

"You're making me nervous," she says. "I wish you wouldn't just stand," she says. "So tell me how I look."

"You look fine," he says. "You look great. I'd buy a car from you anytime."

"But you don't have money," she says, peering into the mirror. She pats her hair, frowns. "And your credit's lousy. You're nothing," she says. "Teasing," she says, and looks at him in the mirror. "Don't be serious," she says. "It has to be done, so I'll do it. You take it out, you'd be lucky to get three, four hundred, and we both know it. Honey, you'd be lucky you didn't have to pay *them.*" She gives her hair a final pat, gums her lips, blots the lipstick with a tissue. She turns away from the mirror and picks up her purse. "I'll have to have dinner or something, I told you that already, that's the way they work, I know them. But don't worry, I'll get out of it," she says. "I can handle it."

"Jesus," Leo says, "did you have to say that?"

She looks at him steadily. "Wish me luck," she says.

"Luck," he says. "You have the pink slip?" he says.

She nods. He follows her through the house, a tall woman with a small, high bust, broad hips and thighs. He scratches a pimple on his neck. "You're sure?" he says. "Make sure. You have to have the pink slip."

"I have the pink slip," she says.

"Make sure."

She starts to say something, instead looks at herself in the front window. She studies their reflection in the window, and then shakes her head.

"At least call," he says. "Let me know what's going on."

"I'll call," she says. "Kiss, kiss. Here," she says, and points to the corner of her mouth. "Careful," she says.

He holds the door for her. "Where are you going to try first?" he says. She moves past him and onto the porch.

Ernest Williams looks from across the street. In his Bermuda shorts, stomach hanging, he looks at Leo and Toni as he directs a spray onto his begonias. Once, last winter, during the holidays, when Toni and the kids were visiting his mother's, Leo brought a woman home. Nine o'clock the next morning, a cold foggy Saturday, Leo walked the woman to the car, surprised Ernest Williams on the sidewalk with a newspaper in his hand. Fog drifted, Ernest Williams stared, then slapped the paper against his leg, hard.

Leo recalls that slap, hunches his shoulders, says, "You have someplace in mind first?"

"I'll just go down the line," she says. "The first lot, then I'll just go down the line."

"Start at nine hundred," he says. "Then come down. Nine hundred is low bluebook, even on a cash deal."

"I know where to start," she says.

Ernest Williams turns the hose in their direction. He stares at them through the spray of water. Leo has an urge to cry out a confession.

"Just making sure," he says.

"Okay, okay," she says. "I'm off."

It's her car, they call it her car, and that makes it all the worse. They bought it new that summer three years ago. She wanted something to do after the kids started school, so she went back selling. He was working six days a week in the fiber-glass plant. For a while they didn't know what to do with the money. Then they put a thousand on the convertible, and doubled and tripled the payments until in a year they had it paid. Earlier, while she was dressing, he took the jack and spare from the trunk and emptied the glove compartment of pencils, matchbooks, Blue Chip stamps. Then he washed it and vacuumed inside. The red hood and fenders shine.

"Good luck," he says, and touches her elbow.

She nods. He sees she is already gone, already negotiating.

"Things are going to be different," he calls to her as she reaches the drive. "We start over Monday. I mean it." Ernest

Williams looks at them and turns his head and spits. She gets into the car and lights a cigarette. "This time next week," he calls again. "Ancient history." He waves as she backs into the street. She changes gear and starts ahead. She accelerates and the tires give a little scream.

In the kitchen Leo pours Scotch and carries the drink to the backyard. The kids are at his mother's. There was a letter three days ago, his name penciled on the outside of the dirty envelope, the only letter all summer not demanding payment in full. We are having fun, the letter said. We like Grandma. We have a new dog called Mr. Six. He is nice. We love him. Good-bye.

He goes for another drink. He adds ice and sees that his hand trembles. He holds the hand over the sink. He looks at the hand for a while, sets down the glass and holds out the other hand. Then he picks up the glass and goes back outside to sit on the steps. He recalls when he was a kid his dad pointing at a fine house high on the hill above the road, a tall white house surrounded by apple trees and a high, white rail fence. "That's Finch," his dad says admiringly. "He's been in bankruptcy at least twice. Look at that house." But bankruptcy is a company collapsing utterly, executives cutting their wrists and throwing themselves from windows, thousands of men on the street. They still had furniture. They had furniture and Toni and the kids had clothes. Those things were exempt. What else? Bicycles for the kids, but these he sent to his mother's for safekeeping. The portable air-conditioner and the appliances, new washer and dryer, trucks came for those things weeks ago. What else did they have? This and that, nothing mainly, stuff that wore out or fell to pieces long ago. But there were some big parties back there, some fine travel. To Reno and Tahoe, at eighty with the top down and the radio playing. Food, that was one of the big items. They gorged on food. He figures thousands on luxury items alone. Toni would go to the grocery and put in everything she saw. "I had to do without when I was a kid," she says. "These kids are not going to do without," as if he'd been insisting they should. She joins all the book clubs. "We never had books around when I was a kid," she says as she tears open the heavy packages. They enroll in the record clubs for something to play on the new stereo. They sign up for it all. Even a pedigreed terrier named Ginger. He paid two hundred and found her run over in the street a week later. They buy what they want. If they can't pay, they charge. They sign up.

His undershirt is wet, he can feel the sweat rolling from his underarms. He sits on the step with the empty glass in his hand and watches the shadows fill in the yard. He stretches, wipes his face. He listens to the traffic on the highway and considers whether he should go to the basement, stand on the utility sink, and hang himself with his belt. He understands he is willing to be dead.

Inside he makes a large drink and he turns the TV on and he fixes something to eat. He sits at the table with chili and crackers and watches something about a blind detective. He clears the table. He washes the pan and the bowl, dries these things and puts them away, then allows himself a look at the clock.

It's after nine. She's been gone nearly five hours.

He pours Scotch, adds water, carries the drink to the living room. He sits on the couch but finds his shoulders so stiff they won't let him lean back. He stares at the screen and sips, and soon he goes for another drink. He sits again. A news program begins, it's ten o'clock, and he says, "God, what in God's name has gone wrong?" and goes to the kitchen to return with more Scotch. He sits, he closes his eyes, and opens them when he hears the telephone ringing.

"I wanted to call," she says.

"Where are you?" he says. He hears piano music, and his heart turns.

"I don't know," she says. "Someplace. We're having a drink,

575

then we're going someplace else for dinner. I'm with the sales manager. He's crude, but he's all right. He bought the car. I have to go now. I was on my way to the ladies and saw the phone."

"Did somebody buy the car?" he says. He looks out the kitchen window to the place in the drive where she usually parks.

"I told you," she says. "I have to go now, Leo."

"Wait, wait a minute, for Christ's sake," he says. "Did somebody buy the car or not?"

"He had his checkbook out when I left," she says. "I have to go now. I have to go to the bathroom."

"Wait," he yells. The line goes dead. He listens to the dial tone. "Jesus Christ," he says as he stands with the receiver in his hand.

He circles the kitchen and goes back to the living room. He sits. He gets up. In the bathroom he brushes his teeth very carefully. Then he uses dental floss. He washes his face and goes back to the kitchen. He looks at the clock and takes a clean glass from a set that has hands of playing cards painted on each glass. He fills the glass with ice. He stares for a while at the glass he left in the sink.

He sits against one end of the couch and puts his legs up at the other end. He looks at the screen, realizes he can't make out what the people are saying. He turns the empty glass in his hand, and considers biting off the rim. He shivers for a time and thinks of going to bed, though he knows he will dream of a large woman with grey hair. In the dream he is always leaning over tying his shoelaces. When he straightens up, she looks at him, and he bends to tie again. He looks at his hand. It makes a fist as he watches. The telephone is ringing.

"Where are you, honey?" he says slowly, gently. He can hear music again.

"We're at this restaurant," she says, her voice strong, bright. "We're having dinner."

"Honey, which restaurant?" he says. He puts the heel of his hand against his eye and pushes.

"Downtown someplace," she says. "It's nice. I think it's New Jimmy's. Excuse me," she says to someone off the line, "is this place New Jimmy's? This is New Jimmy's, Leo," she says to him. "Everything is all right, we're almost finished, then he's going to bring me home."

"Honey?" he says. He holds the receiver against his ear and rocks back and forth, eyes closed. "Honey?"

"I have to go," she says. "I wanted to call. Anyway, guess how much?"

"Honey," he says.

"Six and a quarter," she says. "I have it in my purse. He said there's no market for convertibles. I guess we're born lucky," she says and laughs. "I told him everything. I think I had to."

"Honey," Leo said.

"What?" she says.

"Please, honey," Leo says.

"He said he sympathized," she says. "But he would have said anything." She laughs again. "He said personally he'd rather be classified a robber or a rapist than a bankrupt. He's nice enough, though," she says.

"Come home," he says. "Take a cab and come home."

"I can't," she says. "I told you, we're halfway through dinner."

"I'll come for you," he says.

"No," she says. "I said we're just finishing. I told you, it's part of the deal. They're out for all they can get. But don't worry, we're about to leave. I'll be home in a little while." She hangs up.

In a few minutes he calls New Jimmy's. A man answers. "New Jimmy's has closed for the evening."

"I'd like to talk to my wife," Leo says.

577

"Does she work here?" the man asks. "Who is she?"

"She's a customer," Leo says. "She's with someone. A business person."

"Would I know her?" the man says. "What is her name?"

"I don't think you know her," Leo says.

"May I ask who is calling?" the man says.

"That's all right," Leo says. "That's all right. I see her now."

"Thank you for calling New Jimmy's," the man says.

Leo hurries to the window. A car he doesn't recognize slows in front of the house, then picks up speed. He waits. Two, three hours later, the telephone rings again. There is no one at the other end when he picks up the receiver. There is only a dial tone.

"I'm right here," Leo screams into the receiver.

Near dawn he hears footsteps on the porch. He gets up from the couch. The set hums, the screen glows. He opens the door. She bumps the wall coming in. She grins. Her face is puffy, as if she's been sleeping under sedation. She works her lips, ducks heavily and sways as he cocks his fist.

"Go ahead," she says thickly. She stands there swaying. Then she makes a noise and lunges, catches his shirt, tears it down the front. "Bankrupt," she screams. She twists loose, grabs and tears his undershirt at the neck. "You son of a bitch," she says, clawing.

He squeezes her wrists, then lets go, steps back, looking for something heavy. She stumbles as she heads for the bedroom. "Bankrupt," she mutters. He hears her fall on the bed and groan.

He waits a while, then splashes water on his face and goes to the bedroom. He turns the light on, looks at her, and begins to take her clothes off. He pulls her from side to side undressing her. She says something in her sleep and moves her hand. He takes off her underpants, looks at them closely under the light, and throws them in a corner. He turns back the covers and rolls her in, naked. Then he opens her purse. He is reading the check when he hears the car come into the drive.

He looks through the front curtain and sees the convertible in the drive, its motor running smoothly, the head lamps burning, and he closes and opens his eyes. He sees a tall man come around in front of the car and up to the front porch. The man lays something on the porch and starts back to the car. He wears a white linen suit.

Leo turns on the porch light and opens the door cautiously. Her makeup pouch lies on the top step. The man looks at Leo across the front of the car, and then gets back inside and releases the hand brake.

"Wait," Leo calls and starts down the steps. The man brakes the car as Leo walks in front of the lights. The car creaks and groans against the brake. Leo tries to pull the two pieces of his shirt together, tries to bunch it into his pants.

"What is it you want?" the man says. "Look," the man says, "I have to go. No offense. I buy and sell cars, right? The lady left her makeup. She's a fine lady, very refined. What is it?"

Leo leans against the door and looks at the man. The man takes his hands off the wheel and puts them back. He drops the gear into reverse and the car moves backward a little.

"I want to tell you," Leo says, and wets his lips.

The light in Ernest Williams' bedroom goes on. The shade rolls up.

Leo shakes his head, tucks his shirt again. He steps back from the car. "Monday," he says.

"Monday," the man says, and watches for sudden movement.

Leo nods slowly.

"Well, good-night," the man says, and coughs. "Take it easy, hear? Monday, that's right. Okay, then." He takes his foot off the brake, puts it on again after he has rolled back two or three feet. "Hey, one question. Between friends, are these actual miles?"

The man waits, then clears his throat. "Okay, look, it doesn't matter either way," the man says. "I have to go. Take it easy." He backs into the street, pulls away quickly, and turns the corner without stopping.

Leo tucks at his shirt and goes back in the house. He locks the front door, and checks it. Then he goes to the bedroom and locks that door and turns back the covers. He looks at her before he flicks the light. He takes off his clothes, folds them carefully on the floor, and gets in beside her. He lies on his back for a time and pulls the hair on his stomach, considering. He looks at the bedroom door, outlined now in the faint outside light. Presently he reaches out his hand and touches her hip. She does not move. He turns on his side and puts his hand on her hip. He runs his fingers over her hip and feels the stretch marks there. They are like roads, and he traces them in her flesh. He runs his fingers back and forth, first one, then another. They run everywhere in her flesh, dozens, perhaps hundreds of them. He remembers waking up the morning after they bought the car, seeing it, there in the drive, in the sun, gleaming.

ALMOST IN IOWA

John Irving

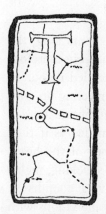he driver relied on travel as a form of reflection, but the Volvo had never been out of Vermont. The driver was an officious traveler; he kept his oil up and his windshield clean and he carried his own tire gauge in his left breast pocket next to a ball-point pen. The pen was for making entries in the Grand Trip List, such things as gas mileage, toll fees and riding time.

The Volvo appreciated this carefulness of the driver; Route 9 across Vermont, Brattleboro to Bennington, was a trip without fear. When the first signs for the New York State line appeared, the driver said, "It's all right." The Volvo believed him.

It was a dusty tomato-red two-door sedan, 1969, with all-black Semperit radial tires, standard four-speed transmission, four cylinders, two carburetors and 45,238 miles of experience without a radio. It was the driver's feeling that a radio would be distracting to them both.

They had started out at midnight from Vermont. "Dawn in Pennsylvania!" the driver told the worried Volvo.

In Troy, New York, the driver used steady down-shifting and a caressing voice to reassure the Volvo that all this would soon pass. Not much more of this," he said. The Volvo took him at his word. Sometimes it is necessary to indulge illusions.

At the nearly-abandoned entrance to the New York State Thruway, West, an innocent Volkswagen exhibited indecision concerning which lane to use. The driver eased up close behind the Volkswagen and allowed the Volvo's horn to blare; the Volkswagen, near panic, swerved right; the Volvo opened up on the left, passed, cut in with aggression, flashed taillights.

The Volvo felt better.

The New York State Thruway is hours and hours long; the driver knew that monotony is a dangerous thing. He therefore left the Thruway at Syracuse and made an extended detour to Ithaca, driving a loop around Lake Cayuga and meeting up with the Thruway again near Rochester. The countryside bore a comforting resemblance to Vermont. Apples smelled as if they were growing; maple leaves were falling in front of the head-lights. Only once was there an encounter with a shocking, night-lit sign which seemed to undermine the Volvo's confidence. LIVE BAIT! the sign said. The driver had troublesome visions with that one himself, but he knew it could be infectious to express his imagination too vividly. "Just little worms and things," he said to the Volvo, who purred along. But there lurked in the driver's mind the possibility of *other* kinds of "live bait"—a kind of reverse-working bait, which rather than luring the fish to nibble would scare them out of the water. Throw in some of this special bait and retrieve the terrified, gasping fish from where they'd land on shore. Or perhaps LIVE BAIT! was a night-club.

It was actually with relief that the driver returned to the Thruway. Not every excursion from the main road leads one back. But the driver just patted the dashboard and said, "Pretty soon we'll be in Buffalo."

A kind of light was in the sky—a phase seen only by duck hunters and marathon lovers. The driver had seen little of that light.

Lake Erie lay as still and grey as a dead ocean; the cars on the Pennsylvania Interstate were just those few early risers who commute to Ohio. "Don't let Cleveland get you down," the driver warned.

The Volvo looked superbly fit—tires cool, gas mileage at 22.3 per gallon, oil full-up, battery water ample and undisturbed. The only indication that the whole fearsome night had been journeyed was the weird wing-mash and blur of bug-stains which blotched the windshield and webbed the grill.

The gas-station attendant had to work his squeegee very hard. "Going a long way?" he asked the driver, but the driver just shrugged. I'm going *all* the way! he longed to shout, but the Volvo was right there.

You have to watch who you hurt with what you say. For example, the driver hadn't told anyone he was leaving.

They skirted the truck traffic around Cleveland before Cleveland could get them in its foul grasp; they left behind them the feeling that the morning rush hour was angry it just missed them. COLUMBUS, SOUTH, said a sign, but the driver snorted with scorn and sailed up the West ramp of the Ohio Turnpike.

"Crabs in ice water to you, Columbus," he said.

When you've come through a night of well-controlled tension and you're underway in the morning with that feeling of a headstart-advantage on the rest of the world, even Ohio seems possible—even Toledo appears to be just a short sprint away.

"Lunch in Toledo!" the driver announced, with daring. The Volvo gave a slight shudder at seventy-five, skipped to eighty and found that fabled "second wind"; the sun was behind them, and they both relished the Volvo's squat shadow fleeing in front of them. They felt they could follow that vision to Indiana.

Early morning goals are among the illusions we must indulge if we're going to get anywhere at all.

There is more to Ohio than you think; there are more exits to Sandusky than seem reasonable. At one of the many and anonymous rest pavilions off the turnpike, the Volvo had a severe fit of pre-ignition and the driver had to choke off the car's lunging coughs by executing a sharp stall-out with the clutch. This irritated them both. And when he made the mileage calculations on the new full tank, the driver was hasty and thoughtless enough to blurt out the disappointing performance. "Fourteen and six-tenths miles a gallon!" Then he quickly tried to make the Volvo know that this wasn't offered as criticism. "It was that last gas," he said. "They gave you some bad gas."

But the Volvo was slow and wheezing to start; it idled low and stalled pulling away from the pumps, and the driver thought it was best to say, "Oil's full-up, not burning a drop." This was a lie; the Volvo was down half a quart—not enough to add, but below the mark. For a sickening moment, past one more countless exit for Sandusky, the driver wondered if the Volvo *knew*. For distance, trust is essential. Can a car feel its oil level falling?

"Lunch in Toledo" hulked in the driver's mind like a taunt; lapsed hunger informed him that lunchtime could have been dawdled away at any of fourteen exits which pretended to lead to Sandusky. God, what *was* Sandusky?

The Volvo, though quenched and wiped, had gone without a proper rest since breakfast in Buffalo. The driver decided to let his own lunch pass. "I'm not hungry," he said cheerfully, but he felt the weight of his second lie. The driver knew that some sacrifices are tokens. If you're in a thing together, a fair share of the suffering must be a top priority. The area referred to as "Toledo" was silently passed in the afternoon like an unmentionable anti-climax. And as for the matter of a falling oil level, the driver knew he was down half a quart of his own. Oh, Ohio.

Fort Wayne, Elkhart, Muncie, Gary, Terre Haute and Michigan City—*ah, Indiana!* A different state, not planted with cement. "Green as Vermont," the driver whispered. *Vermont!* A magic word. "Of course, flatter," he added then feared he might have said too much.

A drenching, cleansing thunderstorm broke over the Volvo in Lagrange; gas mileage at Goshen read 20.2, a figure the driver chanted to the Volvo like a litany—past Nigonier, past Nappanee. Boring their way into the heartland, the driver sensed the coming of an unprecedented "third wind."

Cows appeared to like Indiana. But what was a "Hoosier?"

Shall we have supper in South Bend? A punt's distance from Notre Dame. Nonsense! Gas mileage 23.5! Push on!

Even the motels were appealing; swimming pools winked alongside them. Have a good night's sleep! Indiana seemed to sing.

"Not yet," the driver said. He had seen the signs for Chicago. To wake up in the morning with Chicago already passed by, successfully avoided, out-maneuvered—what a headstart *that* would be!

At the Illinois line, he figured the time, the distance to Chicago, the coincidence of his arrival and the rush hour, etc. The Volvo's case of pre-ignition was gone; it shut off calmly; it appeared to have mastered the famous "kiss start." After the uplift of Indiana, how bad could Illinois be?

"We will be by-passing Chicago at 6:30 P.M.," the driver said. "The worst of the rush hour will be over. We'll drive an hour away from Chicago, downstate Illinois—just to get out in the country again—and we'll definitely stop by eight. A wash for you, a swim for me! Mississippi catfish poached in white wine, an Illinois banana boat, a pint of STP, a cognac in the Red Satin

Bar, let some air escape from your tires, in bed by ten, cross the Mississippi at first light, breakfast in Iowa, sausage from home-grown hogs, Nebraska by noon, corn fritters for lunch . . ."

He talked the Volvo into it. They drove into what the license plates call "the land of Lincoln."

"Goodbye, Indiana! Thank you, Indiana!" the driver sang from the old tune: *I Wish I Was a Hoosier*, by M. Lampert. We will do anything to pretend that nothing is on our minds.

Smog bleared the sky ahead, the sun was not down but it was screened. The highway changed from clear tar to cement slabs with little cracks every second saying, "*Thunk ker-thunk, thunk ker-thunk* . . ." Awful, endless, identical suburbs of outdoor barbecue pits were smouldering.

Nearing the first Chicago interchange, the driver stopped for fresh gas, a look at that falling oil, a pressure check on the tires —just to be sure. The traffic was getting thicker. A transistor radio hung around the gas-station attendant's neck announced that the water temperature in Lake Michigan was seventy-two degrees.

"*Ick!*" the driver said. Then he saw that the clock on the gas pump did not agree with his watch. He had crossed a time-zone, somewhere—maybe in that fantasy called Indiana. He was coming into Chicago an hour earlier than he thought: dead-center, rush-hour traffic hurtled past him. Around him now were the kind of motels where the swimming pools were filled with soot. He imagined the cows who would have woken him with their gentle bells, back in good old Indiana. He had been driving from Vermont since midnight, eighteen and a half hours on the road —with only a breakfast in Buffalo to remember.

"One bad mistake every eighteen and a half hours isn't so bad," he told the Volvo. For optimists, a necessary comeback. And a remarkable bit of repression to think of this mistake as the first.

"Hello, Illinois. Hello to you, half of Chicago."

The Volvo drank a quart of oil like that first tall Indiana cocktail the driver was dreaming of.

If the driver thought Sandusky was guilty of gross excess, it would be gross excess itself to represent the range of his feelings for Joliet.

Two hours of lane-changing inched him less than thirty miles southwest of Chicago and placed him at the crossroads for the travelers heading West—even to Omaha—and South to St. Louis, Memphis and New Orleans. Not to mention errant fools laboring North to Chicago, Milwaukee and Green Bay—and rarer travelers still, seeking Sandusky and the shimmering East.

Joliet, Illinois, was where Chicago parked its trucks at night. Joliet was where people who mistook the Wisconsin interchange for the Missouri interchange discovered their mistake and gave up.

The four four-lane highways that converged on Joliet like mating spiders had spawned two Howard Johnson Motor Lodges, three Holiday Inns and two Great Western Motels. All had indoor swimming pools, air-conditioning and color TV. The color TV was an absurd attempt at idealism: to bring *color* to Joliet, Illinois, an area which was predominantly black and white.

At 8:30 P.M. the driver resigned from the open road.

"I'm sorry," he said to the Volvo. There was no car wash at the Holiday Inn. What would have been the point? And it's doubtful that the Volvo heard him, or could have been consoled; the Volvo was suffering from a bout of pre-ignition that lurched and shook the madly clutching driver so badly that he lost all patience.

"Damn car," he muttered, at an awkward silence—a reprieve in the Volvo's fit. Well, the damage was done. The Volvo just sat there, *pinging* with heat, tires hot and hard, carburetors in hopeless disagreement, plugs caked with carbon, oil filter no doubt choked as tightly closed as a sphincter muscle, etc.

"I'm sorry," the driver said. "I didn't mean it. We'll get off to a fresh start in the morning."

In the ghastly green-lit lobby, arranged with turtle aquariums and potted palms, the driver encountered about 1100 registering travelers, all in a shell-shocked state resembling his own, all telling their children and wives and cars: "I'm sorry, we'll get off to a fresh start in the morning . . ."

But disbelief was everywhere. When good faith has been violated, we have our work cut for us.

The driver knew when good faith had been violated. He sat on the industrial double bed in Holiday Inn Rm. 879 and placed a collect phone call to his wife in Vermont.

"Hello, it's me," he said.

"Where have you *been?*" she cried. "God, everyone's been looking."

"I'm sorry," he told her.

"I looked all around that awful party for you," she said. "I was sure you had gone off somewhere with that Helen Cranitz."

"Oh no."

"Well, I finally *humiliated* myself by actually finding her . . . she was with Ed Poines."

"Oh no."

"And when I saw you'd taken the car I got so worried about what you'd been drinking . . ."

"I was sober."

"Well, Derek Marshall had to drive me home and he *wasn't.*"

"I'm sorry."

"Well, nothing *happened!*"

"I'm sorry . . ."

"*Sorry!*" she screamed. "Where *are* you? I needed the car to take Carey to the dentist. I called the police."

590

"Oh no."

"Well, I thought you might be in a ditch somewhere off the road."

"The car's fine."

"The *car!*" she wailed. "Where *are* you? For God's sake . . ."

"I'm in Joliet, Illinois."

"I've had more than enough of your terrible humor . . ."

"We screwed up at Chicago or I'd be in Iowa."

"Who's *we?*"

"Just me."

"You said *we.*"

"I'm sorry . . ."

"I just want to know if you're coming home tonight."

"It's unlikely I could get there," the driver said.

"Well, I've got Derek Marshall on my hands again, you can thank yourself for that. He took Carey to the dentist for me."

"Oh no."

"He's been a perfect gentleman, of course, but I really had to ask him by. He's worried about you, too, you know."

"Like hell . . ."

"You're in no position to talk like that to me. When *are* you coming back?"

The thought of "coming back" had not occurred to the driver and he was slow to respond.

"I want to know where you are, *really,*" his wife said.

"Joliet, Illinois."

She hung up.

The longer distances take teamwork. The driver had his work cut out for him, for sure.

Bobbing in the indoor pool, the driver was struck with a certain bilious sensation and the resemblance the pool bore to the turtle aquariums in the Holiday Inn lobby. I don't want to be here, he thought.

In the Grape Arbor Restaurant the driver pondered the dizzying menu, then ordered the chef's crab salad. It came. Lake Michigan should be suspected as a possible, ominous source.

In the Tahiti Bar he was served a cognac.

The local Joliet TV station reported the highway fatalities of the day: a grim bodycount—the vision of the carbon-covered carnage sending travelers away from the bar and to bed early, for a night of troubled sleep. Perhaps this was the purpose of the program.

Before he went to bed himself, the driver said good-night to his Volvo. He felt its tires, he felt the black grit in the oil, he sought the degree of damage in a pockmark on the windshield.

"That one must have stung."

Derek Marshall! That one stung, too.

The driver remembered what has been referred to as "that awful party." He told his wife he was going to the bathroom; cars were parked all over the lawn and he went to the bathroom there. Little Carey was staying at a friend's house; there was no babysitter to see the driver slip home for his toothbrush.

A dress of his wife's, a favorite one of his, hung on the back of the bathroom door. He nuzzled it; he grew faint-hearted at its silky feel; his tire gauge snagged on the zipper as he tried to pull away from it. "Goodbye," he told the dress, firmly.

For a rash moment he considered taking *all* her clothes with him! But it was midnight—time for turning to pumpkin—and he sought the Volvo.

His wife was a dusty tomato-red . . . no. She was blond, seven years married with one child and without a radio. A radio was distracting to them both. No. His wife took a size 10 dress, wore out three pairs of size 7 sandals between spring and fall, used a 36B bra and averaged 23.4 miles per gallon . . . *no!* She was a small dark person with strong fingers and intense sea-blue eyes like airmail envelopes; she had the habit of putting her head back like a wrestler about to bridge or a patient preparing for mouth-to-mouth resuscitation whenever she made love . . . oh yes. She had a svelte, not a voluptuous body and she liked things that clung to her, hugged her, hung around her . . . clothes, children, big dogs and men. Wrong. She was tall with long thighs and a loping walk, a great mouth, a 38D . . .

Then the driver's sinuses finally revolted against the night-long endurance test forced upon them by the air-conditioning; he sneezed violently and woke himself up. He put his thoughts for his wife and all other women in a large, empty part of his mind which resembled the Volvo's roomy, unpacked trunk. He took a forceful shower and thought that today was the day he would see the Mississippi.

People actually learn very little about themselves; it's as if they really appreciate the continuous act of making themselves vulnerable.

The driver planned to leave without breakfast. You'd have thought he'd be used to ups and downs, but the early morning sight of the violence done to the Volvo was a shock even to this veteran of the ways of the road. The Volvo had been vandalized; it sat at the curb by the driver's motel-room door like a wife he'd locked out of the house in the drunken night—she was waiting there to hit him hard with his guilt in the daylight.

"Oh my God, what have they done to you . . . ?"

They had pried off the four hub caps and left the cluster of tire nuts exposed, the tires naked. They had stolen the side-view mirror from the driver's side. Someone had tried to unscrew the whole mounting for the piece, but the screwdriver had been either too big or too small for the screws; the work had left the screwheads maimed and useless; the thief had left the mounting in place and had simply wrenched the mirror until it had snapped free at the ball-joint. The ruptured joint looked to the driver like the raw and ragged socket of a man whose arm had been torn off.

They had tried to violate the Volvo's interior with repeated digging and levering at the side-vent windows, but the Volvo had held. They had ripped the rubber water-seal from under the window on the driver's side but they had not been able to spring the lock. They had tried to break one window; a small run of cracks, like a spider web blown against the glass, traced a pattern on the passenger's side. They had tried to get into the gas tank— to siphon gas, to add sand, to insert a match—but although they had mashed the tank-top lock, they had been unable to penetrate there. They had cranked under the hood, but the hood had held. Several teeth of the grill were pushed in, and one tooth had been bent outward until it had broken; it stuck out in front of the Volvo as if the car were carrying some crude bayonet.

As a last gesture the frustrated rapists, the wretched band of Joliet punks!—or were they other motel guests, irritated by the foreign license plate, in disagreement with Vermont? . . . whoever, as a finally cruel and needless way of leaving, *someone* had taken an instrument (the corkscrew-blade on a camper's knife?) and gouged a four-letter word into the lush red of the Volvo's hood. Indeed, deeper than the paint, it was a groove into the steel itself. SUCK was the word.

"Suck?" the driver cried out. He covered the wound with his hand. "Bastards!" he screamed. "Swine, filthy creeps!" he roared. The wing of the motel he was facing must have slept two hundred travelers; there was a ground-floor barracks and a second-floor barracks with a balcony. "Cowards, car-humpers!" the driver bellowed. "Who did it?" he demanded. Several doors along the balcony opened. Frightened, wakened men stood peering down at him—women chattering behind them: "Who is it? What's happening?"

"Suck!" the driver yelled. "Suck!"

"It's six o'clock in the morning, fella," someone mumbled from a ground-floor door, then quickly stepped back inside and closed the door behind him.

Genuine madness is not to be tampered with. If the driver had been drunk or simply boorish, those disturbed sleepers would have mangled him. But he was insane—they could all see —and there's nothing to do about that.

"What's going on, Fred?"

"Some guy losing his mind. Go back to sleep."

Oh Joliet, Illinois, you are worse than the purgatory I first took you for!

The driver touched the oily ball-joint where his trim mirror used to be. "You're going to be all right," he said. "Good as new, don't worry."

SUCK! That foul word dug into his hood was so *public* it seemed to expose *him*—the rude, leering ugliness of it shamed him. He saw Derek Marshall approaching his wife. "Hi! Need a ride home?"

"All right," the driver told the Volvo, thickly. "All right, that's enough. I'll take you home."

The gentleness of the driver was now impressive. It is incredible to find occasional discretion in human beings; some of the people on the second-floor balcony were actually closing their doors. The driver's hand hid the SUCK carved into his hood; he was crying.

He had come all this way to leave his wife and all he had done was hurt his car.

But no one can make it as far as Joliet, Illinois, and not be tempted to see the Mississippi River—the main street of the Midwest, and the necessary crossing to the real Outwest. No, you haven't really been West until you've crossed the Mississippi; you can never say you've "been out there" until you've touched down in Iowa.

If you have seen Iowa, you have seen the beginning.

The driver knew this; he begged the Volvo to indulge him just a look. "We'll turn right around, I promise. I just want to see it," he said. "The Mississippi. And Iowa . . ." where he might have gone.

Sullenly, the Volvo carried him through Illinois: Starved Rock State Park, Wenona, Mendota, Henry, Kewanee, Geneseo, Rock Island and Moline. There was a rest plaza before the great bridge which spanned the Mississippi—the bridge which carried you into Iowa. Ah, Davenport, West Liberty and Lake Mac-Bride!

But he would not see them, not now. He stood by the Volvo and watched the tea-colored, wide water of the Mississippi roll by; for someone who's seen the Atlantic Ocean, rivers aren't so special. But *beyond* the river . . . there was *Iowa* . . . and it looked really *different* from Illinois! He saw corn tassels going on forever, like an army of fresh young cheerleaders waving their feathers. Out there, too, big hogs grew; he knew that; he imagined them—he had to—because there wasn't actually a herd of pigs browsing on the other side of the Mississippi.

"Some day . . ." the driver said, half in fear that this were true and half wishfully. The compromised Volvo sat there waiting for him; its bashed grill and the word SUCK pointed east.

"Okay, okay," the driver said.

Be thankful for what dim orientation you have. Listen: the driver *could* have gotten lost; in the muddle of his east-west decision, he could have found himself headed north—in the southbound lane!

Missouri State Police Report #459: "A red Volvo sedan, heading north in the southbound lane, appeared to have a poor sense of direction. The cement mixer who hit him was absolutely clear about its right-of-way in the passing lane. When the debris was sorted, a phone number was found. When his wife was called, another man answered. He said his name was Derek Marshall and that he'd give the news to the guy's wife as soon as she woke up."

We should know; it can always be worse.

Certainly, real trouble lay ahead. There was the complexity of the Sandusky exits to navigate, and the driver felt less than fresh. Ohio lay out there waiting for him like years of a marriage he hadn't yet lived. But there was also the Volvo to think of; the Volvo seemed destined to never get over Vermont. And there would be delicate dealings to come with Derek Marshall; that seemed sure. We often need to lose sight of our priorities in order to see them.

He had seen the Mississippi and the lush, fertile flatland beyond. Who could say what sweet, dark mysteries Iowa might have revealed to him? Not to mention Nebraska. Or *Wyoming*! The driver's throat ached. And he had overlooked that he once more had to pass through Joliet, Illinois.

Going home is hard. But what's to be said for staying away?

In La Salle, Illinois, the driver had the Volvo checked over. The windshield wipers had to be replaced (he hadn't even noticed they were stolen), a temporary side-view mirror was mounted and some soothing anti-rust primer was painted into the gash which said SUCK. The Volvo's oil was full-up, but the driver discovered that the vandals had tried to jam little pebbles in all the air valves—hoping to deflate his tires as he drove. The gas-station attendant had to break the tank-top lock the rest of the way in order to give the Volvo some gas. Mileage 23.1 per gallon—the Volvo was a tiger in the face of hardship.

"I'll get you a paint-job at home," the driver told the Volvo, grimly. "Just try to hang on."

There was, after all, Indiana to look forward to. Some things, we're told, are even better "the second time around." His marriage struck him as an unfinished war between Ohio and Indiana—a fragile balance of fire-power, punctuated with occasional treaties. To bring Iowa into the picture would cause a drastic tilt. Or: some rivers are better not crossed? The national average is less than 25,000 miles on one set of tires, and many fall off much sooner. He had 46,251 miles on the Volvo—his first set of tires.

No, despite that enchanting, retreating portrait of the Iowa future, you cannot drive with your eyes in the rear-view mirror. And, yes, at this phase of the journey, the driver was determined to head back East. But dignity is difficult to maintain. Stamina requires constant upkeep. Repetition is boring. And you pay for grace.

ROOM TEMPERATURE

Raymond Kennedy

ack replaced the lid on the stove, then went to the door. The snow came up to the doorsill furnished with an icy crust. After looking outside warily, he closed the door, shot the bolt, turned and shuffled back to bed. "Son of a bitch," he said. On the cot lay a magazine, pages thumbed yellow. He had read the stories many times, one of them over and over— a story about a woman whose husband liked to wear dresses. The story made Jack laugh. He sat on the bed, looking at the bolt. He was not himself.

"I got the heebie-jeebies!" he said.

He got up and went to the stove again. Overhead the wind fluttered the tar paper, a sucking sound, like a pulled nail. The flaming log stood on end in the narrow pot of the stove, and he jiggled it ceremoniously with the lid handle, then turned his eyes to the bolt on the door. He did not like the looks of it.

"Contraption!" he said.

He took off his shoes and lighted his pipe. The dog lay beneath the rocker, its side swelling evenly. Later, as the fire cooled, the dog would rouse himself and climb onto the cot. By that time, Jack would be sleeping.

He put his head back against the sack with the coat rolled up inside, puffed his pipe, and pulled the blankets to his chin. The woman in the story was Julia, and the man was Dan, and Jack saw the look on Julia's face as Dan came down the stairway smelling like lilacs and wearing pumps with an open toe. Jack laughed and puffed on his pipe.

Twice during the night he heard noises, the second time plain. It made him sit up, and then get up and put on his pants and a coat over the sweat shirt he slept in. He found a hatchet and hammer in the box, took the hammer and put the hatchet back, and then he went to the door and listened. He drew the bolt all the way back.

He moved forward, the snow shattering like gunshot. The moonlight advanced, lighting up bushes and, beyond them, a man, flat on his back.

Jack had never seen anything like it. All the man wore was a shoe.

"They used to take your money," Jack said. "A man wanted your money and he took it. These filthy bastards are different." The man opened and closed his eyes. "I've seen 'em," said Jack.

He took the bottle, got a tin cup, poured a little whiskey, then went back to the cot.

"I know what I'm talking about," Jack said. "I'm not just talking to hear myself talk. I've seen them and I know what they look like." He looked at the man's face. "It used to be a fellow would want your money, you had a drink or two, and he was waiting for you outside. Listen," said Jack, "I did it myself. What man hasn't? But," he said, lifting a finger, "I didn't take a man's shoes. I didn't take his pants and his hat and his underwear, goddamnit."

Jack lowered himself into his rocker. The stove was glowing now, making popping sounds. He listened to be sure he could hear the man breathing, then sat back and folded his hands on his stomach.

He must have slept hours, and woke to find the man sitting at the table. He sat with his back to Jack, a blanket around him from neck to feet.

"Ten years ago," the man said, "I didn't have a hundred, I had a *thousand* like you."

Jack couldn't make sense of it.

"End up in a dump like this," the man said. He glanced at the ceiling. "And for what?"

The man was raving, Jack decided. He had gotten bad blows on the head.

"How are you feeling?" Jack asked, sitting forward in his chair.

The man turned. "I want something to eat," he said.

"Well, what'll it be?" Jack said. "Oatmeal and coffee, or coffee and oatmeal?"

"Get me some breakfast, some clothes, and a bath."

Jack shook his head. "You can't have breakfast and bath both. The stove's too small. You get one or the other."

The man struck the table a powerful blow. "Goddamnit to hell!" he cried. "I'm lost, don't you understand? I'm lost and cold and hungry and dirty! Look at me!" He opened the blanket. "Are you blind?"

"I hear you," Jack complained, holding up his hands.

"I want a bath! Is that asking too much? I want some coffee and a tub of water!" he cried.

Jack had to laugh, all right. The man was a funny tick. "No oil," he was saying, "no gas, no sink, no lights, no plumbing, no telephone—"

The man spread his hands, taking in the four walls. "An absolute hovel. Anyplace else," said the man, "there'd be someone to shave me. My things would be laundered and folded and laid out." Reaching, he uncapped the whiskey bottle and poured. His eyes followed Jack, who smiled and nodded but went about his business, fetching the coffee bag from the perishables box.

"Come on," the man said, "look at me." He was extending his arms, like a model displaying her garments.

"That's all right," said Jack, not looking.

"This blanket," said the man, "where did you get it?"

"Some men," said Jack, "live one way. Some men live another."

"Oh, that's helpful," the man said, smiling hastily and turning back to the table. He sipped some whiskey from the cup and put his fist to his lips. "Well, my name is Dick," he said, "but you don't call me that." He belched, shaking his head. "No, I don't want any familiarity with you."

Jack was standing with his back to the man. He did not wish to turn around. He looked out the window and across the frosted earth.

"I hope you have some soap—a facecloth, too, and a towel," Dick said. "I won't ask you for your bath salts or talcum or cologne, but I'd like to see myself in a glass." He stood up.

"You'd better wash up first."

Dick pursed his lips, reflecting on it. "So this is where you live," he said, looking out the window. "And out here—this is all yours?"

"Some of it," said Jack.

"I see." Dick puckered his lips, impressed.

"An acre," said Jack.

"Pretty," said Dick, viewing the terrain.

Then, turning about, he took the blanket and flung it aside. Sitting down, Dick began to wash his body, making wet sounds with the washcloth against his flesh. "I have seen the top," said Dick, "and I have seen the bottom. But you know, Jack," his voice growing more familiar, "I enjoyed both."

"You sound well-educated," Jack said.

"That's not what I'm talking about. I'm referring to your **big** shots and bums," Dick said.

Jack made a knowing face. "I knew a bum once." He laughed horsily.

"I'm not talking about beggars," said Dick, shaking a finger. "I'm talking about your bum. A man who knows nobody and owes nobody, but when he has to, will hit you on the head for it. That man," said Dick, mopping under his armpits, "walks the earth on his own two feet, goddamnit. It's like the big shot, only the big shot owns the place and stays put."

"I see what you're getting at," Jack said. He was fishing in the food box and thinking his own thoughts. There were six eggs, some flour, lard, margarine. He made several calculations.

"You see," Dick went on, "the ones in the middle, the accountants and nurses and bookkeepers and cops and schoolteachers and lawyers and laundrymen and such, they're all rats." Here Dick made a broad gesture with his hand, as though broadcasting seed across the surface of the globe.

"Absolute rats," he enunciated. "Are my eggs up?" He shot a swift, sidewise glance at Jack, who had just taken two eggs into his hand and was reaching for the skillet.

"To me," said Dick, "you would be worth ten, fifteen dollars a week. That would be my top-dollar bid."

"You couldn't get me for a hundred," Jack mumbled, at last looking at Dick from the safety of the stove. "Boy, they hit you," Jack marveled, shaking his head. "They hit you left and right."

Dick looked up while working the washcloth in his crotch. "Am I worried about that?" He smiled, showing the spaces in his teeth.

Jack waited, hoping that the man would begin to explain, to tell him something more. But Dick was whistling to himself, lifting a thigh and scrubbing. When he finally spoke, it was quiet. "The filthy honyockers," he said. "The sons of bitches bastards."

"They must have hit you and kicked you all over," said Jack.

"The *reason* you would come so low," Dick added, thoughtful, "is really a tribute to you."

"If you say so," said Jack, popping an egg into the frypan and tilting it to make the lard spread.

"What time does your mail come?"

"I don't get mail," said Jack. "They don't come out here. I have to go for it. But I never get any, so I don't go for it."

"Makes sense," said Dick.

"It's too far, anyway," said Jack.

"What I was getting at," Dick stood up, pointing to the towel on the nail on the door, "was how much better for you to be a bum. I personally couldn't use you. That is, I couldn't fit you in without costing me money." He shrugged his shoulders.

Jack shook his head and grinned. He handed Dick the towel. He wished he were alone with the dog.

While the eggs fried in the pan, Jack fished some pants and a shirt from the suitcase he kept at the foot of his bed.

"Be a good scout," said Dick, "and fetch me a looking glass. And please stop mincing about and avoiding looking at me."

"Here," said Jack, extending the roll of clothes to the man. "Take this."

"Don't hand me everything at once," Dick complained. "Give me the shirt first. Put my trousers and hose on the chair. And keep an eye on those eggs, won't you? And Jack," he said, "do bring me my mirror."

"Where are you going from here?" Jack asked over his shoulder.

"I don't understand the question," Dick said.

"You can't stay here."

The two men considered one another at length. "Have I led you to believe that I *want* to. Great heavens," Dick glanced about, pivoting on his heel, "whatever would I do with myself in such a dump?"

"It's miles out of here," said Jack.

"Miles?" Dick said, his eyebrows lifting. "Miles to *where?* How in the world can you discuss distances without destinations?" Dick's teeth showed as he smiled. "After all, it's not miles from here to the ditch—or to the nearest hillock. I know how to get about. A man is never lost. I, for example," and he placed his pudgy hands flat to his chest, "have never been lost. I have been all over, Jack. I know the continents, the rivers and streams, and I know that the lesser waters flow always to the greater." He eyed Jack shrewdly. "A man has to walk downhill till he reaches water and then downstream the rest of the way. That's simple, isn't it?" he concluded.

"Seems to me," Jack muttered, "you'd follow the road."

Dick shrugged.

Jack had never met the likes of him. Anyhow, the snow was too deep. It was too deep for Jack. And Dick looked very soft.

"Eat your eggs, Dick," Jack said.

"And something else," said Dick, "I told you not to call me Dick! Don't think because you're fixing my eggs you're my favorite." He looked away. "I don't have favorites, and I don't like toadies. You have a job to do, and do it."

Dick, it seemed, was beginning to rave, and Jack had fallen into a reverie. When he came out of it, Dick was staring at him, as though waiting.

"Are you deaf?" he said. "I told you to bring me my shoes!"

So startled was he by Dick's shout, Jack plunged forward in the direction of the suitcase.

"If you were younger, by even that much," Dick made a space between thumb and forefinger, "I might have a place for you. For example, down in the watershops division there's an opening on the three-to-eleven shift for a registered nurse. That's one possibility." Abruptly, Dick put down his fork. "I can't eat these eggs," he said. "They're cold." He thrust away his plate. "No, thank you."

Jack had one shoe in hand but could not find its brother anywhere. He lifted the blanket and peered under the bed. "I can't find the mate," he said, getting up with a sigh. "I think the dog took it."

"Well, give me that one," said Dick, motioning. "Bring it here. I still have one of my own." He showed Jack a peevish look. "I don't need three. While I'm getting dressed," he said, glancing thoughtfully at the ceiling and hunching to zip up his fly, "I want you to make preparations for us. For the trip."

"I'm not going," said Jack.

"We'll see," said Dick.

"No," said Jack, "I don't think so."

"Old knuckle-walking son of a bitch." Dick smiled tolerantly. "Do you have any handkerchiefs or underwear?"

Jack did not answer. He took Dick's plate and scraped the eggs.

"Understand me," Dick pronounced each word plainly, "I will brook no impertinence from you! When I ask you a question, you will reflect momentarily, consider the various sides and angles, and then, having done so, give me a prompt, concise answer. What lies south of here?"

"Woods," said Jack.

Dick smiled and lifted his hands in a gesture that bespoke surprise while conferring a blessing. "A very neat response. You see, that pleases me. What's east?" he whispered rapidly.

"Woods," said Jack.

"North?"

"Woods."

"Town is that way?" Dick pointed.

"That's east," said Jack. "Mountains and woods."

"What was difficult about that?"

"About what?"

"*Showing some intelligence!*" Dick bellowed, his eyes bulging.

Jack retreated a step. As he did so, he heard the sound of Dick breaking wind.

"I'll bet they drove you out here and dumped you," said Dick. "They got tired of your bellyaching."

Jack said nothing.

"We'll head for town," said Dick, tightening his belt. He slapped his waist. "I'll get some money wired in. I might even give you a dollar or two." Dick smiled up at him. "You've been wonderful to me, Jack, and I won't forget it. You've been a prince." Poking his finger into the heel, Dick popped the shoe onto his foot.

"I'm not going," said Jack.

"You gave me your bed, old fellow, and you gave me your board. Should I forget that? Could I?"

"You didn't even sleep," said Jack.

"I don't like being covered up and secured that way," Dick said. "For usually I sleep in a very big bed, the covers arranged in two sets, one tucked in on one side," Dick gestured, "the other tucked in on the *other* side. In that way all the blankets dovetail, you see. Then," he showed Jack a finger of caution, "if anything should occur during the night, I *fling back* the covers and spring directly out of the heart of the bed!" Here Dick lunged forward illustratively and seized the old man. "Now, I've got you, you old honyocker!" he cried.

"What are you doing!" Jack squirmed, but Dick held, encircling the old man in his arms.

"This is my bear hug!" Dick screamed.

"Get away from me!" said Jack, turning his head.

"Do you think I'd leave you behind?" Dick demanded, as he released Jack with a motion that made him reel. "What sort of game do you think this is? Do you want them to come in here, knock you about, smash up your place—probably kill you?"

"No one wants to kill me," said Jack.

"No one wanted to kill *me*," said Dick. "Here, look at me."

He showed Jack his eye. "No one wanted to do that. They didn't *want* to do that. They just did it." He swung his arms wildly. "They'll grab you by the neck and hammer you and hammer you. They'll kick you blue! *They'll kick the stuffings out of you!*" he bellowed again. Then, swiftly, he put his hands lightly to his chest. "*I'm* not staying," he said. "I'm getting out *tout de suite*. And so are you. What do you think I'm paying you for?"

Jack walked away from him. Dick grunted knowingly, sat down, and started lacing his shoes.

Jack wished he could just go outside by himself and sit down on the chopping block for a while. He knew that what was happening could only happen to an old man.

"I'm not trying to alarm you," said Dick, making a bow in his laces. He slapped his knees and stood up. "I don't feel that the road is wise."

Jack did not look at Dick's face. "It's about five miles through the woods to the highway," he said.

"I'll need a coat, of course, matches, a compass, an ax. Would you get that together for me?" Dick went to the window and flexed his arms, a man itching to be on the move. Spotting Jack's mackinaw, he asked, "Is this to be my coat?"

"That's my coat," said Jack.

"Then what am I to wear?"

Jack shuffled to the bed and raised the mattress. Stretched across the springs was a long grey overcoat, moth-eaten and threadbare at cuffs and collar, but Dick was delighted with it, and crossed the room at once. He folded it shut and pressed one side flat to his body and leaned forward like a customer in a fitting room. "No, they'll never keep me down, Jack. They can wreck my businesses and steal my women, but I'll come back." He nodded resolutely. He stood splayfooted, the brown-and-white shoe pointed one way, the black business toe pointed the other. "They chased you out, and you stayed out. You took the count. Now, look at me," he waved at himself, at his coat, pants, shoes. "See what they've done?"

"They got you," said Jack.

"They got me good," Dick acknowledged.

"They got you coming and going," Jack said.

"But I get them," said Dick.

"They get their turn," said Jack, "and you get yours."

"I get them three different ways," said Dick, and he raised a finger for each. "I punch them in the groin. I kick them in the slats, and I knee them in the nuts. *Now*," up came a finger of caution, "I'm not going to go back along that road. No." Dick wagged his finger and smiled. "That's not cute enough for me. You see, they're down there. I know they're down there." Turning, he reached and moved his hand in a broad arc. "I'm going to go *all* the way around them," he said. "That's my plan." He raised his hands, as though trying to frame an elusive concept. "You could have had anything you wanted," said Dick. "But as soon as they put the heat on, you skedaddled. I," he continued, and commenced pacing, "have set aside these few moments to pass along to you, my friend, the word of the world." He leaned close to the old man's ear. "*We don't need you*," he whispered.

"You take the cake," said Jack.

"I'm on my way," said Dick.

"That's okay," Jack waved.

Abruptly, Dick turned and paced to the door. "Show me the route."

Jack took his mackinaw and followed the man outdoors. On the sides of the tar-papered shack the snow lay like a white sea that had come to a stop. Dick was surveying the landscape. "Cedars," he said. "Cedar and birch. That's good." He nodded and pursed his lips. "I like the look of it, Jack."

"I'll walk you to the trees," said Jack.

He went indoors again and fetched his hat and took a final

look at his home. The sun shaft leaning in at the window lit up the numerals on the wall calendar. The stove made popping sounds. All morning long the dog had stayed outside, so Jack got his bowl and put in a biscuit.

"Wonderful," Dick was saying, surveying the landscape. He opened his arms appreciatively. "What composition," he said, "what balance!"

Then they set out for the woods.

"I've been thinking about you, Jack," Dick began. "What you really needed," he said, "was a squaw."

"I had a squaw," Jack replied.

"Someone to blow on the coals, grease you up, repair the kayak."

"There's the road," said Jack.

But Dick had turned his eye to Jack. "Jack," he declared, "I've grown fond of you." He put his hands on his hips. "Oh, you're a *laconic* honyocker, make no bones about it, but you have the dignity of the savage. In my book, the savage is the bum pristine."

Jack made his way past Dick in the direction of the forest. Dick, at length, followed, going gingerly over the treacherous face of the snow, stepping lightly on the balls of his feet. Jack walked on, his steps pointed toward the flank of the dark forest. Julia, he recalled, wore an apricot-colored dress with a brown sash. Her wardrobe was small but select. Dan, of course, had two wardrobes. Jack set to laughing.

"Something funny?" said Dick.

"I was thinking about my friends," Jack said.

"You have no *friends*," said Dick.

"Yes, I do." Jack waited for Dick to overtake him.

"Don't be an ass," said Dick. "How could you possibly? You don't talk, you don't mix, you don't *entertain*."

Jack regarded Dick narrowly from beneath the big hat brim.

"The woman's name is Julia," said Jack, "and the man is Dan."

"That's impossible." Dick looked away.

"No, it's not."

"I say it is," Dick said. "It's so absolutely farfetched that I shall forbid you," he made a forbidding face, "to speak of it again. Where did you meet them and what was the instrument of your acquaintanceship?"

Jack made only a sighing sound.

"Was it at a ball?" asked Dick, half closing one eye.

Jack dropped his eyes.

"Tea?"

Jack shook his head.

"I am not at all pleased with any of this," Dick said.

"You don't have to believe me," said Jack.

"I don't believe you," said Dick.

"It doesn't matter," said Jack.

"Tell me all about them," said Dick, folding his arms ceremoniously. "Tell me about Julia and Dan. Do they call you Jack?"

"You'd better get started," said Jack and, turning, he continued toward the trees.

Dick came along in his wake. "Tell me about Julia and Dan," he said. "It's possible I may know them. Tell me about Dan. What does he do?"

"He wears women's clothes," said Jack.

"For a living?" Dick exclaimed.

"No," said Jack, "just for the fun."

"Fun?" said Dick. "What possible fun could a man get from a thing like that? That doesn't sound like fun to me."

Jack laughed, putting his fist to his mouth, and his laughter evolved into a wheezing cough. Stopping, he took a long handkerchief from his pocket and slowly spat into it.

"A man who would do something like that," said Dick, sternly, "should be strung up by the cojones."

613

"It's just for the joke of it," said Jack.

"He should be beaten to a frazzle," said Dick. "I would take that man by the neck and, believe me, teach him the p's and q's of life. It's disgusting."

"Julia was disgusted at first, too."

"I should think she would be."

"She saw him coming down the stairs," said Jack, "and he was wearing a wig and nylon stockings and high-heeled shoes. She said, '*Dan!*'" Jack laughed lightly as he rolled up his handkerchief with great care, folding it several times, and restored it to his pocket.

"A woman who would marry a man like that," said Dick, "should be taken somewhere and plugged up."

Jack was looking at the wall of trees. The two men walked on in silence, approaching the verge of timber. The evergreens showed themselves coated with ice and stood like a thousand sentries.

"You'll be lost in an hour," said Jack.

"Don't be stupid." Dick dealt the nearest tree a blow with the toe of his brown-and-white shoe.

"It's very heavy," said Jack, glancing away. "First the spruce, then a mile down through hardwood to a stream, then more hardwood, and up again through the evergreen."

"Simple enough," said Dick.

"There used to be a sawmill in there."

Dick planted his hands on his hips.

"You'll see the piers," said Jack.

"I don't think," said Dick, thoughtfully, "I'm going to take you with me." He looked at the old man. "I don't think you could keep up."

"I don't think I'll go," Jack said.

"You old wag," Dick replied. "Are you making fun of me?"

"I think I'll stay here," said Jack.

"It's a good thing I haven't any baggage. Good for you, that is. Have you ever done valet work?"

Jack said nothing. Dick looked in at his eyes, barely visible under the hat brim.

"You have no polish, Jack. Look at the way you're dressed. I'd be the laughingstock of six continents."

Jack was smiling under his hat brim.

"A proper lackey," Dick went on, "is a pale reflection of his employer and master. My man would have to have some get-up-and-go." Dick balled his fist to express the requisite vigor. "Some brains," he said. "Some bounce to him! Up at dawn, brush my shoes, iron my clothes, draw my bath—it's run, run, run, Jack. Work, work, work. Always polite, always discreet, always eager, always smiling. Go, go, go!" He was swinging both fists now, punching the air. "Cables, memos, lime juice, messages, aspirin, slippers, pen and ink, coffee, manicure, go downstairs, go upstairs, polish my shoes, smile, bow, tiptoes, *run!* Meanwhile, I'm reaming your ass. I'm yelling at you, threatening you, abusing you, *Muttonhead! Knuckle-walker!* Come back here! *Not that!* Stand straight! Lickspittle! I'm *yelling,* do you understand!"

"I hear you," said Jack.

"I've become a wild boar! You're terrified! You haven't any go left, no pep. And I want more, more, more!"

"I think it would be too much for me," said Jack.

"It saddens me to turn you down," said Dick.

"I'd rather not work," said Jack.

"It's too bad, because you have a winning way about you." Dick smiled angelically.

They stood facing each other in the shadow of the lower boughs. Overhead, the wind made a deep breathing sound in the branches.

"You see, I would have to keep you out of sight," Dick said. "For that matter, I couldn't think of offering you a wage. Not one penny, Jack." He made a zero of his thumb and forefinger. "Nothing. You'd have to prove yourself. You'd have to come in at the bottom of the picture, maybe as a pot-and-pan boy, or a kind of shock absorber my butlers could shower their spleen against, as when I've given them a stiff reaming and everybody is boiling in the back rooms. No, I don't feel you could stick it. I don't think so. But I may be wrong."

In the way of assenting, Jack shook his head.

"I'm going to leave you now," said Dick, "and make my way in the forest. But I should feel genuinely penitent if I thought that our parting was not genial. You," he pointed out, "want to go, and I, my dear fellow, cannot take you." He squeezed his lips together and regarded the old man placidly.

"I don't want to go," Jack said.

"Because if you didn't want to go," Dick continued, "you would have but seen me to the door. Instead, you have clung to my side every moment, tried to please me in every imaginable way, and even now," Dick stated the point dramatically, "you are five paces ahead of me, like a gundog eager for a day in the field. If you had a tail, I believe it would be wagging." Dick's head popped forward as he laughed uproariously. "Look at you, you old honyocker!" he cried out. Drawing in his chin, he lifted his hand in an imperial salute.

With that, Dick started away, plunging past Jack into the heavy woods. Jack turned to watch him go. Dick's progress was frenzied, his arms pumping, his stride wide-legged and full of purpose. He kicked up snow at every step. He followed a straight line, veering only to avoid trees. Jack went the opposite way, but halted at the edge of the trees. When he looked back, Dick was still in view—a glimpse of his bald head, a blown coat-tail, a puff of snow spotted here and there through the evergreen.

But Dick's path had already begun to lean west. The old man didn't like the look of it. A northwesterly course would open out for eight or ten miles. After a few hours of that, doubt would bring on panic, after which there were forty square miles of wild country to spend all a man's energy.

So Jack started up in pursuit, but moving cautiously, not in haste. He did not want to catch Dick. He wanted to satisfy himself that Dick's angle of flight would land him safely on the flanking northern road. But by now Dick was no longer visible.

Jack stepped forth into the sunlit clearing, following Dick's trail. He made his way across and stood at the point where Dick had reentered the forest. Not ten feet into the timber, just beyond the nearest cedar, Dick's path went utterly awry, his footsteps disappearing behind a tree, then emerging to the side, going away at a bizarre angle. Jack started forward, choosing easier footing. Where Dick had to duck, bend, or even crawl, Jack took a better route. Following the man, and overtaking him, would be child's play for Jack. He blew into his hands and rubbed them together. Twice he anticipated Dick's route, making rapid circuits around hillocks, recovering Dick's footmarks, then hastening forward, when suddenly there, at the foot of a cedar, stood the stranger himself, his hands dangling at his sides. He was bleeding from both nostrils, the blood forming a moustache on his face.

"I suppose you wonder what I am doing here," said Dick.

"I don't like what's happening," said Jack. "I don't like it at all."

"I don't either," said Dick.

"What happened to you?" Jack asked.

"I was running," Dick said. He turned and pointed inconclusively. "Out there."

"You were not running. You were walking."

"Wasn't I running?" Dick widened his eyes.

"You were walking. I was following you!" Jack said.

Dick's face changed. He squinted at Jack. "That was *you* following me?" he said. "*You?* I was running away from *you*,

you old son of a bitch?" he shouted. "Ball-busting old fart!" Dick growled. "I ought to—" He came forward threateningly. "I put all my money on you," said Dick, wheezing. "Everything," he said. "You—stabbed me in the back!"

With a wild light in his eyes, Dick turned about and marched away swinging his arms, expostulating.

"That's the sawmill ahead," Jack called to him.

But Dick made no reply. He did not slow down, nor look around at the stooped figure coming in his wake.

The surface of the river was frozen solid, and snow lay atop the ice. On the near bank of the stream stood a host of derelict piers, each as tall as a man, sheathed in snow and ice.

"Here it is," said Dick, but not for Jack's benefit, for as he spoke he quickened his stride. They were in the clear now, the woods divided as into two separate walls, one behind them and the other opposing them beyond the river. Dick hurried ahead, making quickly for the ruins. When he got to the first pier he ran forward and wrapped his arms around it. "The size of them!" he said.

"It was a sawmill," said Jack.

Dick made a low whistling sound. He hugged the pier, then thrust himself from it and began to pace about among the other uprights.

"What workmanship!" he said, and shook his head profoundly. Then he stood back, his fists planted on his hips, regarding the site in its entirety. "Many a vessel put out from this corner of things." He nodded impressively.

"Used to be a sawmill," said Jack, looking away to the wooden posts standing forlornly at the river's edge.

"Getting chilly?" Dick said.

"It's near zero," Jack said.

"Do you want my coat?"

"I'm too cold even for that," Jack said. He glanced at Dick, then away again, facing upstream. He wanted Dick to understand where they were. "The chief sawyer's shack was by the water. The saws were over there."

Dick studied him with a sidelong eye.

"This is a cove," Jack added.

A silence issued between them.

Jack watched as a single snowflake fluttered down and lit on the yoke of Dick's coat, and then the sky was a shower of snow, the flakes tracing diagonally against the pines on the opposite shore.

"The years have been good to you, Jack," Dick said. "How old are you?"

"I'm seventy-two," replied Jack.

Dick's eyebrows went up. "That's about room temperature, isn't it?" said Dick. "Or is it the heart rate?"

"I think we should go," said Jack.

Dick turned on him, suddenly indignant. "Can't you show any enthusiasm!" He seized Jack by the shoulder and shook him. "It's something about me, isn't it?"

"No," Jack mumbled.

"It is!"

"It's the cold," said Jack.

"It's me!"

"I think I'm freezing. Take me back."

Dick's lower lip began to quiver. "I was proud of you, Jack. Let them have their tycoons and their poets, is what I used to say, because Jack is best of all. And I was your legacy, your hope. You looked at me, a chip placed on the green baize of history. 'Turn the wheel,' you said. 'This is Dick, my hope, my beauty, my chalice.'"

"Let's go," said Jack.

"Now I stand before you." Dick smiled.

Reaching, he took hold of Jack's elbow and gave it an encouraging tug. But Jack could not move. His body, hunched inside the snow-covered mackinaw, swayed forward, but he could not un-mortise his feet.

"Walk with me," said Dick.

Jack shook his head. He could not move his feet.

Dick helped him, his eyes trained on Jack's feet. "That's good," he said.

"I'm moving now," said Jack.

"You're walking like anyone else," Dick said.

Jack lurched forward, tottering like an infant.

"Keep going," Dick said.

"That's better," said Jack, and summoned all his resources. He plunged forward, step by step.

"In a world full of dildos and dumdums," Dick said, "I aspired, Jack. If I hadn't, I wouldn't be here today."

They had reached the first pier. Jack leaned against it and closed his eyes, and slowly lowered himself, clutching the post for support.

Dick watched impassively. "Bushed?" he inquired.

"I think so," said Jack.

"You did all you could," declared Dick.

"Thank you," said Jack.

"No one did more," Dick said.

"I don't know," said Jack. He could not see Dick's face anymore, only the horrid shoes. There was a piping of snow in his trouser cuffs. He would like to have seen Dick's face, but he did not want to move, nor try.

"Solitude is a populous street," Dick was saying. "I know."

Jack opened and closed his eyes. His hands and feet were useless to him, inert save for their shaking.

"Of course," said Dick, "a fellow doesn't have to suffer alone. It isn't necessary. When you go to the top of the mountain, Jack, you need rope," he said, "you need cleats, a lantern, some sandwiches. Other people are brought into it! Porters, runners, photographers, et cetera. No one ever went to the mountain, Jack, without thinking everyone was waiting for him to come back."

Opening his eyes, Jack could see through Dick's legs to the other side of the river. The snow was falling. It was burying him.

"You should have seen us," Dick said. "I was wearing a white swimsuit and green sunshades, and the limousines were lined up from here to Zambesi." Dick paused as though to relish the remembrance of it. "It seems like only yesterday," he added.

When Jack looked again at Dick's legs, Dick was facing the other way. When Dick spoke, his voice was windy and weak.

"I owe it all to you," he said.

Now Jack could see nothing save the snow and the shadow of Dick's legs. Soon, he imagined, a snowflake would move across the open space of his mind. He could hear it approaching. Everything stood still on all sides, until, at last, with the profundity of a vast army drawn up to begin, Dick's left foot began to lift. It came up from the snow, spilling white behind it. He was moving. Saying no more, Dick marched soundlessly away toward the river. Jack watched him go. Now the snow covered his lap and his legs, and in the white screen only Dick stood forth. He did not look back.

Jack sat against the pier, his mind flashing and dimming like sun behind running clouds. He thought he smelled the dog. Then he imagined one of his shoes was missing. Then it all changed, and he was looking across the river. He saw the trees. Then, by the base of a tree, he saw Dick. Then it all changed again. The wind shifted. It came blowing across the river in a sudden white tumult. When it passed, Dick was gone.

THE SEX MANIAC

Hilma Wolitzer

verybody said that there was a sex maniac loose in the complex and I thought—it's about time. It had been a long asexual winter. The steam heat seemed to dry all of the body's moistures and shrivel the fantasies of the mind. From the nineteenth floor of Building A, I watched snow fall on the deserted geometry of the playground. The colors of the world were lustless, forbidding. White fell on grey. Grey shadows drew over the white.

He was first seen in the laundry room of Building C, but it was not clear just how he had presented himself. Was his attack verbal, physical, visual? The police came and they wrote down in books the fiction of the housewives. He was next seen near the incinerators on the sixth floor of our building. He was seen twice by elderly widows whose thin shrieks seemed to pierce the brain. There had been an invasion of those widows lately, as if old men were dying off in job lots. The widows marched behind the moving men, fluttering, birdlike. Their sons and daughters were there to supervise, looking sleek and modern next to the belongings, chairs with curved legs, massive headboards of marriage beds trembling on the backs of the movers. The widows smiled shyly as if their survival embarrassed them.

Now two of them had encountered a sex maniac. Help, they

625

had shrilled. Help and help and he had been frightened off by their cries. I wondered where he waited now in ambush and if I would meet him on a loveless February night.

There were plenty of men in my life that winter, not one of them a sex maniac. The children developed coughs that made them sound like seals barking and the health plan sent a doctor. He was thin, moustachioed, and bowed with the burden of house calls. Bad boys in bad neighborhoods slashed his tires and snapped his aerial in two. Angry children bit his fingers as he pried open the hinges of their jaws. I clasped a flower pin to the bosom of my best housedress, the children jumped on the bed intoning nursery rhymes, but the doctor snapped his bag shut with the finality of the last word. His moustache thin and mean, he looked just like the doctors of my childhood. We trailed after him to the door but he didn't turn around. Never mind. There were policemen to ask us leading questions. There was the usual parade of repairmen and plumbers.

There was the delivery boy from the market. His name is Earl. We coaxed him into the apartment. Just put it down there, Earl. Just wait a minute while I get my purse, Earl. Is it still as cold out there? we asked. Is it going to snow again? Do you think the price-level index will rise? Will I meet the man of my dreams? Will I take a long voyage? But he was a boy without vision or imagination. He counted out the change and hurried to leave.

That night I said to Howard, "Love has left this land." When the children were tucked in behind veils of steam from the vaporizer, he tried to disprove it. We turned to each other in that chorus of coughing and whispering radiators. The smell of Vicks was there, eaten into my hand, into the bedclothes, and the lovemaking was only ritual. It was no one's fault. It was the fault of the atmosphere, the barometric pressure, the wind velocity. We comforted each other in the winter night.

The next day the whole complex was thrumming with excitement. The sex maniac had been seen by a very reliable source. The superintendent's wife came from a mining area in Pennsylvania, a place not noted for frivolity. She had gazed at a constant landscape and she had known men who had suffocated in sealed mines. Her word was to be honored, she had no more imagination than the grocer's boy. After the police were finished, the women of the building fell on her with questions. Did he just—you know—show himself? Did he touch her? What did he say?

She answered with humorless patience. Contrary to rumor, he was merely a white man, not very tall, and young, like her own son. But not really like her own son, she was quick to add. He had said terrible, filthy things to her in a funny, quiet way, as if he were praying, and I saw him in my mind's eye, reedy and pale, saying his string of obscenities like a litany in a reverent and quaking voice.

I wondered who he was, after all, and why he had chosen us. Had he known instinctively that we needed him, that winter had chilled us in our hearts and our beds?

But the superintendent's wife said that he hadn't touched at all, only longed to touch, promised, threatened to touch.

Ahhhhh, cried the women. Ahhhhhh. The old widows ran to the locksmith for new bolts and chains.

The men in the building began to do the laundry for their wives. They went in groups with their friends. Did the sound of their voices diminishing in the elevators remind the superintendent's wife of men going down to the mines?

Did you see him? the wives asked later, and, flinging the laundry bags down, some of the husbands laughed and said, yes, he asked for you, he told me to give you this and *this*, and the wives shrieked with pleasure.

Howard ruined our clothes, mixing dark and white things, using too much bleach. But when he came back from the laundry room it was as if he had returned from a crusade.

"Have you heard anything?" I asked, and he smiled and said, "*You* don't need a sex maniac."

But you *were*, I thought. Your eyes and your hands used to be wild and your breath came in desperate gulps. You used to mumble your own tender obscenities against my skin and tell me that I drove you crazy. I looked at Howard, his hand poised now on the rim of the laundry basket, and I knew that I was being unfair. But whose love is not unfair? When is it ever reasonable?

Perhaps whatever I needed was outside the confines of the building, farther than the outer edges of the complex where I could see the grocer's boy on his bicycle turning in concentric circles toward our building. Artfully, he raised the front wheel as he rode on the rear one, and then the bicycle became level again like a prancing pony. "Whoa," I said against the window-pane, and then I waited for him to come up.

His ears were red from the cold wind. He snuffled and put the bag of groceries on the kitchen counter. He is the sort of boy who won't meet your eyes. His own, half-lidded and secret, seemed to look at my feet. And because I didn't want him to go yet and didn't know what else to do, I said, "Have you heard about the sex maniac, Earl?"

The red of his ears flamed to his face and I thought he would be consumed by his own heat. He answered from the depths of his throat in a voice that might have been silent for weeks. "Whaaa?" he asked.

There was no way to retreat. "The sex maniac," I said. "He stays in the complex. He molests women. *You* know."

Perhaps he did. But if he didn't, then a match had been set to his fantasy. His eyes opened wide and for the first time I saw that they were a bovine brown. Sex maniac, he was thinking, and I watched his face change as the pictures rolled inside his head. Sex maniac! A grocery bag slid across the counter and into the bowl of the sink. But he stood there, his hand paused at the

pocket of his vinyl jacket. Half-nude housewives lay in stair-
wells pleading for their release. Please don't, they begged. For
God's sake, have mercy. His lips were moving, shaping melo-
dies.

I pulled on the sleeve of his jacket. "Listen, did you bring the
chow-chow?" I asked. "Look Earl, the oranges are all in the
sink."

Slowly the light dimmed in his face. He looked at me with
new recognition. "I always take good care of you, don't I?" he
asked.

"Yes, you do," I assured him. "You're a very reliable person."

"What does this here guy do?"

"Who?"

"The whachamacallit—the maniac."

I began to put the oranges back into the bag. "Oh gosh, I
don't know. I never saw him. Who knows. Rumors build up.
You know how they snowball."

"Yeah," he said, dreamy, distant.

"Well, so long," I said. I pressed the money into his relaxed
hand.

"Yeah," he said again.

I guided him down the hallway and out through the door.

That evening the superintendent came to fix the leaking faucet in the bathtub. "Keeping to yourself?" he asked as he knelt
on the bathroom tile.

I was surprised. He usually avoided conversation. "More or
less," I said cautiously.

"You women better stick close to home," he advised.

"Oh, I *do*, I *do*," I said.

"You know what that guy said to the missus? You know the
kind of language he used?" His eyes were a cruel and burning
blue. He unscrewed a washer and let it fall into the tub. He
raised his hand. "Do you know what I'll do if I catch that guy?

Whop! Whop!" His hand became a honed razor, a machete, a cleaver. "Whop! Whop!"

I blinked, feeling slightly faint. I sat down on the edge of the closed toilet seat.

The superintendent replaced the washer and stood up. "You ever see him?" he asked.

I shook my head.

His long horny forefinger shot out and pushed against my left nipple as if he were ringing a doorbell. "Maybe he don't go for a big woman," he said, and lumbered through the doorway.

I sat there for a few minutes and then I went into the kitchen to start supper.

Several days went by and gradually people stopped talking about the sex maniac. He seemed to have abandoned the complex. It was as if he hadn't been potent enough to penetrate the icy crusts of our hearts. Poor harmless thing, I thought, but at least he had tried.

The children's coughs abated and I took them to the doctor's office for a final checkup. He examined them and scribbled something on their health records. "Did they ever catch that fellow?" he asked suddenly.

"I don't think so," I said.

"Did he actually attempt *assault?*" the doctor asked. I must have seemed surprised because he poked at his moustache and said, "I've always had an interest in crimes of a sexual nature."

I dropped my eyes.

"I'm concerned with the psychodynamic origin of their obsession," he persisted.

Aha, I said to myself. I stood up, smoothing the skirt of my dress. His eyes followed my gesture, lingering, and I thought, so here's my chance if I want one. Here's unlicensed desire. Was this where the sex maniac had led me?

"Oedipal complex, all that jazz," said the doctor, but his gaze stayed on my hips and his hands became restless on the desk.

But this wasn't what I had meant at all, not those clinical hands that tapped, tapped their nervous message. I could see the cool competence in his eyes, the first-class mechanic at home in his element, but it wasn't what I needed. He had nothing to do with old longings and the adolescent rise and plunge of the heart. He had no remedies for the madness of dreams or the wistful sanity of what was familiar and dear.

"I once considered a residency in psychiatry," he said, and he laughed nervously and glanced up at his wall of diplomas as if for reassurance.

Nothing doing, I thought, not a chance. But I laughed back just to show no hard feelings. I walked to the door and the doctor followed. "So long," I told him in a voice as firm and friendly as a handshake.

"Keep an eye on those tonsils," he said, just to change the subject.

The children and I went out into the pale sunshine. Filthy patches of snow melted into the pavement.

Home, I thought, home, as if it were my life's goal to get there. We walked toward the bus stop. Everywhere color was beginning to bleed through the greyness and I felt a little sadness. I had never seen him. Not once crouched in the corner of the laundry room, not once moaning his demands on the basement ramp, not once cutting footprints across the fresh snow in the courtyard. It was as if he had never existed. The winter was almost over and I was willing to wait for summer to come again.

Pulling the children along, although there was no one waiting for me, I began to run.

THE GREAT WESTERN CIVILIZATION CAPER

Sybil Claiborne

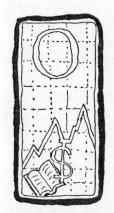

n Monday and Thursday evenings I give a seminar at the New School on the evolution of conglomerates. I am an economist at Crowly and Glim, an expert in all aspects of financial theory, planning and management. In my opinion the economy has many soft spots, the financial outlook is extremely blurred. Eighty-eight percent of my colleagues concur.

The people taking my seminar are junior executives or better. Except for Connie; she is a financial engineer trainee at Berkowitz and Mead and therefore I had strong doubts about her qualifications. I am glad Connie persuaded me to let her take the seminar. She has written a brilliant paper on advance numerical control that has widespread implications.

"Someday I intend to be an internal auditing manager," she says. Knowing Connie, I am certain she will make it. On Mondays and then again on Thursdays I stay at Connie's. We are having an affair.

Connie knows I am married. "In a consumer-oriented economy, marriage is a condition of life," she says. Her outlook is extremely mature.

I live in Westlong, Connecticut, a suburb of Westport. My wife Jean and I are progressive Republicans. We voted for

Nixon with reservations. In my opinion his tight-money policy is merely accelerating prices. On the other hand, we support his family-allowance plan and his fight against pollution.

I love Jean, though she has many faults. She is disorganized, wasteful and indecisive. She worries a lot. When the children were little, she worried about nutrition, contagious diseases, reading readiness and conformity. Now she worries about unwanted pregnancies, her figure and the environment. Her biggest fault is excessive spending. No sooner is an appliance installed than she is dreaming of its successor. "If I had two more speeds I could mill my own flour," she says.

"Any further capital outlay can only be viewed as inflationary," I say.

"If hemlines dip, the girls will need new clothes," Jean says.

"You must exercise some fiscal control," I say. This leads to fights.

Jean lets things go. Our house, for which I paid $50,000 ten years ago and which is worth at least twice that on the current market, is dirty. There is dust under the bed, on Jean's collection of Early American bottles and on the Mies van der Rohe chairs. Many things are greasy: our marble bathroom, the dishes, both handles on the side-by-side refrigerator/freezer. "The dishes are greasy," I say.

"It is the biodegradable detergent," Jean says. Somehow I doubt this. There is a blight on our home, as if we have been using Brand X for all our household needs.

I keep wondering how Jean spends her day. When I question her subtly she says, "I package things for the freezer." But there is nothing in our freezer to corroborate this.

There are certain things I can discuss with Connie that I no longer feel free to discuss with Jean. We have long frank conversations on all aspects of finance. After the seminar, we go to Connie's place. She lives on West Twelfth Street in a two-bedroom, rent-controlled apartment. Her girls are doing their homework. Connie and I are talking. "A return to pre-1966 levels is unlikely," I say.

"High interest rates have curbed capital expenditure," Connie says.

"There is an alarming acceleration of prices," I say.

"Things will get worse before they get better," Connie says.

This kind of talk makes us both very sexy. We touch each other between the legs and wait impatiently for the girls to go to bed.

Connie has three children; Jean and I have three children. All of them are girls. Connie's girls are thirteen, fourteen and fifteen. Our girls are also thirteen, fourteen and fifteen. Connie's eldest, Clancy, takes after Connie. When Clancy finishes high school, she plans to set up a commune on East Sixth Street. "I am certain I can show a five and a half percent yield per annum on the capital outlay," Clancy says. With the Dow-Jones averages continuing to plummet, that is not a bad return.

Bettina, the youngest child, also has a head for business. She sold the largest number of subscriptions to *Reader's Digest* in zip code 10017. Her bonus prize was an all-expense-paid round-trip for two to Guantánamo Bay. She took her father along.

Mr. Hansburger, Connie's ex, is a small-business failure. He was a war-toy manufacturer who could not keep up with the times. "All his weapons were phased out before they hit the market," Connie says. Convinced that the military-industrial complex would iron out the bugs, he produced eleven models of tanks, bombers and missiles that never became operational. Many of them are in Connie's closet, unassembled. It was part of her settlement. "Someday they'll be a collector's item," Connie says. When this happens, she hopes to make a killing.

The middle girl, Lassy, takes after her father. In school, she consistently underachieves. Lassy wants to be a radical anarchist when she grows up, but with her marks I doubt she will make it.

Some nights I help her with her homework. Her greatest weakness is time-distance concepts. "Lassy, pretend you're an astronaut," I say. "How far is it to Mars? How long will it take you to get there?"

"Our space program is counter-productive," Lassy says.

"Do you want the Russians to forge ahead?" I say.

"The planets belong to the people," Lassy says. "Right on."

When she talks like that, I cannot help but wonder whether she is a Communist. Even so, I have managed to raise her percentile six points. Naturally, this pleases me, but it worries me too. My own middle child, Vera, is also an underachiever. At home, I help her with her homework. She is failing Rhythm and all aspects of Communication. "How can you hope to be a cattle breeder if you don't learn to read and write?" I say.

"In a non-linear culture, literacy is an anachronism," she says.

"Success is a habit," I say.

"The entire alphabet makes me like sick," Vera says. She gets this squeamishness from her mother.

What worries me is this: both Vera and Lassy have their hearts set on Sarah Lawrence. Suppose, when they apply, they are competing for the same place. And suppose, because I helped Lassy raise her percentiles, she gets the place instead of Vera. Could I ever forgive myself?

I wake Connie in the middle of the night. "Promise me something," I say. "Promise me that none of your girls will try for the colleges that my girls try for."

She knows instantly what I'm getting at. "Lassy has her heart set on Sarah Lawrence," she says.

"Vera has visited the campus," I say.

"Lassy attended a theatre performance there last April," Connie says.

"Vera had tea at the president's house," I say.

"Vera is more the Smith type," Connie says. I find this remark extremely insulting. We fight. After that I do not spend Monday and Thursday nights with Connie.

At home things are not very pleasant. Jean is testing a home compactor for the planning board that is designed to reduce garbage-disposal problems. The remains of TV dinners are everywhere. Mounds of bones litter the kitchen. The neighbors carry in large plastic bags full of garbage. "Garbage is everyone's responsibility," I say.

"The American people have a right to a clean environment," Jean says.

"The beds are unmade," I say.

"In the absence of population control, we must rely on emergency measures," Jean says.

"Our home laundry got the highest rating in *Consumer Reports*. Yet my underwear is grey," I say.

"Pollution control has a price," Jean says.

I question the girls subtly about their mother. "What does she do all day?" I say. Jackie, the eldest, says, "She spies on me. She is into my things looking for pot and contraceptives." Gloria, the baby, says, "She groped the repairman yesterday." But Jackie is very low on the index of reliability and Gloria has been trying to get Jean and me to get a divorce since her Oedipal days.

I ask Vera. "She crochets edges on the frayed blankets," she says. But like most middle children, Vera is loyalty incarnate.

At dinner, Jean serves canned spaghetti and Drake's cakes. I question the girls subtly about what they eat when I'm in town. "What do you eat when I'm in town?" I say. "Peanut butter on day-old bread," Jackie says. "Instant everything," Gloria says. "Filet of beef Wellington," Vera says. I think her mother told her to say that.

In happier times the entire family cooked together. While I shelled lentils, Jean stood at the stove stirring sauce béarnaise and the girls, in a circle on the floor, peeled shallots while we had long frank discussions on the quality of life, all aspects of financial management, family planning and the state of the world. Now the house is dirty and we eat out of cans and Jean is only interested in garbage.

The strain tells on me. I am tense, keyed up. At the seminar I have lost my brilliance. Someone asks me, "What is the effect of quantitative marketing on the national economy?"

"Nixon is on the right track," I say.

"How do you explain the home-building lag?" Connie says.

"The public is determined to restore the environment," I say.

"Why can't monetary policies be redirected toward fiscal responsibility?" Connie says.

I get an erection and have to turn away. Think about the money squeeze, I tell myself. I think about the money squeeze but it does not help. I am compelled to hold a book in front of me for the rest of the discussion.

After class, I stop Connie. "If Lassy has her heart set on Sarah Lawrence, the place is hers," I say. "Vera would be happier at Cornell."

"I missed you," Connie says. We go home. I am eager to climb into bed with her. I give the girls movie money and Connie and I are alone. "Let's go to bed," I say. In my absence, Connie has taken up knitting. "I just have to finish this square," she says. Hours later, we climb into bed. We make love but I am wary and it is not the same.

It is early spring. Connie and I are alone. The girls are spending the night with Mr. Hansburger. Connie is knitting. I am reading a paper on conglomerates and the third world. Someone knocks at the door. Connie opens it. It is Jean. "I thought so," she says. She looks at Connie and calls her terrible names. Then Connie calls Jean terrible names. A scene follows. "Please," I say, "things are never as bad as they seem."

Jean cries. Connie cries. I fix us all a stiff drink. Jean and

Connie drain their drinks. I quickly fix another. Connie sits down. She picks up her knitting. Jean stares at it. Then she pinches it between her fingers. Fearing another flare-up, I say to them, "Let's discuss this like civilized people."

"What stitch is that?" Jean says.

"A double cable," Connie says.

"Is it hard?" Jean says.

"Once you get the hang of it, it's easy," Connie says.

"Why don't we discuss this like civilized people," I say.

"This is a nice place," Jean says.

"Would you like to see the rest of it?" Connie says.

She shows Jean through the apartment. Jean likes the closets. She spends the night with us.

I am very happy. Jean and Connie are very happy. Connie shows Jean a fancy knitting stitch. Jean teaches Connie how to crochet. We discuss the environment.

It is early summer. I am less happy. Jean and Connie talk about things that do not interest me. "Talk about something I like," I say. "Why don't you make friends of your own?" they say. I am uncertain how to proceed.

Tonight I am alone. Connie and Jean have gone shopping together. I think they are planning a vacation without me.